WHEN SUPPER
WAS ENDED...

WHEN SUPPER WAS ENDED...

AN INSPECTOR HOOD NOVEL

MICHAEL GT STOKES

Matador
Unit E2 Airfield Business Park,
Harrison Road, Market Harborough,
Leicestershire. LE16 7UL
Tel: 0116 2792299
Email: books@troubador.co.uk
Web: www.troubador.co.uk/matador
Twitter: @matadorbooks

ISBN 978 1803135 274

British Library Cataloguing in Publication Data.
A catalogue record for this book is available from the British Library.

Printed and bound by CPI Group (UK) Ltd, Croydon, CR0 4YY
Typeset in 11pt Aldine401 BT by Troubador Publishing Ltd, Leicester, UK

Matador is an imprint of Troubador Publishing Ltd

In memory of Dom Edmund FitzSimons, OSB
(always with a Capital S)

"You cannot really break away from antiquity; it has always been there first and muddied the trail of truth with its own footprints."

Ronald Knox

CHAPTER ONE

Summer 2002

'Who would kill a priest?'

Detective Chief Inspector Henry Hood shook his head in disbelief. 'I take it he is a priest? The habit he's wearing certainly suggests he is.'

'Yes sir,' replied Detective Constable Adrian Swanson. 'He's a priest all right. I recognise him. He's Father Dominic Renville. He lives – or lived – in the Gatehouse. Been here for about two years. I believe he's officially retired but he says Mass most Sundays in the chapel. I'm not a Catholic myself, sir, but my wife is. She's pretty regular in her attendance and I've been with her on the odd occasion. It's definitely Father Dominic.'

Hood crouched down to get a better view. 'And in a place like this.'

Swanson seemed perplexed. 'What exactly is this, sir?' he asked, leaning forward, and peering down at the body of the elderly man lying awkwardly in the deep recess before him. 'It looks like some sort of excavation has been going on.'

Hood got to his feet. 'I'm not sure, and forgive the irony, but I think this is a priest-hole.'

'A what?'

The detective constable looked mystified. Hood pointed to the oak panelling, one section of which had been removed and propped against the far wall next to a damaged oriel window. He had already noted what appeared to be the remains of two wooden boards – about two and a half feet in length and almost a foot wide – leaning against a pile of soil and debris a few feet from the excavation. He also sensed a distinct aroma of dry earth and mustiness mixed with a delicate hint of incense.

'It's a hiding place,' he explained. 'Specially constructed, probably in the reign of Elizabeth the First, to hide Catholic priests from the

1

authorities. Very well done too, from what I can see of it. That panelling'
– he pointed to the oak panelling near the window – 'must have been
fitted later and I suspect a staircase or something would have finished the
job so no one would realise it was here.' He paused and looked around
the oak panelled room. 'There must have been a more accessible entry in
Elizabethan days.'

'But why would anyone want to hide a priest?'

Hood gave the young detective constable a withering look as he
crouched down again. 'Don't you know any history, DC…?'

'Swanson, sir. Adrian Swanson.'

'Of course, forgive me. We haven't worked together before.'

'No, sir.'

Hood explained as best he could. 'In the latter part of the sixteenth
century a Catholic priest could be executed simply for being a priest, if
he were apprehended. And hides like this were designed to try and make
sure they were not caught. Some of them spent days in these uncongenial
spaces while the house was searched from top to bottom.'

Swanson flinched. 'I wouldn't fancy spending any time at all down
there, sir.'

'I don't suppose they did either, but the alternative hardly bears
thinking about.'

Hood's eyes darted about the sides of the excavation as he crouched
down again. The recess was well over six-feet deep and no more than
five and-a-half feet square. The recently hollowed out floor appeared
to be laid directly on to earth. Two sides were partially panelled, the
wood in surprisingly good condition bearing in mind the centuries that
must have gone by since it had been exposed to daylight. The outside
wall, in solid looking sandstone, bore some signs of deterioration but
looked substantial enough. The side opposite was in roughly mortared
brick, topped by a narrow oak beam. There were distinct marks in the
stonework suggestive of supports for a staircase long since removed.
The recess itself, although cramped, would have been just large enough
for two men to conceal themselves in what must have been far from
comfortable conditions.

'There must have been an air shaft somewhere and possibly an escape
passage under the outside wall…otherwise anyone secreted down there
would not have been able to breathe – not for very long anyway.'

Hood got to his feet, his eyes turning to the intricately carved stonework of the vaulted ceiling above. 'Yes, I suspect this place was originally a monastery or convent. This room... it has a very ecclesiastical feel about it, don't you think?' His voice softened. 'Have you heard the expression, "a sense of place?"'

Swanson gave him a blank look and shook his head.

'What the Romans called *genius locus* – a sort of protective spirit that one finds in certain locations or buildings.' He paused then continued softly. 'One can almost hear the monks chanting.'

The detective constable had no idea what his superior was talking about. He shuffled uncomfortably as he looked down again at the dead priest's body. 'It didn't do Father Dominic much good, this protective spirit – whatever it is,' he grunted.

Hood was forced to agree but did not allow the junior officer's comment to interrupt his thoughts. 'Yes. Probably turned in to a fairly grand house after the dissolution. Ironic, isn't it? To find a dead priest in a priest-hole. I wonder what the newspapers will make of that when they get hold of it?'

Swanson hesitated before he replied. 'As you've probably gathered, sir, history is not my specialist subject. But my wife did mention something about a hiding place being discovered here a few weeks ago. I didn't really understand what she was talking about. This is it, I suppose?'

The detective constable looked mightily unimpressed. Hood frowned then smiled. 'Yes, I suppose it is.'

Silence.

Swanson was bursting to ask Hood what he was doing at Easton Grange. He'd heard of the detective chief inspector – who hadn't? A devotee of the works of Charles Dickens who invariably named his major investigations after a Dickens' character or novel, Hood was one of the first mixed-race senior officers in the combined Mid-Shires constabulary. His successful investigation of the Campion kidnapping case – *Operation Christmas Carol* – had achieved huge country-wide publicity, but Swanson also knew that the senior officer standing in front of him was not locally based. Had he been specifically sent to Northamptonshire to investigate the priest's death? He eventually plucked up the courage to ask the question which continued to vex him.

3

'Do you mind me asking, sir, how you got here so quickly? You're not based in this division are you? And I'd not been here that long when you arrived.'

It was a fair enough question and it was certainly true that Hood was well outside his usual area of operations. He had been contacted as he drove back to Leicester from a conference in Oxford – two days of his life he would never get back. These conferences were the bane of a senior officer's life, and only occasionally useful. But he supposed they got him out of the office and away from the mountain of paperwork which was fast becoming his daily diet. The call from the Deputy Chief Constable had come through when he was only a few miles from Easton Parva. It was she who had diverted him to the Grange, as the home of Sir Robert Southall was known. He assumed the local DCI would take over the investigation in due course but the top brass, sensing the killing would quickly hit the headlines, wanted his immediate take on it. He had more than enough to do in Leicester and had no wish to embark on a major inquiry involving the death of a priest in such an apparently bizarre setting. He didn't have the time, although he found the circumstances quite fascinating. He explained his presence to the junior officer.

'I happened to be passing,' he said. 'The DCC wants me to give her a heads-up. She thinks this case is going to attract a lot of publicity – and she's probably right. I shan't be interfering though – once the local DCI gets here. Where is he, by the way?'

'DCI Saunders? He's away, sir. Won't be back until the end of next month. He had a lot of leave outstanding. He's in Australia I believe. His brother lives there, Melbourne, I think. Detective Sergeant Knight is standing in for him at the moment. You know her, of course. She mentions you a lot.'

Hood smiled. He knew DS Knight of old, of course. They had worked together on several major inquiries in Leicestershire and Nottinghamshire, including the Campion kidnapping case. Following her promotion, she had transferred to the Northamptonshire division. It would be good to see her again. But he wondered, silently, whether she would be allowed to head such a potentially complex inquiry in the absence of her DCI. He decided to get as much information as he could from Swanson.

'Do you happen to live around here?'

The junior detective nodded. 'Yes, sir. We've lived in the village for the last three years, since I was married. My wife's family comes from here. I was at home when I got the call. That's why I was asked to attend.'

'That may be helpful – a bit of local knowledge doesn't usually go amiss in a case like this. What about the family who live here? What do you know about them?'

Swanson seemed reluctant to answer. 'We don't have any dealings with Sir Robert or his family, sir...we don't move in those circles.'

Hood gave the junior officer an encouraging smile. 'Come on, Swanson, don't hold back. You must know something about them. I would have thought the people living in a place like this would be the subject of at least occasional comment in the village.'

Swanson overcame his hesitancy and took a deep breath. 'Well sir, it's just village gossip really. The house has always been known as Easton Grange as far as I know, but as you'll have guessed, I don't know anything about its origins.' He smiled and added, 'They sometimes hold concerts in the grounds – my wife and I have been to a couple – but I've only been in the house once before – in this room in fact, and in the chapel, of course.'

'The chapel is the Victorian looking building that abuts this side of the house?' Hood pointed over the priest-hole.

'Yes sir. It's directly behind that wall. But it's not the original church. I remember my wife saying it was built by one of Sir Robert's ancestors over a hundred years ago. You can still see part of the original church in the grounds near the stable yard – not that there's much left of it.'

'Go on,' said Hood. 'You obviously know more than you think you do.'

Swanson cleared his throat, reluctant as he was to say anything about the family which occupied what was by far the largest house in the area. But he revealed what little he knew. 'I don't know about that, sir. I do know that Sir Robert Southall's family has owned the estate for as long as anyone can remember. He used to be very involved in local affairs but he generally keeps himself to himself since his wife died – that was nearly three years ago. Knocked the old boy for six, at least that's what they say, but I suspect he's over it by now.'

Swanson continued with his account as Hood inspected the rest of the room, the detective constable following in his wake. The chief inspector stepped over the police tape which had been placed to secure the area around the priest-hole and prevent unauthorised access. The junior detective did likewise as he tried to keep up with him. It was certainly an impressive room and of significant size. Hood was no expert but he reckoned it must have once formed the inner section of the earlier monastery. The outline of the original construction could still be made out in the variation of the stonework in the vaulted ceiling, despite what appeared to be a more recent addition which opened up the accommodation from what must have been a fairly wide corridor leading in the direction of the ruined chapel to the present-day grandly proportioned reception room. For the most part, the floor seemed to be constructed from oak, but the lengthy section which he surmised had formed one side of the original cloisters had a stone floor which must have survived the reconstruction and extension of the house after it was put to secular use. When he reached the damaged oriel window he came to a halt and waited for Swanson to complete his account of the Southall family.

'Sir Robert has three sons but none of them live locally. The youngest, Maxim, is still at university; the eldest, Michael, works in Brussels, or he did last I heard. I don't know where Philip is, bit of a weirdo by all accounts. Travels around. Never could settle to anything. Sir Robert will be able to tell you more when he arrives.' Swanson looked at his watch. 'The London train should be getting into Wellingborough about now. Mrs Morton phoned him at his club directly after she called us.'

'Mrs Morton?' asked Hood.

'The housekeeper.'

'Sir Robert wasn't here when the priest died?'

'It seems not, sir. He spends quite a bit of time in London. He's something to do with a merchant bank.' His voiced dropped to a whisper. 'Rumour has it that the family were in financial difficulties a few years ago. They sold off most of the estate's land in the mid-nineties.'

'Did they? Very interesting.' Hood grinned. 'See, just as I thought young Swanson, you're remarkably well informed. Anything else?'

Swanson almost blushed. 'That's about it, sir. And, as I said, it's mainly village gossip, if truth were told.'

Hood became serious again. 'Tell me, who discovered the body – the housekeeper?'

'I don't think so, sir. It was an American gentleman who found him according to Mrs. Morton.'

'An American? What's an American doing here?'

Swanson referred to his notebook. 'He's been staying here for a few weeks, or so he says, doing some research for Sir Robert. But I think he's a priest as well. Father John Grantham he calls himself. He's some sort of academic, apparently, from a University in the States. He's with the housekeeper in the kitchen. I didn't think she should be left on her own. She's really upset.'

'You've never met him before – the American?'

'No sir. I didn't even know he was staying here before today. He hasn't been seen about the village, not so far as I'm aware. If he had been, my wife would have spotted him. There's not much gets past her.' Swanson grinned.

Hood smiled. 'I must meet your wife. Now, tell me about the housekeeper.'

'Martha? She's in her late thirties or early forties I would guess. Good looking woman for her age but she hasn't worked here for very long – and she doesn't live in. She tells me she comes in four days a week. Lives in a cottage close to us. It's owned by the estate. Our garden backs onto hers. Today was one of her days off. She only came in this morning after Grantham found the body and telephoned her. Whatever happened had obviously happened by then.'

'Any staff live in?'

'No. Sir Robert gets people in from the village if he has a function – and they're pretty rare these days. My wife used to help out here when she was younger – when Lady Southall was alive. They were quite sociable in those days. Sir Robert was High Sheriff a few years ago. He gave a party for the villagers in the grounds – but there's been nothing like that since Lady Southall died.'

'Has anyone formally identified the deceased?'

'Not officially sir, no. But I'm sure Sir Robert will. And as I said, it's definitely Father Dominic.' He lowered his voice again. 'He'd apparently been dead for some time when the American gentleman discovered him.'

'Had he? We'd better have a word with the housekeeper and this American before Sir Robert gets here.'

'What about SOCO, sir? They'll be here shortly.'

'Well, they'll have to wait until the pathologist has examined the body *in situ*. I don't want the deceased or the priest-hole interfered with before he's examined him. He's on his way I assume?'

'Yes, sir. He's coming from Northampton, Professor Romney. He was in court this morning but he'll be here directly. DS Knight arranged everything. She's already contacted the coroner.'

Hood was relieved. 'Guy Romney, eh? He's a good man. We've worked together before. Mind you, it looks pretty clear that someone's bashed this poor fellow over the head. No sign of a weapon I suppose?'

'No sir. Not that I've noticed – and I've had a good look round.'

'SOCO can start with the Gatehouse, until the pathologist has finished in the priest-hole, although I suppose a couple of them will have to observe Professor Romney's examination of the deceased and take some photographs.'

'Yes sir.'

'What about DS Knight? Is she on her way here?'

'Not yet, sir. She's still in Wellingborough, making enquiries about the deceased and organising the team. I can get her here if you like.'

Hood shook his head. 'No, that won't be necessary. She has her own way of working, and she'll be here in due course, I'm sure. Now, what do you make of this damaged window? Someone's made a right mess of it.'

He pointed to the shattered glass scattered around the oak floorboards. It had obviously been broken from the outside with considerable force. Some of the lead was lying on the floor, misshapen, with pieces of coloured glass still clinging to it. The gap between the remnants in the window would have allowed a hand to pass through and lift the casement stay, enabling it to be opened.

'That's how they got in,' observed Swanson. 'Apparently, Sir Robert doesn't use this wing of the house much at the moment.'

Hood said nothing as he completed his inspection. But he wasn't going to fall for the old broken window routine. It could easily have been an attempt by the killer to mislead. Besides, the window was firmly closed. If the killer had come through it, why did he bother closing it? And from what Hood had observed, anyone could have walked into the house through the front door with comparative ease. All it would have taken was a bit of nerve. And there were other windows through which it would have been much easier to effect an entry. No need to smash your way in through leaded glass. He turned towards Swanson.

'There are three doors which give access to this room, is that right?'

'Yes, sir. There's the door you came through, the door that leads into the present chapel and the old outside door on the far side.' He pointed towards a solid looking oak door of considerable age on the opposite side of the room. 'But that door is never used.'

Hood went over and tried the handle. The door was firmly shut and did not give when he put his full weight against it. In addition to the ancient mortice lock, there were heavy iron bolts at the top and bottom of the door. It would have been impossible to open it from the outside.

'Who has a key to the doors in this room?' he asked.

'I don't know, sir. I'll make inquiries when Sir Robert gets here. But this one doesn't look as if it's been opened in years. And those bolts would prevent the door being opened from outside, even with a key.'

Hood tried to release the top bolt. It would not budge. It seemed to have rusted in the locked position. He had to agree with Swanson; this door had obviously not been opened for decades. He then walked back to the other side of the room and checked the door that led into the present chapel. It was securely locked. 'So, the only way into this room, in the absence of a key, would be through the front of the house?'

'Or through the window, sir. I'll check how may keys there are and who has them. But the window looks the favourite.'

Hood had already dismissed the broken window as being the point of entry but he did not say why. He wanted the keys checked anyway. 'You do that. Now, did the housekeeper tell you what Father Dominic was doing in here?'

Swanson bent down and picked up a piece of broken glass and examined it. 'Some sort of archaeological investigation with the American gentleman. I don't know the details but it looks like he may have been down the hole when he was attacked.'

Hood had his doubts about that. He re-traced his steps back to the hide and looked down at the body. The one thing he had learnt as a police officer was never to assume anything. Assumption was often a significant impediment to getting at the truth. Nothing wrong with speculation, of course. That might well lead to a workable theory, but appearances could be and frequently were deceptive. *Take nothing on its looks; take everything on evidence.* The lawyer Jagger's advice to young Pip in *Great Expectations* had always informed Hood's approach to an investigation. For him there really was no better rule.

'Possibly. We'll have to wait for Professor Romney's take on that. We mustn't jump to conclusions. He could easily have been dumped in there after he was killed elsewhere. And there's not much blood about in the vicinity of the hide given the injury to his head. He must have bled profusely when he was assaulted. Chances are he was attacked somewhere else. If he were, he can't have been brought into this room through that broken window.'

The detective constable did not reply. He was certainly not going to contradict his superior. Hood scratched his head. 'Anything missing?'

'Too early to say, sir. But that painting over the fireplace is worth quite a bit, and it hasn't been disturbed. It was the first thing I checked.'

Hood walked over to the fireplace and looked at the portrait and took hold of the frame. It was still securely fixed to the wall. 'What makes you say it's valuable?'

Swanson smiled. He was on surer ground when it came to the painting. 'Sir Robert asked us for advice on security earlier this year. The officer assigned was Andy Crossley. Well, he was a bit nervous about meeting Sir Robert was Andy, so I agreed to come with him. The old boy told us he was hoping to open this wing of the house to visitors. His insurers wanted the room assessed because that particular painting is quite valuable. I remember he said it had to be specially secured to the wall and alarmed. Perhaps that's why it wasn't taken?'

Hood was not convinced. 'I don't know about that. A professional burglar would have cut it from the frame if this is what he was after. There must be some other explanation for what happened here. How valuable is it?' Hood studied the painting for several seconds.

'Worth about twenty-five thousand, sir. That's what we were told. Not the sort of thing I'd have over my fireplace at home though.'

Hood turned back towards the priest-hole and stroked his chin. *But why would anyone kill a priest?* That was the question that needed to be answered. Had Father Dominic found something more valuable than the painting? Or was he killed because of something he knew or by an adversary from his past? Hood found the whole thing quite intriguing. Something told him that this was not the random action of some would-be burglar. There was more to it than that. The broken window was obviously a smokescreen. He almost regretted that he would be handing the inquiry over to the local team. Investigating the murder of a priest in a house laden with history certainly appealed to him. Much more interesting than any of the cases awaiting him in Leicester.

'Come on, let's speak to the housekeeper and this American. And put a uniformed officer on this door. I don't want anyone coming into this room without my express permission – and I mean anyone.'

CHAPTER TWO

While Swanson organised a police officer to guard the entrance to the room where the body of the deceased was located, Hood headed along another lengthy corridor towards the kitchen. He was beginning to appreciate the size of the task that whoever took over from him would face in identifying the person or persons responsible for the murder of the priest. This was a huge house. Checking all the rooms would be a massive task. Then there were the grounds. He had no idea of the acreage involved, but he anticipated the estate would straddle a great deal more than his own extensive garden in South Leicestershire. Perhaps it was no bad thing that he would be handing the investigation over to someone else by the end of the day. He assumed a more senior officer than DS Knight would be found to head the investigation although he had few doubts himself about her ability and diligence. His mobile phone vibrated as he approached the kitchen. Margaret Knowles, Deputy Chief Constable of Mid-Shires Combined Constabulary, had decided that he should assume permanent overall control of the investigation into Father Renville's death. He was to drop everything he was working on and concentrate on solving the priest's murder. A speedy conclusion was essential.

'I've had the Bishop of Northampton contact me, Harry. He's naturally very concerned about the suspicious death of a priest in his diocese and we need someone of your sensitivity and experience on this one. The Chief agrees. He says you're just the man for the job.'

Hood smiled to himself. Such compliments usually preceded something to his disadvantage. The DCC continued in the same vein. 'And the local DCI is away for several weeks. DS Knight is too junior to be made up to acting Inspector and she hasn't been on a Senior Investigating

Officer course yet. There's no one else immediately available so it's necessary to bring someone in from outside the division. I'm sure you'll agree that a case of this gravity needs a top man. The Chief and I both think you're well suited. It will require your full attention, of course.'

'Wendy Knight's a good detective,' countered Hood. 'And there's my work in Leicester to consider, ma'am. I'm snowed under at the moment.'

The DCC waved Hood's concerns aside. 'This is far more important. Sir Robert Southall, who owns Easton Grange, is a big noise in the county and the press have got hold of it too – I don't know how – but it was mentioned on the local lunchtime news. It's bound to go national, so this will need very careful handling. And your being a Catholic might be an advantage.'

Hood felt it necessary to put up further token resistance. He really did have more than enough on his plate in Leicester. 'But I was on my way back to the office, ma'am. I have a huge amount of work waiting for me there. I've just spent two days at Keble College on this diversity course, time that could have been more usefully spent in my humble opinion. And I need hardly mention, this isn't my division.'

'Not at the moment, no. But that's the other bit of news. Your promotion has come through. Congratulations Detective Superintendent Hood! I'm sorry it's taken so long. In my view, it's well overdue. There'll be a letter in the post.'

Hood was delighted, if not a little resentful. It had certainly been a long time coming. 'When does it take effect?' he asked.

'At the beginning of next month, so that's only a week or so away. I have the Chief's approval to tell you. It will be announced to the press at the beginning of next week but keep it to yourself until then. And given what's happened, it comes at a highly convenient time, but there is a slight catch.' She paused ominously. 'It will mean a move to Northamptonshire. You'll be replacing Maurice Kingston. He's finally on his way. I hope that will meet with your approval? You'll have to put a new team together, of course.'

The news of his promotion caused Hood to forget, temporarily, the complexity of the investigation into Father Dominic's murder. He sounded suitably enthusiastic about his proposed transfer. The change of division did not, in truth, trouble him. He lived close to the Northamptonshire border so it wasn't much of a drive, and he and his wife were considering a move. They now had three children and a bigger house was already on their agenda. That Wendy Knight was already based in Wellingborough was also a welcome incentive.

Knowles continued. 'You'll be based in Northampton rather than Wellingborough, of course; we can't justify having a Detective Superintendent running that rural area. But it will be on your patch. You'll be in overall charge of serious crime for most of the county. It'll be up to you how you organise things.'

'That will include personnel?'

'Naturally. The whole division could do with a shake-up. I think Maurice had started to let things drift. Once you've decided what to do, just clear it with the ACC and Chief Superintendent Coupland; he's in overall charge of the county, so make sure you keep him in the loop. By the way, Andrew Hooper will be taking over from you in Leicester. His promotion to DI has been confirmed.'

'I'm very pleased for him. I'll liaise with him when I get the opportunity. Please give him my congratulations.'

'I will, but this murder investigation is to be given priority, Harry. You can sort out a handover with Andrew later. I mean it when I say this inquiry is to be given your full attention.' She paused to make the point. 'Any news so far? It's definitely homicide is it?'

'It's murder, ma'am. There doesn't seem much doubt about that. I'm about to speak with the housekeeper and some American guest who found the body. And I'm still waiting for the pathologist to get here.'

'That will be Guy Romney, I presume? Professor Kennedy is attending a conference in Berlin. He'll be away for the next week or so. DS Knight has already obtained the coroner's permission for a full forensic *post-mortem* to be carried out. Like you, she believes the priest was murdered.'

'There can't be much doubt about that. I believe Guy is on his way as we speak.'

'Very well. I'll leave it with you. I shall require a daily report on how things are going, certainly for the next few days. I'll take the heat from the press for the first twenty-four hours. There'll be a brief press conference tomorrow morning at HQ which I will handle personally. I don't expect there'll be anything to report of significance. But let me know if there are any developments.'

'Do you want me there as the SIO?'

'That won't be necessary, but I shall want you here next Thursday when your promotion takes effect and you'll have to handle any further press briefings yourself alongside DCS Coupland.' She paused. 'Again, many congratulations. And Harry, remember, the utmost discretion. This investigation will require very sensitive handling. Best of luck.'

Hood switched off his phone and although he was delighted with the news he had just received about his imminent promotion, he adopted a serious air as he walked into the huge old-fashioned kitchen. That he was now in sole charge of the investigation into Father Dominic's death weighed heavily upon him. There would be no excuses if things went awry. The buck would stop with him. He couldn't help wondering if the timing of his promotion was in some way connected with his being put in charge of what would inevitably be a lengthy and difficult inquiry carried out in a blaze of intrusive publicity and media speculation. Still, it was up to him to make sure no errors were made. And working again with Wendy Knight was an unlooked-for bonus. The two of them usually made a winning combination.

As he entered the kitchen, a man and a woman were in whispered conversation sitting at a large pine table in the middle of the room. Hood noted a look of concern in the woman's eyes as he approached. She had obviously been crying and was struggling to control her emotions. The man, tall and slim and in his mid-forties stood, stepped towards Hood, and proffered his right hand in greeting. He was casually but smartly dressed in dark clothing and had a firm grip when Hood shook his hand. Hood noted he was not wearing a clerical collar.

'You must be Chief Inspector Hood? I hope I got your title right? Things are different where I come from. That young detective said you were on your way.'

'That's right. Detective Chief Inspector Henry Hood. I shall be taking charge of this investigation.'

The man nodded as he spoke. 'I'm John Grantham – from Minnesota in the States, John Grantham of the Society of Jesus. This is Mrs. Morton, Martha Morton – she's Sir Robert Southall's housekeeper.'

Hood acknowledged the still tearful individual sitting at the pine table, dabbing her eyes with a tissue. She was a handsome woman with dark brown hair and attractive even features, much younger looking than Hood had anticipated from Swanson's estimate of her age.

'She's very upset,' said the Jesuit, stating the obvious. 'Father Dominic was a good man, a very gentle soul. He will be sorely missed.'

Hood noticed the Jesuit's mid-Atlantic accent. American, yes, but obviously highly educated. Neither did he fit Hood's idea of what a priest should look like. He had the appearance of a Wall Street banker rather than a man in holy orders, not that Hood had ever knowingly met a Wall Street banker, or, indeed, a Jesuit. Then again, the Jesuits were far removed in almost every respect from Hood's conception of a parish priest. He knew they were usually very clever and articulate, that was certainly the reputation of this powerful religious order. Father John Grantham, on first impression, seemed to embody everything Hood had heard about them. The chief inspector pulled out a chair and seated himself at the table, taking out his notebook and inviting Grantham to join him.

'Could I take a few personal details first?' he asked, 'then we shall want to speak to you individually. Standard procedure, you understand.'

'Of course,' replied Grantham, retaking his seat, and answering for both of them. 'As I said, I'm John Edmund Grantham. I'm a member of the Society of Jesus from the Catholic University of the Annunciation, just outside St. Paul in Minnesota. I teach there; I'm an associate professor specialising in the history of Christianity. I've been assisting Sir Robert during my vacation. I should add that I came here initially to research this house. My interest is in the people who used to live here, a recusant English family.'

Hood turned towards the housekeeper who was hesitant when she spoke, obviously still upset. 'Mrs. Martha Morton. I've been here for about seven months, now. I'm separated from my husband – no children. I live in the estate cottage in the village; sixteen Main Street.'

'No other staff?'

She shook her head. 'No, apart from Mrs Bolan and Mrs Pearson who help with the cleaning. They come in on Fridays and on other occasions if required. I couldn't manage a house of this size without assistance.'

Hood nodded and noted down the details. 'I think they'll have to have tomorrow off. I don't want anything touched.' He looked up from his notebook. 'Could I ask who found the body?'

The two looked at each other. The Jesuit replied. 'I did, Chief Inspector. I went into the Long Room – that's what it's known as –

looking for Dominic. There was a phone call for him. That's when I found him. He was already dead, quite cold. I suspect he'd been dead for some time.'

'What time was that?'

The priest paused and looked at the housekeeper. 'About nine-thirty, I think.'

'Who wanted to speak with him?'

'You know, I didn't ask, but I got the impression it was someone from his monastery. That's what was said anyway. I'm afraid I didn't continue the call in the circumstances.'

'His monastery?'

'Yes. He is – was – a monk, although I believe he had resided here for quite some time.'

Hood made a brief note. 'What made you think he would be in the Long Room?'

The Jesuit shrugged his shoulders. 'I didn't. For all I know he could have been back at his cottage or still in the chapel. There isn't a phone in the Gatehouse, you see. Dominic had no use for one. He's had to be fetched before on the rare occasions he's received a call. Sir Robert warned me about it. I went into the Long Room first simply because it was the closest and there's a door there which leads into the chapel.' He looked again at the housekeeper. 'That's where I found him, in the hide.'

Detective Constable Swanson came into the kitchen. He stood awkwardly just inside the door. 'Sorry to interrupt, sir. Professor Romney is here. Should I let him into the room so he can make a start?'

'In a moment. I need to speak to him first.'

'Oh, and DS Knight is on her way. I mentioned you were here.'

'Did you?' Hood smiled and turned his attention back to Grantham. 'Tell me, what did you do when you found Father Dominic?'

'At first I thought he might have fallen. I climbed down the ladder then I noticed the injury to his head. I checked his pulse. Nothing. I could tell he was dead. He was quite cold. It came as quite a shock to see him lying there. I then came in here and called Mrs. Morton, using the phone over there.' He pointed to the telephone fixed to the wall by the door. 'She was off today. You'll understand, chief inspector, I'm not very familiar with police procedures in this country. Mrs. Morton came straight here and we called the police.'

17

'Why did you call the police? What made you think his death was suspicious?'

Grantham answered again, a knowing half-smile on his face. 'The wound to the back of the head, of course. It seemed obvious to me that Father Dominic had been assaulted. He didn't get an injury like that by falling over, did he? And as he was obviously dead, there was no point troubling the paramedics. In the States, it would be the ME who would get the call.'

'The ME?'

'The Medical Examiner – what you call the coroner over here.'

Hood nodded that he understood. 'Well, the coroner has been informed of course, but as this looks very much like a homicide, any inquest will have to await the results of my investigation.'

'I understand. I'm sure Mrs. Morton and I will do everything we can to assist you.'

The housekeeper dabbed her eyes with a second tissue she pulled from a box on the table before nodding her assent. Grantham patted her arm as Hood turned his attention to her.

'How old was the deceased? Do you know?'

Grantham shook his head as the housekeeper replied. 'He was seventy-three last March. I remember because Sir Robert asked me to make him a birthday cake. Not that he made much of the occasion. He kept himself very much to himself. He wouldn't let me do very much for him. He preferred his own company and did most things for himself.'

'Has this priest-hole only recently been discovered?' asked Hood.

'Yes,' replied Grantham. 'Sir Robert was planning to open the east wing to the public. He was having some essential refurbishment done – there was dry rot in some of the panelling – he found the hide when the panelling was removed. He was very excited about it.'

'And Father Dominic? Was he part of the project?'

Grantham frowned. 'Not initially. He knew the hide had been found, of course, but he had very little to do with it to begin with. But I believe Sir Robert confided in him to explain why I was here and he became very interested as did I. We were excavating and trying to establish its original design. Very slowly and carefully you understand. The layout has obviously been altered since it was constructed or adapted. Considerable refurbishment has taken place over the years in the Long Room. There may even have been a staircase over it in the sixteenth century.'

Hood nodded as he recollected the marks in the stonework. Grantham continued. 'Dominic had some experience in archaeology. He told me that some Roman remains were found in the grounds of his monastery when they were preparing to build a new guesthouse. That was many years ago but he played a major role in overseeing those excavations. You see, my expertise is purely academic; his was also practical. He was extremely helpful and very knowledgeable about the period. He read history at Cambridge before he became a priest.'

Hood scribbled a short note. 'Did you work together or separately?'

'As you probably saw for yourself, Mr. Hood, it would have been difficult for both of us to work in the hide at the same time, but we sometimes worked together in the sense that one of us would be in the priest-hole with the other assisting from outside. Yesterday in fact, we spent part of the afternoon together.'

'In the – what did you call it? The Long Room?'

'Yes. I suppose it got its name because of the corridor which runs alongside towards the ruins of the old chapel, all that remains of the original cloisters.' He returned to the subject of the hide. 'We had made quite a lot of progress. You have to understand that when it was first discovered it looked like an attempt had been made to remove any evidence of its existence. It was full of earth and rubble. It has taken a little time to expose it. And we have to examine everything we remove. After so many centuries there's no saying what might be concealed in all that detritus.' He smiled. 'I'm bound to say that the excitement of discovering the hide has taken priority over my research over the last week or two.'

'Have you found anything of significance?'

Grantham's face fell. 'No, not yet, but we haven't finished trawling through it all. It's very painstaking work, you know. We don't want to miss anything.'

'Were you looking for anything in particular?'

Grantham narrowed his eyes. 'What do you mean, exactly?'

'I'm not sure, something valuable, perhaps?' Hood smiled. 'I have heard that these priest-holes have been used in more recent times for hiding things other than priests. I read something years ago where the proceeds of a bank robbery had been located in a priest-hole, somewhere in Lancashire, I believe.'

Grantham grinned, shaking his head as he answered. 'I don't know about that. And we certainly haven't found anything which falls into that category. You have to bear in mind it has been sealed off, probably for centuries. Anything we might find must have been there for at least the same period of time – or longer. That's what makes it so interesting. There's no saying what we might discover.'

'But nothing so far?'

Grantham's enthusiasm waned again. 'No, not that we expect to find anything in particular. I guess there's probably nothing there of significance. But the discovery of the priest-hole is exciting in itself.' He dropped his voice and adopted a confidential tone. 'Sir Robert was hoping to prove a connection with someone quite famous.'

'A link with his family?'

'Oh no. The Southalls did not live here in Elizabethan times. My research shows they did not acquire the property until sometime in the eighteenth century. They're a Somerset family originally.' The priest lent forward. 'I came across a bit of a manuscript in the archives of the *Venerabili* in Rome when I was in Europe over two years ago. It mentioned this house and a monk who was a member of the Powdrell family. My superior had written to Sir Robert to see if I could do some research in his excellent library. I wasn't able to come last summer but I later read in the Society's journal about the discovery of the priest-hole and I remembered what I'd seen in the archive, I just had to come. It seemed a piece of happenstance. That's why I got in touch with Sir Robert directly and he invited me to come and stay. I spend some of my time in Oxford, though. Sir Robert's library is extensive and holds some original documents, but there's material in Oxford that is relevant and helpful.'

'The *Venerabili?*'

'Yes. The Venerable English College. That's what the Italians call it.' He paused. 'You see, Mr Hood, it is already well established that the Jesuit martyr, Edmund Campion, travelled from Northamptonshire into Oxford on his way to London. But his superiors sent him back before he got there. He had a price on his head and the government of the day was determined to capture him. It was too dangerous for him to remain in the south, so close to London. Eventually, they did catch him– he was arrested at Lyford Grange in what was then Berkshire. I believe it's part of Oxfordshire now.'

He stood up and pointed to the huge gothic tracery window which dominated the room. 'How many kitchens have you been in which can boast a window like that?' He spread his arms as he spoke. 'This had been a religious house until the reformation when it was sold off and turned over to secular use but the evidence of its earlier function is everywhere. This was probably the prior's kitchen. The heads of religious houses lived very well in those days, even those who had taken a vow of poverty.' He smiled, looking for a reaction from Hood, but none came. 'Henry the Eighth stayed here, you know, in fifteen twenty-one, when he was hunting in the area.'

'You've established that have you?' said Hood, hardly trying to hide his scepticism. He received a gentle reprimand from Grantham.

'Don't be so cynical, Mr Hood. There's no doubt about it. The King was in the habit of imposing himself and his retinue both on the nobility and religious houses. It was impossible to object. He'd also just been made Defender of the Faith by Pope Leo X.' Hood remained unimpressed. 'But we have indisputable evidence he came here, Chief Inspector,' emphasised Grantham, 'which would satisfy even you.' He smiled in a way that Hood would find increasingly irritating as the investigation into the death of Father Dominic progressed. 'The King, even when pursuing his leisure interests, still had to append his signature to certain documents. His retinue would have included numerous clerks and officials. At that point in his reign, he tended to avoid administrative tasks, leaving the day-to-day work to his officials, but he sometimes had little choice when his signature was required. On occasion, the place where a document was signed was also included. One, still extant and preserved in the Public Records Office, was undoubtedly executed here. The Priory of the Blessed Virgin and Saint Augustine at Easton is identified under the King's signature.'

'I'll have to take your word for that,' replied the chief inspector, anxious as he was to get on with the investigation.

Grantham continued. 'After a few years the estate came into the hands of a recusant family, the Powdrells. We already know that Masses were being said here. Sir Robert was hoping to establish that Campion stayed here on his way south – we know he didn't get this far on his journey back – so if he did seek refuge here it would have had to have been as he travelled down to Oxford. If that could be established, then opening part of the house to paying visitors would prove very popular with certain sections of the public, in particular, Americans. Edmund Campion is very big in the States at the moment, you know.'

Hood had a vague recollection from school of the Campion story but could not remember much of the detail other than that he was once a favourite of the first Queen Elizabeth while he was at Oxford University but fell in her estimation after he left the country and eventually became a Jesuit. He returned to England and went about ministering to recusant Catholics but drew the attention of the authorities who were determined to arrest him. He ended up at Tyburn where he was hanged, drawn, and quartered.

'But has anything beyond conjecture been established so far?' he asked.

Grantham continued. 'Not in respect of Campion, no, but Sir Robert remains hopeful, perhaps too hopeful. It's going to be very difficult to prove and I have tried to curb his enthusiasm. But it is highly likely that priests did stay here – hence the priest-hole.' He smiled. 'It was originally my idea that Campion may have had some connection with this place. Perhaps I did exaggerate a little, but Sir Robert is very keen to research the possibility thoroughly, and there is no doubt that Campion did minister in this county, whether or not it was while he was on his way south.'

'I would have thought it impossible to prove – after all this time.'

'I agree. Exact proof will not be possible. But, the discovery of the hide is definite proof that priests did call here, clandestinely, which is a major step forward.' He paused and took the back of his chair in his hands, looking down at the table before turning and facing Hood. 'Perhaps we are reaching for the sky trying to establish that Campion came here, Chief Inspector, but some persecuted priests must have hidden in that hide, and that number may well have included a Jesuit or two. There is no record of arrests from this house, so if priests were sheltered in the priest-hole it fulfilled its purpose. Unfortunately, I have to return to the States soon, but I shall come back and continue with my research, if Sir Robert will have me. Father Dominic, too, had become quite absorbed with the whole thing – and he was a Benedictine monk, not a Jesuit.'

'So what was he doing here?'

'He was on leave from his Abbey at Melford, trying his hand as a sort of hermit, I believe. Sir Robert let him have the Gatehouse in return for saying Mass on Sundays in the chapel. Sir Robert comes from a family which has been Catholic for several generations, but he had to drive to Wellingborough to attend Mass – until Father Dominic arrived.'

Grateful as he was for the information, Hood was anxious to speak with Professor Romney and had no desire to delay the examination of the deceased. SOCO, too, would be anxious to get on with their examination of the crime scene.

'I'd like you both to make statements to this officer, DC Swanson – separately of course. I must go and deal with the pathologist. By the way, you understand that as this is being treated as a suspicious death, Father Dominic's body will have to be removed for *post-mortem* examination?' Hood smiled towards Grantham. 'What you Americans call an autopsy! Regrettable, I know for a priest, but that's the law.'

Grantham nodded. 'I'll get in touch with Melford Abbey and let them know. I suppose he's their responsibility really.'

'One more thing. When did you last see him, alive I mean?'

The priest looked towards the housekeeper. 'We had supper together, here in the kitchen, yesterday evening. Martha left a cold collation for us. Father Dominic usually fended for himself but as we had spent quite a lot of time together yesterday, I persuaded him to eat with me. I don't think he'd been looking after himself very well. He certainly looked in need of a good meal. He left here around a quarter to seven and eventually went back to the Gatehouse, or so I assumed.'

'When did the two of you finish working in the Long Room?'

'Just after five, I believe. Yes, Dominic went back to the Gatehouse just after five o'clock to get changed and returned at about six. He didn't stay long. And between you and me, he wasn't much of a conversationalist. Something of a change seemed to have come over him since the afternoon. I couldn't quite put my finger on it. He seemed almost excited about something. What it was I have no idea and he certainly gave nothing away. But he seemed fine when we separated.'

'Were you together for the whole of the day?'

'Not all the time, no. I was in the library for an hour or so mid-afternoon. Dominic was working alone in the Long Room, or at least I assume he was. He was certainly there when I came down from the library.'

'And after supper?'

'He didn't say where he was going, but I assumed he intended to return to his cottage after he called into the chapel. He certainly did not say he was going to work in the Long Room and he would have wanted to complete his daily office, either in the chapel or perhaps in the grounds. I guess he would have said something if he intended to return to the hide. I walked with him part of the way, but only as far as the chapel door.'

'How was he dressed when assisting you in the excavation?'

'Just in some old clothes, nothing specific as I remember.'

'But he was in his habit when you found him.'

'Yes he was. I suppose that means he wasn't intending to work in the priest-hole at the time he was attacked?'

'Quite – and we mustn't necessarily assume he was attacked in the Long Room. He could have been dumped there after he was assaulted. Did you see or hear anything suspicious at all yesterday? No strangers about the place?'

'Strangers, no. It was just like any other day, except Dominic had supper with me. My room is in the west wing; I doubt if I would have heard any extended activity in the Long Room.'

'Was he wearing his monk's habit at supper?'

'He was, yes. He was usually in his habit when I saw him about the place. I never recall him leaving the premises, so he hardly ever dressed otherwise save when helping in the hide.'

'Had you arranged anything with him today?'

'Nothing specific, no. He was not regular in his lending assistance. He rather came and went as he chose. But I suppose I did expect to see him in the Long Room at some point today but certainly not in the condition in which I found him.'

'And this morning?'

'After breakfast, which I prepared myself incidentally, I unlocked the front door and went up to the library. No-one else was in the house – or so I thought.'

'The front door was locked last night?'

'Yes. I locked it myself, at about ten o'clock. I knew Sir Robert was unlikely to return by that time. He sometimes comes back unexpectedly, but not as late as that. He trusted me to keep the place reasonably secure, although the key to the main entrance is usually kept in the lock as you can see for yourself.'

'Any other keys that you know of?'

'Dominic had his own keys to the chapel and his cottage. I didn't check if they were in his possession when I found him but I know he usually left his cottage unlocked during the day.'

'So the front door of this house was unlocked until about ten o'clock?'

'I guess so. But I don't think anyone came in. I certainly didn't hear anything.'

'You would have been in your room?'

'Or in the library.'

'And both are in the west wing?'

'Yes. I like to listen to music when I'm relaxing. I use headphones, so as not to disturb anyone else who might be in the house. I know Sir Robert likes silence.' He gave Hood a sideways glance. 'Between you and me he's not very musical.'

'But he wasn't here last night?'

'No. I wasn't anticipating seeing him, but as I said, he does sometimes return unexpectedly. This is his house; he comes and goes as he pleases.'

Hood hesitated and looked around the kitchen. The gothic window mentioned by Grantham took up the middle section of the shortest wall. The Aga, nestling in the chimney piece, seemed to be switched off, no doubt because of the summer heat. Apart from the pine table at which he was sitting, the only other furniture in the room was a large dresser stacked with expensive looking plates and dishes. An American style fridge/freezer and a stand-alone electric cooker were the only white goods. Racks of pans and utensils hung from the ceiling and a shelf on the far wall was weighed down with what Hood took to be more everyday crockery. A Belfast sink and a few cupboards were situated by a mullioned window which overlooked a small kitchen garden.

'Were you aware of the damaged window in the Long Room?' Hood asked Grantham.

'I didn't notice that until after I found Dominic. Sir Robert will be very upset about that. He'd only just had it put in. His family crest was picked out in the stained glass. I believe it cost quite a lot of money.'

Hood finished making his note. 'Thank-you, I shall want to speak to you again, shortly. You seem to be something of an expert on the subject of priest-holes so I shall probably need your assistance. Oh, one last thing. How long have you been staying here?'

'Just under three weeks. Is it important?'

'I don't suppose so. Thank you.'

'By the way, Chief Inspector, although I know a little about priest-holes, I really came here to research the family that used to live here. I wouldn't want to mislead you. I've never actually seen one before, other than in photographs.'

'I'll bear that in mind,' said Hood as he looked towards Swanson. 'Bring me the statements as soon as you're finished.'

'Yes sir.'

Hood excused himself and made for the front of the house. He walked past the portraits lining the walls of the main hallway but only glanced at them. He had more pressing matters on his mind. Guy Romney and his assistant were busy removing items from a Volvo estate as Hood emerged from the front door on to the gravelled drive. Romney looked up.

'Hello, Harry. What have you got for me this fine Thursday afternoon? By the way, you're a bit out of area aren't you. This is Maurice Kingston's patch, isn't it?'

The two men shook hands.

'A seventy-three-year-old priest. He's not easy to get at either. He was found dead in a priest-hole. It's about six feet below floor level. And I'm not out of area, as you put it, I'm being transferred to this division. I'm the new Detective Superintendent, at least I will be from next month.'

Romney smiled. 'So Maurice has handed in his papers at last, has he? Not before time. Well congratulations, Harry. You've been waiting long enough. I suppose the Hamilton case stymied your promotion for a bit? Very unfair of them I thought, you know, to take it out on you.'

'Who knows?'

It was obvious Hood did not want to go there and Romney realised he had touched a sore point. 'Right. I'll put on a forensic suit before I examine the deceased. You've kept everyone away I take it?'

'As far as I know, apart from the killer, the only person who's been in there since his death is the person who found him. That's another priest – an American Jesuit. They'd been investigating the priest-hole, apparently.'

'A Jesuit, eh? Well that's a first for me. A dead priest in a priest-hole found by a Jesuit. We'll have to watch our Ps and Qs!'

Hood smiled. 'I'll leave it with you then, Guy.'

'Before you dash off Harry, what time was the body found?'

'Just after nine-thirty this morning. And he's got a nasty wound towards the back of his head. On present information, he was last seen alive around seven last night. Detective Sergeant Knight is on her way here; she'll have all the details you need.'

'Seven last night?' Romney looked at his watch. 'Thanks, I'll bear that in mind. We'll speak later.'

A taxi drew up as the consultant forensic pathologist entered the house, followed at a respectful distance by his assistant. A tall, distinguished looking man in his middle sixties climbed from the rear of the vehicle. He was smartly dressed in a dark blue three-piece suit. He carried a bowler hat in his right hand and a small overnight bag in his left. Hood approached him somewhat gingerly. The gentleman looked him over in the way the upper classes do. Was he, perhaps, not expecting to meet a senior detective of mixed heritage? Hood was not exactly unused to such a reaction. He had experienced unfriendly attitudes during his police career on more occasions than he cared to remember, more frequently from colleagues than members of the public. Some who were jealous of his rise through the ranks put it down to political correctness, making light of his well-earned reputation for solving the most complex of crimes. His senior detective status had eased the situation but he could not help feeling a slight tinge of apprehension at meeting a member of the aristocracy, as he assumed the owner of Easton Grange to be. He was, it quickly became apparent, worrying unduly. The baronet smiled broadly and greeted him warmly.

'You're Chief Inspector Hood, I take it? I've been speaking with the Deputy Chief Constable as I was being driven from the station. She tells me she's put you in charge here. Terrible business this. Poor Father Dominic. No chance of his death being accidental I suppose?'

'No sir. It looks like he was murdered, I'm afraid.'

'Murdered! And in my home! God rest his soul. He was a good man. Oh, like many priests he could be difficult, but he was essentially a decent cove. I shall miss him dreadfully. He'd been here nearly two years you know. It was a great relief for me to have a priest here after my wife died. Shall we go inside?'

Sir Robert led Hood into the panelled hallway leaving the heavy oak front door wide open. Hood's attention was now taken up by the several portraits he had merely glanced at earlier. He rightly assumed they were paintings of the baronet's ancestors and members of his wider family. He looked at one or two in detail then glanced towards the gallery at the top of the intricately carved staircase where more portraits were displayed in their elaborate frames. There was an obvious space which presumably had once been occupied. He made a mental note as Sir Robert placed his bag and hat on a chair then introduced himself.

'Robert Southall,' he said, extending his hand to Hood, 'the present occupier of this ancient house. It's been in the family for nearly three hundred years. Shall we talk in my study?'

Hood smiled and shook hands with Sir Robert just as a red Mazda sports car drew up outside. Detective Sergeant Wendy Knight alighted and walked towards the entrance, pausing momentarily to take in the beautifully ornate facade of the Grange. Sir Robert turned and faced her as she hesitated at the threshold.

'Good afternoon, sir.' She remained standing at the open door until Sir Robert beckoned her to come inside. 'I'm Detective Sergeant Knight.' She smiled, then noticed Hood. 'Nice to see you again, sir. Swanson told me you were here. A bit out of your way, aren't you?'

'Better get used to it Wendy. I'm being transferred here permanently from next month. I'm replacing Superintendent Kingston.'

Knight almost purred in delight. 'They've promoted you at last. That *is* good news. I shall look forward to working with you again. I'd been informed you're taking over this investigation but your promotion wasn't mentioned.'

'It doesn't take effect until next Thursday,' said Hood.' Let's keep it confidential until then.'

'So you know each other?' observed Sir Robert.

'Oh yes,' replied Hood. 'We worked together in Leicester on the Campion kidnapping case and others.'

'I read about that,' said Sir Robert. 'All over the newspapers as I recall.'

'Yes, sir. It did receive wide publicity.'

'As will this case, I suspect.' Sir Robert furrowed his brow. 'Campion, that was the judge's name wasn't it? His wife and child were kidnapped in order to influence his handling of a trial?'

'Well remembered,' said Hood. 'Not that he succumbed, of course. He contacted me directly and we managed to locate his family before he made any decisions about the case in front of him. But it was a close run thing.'

The Chief Inspector was keen to move on and although he would have loved to chat over old times with Knight he gave his instructions briskly. 'Would you deal with Professor Romney, Wendy? He's just gone through to where the body was found. I take it you're familiar with the details?'

'Yes, sir. DC Swanson has brought me up to speed and I've made some other inquiries of my own. I've informed the deceased's monastery and I've spoken with the coroner. I'll fill you in later.'

Hood nodded his approval. 'Romney will be in the Long Room. You can't miss it if you follow the corridor through to the east wing. Sir Robert and I will join you shortly.' Hood glanced at Sir Robert. 'It would help if you could identify the body, sir; just a formality.'

Sir Robert sighed. 'Of course. Anything to assist.'

Hood turned to face Knight. 'And make sure Guy Romney doesn't leave before I have a word with him. I want to know his preliminary views as soon as possible.'

'Yes, sir,' smiled Knight. 'Feels like old times.'

She took her leave and went in search of the consultant pathologist. Sir Robert led Hood towards his study.

'So your family were not here during the time when the priest-hole must have been constructed?' observed Hood. 'I had a word with Father Grantham before you got here.'

Sir Robert shook his head. 'Oh, no. The Recusancy Acts were being repealed when we came to prominence, if you can call it prominence.' He laughed. 'A judge of the Common Pleas, two members of Parliament, a Lord Lieutenant and three High Sheriffs – not much in over two hundred and ninety years, when you think about it.' He paused. 'You see my title only goes back to the time of Charles the Second. Although I'm the thirteenth baronet, we're not really counted as one of the truly ancient Catholic families – too many heretics in the family tree.' He smiled. 'It was my great-great-grandfather who swam the Tiber, as it were, and converted to Roman Catholicism.' He chuckled. 'Caused quite a scandal at the time, I can tell you. His mother refused to speak to him for years, but she converted too, eventually, just before she died. We've been Catholic ever since.'

'Do you know who lived here when the priest-hole was constructed?' asked Hood

'We do now – thanks to Father Grantham's research. This estate was in the hands of another family altogether in penal days, the Powdrells, distant relations of ours in point of fact. Come into my study and I'll tell you all about it, or as much as I know. Father Grantham's the expert. You really need to talk to him at length.'

'I fully intend to,' said Hood.

CHAPTER THREE

Sir Robert Southall spent over thirty minutes taking Hood through the highlights – and lowlights – of his family tree and the history of Easton Grange. He was briefly interrupted when DC Swanson brought in the statements he had taken from the housekeeper and Father Grantham. Hood put them to one side, waiting for Sir Robert to pause for breath before he glanced at them. The chief inspector found the history of the estate quite fascinating. Sir Robert confirmed what Grantham had said. The house was originally an Augustinian priory of Canons Regular. It had been founded at the direction of King Henry II in the twelfth century, one of many such establishments endowed by the King as part of his penance for the murder of Archbishop Thomas Becket in 1170. Enlarged and rebuilt in the fifteenth century, it had avoided the dissolution of religious houses in 1536 because its annual income exceeded £200 and it fell outside the parliamentary legislation of that year, but as attitudes hardened, and the King's need for money increased, it was dissolved early in 1538 and the occupants expelled. The Prior had eventually been persuaded to accept the surrender of his monastery to Cromwell's Commissioners and was pensioned off together with a few of his senior brethren. The Deed of Surrender, while it was mentioned in Cromwell's surviving letters and papers, had subsequently been lost. The property was then sold and the major part of the cloisters demolished before it eventually came into the hands of the Yelverton family. They were already in occupation of the Manor house a mile or so away and the Grange, as the house became known, was leased to a London lawyer as his country home. After the lawyer's death, it was purchased by Anthony Powdrell in Mary Tudor's time. This branch of the Powdrell family, like the Southalls, originally

31

hailed from Somerset although they had several relatives living in the Midlands. One of the Powdrell brothers was a monk at the great Benedictine Abbey at Glastonbury. History did not relate what happened to him, but Anthony Powdrell and his immediate family remained true to the old faith throughout the reigns of Queen Elizabeth and James the First, although it cost them dearly, both in fines and social position. By the time Charles Stuart came to the throne, the Powdrells were almost destitute but hung on to the estate until William and Mary's reign when they were forced to sell. The house then quickly changed hands several times before Sir Robert's ancestor came into possession in Queen Anne's time.

'The clue is in the name,' explained the baronet. 'A property of this age called "the Grange" usually means that the house or estate was once the farm of monks and this house is no exception. Of course, our present chapel is not part of the original priory, you understand. It was erected by my grandfather as a place for local Catholics to worship and for us to bury our dead. Only part of the transept and the east end of the Priory church remain – the rest was demolished and quarried to extend this house or sold for building material elsewhere. You can still see the remains of the original chapel near the stable yard. I've had the original footprint marked out. The surviving cloister runs down in that direction.'

'And the present chapel?' asked Hood.

Sir Robert smiled. 'Our new chapel, as my grandfather called it, had almost fallen into disuse until Father Dominic arrived. Since my father's time we haven't been able to afford the stipend for a family chaplain and persuading a priest to come here every week proved very difficult so it was only used rarely and then mainly for family occasions. That's why I was so delighted when Father Dominic came along.'

'Father Grantham tells me that he was a monk, from Melford Abbey.'

Sir Robert nodded. 'Yes, he came here with the permission of his Abbot to try his hand as a sort of hermit – the eremitic life, you know. The then Abbot asked me if he could live here. I agreed and allowed him to reside in the Gatehouse, rent free. The only demand I made of him was that he celebrated Mass on Sundays and holy days. He was happy with that. In fact, he would try and say Mass more frequently. Not every day, but two or three times during the week, usually early in the morning at seven. I would go occasionally during the week and every Sunday, of course, unless I was away.'

'So, he was a bit of a recluse?'

The baronet shook his head. 'Reclusive, but not a recluse in the formal sense, no. He would speak to those who attended Mass on Sundays and I had several conversations with him, usually on religious topics. I invited him to dine with me on occasion, but he took me up on it only rarely. He spent most of his time alone, as was his wish.'

'Did he have much of a congregation?'

'Not during the week, no – on Sundays it was different. He was building up quite a following – thirty-five or forty attended – more on the first Sunday of the month when he said Mass largely in Latin.' He smiled broadly. 'The local vicar, Thomas Wide, who has four churches to look after, was rather jealous. Dominic was getting a larger congregation than he was, certainly in Easton Parva.' He paused. 'But I'm on good terms with Wide, despite our religious differences, and he met Dominic on a few occasions. Bit too 'happy clappy" for my taste. But he's a decent fellow and a good Christian; plays a useful hand of bridge too.' He dropped his voice to a whisper. 'I do believe Dominic was trying to convert him!' Sir Robert laughed before continuing. 'On major feast days we had all the trimmings, incense and the lessons sung by one of the ladies, Joan I think she's called, a retired professional singer. She lives in the next village. A couple of the boys from Easton Parva served for him most Sundays. I'm not sure if the Bishop approved of the Latin, but he never interfered. I suppose it will be back to Wellingborough for us now.'

'Won't Father Grantham stand in for him?'

Sir Robert shook his head. 'He's not usually here at week-ends. He goes to Oxford or visits friends. He has been to Mass a couple of times during the week when I have been present, but not at week-ends. He did a post-graduate degree at Oxford and he has friends and colleagues he likes to keep up with. Useful connection that – for his research. Our family archive has a number of gaps in it, so there is material at the Bodleian in Oxford which he finds useful. I suppose he might help out this Sunday if I ask him, but he's going back to the States the week after next. He only came over during his vacation.'

'How did Grantham contact you?'

'It was out of the blue really. He'd read about the Powdrells when he was doing some research in the archives of the English College in Rome.'

'The *Venerabili?*'

Sir Robert smiled. 'You've heard of it, Mr Hood?'

'Not until Father Grantham mentioned it earlier, no.'

Sir Robert continued. 'Well, there was a report in the *Catholic Herald* about our discovering the priest-hole, so it would have been picked up by the Jesuits – they don't miss much.'

He went on to explain that Grantham's superior had written to him the year before – well before the hide was discovered. It was Father Grantham's idea that Edmund Campion may have visited the Grange on his way south. It had never occurred to Sir Robert before Grantham mentioned it, but he conceded that the Jesuit had never suggested it as anything other than a theory.

'But it's not that far-fetched an idea when you think about it. It was known Campion travelled through this county. But he was captured later at Lyford Grange.' He paused and smiled. 'They make a great deal of it at Lyford, even these days. They have a Mass there every December, on Campion's feast day. But I suppose it was always going to be a bit of a long shot proving he came here.' He sighed. 'I thought it would be a selling point when I open part of the house to the public in the autumn if a connection could be established.' He shook his head and his voice dropped. 'But the place will become known for this latest atrocity now. Murder week-ends at the Grange! Not what I had in mind at all.' He let out another but deeper sigh. 'But who would kill a harmless old priest? It doesn't make sense. It really doesn't.'

Hood agreed. 'The very question we have to resolve – and believe me – we will.'

Sir Robert did not sound too optimistic as he replied. 'I hope you're right Chief Inspector, I really do, but I suspect whoever did this is long gone by now. And no doubt I'll have a visit from the Bishop to look forward to.' He chuckled to himself, then added almost jocularly, 'He has no idea what we were about here – though I'm sure he'd have been the first to congratulate me had we got anywhere with our research and proved that Campion had stayed at Easton Grange.' That mischievous twinkle reappeared in his eyes. 'Lyford Grange is not in his diocese!'

It was Hood's turn to express scepticism, echoing the comment he had earlier made to Grantham. 'But how can such a thing be proved one way or the other, after all this time?'

'We were hoping against hope that we might find some evidence during the excavation of the priest-hole. You see, priests in that period travelled in disguise. Very few outside their immediate circle would have known they were priests. Campion went about as a jewel merchant and Father John Gerard – one of the few men ever to escape from the Tower of London – he adopted the style of a country gentleman and card player. He was, it seems, a very successful gambler. His luck continued away from the card table too. He survived, unlike poor Campion.' He paused and leant towards Hood. 'They rarely carried vestments or sacred vessels with them – much too risky. There were exceptions, of course. There's a priest's chest kept at Stonyhurst with a hidden compartment in which liturgical items could be secreted, but it's regarded as almost unique. If a priest were caught in such circumstances he would undoubtedly have been hanged as a traitor. So they were usually provided for them by the households where they stayed. Our priest-hole must have been filled in centuries ago. There's a remote possibility that something might be found. The fact that it's undoubtedly sixteenth century confirms that priests did visit here during penal times.'

Hood begged to differ as to what could amount to evidence. 'But as you say, sir. It's a very long shot indeed, isn't it? To prove a connection with a particular priest, even if he is a canonised saint.'

Sir Robert's enthusiasm was only slightly diminished as he explained further the nature of Grantham's research. He assured Hood that the Jesuit had not attempted to build up his hopes but had researched the whole county in great detail. He'd worked out the probable maximum distances that a man on horseback or on foot could have travelled in those days and considered the various known establishments where priests could stay in comparative safety.

'Travellers were regarded with real suspicion in the time of the first Elizabeth, Mr Hood, so great care had to be taken and progress could be very slow. There's no priest-hole at the Manor, which is hardly surprising. The Yelvertons were Protestant through and through; they'd have turned in anyone they even suspected of being a Jesuit. Father Grantham reckons Campion and his companions may well have had to stay here if they travelled from the north or from Norfolk down into Oxfordshire. There wasn't another safe lodging in the immediate area. Campion would not have risked staying with the Vaux family at Harrowden, not according to Grantham. That house was watched all the time because of its earlier association with him. The third Baron Vaux was also a notorious recusant and suffered imprisonment himself.'

'But it's very speculative, isn't it? Without some actual evidence.'

Sir Robert agreed. 'We can but hope. The Powdrells remained loyal to the old faith well into the eighteenth century – even after they left this place. We know the pursuivants searched this house on several occasions – the records still exist, but no priest was ever captured. And if Campion called here, he'd have been hidden in our priest-hole, along with any evidence that would have confirmed his true vocation.'

'But nothing has been found to prove any of this?'

Sir Robert lowered his head. 'No, not so far. And we would never be in a position to prove beyond doubt that he visited here. Only that it was a probability, so Lyford Grange will always have the advantage. There's no doubt at all Campion was there, given that's where he was captured.' He paused and looked at Hood, his forehead deeply furrowed. 'It has crossed my mind that if Father Dominic really was murdered, he might have been because he'd found something important or valuable. Or would that be mere speculation? And what could it possibly have been to have prompted his killing?'

A similar thought had already occurred to Hood. He was hoping against hope that something would be found during the examination of the Gatehouse. 'What you say is certainly worth considering. Is there anything of value missing?'

Sir Robert shook his head. 'Not that I know of. There are only two really valuable items in the entire house. The painting of the eighth baronet – it's by Joshua Reynolds and that's away in London being cleaned and restored. It was painted some years after the family acquired this estate and is worth a considerable amount of money, although I'm loath to sell it. Then there's the portrait of Sir Christopher Yelverton in the Long Room where Father Dominic was found. As far as I'm aware, it hasn't been touched. That was purchased by my grandfather, late in Queen Victoria's reign.' He smiled and continued with a modicum of pride. 'Do you know, he lived until he was ninety-seven? That's him in the hallway, the large portrait just before the main staircase.'

Hood recollected the painting. It was one of the two he'd studied in a little detail just as Sir Robert was arriving. 'That is a great age. But what about the other paintings? I couldn't help noticing there's a large number of them in the house. And your grandfather's portrait seems to my untutored eye to be very accomplished.'

Sir Robert smiled. 'You have a good eye, Mr. Hood. I'm very fond of that picture myself. But the others of my ancestors and family members? All by jobbing artists, I'm afraid – worth a few thousand at the most. There'd be no market for them, I assure you.' He leant forward again and smiled. 'My grandfather had them all checked out when he inherited. He was hoping to find a Gainsborough. Unfortunately, he didn't. And the artist who painted him is all but forgotten now.'

'And the Reynolds definitely isn't here at present?'

'No. As I said, it's been at the restorers for the last two months.'

'And it hung in the gallery at the top of the staircase?'

'Yes. You noticed the vacant space?'

Hood nodded. 'And you can't think of anything else that might have attracted a thief?'

'There's our collection of chalices and ciboria which are under lock and key in the sacristy safe and the monstrance my father retrieved from the Cathedral in Northampton. That would fetch a pretty penny if it were auctioned. It was designed by Augustus Welby Pugin and made by a well-known Victorian silversmith in Birmingham. My great-grandfather commissioned it to commemorate his marriage and loaned it to the Cathedral some years after the hierarchy was re-established, but it was never used much after Vatican Two. Kept in a box in the cathedral safe. My father got it back with a view to putting it on display with our other liturgical objects.'

'And it's still in your safe now?'

'Yes. It should be. It's insured for ten thousand pounds. It's worth far more than any of the chalices.'

'They're not as valuable?'

'Alas, no. One or two are probably worth a thousand or two. My grandfather and father both collected them, but there's nothing older than early eighteenth century. They hoped to find a pre-reformation chalice, but never did. My father never got round to displaying them. He changed his mind about opening the house to the public, so they've languished in the sacristy safe for years.'

'And the key?'

'I have the only one.' He opened the top drawer of his desk and produced a key. 'I suppose we should check there's nothing missing? I have a list of what should be there in my insurance file.'

'This is definitely the only key?

'Yes. Father Dominic didn't need to go into the safe for anything. He had his own chalice which he kept in a cupboard in the sacristy. It wasn't very valuable. I showed him the contents of the safe once, but he never used any of the items in there, not to my knowledge anyway.'

'And your key is always kept in your desk drawer?'

'Yes. Not very secure, when you come to think about it.'

'Is the desk usually unlocked?'

'I must confess that it is. *Mea culpa.*'

'We'll check the items in the safe,' said Hood. 'Do you know where Father Dominic kept his keys? I don't know, yet, if he had any keys with him when he was found.'

'He certainly had several keys. The keys to his cottage, which he hardly ever locked and a key for the chapel. I think he kept them together on the same key ring which I gave him when he first arrived. He may have had other keys of his own, but I'm not sure about that. He always kept the door locked that leads from the Long Room into the chapel. If his keys were not with him, they would be in his cottage, unless they were stolen, of course.'

'Did he usually use the door in the Long Room to access the chapel?'

'Always, if he were in the house. Not that he was a regular visitor here. He would leave the main chapel door unlocked until dusk in the summer.'

'Anything else that might have attracted a thief?'

'No…unless…' He laughed. 'There's the old story of the so-called Powdrell chalice. But nobody takes that seriously these days.' Sir Robert's tone suggested he was not as sceptical as his words implied.

'The Powdrell chalice?' queried Hood.

'Yes. Although there are some who question its very existence. It was the Powdrell family that brought about my connection with Father Grantham, you see. We hadn't discovered the priest-hole when his superior first got in touch. It was the Powdrells he was researching. If you go back far enough, we have a connection with them, apart from this estate. My great-great grandmother was a Powdrell and a Catholic. Both our families originate from Somerset so I suppose they might have known each other as near-neighbours before the Southall's acquired this estate. I also suspect she was instrumental in my great-great-grandfather converting.'

38

'Did Father Grantham know about the story of the chalice?'

'Oh, yes. It was he who first mentioned it to me. But by the time he got here, it was the priest-hole that took his interest. I deliberately waited until he arrived before starting the excavation. I didn't want to risk damaging anything that might be hidden in there. My gardener gave him a hand with the heavy work.'

'What do you know about this so-called Powdrell chalice?'

'Well, it's a long story and I don't want to detain you unduly, but I suppose it must have belonged originally to the priory. What happened to it is lost in the mists of time. There are references to a chalice in the Powdrell records but it has never been found.'

'Is it known what it looked like?'

'A good question, but not one that is easily answered. There is a description of a chalice in a return made by the Prior to Cromwell's commissioners just before the dissolution, but no evidence that it was seized by them. Thomas Cromwell made very careful records of everything although a significant proportion was destroyed by his retainers when he fell from power.'

Sir Robert was now in his element. He carefully explained everything he knew about Cromwell's attempt to seize the Priory's treasures before his fall from grace and execution in 1540. Apparently, in those days when a great magnate was made subject to attainder, as happened with Cromwell, the King's officers were quickly on the scene to list and seize his property. And Cromwell, the baronet pointed out, had helped himself to several religious houses after they were surrendered or supressed. He had built up a large portfolio, despite the estates he granted to King Henry shortly before his fall in a desperate attempt to preserve his position. Whatever one made of him, he certainly generated immense loyalty in those who served him. Quite a number of documents and other records were destroyed before the King's men could sequester them. In Sir Robert's opinion, some of those documents could well have related to the chalice. But he pointed out that it was believed that the Powdrells still had a chalice in their possession during Queen Mary's reign because a chalice was mentioned in a letter sent by Anthony Powdrell to Abbot Feckenham of Westminster, which still exists and can still be seen in the British Library. Sir Robert continued, his enthusiasm undiminished.

'Queen Mary re-established Westminster as a Benedictine monastery – not that it survived her. Whether it's a reference to the chalice mentioned in the return to Cromwell simply isn't clear. It was not unknown, of course, for the monks to hide their treasures from the commissioners – more than one lost his life for doing precisely that – and it may have been found by the Powdrells when they took possession of the property. Of course, they would have kept its existence to themselves during the subsequent persecution.'

'Or perhaps they sold it,' suggested Hood. Intrigued as he was by Sir Robert's account, he was all for keeping his feet firmly on the ground. 'It sounds like they were in need of money after they were dispossessed. Selling the chalice might have been resisted but eventually they may well have been left with no alternative.'

Sir Robert did not dismiss such a possibility out of hand. 'That could well be the case. But if the chalice had been used by priests during Queen Elizabeth's time to celebrate Mass here, they would have had to have been pretty desperate before they parted with it. It would have been of huge importance to them and deeply venerated.' Sir Robert looked up and smiled. 'They took such things much more seriously than we do today, Mr. Hood. And if they did sell it, there's no record of what happened to it. There are records of the sale of other items of their property, but no mention of a chalice. I should add that this nearly all comes from Father Grantham's research.'

'Would it be valuable?'

Sir Robert smiled again. 'A pre-reformation chalice? It would depend in part on its make-up. The Powdrell chalice was thought to have been fashioned mainly from gold, although I suppose it might have been parcel-gilt. That was not uncommon in those days. And there are a number of other pre-reformation chalices still in existence, though only a few of them are in Catholic hands. I believe Ampleforth has a couple and there is the well-known one kept at their parish in Leyland in Lancashire, a silver one. But they're very unlikely to come on the market, so very difficult to value. Recusant silver, they're sometimes called in antiquarian circles. They would certainly be worth more than the silver content, but hardly worth killing for.'

Hood now engaged in some speculation himself. 'But if the Powdrell chalice remained here during the Elizabethan persecution it might have been used by Edmund Campion, always assuming he came here. That would make it very valuable, wouldn't it?'

Sir Robert said nothing for several seconds. That was a possibility which had clearly occurred to him. He shook his head slowly and spoke in a hushed tone looking wistfully at the chief inspector. 'No, not valuable, Mr. Hood – priceless!'

Sir Robert's words hung in the air until Hood broke the silence. 'And if it were found, who would it belong to?'

Sir Robert hesitated as he pondered the question. 'I'm not sure of the precise legal position, but if it had been hidden here, I suppose it would pass with the property. Possession would certainly be nine-tenths of the law in those circumstances, I should imagine, especially if it had been hidden within the fabric of the building, always assuming, of course, it didn't qualify as treasure trove.'

'So you might well own it?'

'I suppose I might, especially as my ancestors include members of the Powdrell family. And if it were hidden here it would have been secreted simply to protect it from those who would otherwise have appropriated it.'

Hood smiled. 'I suppose the lawyers would have the final say?'

'I suppose they would, but they'd have a fight on their hands I can tell you. But that problem won't arise unless we find it. And if it were found, I could never sell it. That would be sacrilege.' He laughed. 'We're not a particularly well-endowed family, Chief Inspector, and this place is very expensive to run, but I could never solve my financial difficulties by disposing of such a treasure. If it were discovered and displayed here it would be quite a draw – I'd have more visitors than I could manage.' He sighed deeply. 'Anyway, the chances of finding such a treasure now must be very remote. I've never been a gambling man and I'm probably too long in the tooth to start to engage in such speculation now.'

Hood found the story of the chalice quite fascinating. There was a possibility the search for such a valuable artifact could be connected with Father Dominic's murder. Sir Robert was clearly hoping that something of real historical significance might have been hidden in the priest-hole, but, as a detective, Hood had to remain pragmatic and down to earth. He probed further with his questions as he pondered the practicalities. 'If the Powdrells had discovered a chalice, wouldn't they have taken it with them when they left here?'

Sir Robert was loath to consider such a possibility but could hardly discount it. 'I suppose that's the most likely scenario. But if the monks had concealed it so well that it evaded Cromwell's commissioners, the Powdrells may well have decided it was wise to leave it hidden here where the monks had originally secreted it.' He smiled. 'Father Grantham believes there's an outside chance something of interest might have been hidden somewhere in the house, if not in the priest-hole, but I assure you I have no intention of knocking down any walls or excavating anywhere else in the hope of finding something that may not even exist.'

'And apart from the damage to the window in the Long Room, there's no evidence of anything else being damaged or interfered with?'

'Not that I'm aware of, no. Nothing has been found in the priest-hole either, not so far. Father Grantham is not as enthusiastic as he once was but I haven't altogether abandoned hope.'

Hood nodded. 'It might have been the story of the chalice that attracted someone here and led to the attack on Father Dominic. You're sure that neither he nor Grantham had found anything?'

'Nothing has been said to me about finding anything, Mr Hood. And I'm sure it would have been had something been discovered.'

'It's possible that Father Dominic interrupted a potential thief. He could have heard the window in the Long Room being smashed and gone to investigate; then been attacked.'

'I suppose so. But who would kill a priest in such circumstances? And why?'

'I don't know, sir.' He paused. 'We may well have to investigate how well known the story of this chalice is.'

'Whoever is responsible, I hope you catch him and quickly.'

Hood turned to a different subject. 'And you are still planning to open the house – or part of it – to the public?'

'Indeed, I am. I have already expanded the car park in front of the present chapel and I may have to enlarge it further. My eldest son describes this place as a money pit. And he will inherit it after me. What he will do with it I dread to think. The entail ended with my father, so there is nothing I can do to control its destiny after I am gone.' He sighed. 'I've had to work hard for my living all my life – not that I'm complaining you understand. Until recently, I'd always been against opening the house to the paying public, like my father, but the discovery of the priest-hole – and the influence of my son and heir – has caused me to change my mind.'

'You have three sons I believe?'

'Yes. Michael is the eldest. He's a lawyer working in Brussels for the EU. He's very well established, thank God, but still unmarried. I have heard rumours of a French girl-friend but, if she exists, I am yet to meet her. Maxim, my youngest – he's named after Maximilien Kolbe – my late wife's mother was Polish. He's still at Oxford – at Merton, my old college. Then there's Philip…' Sir Robert's voice weakened. 'Do you have children, Mr Hood?'

'Yes, sir. Three – two sons and a daughter.'

Sir Robert smiled. 'I would have liked to have had a daughter, but it was not to be.' He paused. 'But Philip is quite a worry. Never could apply himself to anything, if you know what I mean? Sent down from Oxford – for idleness. I stopped his allowance earlier this year in the hope it would prompt him to do something useful with his life, but I haven't seen him since. I have no idea where he is or what he's up to.'

A pained expression clouded Sir Robert's features as he turned and gazed out of the study window. It was apparent to Hood that the baronet had grave doubts as to whether he had done the right thing, cutting his son off. But he had his reasons, or so it seemed. Philip, he explained, had got himself involved with the drugs scene when at Oxford and the death of his mother had not helped their relationship. Philip was very fond of his mother and missed her dreadfully. His father had supported him as best he could when she died and paid for him to go into rehab but Philip had quickly returned to his old ways. Their relationship had never recovered.

'When was Philip last here?' asked the chief inspector.

Sir Robert adopted a confessional tone. 'It must be about four or five months ago, I suppose. We parted in somewhat bitter circumstances. He was in contact with Michael a couple of months later, touching him for a loan I believe. None of us has had contact with him since, although I have heard it suggested that he's been seen in the village more than once. If that is right, he hasn't been here to this house, not as far as I am aware.'

'Forgive me, but could I ask if Michael let him have anything?'

'Yes, I understand he did. Three hundred and fifty pounds. He wired it to his account.'

'That wouldn't last long these days.'

'No. But to be fair to Michael, he was concerned he would spend it on drugs if he gave him anymore. That's the main reason I stopped his allowance. I wasn't prepared to supplement his drug addiction from my limited funds.'

Hood changed the subject. 'Tell me about your housekeeper, Mrs. Morton.'

Sir Robert smiled. 'Martha? What's to tell? She's been with me about six or seven months now, since the beginning of this year.'

He went on to explain that he'd had a full-time housekeeper until she retired the year before. Now, as it was just him living at the Grange most of the time, he didn't think he could justify replacing her with a full-time housekeeper. Martha was restricted to twenty-seven hours a week. She was fairly flexible as to when she came in and took her days off usually when he was in London or at week-ends. Otherwise, Sir Robert managed for himself. It had worked quite well so far.

'How did you find her?' asked Hood.

Sir Robert was taken aback. 'Good God, you don't think she had anything to do with this, do you?'

'I shall be checking everyone, Sir Robert, including you.'

The baronet smiled. 'Well, I've been in London for the last two days. I stayed at my club in Pall Mall – the Reform. I have the proof in my bag, if you want to see it.'

'Not at the moment sir, later, perhaps. You were telling me about Mrs. Morton.'

'She was advertising her availability in *The Lady* magazine. I got in touch and interviewed her. She'd had a bit of a hard time. Her husband, who sounded like a brute, had abandoned her. She'd been left in dire circumstances. Fortunately, there were no children involved.' He paused and smiled. 'She's also a very good cook.'

'She's not divorced though?' Hood glanced at the short witness statement that Swanson had taken from her.

'Is she not? I never enquired. One doesn't these days. But she's a decent woman and I've no complaints.'

'And she doesn't live in?'

Sir Robert chuckled. 'No, she doesn't. She's a very good-looking woman, Chief Inspector, as I'm sure you've noticed. Despite my age, I didn't want to encourage gossip in the village. She lives in an estate cottage. It's only a few minutes' walk away– once you've negotiated the drive or you can cut through the picket gate at the back of the old chapel ruins. That's slightly quicker.'

Hood quickly calculated that only Grantham should have been in the house at the time Father Dominic must have been killed. Sir Robert reacted with astonishment when the chief inspector made this observation.

'I suppose so, but he can't have been involved, surely? He's a priest. I can't see one priest murdering another.'

'Unlikely, but every possibility will have to be considered. Could I see the letter of introduction you received?'

'Of course.'

Sir Robert opened his desk drawer, rummaged around for a few moments then produced a letter typed on official university headed note paper. Hood read it before handing it back, noting the date. It was obviously written by an educated person.

'I see it's dated over eighteen months ago.'

'Yes. Grantham couldn't get here last summer. Had a number of other matters to deal with, of a personal nature I believe.'

'And you're sure he is who he says he is?'

Sir Robert raised his eyebrows. 'It has never crossed my mind he was anyone else. I was at Stonyhurst, Mr. Hood – in the old days. I think I can recognise a Jesuit when I see one.'

CHAPTER FOUR

Professor Romney climbed awkwardly out of the priest-hole and glanced at Detective Sergeant Knight and two members of the waiting SOCO team as he removed his face mask.

'He's all yours now. You can get a couple of your big strong boys to lift him out of there, after my assistant has taken some more photographs. Not that I suspect he weighs very much. He'll have to be taken to the hospital so I can carry out a full *post-mortem* examination. But I'll give him another look over before he's taken away. It was very cramped and musty down there. One curiosity; there's something in his left hand. Very tightly gripped, too. When he's out of there, we'll take a look.'

'Have you been able to form any opinion as to the cause of death, sir?' asked Knight. 'I'm sure the DCI will want to know what you think as soon as possible.'

Romney wiped his forehead. 'I can't give a definitive view until I get him on the slab, but the injury to the back of his head looks the most likely explanation. He was undoubtedly struck with significant force. I would suggest whoever did it intended to finish the job. It wasn't just to render him unconscious.'

'A single blow?'

Romney frowned. 'Possibly, but unlikely. There's quite a bit of external damage but I won't be able to assess the internal injuries until I've opened him up.'

'So it's not simply a fall?'

Romney shook his head. 'No. I think that's pretty clear. There isn't enough space for him to have struck his head with sufficient force in a fall, even if he collapsed into there. And the position of the major wound tells against it being accidental. No, that head injury is undoubtedly the result of blunt trauma, probably inflicted with a heavy fairly flat object… like a spade. I don't see one about the place though.'

Knight looked about her. She noticed the pile of earth and debris close by, but no sign of a spade or other implement. 'There must be a spade somewhere. One must have been used to excavate all this.' She pointed to the heap of debris, lying on a tarpaulin, presumably to protect the floor.

'Perhaps whoever did this took it away with him?' suggested Romney.

Knight nodded. 'We'll have to mount a search and that'll take time given the size of this place. Any idea as to time of death?'

The forensic pathologist shook his head and smiled. 'I'm always asked that, you know. It's the influence of television programmes I suppose. Unlike fictional pathologists, I can't give you a precise answer, so I'll give you my usual response.' He grinned broadly. 'He died at some point between the time he was last seen alive and when he was found – dead!' He chuckled to himself. 'That should give you a sufficient window of opportunity to pull in no end of suspects.'

The detective sergeant sighed. She'd heard Romney give a similar reply before. 'You can't give us anything more specific to go on?' she pleaded.

'Well rigour is fairly well established; I think it's even passing, so he's been dead for several hours –that's the best I can do for you at the moment. He was found at about half past nine this morning, wasn't he?'

'Yes, sir, about then.'

'And last seen alive around seven o'clock last night?'

'So I understand.'

He looked at his watch. 'And it's nearly half past two now.'

'So he died sometime…before midnight, but that's very approximate; could have been earlier. I'm sorry I can't be more helpful. It's also quite cold down there. I've taken his body temperature but that's not going to help if he's been there for any length of time.'

'Could it have been as early as yesterday evening?'

Romney sighed. He plainly did not want to be pressed for an answer. He nodded. 'Possibly. If he were seen alive just before seven, it couldn't have been before then, could it?'

He smiled again. There was more than a hint of sarcasm in his response. Knight frowned as she realised she wouldn't get anything more definite. She decided to pursue a different tack. 'Was he killed in the hide or dumped after he was assaulted?'

'Too early to say. Not much blood about if he were struck while he was down there and he would have bled freely from his injuries. And I doubt if he died immediately. When I get him to the morgue and opened up, there may be some clues that will answer that question.'

'He wouldn't have died as soon as he was struck?'

Romney shook his head. 'Unlikely. He could even have regained consciousness – despite the mess someone has made of him. It does happen with head injuries, but I'll be able to answer that when we have the brain examined. I'll probably send samples to Professor Alan Durrell at King's College, London. He's a consultant neuro-pathologist. He's usually very helpful in cases like this.'

Romney stood back as the priest's body was lifted from the priest-hole by two police officers and laid gently on to a stretcher. Knight noticed the deceased's left hand appeared to be closed. The pathologist bent over the body and had some difficulty releasing what appeared to be an oval shaped wax object, about two and three-quarters inches in length and just over an inch and a half wide. He stood up and scrutinised it.

'Extraordinary. Any idea what this is, detective sergeant?'

He handed the object to Knight who examined it closely. 'No idea. It seems to have something engraved on it. Perhaps it's some sort of religious keepsake, you know, like a St Christopher?'

After the object had been photographed, she took a plastic exhibit bag from her pocket and placed the item into it. Romney answered her. 'Perhaps? But why was it in his hand? And why didn't his assailant remove it?'

Knight speculated. 'Because he didn't know it was there?'

'Exactly. Now, the fact that it was in his hand suggests that whatever it is might have been discovered shortly before he was assaulted. If it was something he already had with him, it would have been in his pocket – I assume there's a pocket in his habit? And if there isn't, he was wearing trousers underneath. You wouldn't have something as delicate as that in your hand while doing what he was doing, now would you?'

'We'll look into that. But as you observed, he's in his habit. He wouldn't have been working in the priest-hole in his habit, would he?'

48

The pathologist paused then nodded. 'Good point. But perhaps he wasn't working in there? Perhaps he was simply retrieving something he'd found earlier? Something he didn't want anyone else to know about.' He smiled in a knowing way.

Knight grunted her reply. 'That's a possibility, I suppose, but it would help if we knew what it was.'

'Well, you're the detective...'

'Nothing else down there?'

'There was a trowel under the body and one of those little brushes archaeologists use – I've left them there – but the trowel couldn't have caused the injury – far too light.'

Knight held the wax object – still in the exhibit bag – up to the light.

'It's almost transparent and someone has made an attempt to clean it. See, there are bits of earth or debris still embedded in it, but it's definitely been wiped. I'll show it to the DCI. He's with Sir Robert at the moment. He'll want a word before you go, if that's all right, sir.'

'Where is he?'

'In Sir Robert's study. But he was going to ask Sir Robert to identify the body. That may as well be done before he's taken away.'

Knight turned to the officers who had brought the body up from the hide.

'Make sure Sir Robert sees him before he's removed to the morgue.'

She then addressed the consultant pathologist. 'I take it it's OK for SOCO to check out the priest-hole now?'

'Be my guest. There's nothing down there that's going to help with establishing the cause of death, not pathologically speaking anyway.'

CHAPTER FIVE

'You think it might be important, sir? It's not just a religious keepsake?'

Hood examined the unusual item removed from the dead priest's hand which DS Knight had handed to him as they walked towards the Gatehouse. He shook his head before returning the exhibit bag to the detective sergeant. 'I don't know, Wendy. I've never seen anything like it before. But if Guy Romney is right and Father Dominic could have recovered consciousness, if only for a minute or so, he might have taken it from his pocket to comfort himself, especially if he thought he was dying. So it may be completely irrelevant to the inquiry.'

'You don't think he found it in the priest-hole then?'

'That remains a possibility, but I can't see how it could have survived for centuries in all that in-fill, not without sustaining some damage. It looks quite fragile. Hopefully, someone will be able to age it, once we find out what it is.'

'You think it may not have been in Father Dominic's hand at the time he was attacked?'

'Precisely. We simply can't assume that at the moment. And, don't forget, Wendy, he was wearing his habit; so he probably wasn't working in the priest– hole when he was attacked.'

'Yes sir, I appreciate that.' She repeated what Guy Romney had said. 'But suppose he was collecting something that he had found earlier. He might not have bothered changing simply to retrieve it.'

Hood frowned. 'It's all very speculative. We should keep an open mind for the moment. The American priest would surely have known if Father Dominic had found something of interest. After all, they were working together most of yesterday.'

'But not all the time, sir. Grantham was in the library for about an hour after lunch. Father Dominic must have been alone in the Long Room during that time.'

'True, but they were in each other's company afterwards.'

'Perhaps Father Dominic didn't want him to know that he'd found something?'

Hood stopped and smiled. 'Now that really is highly speculative, Wendy. If they were working together they were surely bound to share anything they discovered?'

Knight was not convinced. But she did not pursue the matter further. She had not yet met the Jesuit but she had certainly not excluded him as a suspect. He was alone in the house when Father Dominic had died, or so it seemed. But he had told the DCI that he had neither heard nor seen anything suspicious. She doubted if his being in the west wing was a sufficiently credible explanation. And the wax object was very hard and seemed to her to be pretty robust, not as fragile as Hood appeared to think. But if Father Dominic had found it in the priest-hole, perhaps on an earlier occasion, why did his assailant not remove it from his hand? Until they established what it was and whether it had any intrinsic value it would not be sensible to form a definite conclusion.

Sir Robert identified the body of Father Dominic before it was removed to the hospital in Northampton where Professor Romney would carry out the *post-mortem* examination. The pathologist had promised to inform Hood of his considered findings in writing by the following Monday although both he and Knight were invited to attend the actual examination later that evening. Hood had grimaced and deferred to Knight. He tasked her to attend and obtain the pathologist's interim oral report on his behalf. Like the chief inspector, she had no desire to witness the more intimate aspects of what she well knew would be an intrusive medical procedure, but Hood explained he had other urgent matters to deal with. In truth, he had never regarded his presence at *post-mortem* examinations as necessary or desirable. All would be set out in the official report and he trusted the detective sergeant would be able to explain any unusual features which might arise before the typed report arrived.

The two detectives found the Gatehouse undisturbed save for the activities of SOCO who were still examining the outside of the cottage with scrupulous care. There was no sign of an untidy search or forced entry. The priest's keys were hanging on the hook just behind the kitchen door. They had obviously not been taken by the killer. Hood placed them in a transparent exhibit bag. There were four keys; a Yale, which probably operated the external door lock to the cottage and three others; one was a typical key for a mortice lock, large, and fairly antiquated in appearance, another a smaller mortice key and the fourth, tiny and more elaborate in design, the sort of key Hood associated with a trunk or storage chest. Once they had been tested for fingerprints and DNA he would ascertain their various functions. A shake of the head from one of the SOCO officers indicated that they had not discovered any blood or anything indicating that a struggle had taken place within the cottage.

Father Dominic had seemingly lived very simply. There was nothing of any material value anywhere in the tiny cottage. A Bible and a few religious books, a biography of G K Chesterton, a book of poetry and a statue of the Virgin Mary seemed his only possessions. The small fridge in the kitchen was almost empty. A rather ancient looking piece of cheese, a couple of tomatoes, three eggs and a tub of over-ripe strawberries were all it contained. A few tins of soup and some vegetables were stacked in the adjoining pantry. The remains of a small brown loaf stood on the sideboard. *Father Dominic must have had a very poor appetite.*

Hood climbed the little staircase and opened the door which led into the cramped bedroom. The bed seemed to have been slept in, but even that could not be regarded as a certainty. According to the housekeeper's statement, Dominic always made his bed shortly after awaking. She was aware of the priest's daily routine, although he had always refused her offer to look after the cottage for him and do his housework. The only concession he made was to permit her to take charge of his laundry requirements and to provide him with the occasional loaf of bread or cake if she had been baking. Her repeated offers to do more for him were always politely but firmly declined.

Hood noticed a pair of slippers peeping out from under the bed. *So perhaps the priest had not returned to the Gatehouse after supper with Grantham?* Hood recollected Father Dominic was wearing sandals when his body was found. The clothes he must have been wearing while working in the hide had already been uplifted for transmission to the forensic science laboratory for detailed examination along with his pair of stout walking boots. SOCO would take soil samples from the excavation itself in due course for comparison purposes. Hood took it as read that the traces of soil he was told were visible on the soles of the boots would match the samples taken from the excavation. The sandals along with his blood-stained habit would be sent directly from the morgue to the laboratory.

Hood peered inside the wardrobe. Two pairs of black trousers and a linen jacket were hanging there alongside a couple of white shirts and a heavy– looking knitted cardigan. On the shelf above, a single, slightly grubby, clerical collar and a back collar stud sat next to a woolly scarf. A black coat and a jacket hung on a hook behind the inside of the door. On the bedside table he noticed a well-thumbed copy of Thomas a Kempis' *Imitation of Christ*. Hood smiled and recalled a quotation he had learnt as a youth from this fourteenth century monk. *"Who has a harder fight than he who is striving to overcome himself?"*

He opened the lower drawer. There were several items of clean underwear and two further shirts but nothing of particular interest. A trunk at the bottom of the bed was unlocked. Hood opened it. It was empty. After looking around the rest of the cottage, he and Knight walked back towards the Grange. They did not speak but Hood could not conceal his disappointment that nothing of relevance had been found in the Gatehouse. This really was going to be a difficult investigation. He couldn't even be sure where Father Dominic had been assaulted let alone who had caused his death. He was still deep in thought when Sir Robert came out of the front door of the Grange to greet them. He seemed almost excited and pointed towards the five or six journalists hanging about the entrance gates at the bottom of the drive. A uniformed police officer was keeping them in some sort of order. None was allowed to approach the house or grounds.

'Mr Hood. If you wish to set up some sort of incident room here, could I suggest that you take over the Long Room itself, or, if you prefer, the Gatehouse? I can let you have a key, unless you have found Father Dominic's?'

'We have his keys, but they'll need to be examined by the scientists. An additional key would be useful. Thank you, Sir Robert.'

'I'll see to it. Once your scenes of crime people have finished in the Long Room – and I believe they're nearly through – I can let you have the use of it for as long as you wish. It will certainly be more convenient than my study. I assume you can put phone lines in and all the necessary technical equipment you'll require?'

'That's very kind of you, sir. But I doubt if that will be necessary – as long as we retain access to the Long Room and Father Dominic's cottage as and when required. The Gatehouse will be all we'll need for speaking to potential witnesses. I shall be assembling a specialist team later to go through the in-fill that has been removed from the excavation. And when SOCO have finished, I shall want to examine the priest-hole myself. It may mean removing some of the panelling inside the hide. I hope that's all right with you?'

Sir Robert did not look at all keen. 'I must confess I was hoping that would not be necessary, but in the circumstances I don't suppose I can object.'

'Not really, sir, no. We'll be very careful and do as little damage as possible. We also need to mount a search for a spade or similar implement that may have been used as the murder weapon. Could someone show me where you keep your gardening equipment? The offender may have used one of your tools to attack Father Dominic.'

Sir Robert winced. 'That's a possibility, I suppose. Mr Hitchens only comes in twice a week save for when he was assisting Father Grantham in his own time. He has equipment of his own which he brings with him, but I have some tools stored in the old stables. Mr Hitchens should be here tomorrow to make up for yesterday when he took the day off, but I can show you where everything is kept, if you'll follow me.'

Hood did not show the item concealed in the priest's left hand to Sir Robert. He determined to seek assistance from the American priest first. He assumed, wrongly as it turned out, that Grantham would have greater knowledge of the object than the baronet. As Hood and Knight turned about ready to follow Sir Robert around the side of the chapel towards the rear of the house, the senior scenes of crime officer came out of the front door and called to Hood. The chief inspector waved Wendy Knight and Sir Robert onwards then walked over to his colleague.

'Anything to report, Nigel?' he asked.

'Nothing out of the ordinary, Harry,' came the reply. 'There's a bit of blood but not as much as I would have expected if he'd been killed in or around the priest-hole. The distribution – such as it is – suggests to me he was attacked somewhere else and the body simply dumped in the hide. What we found is certainly consistent with that. I gather from what the pathologist has said that the old boy might have re-gained consciousness. If he did, the smears we found on a piece of the old panelling might have been caused by his moving while he was still bleeding. There's no splatter pattern or anything like that – only smears and droplets. You can certainly proceed on the basis he wasn't struck with anything while he was down there.'

'What about the surrounding area?'

'The position is much the same. There's no evidence of him being struck in the vicinity of the hide while he was bleeding. If Guy Romney is right and he was struck more than once, we'd have found blood splatter – but there's no sign of it. One or two drops near the edge of the recess, but that fits with his being dumped in there after he was attacked elsewhere.'

Hood frowned. 'Anything else?'

'Well, wherever he was when he was attacked there's going to be a fair amount of blood. There'd be blood on his attacker too. If he was struck several times to the head – and it looks like he was – blood would have been distributed over a wide area, unless it was stopped in its tracks by a wall or something solid. But we haven't found any evidence of that and we've checked the whole of the Long Room, the kitchen, and the library. We'll check the other rooms and the chapel tomorrow but I think you're going to have to consider the possibility that he was attacked outside somewhere. We certainly haven't found a trail of blood leading from wherever he was attacked, which is decidedly odd.'

'You know what that means?'

The senior forensic officer grinned. 'I know exactly what that means, Harry. A detailed examination of the entire grounds. I'll need more assistance and it will have to wait until tomorrow. It will be impossible to secure a crime scene that may extend to fifty acres or more. There's no rain forecast so if we do locate where the attack took place the evidence should still be there.'

'No chance of starting this afternoon, I suppose? I know it's getting late but I really need to know where he was attacked.'

The forensic examiner looked at his watch and hunched his shoulders. 'We've almost finished in the Long Room but we need to complete our notes on what we've done so far. I'll see what we can do, but it won't be much today. We'll do a general inspection of the chapel and the immediate area around the house before we leave and cover anything we find. But I don't need to tell you, Harry, it's a major job given the size of the place. If you could get some more officers here, they might be able to reduce the area we need to examine.'

'I'll see what I can do, but we are very short-handed at the moment.'

'Do your best. I'm off to the Gatehouse now to check on what Brendan's team has discovered.'

'I've just come from there. Nothing of interest.'

'So, he wasn't killed in his cottage?'

'It doesn't look like it. Let me have your reports and the photographs as soon as. I must catch up with the others. Unless there's anything else?'

'There is one thing.'

'What's that?'

'There were bits of gravel just inside the front entrance and specks of similar looking debris along the corridor, particularly outside the door in the Long Room that leads into the chapel. Not a lot, but enough to suggest someone or something might have been dragged or carried along there. But no blood. We didn't notice anything at first and it's always possible it's just the result of foot traffic through the house. Cursory examination suggests it matches the gravel from the drive.'

'That's certainly something to think about. Perhaps that's the route the killer took to dump the priest in the hide? Either through the front door or through the chapel. I've already dismissed the broken window as being the point of entry.'

'You'd never get a body through there,' agreed Nigel. 'No bloodstains near that window either, or in the corridor. And as I said, there would have been a lot of blood coming from his wounds.'

'That's definite, is it?'

'As sure as we can be. Odd that there were droplets around the hide but nothing between there and either of the possible entrances. One for you I think, Harry.'

'Thanks Nigel. The chapel doors were locked when I checked them this morning. The main entrance looks like the favourite. Excuse me, but I must catch up with the others.'

Hood walked quickly in the direction taken by Wendy Knight and Sir Robert. He passed the old, ruined chapel and caught them up as they walked under a stone archway and into a cobbled yard. The yard was very extensive and could have provided parking for many vehicles. On one side, a large barn that had obviously been modernised stood with its large glass doors closed and its interior in darkness. The baronet noted Hood's interest.

'That's the barn which my late wife and I modernised some years ago and turned into a venue for wedding receptions and the like. It took nearly a year of arguing to persuade English Heritage to give us the go-ahead. They can be very difficult. Thank God my father got the double glazing in the house done before it was listed. The barn produced quite a good income, but I haven't bothered with it since my wife died. I'll be bringing it back into use when I open the house to the public.'

He then led the two detectives into one of the outbuildings opposite and pointed to a sectioned-off area where a number of gardening tools were tidily stored. Hood made for the two stainless steel spades in the fairly dark corner, one of which had a couple of flies buzzing around the blade. He took a small torch from his pocket and shone it on the implement, reversing it using his handkerchief, so he could examine the flat rear surface.

'Look at this Wendy. That could be blood, couldn't it? SOCO have not been in here yet, have they?'

'No sir, they haven't. Brendan's team will only just have finished in the Gatehouse. I don't know about you, but I got the impression they were about to call it a day.'

Hood spoke decisively. 'Nigel Mullen's team is finishing off in the Long Room. I've just had a word with him. There's nothing to suggest that Father Dominic was killed in the priest-hole or anywhere near it. In fact, everything suggests the contrary. And it doesn't look like he was attacked in the Gatehouse either. We're going to have to piece together his movements as best we can after he left Grantham just before seven o'clock last night.'

'So he must have been killed somewhere else. But where?'

Hood sighed. 'We'll have to work on that basis for the time being. Hopefully, if we get some more officers out here we should be able to exclude most of the grounds from the inquiry. SOCO will then be able to narrow down the possibilities. If he went into the present chapel, he could have been attacked in there or anywhere in the grounds. Nigel will be examining the chapel fully tomorrow.'

'The grounds are very extensive.'

'I know. Over forty acres, excluding the wood and orchard. That's another ten acres or so. Combing through all of that will take forever. But it's more likely he was attacked near the house. He wasn't one for going far.' Hood looked about him. 'Get the team from the Gatehouse over here now. I want them to be on the lookout for bits of glass as well as blood. This spade could have been used to smash the window in the Long Room as well as to attack Father Dominic.'

'Do you think so, sir? If this was used, I wonder why it was put back and not removed altogether? It might suggest that our murderer is familiar with the set-up here.'

'It might,' said Hood. 'On the other hand...' He noticed a metal wheelbarrow a few feet from the spades. 'Is this usually kept here?'

Sir Robert lent forward, anxious to see for himself. 'Here or hereabouts. You'll have to ask Mr Hitchens to be sure. He has the use of it, but the equipment in here belongs to the estate. Hitchens tends to take his tools away with him; he knows this outbuilding is not secure. I've been meaning to do something about it.' He glanced towards the open entrance.

Hood nodded. 'I think that would be wise, sir.' He then addressed Wendy Knight. 'We'd better get SOCO to look at the wheelbarrow, too. Something had to be used to move Father Dominic's body, unless he made his own way to the Long Room.'

Although he would never have admitted it, Sir Robert was finding the investigation into the death of Father Dominic quite fascinating. Desperately sad though he was about the death of the priest, he was an avid reader of crime novels and being in the centre of a real criminal inquiry engrossed him. He was not to know that future developments would undermine his enthusiasm and place one of his own family members under suspicion. 'Why did you pick on that particular spade?' he asked. 'They look much the same to me.'

'The flies, sir. They were interested in that spade because of what I fancy is blood on it. Only a couple of tiny spots by the look of it but the presence of he flies is quite a giveaway if you know what you're looking for. The wheelbarrow will have to be checked for traces of blood too, although I don't see any obvious signs.'

'Neither do I,' said Sir Robert. 'I must say, it would certainly never have occurred to me that the presence of flies on a spade could be of potential significance.'

'Nor to our killer, I shouldn't wonder,' replied Hood. 'Let's hope so. This may give us our first real clue. Tell me, Sir Robert, were either of these spades being used in the excavation of the priest-hole?'

'I'm not sure. Father Grantham will know, but I suppose it's a distinct possibility. The digging out was completed earlier in the week with my gardener's assistance. Examination of the material removed from the hide would require more sensitive equipment.'

'Like the trowel that was found under Father Dominic's body?'

'Precisely.'

Hood looked about the barn-like building. It was fairly dark and cool. Only a single Velux window in the roof and the open entrance allowed in any light and he was forced to use his torch in order to examine the equipment further. The only electric light was near the entrance some distance from where they were standing. 'Can you think of any reason why Father Dominic might have been in this area yesterday?' he asked.

'I can't think why he should have been in here – unless he were returning something he'd borrowed,' replied Sir Robert. 'He did walk around the grounds, particularly the chapel ruins. He was pretty consistent in his perambulations, saying his daily office – but that was usually in the afternoons and early evening. I was always very careful not to disturb him. I know he liked to pray there. He thought it continued the prayer life of the monks who used to live here. I saw him occasionally, usually in the late afternoon, with his breviary walking in the chapel ruins – weather permitting. His face was not usually visible because his head was covered with his cowl – the hooded part of his Benedictine habit – but it was obviously him. It couldn't have been anyone else. No-one has ever visited from his monastery as far as I am aware.'

'Well,' said Hood, 'It was a lovely day yesterday. SOCO will have to examine this whole area around the site of the ruined chapel.'

'That's going to be an enormous job, sir,' sighed Knight, 'but I suppose it will have to be done.'

'And the sooner the better,' added Hood. 'It will be sensible to start with those areas where Father Dominic was known to go. The ruined chapel grounds seems a good place to begin. Secure the immediate area around the ruins. We can expand outwards from there if necessary.'

'Don't overlook that wax object, sir,' said Knight, handing the exhibit bag to the chief inspector. 'Perhaps Sir Robert can help identify it? I'll go and speak with Brendan and his team and get them over here.' She looked at her watch. 'They won't like it but I'll make it clear they have no choice in the matter.'

Hood called after her. 'Blame me if you have to, but I want that spade and the barrow and the immediate area around them examined before they finish for the day. No excuses. If it means overtime, tell them I'll get it authorised. They can examine the chapel ruins tomorrow.'

Knight smiled to herself as she walked away, leaving Hood with the baronet.

Sir Robert's curiosity was aroused by the item mentioned by the detective sergeant. 'A wax object, Mr. Hood?'

'Yes. Father Dominic was clutching it in his hand when he died. I was intending to ask Father Grantham about it, but if you think you can assist?'

'What is it exactly?'

'I'm not sure.' Hood handed over the exhibit bag containing the object.

'Any idea what it might be?'

Sir Robert examined it without removing it from the exhibit bag. An expression of awe spread over his features. He moved to the entrance to the outbuilding so he could see it more clearly. 'Good God,' he exclaimed. 'I can hardly believe it!'

'You recognise it, Sir Robert?'

'I don't recognise it, but I think I know what it is. If this is the genuine article and not a copy, it might have some bearing on your investigation. Come to my study. I have a magnifying glass and a strong light there. Quickly now, this is really exciting.'

Hood needed no further encouragement. He followed Sir Robert who walked at pace, retracing his steps to the front of the house. Wendy Knight caught up with them as they entered. 'SOCO are heading down to the outbuildings now,' she informed Hood. 'I've told them about the spade. They're not too happy about it but they'll check it out before they leave. If it is blood, they'll take it to the lab for further testing.'

'Good. But I think we might be on to something here. I think Sir Robert knows what this wax object might be.' The two officers followed the still excited baronet into his study. 'Please don't remove it from the exhibit bag, Sir Robert,' instructed Hood. 'We shall have to have it tested for prints and DNA.'

Sir Robert nodded but did not attempt to hide his frustration. 'I doubt if anything will come of that. Not if it's been down there for four hundred and fifty years.'

He switched on his desk lamp and took a large magnifying glass from a drawer. He said nothing more as he moved the glass towards the wax object, still in the transparent exhibit bag, and then withdrew it. The smile on his face broadened. 'Don't you see, Chief Inspector? You can still make out some of the lettering on the circumference, although it would be easier to see if it were taken out of the bag.' He harrumphed and glanced at Hood before turning his attention back to the object. 'Look, is that not an 'X' followed by three vertical strokes – Roman numerals for thirteen? Pity most of the other lettering is so difficult to decipher.' He looked up. 'It really would be much easier if we could take it out of this exhibit bag, you know.'

'I think Sir Robert might be right, sir,' ventured Knight. 'The pathologist handled it when he took it from the deceased's hand and I touched it briefly too, as I placed it in the exhibit bag. I suspect that's all that a forensic examination will reveal, apart from Father Dominic's DNA, of course, and we already know he was holding it.'

Hood shrugged his shoulders, removed a packet of latex gloves from his pocket and handed a pair to Sir Robert. 'All right. But put these on, please. There may be something left of evidential value. I don't want to exclude anything at this stage of the investigation.'

Sir Robert struggled to get the gloves on in his eagerness to examine the object. He then removed it from the plastic bag and placed it carefully on the blotter on his desk.

'As I suspected. This is undoubtedly an *agnus dei* – see there's the lamb and you can just make out part of the flag above it. This is really quite remarkable.'

'An *agnus dei?*' queried Hood. He did not pretend to understand Sir Robert's comment. He'd heard the phrase before but never in the context of the description of an object. The baronet did not avert his eyes as he answered.

'Yes. It's what is sometimes known as a sacramental, you know, like rosary beads or holy water.' That term still meant nothing to Hood, although he knew, of course, what rosary beads and holy water were. 'Father Grantham will be able to explain better than me.'

He handed the glass to Hood who took a second pair of latex gloves from the packet and pulled them on. He bent forward and examined the object carefully. He was just able to make out the same marks. He also noted what appeared to be a faint outline of a dragon or serpent in the

Father Dominic's Sacramental [Charlotte Krone]

lower section, placed under what could well have been the crossed keys of St. Peter. He pointed out what he had observed then handed the glass back to the baronet. 'Is it possible to date it?' he asked.

Sir Robert looked up and smiled. 'I doubt if it will bear a date as such but these other marks make it very likely that it comes from the pontificate of Gregory the Thirteenth.' He looked down again as he continued to examine the marks, his excitement quite palpable. 'He was pope at the time Campion was operating in England and if it is a dragon at the base as you suggest, it just happens that a dragon was this pope's motif. He was of the *Boncompagni* family and it appears on his coat of arms, usually with the tail severed. We really must show this to Father Grantham. I'm sure he'll be able to confirm what I say.'

Hood glanced towards Knight. 'Could you find him and bring him here, Wendy? He's probably in the library. Upstairs in the west wing.'

She nodded and left the study. Sir Robert continued his painstaking examination, passing the magnifying glass slowly over each mark.

'You see here, Chief Inspector? Some of the letters can still be made out around the edge. There's the remains of a 'Q' and if I'm not mistaken part of the word *'tollis'* as in *"qui tollis peccata mundi"*.'

He looked up again, his face quite transformed. 'You remember the words from the old Latin Mass, Mr Hood? *"Ecce, Agnus Die, Ecce qui tollis peccata mundi?"*'

Hood shook his head and smiled. 'Not really, sir. I'm very much post-Vatican Two.'

Sir Robert had become quite emotional as he almost fell back into his leather desk chair. He seemed quite overcome as he placed his hand to his head. He spoke quietly and slowly, looking directly at the chief inspector. *'Behold the Lamb of God; behold Him who takes away the sins of the world!'* His eyes were moist with tears as he studied Hood's reaction. 'Comforting words Mr. Hood if you were about to fall into the hands of the pursuivants, don't you think? And afterwards, facing repeated torture and the most barbaric form of execution imaginable.'

Hood nodded. 'It would take a great deal more than that for me to withstand what they went through. I suspect I'd have given up without much of a fight. I'm glad we live in more tolerant times.'

The baronet nodded. 'Yes, our faith is not as strong these days. Most of us would find an easy compromise, I suspect. We would be very accommodating and find a form of words that would ease our consciences and allow us to continue living in relative comfort. But not the likes of Campion and his companions.' He shook his head and smiled. 'There were no grey areas where they were concerned.'

He took out a large, coloured handkerchief from his pocket and wiped his eyes. 'Forgive me, but I find this very moving. It's more than we could ever have hoped for. And there's no saying what it might mean.' He was now fully in control of himself. 'If this is not a keepsake of Father Dominic's and really does date back to the sixteenth century, it could have belonged to a priest who hid here, possibly Campion himself?' He paused. 'Now there's a thought…'

Before Hood could reply, Father Grantham walked into the study closely followed by Wendy Knight. He appeared much calmer than the baronet but he took the object eagerly into his hands after Hood had insisted he first put on a pair of latex gloves. He examined it carefully using Sir Robert's glass.

'Amazing!' he exclaimed. 'This is almost identical to the Lyford Grange *agnus dei*.' He looked at Hood and added, almost cynically, 'Always assuming it's genuine, of course. It's smaller than the Lyford one, though. Where was it found?'

All eyes were on the priest as Hood answered. 'In Father Dominic's left hand.' Hood paused. 'You didn't notice it when you checked his pulse?'

The American Jesuit appeared wary as he shook his head. He pursed his lips and considered his reply carefully then spoke with emphasis. 'No, I did not. I suppose I must have gotten hold of his right wrist. Yes, now I think of it he was lying on his left side so it was his right arm that came to hand. I also checked his neck for a pulse.' He paused then quickly added. 'Not that I took long about it, you understand. He was very obviously dead.'

No-one said anything further until the examination was completed.

'Is it genuine?' asked Hood. 'Sir Robert thinks it may date back to the time of Gregory the Thirteenth.'

The baronet nodded as he stood up and retrieved the object from the priest.

'Possibly,' replied Grantham, 'although I can't exclude it being a copy at this stage. There are modern copies available. This could even

64

be modelled on the Lyford Grange sacramental which certainly does hail from the pontificate of Gregory the Thirteenth.' He paused. 'I wonder where Father Dominic obtained it?'

'There are seemingly two possibilities,' suggested Hood. 'It's either something he'd had for some considerable time or he found it in the priest-hole, perhaps amongst all that in-fill. Either way, he may have taken it in his hand after he had been assaulted, which means he must have recovered consciousness for some little time before he died. The surprising thing is that whoever killed him didn't remove it. I gather from what Sir Robert says that it may be of significant historical interest and therefore of some value?'

'Undoubtedly, if genuine,' agreed Grantham, 'but I think it unlikely it was found in the priest-hole. It could hardly have survived in such relatively good condition in all that detritus. There are many genuine examples of such sacramentals broken into pieces because of their fragility, and many of those are far more recent than this one. We shall have to keep an open mind about that for the moment.'

Hood, of course, had already suggested as much himself to Detective Sergeant Knight, but he was a little surprised that Grantham appeared to be searching for reasons to discount the possibility that it supported Sir Robert's argument that Campion or one of his companions might well have sought refuge at Easton Grange. But he kept his thoughts to himself. Knight was equally troubled but made no secret of her opinion.

'Oh, I don't know, it looks pretty robust to me and it appears to have been recently wiped or brushed. There was a small brush found in the priest-hole, you know. Perhaps Father Dominic found it and was doing his best to clean it up before he was attacked? We should also bear in mind that it could have been inside something which would have given it a degree of additional protection.'

Sir Robert nodded in agreement with Knight. Grantham was unmoved. 'Has anything of that nature been discovered?' he asked with a degree of scepticism.

'No, I don't think so,' said Hood. 'SOCO have found nothing of relevance thus far, traces of blood apart. The in-fill which you'd removed will require further detailed examination, of course.'

'That will take some time,' said Grantham. 'I made a cursory examination of it, but nothing of interest was found. Many of the surviving *agni dei* are protected by cases which preserved them. This one has no such protection. I find it difficult to believe that it could have survived in such good condition if it has languished in the in-fill from the excavation for hundreds of years.'

Hood noted the correct use by Grantham of the Latin plural for *agnus* but was equally firm in his response. 'Nevertheless, it will have to be done. And the sooner we start, the sooner we'll finish. I'll organise someone to supervise the examination. Perhaps you would assist the officers, Father? It might help if you could explain the sort of things we should be looking for.'

'Of course, I shall be happy to help, but I'm sure we would have noticed anything as obvious as a protective container during the initial excavation, no matter how small. I doubt if anything significant will be found now.'

Knight intervened. 'It could have been wrapped in a cloth or something. That would have afforded sufficient protection, wouldn't it?' She was not minded to abandon the possibility that the sacramental had been discovered by Father Dominic in the priest-hole.

Grantham nodded. 'Perhaps it would. But we haven't come across anything like that either. Even a tiny piece of cloth would have been pretty obvious. In any event, if it is genuine, it won't necessarily help us in establishing that Campion came here.' The Jesuit adopted a didactic tone. 'The Lyford Grange *agnus dei* is generally accepted as having belonged to him and there is no doubt that he stayed there. You need to bear in mind, Chief Inspector, that once Campion knew he was in danger of being arrested, he would have removed anything that could have led to his being identified as a priest. So he would have hidden his *agnus dei*; that would have given him away immediately. That, no doubt, explains its being found at Lyford. You must also remember that merely possessing such an item could have led to imprisonment or worse. Cuthbert Mayne, who was executed in fifteen seventy-seven, was found with such an object. That was good enough to prove he was a priest.'

'That's right,' confirmed Sir Robert. 'He was the first of the seminary priests to be martyred. Bringing such items into England in those days was very high risk because of their papal origins. Most of them had actually been blessed by the Pope.'

66

A brief silence ensued before Hood spoke. 'So the one from Lyford Grange is still extant?'

'Most certainly. It's kept at Campion Hall in Oxford. I've seen it,' said Grantham. 'This one is very similar but smaller and may well hail from the pontificate of Gregory the Thirteenth as Sir Robert suggests – those marks make that a real possibility – but it's unlikely Campion had two such objects.'

'Why do you say that?' asked Sir Robert as he cradled the sacramental in his still gloved hands. 'Campion frequently travelled with a companion, didn't he? And the Lyford Grange *agnus dei* wasn't found until nineteen fifty-nine – in the attics as I remember. If this were found by Father Dominic in the priest-hole, there can be little doubt it's been down there since the sixteenth century.' He looked up. 'We may have the better claim.'

The Jesuit smiled indulgently. 'If it is genuine – and I'm not saying it isn't – it may support the notion that priests were lodged here during the reformation period, but we already know that. It doesn't prove that Campion was one of them. These sacramentals were fairly liberally distributed – to the laity as well as priests. We must also remember that as there's no evidence of any priest being arrested from this house, there would be no reason for him to leave his *agnus dei* here – so if it were found in the priest hole it may simply have been mislaid. We know that the house was searched – more than once. It's possible, I suppose, that if a priest were hiding here over a lengthy period he may have dropped it or misplaced it. It was not unusual for an escape to be mounted while another part of the house was being searched. And this is a sizeable mansion. It could have been lost in all the excitement of the getaway.' Grantham noted the look of dismay appearing on Sir Robert's face. 'I'm sorry to play devil's advocate, Sir Robert, but I don't want to build up your hopes only to have them dashed in the future. We must scrutinise the evidence quite dispassionately and not jump to unjustified conclusions, great though the temptation may be.'

Hood could hardly disagree with Grantham's sentiments. Was that not what he always insisted on in a criminal investigation? Proper scrutiny of the available evidence and the drawing of only irresistible inferences. Guessing or assumptions based on wishful thinking only impeded the route to the truth.

Knight, on the other hand, was not convinced by Grantham's explanation. Hood had always enjoyed working with her because she usually took an independent line and looked at the evidence from a quite different perspective. On occasions her insights had proved helpful and, more importantly, correct.

'But surely, a priest who escaped during a search by the authorities would have been very careful to ensure he had his *agnus dei* with him? How would he prove to sympathisers who did not know him that he was in fact a priest?'

Grantham answered her immediately. 'Possession of such a sacramental was hardly conclusive evidence that the holder was a priest; certainly not to other Catholics. The authorities, on the other hand, would certainly have used it as evidence to support such an allegation, but that was purely political. Any indication of support for the papacy was regarded then as treasonous. You may well be right when you say that greater care would have been taken with such an object so it's unlikely to have been lost. The balance of the evidence must suggest that Father Dominic had come into possession of it elsewhere. It's merely a co-incidence that he had it with him when he was killed.' He looked at Hood, knowingly. 'Co-incidences do occur, do they not, Chief Inspector?'

Hood did not reply but Sir Robert was not yet finished. He was not one for giving up. 'If it did not belong to a priest, it's always possible it belonged to the householder. One of the missionary priests could have given it to a member of the Powdrell family. You've just said they were fairly liberally distributed.'

'True,' replied Grantham, 'but that hardly advances the theory that it belonged to Campion or one of his companions.' He smiled. 'Perhaps we should first investigate whether Father Dominic was known to possess such an item before he was killed? That seems to me to be the obvious and logical place to begin. If he already had it and carried it with him, the fact that it was found in is hand may be explained by an understandable wish to comfort himself as he lay dying.'

Hood was forced to acknowledge the point that Grantham made but he did so merely by nodding his head. No-one spoke for some little time. Sir Robert placed the sacramental on his desk and took a few steps towards the window, trying very hard to hide his frustration. Hood looked at him then at Grantham.

'Tell me, Sir Robert, had Father Dominic ever spoken of such an object?'

The baronet turned and shook his head. 'Never. And I did speak with him on religious topics from time to time. I certainly never saw this or anything like it before today.'

Hood turned to Grantham. 'Very well. We'll do as you suggest, Father. I suppose Melford Abbey is the obvious place to begin. That will mean contacting the monastery. Could you make the necessary arrangements?'

'No need for that, Mr. Hood. Remember, I told you earlier I would contact Melford. Well, I did as I promised. The Abbot is sending the Prior, Father Lawrence Milmo. He should be here tomorrow.'

CHAPTER SIX

Hood telephoned the pathologist the following morning. Professor Romney had completed the *post-mortem* and was in the middle of preparing his report.

Father Dominic had died, Hood was informed, from significant blows to the top and back of his head. His skull had been fractured in two places. Romney considered it clearly established that the priest had been struck several times. As the pathologist had indicated would be the case when he first examined the body at Easton Grange, a section of the brain had been removed and sent to the consultant neuro-pathologist in London. Romney suggested that Hood should work on the basis, unless and until contrary evidence was received, that Father Dominic had not died immediately. He thought it possible that he might have re-gained consciousness and could have moved of his own accord, at least for a limited distance and period of time.

'Could he have staggered to the Long Room from wherever he was attacked, then fallen into the priest-hole himself?' asked Hood.

'I can't exclude that possibility, not yet,' Romney replied. 'A great deal will depend on where he was attacked. I doubt if he could have made much ground under his own steam after sustaining the injuries I saw, but it's not unusual with head injuries for the victim to regain consciousness. I have known cases where a considerable distance has been covered before death ensues, but I doubt if this individual would have survived for long given the extent of the damage I found. But we must await the report from London before a firm opinion can be reached.'

'How long will that take?'

'Could be several weeks, he's a very busy man is Professor Durrell. I've asked him to expedite things but I expect everyone asks him to do that.'

Hood let out a lengthy sigh. He didn't have several weeks. The DCC expected an arrest within days. 'So, he was possibly still alive when he landed in the priest-hole?'

'Probably, not certainly.'

'Any other injuries?'

'Bruising, which is probably related to the attack – defensive injuries to his right arm – and a couple of marks on his legs which could well have been made as he landed in the hide. No older bruising and no sign of any existing underlying disease. He was underweight of course, fifty-eight kilos – that's just over nine stone in old money. And he was nearly five-eleven in height. But it looks like he was pretty fit for his age. By the way, he'd eaten some salmon shortly before hie died. I found undigested food particles in his stomach.'

'But there's nothing to suggest he was attacked where he was found?'

'Can't help you with that, Harry, though there wasn't much blood in the hide, certainly not what I would have expected to find had he been struck while he was bleeding. He certainly ended up in there and probably died there, but where he was assaulted is not something I can express a firm opinion about, not at this point. But, if you really want my take on it, I don't think he was struck while he was in the priest-hole. No blood splatter; not that I noticed. SOCO should be able to confirm that for you.'

Hood recalled what Nigel Mullen had told him. His own experience of crime scenes was to the same effect. He would have expected clear evidence of blood splatter in the form of tiny droplets had the priest been attacked while he was already bleeding. He turned to his next question. 'The defensive injuries to his right arm. That might suggest that he turned and faced his attacker at some stage during the assault?'

'That's the most obvious explanation. He could have been struck from behind, turned and raised his arm to protect himself. The original blow may not have been potentially lethal, but if he looked round and saw who was attacking him, it may explain why several further blows were struck with lethal intent.'

'That could suggest he recognised his attacker?'

'Could well be the case. The subsequent blows seem to have been delivered with real intent.'

'There was definitely more than one blow to the head?'

'Absolutely. At least three I would say, but I can't speak as to the precise order. It's quite possible that one blow was from the side. The external damage was not as prominent in that area compared with the wound to the back of his head, but there was a considerable subdural haematoma which would have put immediate and considerable pressure on the brain. The damage to his skull is extensive. You should also bear in mind that he may have been struck after he fell to the ground. He was above average height and at least one of the blows appears to have impacted more towards the top of his head.'

'Anything else?'

'I found a couple of pieces of what look like black thread or fibres in the wounds. Very similar to the makeup of his habit. They've been photographed and his habit taken to the lab along with the other clothing he was wearing.'

'Embedded?'

'Yes. I had to dig a little to get them out.'

Hood swallowed hard. 'Definitely from his habit?'

'I would say so. The scientists will have the final say, of course. There's a sort of hood which forms part of his monk's habit; his head could even have been covered during part of the assault. There's a slight suggestion of the weave of the cloth in one of the larger blooded marks to the top of his head.'

Hood reflected on what Romney had said. 'I suppose if he'd been saying his office, he may have had the cowl over his head. I'm told he sometimes did that in the evenings.'

'There was a lot of dried blood on the inside of that part of his habit, so you may be right. I have photographed in close-up the impression the material seems to have made. You'll get the results at the end of next week from the lab. I pointed out the urgency. His cowl was not covering his head when I saw him *in situ,* though. That much is certain.'

'I suppose there's always a chance the killer may have inadvertently transferred his own DNA on to the deceased's clothing?'

Romney agreed that was a possibility. 'You might get lucky with that Harry, but if the priest was attacked with a spade or a similar implement as seems likely, there may have been no physical contact. But I've taken the usual samples from his hands and fingernails and other areas of his body.'

'As the deceased ended up in the hide, unless he got there under his own steam, there must have been some contact, surely?'

'That'll be another one for the scientists, but I certainly wouldn't rule it out if he was carried or otherwise transported to the priest-hole. As I said, you might get lucky, assuming the killer's DNA is on the database, of course. If it isn't, you'll have to rely on other means to identify him in the first place.'

Hood hesitated before he asked his next question. 'Any further thoughts about when he died?'

Romney was more forthcoming than he had been with DS Knight. 'You know how I feel about time of death, Harry, but my best guess, and it's not much more than that, is between about nine and eleven on Wednesday evening, but don't hold me to it.'

'Thanks Guy. And your report?'

'As soon as it's typed up, you'll have it.'

CHAPTER SEVEN

'What have we got so far, Wendy?'

Hood had assembled his small team of detectives at Wellingborough Police Station on Friday morning. *Operation Monks*, as he had christened the inquiry – after the scheming and dissolute half-brother of *Oliver Twist* – was now very much underway. After disclosing Professor Romney's oral report, amplified by Wendy Knight's comments from her own observations when she attended the *post-mortem*, he turned to the detective sergeant, anxious to hear of any progress made since the day before.

'SOCO are back at Easton Grange and in larger numbers. We managed to find another six uniformed officers to help in identifying where Father Dominic might have been attacked. Chief Superintendent Coupland was very helpful. The publicity this case is receiving should continue to assist when it comes to additional resources. DC Swanson has also discovered something that may be of assistance.'

She looked at the detective constable. He cleared his throat before he spoke and glanced at his colleagues before addressing Hood. 'Well, it was my wife really, sir. She reckons she saw Philip Southall in the village yesterday afternoon. He called into the village shop just after lunch time. It's been confirmed by young Janice Barton who served him.'

'What did he buy?' asked Hood.

Swanson looked at his notebook. 'A cheese and tomato sandwich and twenty Benson and Hedges.'

'What about Janice? Did he say anything to her?'

'She doesn't really know him, sir. She simply served him. Philip hasn't lived here since she started at the shop, so I don't believe she knew who he was until the wife told her, but she's since identified him from a photograph. My wife followed him outside because she was a bit worried about him. He didn't seem to be himself. She wanted to ask him about Father Dominic.'

'Did she manage to speak to him?'

'No. He seemed very much absorbed in himself. He ignored her. She also noticed something else she thought was a bit odd. If you remember sir, it was very warm yesterday, but he was wearing a heavy looking brown coat.'

'Was he? As you say it was very hot yesterday, a bit warmer than today. Your wife knows him quite well, does she?'

'Oh yes. They're about the same age and Philip used to attend some of the social evenings in the village hall when he was younger. That was before he went to Oxford. She hasn't seen much of him since then.'

'Was he carrying anything?'

'Not that she noticed, no. He was walking in the direction of the Grange, but Helen went back into the shop after he declined to speak to her.'

Wendy Knight interrupted. 'We were at the Grange about that time yesterday, sir. He certainly didn't put in an appearance there.'

Hood considered what he had been told. The last thing he wanted was one of Sir Robert's family members coming under suspicion but, as always, he would follow the evidence, no matter how things turned out. The truth usually emerged if that principle were applied whatever the circumstances. He answered Wendy Knight's question as truthfully as he could.

'Not that we saw, no. But it's a large house and the grounds are extensive. He could have been somewhere in the grounds or in one of the outbuildings.' He paused. 'I think I should get over there. The priest from Father Dominic's monastery will be arriving later today and I need to speak to him. We need to find out as much as we can about the deceased. A fellow monk will be best placed to give us all the information we need. Wendy, you'd better come with me. I want the officers who are trying to find where Father Dominic was attacked to look out for signs of someone rough-sleeping. There must be a dozen or more locations where Philip might have put his head down. We shall have to treat him as a person of interest from now on. He could well have been in the village before the attack on the deceased took place. It may be merely co-incidental, but it puts him near the top of our list of suspects.'

'Not much of a list at the moment,' said Knight with a frown.

'Where did we obtain the photograph?' asked Hood.

'From Sir Robert's study,' she replied. 'He was obviously concerned why we wanted it but he handed it over without complaint.' She paused. 'Would Philip not have stayed in the house if he were in the area? He still has a room there.'

'I doubt it. He and his father don't exactly see eye to eye at the moment. I shall have to inform Sir Robert, of course. He may have caught sight of him if he's been hanging around the place. Not that he's mentioned it.' Hood frowned. 'I must confess I'm not exactly looking forward to that conversation.'

'And the photograph, sir?'

'Release it to the media. We need to find Philip, even if it's just to exclude him.'

CHAPTER EIGHT

It was almost half-past two on Friday afternoon when the Prior of Melford, the Very Reverend Lawrence Milmo, OSB, arrived at Easton Grange. He had driven himself from Buckinghamshire in the monastery's somewhat ancient S40 Volvo. He parked it carefully where directed by Sir Robert, who greeted him warmly before leading him into the house and into his study where Hood was waiting. The chief inspector had earlier mentioned Philip being sighted in the village to Sir Robert, but the baronet had informed him he had seen no sign of his son around the Grange. Hood had noticed that a shadow cast itself over Sir Robert as soon as he mentioned Philip's name. He had sighed deeply and shaken his head.

'I pray he had nothing to do with what has happened here.'

'We won't be able to exclude him until we find him,' said Hood. 'If you do have any contact with him, you will let me know?'

The baronet nodded. Reluctant though he was to concede that his son had anything to do with Father Dominic's death, he knew where his duty lay. 'I will assist you in any way I can, whatever the consequences.'

Father Grantham had pleaded a previous engagement in Oxford and had left before the Prior arrived, so only Hood and Sir Robert were in the study as Mrs Morton brought in a tea tray replete with toasted muffins for which Father Milmo was profoundly grateful. She had volunteered to work over the week-end and already prepared a room in the west wing for the distinguished visitor. Wendy Knight was busying herself in the grounds, supervising the examination of the outbuildings and other locations were Philip may have spent the night.

The Prior was a fairly tall, middle-aged man whose hair had seemingly gone prematurely powder-white. He was dressed in black trousers and a light– coloured linen jacket. Like Father Dominic, he did not sport a clerical collar and although it was not as warm as the previous day, his feet were swathed in what appeared to Hood to be a pair of very old sandals. At the same time, he exhibited an otherworldliness that the chief inspector found quite endearing, apart from when it came to the muffins, which the monk demolished with relish, much to the amusement of Sir Robert.

'I had no lunch,' he explained, eying the baronet as he took the last muffin from the silver serving dish, replacing the cover sharply. 'I called to see Father Dominic's sister on my way here. She lives a few miles south of Milton Keynes.' Hood noted just the slightest hint of an Irish accent.

'He has a sister? He never mentioned her,' said Sir Robert.

'Oh yes. And a brother, but he lives in America. We shall have to contact him, I suppose.'

'Do you know where in America?' asked Hood, eyeing the last muffin on the monk's plate jealously. He, too, had not had any lunch.

'The last address we have is in Bryan Mawr in Pennsylvania,' replied the Prior, 'but he may have moved for all I know. He hasn't been in contact with the abbey for several years. He came over about six years ago when Dominic was made titular Prior of Chester. We had a little party following an ecumenical service in Chester cathedral.' He smiled benignly and took a large bite from the remaining muffin. 'These really are very good!'

Hood, who had previously restricted himself to a single muffin, waited until the last one had been consumed before continuing with his questioning. 'When did you last have any contact with Father Dominic?'

The Prior wiped his lips with a linen napkin bearing Sir Robert's coat of arms. 'I rang to speak to him yesterday morning – but of course I didn't. I had not spoken to him for several weeks before then. The Abbot had charged me with maintaining contact with Dominic, although we spoke only very occasionally. On Thursday the line seemingly went dead.' He paused. 'I suppose that must have been when he was found?' Hood nodded as the Prior continued. 'The Abbot was hoping he would agree to attend the service at Chester again – it's a biennial event. He declined to come the year before last.'

'Why Chester?' asked Hood. It's a long way from here.'

The Prior paused and looked at Sir Robert before explaining. 'Dominic's appointment as titular Prior was made by the President of the English Benedictine Congregation as an acknowledgement of his years of service in the habit. There are a number of such appointments – a slight remonstrance against the reformation, you see, and an attempt to continue the tradition of our old monasteries – many of which now serve as Anglican cathedrals. It's purely honorary, of course, but it is expected that the holder puts in an appearance when requested; and the authorities at Chester are very keen to continue their association with our Abbey. The Cathedral was once a Benedictine monastery.' He hesitated before continuing. 'You see Dominic had rather gone into his shell over the last few years – that's why the Abbot agreed to his coming here to try his vocation as a sort of hermit. We hoped he would eventually return to the monastery when he had resolved whatever it was that troubled him.' He paused. 'We certainly did not anticipate he would return in such circumstances as these.' The Prior took a sip of his tea.

'Do you know why Father Dominic retreated into his shell, as you put it?' asked Hood.

'I'm not sure. He was very guarded and a very discreet and private person. He had rather turned inwards on himself, if you know what I mean? We had all noticed a change in him after he returned to the monastery from our parish near Buckingham. He was parish priest at Our Lady and St. Thomas More for five years.'

'Do you know why he left the parish? Was it his decision or someone else's?'

The Prior smiled. 'I have to be very careful what I say, Mr Hood. Only the then Abbot would have known the full story – and he died last year. The decision would have rested ultimately with him, of course, but I understand that Dominic had asked to leave his parish.'

'And you don't know why?'

'No, but it did coincide with an unfortunate incident involving one of our novices.'

Sir Robert looked at Hood as the Prior cleared his throat. 'This is highly confidential, Mr Hood, and it does not affect Dominic's character in any way. I want to make that clear at the outset.' He said nothing more for several seconds. 'The novice in question was a very handsome young man. His name was Ambrose Harcourt. He came to us straight from Oxford where he read law, at Lincoln College I believe. First class brain. He'd stayed on for an additional year to get his BCL. I suspect he'd have made a very good lawyer. But he wanted to try his vocation. He'd been with us for just under eighteen months. He survived his period as a postulant but was hesitant about proceeding further. Fortunately, as things turned out, he had not made any irrevocable vows. He went to the parish to assist Dominic – his curate had been injured in an accident and was undergoing a lengthy period of rehabilitation. It was quite exceptional for a novice to be allowed to help out in a parish, but things are much more flexible than they were in my day and the Abbot thought it might assist Ambrose to be away from the monastery for a while. Things did not work out as planned. Ambrose became very popular very quickly, particularly with the young women parishioners.'

He sat back in his chair and took another sip of tea then looked directly at the chief inspector. 'It's one of the tribulations we sometimes encounter, Mr. Hood. The celibate is sometime seen as something of a challenge by members of the opposite sex, and for all I know these days, by members of the same sex.' He grinned, sheepishly. 'It's not a problem I have ever encountered, but Ambrose fell into a quite different category. He'd only been at the parish for three months when he disappeared with another parishioner's fiancée. It caused quite a scandal locally. The gentleman in question – they were due to be married four months later by Dominic – caused quite a fuss and blamed the parish priest. He thought Dominic should have prevented it. Rather unfairly, I think, in the circumstances because Dominic knew nothing about it until Ambrose had taken off.' He sighed. 'We've never seen him since. He wrote to the Abbot apologising, but never returned to the monastery. The last we heard, he and the lady were married and living somewhere in France. I believe they run a small hotel near Dinard.'

'Do you remember the parishioner's name?'

'I'm afraid I don't, but it shouldn't be too difficult to find out – I'm sure Dominic discussed it with his curate. He'll probably remember if you think it worthy of consideration. And there's bound to be something recorded at the Abbey. Letters were written to the then Abbot and I believe the disappointed gentleman made a complaint to the Bishop.' The Prior looked about him and placed his cup and saucer on the tray on Sir Robert's desk. 'Yes. This man –whoever he was – was very angry about what had happened. Understandable I suppose, but he took things too far. He certainly stopped attending church, but only after he'd interrupted Mass on a couple of occasions. I think Dominic was forced to involve the police, so there should be a record of his identity and whereabouts with them too.'

'A different constabulary,' said Hood. 'But we can check. And you think this might have been what affected Father Dominic?'

'In part, yes. He certainly felt responsible for Ambrose abandoning his vocation. I think he thought he should have been there for him. But he took far too much on himself in my opinion. It simply wasn't his fault.' He paused. 'Dominic had been in charge of the novitiate when I joined the monastery. He was an excellent novice master.'

'Can you think of anything else that might have caused him to leave the monastery and come here?'

The Prior shook his head. 'Whatever it was would have been discussed between him and the then Abbot – and remained confidential. As I said, he died last year. There will be nothing recorded, but I cannot think of any scandal touching Dominic.'

Hood shifted uncomfortably in his chair. He did not want to ask the next question but knew that he had no alternative. 'There's a school at the Abbey, isn't there?'

The Prior hesitated and frowned as he answered. 'Yes, and Dominic did teach in the college – but that was years ago. History was his subject as I recall. He also taught Latin to first-year pupils.'

'Were you a pupil at the college, Father?' asked Hood.

The Prior shook his head. 'No, my parents couldn't afford the fees. My family came over from Cork in Ireland when I was about nine years old. I went to the local grammar school then on to Cambridge. I have a first-class honours degree in chemistry, believe it or not.'

'And you know of no complaints involving Father Dominic when he was a teacher?'

The Prior reacted with a degree of irritability. He stood up and took a couple of paces before facing Hood as he answered. 'No. As far as I am aware, Dominic never breached his vow of chastity. He was always scrupulous about such things. I know there have been scandals in respect of some priests and religious, but not at Melford and certainly not in the case of Dominic. We also take safeguarding at the college very seriously.'

'I'm sorry,' said Hood. 'But the question had to be asked.'

The Prior nodded as he resumed his seat. 'Forgive me, but one does get a little tired of such suggestions.' He smiled. 'You have your job to do of course – and I am here to assist in any way I can.'

Hood took the sacramental discovered in the dead priest's hand and handed it to the Prior who removed his spectacles from his breast pocket before scrutinising it, initially, through the transparent bag

'You can take it out of the exhibit bag. It's been swabbed for DNA and dusted for fingerprints,' said Hood.

The Prior put on his glasses as he carefully removed the object from the bag and studied it for a few moments. 'An *agnus die*, I believe,' he said looking up at Hood and removing his spectacles.

'Could I ask, have you seen such a thing before?'

'Of course. I have one myself, but not as elaborate or as ancient as this one.' He smiled. 'You can pick up pale imitations of this in Rome for a few euros. But this is something else.' He looked up. 'Where has it come from?'

Hood did not answer the Prior's question immediately. 'Have you seen such an item in the possession of Father Dominic?' he asked.

The Prior shook his head. 'No, I haven't. Was this his? I'm sure he would not have kept such a thing to himself if it were.'

'Not even in his guarded and inward-looking period?'

The Prior replied emphatically. 'No. You must understand, Chief Inspector, Dominic was an accomplished historian. If he came across something like this, he couldn't have kept it to himself. He just couldn't have. That would have been completely out of character. Knowing him as I did, he'd probably have written an article about it for the *Melford Recorder* – that's the annual magazine we publish, essentially for former pupils of the college.'

The Prior put on his spectacles again and continued to examine the sacramental. 'Sir Robert believes this dates back to the sixteenth century,' Hood pointed out.

The baronet nodded his agreement. The Prior looked up. 'I'm sure he's right. I'm no expert, but it bears a striking resemblance to the sacramental found at Lyford Grange, the one that's associated with the Jesuit, Edmund Campion. This one is smaller but equally significant, always assuming it's genuine.' He continued to examine the sacramental then smiled and handed it back to Hood. He removed his spectacles and replaced them in his breast pocket.

The chief inspector paused and glanced at Sir Robert as he disclosed where it had been discovered. 'It was found in Father Dominic's hand. He may well have discovered it in the priest-hole he and Father Grantham were excavating.'

The Prior appeared unsure how to re-act. 'Who is this *Father Grantham?*' he asked.

'An American academic and Jesuit. He's been assisting Sir Robert in researching the priest-hole and the family who used to live here in penal times.'

'I don't know a priest of that name,' replied the Prior. 'But if he's an American, there's no reason why I should.' He frowned. 'Is he still here?'

'Yes. But he's away at the moment – in Oxford. He'll be back after the week-end. He discovered Father Dominic's body. I thought he spoke to the Abbot to report his death.'

'You mean *that* John Grantham?' The Prior looked slightly disconcerted. 'I've heard the name, of course, but I didn't realise he was a priest. Father Abbot certainly didn't say he was a priest. How very odd.'

'He didn't tell the Abbot he was a priest?' Hood did not try and hide his surprise.

'If he did, that was not conveyed to me. Some confusion perhaps? I think I should meet him? If he found Dominic's body, there are a few things I need to ask him.'

'Such as?' asked Hood.

'Nothing out of the ordinary Mr. Hood. I was not aware before you told me, that the person who found Dominic was a priest. That is a comfort in a way. Too late for the *viaticum* but he would have observed the usual practice and commended his soul to God. Presumably he has told you as much?'

'Forgive me,' replied Hood. 'I must keep what witnesses may have said to me confidential.'

The Prior nodded. 'He's a witness is he? Yes, I suppose he is if he discovered the body. As you please, but if you have no objection, I shall ask him the same question myself. Perhaps you could direct me to him when he returns?'

'In due course,' replied Hood. 'But I would be grateful if you would first explain to me what you know of sacramentals, like the one we have here. You see, I'm a Catholic, but I must confess, I'd never heard of them before.'

'That doesn't surprise me. Sacramentals like this have rather gone out of fashion. Originally, they were made from the wax from the paschal candle from St. Peter's in Rome and blessed by the Pope– in the first year of a pontificate – sometimes repeated every seven years if a pope reigned that long. But the practice was abandoned by Paul the Sixth and has not been resurrected, as far as I know. Pity really; plastic imitations are now sold to tourists. Nothing like this one, mind you. This one looks like the real thing.'

Sir Robert, who had said nothing, a condition Hood had imposed when he agreed he could be present during the conversation with the Prior, begged to speak. Hood nodded his consent. 'The marks on it appear to suggest it comes from the pontificate of Gregory the Thirteenth. Do you really think it's genuine?'

The Prior nodded vigorously. 'As I said earlier, I am not an expert, but it looks genuine enough to me. Do you really suppose Dominic found it in the priest-hole? Surely, if he did, he'd have mentioned it to Grantham?' He paused. 'You must let me see this priest-hole, Sir Robert, or is it a crime scene and out of bounds?' He looked at Hood who shrugged his shoulders.

'I don't see a problem with that, providing I am there when you inspect it. We'll be examining it ourselves shortly, now that scenes of crime have almost finished in the house.'

Sir Robert rubbed his hands together. 'Excellent. I believe Father Milmo has experience of other priest-holes.'

The Prior nodded. 'I most certainly do. I suppose you might say it's a hobby of mine. I have seen and inspected a number of the well-known ones. Baddesley Clinton, Moseley Old Hall in Staffordshire, Scotney Castle, but my favourite is Harvingtom Hall near Kidderminster. There are several hides there. Perhaps I will be able to add this one to my list?'

'I'd like you to take a look around the Gatehouse first, if you don't mind,' said Hood. 'Father Dominic seemed to have few possessions, but you may be better placed to recognise if there is anything missing.'

'Of course,' replied the Prior. 'Shall we do that now?'

'One last question before we do, Father. Was Dominic right or left-handed?'

The Prior thought for a moment. 'Right-handed.' He smiled. 'He was not one for computers, although he understood how to use a word processor. Dominic much preferred pen and ink. Beautiful copperplate handwriting he had. It was always a pleasure to read a letter from him.' He sighed. 'Something else I will miss.' He then smiled. 'My own handwriting, I regret to say, is quite deplorable.'

CHAPTER NINE

Hood and the Prior made their way to the Gatehouse, leaving Sir Robert in his study. When they arrived, the Prior went into each room and examined the few items Father Dominic possessed while he was alive. He explained the absence of personal property.

'We Benedictines take a vow of poverty, Chief Inspector. I'm not as surprised as you that Dominic managed with so little. Mind you, some of my brethren are very imaginative when it comes to justifying possession of certain items, despite their vows.' He smiled. 'Dominic, however, was not of that number.'

As he came downstairs, having looked around the bedroom, the Prior appeared concerned. 'There is one thing that appears to be missing; Dominic's breviary. I would have expected to have seen it in his bedroom if he'd returned here. And I haven't noticed it anywhere else in the cottage.'

'He definitely had a breviary?'

'Oh, yes. He'd have used it every day, several times to say his office.'

The Prior pulled his own breviary from his pocket. 'See what I mean.'

Hood nodded. 'If it's not here, he must have had it with him when he was attacked.'

The Prior seemed surprised. 'It wasn't with him when he was found? I can't imagine that Dominic would have left it anywhere, not intentionally anyway.'

'We haven't found it. If we can locate it, it might help pin-point where he was attacked. He could well have dropped it when he was assaulted.' Hood paused. 'Tell me, Father, if you were living here where would you say your office – on a nice warm summer's evening?'

'Probably outside, somewhere in the grounds, perhaps? The ruins of the old chapel would seem an obvious location. Were he at the monastery, the last office of the day would have been compline. We usually sing it at about half-past eight in the summer, vespers would have been earlier, at about six o'clock.'

'We know he was with Grantham until just before seven o'clock. They had supper together in the kitchen.'

'Did they? Supper with a Jesuit, eh? He would have needed to pray after that.' The Prior smiled. 'I'm joking, of course. There's always been a bit of rivalry between our respective orders, but we are quite friendly these days.' He hesitated and assumed a serious air. 'Does that mean that Grantham was the last person to have seen Dominic alive?'

'Apart from his killer, yes.'

'So you've excluded the Jesuit from your list of suspects?'

'I haven't excluded anyone – yet. But my sergeant has checked his passport and Sir Robert has no concerns as to his identity.'

'Does he often go away at week-ends?'

'Every week-end, apparently. But he's only been here for three weeks.'

'He's never said Mass in the present chapel?'

'I don't think he has, no. He's never been here on a Sunday – not according to Sir Robert.'

'Don't you find that a little odd, Chief Inspector? He's happy enough to stay here during the week – no doubt at Sir Robert's expense – but he's never here at the week-ends. What does he get up to I wonder?'

'He usually goes to Oxford. He has friends there and he was a post-graduate student at Christ Church a few years ago. He also uses the library there for research.'

'You've checked all this, I assume?'

'Not in any detail, no. Do you think we should?'

The Prior shook his head. 'Forgive me, I am not casting stones at anyone. It's just that if I were a guest here – and a priest – I would feel some obligation to stay and say Mass this Sunday, not go trooping off to Oxford to spend the week-end with my friends. But then, an American Jesuit may have different priorities.'

Hood was not so sure. 'He knew you were coming, of course. It was Father Grantham who made the arrangements for you to be here.'

The Prior relented. 'Ah, I'd overlooked that. And Sir Robert has already asked me to say Mass on Sunday – at eleven o'clock. Perhaps you should come, Mr Hood? I suspect there'll be quite a few people in the congregation in view of what's happened. Could be a full house.'

'We usually go to Mass in Market Harborough – Our Lady of Victories – but as you say, it might be worth the journey. There should be several people in attendance who knew Father Dominic.'

'I wonder if the murderer will be there?'

Hood smiled. 'That would be too much to hope for.'

'Stranger things have happened, and this is a very strange set of circumstances, don't you think?'

Hood looked at his watch. 'Would you mind coming to the old chapel grounds with me? If we can find anything resembling a breviary, you may be able to identify it.'

The Prior needed no second invitation. 'If you have no objection? I wouldn't want to get in your way. I noticed there were several police officers combing the grounds. They haven't found anything yet?'

'No, but it's a very large area that needs to be searched, several acres. They should be moving into what remains of the old Priory church about now.'

'I noticed there's a large wooden cross set in the ground – probably where the altar used to be. I suspect that Father Dominic would have walked around that area when saying his office.'

'We'll check it out, unless it's already been done.'

The Prior responded with enthusiasm. 'Lead the way, Mr Hood. I feel rather like Chesterton's Father Brown, you remember, the sleuthing priest? A work of fiction he may have been but he always solved the case. I wonder what he would have made of Father Dominic's murder?'

★ ★ ★ ★

All that remained of the ancient Priory church was a section of the transept and a significant portion of the east end which formed a distinctive arch, together with an accumulation of stones that had once formed the outside wall. A sizeable fragment of a huge, mullioned window had been cemented onto the stones giving some considerable height to the ruins and the boundary had been marked to give an impression of its former proportions. Every few feet a piece of solitary sandstone rested where the walls had once stood but overall it lacked the atmosphere of monastic sites where a greater portion of the buildings had survived. The central area resembled a carefully tended lawn save for a few flagstones believed to be part of the original floor. They were seemingly too deeply embedded to be removed. On one of the larger grey slabs a worn Latin inscription, no longer discernible, marked the assumed location of the grave of a fourteenth century Prior. A wooden cross about five and a half feet tall was securely positioned where it was thought the altar had once stood. Father Milmo crossed himself as he and Hood stepped over the curtilage. A young constable approached them.

'Excuse me, sir,' he said, eagerly. 'I think you should see this.' He led the two men towards the wooden cross and pointed to the back. 'Could that be blood, sir?'

Hood leant forward, then knelt on the ground and looked closely where the constable indicated. He nodded. 'It could indeed.'

He stood up as the Prior put on his spectacles as he, too, scrutinised the stains.

'Well spotted, constable,' said Hood. 'Have you noticed anything else?'

The young officer looked very pleased with himself and smiled broadly. 'Not so far, sir, no. We've only just started in here. DS Knight told us to check the outer area first. Nothing of interest there so far.'

'You haven't come across a book by any chance?' asked the Prior, who took a few steps towards the remains of the east end as he removed his spectacles and started examining the gaps between the stones.

'No, sir' replied the constable. 'No-one said anything about a book.'

The Prior turned and pulled his breviary from his pocket. 'Something like this?'

The constable glanced at the breviary and shook his head. 'Nothing like that, sir, but I'll keep an eye open.'

Hood dismissed him and he went on his way. The chief inspector noticed Wendy Knight walking quickly towards them from the direction of the stable yard. She was slightly out of breath when she arrived. Hood pointed to the marks on the cross.

'That could be blood, Wendy,' said Hood. 'Get the boys from SOCO over here. I want samples taken. And this whole area will need to be covered. I don't want to risk losing any evidence if there's a change in the weather.'

She nodded. 'I've just heard from Nigel Mullen, sir. They did find a couple of tiny splinters of glass on that spade. And some blood; initial tests show it's the same group as Father Dominic's.'

'DNA?'

'Too early to say. It'll take about a week or so before we hear anything, always assuming there's enough to carry out the tests. And I persuaded them to treat it as high priority and have it fast-tracked.'

Hood stroked his chin. 'It's looking like the spade is the murder weapon. I take it the glass will be compared with glass from the broken window in the Long Room?'

'Yes, sir. That may take a bit longer, but Nigel has taken samples from the window. The glass from the spade and the samples are on their way to the lab. I've appointed DC Bradley as exhibits officer for the time being.'

'Bradley? I don't think I know him.'

'Mark Bradley. Inexperienced, but very keen. He's going to the library in Northampton after he's taken the exhibits to the lab. I want him to look into the history of the estate. There are records here but I'm told there are some ancient plans and other documents preserved in the County Library which may assist.'

The Prior was now several feet away from the two detectives as he continued to scrutinise the remains, carefully checking the gaps between the stones. Hood pointed towards the cross. 'I want this photographed *in situ* then removed to the laboratory. The angle of those marks may well be important. They don't look like smears to me, more like splatter. This could be the very spot where Father Dominic was attacked.'

The Prior suddenly called to Hood. 'Chief Inspector. I think I've found it.' Hood and Knight joined him. 'This must be it; Dominic's breviary. It's been placed between those two stones. I didn't notice it to begin with. It's very well camouflaged.'

'Neither did anyone else, or so it seems.' He eyed Wendy Knight pointedly. His tone was quite sharp.

'We hadn't got round to this area yet sir, and, to be fair, we didn't know anything about the deceased having a book.'

'A breviary,' corrected the Prior.

'Well, we do now,' said Hood.

He put on a pair of latex gloves and carefully removed the book. He turned over a couple of pages. There was no sign of any blood, but the deceased's name was written in perfect copperplate handwriting on the second page; *"Dom Dominic Renville, OSB"*. Hood closed the book and took a transparent exhibit bag from his pocket. 'Now, how did that get there I wonder? It seems to have been placed in position with some care. It's certainly not ended up there accidentally. Someone must have put it there deliberately.'

'No blood on it either by the look of it,' observed Knight, 'it must follow that he wasn't holding it when he was attacked.'

'I agree,' replied Hood. He started to place the breviary inside the exhibit bag.

'Could I make a suggestion?' said the Prior. He was well into Father Brown mode, his eyes darting from Hood to Wendy Knight. The chief inspector had no objection as he refrained from closing the exhibit bag. 'The bookmark, that red ribbon. It might tell us where Dominic was reading from before he was attacked. And that may give us some idea of the time he last used it. If he were interrupted by someone, he'd have marked where he was up to using the ribbon before he closed his breviary.'

'Unless he was attacked suddenly and without warning.'

'But if Dominic placed his breviary where I found it, it suggests he wasn't attacked suddenly.' The Prior paused and looked first at Wendy Knight and then at Hood. 'Perhaps he knew whoever approached him?'

Hood nodded, recalling what he and Professor Romney had speculated. 'That's a possibility, I suppose. Would he have definitely marked where he was up to?'

'Yes. I think so. We Benedictines are meticulous in saying our daily office, and Dominic was a stickler. If he were approached by someone, someone he knew, someone who wanted to speak with him, it would have been second nature to him to put his breviary down somewhere; it would be an indication that he was giving whoever it was his full attention. He was always very insistent that a monk should give his full attention to anyone seeking help. That's what he taught me when I was a novice. I have never forgotten it.'

Hood passed a pair of latex gloves to the Prior and removed the breviary from the exhibit bag. 'You're the expert, Father,' he said. 'Perhaps you would look for us?'

The Prior took the breviary eagerly into his gloved hands and, using the ribbon bookmark, turned towards the back of the book. 'There, just as I thought. Vespers.' He looked up and explained what he meant. 'He hadn't got as far as night prayers; that could be significant, couldn't it? And he'd probably say those back at his cottage before retiring for the night.'

Hood was grateful. 'Not conclusive, but everything helps. For present purposes then, we should proceed on the basis that he was attacked sometime between, say, seven-thirty and eight. If he did go back to his cottage first, he would probably have been there for only a brief period.'

'That would seem a reasonable hypothesis,' said Knight, 'and it just about fits in with Professor Romney's somewhat extensive estimated time of death.'

'So far as he has one,' said Hood, ruefully, 'but he's now putting his money on Dominic dying well before midnight on Wednesday. I want this whole area carefully examined and preserved. Although it seems Father Dominic was attacked near this cross, he might have been able to make some distance away from his attacker only to be struck again somewhere else, probably close by.' He looked about him. Three or four shirt–sleeved officers were searching the outer perimeter of the chapel. 'Get them in here Wendy, down on their knees.' He cast a sideways glance towards the Prior. 'I don't want them praying, mind you, but I don't want them missing anything either. A fingertip search and a careful plan produced of anything found showing its precise location, no matter how insignificant it may seem, understood?'

'Yes, sir.'

'Speaking of knees,' said the Prior, handing the breviary back to Hood, 'I must get back to the present chapel. I promised Sir Robert I would say Mass this evening. Please let me know if there are any developments.'

CHAPTER TEN

On Saturday morning Hood and Knight attended a specially convened sitting of the Coroner's court in Northampton. Hood gave evidence briefly in the crowded court room and informed the coroner that Father Dominic had undoubtedly been the victim of foul play. A loud murmur went around the courtroom as he informed the coroner that the monk's death was being treated as murder by a person or persons unknown. The coroner then adjourned the inquest until Hood had completed his investigation into the killing. The chief inspector was then obliged to make a short statement outside the court to the assembled journalists and TV crews which added nothing to what was already known. Their understandable interest in the death of Father Dominic and the reluctance of Hood to add anything further caused some of them to jostle the two detectives as they made their way from the court steps, demanding answers and speculating as to what might have happened at Easton Grange. 'Was Sir Robert's son under suspicion?' they demanded to know. 'Has he handed himself in yet?' They were aware, of course, that Philip Southall's photograph had received massive publicity over the previous twenty-four hours together with a request that he made himself known to the police. Hood had little option but to stop and address them further, promising that a press conference would be arranged during the week when hopefully he would have something positive to disclose about his inquiry into the death of the priest. He otherwise repeatedly answered "no comment' to their questions other than to state that Philip Southall was indeed a person of interest but there was as yet no evidence that he was involved in the killing. He had been seen in the village the day after the murder and Hood wished to speak to him to exclude him from the inquiry. He and Knight then retreated to the comparative safety of his car and drove to Wellingborough Police station.

The two detectives relaxed in Knight's makeshift office on the first floor. The decorators were in and accommodation in the police station was restricted

'Any sign of Philip?' Hood asked Knight. No journalists had followed them although Hood had noticed a *Central News* van parked half on the pavement fifty yards along Midland Road. He had taken over the detective sergeant's desk leaving her standing by the open window. She adjusted the blind and looked out over the street.

'No sir. He's been asked to make contact with us, but I don't suppose he will, not if he's responsible. And his photograph is everywhere. It was even on *Breakfast News* this morning. Do you think he could be our man?'

'I don't know. If he is, Sir Robert's going to be very upset. We've got a good set of prints from the spade. They don't match anything on record.'

'They could well be his, then. Detective Sergeant Wilson is our local expert. He's back from leave this week-end. We'll know more when he's looked at them.'

Hood sighed. 'But we'll have to locate Philip whatever the consequences may be for his father before we can be certain. He presumably knew Father Dominic and he's been to the Grange on at least a couple of occasions while the priest was living there. Is the photograph of him up to date?'

'Sir Robert says it's a good enough likeness.'

She pointed to the file on the desk. Hood picked it up, removed the photograph and perused it. 'Good looking boy.'

'Hardly a boy, sir. He's twenty-five. In fact, he'll be twenty-six in two months, according to his father.'

Hood placed the photograph back in the file. 'Nothing on record? That's definite?'

'No. No previous. I've checked the PNC.'

. 'Do you think we should be looking at the other two sons?'

'I've got Swanson on to that, simply to exclude them. It seems pretty clear that Michael was in Brussels at the time and young Maxim is being spoken to this morning by Thames Valley. Swanson reckons he has a pretty good alibi. He'd been playing cricket for the university most of Wednesday. They won by two hundred runs apparently, and the celebrations went on well into the night. He has more than a dozen witnesses who can vouch for him.'

Hood stretched his arms and supressed a yawn. He'd had very little sleep since the investigation began. 'You seem to have everything under control, Wendy. How did Bradley get on at the library?'

'Nothing we didn't know already. There wasn't anything in the records about a priest-hole at Easton Grange, but that's hardly surprising. The whole point, I suppose, is that such things should be secret and not recorded anywhere. I don't suppose whoever constructed it applied for planning permission.'

'Very droll,' replied Hood, with a smile. 'Where is he now?'

'He's getting some drawings of the estate copied at Campbell Square. They might assist. Otherwise, we'll have to rely on Sir Robert's account and anything Father Milmo can add, and Grantham of course. Bradley did establish that the Powdrells sold up in sixteen hundred and ninety-four. Can you believe that the whole place was valued at only fourteen thousand pounds? And it extended to over five hundred acres back then.'

Hood was not surprised. 'But fourteen thousand pounds in those days would be worth a hell of a lot more than today. The average wage then was only a few pounds a year. I suspect the place is worth well over a couple of million now, despite the reduction in the land.'

'And the rest,' added Knight, cynically.

Hood smiled then started to go through the witness statements that had been assembled. After he'd read three statements, including Sir Robert's, he looked up. 'There's definitely nothing missing from the house?'

'Not according to Sir Robert. I've double-checked what he said to you.'

'And you've checked the chalices and the monstrance in the sacristy safe?'

'I did it myself. They were all there – all thirteen, plus the other thing.'

'How did you carry out the check?'

'I just counted them. Sir Robert said there should be thirteen and that's how many were there, plus the, er, monstrance.'

'I think we should have them photographed, individually. Arrange to have it done with Sir Robert present. I would like him to look at each one in detail. His insurance documents give a brief description but I doubt if anyone but he could distinguish one from another. I don't want to overlook anything in a case of this nature, Wendy. The DCC is breathing down my neck on a daily basis.'

'As you wish, sir. I'll organise a photographer for next week.'

Knight sat down on one of only two other chairs in the room, placing her jacket on her knees. 'I have had one thought, sir.'

'Mmm?' Hood continued reading.

'Perhaps whoever killed Father Dominic wasn't interested in anything in the house? It could have been something personal.'

Hood looked up and placed the statements he had been reading neatly together. 'That's a possibility and I have it fully in mind, but I can't get it out of my head that Father Dominic found something, something valuable, apart from the sacramental we discovered in his hand.'

'Isn't that valuable in itself?'

'Undoubtedly, and it looks like it's a genuine sixteenth century piece. I have no idea how much it's worth and neither has Father Milmo, nor Grantham. Such things just don't come on the market.'

'But at the end of the day, it's only wax. It can't have much intrinsic value.'

'I don't think that matters; it's its history that makes it valuable – and the possibility it belonged to someone of distinction, perhaps even a saint.'

He stood up and walked towards the window which he opened to its full extent. He continued to think aloud as he looked out towards the town. The *Central News* van was departing, headed as Hood later discovered, for Easton Parva. 'But it wasn't taken, was it? The killer couldn't have known the priest even had it. Had he realised it was there he would have removed it. No, if the motive were theft, it was something else entirely, and something much more valuable.'

He turned and faced Wendy Knight as she answered him. 'But if Father Dominic was in the ruins of the old chapel when he was attacked, it doesn't look as if the killer was necessarily a thief, does it?'

Hood sighed in exasperation as he returned to the desk. 'It could have been someone with a grudge, I agree, but I don't know Wendy, there has to be more to it than that.'

Was Hood allowing his imagination to get the better of him? The sacramental could be wholly irrelevant, as he had admitted to Knight the day before. But surely the death of a priest in these somewhat bizarre circumstances couldn't be as simple as that? Or could it? Someone from his past holding a grudge against him? Knight took a more down to earth approach.

'But if Father Dominic had found something, Grantham would surely know about it? And he's very clear that nothing had been discovered. Remember what you told me Father Milmo said? Father Dominic was a historian; he simply couldn't have kept it to himself if he'd found something.'

'But he didn't tell Grantham about the sacramental. That's surely significant, wouldn't you say? Always assuming he found it in the hide, of course.' He paused as if in thought. 'I do wonder why he doesn't seem to have mentioned it to Grantham, though. Interesting isn't it? Do you think we need to speak to Father Grantham again?'

'Perhaps he intended to tell Sir Robert first?'

Hood nodded. 'That's a possibility, I suppose. Pity he was in London.'

Knight said nothing for some time. She then decided to raise a suspicion she had kept to herself since the beginning of the investigation prompted by the fact that Grantham was alone in the house at the time the murder must have taken place. Could it have been an inside job? She hesitated before disclosing her suspicions. 'Could Grantham be lying? Could Dominic have told him he'd found something or even shown him? Not the sacramental, something else, something of real historical importance and much more valuable?'

Hood frowned. Such a possibility had never really occurred to him. If Grantham were responsible and knew about the sacramental, he'd hardly have left it in Father Dominic's hand. 'I don't know Wendy. They were working together on Wednesday afternoon. Surely, Grantham would have seen anything that was discovered.'

'Supposing he did. Supposing something really valuable was discovered. Perhaps it related to that Jesuit martyr Sir Robert mentioned and Grantham wanted it for the Jesuits. Could he have been tempted to keep it? The Jesuits do have a bit of a reputation, don't they?'

Hood smiled. 'Do they now? You're sure you're not buying into anti-Jesuit propaganda? The myth of the sly Jesuit?' He paused and almost laughed. 'Go on Wendy; let your imagination soar.'

Knight frowned. *Was the DCI making fun of her?* But she did as he asked.

'Well sir, you always taught me not to think in straight lines. He may be a priest but everyone is open to temptation, aren't they? Grantham would definitely have known that Father Dominic couldn't have kept it to himself if anything had been discovered. He was bound to speak about it.'

Hood continued to look faintly amused. 'So he killed him to keep him quiet, did he?' He laughed. 'You do have a suspicious mind, Wendy, which is all well and good. And I don't mind a bit of cork-screw thinking if it results in something useful which moves the inquiry on.' He paused, unable to keep a straight face. Knight was not amused. Hood noticed her expression but continued in much the same vein. 'You're not *seriously* suggesting that a Jesuit priest would stoop to killing the man assisting him in this important enterprise, and he a priest too? Over an historical artefact? He was almost laughing openly. 'Where, I wonder, did he do the dirty deed? Not in the Long Room, not according to SOCO. Perhaps he tricked Father Dominic into going into the chapel grounds and crept up on him while he was saying his office, spade in hand?'

Wendy heaved a sigh. She realised her suspicions were, perhaps, a little far-fetched. 'I'm sorry sir. It's highly speculative, I know. But perhaps we need to think out of the box sometimes. And, if he has stolen something, he's had every opportunity to spirit it away by now.'

Hood continued to smile but then adopted a more serious tone. 'To Oxford you mean? Let's speak to him first, shall we? He should be back tomorrow evening or first thing on Monday. You can make yourself available?'

'You want me there, sir?' Wendy was not exactly sulking but her eagerness to pursue Grantham as a possible suspect was certainly plummeting.

'Yes, I certainly do. The housekeeper needs speaking to again as well. You can tackle her on your own. She should be able to give us a bit more background about life at Easton Grange. Housekeepers usually know more than they let on.' He smiled. 'Pity Sir Robert didn't keep a butler. We'd have the full cast for a Victorian melodrama.' He then became deadly serious. 'I'm sure young Swanson did his best, but the statement he's taken from her has a few gaps that need filling.'

'I spoke to her briefly yesterday while you were with Sir Robert and Father Milmo. She didn't have anything useful to say, although I did pick up that not everything was right with her. I think Father Dominic's death has hit her very hard.'

'Has it? Well, that's understandable, I suppose. Have another word with her. Push her a bit harder. I'm sure she can add to what she's already told us.'

'And Sir Robert?'

Hood chuckled to himself. 'I think he's in the clear. He was at his club in Pall Mall. There's no doubt about that and I somehow don't see him wielding a spade and killing his own priest. His son however is another matter.' He paused. 'Any other likely candidates?'

'We've already checked up on the former parishioner, the one who caused Father Dominic trouble a few years ago. There's no way he can have been responsible. He's in a secure hospital – Marlborough House in Milton Keynes. He was sectioned after committing a serious assault on a nurse at A and E in Aylesbury eighteen months ago. He's a restricted patient and only allowed out when escorted by a member of staff. He was definitely in the hospital on Wednesday night.'

'We're not exactly making much progress are we?' sighed Hood. 'Running out of obvious suspects fast, Jesuits apart.'

There was a twinkle in his eye as Wendy tried her best not to look too embarrassed. He returned to the statements on his desk. After a few moments she interrupted him. 'I've had a few thoughts about the book, too. The one that was found in the stonework behind the cross.'

'The breviary.'

'Yes sir, the, er, breviary. I was thinking that perhaps Father Milmo is right and Father Dominic put it there himself? SOCO are photographing the book where we found it. It seems to me that the layout of the stones makes a sort of shelf where something could be put, temporarily.' She stood up to demonstrate what she meant. Hood looked up then sat back in his chair and listened to Wendy propounding her theory.

'Suppose whoever approached the priest was someone he knew? There he was, reading from his…breviary when this person approaches him. Whoever it was wanted to speak to him urgently, so he placed his breviary instinctively in a convenient spot so they could converse and he could give this person his full attention, just like Father Milmo suggested. If you stand by that section of the wall, it's quite natural, just a couple of arms lengths from the cross. I've stood there myself. Now, Father Dominic was a few inches taller than me, but it seems likely that's how it got there.' She paused. 'And the bloodstaining on the cross suggests he must have been in that approximate position when he was first attacked.'

'You mean no blood was cast in the direction of the breviary?'

'Exactly, sir. SOCO are there this morning double checking, but there was no obvious bloodstaining other than on the cross and on the grass some several feet away.'

Hood started to show some interest in what his detective sergeant was saying. He didn't have the heart to tell her he had already reached a similar tentative conclusion himself. 'The cross is about 6 feet from the stonework, right?'

'Yes, sir. One hundred and eighty-six centimetres to be exact. Just over six feet.'

'And the blood on the grass?'

Wendy checked her notes. 'Two hundred and thirty-seven centimetres from the base of the cross in the other direction. The blood was spread over an arc and there was quite a bit, which suggests Father Dominic was already bleeding when he was struck again. The distribution is consistent with a second or further strike with whatever weapon was used. And although it's not easy to be exact because it's on grass, there seems to be more blood in this area than on the cross.'

'No other spots of blood?'

'No, sir. SOCO have found no sign of a trail in the direction of the house or inside the house except in and around the hide. I have requested they check again, just to be sure.'

Hood picked up a pencil and, in the absence of a detailed plan which was still awaited, drew a sketch of the area from memory marking the approximate position of the cross, the back of the ruined chapel and the bloodstains. 'But wouldn't the head injuries suggest he was struck from behind?'

'That's easily explained, sir. He spoke with whoever it was, then turned to walk away. Then the killer struck him when he wasn't expecting it.'

'So he forgot his breviary?'

'It's perfectly possible, if he wanted to get away from whoever it was. His breviary might not have seemed that important.'

'So, whoever did this will be heavily bloodstained?'

'I imagine so, until he cleaned himself up.'

'Which even the most stupid assailant would make sure he did.'

'Yes, sir. Which explains why there was so little blood on the spade. The killer thought he'd cleaned it but not being forensically aware and probably in a state of panic, left a speck or two on it.'

Hood undid his top button and loosened his tie. It was going to be another very hot and slow day. 'So your theory is that whoever it was who attacked Father Dominic was probably known to him, as our sleuthing Prior suggested yesterday. That number would include Philip Southall.'

'Yes, sir. It makes sense when you think about it. Father Milmo may well be right. I suppose it could have been one of those attending the chapel on Sundays. Father Dominic had a fair following according to Sir Robert. And he would have got to know the regulars.'

'But where did the spade appear from?' asked Hood.

'If the spade is the murder weapon, perhaps it was just left lying around.'

Hood shook his head. 'Not according to Mr Hitchens, the gardener. He's almost obsessive about putting the estate's equipment away when he finishes for the day. He treats them like his own. He's never seen any tools lying about the place. He even insisted that Grantham put anything away he borrowed. Apparently he helped out on one of his days off in clearing the hide and made sure all the tools were put away.'

'But he wasn't there on Wednesday, was he?'

'No, and apart from the two priests, who would be using a spade? Grantham said he hadn't borrowed a spade for a couple of days. They'd finished the digging out the previous Monday. It's all set out in his witness statement.'

He pointed to the file on the desk. Knight continued. 'But the spade was probably used to smash the stained glass window as well. The murderer and the person who caused the damage could well be one and the same?'

Hood did not dismiss that possibility. It had already occurred to him as the most likely explanation for what had been found on the spade. His initial take on the broken window that it had been damaged simply to mislead seemed to be well established.

'That's probably right, Wendy. We shall have to await the results of the tests to confirm it, but it's our best guess at the moment. Whether the window was smashed before or after the killing, though, we simply don't know. It could have been put in to make it look like a burglary had taken place, and putting the body into the priest-hole might have been done to suggest Father Dominic was attacked in the Long Room, which excludes Father Grantham as a suspect, don't you think? He'd hardly have left the body where it could be so easily found, and in a location so closely connected with him.'

Wendy Knight had to admit that if Grantham were involved, he'd hardly have dumped the body somewhere so obviously associated with himself. If he were involved in stealing something Father Dominic had found, it didn't follow that he must have been the killer too. 'Thank God, for forensics, eh sir?'

'As you say, Wendy. It's the forensics that make it clear he was *not* attacked in the Long Room. Our killer obviously has no understanding of the science. But whoever killed him might have wanted it to look like he was despatched in or around the priest-hole for his own reasons.'

Wendy contemplated what those reasons might be but nothing occurred to her. 'Funny that Father Grantham never heard anything.'

Hood smiled. The detective sergeant had not entirely abandoned her theory that the Jesuit might be involved in some way, even if he were not the killer. Hood pointed to a likely explanation. 'Not necessarily. His room is in the west wing. It's quite a distance from the Long Room. He also listens to music when he's relaxing. He's very keen on Mozart, apparently. And his room is at the front of the house. You can't see the old chapel from his window.'

Wendy sighed. 'Isn't Father Milmo saying Mass in the chapel tomorrow?'

'He is, at eleven o'clock; perhaps we should be there? He did invite us.'

Hood's mobile phone buzzed. He listened for a few seconds then pulled on his jacket and placed the phone in his breast pocket. He was suddenly quite animated. 'Well, that's something I wasn't expecting, Wendy. Philip Southall has just walked into Campbell Square Police Station in Northampton and admitted responsibility for what happened at Easton Grange. I think we'd better get over there and quickly.'

CHAPTER ELEVEN

'He's in the medical room, at the moment sir,' said the custody sergeant as Hood and DC Knight arrived at Campbell Square. 'He's not asked for a solicitor, by the way, although I told him he was entitled to one.'

'Have you contacted the duty solicitor?' asked Hood, briskly.

'I have, sir. But it's Saturday. No saying who'll turn out on a Saturday.'

'Well, I'm not keen on interviewing him without a solicitor. Not in a case like this. What did he say when you made the decision to detain him?'

The sergeant picked up the custody record from his desk and handed it to Hood. 'He didn't say much, just that he'd done it. And he didn't volunteer what "it" was. Mind you, he looked pretty shell-shocked when I told him he was being detained on suspicion of murder. DC Bradley reckoned there was sufficient cause to detain him and I agreed.'

Hood glanced at the custody record before handing it back to the sergeant. 'Bradley was here when Southall walked in, was he?

'Yes sir. I authorised the suspect's detention at eleven seventeen precisely.'

'Where is Bradley now?'

'He's just popped out the back for a smoke. Detective Superintendent Kingston doesn't allow smoking in the building, except in the cells. We'd have real problems with some of our customers if it was banned there.'

'Southall didn't say anything further?'

'Nothing, sir. Not even "no comment."'

'He's been fingerprinted and photographed?'

'Yes sir. DC Bradley organised that too. The suspect was cooperative enough. He's also given a DNA sample. He seemed pretty eager to do so when murder was mentioned.'

'What condition was he in? He may have been living rough for the last few days.'

The sergeant took a deep breath. 'He looked pretty unkempt and he could certainly do with a shower. Mind you, it's very hot today. His clothing has been seized too. He's in one of those paper forensic suits, but we haven't let him shower in case there's anything on his body that might be relevant. But I don't want him stinking out one of my cells, not if it can be avoided. There's no air conditioning down there you know, sir.' He gave the chief inspector a knowing look as he spoke.

'No air conditioning anywhere in this place, is there?' said Hood. sarcastically. He did not wait for an answer. 'Has he been examined by the FME?'

'In with him now, sir. Dr Hussain. She should be through shortly.'

Hood nodded. 'I think we'll leave him for the moment, until a solicitor arrives. Is there an office we can use?'

'On the next floor, sir. It'll be your office from next month, but the Superintendent isn't coming in over the week-end so there won't be a problem with you using it. There's a few cardboard boxes in there. He's started packing up already. Can't wait to get away from us it seems.' He smiled. 'I've been told to give you every assistance. Let me know when you want to see this fellow and I'll make the necessary arrangements. Constable Newman will show you the way.'

★ ★ ★ ★

It took the duty solicitor another twenty minutes to arrive at Campbell Square and he required half an hour to speak to Philip Southall before the interview could begin. Hood gave him a brief summary of the limited evidence the police had assembled. The solicitor, an inexperienced but eager young man, wisely refrained from commenting. Philip Southall, still in the white paper forensic suit, looked a forlorn sight as he slumped in his chair in the basement interview room. He didn't appear to have shaved for a few days and there were dark circles around his eyes. After the suspect was cautioned, Hood began his questioning. DC Bradley had been allowed to sit in with DS Knight, but Hood had told him he was to say nothing. He sat in the corner with his notebook ready, keen to learn how an interview in a murder case should be conducted.

'What did you mean when you came in here this morning and said you had done it? Done what?'

Hood got straight to the point. He saw no reason for shadow boxing or futile preliminary skirmishes. Philip Southall looked at his solicitor before he answered. 'I have advised Mr Southall to say nothing, but I believe he wants to make one thing clear, at the outset.' He glanced towards his client. 'Go on, Philip.'

Philip Southall spoke slowly, looking Hood straight in the eye. 'I haven't killed anyone. That's not what I meant. I knew nothing about Father Dominic's death until I came in here this morning.'

'It would help if you told us what you meant, then.'

He sighed and looked briefly at his solicitor who shrugged his shoulders. 'It's up to you, Philip. I can only advise you.'

The suspect exhaled loudly before he spoke. 'The window. I broke the window.'

Hood shot a knowing look towards Knight. She did not react. Hood then concentrated his gaze on the suspect. 'How did you break it? You don't appear to have cut yourself, not according to the doctor who's just examined you.'

'I used a spade. I got it from the outbuilding where the gardening tools are kept.' He placed his head in his hands.

'But why did you break the window? Your father had only just had it put in. It cost him a lot of money. You don't look to me like a mindless vandal.'

Philip raised his head and half-smiled. 'That's why I did it.'

'Could you explain what you mean?'

The solicitor intervened. 'Philip, don't forget what I advised. You don't have to answer any of these questions. Remember, this is a murder investigation. You have the right to remain silent. We've had very little disclosure so far.'

Philip shrugged his shoulders. 'I don't see the harm in telling them why I broke the window.'

'Well, it's up to you, but my advice stands.'

Philip acknowledged his solicitor, then turned to Hood. He leant forward as he gave his explanation. 'My father refused to let me have any more money. He even stopped the paltry allowance he'd previously given me, yet he spent over five grand on a bloody window.' He sat back in his chair and folded his arms. There was an angry look in his eyes. 'That's why I did it.'

He continued to glare at the chief inspector who said nothing for several seconds. The silence was broken when Hood asked him a question he was not expecting.

'Are you still using drugs?'

Philip looked at his solicitor again. The solicitor shook his head.

'No comment,' said Philip.

Hood knew from the FME's brief report there were no recent indications that he had been injecting illicit substances, but Hood appreciated there are other ways of ingesting them. Neither did Philip Southall appear to be suffering any withdrawal symptoms. Hood considered it appropriate to continue questioning him. 'When did you break the window?'

'I'm saying nothing else – on the advice of my solicitor.'

Hood stood up and walked around the room in silence before resuming his seat. He heaved a sigh then looked directly at Philip. 'If you didn't kill Father Dominic, it would help us if you told us *when* you broke the window. You see, the spade you had in your possession could have been the very thing the murderer used to kill the priest. And in view of what you've just admitted, the fingerprints we found on it are probably yours.'

Hood turned towards DC Bradley. 'Go and see if the results have come through on the prints on the handle of the spade, will you?'

Hood was bluffing. He knew the fingerprint expert would not be examining the evidence before Sunday morning when he came back from leave. All they knew at the moment was they did not belong to anyone on record. And no comparison had yet been made with the prints Philip Southall had given on his arrest. Bradley, anxious to play along with the chief inspector, put his notebook away and left the room without saying a word.

'I take it you weren't wearing gloves when you smashed the window?' continued Hood.

Philip looked at his hands and shook his head. Panic was setting in. He looked plaintively towards his solicitor who leant forward in his chair as he complained to Hood. 'You never mentioned that to me, Chief Inspector when you were giving me disclosure. Can you establish that the same implement was used to kill this priest and to smash the window?'

Hood's reply was curt and to the point. 'We haven't had a response from the scientists yet. As I hope I made clear, it's only supposition at the moment and we've only just taken your client's prints. When we have any actual evidence, you'll be the first to be informed.'

Philip continued to appear agitated. When he eventually replied to Hood's question, his voice betrayed what seemed to be genuine alarm. 'No. I had nothing covering my hands. I wanted my father to know it was me. I assumed he'd call in the police and that my prints would be found on the spade. But I didn't kill Father Dominic. I know nothing about that.' His panic increased. 'I wouldn't do anything like that. For God's sake, you can't think I would kill a priest? What do you think I am?'

Hood's eyes darted around the room; he noticed the solicitor was displaying concern. Was he going to stop the interview and ask to speak to his client in private? Hood pressed on. 'Tell me, what time was it when you broke the window?'

As Hood had anticipated the solicitor intervened. 'Philip, I advise you not to reply. We need to see the evidence before you say anything which may incriminate you.'

His client ignored him. He almost shouted his reply. 'I didn't kill Father Dominic. I don't care about the evidence. How can it incriminate me? I didn't do it.' He was now breathing rapidly as he ignored his solicitor and answered Hood's question. 'I don't have a watch but it must have been between half-past seven and eight o'clock on Wednesday evening, probably nearer eight. I remember it was still light. The sun had not gone down.'

'Did you see anyone about the place?'

'No, I don't think so.'

'You didn't see Father Dominic?'

'Not when I broke the window, no… but I saw him a bit earlier.'

'How much earlier?'

'Twenty minutes or so. He was walking back to his cottage from the chapel.'

'From the chapel? You mean the present chapel, not the grounds of the ruined church?'

'The new chapel, yes, not that it's that new, but my father calls it that.'

'Did he see you?'

'I don't think so. I wasn't making my presence too obvious.'

Knight intervened. 'Why not? If you wanted your father to know you'd smashed the window, why not let Father Dominic see you doing it?'

Philip paused then smiled. He was now much calmer. He spoke quietly. 'Cos he'd probably have talked me out of it. That's the way he was. I hadn't smashed the window at the time I saw him. I waited until he had gone into his cottage. I hung around for quite a bit before I did it. I didn't want to involve him. That wouldn't have been fair.' He continued smiling as if he were remembering something from the past.

'When did you last speak to Father Dominic? asked Hood.

'About a month ago. He heard my confession. I promised him I'd try and quit the drugs scene completely.'

'Where did he hear your confession?'

'In his cottage. My father didn't know I'd been there. He was in London, or so Father Dominic informed me. I'm sure he wouldn't have told my father he'd seen me. He was very good about that, you know, keeping confidences.'

'Did you keep your promise?'

He looked down. 'I tried, I really did, but I'd had some gear on the night I smashed the window.'

'What exactly?'

'Only some weed. I haven't used heroin or cocaine for over four months, not that my father would believe me. It was Father Dominic who encouraged me to get off hard drugs.'

'Where did you leave the spade, after you broke the window?'

Philip hesitated before he replied. The solicitor repeated his advice, but Philip waived him away. The solicitor shook his head, sat back in his chair, and folded his arms. He was beginning to think his presence served no purpose.

'I didn't put it back, I remember that. I just threw it down.' He continued slowly as if he were genuinely trying to recall his actions. 'Yes, I remember now. I still had it with me when I thought I heard a car turning into the drive, so I headed for the picket gate at the back of the ruined chapel and made myself scarce. I thought it might be a taxi with my father in it.'

'Did you actually see a car?'

'No, but I definitely heard one. There's a lot of excess gravel at the entrance gates; it was very quiet that night so it was easy to hear a car coming up the drive. I ran towards the picket gate that leads to the village. I wasn't going to go down the drive in case it was my father. I didn't actually see anyone.'

'Where did you leave the spade? It may be very important.'

Philip appeared to be concentrating hard. 'I wasn't thinking about it that much. I doubled back through the old chapel grounds and just let it go.'

'Did you lean it against something or just drop it on the ground?'

'I must have just dropped it. I was somewhere near the wooden cross when I let go of it. I was…'

Hood interrupted. He regarded that answer as highly relevant. 'Why did you not leave it by the window you'd damaged. You say you wanted to be caught. Why take it with you?'

Philip gave Hood a curious look. 'I don't know. I think I just panicked when I heard the car coming up the drive.'

Hood glanced at DS Knight before he continued. She raised her eyebrows and shrugged. *Here was the suspect admitting he'd left what could well have been the murder weapon close to where Father Dominic was attacked. Did he realise what he was saying? Did he know the deceased's blood was on the back of the wooden cross?*

'Where did you go after you dropped it near the cross?' asked Hood.

'Through the picket gate, then into the village. I hung about for a bit then I walked to the farm a mile or so down the road. The Robinson place. I slept in their barn overnight.'

'Anyone see you?'

'I hope not. I've slept there a few times when I've been in the area.'

'But you have a room in the Grange, don't you?'

He lowered his eyes. The tone of his voice changed. 'What if I do? I don't use it. That would mean having to see my father. I have a few things stored there but I haven't been in my room for several months.' He spoke with feeling. 'I know I'm not welcome there.'

Hood looked at him intently. He said nothing for some time, then he pressed the suspect hard. 'Your story has a number of obvious logical flaws. You tell us you wanted your father to know you had broken his very expensive stained-glass window, but you made yourself scarce when possibly two individuals could have confirmed that you were responsible; Father Dominic for one, and whoever was coming up the drive.'

Philip smiled. He had no difficulty answering. 'I wasn't going to make it that easy for my father, Mr Hood. I wanted him to fret. I wanted him to worry. I wanted him to think anything other than that I had done it, so that when he eventually discovered it was me, it would make an even greater impact upon him.'

Hood frowned. 'And there's a second problem. Your fingerprints are not on record. How could you be connected with events on Wednesday night at Easton Grange? Until you came into Campbell Square this morning and you were required to give your fingerprints, we had no way of connecting you with the damage to the window. No witnesses. Nothing that pointed to you. Only your recent admission.'

Philip appeared surprised. 'But I thought they were on record. I was done for possession of cannabis about five years ago. I was given a conditional discharge by Reading Magistrates' Court. I'm sure the police took my prints.'

Hood looked at Knight. 'No record of that conviction, sir,' she said, shaking her head. 'I definitely checked on the PNC. Must be a bureaucratic error or perhaps a court oversight in reporting it.'

'I don't suppose you remember the date?' asked Hood, wearily.

'No, I don't. I know I'd just finished my first year at Oxford. I'd been at a music festival, near Newbury I think it was. That's where I was nicked. Most of my friends who were also using got a caution but I definitely appeared in court. I was originally charged with possession with intent to supply, but there was a cock-up with the evidence. The drugs I was supposed to be supplying apparently went missing. They couldn't find them. I remember the Magistrate was furious. My case was put back for half-an-hour and they then accepted a plea to simple possession. I'd admitted that when I was interviewed. I was conditionally discharged for twelve months.

'Did you tell your father about this conviction?'

'Of course I didn't. I didn't tell anyone. Not even my then girlfriend knew about it. But if there's no official record, that's fine by me.' He smiled and looked at his solicitor. 'Does that mean I'm of good character?' he asked.

The solicitor did not reply. Hood made the position crystal clear. 'You're not of good character Mr Southall, no. You've just admitted smashing a window worth over five thousand pounds.' Philip stopped smiling. 'And I don't imagine that your father will be very happy when he finds out you caused the damage.'

Philip's tone hardened. 'That's exactly why I did it.'

Hood gave Philip a severe look. When he spoke there was an edge to his voice which had not been apparent before. 'You really don't like your father do you?'

Philip dropped his head. He did not answer.

Wendy Knight continued the questioning. 'You were in the village on Thursday, remember? You were seen.'

He looked up and smiled. 'Was I? Yes. I called in at the shop for some cigarettes sometime in the afternoon.'

'And a sandwich?'

Philip smiled and nodded. 'You have been thorough.'

'You saw Helen Swanson in the shop.'

'Yes, but I didn't speak to her. She's married to a police officer, you know.'

'Surely you must have heard about Father Dominic? His death was reported on the lunchtime news. And it's been all over the media since.'

Philip shook his head. 'No, I knew nothing about it until I came in here this morning. I don't listen to gossip or the radio and I didn't see anyone to speak to in the village apart from Helen and I said nothing to her or she to me.'

'Wasn't it being discussed in the shop?'

'If it were, I didn't pick it up.'

Hood leant back in his chair. He was beginning to think that Philip might be telling the truth; either that or he was spinning a carefully contrived yarn to explain the evidence against him. He took up the questioning. 'Why did you come in?'

'To confess to the window, of course. I was beginning to think my father wasn't going to report it, so I came in. When I admitted it, I knew you would have to speak to him about it. He's had three days to fester.'

'But not the killing?'

Tears started to form in Philips eyes. He shook his head vigorously. 'I didn't kill Father Dominic. I regarded him as a friend. He was someone I could talk to. He wasn't like my father. He would listen. He was very good at that, listening.' He looked plaintively at Wendy Knight. 'He didn't try and make me do anything or judge me. He said how I chose to live my life was up to me.' He paused and leant forward. 'I couldn't do anything like that. To kill a priest!' He shook his head again. 'And Father Dominic? No. I didn't do it.'

'And you didn't talk to him on Wednesday?'

Philip did not reply for some time. He looked towards his solicitor who simply shrugged his shoulders. 'I admit I called at the Gatehouse earlier in the day, but he wasn't there. There was no sign of him.'

'You agree you were in the grounds on the day he was killed?'

Philip looked up, a sarcastic grin crossed his features. His tone was much sharper. 'I've already admitted that.'

'But this is much earlier. When we know that Father Dominic was working in the Long Room with Father Grantham.'

Philip appeared surprised. 'Who's Father Grantham?'

'You'd never seen him around the place?'

'Never. Who is he? Is my father collecting priests for a hobby?'

He attempted to laugh. Hood did not respond but continued with his questions. 'Tell me, Mr Southall, did you look for Father Dominic when he wasn't in his cottage?'

'No. I didn't want to risk bumping into my father. I know he spends a few days a week in London, but I had no idea whether he was at home or not that day.'

'Did you want to see Father Dominic about anything in particular?'

Philip paused before he answered. 'No. Just a chat. He'd told me I could call in anytime. If he'd been there I probably wouldn't have broken the window. As I said, he'd have talked me out of it.' He looked down. 'He was trying to mediate between my father and me.'

'Did he ever give you any money?'

Philip had the grace to appear embarrassed. 'The odd pound. He didn't have much and I didn't like borrowing from him. I believe he received a small monthly allowance from his monastery. And I always paid him back. I want to make that clear.'

'Why were you heading towards the Grange after you left the shop on Thursday afternoon?

'Was I?'

'Helen Swanson saw you walking in that direction.'

'Did she? Well, I didn't go into the grounds or the house if that's what you're suggesting. I was heading for the main road which is in the same direction.'

'Where did you spend Thursday night?'

'In Northampton.'

'Where in Northampton? Where have you been living over the last few weeks?'

Philip looked suspiciously towards Hood before he answered. 'Here and there. I do have one or two friends, you know. And there's a squat here in the town, just off the Barrack Road. Blenheim Street I think it's called. Opposite the off-licence. I was there last night too.'

'You'd rather stay in a dump like that than return home?'

'So it seems.'

'How did you get to Northampton from Easton?'

He held up his thumb. 'Hitch-hiked. I do it all the time. It's surprisingly easy. That's why I was heading for the main road when Helen saw me. Not much chance of getting a lift in the village.'

'I understand you haven't told your father you've been arrested? You declined the offer to phone him.'

'I thought he'd find out in time anyway, once I confessed. And I don't want to see him. We'll only end up having another row.'

Hood looked him in the eye. 'You do realise that on what we have so far, you were probably the last person to see Father Dominic alive?'

'Apart from the killer, you mean?'

Philip was quick to make the point. Hood nodded. 'Apart from the killer, as you say. But we shall have to treat you as a prime suspect, Mr Southall. The evidence puts you at the scene and in possession of what appears to be the murder weapon. We're still awaiting results from the lab. They'll confirm it one way or the other very soon. But we already know that the blood found on the spade is the same group as Father Dominic's. His is not a particularly common grouping. Do you know your own blood group?'

'Can't remember, but the doctor took a sample from me. You'll know soon enough.' He became visibly upset again. 'But I didn't do it! Why would I want to kill Father Dominic? He and I...'

Hood interrupted. He itemised the factors which told against Philip. 'You've admitted breaking the window with the spade. They're probably your fingerprints on the handle. You were in the vicinity at the relevant time and we are pretty sure that the spade *you* used to break the window was used to kill the priest. It's not looking good, is it?'

'I didn't do it.'

'So you say. We'll continue with our inquiries and I shall want to see you again.'

Hood stood up, stated the time, and switched off the tape recorder. Philip looked at his solicitor and repeated his denials to himself several times. He then looked at Hood. His tone was again desperate. 'You do believe me, don't you?'

'It's not me you need to convince. As I said, you are and will remain a suspect, certainly for the time being. And I shall have to speak to your father about what you've told us.'

Philip dropped his head. He hardly dared raise it. 'You're not going to charge me then?'

'Not yet, no. We'll have to check a few things first. In the meantime, you'll be kept here in custody.'

Philip became emotional. He looked up. Tears formed in his eyes once more. 'For how long? I only broke a bloody window.'

'Too early to say. Your solicitor will advise you as to the position. It will assist you getting bail, always assuming bail becomes appropriate, if you can provide us with a permanent address. We can't have you wandering about the county, you know. I need to know where you are, twenty-four-seven. Will your father have you back home?'

Philip shook his head. The reference to bail had raised his spirits briefly but the mention of his father plunged him back into despondency. 'I don't think so. Not when you tell him I broke his precious window.'

CHAPTER TWELVE

'What do you reckon, Wendy? Is he our man?'

Wendy Knight shook her head. 'I must say, I have my doubts, sir.' She smiled. 'But I'm open to persuasion. It looks like he didn't know that Father Dominic had been killed when he came into Campbell Square this morning. Either that or he's an extremely good actor. He'd hardly have come in and admitted using the spade to break the window if he were the killer and had used the same spade to attack the priest.'

Hood had taken Knight to a convenient public house for a late lunch and a drink. They occupied a small table in the lounge bar well away from flapping ears. Hood was hungry and demolished a chicken mayo sandwich with gusto as he listened to his sergeant. When he had finished he wiped his mouth with a paper napkin and took a generous swig of his pint of lager. 'That's better. Are you sure you don't want anything to eat, Wendy? My treat.'

'No thanks, sir. I'm not particularly hungry. The drink is fine.' She paused, looked around the lounge bar, then leant forward over the table.

'As I said, sir, I have very real doubts that Philip is our killer.'

Hood wasn't going to admit it – not yet – but he had similar doubts himself. 'You may well be right. But he's got himself into a very tricky position, hasn't he? The scientific evidence is pretty strong, assuming they're his prints on the spade, and even if they're not, he admits he used it to break the window. In the absence of any other suspects, the evidence is pointing decidedly at him.' Hood looked down. 'God only knows what his father is going to say. I'll have to speak to him, of course.'

'But what could his motive be? Why would he want to kill Father Dominic? He seems to have been very fond of him, in his own way.'

Hood shrugged his shoulders. 'We don't have to prove motive, Wendy. Perhaps Father Dominic heard the window breaking. If he was in the old chapel grounds saying his office, or still in his cottage, he was bound to have heard it going in. It's very quiet there in the evening and the noise must have been considerable.'

'But not so loud that Grantham would hear it?'

Hood smiled. The detective sergeant was not letting go of her suspicions about the Jesuit. 'Remember Mozart and the distance to the west wing. And he uses headphones. I doubt if he'd hear anything wearing those, the music apart.'

'Yes, sir,' answered Knight, not even attempting to hide her reluctance to agree with the chief inspector who put a contrary view of the evidence to her.

'Perhaps Dominic challenged Philip and a row broke out. Philip lost his temper and hit him with the spade. It would fit with our theory about the killer knowing the priest and it explains the presence of the spade. If Dominic saw Philip, he'd also see the spade and wouldn't necessarily regard it as a threat even if he'd heard the window go in.'

'But he says he never spoke to Father Dominic?'

'Of course he does. But why should we believe him?'

Neither said anything for several seconds.

'And the breviary?'

'What about it?' asked Hood, taking a further drink.

'How did it end up where we found it? It's a fair way from the broken window to the back of the ruined chapel.'

'As you suggested earlier, Father Dominic probably put it there himself before he spoke with his killer. He could have caught up with whoever it was who killed him at that point after he'd heard the window going in. And Philip agrees that's where he abandoned the spade. He's put himself at the very spot where the priest was attacked.'

'That's what I mean sir; he's providing some rather damning evidence from his own mouth, if he is responsible. That crossed my mind when we were interviewing him. Why would he do that if he's the killer? Surely, he'd not put himself anywhere near where it happened. He didn't take much notice of his solicitor's advice either. Most guilty men simply clam up, especially when advised to by a lawyer.'

Hood considered his response. He looked around him and leant forward before he continued. 'I have come across something like this before, Wendy. A killer who provided pretty powerful evidence against himself as a defensive strategy. He made it appear he was guilty from his own mouth, knowing that some evidence would emerge which suggested someone else was responsible. Evidence that he had carefully prepared and made sure we eventually discovered. It almost worked too. It was quite a *cause celebre*. I'll tell you all about it sometime.'

'Is Philip up to that sort of thing? He seems to have deliberately left his prints on the spade. And the spade was recovered in the outbuilding. Not very clever if he used the spade to kill the priest to leave it there with his prints on it.'

'How did the spade get back to where we found it?' asked Hood. 'That's not where he said he dropped it.'

'Someone must have known that's where it was usually kept,' replied Knight. 'And the outbuilding is insecure. The killer must have known that.'

'Then the killer must have put it there,' said Hood. 'There isn't another rational explanation. The window was broken at some point, but whether it was before or after the killing we don't yet know. If it occurred after Father Dominic was attacked there may be some blood on the pieces of glass left inside the Long Room.'

'Always assuming the same spade was used?'

'That looks pretty clear, don't you think? The priest's blood and glass that must have come from the broken window on the same implement.'

Knight took a sip of her mineral water. 'If Philip is responsible for the killing, my money's on the killing taking place first. An unpremeditated killing followed by a desperate attempt to make it look like a burglary gone wrong.'

'Let's consider that further, shall we?' said Hood. 'How did he get the dead priest into the house? It certainly wasn't through the broken window. And why go to the trouble of dumping him in the priest-hole?' Hood was quite happy to switch to highlighting features of the evidence in Philip's favour. It was a favourite ploy of his and kept his junior officers up to the mark. Knight answered him.

'He has a key to the side door just off the main hall. The adjacent corridor leads to the Long Room. Father Dominic probably told him about the priest-hole. Anyone else would presumably have to risk carrying the body through the main entrance or through the chapel.'

'With only Grantham as a potential witness.'

'Yes, sir. But he'd have been absorbed in his Mozart wouldn't he? And Philip didn't know that Grantham was in the house. He admitted as much.'

Hood laughed. 'You really have it in for Grantham, don't you? He was in the house so must have been involved. Is that what you're saying?'

'Not really, sir, no. But he had as much opportunity as Philip, if not more. I don't think we can exclude him as a suspect, not yet.'

Hood shook his head but continued smiling. 'But we're not going to find his fingerprints on the spade handle. Neither has he admitted wielding it and breaking the window; Philip has.'

The detective sergeant nodded but did not reply. She tilted her head allowing her hair to fall back off her shoulders. Hood wandered if she realised how attractive that made her look. Was she doing it deliberately? Several men propping up the bar had noticed her and were paying the two of them more attention than Hood thought appropriate. 'When will we have the full fingerprint report?' asked Hood.

'Tomorrow sometime. DS Wilson is back from leave tomorrow. He's our local expert on fingerprints.'

'If there's only Philip's prints on the spade we are going to have to consider charging him.'

'Before we get the DNA analysis?'

'We can only hold him for a limited period of time. And there's real pressure from the fourth floor to make headway in this inquiry. I had to give the Deputy Chief an update by phone first thing this morning. And there were TV cameras outside Easton Grange earlier too, according to Swanson. We need to make progress.'

Wendy shook her head. 'But charging the wrong man isn't progress, is it? Poor Sir Robert. It will destroy him if Philip really is responsible.'

'If he's the killer, that can't be helped.'

'Can't we hold off for a couple of days, sir? I'm not at all sure Philip's our man. There's a long way to go with this investigation. We could always bail him.'

'You really do think he could be innocent?'

She frowned. 'Not for the window, no. He definitely did that, or why admit it? We could charge him with criminal damage and get him remanded if you don't want him out on bail.'

Hood smiled. 'And what if his father refuses to press charges? If I know Sir Robert, there's every chance that's what he'll do. I don't think it's even occurred to him that Philip might be responsible for breaking his window.'

'I'd be pretty miffed if it were my window. I suppose he targeted that particular window because of his father's coat of arms being so prominently displayed in the glass?'

Hood nodded. 'Along with the family motto, *Orbis non sufficit.*'

She smiled. 'My Latin is terrible, sir. Non-existent in fact.'

'Mine is not what it was, but it's quite simple. It means "The world is not enough."' He smiled. 'Ring any bells?'

'Isn't that the title of a film? Pierce Brosnan as James Bond if I recall correctly.'

Hood smiled. 'If it is, I think the motto came first.'

'Do you think he was attacking the motto rather than the coat of arms?'

Hood shook his head. 'I think he was motivated by the cost. He'd discovered somehow how much had been laid out by his father. Remember, he knew it had cost five thousand pounds which is pretty accurate for a guess. Perhaps Father Dominic told him?'

'Why would his father not prosecute him?'

Hood finished off his pint. 'Have you heard of the parable of the prodigal son, Wendy?'

'Heard of it, of course, but I don't remember the details. I'm not very religious, as you know, sir.'

'Well, I suspect that Sir Robert will turn out to be like the father in the parable who forgave his younger son, despite his profligacy. He might not go as far as killing the fatted calf for Philip, but I doubt if he'll prosecute even if his insurers put pressure on him.' He smiled. 'I must confess, I've always had a sneaking regard for the older brother in the parable. The responsible one who stayed at home, caused no trouble and worked hard for little reward. It's hardly surprising he felt miffed at his father's welcome home party for his dissolute sibling.'

Wendy raised an eyebrow as one of the men at the bar tried to catch her attention. She had left her jacket at Campbell Square and looked very eye-catching in her colourful summer dress which revealed her toned arms and emphasised her slim figure. Hood noticed the interest. 'Drink up,' he said. 'There are too many eyes and ears in here. Let's get back to the station.'

Wendy took a final sip of her sparkling mineral water and the two of them left the pub through the nearest exit. Was that a wolf whistle she heard as she passed through the door? She continued to think aloud as she and Hood walked slowly back to Campbell Square in the late-afternoon sun. 'It's not out of the question, I suppose, that Father Dominic staggered to the Long Room after his assailant had left. Professor Romney agrees it's a possibility, if somewhat remote. Perhaps he thought Grantham would be there. He'd obviously be looking for help and the only person he knew who could do anything for him was Grantham. He would have known Sir Robert was away in London and that the housekeeper had left for the day.'

Hood always found Wendy's take on the evidence useful. She made a valuable sounding board as he propounded his own views and he had the good sense to listen to hers, whether he agreed with her or not. Two heads were invariably better than one.

'But why go to the Long Room? It would have been more sensible to call for help as he came into the house from the chapel grounds rather than going through to the Long Room. And it's quite a distance from the ruins of the old chapel. No blood was found in the hall or the corridor either. Much more likely that the killer dumped him where he was found. Yes, there's no getting away from it. The solution to this mystery lies somewhere in that room. I intend to have a good look at the priest-hole tomorrow, now that SOCO have finished with it. Father Milmo is desperate to examine it too. He probably knows more about these things even than Grantham. I shall be taking full advantage of his expertise, I can tell you.'

Wendy nodded and continued to speculate. 'As you say sir, no bloodstaining was found inside the house except in and around the hide in the Long Room, which is a bit odd if Father Dominic got there under his own steam. He must have been bleeding quite heavily from the wounds to his head. And there was a lot of blood on his habit, according to the pathologist.'

'What are you suggesting, Wendy? That he was wrapped in something before he was dumped in the priest-hole?'

'He must have been. How else do you explain the absence of any blood on the route from the old chapel? And Nigel did find traces of dust and particles of gravel which match the surface of the drive and parking area.'

Hood pondered what she had said. 'An interesting theory. But is there any evidence to support it?'

'Well he wasn't very heavy, was he? He wouldn't have proved much of a burden to carry and his habit would have absorbed most of the blood, especially if his cowl had been over his head, and that's where most of the blood was found when his clothing was examined.'

Hood could hardly disagree. 'We'll learn more when the scientists have examined everything in greater detail, I suppose.'

'By the time he was found he must have been dead for hours. If his cowl had been over his head, the blood would have dried and caused it to stick, surely?'

Hood nodded. 'Guy Romney did find what looks like an impression of material in one of the bloodied marks left on his head. He's had it photographed. We should get a copy in a day or two. He could well have had the cowl over his head when he was struck.'

'So it could be pure chance that no blood dripped as he was carried to the priest-hole?'

Hood shrugged his shoulders. 'I don't know, Wendy; that could well be the case, but it's very unlikely. Some blood must have fallen, unless he was wrapped in something. Whoever killed him would have had to move pretty quickly. The Grange is hardly the centre of the universe, but the killer would still have been concerned about being seen. It was a fine summer evening. There was a chance he might have been seen by someone. Blood dripping from the wounds would not have been his priority. We need to question Grantham again when we have the pathologist's report. We should have a typed copy of Guy's preliminary findings on Monday.'

'Along with the photographs.' She grimaced as she recalled what she had witnessed at the post-mortem. She then pointed to another negative feature of the evidence. 'And if Philip did kill him, he wouldn't have anything available to wrap the body in, would he? After all, he didn't go there with the intention of killing anyone. If he did it, it must have been a spontaneous act. Someone else, like whoever was in the car Philip heard, might have had a rug or something available in his vehicle. I keep a rug in my car.'

Before Knight could answer, Hood stopped in his tracks. He put the flat of his hand to his forehead. 'His coat! We've overlooked his coat.

Swanson's wife noticed he was wearing a heavy coat when he was seen in the village shop on Thursday afternoon. She remembered it because it was so hot.'

Wendy pulled a face. She had overlooked it too. 'That's right, sir. And he wasn't wearing it when he came into Campbell Square this morning. I'm almost sure there was no coat listed amongst the property taken from him.'

'If he'd used it to wrap the body in, it's inevitable some blood would have been transferred on to it and afterwards on to his own clothing, especially as he was seen wearing the coat on Thursday afternoon – after the killing had taken place.'

'No obvious bloodstains on the clothing he was arrested in. But it's all gone to the lab for a full examination.'

'Would the absence of bloodstaining put him in the clear? Blood would inevitably have got onto him during the assault if he did kill Father Dominic. If he did it, he'd have had to clean himself up somehow… and somewhere. As far as we know he hasn't a permanent address or anywhere he could go.'

Hood was trying his best to remain detached as always. He was a great believer in letting the evidence lead him to a conclusion. Not like some detectives of his acquaintance who used their gut instincts to identify a suspect and then tried to fit the evidence in to justify their theories. As they arrived at the steps leading up to the police station he paused as Wendy answered him.

'Where would he have done that, sir? He had nowhere to go apart from the Grange and we know he didn't go to his room there. And he's no fool. He'd be stupid to continue wearing the same clothing.'

'Perhaps he had a change of clothes somewhere other than at the Grange, but where?'

They walked up the steps and into the police station. Wendy had previously organised a search of the bedroom Philip used when living at the Grange but nothing had been found. There was certainly no sign of blood. And the room was still available to him. A key to a side door to the Grange was still in his possession when he was arrested. Wendy continued to think aloud as they approached the custody desk. Overlooking Philip's coat was causing her noticeable embarrassment. It was no comfort that the DCI had missed its possible relevance too.

'We need to find his coat, sir. It could be crucial evidence, either way. He may have left it somewhere because it's so warm, or if he's our killer, got rid of it. We also need to organise a search of the barn where he spent Wednesday night and that squat off the Barrack Road he mentioned. I've already tasked Bradley with finding the squat, but I haven't heard from him yet.'

Hood nodded his agreement. He stopped in front of the custody desk and addressed the uniformed sergeant. 'Let me see the custody record for Philip Southall would you?'

The sergeant turned and opened his filing cabinet, pulled out the relevant document and handed it to Hood who scrutinised it with care.

'You're right about the coat Wendy. He didn't have it with him when he came in, just a hooded top.' Hood sighed in frustration.

'It was very warm this morning,' volunteered the overly perspiring custody sergeant, despite being in his shirt sleeves. 'Not really the weather for a coat, sir.'

'Yes,' replied Hood. 'It's very warm. But not as hot as it was on Thursday, eh Wendy?'

'No, sir.' Knight dropped her head.

Hood handed the custody record back to the sergeant and indicated for Wendy to follow him upstairs. He opened the door to his room, as he now regarded it, but did not sit down at his desk. He paced the room, annoyed with himself at overlooking the possible significance of Philip Southall's coat.

'Instruct Swanson to search the barns at the farm where our suspect says he spent the night. He should be able to manage that. He's probably familiar with it. It's only a mile or so from the village.'

'Yes, sir.'

Wendy Knight was still deep in thought as she grabbed her mobile and made a call to Swanson. She was no longer fighting Philip's corner as keenly as before. The coat seemed to have assumed real significance; the fact that it had been overlooked causing her, perhaps, to give it undue weight. She paused as Swanson answered her call. She quickly gave him his instructions then put through a call to DC Bradley. He did not respond. 'No show from Bradley, sir. But he may have gone off duty by now. He started very early this morning.'

Hood harrumphed. 'No-one on my team is ever off duty, Wendy.

Leave a message. I want that coat found. And he shouldn't have gone off duty without reporting how he'd got on.'

Wendy did as she was asked. Hood eventually stopped his pacing and slumped in the chair behind his desk. He was already counting in his own mind a number of potential evidential problems if Philip were the murderer. 'But if he is the killer, how would he have known the spade had been discovered? We never announced that.' He looked pointedly at Wendy. 'Did we?'

Wendy looked down and appeared slightly embarrassed. 'Not that we'd found the spade, no sir. But the press office did indicate we had found what we thought was the murder weapon. It was on the late news last night and again this morning.'

Hood was furious. He had not seen the television news. He'd gone straight to his bed after driving home the evening before. He had left dealings with the press to Knight. He stood up and walked towards the detective sergeant.

'What! How did that happen? Who is responsible? It's basic procedure to keep such matters confidential not to tell all to the press, not even our own press office.'

Wendy Knight tried to explain. 'This is a high-profile case, sir. As you mentioned earlier, the DCC wanted an update this morning. The press office has been equally demanding, pushing us for information. Central News is highlighting the investigation. Someone on the team must have mentioned it. I gave instructions that everything relating to the media had to come through me and I certainly did not include it in the written briefing I handed over. You've seen a copy of it. You approved it. That was all that was disclosed by me.'

Hood was still beside himself with anger. 'It's not your fault, Wendy.' He paused and did his best to calm himself down. 'So, Philip Southwell may have picked up from the news that the murder weapon had been found. And if he is the killer, he'd have known it was the spade that was used and so in he comes and admits the damage, realising his prints were probably on the handle.'

Wendy nodded apprehensively. 'It's a possibility, sir. No-one other than the killer could have known that a spade had been used to kill the priest. But I do wonder why he didn't wipe the handle or why he put it back with the other tools.'

'Isn't that the obvious place to put it? Sitting alongside other gardening equipment it wouldn't stand out. At least it wouldn't have, had a better job been made of cleaning it.'

'Perhaps that's why the killer put the spade there; to suggest that Father Dominic had been murdered by someone with intimate knowledge of the estate? But surely Philip would have wiped the handle? He wouldn't have been concerned about the window anymore and wanting his father to discover what he'd done, not after he'd killed the priest. It doesn't make sense for him to have left his prints on the spade or to put it back in the stable.'

Hood acknowledged what Knight had said but he remained annoyed with himself that he had overlooked the coat. He couldn't get it out of his head. She tried to soothe his ego. 'Good job you noticed the flies, sir.'

Hood grunted. He was not in the mood for compliments.

Wendy dared to underline what she had said. 'It's still a bit odd, sir, isn't it? As you say, putting the spade back indicates a degree of intelligence. Not cleaning the blade properly and not wiping the prints from the handle doesn't!' She paused briefly. 'It's almost as if two different individuals were involved.'

Hood grunted again. 'Let's not go there Wendy. One suspect at a time. And if Philip Southall is playing a game with us, it's going to prove a very high risk strategy.' He was now much calmer. 'And Wendy, find out who spoke to the press officer. Whoever it was, he's off the team. No excuses. I simply can't have this.'

'Yes, sir.'

But doubts still nagged away at the detective sergeant about Philip Southwell being the killer.

Why would he dump Father Dominic in the priest-hole? And return the spade to the stable? Surely, if he were the killer he'd have got rid of it along with the rest of the incriminating evidence?

CHAPTER THIRTEEN

'Yes, Swanson. What did you find out at the farm?'

Hood was still in the Superintendent's room at Campbell Square, his mobile phone in his hand. He really should have been home hours ago. He was beyond imagining what his wife would say when he eventually returned. She was pleased about his upcoming promotion but would be expecting him to work more regular hours given his new status. He had assured her that would be the case when his promotion took effect the following month. He was not at all sure that she believed him. He had never been one for sitting behind a desk and working 9 to 5. Wendy Knight was going through further statements which had been taken during the door-to-door inquiries in Easton village. She had failed to discover who had leaked information to the press office and the press officer was being deliberately obstructive in identifying her source. 'Just something I picked up,' she asserted when Wendy spoke to her over the phone. 'And I didn't see any harm in mentioning that the murder weapon *may* have been located. It was not a definite statement, just a possibility.' Hood decided to leave it to the Deputy Chief Constable to sort out. He'd put in his complaint but now wanted to get on with the investigation.

Wendy Knight assumed a very low profile as Hood paced the room while he spoke to Swanson. The signal was not of the best and he had difficulty in hearing everything Swanson was saying. It all added to his ill humour.

'Nothing found at the farm, sir,' said the junior officer in a matter of fact way. 'And the farmer didn't know anything about anyone sleeping in any of her outbuildings. She's a widow and keeps two dogs who have the run of the yard at night. Big buggers they are too. I wouldn't want them running towards me in the middle of the night, I can tell you. She never heard a thing, and the dogs were pretty noisy when I turned up. Really made their presence felt. She had to put them into the house to stop them barking at me.'

'You nevertheless checked the barns, I hope?'

'Yes sir, all three of them.'

'No sign of anyone bedding down there?

'No sir, nothing.'

'Nothing at all?' repeated Hood. 'No clothing, no bloodstains?' He exhaled noisily.

'Not that I could see, sir, and I had a good nosey round. Mrs Robinson was very cooperative. I was there for over an hour.'

'And you're sure you got the right farm?'

Swanson sounded almost offended but he knew his place. 'Yes sir. It's the only one in the immediate area. Washbrook Farm is the next one and it's a good three miles farther on. I doubt if he legged it that far.'

'What about the Manor. That's within walking distance isn't it?'

'Only the house there now, sir. Mrs Robinson's late husband bought the land decades ago. No barns at the Manor nowadays apart from a couple of garages – and they're kept locked.'

'So, Philip Southall may not be telling the truth about where he stayed on Wednesday night?'

'Looks like it, sir. Perhaps we should get SOCO to the farm to check the barns out thoroughly?'

'I'll bear that in mind, but they're still very busy at the Grange and resources are limited. Anything else?'

'There is one thing, sir, that I think I should mention.'

'What's that?'

'Well I don't know if anything'll turn on it, and it's nothing to do with the farm. It's my wife.'

'Your wife?' Hood raised his eyebrows and glanced towards Wendy Knight.

'Yes, sir. She reckons she saw a man leaving Mrs Morton's cottage this morning. As you know, our rear garden abuts her cottage garden and the wife reckons she saw a man coming out of the back door. Not long after six o'clock. She couldn't sleep and had gone downstairs to make herself a cup of tea.'

'Did she recognise him?'

'No, she only caught a glimpse and she didn't see his face. He moved like lightening, apparently. Tall and slim is all she can remember by way of a description. Dark clothing too. Left through the side-gate. She only mentioned it to me at tea-time when I got in. I don't suppose it means anything?'

Hood had a different opinion but he had no intention of disclosing his thoughts to a junior officer. 'I don't suppose it does, Adrian, but thanks anyway. Oh, and remember, I want you at the chapel tomorrow morning. Bring your wife with you. I would like to meet her and I shall want to take a statement from her about what she saw, just a formality you understand.'

Hood switched off his phone and caught Wendy Knight's attention. 'What do you think of that, Wendy?'

She looked up from the statements she was perusing. 'Progress, sir?'

'Could be. Young Swanson's wife – she saw a man leaving Martha Morton's cottage early this morning, and by the back door. Now, I wonder who that could be?'

'How early?'

'Six o'clock. Or shortly afterwards.'

'That's very early. Who was it?'

'She only caught a glimpse and didn't recognise him.'

'You don't think it could have been Philip Southall? Did Swanson find anything at the farm to support Philip's story that he spent Wednesday night sleeping in a barn?'

'No he didn't. Quite the contrary. And the farmer keeps two dogs. They have the run of the place at night. Barked like mad when Swanson turned up. And the farmer heard nothing on Wednesday night. Neither did the dogs, presumably? Doesn't sound like Philip Southall is telling us the truth about where he spent the night.'

Wendy was intrigued. 'Could he be the man Helen Swanson saw? He didn't walk into Campbell Square until the middle of this morning. Plenty of time to get from Easton Parva into Northampton, even if he had to thumb a lift.'

'My thoughts exactly. Her cottage would prove the ideal place for him to stay when he was in the village. We need to speak to Mrs Morton before we interview Philip again. If she's in some sort of relationship with him, we need to know.' He smiled. 'I can understand him not mentioning it.

His father would go ballistic if it's true. And she is a beautiful woman with no man in her life at the moment, as far as we know.'

Wendy frowned. 'Handsome, I would say, rather than beautiful. She's thirty-nine but looks younger.' She held up the witness statement she had just finished reading. 'Swanson asked her date of birth – very politically incorrect.'

Hood chuckled but was not going to quibble. 'Handsome if you must, but I suspect there's many a man who would have no problem adopting my description.'

'And he did say he had friends in the area?' added Wendy. 'This could open up a whole new area of the investigation.' She then paused and her tone changed. An obvious drawback flashed into her mind. 'But sir, Helen Swanson knows Philip. They almost grew up together. If it were him, she'd surely have recognised him? And Martha Morton is a good few years older. Would he really be interested in an older woman, or she in him?'

Hood's keenness waned but only slightly. 'I see what you mean Wendy.' He smiled. 'But we must still check it out.' He perched on the edge of her desk. He seemed to have forgotten the leak of information to the press office. 'It depends on the nature of the possible relationship, doesn't it? As I said, she's very, eh, handsome, very handsome indeed. Might appeal to a young man's fancy, if only temporarily, and he may have been more interested in the cottage. It would give him somewhere to change his clothes and to spend the night. And as far as Helen Swanson not recognising him is concerned, she'd hardly have expected to see Philip Southall coming out of the housekeeper's back door, so it may simply mean that it didn't occur to her that it could have been him. He fits her admittedly vague description. He's tall and fairly slim. Identification is dodgy at the best of times. People are influenced by what they expect to see as much as anything else.'

DS Knight was not wholly convinced. 'I was at her cottage late yesterday afternoon and I didn't see any sign of anyone else being there and she never mentioned anyone. I didn't carry out a search, of course. I had no reason to do so. If he has been staying there, he would presumably have left some clothes about the place?'

Hood nodded. 'If Philip has been calling on her, she'd have no more reason to mention it than he would. She would want to keep such a relationship secret.'

Wendy remained doubtful. 'He didn't look as if he'd spent the night anywhere very comfortable, did he?'

Hood was forced to agree. 'Possibly not.'

'What do you propose, sir?'

Hood looked at his watch. 'It's nearly six-thirty. I really should be getting home, but I think we should get someone over to Easton Parva to see her now, not wait until Monday morning. The clock is running on Philip's detention. I should be able to get a twelve hour extension easily enough, but the twenty-four hours will be up just after eleven o'clock in the morning. An extension gives us until about a quarter past eleven tomorrow night. We really don't have much time to waste.'

'So no further interview tonight?'

'No. You can inform his solicitor. No point dragging him in. There's still a few things we need to check and I still haven't been able to speak to Sir Robert. He hasn't answered the phone when I've called him.'

'So he doesn't know his son has been detained?'

'Not yet, no.' He paused. His eyes met hers. 'Not unless the press office has informed him, of course.'

Knight swallowed hard and looked away just as her phone buzzed. It was DC Bradley. She listened to what he had to say then repeated to Hood what he had told her. 'Bradley's on his way in, sir. It seems he didn't go off duty after all. He's come up with something from the squat off the Barrack Road.'

'So he's responded at last. Does he say what it is?'

'It looks like it could be Philip's coat.'

Hood's face was a picture. 'That I have to see. How long will he be?'

'He should be here in ten minutes. If you want to get off, I can see the housekeeper. It's almost on my way home.'

Hood nodded. 'I'll hang on for him. You get off and see Martha Morton. Let me know if she says anything useful. And, Wendy, ask her if you can look around the place. If she refuses, threaten to get a search warrant.'

'Do we have sufficient grounds, sir?'

'Let me worry about that. And she won't want to appear obstructive. If you have to, lean on her. You get off now.'

The detective sergeant grabbed her jacket and bag and left the room. Hood watched her go, then after a moment's hesitation, picked up the phone on his desk and rang his wife. He was going to have to explain yet again why he would be late home.

CHAPTER FOURTEEN

'Good work, Bradley. If this is Philip Southall's coat it will add significantly to the evidence. Tell me, what was this squat like?'

DC Bradley was feeling very pleased with himself. He had joined the police service after spending what he considered to be two wasted years in retail management. Three years in uniform followed before he was accepted into CID. He was anxious to make his mark and regarded his recovery of the coat as his opportunity to impress the chief inspector. *Was it possible that he had discovered the key to the entire case?* He could hardly contain his enthusiasm as he answered the DCI, seizing the chance to highlight his prowess as a detective. He underlined in some detail the efforts he had made to locate the squat. 'As you would expect, sir, bit of a dump. It took me a while to find it. There were several options, given the state of the street. It's in a terraced house not far from the Cathedral. The front door was hanging off its hinges, so it's quite insecure. There were a couple of druggies in there when I went in. I couldn't get much out of them. They were very incoherent, if you know what I mean?'

'And the coat?'

'One of them claimed he'd been given it by someone this morning. It was the only decent bit of kit in the whole place. He was actually wearing it, and in this weather too, but he was shivering a lot. It was also quite cold in there compared with outside.'

'Druggies seem to feel the cold for some reason.' Hood shook his head. 'I've never understood why.'

'They didn't look too well nourished, sir, the pair of them, but I suppose that goes with the territory if all your money goes on illicit substances.'

'The coat,' said Hood. 'You persuaded him to hand it over?'

'Yes, sir. It looked a good fit for the suspect so I seized it and gave Mr Smith, as he called himself, a receipt. I told him he could have it back when we've finished with it.' Bradley grinned as he spoke. 'That won't be his real name, of course.'

'I'm sure it isn't,' answered Hood. 'And I suspect he was long gone seconds after you left. Remind me, when did he say he was given it?'

'This morning. I suppose I could have arrested both of them for possession of drugs, but I thought the coat was more important. There were several syringes lying about the place. So it's not just a bit of cannabis smoking that's been going on there. They were a couple of real smackheads, no doubt about it.'

'You were quite right,' said Hood, approvingly, as he put on a pair of latex gloves. 'I'll suggest that the drugs squad pays a visit and checks the place out, though I suspect they know about it already. This person who gave it to him. Did he say anything about him?'

'He said it was a man, but he didn't know him. He couldn't remember when he'd turned up at the squat either.'

'So, he didn't confirm that whoever gave it to him had spent the night at the squat?'

'No, sir. But, to be honest, I don't think he knew what day it was. And there are several rooms in the house. It's possible he didn't see whoever gave it to him until this morning.' He paused. 'He'll not make a very reliable witness.'

Hood laughed. 'If we ever find him again.'

He began to examine the heavy brown overcoat with care. His gloved hands checked the entirety of the garment as he scrutinised each mark and tear and looked carefully at the lining. He observed that on the inside of the collar a name tag had been torn off and one of the large shank buttons was missing from the front. He then turned the sleeves inside out. But it was the areas of staining that were of most interest to him. 'I think you're right,' he said, breaking off from his examination and looking towards Bradley. 'These look like bloodstains on the inside of the right arm. And that looks like a smear of blood on the front left side, near the missing button.' He pointed to an obvious stain about an inch and three-quarters in diameter.

DC Bradley nodded his head in agreement. 'It also looks like an attempt has been made to sponge off some other marks or stains as well.'

He had observed areas on the lower section of the coat where the colour had seemingly faded in irregular shaped patches.

'You could well be right, Bradley, always assuming the original stains were in fact blood.'

'No doubt that there's blood on it, sir. Both of the two obvious areas have field-tested positive; the other faded areas will require more sophisticated testing. And we know Southall was wearing a coat like this after the killing took place. It fits the description given by the witnesses in the shop.'

Hood removed the coat from the table and held it up. 'About the right size for our suspect, wouldn't you say?'

'Yes sir. As I said, he's about my build and height and it would fit me all right. Not that I've tried it on, of course.'

'Expensive looking too. The label on the inside pocket shows a London tailor if I'm not mistaken; Saville Row no less?'

'We can check that sir, if he denies the coat is his.'

'He'll not do that. His DNA will be all over it. I don't suppose the stains have been grouped yet?'

'No.'

'It's too much to assume at the moment that this is Father Dominic's blood, of course? We already know that he was A negative and our suspect is B positive, so there'll be no confusion even at the grouping stage.'

'Let's hope it gets us somewhere, sir.'

'It should. Of course, it's not out of the question that it's our suspect's own blood, although not shed recently. He had no injuries when he was examined by the FME earlier today. As I hope you know, bloodstaining like this is virtually impossible to age. The scientists will have to determine whose blood it is which will hopefully help to establish how it got there and, perhaps, when.'

'Yes sir. DNA testing will take a few days but I'm told we'll have the blood grouping shortly. They'll do the grouping first, before they decide whether it's worth testing for DNA.'

'Excellent. Photograph it and get it all off to the lab pronto. The suspect's sample has already been sent. And Bradley, whatever the result of the grouping tests, I want a full DNA profile. The coat itself is to be tested along with the various areas of staining. I want it clearly established that Philip Southwell has worn this coat whoever shed the blood.' He paused. 'I can't wait to hear his reaction when I put all this to him tomorrow.'

CHAPTER FIFTEEN

Hood saw Sir Robert in his study immediately after Mass on Sunday morning. The baronet seemed very disheartened when he was informed his son was in police custody, suspected of killing Father Dominic. Not that he was surprised that Philip had been arrested. He'd heard on the radio that a twenty-five –year old man with a connection with Easton Parva had been detained and was "helping police with their inquiries". The BBC had been particularly discreet and not named Philip, although his name and photograph had appeared in all the tabloid newspapers that morning as someone the police wanted to interview. Sir Robert had not seen a newspaper, but something told him it had to be his son. He'd also picked up from his housekeeper that Philip had been spotted in the village on Thursday afternoon, so he was expecting the worst. Hood's verifying that it was Philip who was in custody on suspicion of murder merely confirmed his fears.

As the chief inspector had anticipated, Sir Robert immediately indicated he would not press charges in respect of the stained-glass window, saddened though he was that his son could have perpetrated such a deed. That Philip might also have been involved in the murder of a priest rendered his concerns about the damage to his window very much of secondary importance. In truth, he blamed himself. It probably would not have happened if he had not stopped Philip's allowance. At least, that was what he told himself. Hood was as sympathetic as he thought proper and did his best to assure Sir Robert that he would continue to investigate the matter neutrally without forming any adverse view of Philip unless the evidence drove him to it. He observed that there were aspects of Philip's account which told against him being the killer, always assuming he was telling the truth. The baronet seemed easier in his mind when Hood informed him that Philip had vehemently denied responsibility despite admitting damaging the window.

'I am very conscious of your consideration towards me, Mr Hood.' said Sir Robert. 'Philip has had his problems, particularly since his mother died, but I have invariably found him to be truthful even when circumstances have initially told against him. Indeed, he's almost boastful in revealing exactly what he has done – or not done. And I cannot think why he would want to harm Father Dominic. They were always very friendly, so far as I was aware.' He smiled. 'I sometimes thought they were in cahoots with each other – against me.' He paused. 'Poor Philip. He took his mother's death very hard, you know. She was always much closer to him than I was.' He shook his head. 'I do not know how I could go on if it is proved he murdered Father Dominic.'

Hood pointed to a positive feature of the investigation in an attempt to raise Sir Robert's spirits. 'My sergeant doesn't think he did it, if that is any consolation, sir. And she has demonstrated remarkably good judgment in the past. We should know a little more later today when we have the fingerprint report.'

Hood then produced a photograph of the coat that had been recovered from the squat in Northampton. Sir Robert scrutinised it carefully.

'That could be Philip's coat. He's had one like that for several years. My London tailor made it for him.'

'Saville Row, sir?'

'Yes, how did you know that?'

Hood smiled. 'There's a label on the inside pocket.'

Sir Robert nodded. 'Of course. Does this incriminate Philip in some way?'

'Too soon to say. We believe he was wearing this coat on the day after the murder, despite the warm weather. And there are certainly blood stains on it.'

Sir Robert slumped in his chair. 'Please, Mr Hood, don't tell me the blood is Father Dominic's.'

'We are awaiting the grouping results. We should have them later today. DNA will take a little longer.'

Sir Robert seemed slightly relieved. 'And if the blood is not Father Dominic's?'

'Then the coat will not figure any further in the investigation.'

'And Philip?'

'He won't be quite out of the woods, I'm afraid. We're pretty sure his fingerprints are on the murder weapon.'

Sir Robert sighed. 'The spade you located in the stables?'

'That's the one. Philip admits he used one of the spades to smash the window. It would, perhaps, be asking too much to conclude someone else used the same spade to kill Father Dominic. That would be a remarkable coincidence, don't you think? And we are pretty sure the same spade was used to commit both offences.'

'But it's not impossible that two different people used it?'

'Not impossible, no. But highly unlikely.'

Sir Robert looked down and exhaled heavily. Hood tried again to reassure him. 'Patience, Sir Robert. I know how painful this is for you. We'll know a lot more by the end of today.'

Hood looked up as Wendy Knight appeared at the study door with Father Milmo, still in his monk's habit. He had just demonstrated to her the position of his cowl when it was covering his head. Knight had not attended Mass. She had been busy dealing with other matters and had information she needed to relay to the chief inspector. Sir Robert put on a brave face as he addressed the Prior.

'Thank you for what you said about Father Dominic in your homily; I believe you caught him just about right. I think it went down very well.'

'It's the least I could do,' replied Father Milmo, 'after all, he was one of ours. The reading from the Book of Wisdom was highly appropriate, don't you think? *The souls of the righteous are in the hands of God and no torment shall ever touch them.*' He looked directly at Hood. 'Any progress on the investigation, Chief Inspector? I was concerned to read that young Philip has been arrested. I'm sure there must be some mistake.' He continued to look at Hood then glanced sympathetically towards Sir Robert.

'I think I've probably said too much already,' replied Hood. 'I shall be interviewing Philip again later today. I'll hopefully understand more about the case by then, but it doesn't follow that I shall be able to disclose any more to you than I have already.' He turned to Wendy Knight. 'How are the interviews going with the congregation? Anyone refusing to cooperate?'

'No sir. Quite the opposite. They're all being very helpful. Over fifty of them, excluding children .'

'And you've taken a statement from Mrs Swanson?'

'Yes, sir. I have it here.' She held it up. 'I took it as soon as I arrived.' She did not mention that she had also spoken to the housekeeper the evening before, not in front of Sir Robert.

'Any sign of Father Grantham yet?' asked Hood'

'No.'

'He doesn't usual get back until fairly late or until Monday morning,' interjected Sir Robert. 'I don't usually see him before breakfast, if I see him at all.'

'I'm a little surprised he wasn't here for the Mass,' observed the Prior, 'given the circumstances. But no doubt he has other things to attend to in Oxford.' His tone of mild disapproval suggested otherwise.

'A word, please,' said Hood taking Wendy Knight by the arm. 'I'll be in touch, Sir Robert, when I have anything I can properly tell you about Philip. I'm sure you will understand that some things, however, have to remain confidential.'

'Could I see him?' pleaded Sir Robert as Hood made for the door.

'Not at the moment, no. Perhaps later when things are clearer, always assuming he's willing to see you. He didn't seem too keen when I spoke with him yesterday. Before I forget, if he were to make bail, and I am not promising anything, could he stay here? He will need a suitable address where he can be contacted and I'll need to know exactly where he is twenty-four-seven.'

'Of course, always assuming he's willing.'

Hood smiled. 'He might prefer it here to Leicester prison or Woodhill.'

Sir Robert visibly wilted.

'Chief Inspector,' said Father Milmo, 'what about examining the hide. I'm really looking forward to that. You mentioned we could inspect it after Mass.'

'Would half an hour be convenient?' asked Hood. 'I have a couple of matters I need to speak to Detective Sergeant Knight about first.' He looked at his watch. 'I'll see you in the Long Room at ten-past one, if that is convenient to you. You too, Sir Robert, if you're minded to assist. I'm conscious of your concerns about further damage being caused to what is undoubtedly an important historical site. It might be helpful if you're there before we remove anything so that you know exactly what we are about.'

The Prior seemed very excited, Sir Robert less so.

'I'll go and change immediately,' said Father Milmo. 'I'm really looking forward to inspecting this priest-hole, always assuming that's what it is.'

CHAPTER SIXTEEN

'What did Martha Morton have to say, Wendy? Anything useful?'

Knight looked slightly apprehensive before she answered. 'I asked her about the man who was seen leaving her cottage early yesterday morning as you requested. She was very reluctant to say anything, but when I informed her he'd been spotted, she became more cooperative.'

'You didn't tell her by whom the man had been seen?'

'I certainly did not. She did ask, but I refused to say. Mind you, she could well have worked out it must have been either Swanson or his wife.'

'What did she tell you?'

'It was her estranged husband.'

'At that hour of the morning?'

' Yes. He was on his way up north. This is the only occasion he's been to her cottage, apparently. She told me that at one point he wanted her to take him back. Been bothering her sister in London for several months. Now he's changed his mind and agreed to a divorce. Probably moved on and found someone else.'

'So, it wasn't Philip?'

'No, sir. Not if she's telling the truth. But there was definitely something worrying her. She told me she's thinking of handing in her notice and leaving the Grange. She's not said anything to Sir Robert yet, but Father Dominic's death seems to have affected her. Unless, of course, there's something else. She became quite tearful towards the end of our conversation.'

'Did she allow you to have a look around the cottage?'

'Yes, sir. No problem. Told me to look wherever I wished. There are two bedrooms. No sign of a man staying there. I checked the wardrobes and the drawers in both bedrooms and looked in the bathroom. Nothing to report.'

'When is her husband visiting again?'

'I asked her that, of course. He isn't; she hopes she won't see him again. She certainly doesn't expect to see him before this investigation is completed. The divorce is in the hands of her solicitor who's local.'

'Does her husband know about Father Dominic's death?'

'Yes. She told him all about it. He'd also read about it in the newspapers.'

'You obtained his name, I hope?'

'Roger Andrew Morton. She said she couldn't recall his exact date of birth. But he's forty-six years of age and lives in London.'

'Nevertheless, I want him traced and spoken to. If he's been in the village in the last week we need to eliminate him from the enquiry. Get the Met on to it. Does she know his address in London?'

'No sir. She thinks he lives in Stoke Newington but she's not sure. That's what concerned me. She was very cagey when I asked for any details about him. But if they are getting a divorce her solicitors must have a contact address. It might assist if you have a word with her. She might open up a bit more if you were to question her, senior officer and all that.'

Hood nodded. 'If you think that will assist, I'll speak to her later today, if I have a moment, otherwise it will have to be tomorrow. Now, what about Mrs Swanson? You've taken a statement from her?'

'I have.' Knight handed over the witness statement. Hood started to peruse it.

'I noticed her in church with her husband,' he said. 'She looks an intelligent woman. I'll have a word with her myself later. We have a lot on today and don't forget, we have to get back to Campbell Square to interview Philip.'

'All she can say is the man definitely *wasn't* Philip Southall. She said she'd have recognised him if it had been him, even though she didn't see the man's face. She was quite definite about it. She reckons she would have noticed the way Philip moves.'

'The way he moves?'

'Yes, sir.'

Hood sighed as he handed the statement back to Knight. 'And the fingerprint report?'

'Sergeant Wilson came in early. He isn't officially back on duty until tomorrow but he appreciated the urgency. He's found something unusual. He's coming over to see you.'

'Did he say what it was? If he's taking the trouble to drive down here on a Sunday afternoon, it must be significant.'

'More than one set of prints apparently on the spade handle. Both have been identified.'

'Did he say who's?'

'Yes, sir. Philip's, as we expected, but there are other prints. One is smudged but the other one is clear enough.' She hesitated. 'They're Father Dominic's.'

Hood gasped in surprise. 'Father Dominic's? How can that be? How could his prints be on the spade handle?'

'I don't know. Perhaps he tried to fight off his killer?'

'By grabbing the handle? I don't think so. He would have been at the business end of the spade. His injuries make that abundantly clear.'

'Or they might have been old prints from when he used the spade to dig out the priest hole?'

'Possibly. It means that the positioning of the fingerprints could be crucial.'

'That's why DS Wilson is coming over. He's already photographed and enlarged the relevant marks. He'll be bringing copies with him.' She dropped her voice and grinned a little awkwardly. 'He thinks it may affect the case against Philip.'

'Does he, indeed?' Hood sighed in frustration. 'What about the blood grouping from the stains on Philip's coat?'

'No information on that yet. It is Sunday, sir. I've been promised the results before we interview our suspect again this evening.'

Hood looked at his watch. 'When will Wilson get here?'

'He's waiting for the photographs of the marks to come through. As it's the week-end there's a bit of a delay, but he said he should be here by mid– afternoon.'

'Time to inspect the priest-hole, then. I don't want to keep the Prior waiting. I'm hoping something will turn up when we examine it. Lucky we have a bit of an expert on priest-holes in Father Milmo.'

'Yes, sir. You still think the solution to this case lies in the Long Room?'

'I could be wrong, Wendy, but my instinct tells me there's something significant about that priest-hole. There's something hidden there – or there was – which will point us to the truth. I'm sure of it. It just needs exposing.'

Knight did not share Hood's confidence. Was the DCI working by instinct rather than evidence? She articulated her concerns. 'SOCO didn't find anything apart from some bloodstains.'

'They're not experts on priest-holes, and they were looking for blood not examining the design and function of the hide. Experts on this sort of thing are very few and far between. That's why I'm relying on Father Milmo.'

'It's a pity Father Dominic didn't leave any clues behind for us, apart from the sacramental.' She smiled. 'No chance of a dead priest telling us anything, I suppose?'

'No Wendy. I'm afraid it doesn't work like that.'

'God moves in mysterious ways, eh, sir?'

'He certainly does.'

CHAPTER SEVENTEEN

Hood authorised the removal of the police tape from around the priest-hole as the Prior, now dressed in a short-sleeved blue shirt and charcoal grey slacks, visually inspected it. He did not descend the ladder and go down into the hide. Not yet. Neither did he seem particularly impressed. His eyes darted about the recess and alighted on the marks in the stonework suggestive of a staircase long since removed. He turned and addressed Sir Robert who was standing several feet back from the hide. 'I did hear talk of a couple of wooden boards,' he said, quietly. 'May I see them?'

'They're over there,' said Sir Robert, pointing to the side of the pile of soil and debris.

'They've been examined for prints and DNA,' added Hood. 'so feel free to examine them.'

Father Milmo took a few steps back and cast his eyes over two ancient looking planks; two pieces of oak with an iron hinge holding them together. 'Now that is interesting,' he said. 'What do you think of that Mr Hood? It hardly fits the description of what some have described as a trapdoor does it? But I suspect they performed a similar role. I take it this is all there is?'

'I believe that's all that was found.'

'Well, it tells us something.'

'It does?' replied Hood, his curiosity aroused.

The Prior pointed to the marks in the stonework which Hood had observed when he first examined the hide when the body was still *in situ*. 'There was obviously a staircase against that wall. You can see the marks where the supports rested. I'm pretty sure those two pieces of oak formed part of the staircase itself. Not really a trapdoor; that old hinge suggests to me that entrance to this pit – for want of a better description – was obtained by lifting the treads of the staircase. That's what these were. A simple but effective arrangement, not uncommon in houses of this age.'

He picked up the two pieces of wood and demonstrated what he meant. 'Do you see? Obviously the treads were wider and longer when first put in place. What is left is only part of the original. Much of it has rotted away. Where was this found?'

'I believe it was buried in all the in-fill,' volunteered Sir Robert. 'That is what Father Grantham told me.'

The Prior took the few steps back towards the hide. 'That apart, I must say, this does not at first sight suggest it was constructed by one of the master carpenters operating during the period. It's really just a hole in the ground.' He looked towards Sir Robert who appeared perturbed. 'Is there a cellar underneath this room?' he asked.

'No,' replied Sir Robert. 'There is a large cellar underneath the west wing. The west wing was added in the eighteenth century but there's nothing under this part of the house.'

'And this room is part of the original building?'

'Oh, yes. The old plans I once examined in the County Library suggested this was the inner hall of the original priory. Most of the cloisters were demolished, but the surviving section, which is where the stone floor begins, is part of the corridor which led to the original priory church, what we call the old chapel.' Sir Robert digressed. 'I've always supposed that's what explains it's length. It was my grandfather who christened this the Long Room and the name has stuck.' He paused and glanced towards Hood then smiled. 'He was a life-long member of the MCC. I used to play cricket in here myself with my sons in the bad weather, when they were younger. The wicket was at the far end where the original cloister ended.' He chuckled to himself. 'The stone floor meant it didn't take spin, of course, but it didn't affect Maxim's love of the game. He plays for his university now. He's a very decent bowler.'

The Prior, a keen cricketer in his youth, smiled but moved on quickly. 'And the staircase that used to be here? Where did it lead?'

'Of that I am not sure. Father Grantham thought it may have led to the Prior's accommodation. But the refurbishment of the house has removed all evidence of it.'

'The Prior's living quarters?' Father Milmo nodded. 'That's probably right. This was an Augustinian priory. Father Grantham would know that. Augustinians in England, certainly in this house, were governed by a Prior, not an Abbot.'

'I think Father Grantham has researched the history of the former priory pretty exhaustively,' suggested Sir Robert, defensively.

Father Milmo did not comment further, but Hood noticed he was obviously unimpressed. 'You don't think much of this as a priest-hole then, Father?' he said, glancing apprehensively towards Sir Robert.

The Prior nodded. 'It doesn't appear to me to be anything like as sophisticated as some I have seen. Certainly it wasn't created by Nicholas Owen, the famous Jesuit brother who is now a canonised saint. Tortured to death he was in the Tower of London by a sadist by the name of Topcliffe. I've seen some of Brother Owen's hides elsewhere. They are usually very state-of-the art.' He smiled and dropped his voice as if he were revealing something of a confidential nature. 'They do say that some of his work is yet to be discovered, because it's so carefully incorporated into the buildings in which he worked. What would I give to find one of his hides!' He shook his head. 'No, I'm afraid this doesn't live up to my expectations at all.' Sir Robert appeared downcast as the Prior continued. 'As there is no cellar here, it appears simply to have been dug out, directly into the earth. It's almost as if it were intended to hide something valuable, not designed to conceal a priest. There's no indication of an air shaft, unless it was removed when it was filled in. And the absence of any obvious escape route is a problem, too. I wonder, though, whether further excavation might lead to the discovery of a passage way or similar, a means of escape for anyone hiding here?'

Sir Robert's spirits rose. He'd started to think the Prior was about to write off his priest-hole as a mere pit, but his mention of a possible escape route reassured him. He determined he would extend the excavation after Father Dominic's murder was solved.

The Prior then pointed to the panelling fixed to only two sides of the recess. 'That's very odd, though. Why would anyone go to the trouble of securing what looks like fairly expensive oak panelling to two sides of what otherwise might be regarded as a simple pit? And I suppose the staircase must have hidden the whole thing from sight.'

Sir Robert's spirits plunged once more. There was that mention of a simple pit again. He intervened. 'I think the staircase must have been removed when the hide was discovered and the Long Room panelled, and that was many years ago. We know the oak panelling in this room is mid-eighteenth century. I suspect it was put in when the west wing was constructed.' The baronet pointed to the larger piece of oak panelling that had been removed to expose the hide. It was still leaning against the wall where Hood had first noticed it, close to the now boarded-up oriel window.

'It was when we removed the panelling that we discovered what I took to be a priest-hole,' added Sir Robert. 'I was worried about extensive dry rot in this room. If it hadn't been for the refurbishment, we would never have found it. There was enough of it exposed to demand further investigation.'

'The in-fill we see over there didn't reach the top then?' queried the Prior.

'Oh, no,' said Sir Robert. 'At least eighteen inches was clearly visible. It had probably settled over the years because we could see the upper section of the panelling quite clearly. That's why we decided to excavate.'

Hood looked at his watch. He was anxious to make progress before Detective Sergeant Wilson arrived. He interrupted. 'But it sounds from what you have said, Father, that you don't believe it was used to hide priests during penal times?'

Sir Robert appeared utterly dismayed by Hood's question but relief was to follow quickly.

'That's not what I said.' replied the Prior, sensing Sir Robert's disquiet. 'I'm sure priests were hidden here. Otherwise the pursuivants would not have searched the house, as we know they did, and the hinged stair tread is pretty powerful proof. No, I was speaking of its original purpose. It was undoubtedly adapted and used as a priest-hole in the late sixteenth century, but I suspect it was constructed before the persecution, perhaps by the monks themselves.'

'By the monks? Why would they have done that?'

'I should correct myself, although I don't want to appear to be engaging in pedantry. This was a house of Augustinian Canons Regular, who are not regarded as monks in the sense we Benedictines are accepted to be monks. Their rule was less rigid. Before the dissolution, while they lived here in community and would have been regarded as monks by most people, certainly by Cromwell when the Priory was dissolved, their spiritual labours were largely carried out outside in the locality, not in the Priory itself. They probably provided priests for the local churches and ran a school…'

Hood interrupted again. He was not over interested in whether the previous occupants of Easton Grange were correctly labelled monks or canons. 'What you are saying is that you believe this was originally constructed to hide *something* rather than someone?'

The Prior temporarily abandoned his history lesson. 'You have it in one, Mr Hood. The question, of course, is what? It was not uncommon for the treasures belonging to religious houses to be hidden from Cromwell's commissioners who tried to seize them before houses were dissolved. The King was very short of money. The Treasury was bare, given all he spent on pointless wars against France and Scotland. The monasteries were regarded as fair game for plunder, I'm afraid. Their gold and silver plate was purloined and melted down to be turned into coinage. Any jewels were stripped from chalices and even from books and sent to the King's treasury at the Tower of London. In many cases the superiors handed their treasures over in an attempt to preserve their way of life only to realise later they had been duped. They were eventually turned out, many with a small pension. Those who did not cooperate fared less well. The superiors were not infrequently hanged and the lesser brethren violently expelled.'

'You will recall that is effectively what I told you Mr Hood, when we first met,' said Sir Robert.

'Yes, indeed you did.' Hood paused then engaged in some speculation of his own, anxious as he was to push things forward. 'Have you heard of the Powdrell chalice, by any chance, Father?' He glanced at Sir Robert who was growing increasingly excited. The Prior's expression revealed his previous lack of knowledge of the Powdrells or a chalice before he answered.

'No, I have not. It sounds very interesting. Does it have a connection with this place?'

'If it still exists, it certainly does,' enthused Sir Robert, who then repeated the story he had told Hood on the day Father Dominic's body had been discovered.

'This is really fascinating,' replied Father Milmo. 'I'm surprised it is not more widely known. Tell me, is there any record identifying the canons who were living here at the dissolution, the Prior apart? I'm aware he was one Robert Pritchard, but what happened to him after this place was closed is not recorded anywhere, so far as I'm aware. He was awarded a small pension, but where he went when he left here is simply not known.' He looked at Sir Robert. 'As you may have gathered, I've been doing some research myself. Your library is very well furnished with books and original documents. I was up very early this morning. But I haven't heard of this chalice before. Does it still exist?'

Sir Robert gave a slight bow. He was, it had to be said, very proud of his library. He took it upon himself to answer the Prior's question. 'The Powdrell chalice may be just a story. Father Grantham will know more about it. He's been researching the Powdrell family who lived here in penal times, at least he was until he was shown the location of this hide. Then he seemed almost to forget about his research altogether. He became quite fascinated with the priest-hole. He and Father Dominic carried out the whole of the excavation themselves, with help from Mr Hitchens.' He paused. 'I am correct to continue to describe this as a priest-hole, am I Father?'

'Perfectly correct,' smiled the Prior. 'I have no doubt it was used for that purpose.'

Sir Robert seemed much happier. He smiled and acknowledged the Prior with a wave and moved closer to the recess.

'We do seem to keep coming back to Father Grantham, don't we?' continued the Prior. 'Pity he's not here. I'm sure he'd have been very interested in investigating this *priest-hole* further.' He emphasised the words and nodded towards Sir Robert.

Hood eventually broke the silence that followed 'It occurs to me,' he said (he was being deliberately provocative) 'that if this was originally constructed to hide valuables belonging to the Priory before the dissolution, whoever filled it in must have removed them, which may explain why nothing has been found. From the size of this excavation, there must have been things hidden here much larger than gold and silver plate.'

Father Milmo did his best to elaborate. 'It was not only plate and jewels that were hidden, Mr Hood. Much larger pieces were secreted once it became known how much desecration was going on around the country. Rood screens, lecterns and statues were destroyed by the thousand. I'm afraid the vandalism knew no bounds. The monks – and canons – proved very ingenious in protecting their treasures. At Newstead Abbey in Nottinghamshire, originally another Augustinian priory, they hid an ornate lectern in their lake! It wasn't recovered until well into the eighteenth century and I believe it can now be seen in Southwell Minster.' He smiled. 'Perhaps the Augustinians who lived here, like their brethren at Newstead, tried to preserve their treasures, hoping for better times.'

'There was only a small pond here,' advised Sir Robert, with a sardonic grin.

'Which might explain what we see here,' said the Prior. 'But the chances are that after the priory was dissolved and given over to secular use, such items, once discovered, were sold or destroyed.'

Wendy Knight, who had remained silent to this point, suddenly intervened.

'Are we not overlooking the wax object found in Father Dominic's hand? If he discovered it in this priest-hole, does that not suggest that whoever filled it in centuries ago did not remove everything of value, possibly because they didn't look hard enough?'

The Prior indicated his agreement. 'An excellent observation, Detective Sergeant, if I may say so. Which brings us back to the oak panelling *inside* the hide. Now that is quite remarkable and highly unusual. I have never seen anything quite like it before, not executed as well. It is not part of the original structure of the house. I suppose that it could have been put in during penal times to make it more congenial for those who were hidden here, but I wonder?' He shot a glance at Sir Robert. 'Is there any prospect of removing the panelling, or at least giving it a very close inspection?' He approached the ladder that was still in place. 'Would you mind if I take a look?'

'You must ask Mr Hood. He's in charge here,' answered Sir Robert, reluctant as he was to countenance any damage to the hide.

Hood nodded his approval as the Prior quickly descended the ladder. 'Now,' he added, before he touched anything. 'Can you tell me the position of Father Dominic's body when he was first found in the hide?'

Hood thought that an odd request, but he saw no harm in disclosing the information. 'I think we can do better than that. Wendy, the photographs.'

Knight opened the file she was carrying and produced two photographs which showed the precise position of the deceased priest. His left hand, in which the sacramental had been found, was tucked under his body, his right arm stretched out, pointing towards the middle of three panels on the south side of the hide. She handed the photographs to Hood who glanced at them then passed them down to Father Milmo.

'You must bear in mind that Grantham checked Father Dominic's pulse using his right wrist while he was lying down there. His right arm may not have been replaced in exactly the same position in which he was later found.'

'Thank you Mr Hood,' replied the Prior. 'I shall make due allowance for that, but if Father Dominic were conscious when he was lying in here, he may have been pointing purposively towards this section of panelling.'

That was something that had certainly never occurred to Hood. He had not regarded the position of the body as being of any real significance. He had assumed that Father Dominic had simply been dumped in the priest-hole. Father Milmo then removed a small hammer from his pocket, about six and a half inches in length. It resembled a reflex hammer, the medical instrument used by practitioners to test deep tendon reflexes. He smiled as he held it up for the others to see. 'I never go anywhere without this. Not if there's a priest-hole in the offing.' He handed the photographs back to Hood and knelt down on the dry earth floor. Using his hammer, he began to tap the wooden panels on the north side, starting with the centre one. He asked for silence as he went about his task, listening carefully for any difference in the sound reflected from the wooden surfaces. The others stood in silence for what seemed like an eternity, straining to listen. Eventually, the Prior spoke.

'I didn't detect any difference,' he sighed.

He then turned to the panelling on the south side and repeated the procedure, concentrating on the middle section.

'I don't know whether you detected anything, but I fancy I heard a difference in the sound reflected from the centre panel when compared with the two outer panels. Did any of you catch a similar distinction?'

'Sounded much the same to me,' murmured Hood, who was now kneeling at the edge of the excavation. The others agreed with him.

'I suppose I have the advantage being down here and closer to the panels. Will it be too much to ask permission to remove the middle section? Am I to assume that is a tiny blood stain to the left?'

'It is,' replied Hood, 'but it has been examined and photographed. You can ignore it. It should be perfectly safe.'

The Prior nodded. Hood turned and signalled to Sir Robert who approached the edge of the recess with some trepidation. Hood gave his approval for the panel to be removed if necessary and Sir Robert gave his blessing. 'By all means,' he said. 'But try and do as little damage as possible. That panelling has been undisturbed for over four hundred years.'

The Prior put the reflex hammer down and ran his hands over the middle panel, pressing and probing at the edges then applying considerable pressure to the centre. He looked up. 'I don't think that can be right, Sir Robert. This panel has been interfered with much more recently.'

Sir Robert's spirits rose. Both he and Hood were now leaning over the edge of the recess as Father Milmo started applying pressure to the outer panels, detecting no movement at all. They seemed firmly secured and did not give way, no matter how hard he pressed against them. He repeated his examination of the panels on the other side of the hide. None showed any sign of movement. He turned once more to the centre panel on the south side. 'This panel is moving ever so slightly,' he said. 'There appears to be nothing very solid behind the middle of it. The outer sections seem unyielding. I suspect this centre panel was designed to move in some way. Does anyone have a torch?' ·

Hood needed no second invitation. He climbed down the ladder and crouched by the side of the Prior, one knee on the floor. Taking out the small torch from his inside pocket which he invariably carried, he shone it against the bevelled edges of the centre panel. He then pressed his fingers along the perimeter following the line of the panel both horizontally and vertically. 'I do believe you're right, Father. I wonder if there is some mechanism that would cause it to open?'

He shuffled back, allowing Father Milmo to repeat the exercise. The Prior attempted to slide the panel, one way and then the other. All of a sudden, it slid rapidly to the right, revealing a niche carved out of the earth about eighteen inches square. Hood, startled by what had occurred, quickly got to his feet.

'Jesus, Mary and Joseph,' whispered the Prior under his breath. 'What have we here?'

Hood dropped to his knees again and shone his torch into the niche. It was no more than twenty inches deep, without any lining. The earth had become as hard as concrete over the years. But it was empty. If something had been hidden there it had been removed.

'Anything there?' shouted Sir Robert, desperate to see what was happening.

'Nothing,' replied the Prior, who did not try and hide his disappointment.

'Not quite,' called out Hood, inserting his torch well inside the niche 'There is dust and other debris in here. Wendy, are there any scenes of crime officers still here?'

Detective Sergeant Knight approached the edge of the recess. 'Yes, sir. There's still a couple double-checking the old chapel grounds.'

'Get them over here immediately.'

Knight scurried off. Hood stood up and helped the Prior to his feet. 'We must postpone further examination until SOCO have taken samples from inside this hiding place. This remains a crime scene, after all. I must ask you to climb out now, Father. Don't worry, you'll have every opportunity later to examine the rest of the hide.'

The Prior did as he was asked. He was disappointed the niche was empty but nothing could dispel the excitement that he had discovered what could only have been a separate hiding place constructed by the Augustinian Canons who had once resided at Easton Priory. Sir Robert was equally thrilled. For a few seconds the plight of his son was pushed to the back of his mind. But then his unease returned. Would this empty niche help in showing his son's innocence?

Hood was not without a degree of exhilaration himself. His instincts had proved right. Perhaps something valuable had been hidden in the priest-hole? SOCO's earlier examination had revealed the presence of blood which had already been established to be the same group as Father Dominic's, but no prints had been found on any of the panelling. The whole area had been thoroughly swabbed and the results sent for DNA analysis, but SOCO had failed to locate the moving panel. *Had Father Dominic discovered it? Had there been something hidden there, something valuable? Something so valuable that it was worth killing for?* Hood now needed to speak to Father Grantham as a matter of urgency. If Father Dominic had discovered the niche, Grantham must have known about it, surely? As he climbed out of the priest-hole, he instructed those standing around they were to say nothing to anyone about what had been discovered. No exceptions. Grantham, in particular, was not to be told about it. It was essential that the hiding place within the priest-hole remained as secret as it had been for over four centuries.

'I must insist,' said Hood. 'This could be crucial to the investigation of Father Dominic's murder.'

Both Sir Robert and the Prior undertook to keep the discovery to themselves and made their way to the study where Hood indicated he would join them. One of the uniformed officers patrolling the entrance gate to the Grange was detailed to control entry to the Long Room. He was not told why and he was instructed to keep away from the priest-hole itself. Hood taped off the immediate area afresh and was finishing the task when the two SOCO officers arrived with Knight.

'Missed something, did we?' said one of them, somewhat flippantly, as Hood pointed to the open panel. 'Nigel won't be very happy.'

'No-one will be looking to blame you,' Hood assured him. 'But I want that niche photographed and samples taken from the debris and dust inside it. The traces of soil or whatever that was found on the sacramental are to be compared with the soil and debris inside there, understand?'

'You think the wax thing may have been hidden in there?'

'There's a chance that it could have been,' replied Hood. 'Now get on with it. I need the results as soon as possible.'

The two men nodded and prepared to change their forensic suits to avoid any risk of contamination of the hide. Hood's thoughts were racing.

If the sacramental were found in that niche, a pound to a penny there was something else in there with it, something even more valuable. The question was, what was it and where had it gone? Could it have been the legendary Powdrell chalice? Father Grantham would certainly have some questions to answer when he returned from Oxford.

As the two SOCO experts climbed down into the priest-hole, Hood made his way towards Sir Robert's study where the baronet and Father Milmo were waiting. Knight remained in the Long Room to observe SOCO going about their work. Hood gave her instructions to report back to him immediately if anything of relevance emerged. There was a certain lightness in his steps as he headed towards the study. Things were beginning to move in the right direction at last.

CHAPTER EIGHTEEN

Hood had almost reached Sir Robert's study when his mobile phone buzzed. It was Detective Sergeant Wilson who had found his way to the Grange and wanted to know where he should meet with the chief inspector. Hood directed him to wait at the main entrance to the house. He promised he would join him there in a few minutes. He popped into the study where Sir Robert and the Prior were drinking coffee prepared by the housekeeper. She was just about to leave with her tray as he walked through the study door. She glanced at Hood, giving him a weak smile, but she said nothing. Had she noticed the excitement that was so evident on the faces of Sir Robert and Father Milmo? 'I will join you in about twenty minutes,' Hood informed them. 'There's something I must see to immediately.'

'I'll make some sandwiches for you,' said Mrs Morton, blandly, as she departed and headed for the kitchen.

Hood made his way through the entrance hall and joined DS Wilson at the front door. He pointed towards the Gatehouse where the two men would be able to speak in comparative privacy. Duncan Wilson, an experienced fingerprint expert approaching retirement, had a file with him which he opened on the tiny kitchen table inside the cottage. He first produced some photographs which had been taken by Nigel Mullen's team who had first examined the spade and dusted it for fingerprints.

'These are the photographs taken by SOCO,' he said, pointing out three distinctive fingerprints highlighted on the handle of the spade. One was almost perfect and he had found no fewer than twenty-one characteristics which matched Philip Southall's sample. The other two were partial prints but he had counted over sixteen similar characteristics; further evidence that Philip Southall had handled the spade.

He then produced several other photographs which he had taken earlier in the day. They were sharply focused and showed the handle of the spade close up and in greater detail. 'You can see there is another print which slightly over-rides the best of the three Southall prints.' He directed Hood's attention to the area he had under consideration. 'I'm quite sure this print belongs to the deceased. There is another one on the left of the underside of the handle. Although it's smudged, there's no reason to doubt it was made by the same person. Only twelve characteristics, but it would be a quite amazing coincidence if it were put there by someone else.'

'So, Father Dominic handled the spade at some point?'

'Not at some point, sir. He must have handled it *after* Southall.' He pointed again to the overlapping print. 'It's what we in the trade call an overprint. The deceased's print was applied after Southall had left his right middle-fingerprint on the handle. There's no doubt in my mind. It's definitely on top of Southall's fingerprint. It's the deceased's right index finger.'

'How do you interpret that?' asked Hood, his expression making it quite evident he would not welcome the answer he anticipated was coming.

'While it's always possible the deceased's print got there during a struggle to get control of the spade, I think that's most unlikely. It's pretty clear what's happened, in my opinion. Your dead man was hardly physically strong; he would have been in no position to fight off his attacker. It's likely that he merely handled the spade by picking it up after Southall had put it down. It's the most obvious and the simplest explanation for the positioning of the marks. It can't be satisfactorily explained otherwise.'

Hood breathed in then sighed deeply. 'I suppose the simple explanation is often the true one. Any sign of blood in any of the prints?'

'Not that I can determine, no. And SOCO did all the usual tests. The lab may come up with something different but I think it highly unlikely.'

'So, Father Dominic picked up the spade by the handle after Southall had caused his prints to appear on it?'

'That's about it, yes. And before there was any blood flying about. I only got a brief account of what your suspect said to you in interview but he could well be telling the truth. If he used the spade to smash the window, then abandoned it, the deceased must have simply picked it up, possibly propped it up somewhere *then* come across his killer…'

'Who, unlike Philip Southall had the wit to wear gloves.'

'Exactly, sir. He may even have caused some of the prints to become smudged.' He paused momentarily. 'But what I found is certainly consistent with what your suspect told you. I don't think it would be possible to prove the contrary.'

Hood said nothing for several seconds. 'Anything else?'

'No, sir. There was nothing discernible on the wax object, what do you call it?'

'A sacramental or *agnus dei*.'

'That's it, yes…the sacramental. Nothing at all. You'll have to rely on DNA for that.'

'Well, thank you, Detective Sergeant. You've not exactly made my day but I can think of one person who'll be pleased by your conclusions. Will you let me keep these photographs? I'll take good care of them.'

Wilson nodded. 'No problem. There are copies back at the factory. I'll get back, if I may, sir. I've several other cases awaiting examination. It's always the same when I've been off for a couple of weeks. And I may as well work the full shift.'

'And take a day off in lieu?'

Wilson smiled. 'With your permission, sir, yes. I hear you're to be the new Detective Superintendent from Thursday, now that Maurice Kingston is retiring. Word gets round quickly at Campbell Square.'

CHAPTER NINETEEN

Hood was about to leave the Gatehouse when Wendy Knight appeared. Her expression told all. He sensed that what she was about to disclose would be along the same lines as what he had just heard from Duncan Wilson.

'They've just rung through the grouping tests on Philip Southall's coat, sir. Both areas that were tested gave the same group result – AB. It isn't Philip's blood and it isn't Father Dominic's. It looks like Philip could well be telling the truth.'

'I guessed as much. Duncan Wilson's conclusions on the fingerprints on the spade handle also support Philip's account. It looks like we're going to have to let him go. Wilson found Father Dominic's fingerprint on top of Philip's. It looks like the deceased handled the spade after Philip had put it down.'

'That's what he said, isn't it? That he abandoned the spade near the wooden cross as he went through the old chapel ruins. Father Dominic must have picked it up then his killer got hold of it and attacked him.'

'The evidence now suggests that is the most likely explanation for what happened. The question is who?'

'We bail Philip then, do we sir?'

'Yes, although his father won't press charges in respect of the window, not unless we can persuade him. Perhaps you should have a word with him?'

'I don't think he'd take much notice of me.'

'Oh, I don't know. He seems to like you. You're the one who supported his theory that something had been found in the hide, remember?'

Knight almost blushed. 'It's his window sir, and it's not in a public place. Up to him, isn't it?'

'I suppose so.'

'So we're back to the beginning?'

'Not quite. I shall be having serious words with Father Grantham as soon as he gets back from Oxford. And we'll speak to Philip again before he's bailed. We'll have to disclose to his solicitor the results of the blood tests and fingerprint examination, of course.'

Knight beamed. 'You mean I might not have been quite so off-field as you thought.'

Hood nodded. 'Your instincts about Philip seem to have been right. As for Grantham, I shall remain wholly neutral, for the time being. He will certainly have some further questions to answer. That niche we've just uncovered has not been closed up for the last four-hundred and fifty years. Someone found it recently and probably removed whatever was in there. Grantham has to be the prime candidate, unless Father Dominic discovered it and hid whatever was in there elsewhere.'

'Would he have wanted to keep anything he discovered from Grantham?'

'I don't know, Wendy. Perhaps he didn't trust him? He never told him about the sacramental, otherwise that might have disappeared as well. I want you to look into Grantham's background. Check with his university and the Jesuit authorities there. Sir Robert mentioned some personal difficulties which prevented him coming here last year. I want to know what they were.'

'It won't be easy, sir. I rang his university in the States on Friday. It's vacation time. There was no-one available to speak to who knows much about him'

'Did you? Well try again and keep trying until you get somewhere. I want to know as much as possible about this Jesuit before I speak to him tomorrow.

CHAPTER TWENTY

Philip Southall was now dressed in the casual clothing his father had sent with Hood to Campbell Square police station. The chief inspector had disclosed in outline the fingerprint and blood grouping evidence to his suspect's solicitor before the interview began. The solicitor had also been shown a photograph of the brown coat recovered from the squat. He did not dispute it belonged to his client.

'It seems you were telling us the truth,' said Hood after Philip had been cautioned. 'The blood on your coat; it was neither yours nor the priest's. Why did you get rid of it?'

Philip half-smiled. 'I didn't get rid of it. Not in the sense you're suggesting.' He shrugged his shoulders. 'I just gave it to one of the people at the squat. He was shivering with cold, despite the warm weather. He was very far gone. It seemed the least I could do and I didn't need it. I have other coats back at the Grange.'

Hood shook his head and smiled. 'Just a good Christian gesture, was it?' Philip did not respond other than to look away. 'When did you first come across this man?' Hood continued.

'It was on Saturday morning, just before I left. I'm not sure he was even there the night before.'

'So you didn't spend the night with him in the same room?'

'No, I was upstairs. He was with a woman downstairs when I saw him. They'd been shooting heroin; that much was obvious. I was trying to keep away from hard drugs.'

Hood seemed satisfied with the explanation. 'But you're not quite out of the woods yet, you know. There's the question of the damaged window.'

Philip dropped his head. 'I've admitted to that. I suppose my father's furious about it?'

'The broken window is the least of your worries, Mr Southall. As you know, it places you in the immediate area where Father Dominic was attacked and killed and at approximately the right time.'

Philip frowned. 'That had nothing to do with me. The fingerprint evidence proves that, doesn't it? It shows I was telling you the truth. Father Dominic handled the spade after I'd put it down. Someone else must have picked it up after him. He'll be your killer.' He paused. 'My solicitor has explained it all to me.'

He nodded towards his lawyer who smiled in response and looked towards Hood. 'That being the case, Chief Inspector, there would seem to be no basis for keeping my client in custody any longer.'

Hood nodded. 'I agree. I intend to bail him, shortly.' Philip sighed in relief.

'But I was hoping your client might like to try and assist us further. From what he said to us yesterday, he was very fond of Father Dominic. He'll surely want to help us catch his killer.' Hood looked at Philip and raised an eyebrow.

'But I've told you everything I know. If I knew anything more I would tell you. Honestly I would.'

Hood persisted. 'If we could go through events again, you might remember something, however trivial. This car you heard coming up the drive, for instance, did you get any sort of look at it?'

Philip sat back in his chair. He looked at is solicitor, who shook his head. 'I can only advise my client to answer further questions if this interview ceases to be under caution. If you are now seeking my client's help as a potential witness rather than as a suspect, then the interview under caution should be terminated.'

Hood leant over the table and switched off the recording equipment. 'Does that help?'

Wendy Knight, who was sitting next to Hood, appeared troubled. 'Is that wise, sir.'

Hood did not reply. The solicitor smiled. 'Go ahead. I'm sure Philip will give you any help he can.'

Knight frowned and took out her notebook and pen. She would now be obliged to note down anything Philip might say.

161

'This car,' said Hood. 'Did you get any impression of it at all?'

'I told you last time, I never saw it. It was because I heard it turning into the drive that I took off. I thought it might have been a taxi with my father in it. You can't see the entrance to the drive from where I was standing.'

'What about the sound of the engine? Did it sound like a taxi? Was it a diesel engine?'

Philip thought for a moment. 'I honestly couldn't say. But I don't recall it sounding like a diesel, now I come to think about it.'

'Where did you go?' asked Knight, 'after you heard it turning into the drive.'

'Like I told you before, I went across the grounds of the old chapel, through the picket gate and into the village. I had a cigarette and hung about there for a while. Then I set out and walked to Robinson's farm. I spent the night there in one of the barns.'

'What about the dogs?' asked Hood, showing a degree of cynicism. 'I'm told Mrs Robinson keeps two quite aggressive dogs who have the run of the place at night.'

Philip grinned. 'You mean Ronnie and Reggie? They know me well enough. I'm very good with dogs. I don't know why, I just am. Must be a gift. They just seem to like me. I've never had any trouble with them. They spent the night with me in the barn. Never made a sound. I left at about six o'clock.'

Knight smiled as Hood continued. Another explanation which neither she nor he had anticipated. 'And you neither saw nor heard anything suspicious after you left the grounds of the Grange?'

'Nothing. I slept for a few hours. I was very tired. Those straw bales are quite comfortable.'

'You told us before that you were unaware that there was another priest staying at the Grange?'

'That's right. I never met him nor saw him around the place.'

'Father Dominic never mentioned him?'

'No. Was he there the last time I spoke with Father Dominic?'

'I don't think he was,' interjected Knight. 'Tell me, how long did it take you to walk to the farm?'

'No more than half an hour. I wasn't exactly rushing and it's not too far.'

'A mile and a half, approximately,' said Knight. She looked at Hood. 'I got Swanson to check it in the car, sir.'

'As far as that?' said Philip. He seemed surprised.

Hood continued his questioning. 'Did anyone see you as you walked through the village towards the farm?'

Philip paused as if he were thinking hard. 'I don't think so. There was no one about as I finished my cigarette. I remember there was someone in a rear garden in one of the cottages. I did hear a door slam and someone shouted as I walked past, but I couldn't say who it was. I also remember a car going past me at some speed just before I got to the farm, but I dodged behind a tree so I wasn't seen.'

'Why did you do that?'

'I was about to climb over the farm gate. I didn't want anyone to see me going into the yard.'

'Just a moment,' said Hood. 'If you'd reached the farm, that must have been, what, well over half an hour *after* you heard the car turning into the drive at Easton Grange?'

'I suppose it was. Possibly longer. As I said, I wasn't in a hurry. Nearer forty minutes I would have thought before I saw the car. I stopped to relieve myself at one point.' He paused. 'Do you think this was the same car?'

'It's a possibility. Did any other cars pass you?'

'Not that I recall. I remember a motorbike, but he was going in the other direction.'

'Getting back to the car you say you saw, did you get much of a look at it as it passed you?'

Philip thought for a moment. 'I didn't see the driver. He'd already passed me when I looked up, but I can tell you the make of the car.'

'You can?' The two detectives looked at each other.

'Yeah. It was a Jag. Like the one in the TV series. Same colour too.'

Hood was now very interested. 'Which TV series?'

'The one with John Thaw. You know, *Inspector Morse*. It was one of those old fashioned Jaguars. Maroon. I'm positive about the colour. It was still light when it passed me. The sun still hadn't quite gone down.'

'Any idea of the time?'

'No. But the headlights weren't on; I remember that.'

Hood looked at Knight. She was about to surprise him again, this time with her knowledge of Jaguar motor cars. 'A Mark Two Jaguar, sir. My father had one years ago. In the novels, Morse drove a Lancia, as I recall, but when they made the TV programmes, they thought he should drive a British car. Only the Jaguar features in the TV series.'

'You're very knowledgeable,' said Hood.

'One of my favourite programmes, sir.'

'Really? I always thought Morse was a lousy detective. Worked by instinct instead of evidence. Let's not make a similar mistake.'

Wendy Knight smiled. She concentrated her gaze on Philip. 'Are you sure it was a Mark Two? Could it have been an 'S Type?'

'I take it there's a difference?' asked Hood, a broad smile on his face.

'Oh yes, sir. Quite definitely. The 'S Type' has a look of a Mark Two but it's a later model. I would spot the difference straight away. Others might not.'

'I certainly wouldn't,' confessed the chief inspector.

Philip shrugged his shoulders. 'I'm not really into cars. All I can say is that I thought it looked like the car in the TV programme. It was definitely the same colour. I even noticed that the roof was different; black, as I remember, just like on the TV. I haven't seen *Inspector Morse* for some time, but I remember the car that he drove. The one that went past me was going pretty fast too. He wasn't hanging about.'

'He?' queried Hood.

Philip shook his head. 'I didn't see the driver. I couldn't say whether it was a man or a woman. It went past me too quickly. It was out of sight before I got over the gate. I had to wait for the dogs before I climbed over, you see, to let them know it was me, otherwise they'd have made a right racket.'

'Any passengers?'

'I got the impression there was no one apart from the driver in the car, but I couldn't swear to it.'

'If we show you some photographs of the Mark Two and the S Type, do you think you could spot the difference?'

'I don't know, but I'll have a go. Anything to help.'

Hood glanced towards Wendy Knight.' 'I shall ask Detective Sergeant Knight to organise that. Now the question arises, what are we going to do with you in the meantime?'

The solicitor intervened. 'You've already said bail is in order, Chief Inspector.'

'Yes. But we need to know where Philip will be,' insisted Hood. 'It's in his own interests as well as ours.' He paused and eyed the former suspect. 'Your father is prepared to have you back home.'

The solicitor frowned. 'Is that really appropriate? Sir Robert is the complainant in respect of the criminal damage unless, of course, he drops the charge. And the murder of the priest took place there. That's still under investigation.'

Philip looked away and let his chin fall into his chest. Hood was not prepared to disclose what Sir Robert had indicated about abandoning the charge, not yet.

'Is there anywhere else he can go?' asked Hood.

The solicitor looked at his client. Philip shook his head. Hood continued. 'I agree it would be unusual, but as Philip has admitted the damage, I don't see it as a problem if his father doesn't. I won't be bailing him on the murder allegation, just the criminal damage – but he must understand, if any new evidence emerges in respect of the killing, he'll be re-arrested. I agree that the evidence at present does not justify his remaining in custody. He will have to stay out of certain areas, of course, the Long Room in particular.'

'I have already advised him of the position, Mr Hood, but I doubt if anything will emerge in the future that implicates my client in the killing. He simply seems to have been in the wrong place at the wrong time.' He paused. 'In the event of Sir Robert not pursuing the criminal damage charge, I assume my client will be released unconditionally?'

Hood was quick to respond. 'It's not entirely his decision, as I'm sure you're aware. Your client has confessed to the offence and the scientific evidence is likely to confirm his admissions. I don't need Sir Robert as a witness.' Hood paused, a smile appearing on his face. 'But I suppose there's every chance the CPS may not consider it in the public interest to pursue the matter if that is Sir Robert's concluded view.' He glanced at Philip. 'They are family after all.'

'I get your drift,' replied the solicitor. 'I suppose it's a little early for a final decision?'

Hood nodded. The two were clearly of the same mind.

'Do I have a say in this?' asked Philip, raising his head. 'I've admitted what I did but I'm not going home to have a row with my father about it. He's going to be pretty pissed off with me, isn't he?'

'I don't think it will come to that,' responded Hood quietly. 'I've spoken to your father at length. He wants to help. He's not going to be confrontational with you, especially if I were to tell him you are helping us in the investigation into Father Dominic's death.'

Philip almost smiled. 'Is what I have said of some assistance then?'

'Too early to say, but it may well prove valuable. There can't be too many maroon Mark Two Jags about. We shall certainly be looking for the driver, although he may well have nothing to do with what happened at the Grange.'

He turned towards Wendy Knight. 'Are there any CCTV cameras around Easton Parva? Or speed cameras? I've heard that Northamptonshire is inundated with speed cameras?'

'I'll check, sir. Nothing in the immediate vicinity of Easton Grange, I know that. But there is a speed camera on the Wellingborough Road half a mile or so before the village, but that's on the opposite side to where Philip was walking. I'm pretty sure there's nothing between the Grange and Robinson's farm. It's not the busiest stretch of road.'

'Well, I want the whole area checked. There's always a chance this car came from the Wellingborough side initially. If the driver is a local, he may have taken the route he did to avoid the cameras.'

'Bit of a long shot, sir,' offered Knight. 'We have no evidence this car went into the grounds of Easton Grange.'

'I know, but every piece of evidence is to be examined.' He paused. He didn't think it appropriate to say anything further in front of Philip and his solicitor. 'You can take Mr Southall and his solicitor to the custody sergeant. He knows what to do. Philip can be bailed subject to reside at his father's address. No other conditions are necessary save to exclude him from the Long Room and the old chapel grounds.'

The solicitor and his client stood up.

'Thank you, Chief Inspector,' said the lawyer. 'If I may say so, you have been very fair and wholly professional. I'm sure Philip is grateful.'

Philip grunted his appreciation. The two men made for the door followed by Knight. After they had passed into the corridor, the detective sergeant stepped back into the room.

'Of course, sir, if this car did travel up the drive at Easton Grange,

Father Grantham might have seen it. His room overlooks the entrance, as does the library.'

Hood grinned. 'Exactly. Another question to add to the list for tomorrow when he gets back from Oxford.'

CHAPTER TWENTY-ONE

Detective Sergeant Knight returned to Northampton after dropping off Philip Southall at Easton Grange. Although his lawyer had volunteered to drive him home, Hood wanted to know how father and son reacted when they saw each other so Knight was prevailed upon to deliver him. Hood telephoned the baronet to inform him of his son's arrival as the detective sergeant set out. The middle son of Sir Robert Southall was strangely silent during the journey but Knight later reported to Hood that the reconciliation had gone much better than she had anticipated. Sir Robert was waiting, anxiously, at the front gates. Philip initially hesitated when he got out of the Knight's car. His father then walked towards him and embraced him. The two then walked up the drive together then disappeared into the house arm in arm. Knight decided not to intrude and left without saying another word other than to explain the bail conditions to Sir Robert.

'That's something, I suppose,' said Hood. 'We have, at least re-united Sir Robert with his wayward son.' He smiled benignly. 'Just like in the parable. His father saw him while he was some way off, went to him, embraced him and, I'm sure, forgave him. I think we can remove young Philip from our list of suspects. You were right about him after all, Wendy.'

'Not much of a list then, sir, if we take him off it.'

Hood's smile disappeared. 'I thought you always had your doubts about him? Don't tell me you've changed your mind?' He gave the detective sergeant a plaintive look.

'I've never been convinced he's responsible, no, but then I remembered what you said about that earlier case, where the suspect provided evidence against himself in the hope that something only he knew about would later clear him. You said it almost worked, too.' She paused and ran her hand through her hair. 'I just think it may be slightly premature, to remove him from our list, that's all, but I agree he's probably not our man. He didn't come across to me as a cold blooded killer.'

'Those were very unusual circumstances,' said Hood, referring to his previous investigation. 'It was a quite bizarre case, although we did get a result in the end. This case is quite different. How could Philip have known that Father Dominic had handled the spade before it was used to attack him?'

'It's not inconceivable, sir. If Philip is responsible, he might have seen Father Dominic do exactly that. He was in the immediate area, after all. And even if he didn't witness it, if he left it near the cross in the old chapel like he said, Father Dominic could well have picked it up for some reason. Perhaps to put it away? Then Philip attacked him, possibly wearing gloves.'

Hood remained highly sceptical. 'That sounds like a premeditated killing to me. Just think about it for a moment. He puts his fingerprints on the spade, quite deliberately, when he uses it to smash the window then puts some gloves on to attack the priest? That doesn't sound like the Philip Southall we interviewed, does it?' Hood smiled. 'You're not really changing your mind, are you Wendy? I'm pretty sure Philip is innocent. Think of the risks he'd be taking coming into Campbell Square if he's responsible. Even if he'd picked up in the media reports that the murder weapon had been recovered, how could he possibly have known that the priest's fingerprint would be found over one of his? That simply couldn't be foreseen by anyone.'

'Perhaps he's just been lucky, sir?'

'You think so? No one can be that lucky, surely? And from what he said, it wouldn't have bothered Philip very much if Father Dominic had seen him break the window. That would hardly have caused him to attack him. But if we can locate this car it will prove he's being truthful about something of potential importance. He was very precise about the make and colour. He even remembered it had a black roof.'

'Some of the two point four models were manufactured with a black vinyl roof covering, just like the model used in the TV programme.'

'So we're looking for a two point four model?'

'Yes, sir.'

'But we have no clue as to the registration number.'

'No, sir. Though I suspect it won't be the registration number of Inspector Morse's car in the TV programme; 248 RPA.'

Hood smiled. 'Is there any subject upon which you are not brimming with information, Wendy?'

She laughed. 'I'm sure there are hundreds of things of which I know absolutely nothing. But that number has always stuck in my mind for some reason. Comes of watching too much TV, I suppose. Perhaps I need to get out more?'

'How is the search for this Jaguar progressing?' asked Hood.

'Bradley's on to it. Philip has already identified it as the two point four, so we can forget about the 'S Type' or other Mark Two models.'

'We can restrict the search to that specific model and colour can we, at least to begin with?'

'I think so, sir. I showed Philip the photos before I dropped him off at Easton Grange. Bradley will be checking all the cameras within a five-mile radius. It will have to be tomorrow though. Can't get access to all of them, not at this time on a Sunday. The five-mile radius limits the available cameras to a dozen or so. If he finds nothing, we'll extend the area. But they're nearly all speed cameras. If the driver kept to the speed limit, we won't find anything.'

'He certainly didn't keep to the speed limit when he passed Philip Southall. He probably panicked. Wanted to put distance between himself and the crime scene as quickly as possible, always assuming he's the killer, of course.'

Wendy Knight hesitated before she replied. She didn't relish even a mild further put-down from her chief inspector. 'Perhaps Father Grantham will be able to help? As I mentioned before, if this car did enter the drive, it presumably left the same way. Could he have been so engrossed in Mozart that he didn't hear it on either occasion? And if he glanced through his window he was bound to see it. It was still daylight. A sunny evening if you recall?'

Hood smiled. Knight's cynicism amused him. She was like a dog with a bone. She was not for letting go of her suspicions about Grantham. Hood stood up and stretched his arms. 'We will certainly ask him, but I think we'll call it a day for now. My wife will be forgetting what I look like. And I think you should go home too. You do have a home to go to I take it?'

'Yes, sir, I do. Not far from Easton Parva, in fact. Do you still think the killing has something to do with the priest-hole?'

Hood nodded. 'I'm not as convinced as I was, but I'm sure Father Dominic found something apart from the sacramental we discovered in his hand. It's perfectly possible we could be investigating two quite distinct incidents, but for the moment we'll proceed on the basis that there's some sort of connection. I'm not saying I know what it is, mind you, unless of course, your suspicions about Grantham prove to be correct. And I have to concede, I have had a thought or two about him myself.'

'Really, sir?'

'It's probably nothing. Just something Father Milmo said on Friday that I can't seem to get out of my head. He wondered why Grantham had never offered to say Mass, given he's been here for three weeks, not even after Father Dominic was killed. His letter of introduction also referred to him simply as "John Grantham." Remind me to show it to you. Sir Robert has it in his desk.'

'Perhaps that's just the way American Jesuits do things; informally?'

'You may well be right, but we need to push for information from his university in America. Those personal difficulties Sir Robert mentioned which delayed his arrival at Easton Grange still haven't been disclosed. I don't want to appear intrusive, but we need to know what those issues were.'

'If it matters, sir, his university in Minnesota will know the true position. I'll redouble my efforts. I'll keep phoning until I get to speak to someone in the know.'

'You do that, Wendy. If you get no joy from the States, it might be worth making a few discreet inquiries at Oxford. Grantham seems to spend a lot of time there. The porter at Christ Church, for example, he should be a good starting point. And don't overlook the Jesuit's own establishment – Campion Hall I believe it's called. It's in Brewer Street. But, Wendy, be very careful. I don't want this rebounding on us. The DCC won't like that one bit.'

'Yes, sir. Tomorrow?'

'Yes. I'd like to be fully briefed before I tackle Grantham. Go down first thing and give me a ring if you find out anything useful. Speak to Detective Inspector Ambler at Thames Valley. He'll give you a steer on who you should speak to if the porters don't come up with anything.' He hesitated. 'Grantham won't be an easy person to interview, that much is clear. He'll be quite a challenge. Let's make sure we know as much about him as possible.'

CHAPTER TWENTY-TWO

'Have we got anywhere tracing this Jaguar?' asked Hood as he addressed his team at Campbell Square police station on Monday morning. He had transferred the enquiry from Wellingborough to Northampton. The redecoration of the police station in Wellingborough had become too much of an intrusion and as he was due to take up his position at Campbell Square in a few days' time it proved a more convenient location. The incident room he had established on the first floor adjacent to his own office was now occupied by all the members of his team with one exception. Wendy Knight was absent having driven to Oxford earlier that morning.

Bradley shook his head. 'Nothing so far, sir. I've extended the area to ten miles but there's no sign of a maroon Jaguar of that type. If he drove on any of the roads we've covered so far, he must have kept to the speed limit.'

'What about the ANPR cameras?'

'They're designed to read registration numbers and we don't have a registered number for this vehicle. There are only a couple of cameras in this area and they're on the main road. But we are tracing every Mark Two. It will take some time, but once we have the reg. number we should make progress. Once its spotted, it will be tagged and we can then determine its movements.'

'Do we know how many Mark Twos are still on the road?'

'More than you would think, sir. Swansea's confirmed there are six hundred and fifty seven Mark Twos presently registered with them'

Hood whistled through his teeth. 'As many as that?

'Yes, sir.'

'How many are maroon in colour?'

'They're letting me know when they complete the check, but it's a very popular colour because of the TV programme. But we should have most of the information we require by later today.'

'Could I make a suggestion,' piped up DC Swanson, looking around at is colleagues.

Hood nodded. 'Go ahead, Adrian.'

Swanson seemed a trifle self-conscious as he replied. 'Well it was my wife, sir, who mentioned it actually.'

A well-meaning but distinct groan went round the room. Swanson took it in good heart but ploughed on. 'She suggested asking members of the congregation who attended services at the chapel at Easton Grange. She remembers an old fashioned maroon car parked there during Mass a few weeks ago. She can't place the driver and she's not sure it was a Jaguar, but she remembers a car of that style and she remembers the colour. She's very clear about the colour. She only saw it the once.' He paused. 'It's only a suggestion, sir, but something might come of it.'

Hood regarded Swanson's contribution as helpful. 'Does she remember precisely when she saw this car?'

'Two or possibly three weeks ago. She says it hasn't been back since and she doesn't remember seeing it before then. Just a one-off.'

'And it wasn't there yesterday?'

'No, sir. It wasn't. She's quite definite about that.'

'Did she see the driver at any stage, perhaps when he was leaving?'

'No, sir. She remembers the car was still there after she started to walk home. The other cars had all gone by then. She'd stayed behind for a few minutes to help with the flowers. When she left the chapel, the car was still there. That's why she remembers it.'

'So this person, whoever it was, also stayed behind for some reason?'

'Yes, sir.' He paused. 'Perhaps to speak to Father Dominic?'

Hood nodded. 'Did she see where Father Dominic went after Mass?'

'No, sir. All she can recall is that he wasn't in the sacristy when she went in there and he wasn't outside the chapel when she left. He could have gone back to his cottage. He occasionally saw members of the congregation in the Gatehouse if they wanted to speak to him in private. He was a good listener was Father Dominic.'

'That would seem to be a distinct possibility. Pity there's no CCTV at the Grange. I don't suppose she remembers the registration number of the car?'

'Sorry, sir, no she doesn't.'

Hood looked at the group of officers assembled before him. They anticipated what was coming. 'Listen up. This means re-interviewing all those who gave statements yesterday, I'm afraid. This vehicle was not part of the inquiry yesterday; it is now and I want it found, and quickly. And we can't wait for next Sunday. We have the names and addresses of those who made witness statements yesterday. Visits must be made to their homes or places of work today. I want the results by first thing tomorrow. This is to be given priority.' He turned towards Swanson. 'Adrian, I would like to speak to your wife myself. Will she be at home now?'

'Yes, sir. She should be there. She had no plans to go anywhere until four o'clock. I'll get her to come to the Grange.'

'Excellent. We'll go there immediately.' He looked up and addressed the other officers as they made ready to leave. 'In the temporary absence of DS Knight, the rest of you divide the work up and get on with it. All statements are to be handed to DC Renfrew. He will collate them and let me have a summary by tomorrow evening at the latest, earlier if something of relevance turns up. We must find this man – I assume it's a man – without delay. There are photographs available of a maroon Mark Two Jaguar. Take a copy with you. It might jog a few memories.'

Hood's mobile buzzed. It was Wendy Knight. He asked her to wait as he addressed the team. 'Right, get to it.' He then turned away from Swanson and Renfrew and concentrated on Knight's call. 'What do you have for me, Wendy?'

'Well, sir, Grantham is definitely who he says he is. He was ordained over nine years ago. He also has a D Phil from Oxford. He was awarded it in nineteen ninety-seven.'

'Did you speak with anyone at Campion Hall?'

'Yes, sir. There weren't that many people about and the Master is away, but I was introduced to the archivist. He was very helpful. Grantham has been to Campion Hall on several occasions and he attended Mass in the chapel there yesterday.'

'But he didn't say Mass himself?'

'That's what I was told. He's also inspected the other sacramental; the one connected with the saint from Lyford. He was given permission to photograph it.'

'Was he? That's hardly suspicious. I should, perhaps, have organised that myself. He told us it was kept there, if you remember?' He paused. 'Well done, Wendy. Do you think we can now eliminate him as a suspect?'

'I wouldn't go as far as that, sir. I got the impression there's something about Grantham that no-one's prepared to talk about. I can't put my finger on it, but there's something going on in the background, something that's being kept highly confidential.'

'We will still have to speak to him, then?'

'Rather you then me, sir. I don't fancy questioning a Jesuit.'

'OK, Wendy. Get back to Easton Parva as soon as you can. I'm still at Campbell Square. I'm about to set off for the Grange with Adrian Swanson. There may be a development on the Jaguar front.'

'Really, sir. Has it been located?'

'No, but Helen Swanson thinks she saw a similar car at the Grange two or three weeks ago after Sunday Mass. Only the once, mind. She never saw it again. I'm on my way to see her now. I shall arrange to speak to Grantham while I'm there, but I'll wait until you get back before I interview him. I want you with me.'

'Safer with the two of us, eh, sir?' She laughed.

'It won't be easy questioning him. I certainly want someone with me. And I'd prefer it to be you.'

Knight hesitated. 'If you say so, sir. Do you want me back immediately? That Inspector friend of yours has invited me for lunch, but I'm sure he'll understand if I have to get back. I should get to the Grange in just over an hour. The traffic in Oxford is unbelievable.'

'So you've spoken to DI Ambler?'

'Yes, sir. He was very helpful. It was he who introduced me to the archivist. It turns out he's his uncle.'

'It's a small world. A happy coincidence that.'

'Yes. By the way sir, the archivist showed me the sacramental that's kept at Campion Hall, the same one that Grantham has inspected. It is remarkably similar to the one we found in Father Dominic's hand, if somewhat larger. Grantham must have been making a comparison between the two. The archivist would like to see the one we have when convenient. He thinks it could be an important find.'

'It looks like ours could be the genuine article, then?'

'So it seems. I'm sure Father Dominic must have found it in the priest-hole, probably in the niche that was uncovered yesterday. I've never bought into what Grantham said. He was far too quick to dismiss the possibility that it was found by Father Dominic during their examination of the hide.'

'Let's hope the forensic boys can establish as much. To be fair to Grantham, he was sceptical that it could have survived in all that in-fill. He presumably would adopt a different stance if it had been protected in the niche? And this archivist, he sounds worth following up. I don't know why I didn't think of him before. We must show him our exhibit and get his views about it.'

'Yes, sir. He'll be delighted to assist. He's read about the case in the newspapers as have most people here. They're all talking about it in Oxford.'

'They're all talking about it around here too, and I include the Deputy Chief Constable in that. I have to go to HQ on Thursday. That's when my promotion takes effect. She'll not be happy about the rate of progress.'

'It's been less than a week, sir. She can hardly complain. Let's hope you get somewhere with Grantham.'

'And that we find that Jaguar. Bradley hasn't got anywhere yet. You, on the other hand, have done well, Wendy. Get back as soon as you can. Sorry about the lunch date. I'll make it up to you.'

'Thank you, sir.' She hesitated. 'But we still don't know for sure whether there was anything else hidden in the priest-hole, do we?'

'No. But something tells me there was. And I suspect Grantham knows more than he's letting on. Let's hope he's prepared to be more helpful when we speak to him.'

'Should be an interesting interview, sir.'

'It should indeed. Anything else?'

'It is true that he has been coming here to Oxford at week-ends. I checked the records at the porter's lodge. He seems to be telling the truth about that.'

'Is he? I'm glad to hear it. Get a copy of the record, will you?'

'Already done, sir. See you shortly.'

CHAPTER TWENTY-THREE

Hood and Swanson arrived at Easton Grange just before two o'clock. A uniformed officer opened the gates which had been closed to keep the much reduced posse of reporters and photographers at bay. The TV vans which had previously partially blocked the highway and caused resentment in the village had departed. Hood had repeated his promise to hold a press conference at the local police HQ later in the week which had placated the news hounds. The DCC was keen that real headway should be made before another press conference took place, putting further pressure on Hood's investigation.

Swanson walked to his home to get his wife while Hood knocked on the door of Sir Robert's study, having first checked that the Long Room remained under secure guard.

'How is Philip?' he asked.

Sir Robert looked at his watch and invited Hood to sit down. 'He's still resting, despite the hour. The poor boy was quite exhausted when he got here last night. I don't think he'd slept at all while he was in custody. We stayed up talking for a couple of hours as well, so I thought it best not to disturb him. I can call him if you want to speak to him. I think he's up and about, but still in his room.'

'No. That won't be necessary. I shouldn't really speak to him other than in the police station. He's still facing a possible charge of criminal damage.'

Sir Robert appeared surprised. 'The window? But I don't intend to press charges. I thought I'd made that perfectly clear.'

'And that will be the most likely outcome, sir. But for the moment, I think you'll agree, deferring a final decision is in Philip's best interests. It means he has to stay here as a condition of his bail.'

Sir Robert smiled and nodded his appreciation. 'Ah, I see what you mean. You're probably right. Is there anything else I can help you with?'

'There is one matter you may be able to assist me with. It's a bit sensitive. What do you know about Grantham?'

Sir Robert laughed. 'Father Grantham? I don't think I can tell you anything more than I already have. And you've taken a statement from him, haven't you?'

'DC Swanson interviewed him, but I want to go into things in a little more detail. I've run a check on him at Oxford. But I would like a bit of a steer before I speak to him. Anything at all you can add will be helpful. By the way, have you seen him this morning?'

The baronet suddenly became serious. 'I haven't, no. He, er, didn't come in for breakfast. That's not entirely without precedent, but I did receive one unwelcome communication this morning.' He handed a piece of paper to Hood. 'Martha Morton has given in her notice. She would like to leave at the end of next week. Poor woman has been upset by events here. Understandable, I suppose. But I shall miss her, and she'll not be easy to replace.'

Hood quickly read the letter. 'Have you spoken with her?'

'Briefly, at breakfast. I've asked her to give it further thought, to sleep on it, but I suspect she means to go. She declined to take her letter back.'

'I'd like to keep this, if I may?'

Sir Robert nodded. 'Be my guest.'

'While we are on the subject, could you tell me why you chose to employ her?'

Sir Robert shrugged. 'She seemed quite suitable, despite never having worked as a housekeeper before. Besides, there was another very good reason for taking her on.' He smiled broadly. 'She was the only person advertising her availability.'

Hood responded with a grin then raised an issue that troubled him. 'Remind me, sir, isn't Grantham due to go back to the States at the end of next week?'

'Yes, I believe he is.'

'At about the time your housekeeper's period of notice will expire.'

Sir Robert reacted with surprise. 'You don't think there's a connection, between Grantham and Mrs Morton, surely?'

'I don't know.' Hood hesitated, pulled his chair closer to the desk behind which Sir Robert was sitting and spoke in a hushed tone. 'Tell me, have you ever doubted his standing as a priest?'

Sir Robert appeared puzzled. 'No, such a thought has never crossed my mind.'

'I must confess, it crossed mine, if only briefly. But his ordination has been confirmed by the Jesuit authorities in Oxford. It was something Father Milmo said about him never having said Mass here, even after Father Dominic's death, that raised a suspicion. And I noticed his letter of introduction simply referred to him as John Grantham.'

Sir Robert appeared slightly uncomfortable. 'It did, yes, but these days the Jesuits can be very informal. They seem to eschew the traditional ways of doing things, which is a pity. Grantham seems quite different from the ones who educated me at Stonyhurst. But that was a long time ago. Things have changed almost out of recognition.' He smiled. 'And he is an American, of course. That must count for something.'

'But you do hear of some men giving up their vocation these days, even Jesuits,' said Hood. 'Could Grantham be considering leaving the priesthood?'

Sir Robert now appeared very concerned. 'That certainly does happen. But do you really think Grantham might be considering his future as a priest? A school friend of mine who became a priest gave it up after seven years or so. He's married with five children now. Teaches at Downside I believe.'

Hood raised a rather delicate point. 'And there's not infrequently a woman involved when a priest seeks to be laicised, isn't there?'

Sir Robert almost gasped as he put two and two together. 'Good God. Grantham and Martha Morton? I can't believe that, Chief Inspector. Do you have any evidence for such an insinuation?'

'It's not really an insinuation, just a passing thought.' Hood paused and changed the subject, much to the relief of Sir Robert. 'It was Grantham who first mentioned the Powdrell chalice to you, wasn't it?'

'Yes. I had some understanding of the history of this place but it was Grantham who galvanised me into concentrating on the Powdrells. I knew the name, of course. You will remember my great-great grandmother was a Powdrell, but the story of the chalice came from him. The discovery of the priest-hole got us all very excited, but if Father Milmo is right, the hide was in place well before they came here.'

'As a secret hiding place for the monks' treasures, yes. And it must follow that Grantham would have known the story of the Powdrell chalice before he came here.'

'It was definitely he who told me about it. I'd heard of a chalice which was connected with the Priory, of course, but not one specifically associated with the Powdrell family, unless they are one and the same. Grantham was very persuasive. Almost everything I told you at the outset of your investigation came from him. He seemed very well informed.' Sir Robert hesitated. 'You think that's what he's been searching for? That he was so keen to examine the priest-hole in order to get his hands on the chalice? But he's always sounded so sceptical about finding anything.' He paused and a look of horror appeared on his face. 'My God, you don't think he's actually found it?'

Hood frowned. 'Frankly, Sir Robert, I don't know. The search for a historic artefact seems the most likely link to the murder, especially as Father Dominic and Grantham were both involved in exposing the hide.'

Sir Robert stood up and moved from behind his desk. He was clearly perturbed. 'What do you propose to do, Mr Hood? I don't think I could bear any further scandal at the Grange. Please tell me that you don't think Grantham had anything to do with Father Dominic's death. That would be too much to bear.'

'I don't know, sir, but when he puts in an appearance, I intend to interview him. He *is* back from Oxford, is he?'

'As I said, I haven't seen him today, but I know he's here. I'll make enquiries, if you wish?'

'Don't trouble yourself, Sir Robert. I'll find him for myself. By the way, is Father Milmo still about?'

'Yes. He said Mass this morning in the chapel.' He paused and looked rather sheepish. 'I'm afraid I missed it. I overslept slightly, the result of staying up late talking with Philip, but he's about the place.'

Hood smiled. 'You and Philip are friends again, then?'

Sir Robert sighed with relief. 'I believe we are. I'm very grateful to you Mr Hood. It's odd how things turn out. I do hope you are able to solve Father Dominic's murder soon and remove any suspicion that Philip was involved.'

'I believe we are making progress, due in part to Philip's assistance.'

'He's been helpful? That's good to hear.'

'But you will make sure he stays out of the Long Room? There's a uniformed officer on duty there during the day, but he mustn't interfere in anyway with my investigation. DS Knight had doubts about bailing him here. I was taking a bit of a risk, but I hope he'll cooperate.'

'I'll make sure he does, Mr Hood.'

A knock on the study door drew the chief inspector's attention. It was Detective Constable Swanson.

'My wife is here, sir. Where would you like to speak to her?'

Hood glanced towards Sir Robert. 'The Gatehouse would be convenient, if that's all right with you, Sir Robert?'

'Go ahead, Mr Hood. You have the key I gave you? Feel free to go wherever you please.'

CHAPTER TWENTY-FOUR

'So it was definitely a car like this?'

Helen Swanson carefully studied the photograph of a maroon 2.4 Jaguar Mark 2 which Hood had placed on top of his file on the kitchen table in the Gatehouse. DC Swanson stood a little way back, his notebook in his hand.

'As far as I can remember, yes, but I don't know a lot about motor cars. I haven't passed my driving test yet.' She giggled with embarrassment.

'But you are learning, aren't you, love?' said her husband, coming gallantly to her rescue.

'Yes,' she said, composing herself. 'Actually, I have a lesson at four o'clock. I really need to get a licence living out here. The bus service is pretty poor. Only two a day. And I shall need a car soon.' She eyed her husband and smiled.

'Anything else you remember?' asked Hood. He invited Mrs Swanson to sit down then joined her at the table.

'It definitely had a black roof, just like this one in the photo, but I'm sorry, I can't recall the registration number. I don't think I ever looked at the car too closely, but I did notice it wasn't in very good condition. The paintwork looked in need of attention.'

'Have you given any more thought to the precise occasion when you saw it?' asked Hood.

'It was definitely this month and it was my turn to do the flowers, or was it?' She hesitated. 'Trouble is, I stood in for Mrs. Burgess one Sunday – she was away on holiday. We usually remove the flowers after Sunday Mass. Father Dominic didn't like them to be left on the altar during the week. Sir Robert usually provides them in summer from his garden so the ones that are still in good condition are removed and placed on Lady Southall's grave.'

'Can you help with the particular Sunday you're talking about?' asked Hood.

'It's just come to me,' replied Mrs Swanson. 'It *was* three Sundays ago; yes, it was the first Sunday in the month. That's when Father Dominic said Mass mainly in Latin. We get a few more people in on those occasions. The driver of this car must have been one of them. I've never seen the car before or since.'

Hood took out his diary. 'Yesterday was the twenty-eighth. The first Sunday in July was the seventh.' He paused. 'Was it definitely the seventh?'

'Yes, Mr Hood. It was the day Father Dominic said Mass in Latin. That's always the first Sunday in the month.'

Hood shuffled a few statements from the file on the table, placing one statement separate from the others. 'Have you ever met Father John Grantham, Sir Robert's guest?'

Helen Swanson looked at her husband before she replied. 'No, Mr Hood. I didn't know he was staying at the Grange until Adrian told me, and that was after Father Dominic had died.'

'But you knew about the discovery of the priest-hole before then?'

'Oh, yes. Father Dominic told us all about it. It was that same Sunday. His homily was about the persecution of priests in Elizabethan days. That was the context for introducing the unearthing of the priest-hole to us. He sounded very interested in it. Quite enthusiastic in fact.'

Hood nodded his appreciation. 'So, whoever owned the maroon car would have heard about it at that Mass, assuming he was present?'

'Yes, I suppose he would. It would have been difficult to miss. I don't like to say anything critical of Father Dominic, but his sermon that Sunday was much more interesting than usual.' She looked at her husband and grinned.

Hood smiled in response. 'Did Father Dominic ever mention the priest-hole again?'

Mrs Swanson hesitated. 'I don't think so, no. I can't even recall what his sermon a week last Sunday was about, I'm ashamed to say.'

'And he never mentioned who was helping with the excavation?'

'No. He never spoke about it again.' She paused then looked up. 'I do remember he said in his sermon that Sunday that he was hoping that something might be found, something from the sixteenth century.'

Hood reacted immediately. 'He did?' He picked up the statements made by other members of the congregation and started to peruse them.

'Yes. He didn't go into any detail but I got the impression he was hoping to find something.'

'Something that might be hidden in the priest-hole?'

'I suppose so, yes.'

Hood cast a glance towards Adrian Swanson, a puzzled look on his face. 'I don't recall reading in any of these other statements that Dominic said he was hoping to find anything in the hide?'

'No, sir. Neither do I.'

'You're sure he said that, Mrs Swanson? That something might be found in the hide?'

'Yes. That was certainly the impression I got from what he said.'

'Has Adrian mentioned to you that something was found in Father Dominic's hand?'

She did not reply but looked down. Her husband intervened. 'I did ask Helen if she'd heard of the sort of sacramental that was discovered. What with her being a Catholic and everything.'

Hood looked at her. 'Have you ever heard of an *agnus die*?'

She shook her head. 'No I haven't. I had no idea what such a thing would look like before Adrian told me about it.'

Hood sighed and placed the statements back in his file. 'You've been very helpful, thank you. You must remind Adrian to let me show it to you in due course, if you'd like to see it?'

She nodded and took hold of her husband's hand.

Hood then changed the subject. 'Do you have any contact at all with Mrs Morton, Sir Robert's housekeeper?'

Helen Swanson was pleased the conversation had moved on. 'Not really, no. I know she doesn't come to Mass, not even yesterday, so I don't think she can be a Catholic. I have seen her in her garden occasionally. As you know, her cottage is directly behind our house. I think I've said "Good morning" to her a few times, usually when I'm hanging out the washing, but that's about it. She keeps herself to herself. I've never even seen her in the village shop. I think she drives into Wellingborough or Northampton to do her shopping.'

'She has a car?'

'Oh, yes. A red one.'

Her husband smiled. 'A Vauxhall Corsa, sir. I noticed it wasn't there this morning when I set out for Northampton.'

'It's there now,' contradicted his wife. 'I saw her putting it into her garage about eleven o'clock this morning.'

Hood smiled broadly. He was beginning to think that Helen was the real detective in the Swanson family. 'Did you ever visit the priest-hole, after Father Dominic mentioned it?'

'Oh, no. I knew where it was – in the Long Room – Father Dominic told us that much, but I don't think anyone from the congregation ever saw it.'

'But you know the set up inside the house, don't you?'

Helen hesitated. 'More or less, yes. I used to help out there in the old days when Lady Southall was alive. But I haven't been anywhere apart from the chapel for years.'

'You can get from the chapel directly into the Long Room, I believe?'

Helen Swanson looked at her husband again. 'Yes, you can. Through the sacristy. But Father Dominic always kept the door locked and he never left the key in the lock. He always had it with him.'

'How do you know that?'

Helen Swanson smiled. 'I must confess, I tried the door after I'd sorted the flowers in the church that Sunday. I'd gone into the sacristy to put a couple of vases away. There was no one there so I thought I'd just take a peep at the priest-hole, but the door into the Long Room was definitely locked.'

'That was on the seventh.'

'Yes, I'm sure it was the seventh.'

'You never asked anyone to be allowed to see it?'

'Oh, no. It sounded as if there wasn't much to see, anyway. I was waiting until the work was finished. I would certainly have asked Father Dominic then. Quite a few of us wanted to see it.'

'Did you ever notice any work being done in or near the Long Room?'

'No, the main entrance to the chapel is some distance from there. We never went into the house.'

'And the progress of the work was never mentioned by anyone?'

'Father Dominic had said it would need excavating, but I had no idea how much work had been done on it at that time.'

'Father Grantham didn't arrive here until the ninth. So he's been here about three weeks. You're sure you've never seen him?'

'Quite sure. Another priest here would have been quite a talking point, but until Adrian mentioned him, I didn't know anything about him and neither did any of the other regulars. He's never been seen in the chapel to my knowledge, not on a Sunday. You'd have expected him to help out, especially two weeks ago when Father Dominic had quite a bad cold. He was not at all well. I was beginning to think he wouldn't make it to the end of Mass, but he recovered pretty quickly. He was fine last Sunday, a week ago I mean.' She dropped her head, realizing that was the last time she'd seen Father Dominic. 'Now, we'll never see him again.' Her eyes filled with tears. 'I shall certainly miss him. He was a lovely man and a good priest.'

Her husband put his arm around her and comforted her. Hood waited a few moments while she wiped her eyes with a handkerchief before he continued. 'The person you saw leaving Mrs Morton's cottage; you've said you're sure it was *not* Philip Southall.'

Helen took a deep breath. 'Definitely not.'

'But you didn't see his face?'

'It wasn't Philip. I'd have known him anywhere. I didn't need to see his face. He didn't move like Philip.'

'Could you describe this man? I take it, it was a man?'

'Oh, it was a man all right. I told Sergeant Knight everything I could.'

'Tell me.'

'Well, he was tall. At least as tall as my husband. Fairly slim. Dark hair and wearing dark clothing. I didn't get the impression he was wearing a coat. He seemed to be in a suit and moved very quickly. I only had him in view for a few seconds before he went through the gate.'

Hood picked up his file from the table. 'That description would fit someone else of interest. I may call upon you again, Helen. Ever attended an identity parade?'

'No, sounds exciting.'

'I'll let you know. Thank you for your help.' He smiled. 'Ever considered joining the police? We could do with more people as observant as you.'

Helen laughed, nervously. 'I did, actually, a year after I graduated but I met Adrian and after we married things just moved on.' She took hold of her husband's arm firmly and snuggled up to him. 'You see Mr Hood, we are expecting our first child, in about five months.'

'Congratulations,' said Hood, beaming. 'That's very good news. But I'm afraid I shall have to drag Adrian away for the present. Duty calls.'

CHAPTER TWENTY-FIVE

As Hood left the Gatehouse, he saw Father Milmo in the distance, hurrying towards the front of the Grange. He acceded to Swanson's request that he be permitted to walk his wife home before returning to duty.

'Glad to have caught you, Father. Have you seen Grantham? I need to speak to him urgently.'

Hood was surprised by Father Milmo's reaction. He was not his usual cheery self and a little abrupt. He sounded very serious when he replied.

'Yes, I have. I saw him after Mass this morning.'

'Do you know where he is now?'

'I don't, no. Have you tried the library? He's usually spends his time up there according to Sir Robert, now that the hide is out of bounds.'

Hood leant his head to one side and looked at the priest with increasing unease. 'Yes, I'm sorry about that, but it won't be for much longer.' He paused. 'You don't seem your usual self, Father. Is something troubling you?'

The priest hesitated. 'No, just re-arranging my priorities, Mr Hood. I think it better if I keep out of your way and let you get on with your inquiries from now on.' He smiled. 'I feel I may have been intruding.'

Hood continued to look puzzled. 'I thought you were quite enjoying the investigation, despite the tragedy which brought it about. And I have to confess, you have been very helpful. We would not have found Father Dominic's breviary as quickly as we did if it hadn't been for you. And it was your expertise that led us to uncovering the niche behind the panelling in the hide.'

Father Milmo acknowledged Hood's gratitude. 'I'm glad I could help. Like you, I'm determined to do anything I can to help to find Dominic's killer and I remain more than happy to continue helping you with the priest-hole, but in other respects I'm afraid my priestly obligations must take precedence. I need to concentrate on those. I feel I have been rather neglecting them of late.'

Hood was confused. *What priestly obligations was the Prior talking about?* He decided to take the bull by the horns.

'Has Grantham said something which upset you when you spoke to him earlier today?'

'No, not at all.' He paused. 'Look, Mr Hood, I'm afraid I can't answer any further questions about Father Grantham. I'm sure you are more than capable of interrogating him. You hardly need my assistance.'

'He's ripe for interrogation is he?'

Father Milmo looked away and shook his head. 'That's not for me to say, Mr Hood.'

Hood gasped in exasperation and surprised himself by his directness. 'You wouldn't know whether Father Grantham is by any chance thinking of abandoning his vocation?'

Father Milmo did not respond. The nature of Hood's question appeared to have startled him. He remained deep in thought and did not reply.

'Don't you have any comment to make?' asked Hood.

'No, Chief Inspector, I don't.'

Hood exhaled loudly, his frustration only too evident. 'Has something happened between you and Grantham? Has he said something about the priest-hole? Does he know that something was hidden there, in the niche we discovered yesterday?'

Father Milmo took a couple of steps away from Hood then turned and faced the chief inspector. 'I would be grateful if you did not press me further, Mr Hood. You will have to speak to him yourself. And so far as the niche is concerned, I followed your instructions. I never mentioned it to him. As far as I'm aware he knows nothing of what we uncovered yesterday.'

The penny suddenly dropped with Hood. 'He's been to confession with you hasn't he?'

Milmo smiled. 'Has he? I'm afraid I cannot comment about such matters, as you should know. And you should not draw any conclusions from what I have said, either.'

189

'If he's said anything about the killing of Father Dominic, I need to know.'

'I'm sorry, Mr Hood. I cannot help you.'

'There must be something you can say?'

'I'm sorry, no.' The priest paused and looked about him, obviously anxious to avoid further mention of Grantham. He then faced Hood. 'Do you still think there's a connection between Dominic's death and the priest-hole?' he asked.

'I haven't yet dismissed that as a possibility. Especially if something were found there apart from the sacramental.'

'Well, the niche was empty. There was nothing there, unless Dominic found something and hid it away somewhere?'

'If he did, it's been very well concealed. Where would he have hidden anything he found? And why wouldn't he tell Grantham?'

The Prior sighed but did not answer. He took another step away from Hood and looked up into the sky. He smiled. 'I wonder, where would a wise man hide a leaf?'

Hood appeared puzzled. Was the Prior trying to tell him something in coded language? 'A leaf? Why would anyone want to hide a leaf?'

The Prior smiled. 'A question asked and answered by that sleuthing cleric, Chesterton's Father Brown, Mr Hood. Look, I really must get on. I suggest you have a look at the novels. They're all fairly short stories. You might learn something to your advantage. Now, if you'll forgive me, I have to telephone my monastery. I have been pressing the coroner to release Dominic's body, thus far without success. We have to make arrangements for his funeral. It's unlikely to take place before the week after next. I'd be obliged if you could have words with the coroner. The *post-mortem* has been completed. Is there any reason why we cannot bring him back to Melford?'

'I'll see what I can do, but these things take time. It may be a few days yet.'

'Thank you. Hopefully, you'll have solved his murder by then and be able to attend his funeral.'

'Of course I'll attend his funeral... but solving the case is another matter altogether. I suspect there's a long way to go.' He paused. 'Perhaps we can speak later about the priest-hole?'

'About the priest-hole, yes.' The Prior paused, relaxing a little. 'I think it might be sensible to continue with the excavation. I suspect there will have been some form of passageway that led to the outside. The exit has probably been covered now by the adjacent Victorian chapel, but the original brick or stonework will probably still be there if we dig deep enough. I'm sure there would have been some means of escape while the house was being searched.'

'That will probably require Sir Robert's permission. It's not really relevant to my investigation into Dominic's death.'

'I'll raise it with him, but I suppose any further work will have to await your resolving Dominic's murder?' Hood nodded. 'By the way, Mr Hood, Wednesday is the feast of St Ignatius Loyola, founder of the Jesuits. I shall be saying Mass at five o'clock in the chapel. I forgot all about the date and failed to mention it yesterday. I really should keep a diary. It was, er, Father Grantham who reminded me, actually. I suggest you come. I expect he'll be there too.' The Prior smiled.

The mention of a diary jogged Hood's memory. 'You don't happen to know if Father Dominic kept a diary?'

'I don't know. I don't suppose he had much use for one, certainly not since he came here. Didn't you find one in the Gatehouse?'

'No we didn't. And it was thoroughly searched.'

The Prior mused on the matter. 'There is a calendar in the sacristy with the odd note on it. I suppose he might be responsible for some of those jottings. I suggest you take a look.'

CHAPTER TWENTY-SIX

'What have you got for me, Guy?'

Hood was walking towards the Long Room with Wendy Knight, his mobile to his ear. He'd arranged to see Grantham at four o'clock. The call from the consultant forensic pathologist had been eagerly awaited. Guy Romney began in his usual business-like manner.

'I've faxed a copy of my interim report to your office in Northampton, Harry. Nothing beyond what I've already told you really, but there is one additional development you ought to know about. I had a drink last night with a fellow medical student of mine from way back, Martin Egerton. He's done very well for himself. He's a top neuro-surgeon now in London. I hadn't seen him for over five years. In view of the likely delay in getting a result from the brain samples I've sent to Professor Durell, I showed him the *post-mortem* photographs. He was very clear in his opinion after he'd looked at them.'

Hood was eager to learn of any developments in respect of Father Dominic's injuries. He stopped and listened intently. 'What did he tell you?'

Romney quoted the exact words Egerton had used. 'After the deceased received the injuries from which he died, he didn't get up again, not of his own accord anyway.'

'He's sure of that is he?'

'Absolutely. Remember, he's used to dealing with the living, Harry. My patients are all dead. Far less trouble, of course, but you'll have to go a long way to find anyone better qualified to pronounce on the progress of brain injuries.'

'And he can tell all that from the photographs?'

'He can, with a little assistance from me about what I found at the *post-mortem*, of course. There's no doubt about it. He's prepared to make a statement to confirm it.'

'But that means if Father Dominic survived the initial attack, the subsequent blows would have felled him, permanently. And as we know, they were all delivered in the grounds of the old chapel.'

'Exactly. You can forget what I said about him making his own way to the Long Room. It was always a remote possibility but according to Martin, that simply could not have happened, not in this case. Someone, presumably his killer, must have dumped him in there. Why, I have no idea. That's more your department.' He paused. 'Martin is not saying he definitely died in the chapel grounds; he may not have died for some time. I got that right, at least. But he would not have been capable of moving for himself.' He paused again. 'I know you're very busy, Harry, but if you can make it, I'm having lunch with Martin tomorrow in Oakham. He's more than willing to explain it all to you personally.'

'Oakham?'

'Yes, it's not that far, and it will be well worth it.'

'Why Oakham?'

'He's visiting his old mum. She lives there in a residential home. He's a very busy man, you know. Difficult to pin down otherwise. Hardly out of the operating theatre. So this is your best chance of speaking to him. And it's a decent enough restaurant. Bring that nice detective sergeant with you. She can take his statement. We'll make it a foursome. The Queen's Head. One o'clock.'

Hood did not require long to consider the invitation. 'One o'clock, then Guy. I'll see you and Martin Egerton on the dot at one.'

Hood switched off his phone and continued to walk with Knight into the Long Room. He handed her his file then went straight towards the heap of soil and debris that had been removed from the hide. Wendy Knight followed.

'I've tasked Adrian Swanson to supervise the examination of all this, although I don't suppose he'll find anything. Whatever was hidden in the hide was probably secreted in the niche, but we'd better check it out. He should be here in a minute or two.'

He walked to the edge of the hide and pointed to the still exposed niche and shook his head. 'I'm certain that Father Dominic found something in there, but what it was and what happened to it, I simply don't know.'

'If he did, surely his fingerprints would have been found on the panelling. But SOCO found nothing.'

'Perhaps the panelling was wiped? Whoever found whatever was hidden there probably removed any evidence of the niche being discovered?'

'But why would he or Grantham for that matter wipe the panelling? It was hardly a crime scene until after Father Dominic had been dumped there. And what was it that might have been found?' added Knight. 'Could it have been this Powdrell chalice everyone is talking about?'

'Ah, if only it were. Sir Robert would hardly be able to contain himself.'

'But even Sir Robert doesn't think it would be worth killing for.'

Hood did not reply. He then returned to the heap of spoil, picking up a handful of dirt and letting it fall through his fingers. Wendy Knight pulled a face. She was glad she hadn't been asked to carry out the sifting task.

'We won't be able to speak to Grantham in here with all that going on, will we? Looks like it could be a bit messy.'

'I agree,' said Hood. 'I have no intention of interviewing him here. But I want him to see what we uncovered yesterday and I particularly want you to watch his reaction. I suspect he already knows about this niche, whatever he may say. We'll then go up to the library.'

'The library? Why not the police station?'

'I don't want to make this too formal, not yet. It will do us no good if he clams up and asks for a solicitor. We'll continue treating him as a potential witness for the time being.'

'But why the library, sir?'

'Remember what you said to me yesterday? There's a good view of the drive from there. If that Jaguar came up the drive last Wednesday evening, chances are he must have seen it or at least heard it, whether he was in the library or his own room. Both overlook the drive. And he was the only person in the house. He's already admitted that.'

'He never mentioned seeing or hearing anything in his witness statement.'

'Quite. I think there are a few things Grantham didn't mention in his witness statement. But I suspect he knows more than he's letting on. Perhaps he just doesn't realise it?'

He edged towards the hide, then turned and glanced at the detective sergeant.

'By the way, Wendy, that lunch I promised you has come around sooner than I expected.'

She smiled. 'Really, sir?'

'Yes. You and I are meeting up with Guy Romney tomorrow and a top neuro-surgeon, a fellow called Egerton. That was Guy on the phone. We can forget about Father Dominic making his own way to the Long Room after he was attacked. There's no way he could have managed that, not according to Egerton. He's a top man who knows his subject as well as anyone. We can now proceed on the basis that after Dominic was felled in the old chapel grounds he didn't get up again. Someone picked him up and dumped him in the priest-hole. And the regulars who attend Mass here were told about the discovery of the hide before Grantham arrived at the Grange. Helen Swanson remembers Father Dominic referring to it in a sermon. It follows that everyone who attended Mass that day would have been aware of its existence, including whoever was in that Jaguar.'

Knight hesitated. 'If it was that Jaguar, sir?'

Hood smiled. 'Of course.'

'Do we have the date? For the Sunday in question?'

'We do. The seventh of July. The first Sunday in the month. Father Dominic always said Mass in Latin on the first Sunday of the month. That's why Helen remembers it.'

'So if we locate this Jaguar?'

'We may find our killer.'

'Grantham's in the clear, then?'

'Not yet, he isn't, but we have no evidence at the moment that he had any involvement, but there could be more than one person responsible for this murder. And, as you said the other day, the killing and the removal of something valuable from the hide may not be connected. It could simply be a coincidence. But Grantham is going to have to explain his behaviour in relation to the hide and whatever was discovered in that niche. I can't believe that if Dominic found something he didn't tell Grantham about it.'

'I doubt if Grantham will admit anything. He always seems very self-assured.'

Hood was inclined to agree. 'There's another development you need to know about, Wendy. I saw Father Milmo earlier. Although he didn't confirm it, I suspect that he heard Grantham's confession this morning when he got back from Oxford. Father Milmo cannot, of course, reveal anything Grantham may have said. It will remain absolutely confidential. I'm sure even you must have heard of the seal of the confessional?'

'Yes, sir. I have. But if he admitted something criminal?'

'It doesn't matter what he admitted. The good Prior will not even confirm that he heard Grantham's confession.'

'But is that legal? Can't he be required to disclose what Grantham said?'

'As far as I am aware the position of priest and penitent has not been authoritatively decided. But if in strict law the privilege does not exist, I believe the usual practice is that a priest should not be required to give evidence of a confession made to him in such circumstances. I had a word with the CPS earlier.'

'And I suppose whatever he confessed may have nothing to do with the murder of Father Dominic?'

'That may well be the case.'

Wendy Knight had a sudden thought. 'But why would he choose to go to confession this morning, unless he had something to confess that had some relevance to events here? Something he knew about and felt he needed to discuss in confidence with another priest. Something he anticipated was about to be exposed.'

'Like the secondary hiding place in the priest-hole? I don't know Wendy, but you may have hit on something without realising it?'

'I have?'

'Never mind why he chose to go to confession this morning, the real question is why he chose to use Father Milmo as his confessor? He's been in Oxford all week-end. Why not go to confession there? He must have every opportunity to use a confessor in Oxford. And he must, if he's still pursuing his vocation, be making regular visits to the confessional, far more often than the likes of me.'

'I see what you mean, sir. If he did go to confession this morning, confessing to Father Milmo takes Milmo out of the equation, so to speak. It silences him. We'll get no further help from Father Milmo now.'

'You have it in one, Wendy. For an agnostic, you've picked up the concept very quickly.'

She smiled. 'Saw it in a Hitchcock film, sir. "*I Confess.*" Montgomery Clift, as I remember.' She explained the plot of the film. 'A murderer confesses to a priest that he has killed someone. Knowing the priest cannot reveal the secrets of the confessional, he then tries to frame the priest. I thought it a bit far- fetched myself.'

'Why? Because the priest couldn't tell?'

'Oh, no. I got that all right. But it was set in a very Catholic part of Canada, Quebec I think. It simply never occurred to anyone that the poor priest couldn't say anything because the killer had confessed what he'd done. The priest couldn't even say anything when he was put on trial and accused of the murder. He was very nearly convicted too. They must have been very dumb not to have worked out why he couldn't reveal anything.'

'Do you think that is what has happened here? And that Grantham thinks we are too dumb to work it out?'

'It's a possibility, sir. But we have the advantage.' She smiled. 'We're not as dumb as he may think.'

Hood laughed. 'We must bear in mind that Father Milmo didn't actually confirm that Grantham had been to confession. Perhaps he just wanted to speak with a priest who wasn't a Jesuit? That would be understandable if he is thinking of abandoning his vocation.'

'Nothing to stop us asking Grantham whether he's spoken to Father Milmo, though?'

'No, but I don't want Grantham thinking that Father Milmo has revealed anything to us, because he hasn't. It wouldn't be right to give a false impression. That could come back and bite us if Grantham ends up being charged with anything.'

'I think I'll leave this one to you, sir. I don't want to blunder in. But in the circumstances, perhaps it would be better to interview him formally at the police station? There'll be a recording then of everything he says.'

Hood pointed to DC Swanson who had just appeared in the corridor that led to the Long Room. Hood started to walk towards him, followed by Knight

'If we have reasonable cause to arrest him, we shall. The interview will then continue in Northampton. But I want him to see the drive from the library window first. That's where he said he was after supper on Wednesday evening.'

'Listening to Mozart.'

Hood gave Knight a wry grin. 'It means, of course, you're going to have to take a full note. Look, hold off Swanson until Grantham gets here, will you? Have a quick word with him.'

Wendy checked her watch. It was almost four o'clock. DC Swanson was now in the room, dressed in a pair of oil-stained overalls.

'Give us five minutes, will you Adrian.'

DC Swanson paused and raised his hand. As he turned and made his way back towards the corridor, Grantham appeared. He was smartly dressed as usual in a dark shirt and black trousers. He had sandals on his feet. His expression was not that of a troubled individual. Hood braced himself. 'Good afternoon, Father Grantham.'

Grantham responded with a nod, heaved a sigh, hesitated for a few seconds then walked slowly towards the hide, crouching down and visually inspecting the exposed niche. He said nothing. Knight watched him closely but he gave nothing away. His facial expression did not change as he got to his feet and addressed the chief inspector.

'I see you've made some progress, Mr Hood. That looks very interesting. A secondary hiding place.' He spoke in his usual confident manner.

'More than you think,' replied Hood. 'Detective Sergeant Knight has just returned from Oxford.' He looked directly at Grantham but the Jesuit's expression remained the same. Disappointed that his comments had seemingly failed to draw anything useful from Grantham, Hood continued. 'I want you to have a good look at this hide, particularly the section we uncovered yesterday. Do you see the niche? Pity you weren't here when we discovered this additional hiding place, but unfortunately there was nothing in there. Quite empty. Our excitement turned quickly to disappointment. The niche was hidden behind the panelling, as you can see. Remarkable bit of construction for the sixteenth century, don't you think? Someone went to a lot of trouble to create a very safe hiding place? I wonder why?'

Grantham did not react. He simply stared at the niche then turned towards Hood as he replied. 'As I said, it's very interesting. I would like to take a closer look sometime. Do you think there was something hidden in there? Perhaps that's where the sacramental was found?'

Hood sidestepped the question. 'We'll go up to the library, now, if you don't mind? Nice and private there. I have a few questions I want to put to you. I hope you are still prepared to assist me with my inquiries?'

'I'm at your disposal,' replied Grantham. 'Lead the way, Chief Inspector.'

CHAPTER TWENTY-SEVEN

Hood and Knight had been in the library at Easton Grange before but had never lingered there. It was a large room with four double-glazed sash windows overlooking the lawns that reached almost down to the narrow country road which wound its way past the house and through to the village beyond. Leather bound books, all carefully arranged on the oak bookcases, lined three of the four walls. A large marble fireplace, never used Hood had been informed, interrupted the flow of books on the longest wall. It had been retrieved by Sir Robert's grandfather from a French chateau in the Loire valley which was in the course of being demolished. It looked out of place, being from a different period than the house.

The drive, clearly visible from the windows, which led up to the front of the house was slightly wider than the public highway, with room enough for two vehicles to pass. It was dressed in Cotswold bluff coloured gravel which had accumulated in deep drifts around the wrought iron gates, causing vehicles coming into the estate to make a distinctive crunching sound as they negotiated the entrance. One of the windows was half open, allowing a gentle breeze to diffuse the late afternoon heat. As Hood removed his jacket and placed it on the back of a chair, he noticed that the occasional vehicle passing on the road below could clearly be heard. He also spied a small music centre and a pair of headphones next to several volumes scattered on the large oak table in the centre of the room.

Grantham had followed the two detectives into the library. He remained standing. Knight gave him a knowing look as she placed the case file on the table, pulled out a chair and invited him to take a seat. Hood sat directly opposite, opening the file and removing the photograph of a Jaguar Mark 2 and placing it on the table. He said nothing. Grantham, too, was silent, betraying not the slightest hint of nervousness. Knight took out her notebook and sat a few feet away at the end of the table. *How,* she wondered, *would the chief inspector begin this interview?* Hood cleared his throat.

'It seems, Father Grantham, that we were all labouring under a slight misapprehension?' Hood looked up and smiled. Grantham did not respond other than by raising an eyebrow. Hood continued. 'If anything were hidden in the priest-hole, it must have been concealed in the niche, not in the in-fill. Do you think that tells us anything?'

'More than you think, Mr Hood.'

The Jesuit gave the chief inspector a languid look. Hood glanced towards Knight to check that she had noted the reply. It had not gone unnoticed that Grantham had used the same expression the chief inspector had employed in the Long Room minutes before.

'What do you mean?'

Grantham shook his head gently then looked down. 'It makes it more likely that Father Dominic did find the sacramental in the priest-hole as I mentioned earlier. It would clearly have survived intact in the niche. It causes me to revise my earlier opinion.'

'But you were unaware of its existence until it was found in Father Dominic's hand?'

Grantham look directly at Hood. 'I see no reason to revise the answer I gave when you asked me last week. I had never seen it before you showed it to me in Sir Robert's study.'

'So, Father Dominic never mentioned finding it to you?'

'No, he did not. Why he did not I have no idea. But I have already told you this. Why am I being asked again?'

'There have been developments.'

'Concerning me?'

'Detective Sergeant Knight was in Oxford this morning.'

'You mentioned that when we were in the Long Room. Is it of any consequence?'

'She visited Campion Hall.'

Grantham smiled. 'I trust she was properly received.'

'Yes. She was introduced to the archivist.'

'Edwin Ambler?'

'Yes. He informed her you had examined and photographed the Campion sacramental.'

'I have. As part of my research. I was a little surprised that you had not done so yourself, Mr Hood. I did inform you of the similarities between it and the sacramental found in Dominic's hand.'

Hood coughed. 'Yes. I was intending to take a look at it.' He paused. 'It seems you were correct. The two are very similar and appear to come from approximately the same period.'

'Certainly from the same pontificate, yes. But I have not seen the two side by side. I would certainly like to do so.'

Hood moved on. 'My sergeant was also informed that you attended Mass at Campion Hall yesterday.'

Grantham glanced towards Knight. 'Was she? Does that surprise you? I attend Mass every Sunday, and on other occasions too. I hope you are not suggesting there is anything incriminating about that?'

'Could I ask why you didn't say your own Mass? You've never said Mass here, either have you? I was brought up to believe that a priest should try and say Mass every day?'

Grantham hesitated before he replied. He strummed his fingers on the table. 'I have made a decision not to say Mass at the moment or engage in other priestly functions.'

'Would you like to tell me why?'

'No, I would not. My reasons are personal and not relevant to your investigation.'

Hood looked at him intently. As he had anticipated, Grantham was not going to be an easy person to question. That he refused to reveal why he had ceased to celebrate Mass served only to add to Hood's suspicions. 'But you still call yourself Father Grantham, don't you?'

'What if I do? I am still a priest and still a Jesuit.'

'That sounds rather ominous, if I may say so? Are you considering giving up your vocation?'

Grantham's tone did not alter. 'You're trespassing on what I consider to be personal territory, Chief Inspector. It is no business of yours and has no bearing on Dominic's killing.'

'You surely understand why I ask the question? You found Father Dominic's body...'

Grantham interrupted. 'Oh, and you subscribe to the notion that he who finds the body must come under suspicion? I was also the last, apart from his killer, to speak to him. So I am doubly suspect am I? I thought you were a better detective than that Mr Hood. This isn't an episode of *Columbo* you know; this is real life.'

'And death,' added Hood.

Grantham nodded, solemnly. 'I have not forgotten. I'm as keen as you to find Dominic's killer. But you are wasting your time if you are considering me as a suspect. I can't think what I can have done to draw suspicion on myself.' He smiled. 'But I suppose everyone sees what one appears to be, few if any really know what one is and those few dare not oppose themselves to the opinion of the many.'

Hood appeared puzzled. *Was this Grantham being Jesuitical* 'Is that a quotation?' he asked. 'Ignatius Loyola, perhaps?'

Grantham laughed. 'Hardly, Mr Hood. Niccolò Machiavelli, actually. Not quite as he originally penned it, but it makes the point, I think.'

Hood frowned. 'You have never attended Mass here on a Sunday. I suppose that's why you went to Oxford every week-end?'

Grantham smiled and shook his head. 'That is not the reason I go to Oxford at week-ends. There are other reasons for that, wholly innocent reasons. I suppose Dominic's death would have raised the issue had Father Milmo not appeared. I may well have had to revise my position and come to a decision earlier than I wished.'

'Revise your position? What do you mean?

'As I said, Chief Inspector, that is a personal matter of no relevance to your investigation.'

Hood was getting nowhere. A change of tack seemed necessary. 'Did Father Dominic know you had decided not to carry out any priestly functions at the present time?'

Grantham did not immediately answer. He sighed before he said anything. 'Yes, he did.'

'How did he find out?'

'I told him, in confidence, of course. He had invited me to say Mass here during the week.'

'You told him?'

'Correct. As I said, I told him in confidence.'

'In the confessional, you mean?'

'I really can't say, Mr Hood.' He paused ominously then looked directly at the chief inspector. 'What I can say is that he respected the confidential nature of what I'd revealed to him. He was a good man and a good priest, a far better priest than I suspect I could ever be. Not that I had a great deal to do with him, you understand. He only really got involved with the hide recently and he was not physically strong. I did the bulk of the excavation myself with the help of Mr Hitchens, Sir Robert's gardener. He did most of the heavy work on one of his days off. He was quite excited about it and was pleased to help. He and Dominic got on very well together.'

'That was on the Monday before Father Dominic died, I believe?'

'Yes. We finished the heavy work on Monday afternoon.'

'But Father Dominic knew the priest-hole had been discovered before you arrived here?'

'Of course he did. He also knew that Sir Robert was awaiting my arrival before the main excavation began.'

'Dominic apparently mentioned the discovery of the hide in a sermon he gave on the seventh of July, before you arrived here.'

'Why should he not? He was, after all, a historian. It would have been perfectly natural for him to do so.'

Hood extracted Grantham's original witness statement from the case file and glanced at it. 'You have previously stated that Father Dominic was with you for most of Wednesday last and that you and he had supper together.'

'Yes.'

'Mr Hitchens was not there that day?'

'No. It was his daughter's graduation. He was up in Leeds, I believe.'

'And you found nothing of interest in the hide after it had been completely exposed?'

'That's right. If you look at what I said in my statement, Mr Hood, you will see that I specifically restricted my observations to what I personally had witnessed. I was very careful how I put things. I said nothing about Father Dominic's activities when I was not present. How could I?'

The chief inspector read through that part of the witness statement again. 'But if you were working together…?'

'We were not in each other's company all the time. If you read on, you will see that I made it perfectly clear that I left him in the Long

Room while I was engaged in a telephone call in here.' He pointed to the telephone on a separate and smaller table in front of one of the windows.

'But you can't have been away for long, simply making a phone call?'

'Again, Mr Hood, if you read through my statement you will see I did not mention the length of time I was away from the Long Room, and the young detective who took my statement never asked me.'

'You could have volunteered the information. I assume your attention was drawn to the caption at the head of the statement before you were asked to sign it?'

'Yes. But if you remember, I told you when we first spoke on Thursday morning that I had been apart from Father Dominic for about an hour. I didn't repeat that in my statement because I didn't think it was relevant. And as the call related to my personal position within the Jesuit order, I wasn't going to give any further details unless it became necessary. And I am, I would point out, mentioning it to you now.' He sighed and looked away for a moment. 'If you must know, I was speaking with my superior in the States. As it was an international call I didn't want to burden Sir Robert with the expense. My superior called me at a pre-arranged time. I had to speak to him that afternoon because he was going to Rome the following day. I'm sure the fact of the call will be recorded somewhere, though not, of course, what was said.'

'Was this a lengthy call?'

'At least forty minutes I would say. We had a great deal to discuss. I then went down to the kitchen and took some iced tea that I had made earlier-American style – from the ice box. It was very hot on Wednesday afternoon, as you will recall. Dominic was very grateful. I don't think he'd drunk iced tea before. I do believe he enjoyed it.'

'So you were away from the Long Room for some time?'

'I suppose I was. About an hour I would think, certainly no longer.'

'Had anything changed when you returned?'

'Not that I noticed. It was exactly as it had been before I left.'

'Did Father Dominic say anything?'

'Other than thanking me for the iced tea, no.'

'How much longer did you stay in the Long Room?'

'About an hour I would say.'

'And what, exactly, were you doing?

'We sat down and drank the iced tea and shared what we knew about this house and the family who used to live here. Dominic also told me what he knew of the dissolution of Glastonbury Abbey. There is a link between Glastonbury and the Powdrells.'

'Father Dominic had heard of the Powdrell family?'

'Of course he had. But, before you ask, he had not heard the story of the Powdrell chalice, not before I mentioned it, which is hardly surprising. He was not aware of the documents I had discovered until I told him about them some time earlier. We then went through the spoil and debris from the excavation, not as carefully as perhaps we should have done, but time was getting on. A more careful search was planned for later. We found nothing. I had already discovered the remains of the staircase treads two days before as Mr Hitchens will confirm.'

'You knew what those pieces of oak were?'

'We both had a good idea. There was probably a staircase over the hide at one time.'

Hood returned to the issue of the heap of soil and debris. 'My officers are going through the spoil now, very carefully.'

'I'm pleased to hear it. I hope they have better luck than we did.'

'What about the priest-hole itself? Did you examine it further?'

'I don't believe I went down there again. In fact, now that I remember, Dominic was quite keen we should leave it until I took some photographs of the panelling that we had fully exposed. He may well have continued to examine it in my absence, but as far as I am aware, he had not discovered that the centre panel could be moved. If he had, he did not tell me.'

'Did you take any photographs?'

'Unfortunately, I had left my camera in Oxford. I was going to take the photographs today. I remembered to bring it back with me this time. But I suppose as it is what you call a crime scene, several photographs will already have been taken?'

'You can rest assured that they have. And a full forensic examination carried out.'

'I thought that would be the position.'

Hood looked Grantham directly in the eye. 'Tell me, had you seen the niche behind the panelling before today.'

Grantham did not hesitate before replying. 'No, not until today. That was the first and only time I have seen it. I thought I had already made that clear.'

'And Father Dominic never mentioned finding it?'

'He said nothing to me. I was unaware of the existence of the niche until I saw it a few minutes ago. Father Milmo never mentioned it when we spoke earlier.'

'I had asked him not to.'

'Well, he did as you requested.'

'Do go on.'

'Dominic and I had both examined and cleaned the panelling on Wednesday morning. We would not have taken any more intrusive steps without consulting with Sir Robert who was away. We would have gotten his permission before damaging anything. You were obviously more successful. Dominic was keen that we wiped down the area of panelling we had examined. It needed cleaning and he didn't want there to be any marks left where we had pressed against it or from the spoil we had removed.'

'Did he say why?'

'No. But it seemed the natural thing to do. We wanted it to look its best for the photographs, although I didn't take any for the reason I've just mentioned.'

'I did wonder why no fingerprints were found on the panelling,' said Hood.

'We were both anxious not to leave any marks on the panelling after cleaning it. Perhaps if we had taken a more robust approach, we may have found the niche before you did.'

'Actually, it was Father Milmo who exposed it.'

Grantham nodded. 'That does not surprise me. He has considerable experience of such hides.'

'You thought there might be something behind the panelling when you were examining it?'

Grantham smiled. 'We couldn't be sure after all this time. But, I suppose, it was always a possibility. Whoever placed the panelling there must have been an expert carpenter, but many of the monks in those days were highly competent craftsman. After all, their predecessors built the priory.' He paused and looked around the library. 'The panelling could have been put in to provide some support for the excavation, but it was so well done, it certainly occurred to me and, I should add, to Dominic, that it might have served another purpose.'

'So you think the monks constructed it?'

He shrugged his shoulders. 'If they did, it must have been adapted later as a hiding place for priests. I believe Father Milmo is pretty sure that is the case and if you recall what I said to you last Thursday, I suggested it could have been constructed or *adapted* later to provide a safe hiding place.' Hood nodded as Grantham continued. 'Having now seen the exposed niche, I see no reason to disagree with him. And I have always been aware that in some religious houses, the monks took care to hide their treasures from the commissioners when dissolution became likely. Dominic was of the same opinion. He was very knowledgeable about such matters. That's why he examined the panelling so carefully. I watched him as he did so.'

'You never mentioned any of this in your witness statement.'

'I didn't think it was relevant to the matter in hand. I have never made any secret of it, as Sir Robert will confirm.'

'It's a very small niche that we uncovered yesterday.'

'So it would appear.'

'What sort of things might have been hidden there, I wonder?'

Grantham took a deep breath. 'Gold or silver plate, jewels, anything.'

'A chalice, perhaps?'

Grantham smiled. 'Perhaps.' He remained perfectly poised, giving nothing away.

'The Powdrell chalice?' added Hood. 'Is it possible it was hidden there?'

Grantham gave a wry smile. 'Ah, the Powdrell chalice. I thought we'd come back to that. I think finding the Powdrell chalice would have been too much to hope for, Mr Hood. But anything could have been hidden there – or nothing.'

'What do you know of this so-called Powdrell chalice?'

Grantham began his account with undisguised enthusiasm. 'Not a great deal, but no-one does. It isn't certain if it still exists. My research shows that a member of the Powdrell family was a monk at Glastonbury, the great Benedictine Abbey in Somerset. But what happened to him is not recorded anywhere as far as I know. Sir Robert's family originally came from Somerset though, and one of his ancestors married a member of the Powdrell family.' He pointed to one of the books on the table. 'That much is recorded in his family history. Whether that is a coincidence or not I cannot say. I mentioned all this to Sir Robert shortly after I arrived here.'

'Did you find out about the Powdrells while researching for your doctorate?'

Grantham shook his head. 'Oh no, it was much later. I came across a document, quite by chance, in the archives of the Venerable English College when I was in Rome well over three years ago, as I think I told you on Thursday. Their archive needs a through re-organisation by the way. The document I found mentioned that a member of the Powdrell family had been a monk at Glastonbury. That was confirmed by a further document I found in the British Library some months later.'

'This research was your own project? No one else was involved?'

'Entirely my own. The Jesuits, as you know, are great educators. We are encouraged to engage in research and I travelled to Rome and England during periods of leave from my University. For most of the last two years, however, I have been in the States. I was busy with my teaching programme and had some personal issues to deal with. That is why I could not come here last summer. I was refused permission by my superiors. We Jesuits are subject to a vow of obedience.'

'This document you found in the British Library, what was it, exactly?' asked Hood.

Grantham's eyes lit up. He was more than happy to disclose what he had discovered. 'It was, and is, a list of the monks who were eligible to vote at the election of their Abbot at Glastonbury. It's amazing it survived all these years but it's still there in the British Library. You English are marvellous at preserving your history, but Glastonbury was, perhaps, the most splendid and certainly one of the richest of all the Benedictine houses in England. That may explain the document's survival. The last Abbot of Glastonbury, despite his reputation and his great age, was hanged on Thomas Cromwell's orders. Cromwell had him tried on a trumped-up charge of treason, but the real reason he was executed was because he and most of his monks were not inclined to surrender their monastery and therefore had to be forced out. Numerous complaints were made against them, including denying the King's supremacy of the Church and, on a more practical level, that they had hidden some of their treasures from the commissioners who were busy expropriating the monastery's valuables. What the King laughingly described as their "superfluous plate." I think the record, in Cromwell's own hand, shows eleven thousand ounces of silver being confiscated as well as an unrecorded amount of gold. Other valuables were found hidden in the fabric of the building including I would point out, a golden chalice, and the rest, as they say, is history.'

'Could that chalice have been the Powdrell chalice?'

Grantham shook his head. 'Obviously not. The commissioners seized it. It would never have found its way back to the monastery or anywhere else. Probably melted down or sold.'

'But you think that some of the other Glastonbury treasures may have eluded Cromwell and been hidden other than in the monastery?'

Grantham nodded. 'I am not alone in that opinion. Dominic certainly thought so. And it is a fairly common view amongst those who are interested in the period. There is very little left of Glastonbury. The monastery was carefully searched and stripped of all its treasures even before the poor Abbot was executed. Nothing will be discovered there now.' He paused and shifted in his seat. 'But one must not jump to conclusions. The imagination is a dangerous faculty in a historian, Mr Hood. The historian's function is to interpret history, not to make it. That is why I have always restrained Sir Robert when it comes to speculating whether Edmund Campion came to this house.'

Hood reflected on what Hood had said, but he was more interested in the Powdrell chalice than Campion's exploits. 'And this chalice could be one of those valuables hidden by the monks from Cromwell's men?'

'It's a remote possibility. If it had been hidden at Glastonbury it would have been found; if it were spirited away, it could be anywhere. I believe Sir Robert has told you of a chalice which is mentioned in a letter, which also survives, a letter sent to the last Abbot of Westminster from Anthony Powdrell in Mary Tudor's reign.'

Hood nodded. 'He has.'

'But whether that chalice, if it still exists, came from Glastonbury simply isn't known.' He smiled. 'I like to think it's just possible that Powdrell, having been expelled from his monastery, managed to smuggle out some of the treasures which later came into the possession of his family, but I suspect that is wishful thinking on my part, which as a historian, I must guard against.' He sighed. 'It would have been a very risky thing to do. Had he been caught he would certainly have been hanged.'

'So, the chalice may have had nothing to do with the Augustinian priory that used to be here? It may have originated in Glastonbury?'

'Quite. On the other hand, who knows? This priory was dissolved before Glastonbury. That much is clear. Perhaps the Powdrells simply took advantage of the hiding place prepared by the monks? I say monks, but as you we know, this was an Augustinian house; those who resided here are properly described as canons rather than monks.'

Hood recalled what Father Milmo had said before the niche was discovered. 'I don't suppose that distinction makes any difference to what happened to them?'

'Not at all.'

'And I suppose the chalice became known as the Powdrell chalice after the monk who saved it?'

'I suppose so, or after the family which preserved it; always assuming it still exists, of course.'

'And this Father Powdrell's name definitely appears on the document you discovered in the British Library?'

'His name in religion, yes. Aidan, that was the name he was given. Not that he had the opportunity of exercising his vote.'

'He didn't?'

Grantham was in his element. 'No, the last election of an Abbot at Glastonbury was some years before the dissolution, in fifteen twenty-five. The monks, after careful consideration and much prayer, decided to allow the Cardinal of York to choose the next Abbot. That sometimes happened in those days, *per formam compromissi,* in the original Latin.' He smiled in that superior way of his. 'Perhaps it was thought that Wolsey would provide them with his protection if they gave him the privilege of appointing the new Abbot? He chose Richard Whiting, a monk of the highest reputation and great learning. He was beatified by Pope Leo the Thirteenth in the nineteenth century, you know, although he had not initially opposed the King's supremacy and had lent his support to the annulment of Henry's marriage to Queen Catherine. He was not alone in doing so, of course, but it did not save him in the end.'

'Wolsey could not protect him?'

Grantham almost laughed. He shook his head more vigorously. 'Wolsey fell from favour some years before, in fifteen twenty-nine and died the following year. Glastonbury survived until the end of fifteen thirty-nine. It had originally been given a clean bill of health by Cromwell's commissioners, but that view was quickly revised and reversed. There were too many greedy men with greasy palms anxious to get hold of the Abbey's lands. No one stood up for the monks. They were regarded as dispensable.'

'And Aidan Powdrell?'

Grantham shrugged his shoulders. 'It would seem that he survived the dissolution; there is no evidence to the contrary. He was certainly not one of the monks executed with his Abbot. You see, Mr Hood, there were several branches of the Powdrell family living in the Midlands in those days. It would have been perfectly natural for him to seek refuge with one of them. They've all died out since then. I think Sir Robert's family can truly claim to be the only surviving descendants.'

Hood may not have appreciated the gap in time between Wolsey's death and the dissolution of Glastonbury but having had it drawn to his attention, he quickly spotted a possible flaw in what Grantham was saying. 'But the Powdrells did not reside here at Easton Parva at that time, did they?'

Grantham let out a deep sigh. 'No, not in this house, not until fifteen fifty-five according to my research. That's where the trail goes cold, unfortunately. The Abbot of Glastonbury was hanged, drawn and quartered in November fifteen thirty-nine. Aidan Powdrell must have left the monastery before then. The destruction of the Abbey was already underway. That gap of fifteen years is a real problem. If he did bring anything valuable from his monastery, it is impossible now to say what it was or what happened to it. But he could not have brought it directly here. The chalice referred to in the letter to the last Abbot of Westminster in fifteen fifty-six may have come from Glastonbury, but it will not admit of certain proof even if it were found. It would be impossible to establish its origins after all these years.'

'Or, presumably, its value?'

'That must follow. The commercial value would be dependent in large part on its makeup, but its historic and religious value would be considerable, particularly if a link with Glastonbury could be established.'

'And if it were in the possession of the Powdrells when they lived here and gave shelter to priests, it could have been used by one of them, perhaps even by one of those who was subsequently martyred?'

Grantham smiled. 'That's a possibility, even Edmund Campion might have used it to celebrate Mass, but again, very easy to imagine but difficult if not impossible to prove.'

'And if Campion had celebrated Mass with it, as Sir Robert hopes, it would be worth even more?'

'Undoubtedly, but as I say, impossible to prove.'

'But not worth killing for?'

Grantham gave Hood a bemused look. 'Is anything worth killing for, Chief Inspector? Even today, murder remains a grave sin as well as a serious crime.'

Hood did not answer. He turned again to the question of the sacramental found in Father Dominic's hand.

'That *agnus dei* that Dominic was holding in his hand cannot have anything to do with Glastonbury, can it?'

Grantham nodded. 'I agree. When Glastonbury was dissolved, the chair of Peter was occupied by Paul the Third. As we have already established, the sacramental found with Father Dominic, if genuine, comes from a much later pontificate; Gregory the Thirteenth was Pope when it was made. Glastonbury was long gone by then.'

'You say, if genuine. As you have examined the sacramental which is kept at the Jesuit house in Oxford, do you have a decided view now about Father Dominic's?'

'I have a provisional opinion. I would like to carry out a direct comparison between the two but I suppose that will not be possible until this murder is solved?'

'You suppose right, although I may ask the archivist at Campion Hall to compare the two. He's quite an expert, I understand.'

'An excellent idea, Mr Hood. He's a very knowledgeable individual. In the short time I have known him, I have always found him to be very insightful.'

'And your provisional opinion?'

Grantham cleared his throat. 'I am coming round to the view that Father Dominic must have found the sacramental in the hide – in the niche. There is no evidence that he possessed such an item before the hide was discovered. Father Milmo has confirmed as much.' He nodded towards Wendy Knight. 'Your sergeant was right from the beginning. Having examined the sacramental at Oxford, I have to concede they are remarkably similar. I would argue now that the one found in Dominic's hand is genuine, not a recent copy, although smaller than the example at Oxford. What I don't quite understand is why Dominic didn't tell me he'd found it.' He looked at Hood and smiled. 'Do you think he didn't trust me? If he didn't, I find that very disappointing. Perhaps he had something against the Jesuits?' He smiled broadly.

Silence. Hood was making no progress, although he found the history lesson very interesting. He decided to try another approach.

'Of course, if he'd found something larger, something he couldn't keep in his pocket, he must have hidden it somewhere else.'

'I suppose he must, but he didn't say anything to me. And if he had found something, why not leave it in the niche? If he were the only person who knew about the niche, there was surely no better hiding place available to him?'

Hood took a deep breath and picked up Grantham's witness statement again. He perused it until he reached the end. He looked up. 'We have searched everywhere and have found nothing. Perhaps he hid whatever it was elsewhere because he thought you might continue with the examination of the hide in his absence?'

'Possibly, but it's surely more likely that Dominic found nothing else there, just the sacramental? If the Powdrell's were aware of any truly valuable treasure they would surely have taken it with them when they were forced to sell this place?'

'Always assuming that generation of the family knew something was hidden here,' cautioned Hood. 'But, if they were in desperate financial circumstances and knew of a valuable chalice, they may well have sold it, I suppose?'

Grantham agreed. 'I haven't come across any evidence of such a sale. But the Powdrell records that do remain are far from complete, so what you suggest may well have come about.'

'Can you think of a reason why something valuable might have been deliberately left here hidden in the niche?'

'The circumstances of the family's departure from here are not fully recorded. There is some evidence of a forced sale of items of their property following pressure from their creditors so they may have concealed religious items to avoid them falling into the wrong hands in the hope that better times would come.' He smiled cynically. 'They didn't, of course, not for two centuries.'

The chief inspector heaved a deeper sigh as he recalled Sir Robert's comments when he first revealed the possibility of the Powdrell chalice surviving the dissolution. If such a chalice did exist, it would certainly have been deeply venerated. Allowing it to fall into the wrong hands would have been regarded as close to sacrilege and might explain why such a treasure was carefully hidden and not removed when the family departed from the Grange.

'Anything else I can help you with Chief Inspector?' asked the Jesuit, sensing that Hood was fast running out of questions.

Grantham's continuing calmness was beginning to irritate Hood. He seemed to have an answer for everything. The chief inspector produced the photograph of the Jaguar Mark 2 and passed it to Grantham who glanced at it before handing it back.

'Did you see a car like that on Wednesday evening after Father Dominic had left you?'

Grantham took up the photograph again and studied it at greater length.

'Not that I recall, no.'

'We have reason to believe it came onto the drive between seven-thirty and eight when you were the only person in the house. The sound of vehicles does carry, and the excess gravel at the entrance tends to announce the arrival of a motorised vehicle as it passes through the gates. Difficult to miss I would have thought?'

Grantham shrugged his shoulders. 'I was probably listening to Mozart wearing my headphones. I doubt if I would have heard anything.'

Hood could no longer contain himself. 'Always Mozart, is it? Never Bach, or Wagner?'

Grantham pulled a face. 'Wagner? Far too loud.'

Hood pointed to the open window. 'Did you have the windows open on Wednesday?'

'During the afternoon, yes. They were all open. I closed them sometime in the evening. I can't remember the precise time, but I definitely closed them. Sir Robert insists everything is closed and locked up before we retire for the night.'

'You heard neither a motor car on the drive nor the window in the Long Room going in?'

'Not that I recall, no. But I can't say I've ever noticed any vehicles negotiating the drive although I'm sure they must have done when I've been in here. If I am reading, Mr Hood, I become quite disconnected from what is going on around me, whether I have my headphones on or not. I rather regard it as a form of academic dissociation.' There was that superior smile of his again. Hood merely frowned.

'Did you see anyone in the grounds at any time on the twenty-fourth?'

'I don't think so. I saw no-one after accompanying Father Dominic to the chapel door. I understand that Sir Robert does not object to the villagers walking in the park in the summer months, but I don't recall seeing anyone. Some even drive here, then leave their vehicles while they walk in the grounds and the woodland at the edge of the park, so a car coming into the grounds might well be perfectly innocent.'

Hood had to concede such might be the case as he continued to press Grantham. 'Was there any sign of damage in the Long Room when you accompanied Dominic to the chapel door?'

'Not at that time, no. I didn't notice the damage to the window until the following morning.' He sighed. 'We have already been over this ground, Mr Hood.' The Jesuit was showing just a trace of irritability.

'What time was it when you saw Father Dominic open the door to the sacristy?'

'I can't be precise. Between twenty to and a quarter-to-seven, possibly a little later.'

'Tell me, did Father Dominic have to unlock the door?'

'I believe he did, yes. I recall that the door is usually kept locked. He must have had the key with him, but I remember he didn't lock it behind him after he went through. I never had a key, of course. If I wished to visit the chapel, as I did from time to time, unless the sacristy door was already unlocked, I used the main entrance in the grounds.'

'Interesting. You're sure the door was not locked after he went through?'

'He didn't lock the door, I'm sure of it. It's a very noisy lock. I'd have heard it.'

'Someone locked the door. It was definitely locked when his body was found. I checked it myself.'

'You have the advantage of me; I never checked it. Perhaps Dominic locked it later before leaving through the other door?'

'Did he say why he was going into the chapel?'

The question amused Grantham. 'No. He was a priest, Mr Hood. It's hardly unusual for a priest to go into a chapel. Perhaps he wanted to pray and as I said in my statement, he usually prepared for his Mass the night before. He simply said, "Goodnight and God bless." They were his last words to me.' Grantham became slightly emotional. Hood waited.

'Did he have anything with him?'

Grantham paused as if in thought. 'His breviary. Yes, he had his breviary with him. But he usually had his breviary with him. He placed it on the kitchen table when we were having supper.'

'You didn't see him again?'

'Not until the following morning when I found him in the priest-hole. After he went into the sacristy, I walked up the stairs to the library. I stayed there, or in my room, until I came down just before ten o'clock to lock the front door.'

'You told me last Thursday that you felt for his pulse when you found him.'

'Yes, but he was dead and had been for some time. He was quite cold. It was very traumatic for me, you know, Mr Hood, to find Dominic lying there. He seemed shockingly out of place in the priest-hole, if you understand my meaning. It had never occurred to me that I would find him there, dead.'

'Did you alter the position of his right hand after you checked his pulse?'

'No, I was very careful to replace his hand in exactly the same position that I found it. That comes of reading my father's cases I suppose. He hoped I would follow in his footsteps and become an attorney, but I didn't. I discovered a different vocation then found academia too interesting and far too comfortable.'

'His right hand was pointing towards the centre panel. Did you notice that?'

'No. Did you Chief Inspector?'

Hood grunted in frustration. 'What about his cowl? Was that covering his head?'

'I don't think so. I assure you I did not alter anything. As soon as I had established he was dead, I climbed out of the hide and rushed to the kitchen to phone the housekeeper.'

Hood was getting nowhere fast. Grantham seemed to be getting the upper hand. The chief inspector changed the subject. 'Tell me, did Father Dominic have a diary?'

'A diary? Oh, yes. He had one of those small pocket diaries. He produced it briefly while we were having supper together. He wanted to check which day of the week the feast of our founder, Ignatius Loyola, falls on. It is this coming Wednesday. Have you not located his diary?'

'No, we have not. But Father Milmo reminded me there's a calendar which is kept in the sacristy. Were you aware of that?'

'I don't remember seeing that, no.'

Hood produced the calendar from the file. 'There are two initials marked on the twenty-sixth, two days after the murder. H and N. Do they mean anything to you?'

Grantham shook his head. 'I suppose they could be the initials of someone Dominic intended to mention in his Mass that day.' Grantham flicked through the pages of the calendar. 'I see there are one or two similar markings earlier.'

'Yes. But nothing after the twenty-sixth.'

'So it appears.'

'Any idea who those initials could relate to?'

'I'm afraid not, Chief Inspector. One of those who attended the chapel, perhaps? But it does look like Dominic's writing. He had a fine hand. He made several notes during our excavation. I still have them.'

'Perhaps you could let me have them, for comparison purposes?'

'Of course.'

Hood recovered the calendar and replaced it in his file. He then removed the record of Grantham's accommodation at Oxford.

'You seem to have stayed every week-end at Christ Church?'

'For the last three week-ends, yes. I spent the week-end before I came here at Oxford too. Does that implicate me in some way?' There was a bemused smile on Grantham's face.

Hood continued. 'Why not stay at Campion Hall?'

'I prefer Christ Church. I suppose I could have stayed at Brewer Street, but I chose Christ Church. It is vacation time. There were plenty of rooms available. And I studied there for my doctorate.'

'And the cost?'

'I am technically paid a salary for teaching at my university in America, but as I have taken a vow of poverty, I do not receive it. But my reasonable expenses are otherwise provided for. I do not have any financial problems, certainly not of that nature. My late father was a very successful trial attorney, what you call a barrister over here. Giving up my inheritance is one of the factors I have to weigh in the balance.'

Grantham went on to explain that were he a secular priest, that would not be an issue. He told Hood that his father died in September the previous year and had left a considerable estate. As his only surviving relative, apart from a few distant cousins, he felt it was his duty to wind up the estate which would take a very long time. For a lawyer, his father had not left his affairs in the best of order.

'And your inheritance is a factor as regards your future, is it?' inquired the chief inspector

Grantham did not reply. Hood sighed in exasperation and looked at the copy bill from Christ Church. 'You appear to have stayed on Friday and Saturday only this last week-end.'

'Yes.'

'But the previous week-ends you were billed for three nights, Friday, Saturday and Sunday.'

'Yes.'

'Why did you return yesterday?'

'Because I wanted to be here and available this morning. There is a murder inquiry going on, isn't there? I thought I should be here. That is why I borrowed Martha's car.'

'Have you used her car previously?' Hood asked.

'No, the necessity hasn't arisen. The week-end before I used the bus to get to Oxford, but I got a lift back from one of the fellows at Christ Church who was travelling to Kettering. I can let you have the details if you wish to check. And don't worry, Mr Hood, I hold an international driving licence and took out insurance for the week-end. The certificate should be in the post. I also managed to drive on the left without difficulty. I did spend three years in Oxford while studying for my doctorate so I am quite used to many of your English ways.'

Hood changed the subject again. 'You didn't come into breakfast this morning?'

Grantham shifted in his chair. His patience was running out. 'No, I didn't. I wasn't hungry. I don't think Sir Robert regards attendance at breakfast as compulsory.'

Hood heaved a sigh. 'How well do you know Martha Morton?'

'Martha?' Grantham appeared surprised that the housekeeper was being introduced into the discussion. 'Hardly at all. I suppose we get on well enough; she did let me borrow her car.'

'Was that at her suggestion?'

'No, I asked her if it might be possible because I wanted to get back on Sunday evening. I was aware there were no buses after mid-day on a Sunday. Martha had agreed to work over the week-end given the circumstances; she didn't need her car.'

'Did you know her before you came here?'

'No. How could I?'

'Have you ever been to her cottage?'

'Apart from going there to pick up her car, I have been there twice, I think. On both occasions after Dominic was killed. She was very upset, understandably as you saw for yourself on Thursday. We discussed what could have caused anyone to kill Dominic. I gave her whatever support I could.'

'We have a witness who saw a man leaving her cottage very early on Saturday morning. He fits your description.'

'Do you indeed? But I was in Oxford on Saturday morning and I do not have the power of bi-location. I had breakfast in college at about half-past eight. Several people saw me, including the Dean. We had a spirited conversation about the foundation of the Oxford diocese. It used to be part of the see of Lincoln, you know, before Henry the Eighth's time.'

Hood eschewed the history lesson. 'Half-past eight? Anyone see you in college before then?'

'I don't know, they may have done. We were a very small party at breakfast.' A smile played on his lips. Hood moved on.

'You have seen Father Milmo since you returned from Oxford?'

'Yes, I met him for the first time this morning, after he had said Mass.'

'Was there a particular reason then why you went to the chapel this morning?'

'To see Father Milmo, of course. I had been informed he wanted to speak to me about Dominic. I also gather he's a bit of an expert on priest-holes. He certainly seemed to know a lot about them and unlike me, he's seen many examples in other houses.'

'Did you discuss anything else?'

'I asked him about Father Dominic's funeral. I was hoping to attend, but I gather it may well not take place until after I have returned to the States.'

'Is that all, or were other things discussed?'

'Not that I'm at liberty to disclose, no.' He furrowed his brow. His patience was about exhausted. 'Mr Hood, while I am happy to assist you in any way I can, I'm getting the distinct impression you think I may have had something to do with Dominic's death. I can assure you I had no involvement at all. My conscience is clear.'

He smiled that supercilious smile of his. Hood slammed the file shut, stood up, pulled on his jacket and walked away from the table. He stood looking through the window for fully a minute. Letting out a deep sigh, he turned and set his sights on Grantham who was still sitting calmly at the table, gently strumming his fingers. 'Oh, believe me, Father, if I had any evidence you were involved, I'd have arrested you and taken you to the police station for formal interview.'

The smile vanished from Grantham's face and he suddenly became serious but without appearing over concerned. 'With an attorney and everything?' he queried. His smile gradually returned.

Hood breathed out slowly and recovered his composure. He returned to his seat. 'Yes, but I don't consider that necessary – not at the moment.'

Grantham continued to look unconcerned. 'I'm pleased to hear it. I hope it will never be necessary.' He then smiled more broadly. 'I might have had to plead the fifth!'

Before Hood could react, a car turned into the drive, crunching the gravel noisily as it negotiated the entrance. The sound carried into the library. Knight stood up and walked to the window.

'Looks like Bradley, sir. Driving too quickly as usual. The uniformed officer opened the gates for him.'

Grantham looked up. He was suddenly quite animated. He got to his feet and walked towards the open window. 'That sound, Chief Inspector. I *have* heard it before. I remember now. I did hear something like that and I believe it could well have been on Wednesday evening. But it wasn't at the time you mentioned. It was much later. In fact, it was dark. Yes, I remember now; I removed my headphones, I looked through the window and saw the taillights disappearing through the gates. I thought for a moment it must have been a taxi leaving after dropping off Sir Robert, but it wasn't. When I went downstairs to attend to the front door it was still unlocked. So it must have been sometime shortly before ten o'clock. There was no sign of Sir Robert, of course. He would have locked the door had he come in.'

'Did you get a look at the vehicle?'

Grantham drew in his breath. 'No. I didn't really think anything of it at the time.'

'You didn't hear a similar sound earlier? As you said, it wasn't Sir Robert returning, whoever it was must have entered the grounds in the same way. There isn't another entrance or exit, not for vehicles.'

Grantham shook his head. 'No, I didn't hear anything earlier; I'm sure of it. But there was something else. I remember I went down to the kitchen to make myself a cup of coffee. I was halfway up the stairs carrying my coffee when the telephone rang. I continued up the stairs and came in here, but whoever it was had rung off by the time I picked up the phone.'

'What time was that?'

'I can't be sure, but it must have been around nine o'clock or shortly afterwards. Certainly well before I had heard a vehicle on the drive. That was at least half an hour later, probably longer.'

'And that was definitely on Wednesday last?'

'I'm pretty sure it was, yes. It was definitely on one of the evenings when Sir Robert was not here.'

'Can you recall which way the car turned as it negotiated the exit?'

Grantham took his time before replying. 'To the right, yes, towards the village.'

Hood stood up and beckoned to Wendy Knight. He obviously thought he was on to something. He whispered to her and she left the room.

'Just wait here a few minutes, Father, if you would. I want to conduct a little experiment.'

CHAPTER TWENTY-EIGHT

'He's a cool one, isn't he, sir?'

Wendy Knight was alone in the library with Hood after what he considered to have been a most unsatisfactory interview with Grantham. Hood was far from happy, his frustration evident. 'He certainly is. Do you think he was telling us the truth?'

'I don't know. He's very plausible and *very* self-confident. Part of his training as a Jesuit, I suppose.' She gave Hood a knowing look. 'I was more than a little suspicious when he suddenly remembered a car going down the drive on Wednesday evening. He'd never mentioned that before. It occurred to me that he may have said what he did because you'd put the idea into his head.'

'You mean he said he'd heard something because he thought that's what we wanted to hear?' Hood shook his head. 'But the time doesn't fit with what Philip said. It's far too late and the car was travelling in the opposite direction. I'd mentioned the time we are interested in to him earlier in the interview.'

'You did, yes. But that doesn't mean Philip isn't telling the truth. Perhaps you were making more progress with Grantham than you thought. Suddenly remembering he heard a car on the drive, whatever the time, does cast suspicion away from him.'

Hood was not so sure. He pushed the case file away and stood up. 'It's a possibility, I suppose, but the little experiment I conducted did bear out what he said. When Bradley drove down the drive quickly, the sound carried easily into the library. When he drove *slowly* in the opposite direction – towards the house – we could hardly hear a thing, even with the window open. Certainly not after the car negotiated the entrance. If the Jag arrived in similar fashion, Grantham may well not have heard it.'

'But speed has little effect as a vehicle turns through the gates. The excess gravel is mainly there. I don't know about you, sir, but I could still make out that a car was on the drive heading for the house, at least when the window was open.'

'But we were specifically listening for the sound, weren't we? It didn't quite replicate the circumstances which existed on Wednesday evening. And when we repeated it with the window closed...'

'I have to admit, I didn't really hear anything, not with the double glazing.'

'So, he's probably telling the truth.' Hood pondered the situation before adding, 'but as you said, it doesn't fit with what Philip Southall said. He thought it was before eight when he heard the car entering the drive. It can't have been here until around ten o'clock before it left, can it?'

'Not if Philip saw it as it passed the Robinson farm, no. That was much earlier, unless his timing is off. Of course, we have no idea if it was the same car.'

Hood sighed. 'On reflection, Wendy, I don't see why Grantham should lie about what he heard, but it's always possible that he got the wrong night.'

Knight smiled. 'They're not exactly rare these Mark Two Jags. Then there's the phone call? Who, I wonder, could that have been?'

'Look into it will you?'

'Yes, sir. You believe him about the phone call?'

'I don't see why not.'

'Aren't the Jesuits known for equivocation?'

Hood laughed. 'Where on earth did you get that from, Wendy? I can't see why Grantham would make up an unanswered phone call. What good would that do him? And he must appreciate, it can be checked. Get Renfrew on to it.'

'Oh, I've been reading up about them, the Jesuits. They're supposed to be the elite troops of the church. Very clever and very powerful and influential, although it's thought they've gone a bit radical in recent years. Perhaps that explains why none of them has ever made it to Pope!'

'Is that right?'

'That's what I read. In over four hundred and fifty-years, there has never been a Jesuit pope.'

'I wasn't aware of that.' Hood smiled. 'I don't suppose Grantham will make it either. But I suppose one of them might, one day.'

Hood continued to smile but could not shake off the feeling that the interview had not produced anything really constructive. He walked towards the still open window and looked out. 'Did you check when sunset was on the twenty-fourth?'

'Yes. Officially nine minutes past nine, but there'd still be some light until about twenty to ten. There wasn't much of a moon that night.'

Hood sighed. 'I'd still like to know what these personal issues are that Grantham is keeping to himself.'

Knight hesitated. 'You don't think he could have a lady friend, do you, sir?' She grinned, cheekily.

'That's an old fashioned way of putting it. It's true there are priests who give up because they can't handle celibacy. Sir Robert told me of one he knows. Perhaps we should ask Grantham directly?'

'Rather you then me, sir.'

Hood frowned. 'Of course, his inheritance could cause problems for him, I suppose. He has taken a vow of poverty.'

'Would that be a problem? It's the sort of problem I could do with and I haven't taken any vows. More likely there's a woman in the background.'

'Who?' Hood looked directly at Knight then grinned. 'Not Mrs Morton?'

'Mrs Morton is a very, eh, handsome woman, sir. You said as much yourself, but I somehow can't see him taking up with her.'

Hood smiled. 'Very handsome, and I don't think we can build a case solely on the basis that they will both be leaving Easton Grange at about the same time.'

Knight continued to speculate. 'Someone he's met at Oxford, perhaps? Maybe that's his problem. He's fallen in love. It does happen.' She smiled. 'Why don't you ask him directly, sir.'

'Not at the moment. We have no evidence that aspect of his personal life has any connection with this homicide. And if it has, we need something concrete before raising it with him.'

Hood smiled. He'd always had considerable respect for the priesthood. He had never made light of the sacrifice becoming a priest entailed. Not easy to explain the concept to an agnostic like Knight but he did his best. 'Becoming a priest, Wendy, particularly a Jesuit, is very far from easy. Apart from the intellectual demands and the years of training, they are obliged to give up everything the rest of us regard as desirable and necessary to live a contented life. Celibacy is a hard ask for most men which may be one of the reasons why there are so few vocations these days. But I think there's a greater issue than celibacy.'

'You do?'

'Undoubtedly. We live in an age of increasing religious scepticism. Most people would think it decidedly odd to give up so much in pursuit of something they regard as wholly imaginary.' He paused and looked down. 'I know I could never have abandoned the prospect of marriage and children and the happiness it has brought me. I simply wouldn't be me living alone without my Sarah. She and the children make me complete. I don't think I could do this job were it not for the stability they give me. I couldn't manage without Sarah. I consider myself truly blessed.' He paused. 'You should try it yourself, Wendy, marriage, I mean.'

She smiled mischievously. 'Haven't met the right man yet, sir. Like the Powdrell chalice, I'm not sure he actually exists. And I don't see the point of celibacy myself. Ordinary vicars can get married, can't they?'

'Catholic priests are not ordinary vicars, Wendy. The idea is that they belong wholly to Christ and not to themselves. Becoming a priest is the consecration of their whole being. There is no room for any other deep relationship. And I don't think they look at what they give up; it's what they gain that motivates them. That, at least is the theory. And the great majority, in my experience, put it into practice.'

'Sounds very demanding?'

'It is. Perhaps that's the problem Grantham has? He can't make that sort of commitment anymore.'

'A man would have to be very sure about things before entered into such a way of life. Grantham must have thought he could at one time?'

'I suppose he did, when he was younger. I wonder if it's something more than the demands of celibacy, though? Is he undergoing a crisis of faith? He's stopped saying Mass for the moment. Something must be troubling him.'

Knight shook her head. 'I doubt that's the explanation. *Cherchez la femme*. That will be his personal issue. I would put money on it.'

Hood smiled. 'You could well be right. Most of the calamities in the world have their origin in a man's infatuation with a woman. And it's a commonplace in our business, of course. But we don't want to get diverted. The discovery of the priest-hole and the death of Father Dominic may not be connected and Grantham's personal difficulties may be completely irrelevant, whatever they may be.'

'So, you're coming round to the view that it might have been something personal? The killer might have had a grudge against Father Dominic?'

Hood sighed. 'I don't know. I really don't. I do know that we need to redouble our efforts to locate that Jaguar, if only to exclude the driver from the investigation and we need to find whatever was hidden in that damn niche.' He slammed his hand down on the table in frustration.

Knight did not respond for a few seconds, then tried to move matters on.

'By the way, sir. Bradley's still waiting downstairs. He wants a word.'

Hood turned and looked at Knight, his eyes alert to any indication of progress. 'Has he got somewhere tracing the Jag?'

'Not really, no. He's says he's got some information that should be helpful, but he hasn't identified the vehicle we are looking for, not yet. He was taking a call when I left him.'

Hood stretched out his arms and supressed another yawn. 'I'll see him in a moment. What about the housekeeper?'

'She was pretty shaky when I last spoke to her. If you have a word, you might get somewhere.' Knight looked at her watch. 'Time is getting on, sir. And it's my night for the gym. What about Bradley? Will you see him first?'

Hood nodded and walked back to his chair on the other side of the table. 'Let's have him in then and line up the housekeeper. I'll see her after I'm done with him. Oh, and Wendy, find out how we're getting on interviewing the regulars from the chapel. Someone apart from Helen Swanson must have seen that maroon Jaguar on the seventh.'

CHAPTER TWENTY-NINE

'Tell me that again,' said Hood.

Bradley placed the piece of paper he'd been clutching on the table. He could hardly get his words out.

'I've only just heard about it, sir. The information came from DC Renfrew moments ago. He's on his way here with the witness statements. I noted down the reg. numbers which he gave me over the phone. The Jaguar has to be one of these.'

Hood looked at the scrap of paper and noted there were several vehicle registration numbers jotted down in no particular order. 'But the boy's not sure which it is?'

'No, sir. He can't remember. You'd think he'd have recalled a Mark Two Jaguar?'

Hood shrugged. 'Why should he? Perhaps he's more interested in the numbers than the cars? One index number does stand out, of course, as more likely to relate to a classic car.'

'Yes. sir. I've underlined it for that reason and I'm waiting for a response from Swansea. I've already phoned it through, 132 AX.'

'Good man. So, who is this boy who takes down car numbers? I wasn't aware anyone did that these days.'

'Young Francis Gilbert; he lives this side of Blisworth. His mother brings him to the chapel most Sundays and they were here on the seventh. She's fairly sure of the date. Apparently, he took down the numbers of several cars that were here that day while she was talking to someone after the service. We can check them all out.'

Hood smiled. 'Do we know why he took them down?'

'He's in competition with some of his school friends. They've started collecting car numbers but in consecutive order. He'd been looking for the number 132 for some time. He's up to 148 at the moment. Apparently, it's crucial that the numbers are collected in the right order. He can't use a number he's seen earlier and make use of it when he needs it. That would be against the rules. That's why he took down the other numbers – to prove that he was sticking to the rules.'

Hood rolled his eyes. 'Fairly harmless, I suppose, if that sort of thing amuses you. More importantly, does his mother remember the Mark Two Jaguar?'

'No sir, she doesn't. She has no recollection of it at all. It was a good job the boy was there when Bill Renfrew was speaking with her, otherwise we may never have known about this. He'd just got in from visiting his grandfather.'

Bradley's mobile phone vibrated. He glanced towards Hood who nodded. Bradley took the call.

'Well?' said Hood, impatiently.

Bradley repeated what he was being told by DVLC as Hood made a note of the details. 'A midnight blue Mark Two Jaguar, registered keeper, Arthur William Henry Newby, The Old House, Stanton Harwood. Has there been any change in the registered details? Colour? No. Thank you. If you would let me have an official printout. OK.'

'It's the wrong colour,' said Hood. He sounded disheartened. 'The boy must have got it wrong.'

'Not necessarily, sir. That's what I was here to tell you before I got Bill Renfrew's call. I visited a classic car dealer earlier today over Kettering way. The principal is a Mr Jack Jennings. He was very cooperative. He tells me it's by no means unusual for cars like the Mark Two to be resprayed in a different colour.'

'In which case Swansea should be notified and the registration details amended, am I right?'

'That's what should happen, yes, sir; but it is not always done. The back street boys leave it to the customers to deal with and I suppose some of them never get round to it. These classic cars don't do much mileage. The owners only tend to take them out on high days and holidays.'

'So this blue Jag might now be maroon, is that what you're suggesting?'

'It's a possibility, sir.'

'But would the owner of a valuable classic car trust it to the back street boys as you call them?'

'Depends on the circumstances, sir. This one was only registered to Mr Newby six weeks ago. Perhaps it was re-sprayed before he bought it?'

Hood thought for a moment, then acted. 'Where is this place Stanton Harwood? I've never heard of it.'

'No reason why you should have. It's not too far away. A hamlet more than a village. Off the Grendon Road. It doesn't usually figure in the crime statistics.'

Hood paused. 'There's only one way to find out about this Jaguar. You have your car here?' Bradley nodded. 'What are we waiting for?' Wendy Knight was standing in the corridor with a nervous looking Martha Morton. Hood acknowledged the housekeeper. 'I'm sorry, Mrs Morton, something urgent has just arisen. I have to go out. I'll see you tomorrow, if that's convenient.' He looked towards Knight as he handed her the case file. 'Don't forget tomorrow, Wendy. We are seeing Guy Romney in Oakham. I'll ring you later.'

CHAPTER THIRTY

The hamlet of Stanton Harwood stands on a rise half a mile from the Grendon Road surrounded by ancient oaks and ash trees and overlooking fields of wheat, barley and, regrettably, oil seed rape, which, in season, scars the landscape with a bright yellow rash. The tiny cottages at the entrance to the hamlet, built in the local stone and discreetly hidden behind the lush hedgerow which borders the narrow twisting road, are suggestive of a community unchanged in decades. But a large, modern house of deplorable design, a hundred metres farther on, shatters the feeling of timelessness the casual visitor might otherwise have savoured. How it escaped the scrutiny of the local planning authority is not known. Money must have changed hands; that's the opinion of those who dwell in the cottages opposite. It certainly jars the senses, but harmony is quickly restored by a line of pretty former alms-houses with carefully tended and well-stocked front gardens. Geraniums and petunias cascade in streams of colour from the little window boxes fixed below the white painted leaded windows. A disused Wesleyan chapel opposite is in the throes of being converted into a home more in keeping with its neighbours but the largest house in the village, fewer than two hundred metres farther along the road, dominates the surrounding properties as it has for over two hundred and fifty years. Constructed from dressed Northamptonshire ironstone under a Welsh slate roof, the three-storey property is not as impressive as Easton Grange but would nonetheless strike any visitor as the home of someone of wealth and influence.

Bradley drew his Mondeo to a halt outside the mansion which rose defiantly behind its creeper-covered stone walls. He hesitated, unsure whether he should drive through the ornate but open wrought iron gates into the gravelled courtyard. A brass plate, discoloured but still legible and fixed to the wall, announced that this was, indeed, "The Olde House, Stanton Harwood". Hood noted the addition of the letter "e" then gave the detective constable the nod. Bradley pressed the accelerator and, moving slowly forward, passed through the entrance and parked in front of a closed and chained wooden gate which barred access to the outbuildings at the side and rear of the house. There was no sign of a Jaguar Mark 2 or of any vehicles. Hood stepped out of the Mondeo and looked over the gate as a liver and white springer spaniel, barking but wagging its tail vigorously, jumped towards him but failed in its repeated attempts to leap the barrier. Hood patted its head then retreated, but not before he noticed the two barns beyond, their doors seemingly firmly shut. *Could the Jaguar Mark 2 be hidden in one of them?*

Bradley followed the chief inspector towards the front entrance. Hood pulled the chain to the left of the solid oak door. A bell could be distinctly heard ringing inside the house. He glanced at his watch. It was approaching six o'clock. He appreciated he should have been home an hour before. It was his daughter's birthday and he had assured his wife he would not be late. Another broken promise. He had been on the go since well before eight o'clock that morning, but the chance of locating the maroon Jaguar Mark 2 drove him on. He could hear movement inside the house but no one came to the door. Impatient, he pulled the chain a second time and instructed Bradley to follow his lead and exercise discretion once inside. No specific details of the circumstances surrounding the death of Father Dominic were to be disclosed. Bradley nodded that he understood. Eventually, the door was opened by a tall, slim, attractive, middle-aged woman with greying hair, dressed in a well– tailored two-piece suit, a double string of pearls arranged carefully around her neck in the form of a choker. She looked at Hood disapprovingly. He had his warrant card in his hand, ready to identify himself.

'What do you want?' she asked, her tone unfriendly. 'Whoever you are, you've called at a most inconvenient time. My husband and I are about to have supper. Can you not telephone and make an appointment? We are in the book, you know, and my husband is not a well man.'

'I'm sorry to hear that,' replied Hood, raising his warrant card so she could see it. 'I'm Detective Chief Inspector Hood from Mid-Shires Constabulary. This is DC Bradley. I take it you are Mrs Newby?'

'What if I am? And it's no good showing me that. I haven't got my glasses with me. Is it my husband you want to speak to or me?'

'If possible, I would like to speak, briefly, to your husband. We are checking Mark Two Jaguars. Mr Newby is the registered keeper of one.' Hood glanced towards Bradley. 'Remind me of the registration.'

'132 AX, sir.'

'What of it?' replied Mrs Newby. Was that a look of concern in her eyes?

'May I speak to him, please, madam,' said Hood. 'It is important.'

Mrs Newby was not backward in showing her displeasure. She stepped forward and glanced at Bradley's Mondeo, sniffing her disapproval. 'This is highly inconvenient, Chief Inspector, but I suppose you had better come in. I'll speak to my husband and find out if he will see you, but I'm not guaranteeing anything.' She opened the door wider and Hood and Bradley instinctively wiped their feet on the mat which Mrs Newby pointed to then ventured into the capacious hallway. She showed them into her drawing room and invited them to sit down. 'Wait here, please,' she added, her tone still far from friendly. 'But I warn you, he may not feel up to seeing anyone at the moment. He has been *very* ill.'

Hood's eyes met Bradley's. 'Doesn't sound too hopeful, sir?' said the junior officer after Mrs Newby had left the room.

'Let's wait and see, shall we? And remember what I said. You are here to observe, to listen and to learn.'

Bradley nodded. Hood looked around the well-furnished and extensive drawing room. A huge mirror, hanging over the marble fireplace, reflected the painstakingly coordinated soft furnishings. A tastefully arranged flower display dominating the centrally positioned coffee table. Despite the money that must have been spent in creating such an ambience, the room lacked a homely feel, reminding Hood of the lounge of a boutique hotel where he had once stayed in the west country. Bradley hesitated before sitting down on the comfortable sofa. He picked up a classic car magazine from underneath the coffee table and flicked through the pages until he found an advertisement for a Mark 2 Jaguar, silver in colour. No price was indicated. He looked at the date on the front cover; June 2002, and made a mental note of the advertiser. The magazine must have been printed long before the events the police were investigating. Hood remained standing. He studied a photograph of an attractive young girl seemingly in her late teens enclosed in an elaborate silver frame. Looking around the room, he noticed three other photographs of the same subject, in different poses. A daughter, perhaps? He was distracted by the dog barking again. He glanced through the sash window but saw no one.

Three minutes later, Mrs Newby returned, pushing a wheelchair. A dark-haired man, prematurely balding and seemingly in his fifties, wearing casual trousers and a sweater that seemed too large for him, sat uncomfortably in the chair. His face was deeply lined and his expression matched that of his wife. He looked quite out of place in the wheelchair that was obviously designed for a much smaller person, his feet dangling over the foot rest. 'Don't fuss woman,' he barked as his wife applied the brake. He strained forward and held out his right hand to the chief inspector. Hood took it. It was weak and flabby and quickly released.

'I'm Arthur Newby. What can I do for you? My wife and I were about to have dinner.'

Hood noticed he was wearing Oxford brogues on his feet and a shirt and tie under the sweater. 'I'm sorry to disturb you, Mr Newby. My colleague and I are making *routine* enquiries into a Jaguar Mark Two, registered number 132 AX. According to DVLC at Swansea, you are the registered keeper.'

'I own such a vehicle. Is there a problem with it?'

'What colour is it may I ask?'

Newby hesitated and cleared his throat before answering. 'Colour? As you've traced it to me, I assume DVLC will have informed you of the colour.'

'I'd like to hear it from you, if you don't mind?'

Newby turned in the chair and looked at his wife. She answered for him.

'Dark Blue.'

'You've not changed the colour?'

'Why should I want to do that?' said the husband, shrugging his shoulders. I haven't done anything with it yet. I've not owned it for very long.'

'Do you use the Jaguar regularly?'

Mr Newby shook his head. 'No, I bought it as an investment. I've only had it for about six weeks. I usually drive a Range Rover. That's almost

233

new. Black in colour, if that helps you.' There was a touch of sarcasm in Newby's reply.

'But it is roadworthy? The Jaguar I mean.'

'Just about. It has an MOT certificate that's good until the end of October, but it needs a lot of work. It should be worth quite a bit when it's fully restored.'

'So you have driven it?'

'I had a test drive before I agreed to buy it. Got a couple of grand off the price because of its condition.'

Hood moved on. 'Are you familiar with Easton Grange? It's about eleven or twelve miles from here, just outside Easton Parva.'

'I know it, yes. Why do you ask?'

'We are investigating a matter which concerns events there. Could I ask, are you by any chance a Roman Catholic?'

The question drew a puzzled look from Newby. It surprised Bradley too. What had this man's religion to do with anything? Newby took a deep breath before answering. 'That's a very personal question. What business is it of yours?'

'I'd be grateful, nevertheless, if you would answer, Mr Newby. I don't ask these questions for the good of my health, you know.'

The wife intervened. 'I don't want you upsetting my husband, He's recovering from a very serious illness. If you must know, he was brought up as a Catholic but has not practised his religion for many years. Not since…' She became slightly emotional and her husband took hold of her hand. 'Not since our daughter, Hannah, died. And that was many years ago, nine, to be precise. She wasn't quite seventeen years of age.' She added, somewhat flippantly, 'I'm Church of England myself, if that's of any interest to you.'

'Could I ask what happened to her?' said Hood. He sounded genuinely interested.

Mr Newby looked away in obvious distress as his wife took up the story, her tone embittered. She released her husband's hand before she spoke. 'We never found out the full details. She was found dead by the side of the road. Hit and run, we were told. No one was ever prosecuted, despite my husband's efforts and complaints. The police got nowhere with their investigation. They were quite useless. We have never had closure.' She glared at Hood as if he represented the incompetent police officers in question.

'Is this her photograph?' asked the chief inspector, pointing to the larger picture frame on the mantelpiece.

'Yes. As you can see, she was a quite beautiful girl. Quite beautiful. It's all so unfair. We had no idea what she was doing on that road. She had no reason for being there. The police thought she had been dropped off by a friend, but we were unable to locate anyone who would have done such an irresponsible thing. It's nearly a mile from here to where she was found. She would have had no reason to get out of a car so far from home unless something untoward was happening in the vehicle.' Mrs Newby became even more distressed and wiped a tear from her eye then gradually composed herself. 'She had been to a function at Lonsdale Hall, a school friend's seventeenth birthday party. My husband went looking for her when she didn't telephone. Then we got the news. We were quite devastated, as I'm sure you'll appreciate.'

'I'm sorry,' said Hood. 'I have a daughter of my own. You have my sympathy.'

Silence.

'Do you have any other children?'

'No,' replied Newby, sharply. 'She was our only child.' He again took his wife's hand but she pushed it away.

'Could we see the Jaguar?' asked Bradley, breaking the silence which followed. Hood shot a sharp look in his direction. Had he not instructed him to remain silent?

'It's not here,' replied Newby. 'It's being, er, serviced and restored at a specialist garage in Banbury.'

Hood raised an eyebrow. 'Banbury? How long, may I ask, has it been there?'

'It was transported there on Friday,' said Mrs Newby, interrupting again. 'But it was booked in over three weeks ago. They are very busy – and expensive.'

Hood nodded. 'So, no chance of our looking at it, then?'

'Not tonight, no.'

Bradley could not hide his frustration at the chief inspector's gentle handling of Mr and Mrs Newby. Was it not obvious that the Jaguar had been removed because it was the car the police were seeking? It had probably been re-sprayed and any forensic evidence destroyed. The young detective could hardly credit his superior's seemingly unhurried and casual approach.

'You still drive?' asked Hood, addressing the husband, 'despite your illness?' His manner did not change regardless of Bradley's evident exasperation.

'I'm in remission,' said Newby, much relieved. 'Believe me, it was touch and go. A few months ago I was informed my cancer was terminal. It turns out they got it wrong. So much for experts, eh?'

He went on to explain that the chemotherapy seemed to have done the trick. The treatment had been intrusive and exceptionally burdensome but he was happy with the result. He was, he thought, in a much better position than he could ever have anticipated. 'But I'm not out of the woods yet.' he added. 'It could still return. But so far, so good.' He glanced towards his wife. 'I never gave up my licence. I'm growing stronger all the time and, yes, I still drive, despite this chair which my wife insists I use around the house. I'm not yet an invalid.'

'Have you ever been to Easton Grange in your Jaguar?' asked Hood.

'Not that I recall. I know it, of course. We are acquainted with Sir Robert Southall. He was High Sheriff a few years ago. We attended a reception there.'

'Let me ask the question again. Have you been to Easton Grange in the last six weeks, whatever vehicle you may have been driving at the time.'

Newby exchanged glances with his wife before answering but was firm in his reply. 'No.'

'Do you know a priest by the name of Dominic Renville? A Benedictine monk from Melford Abbey. He's been living at the Grange for almost two years.'

'The priest who was found dead at Easton Grange?' interrupted Mrs Newby, showing a trace of excitement. 'We saw that on the TV news. Wasn't he found dead in a priest-hole – whatever that is?' Hood nodded. She looked pointedly at her husband then adopted her previous unfriendly manner. 'You have never had any dealings with him have you Arthur?'

'Absolutely not.'

'Have you ever lent your Jaguar to anyone?' asked Hood.

'Certainly not. It's hardly left the barn.'

Mrs Newby interrupted again. 'We haven't really socialised since my husband's illness was diagnosed, Chief Inspector.'

'May I ask when that was?'

'Last October. He's had two operations as well as an extensive course of chemotherapy. It's not been an easy time.'

Hood continued in sympathetic mode although he was getting a little tired of Mrs Newby's interruptions. 'Could I ask what you do for a living, Mr Newby?'

'You may. I am a company director. I have several business interests. Look, what is all this about, Chief Inspector? My dinner is getting cold.'

'My husband is also a JP,' added Mrs Newby, pointedly. 'He's been a magistrate for over fourteen years, one of the longest serving members of the bench in the county. I should also add that my bridge partner is the wife of the Assistant Chief Constable, not that I've been particularly active in that direction since my husband's illness.' She paused, but only briefly. 'You should also be aware that Arthur will be High Sheriff of the county next year. We have several friends in what used to be known as high places. You should bear that fully in mind.'

If those comments were intended to impress Hood or intimidate him, they had no effect. He had never allowed himself to be influenced by those who considered themselves his social superiors, or part of the so-called establishment, but he curtailed further questions despite Bradley's obvious desire to continue the interview. *Why was the DCI being so deferential?*

'It seems that we may have been misinformed, We'll leave you now. I'm sorry to have troubled you. If you could just let me have the details of the garage in Banbury, I can get someone to run his eye over the Jaguar in the next day or two so as not to trouble you further. Enjoy your dinner.'

'Bensons. It's on the Southam Road,' replied Mrs Newby with a self –satisfied grin. 'I'll see you out.'

Hood took a couple of paces towards the door, as if he were about to leave. He then turned and looked directly at Newby. 'By the way, Mr Newby, can you remember where you were last Wednesday evening, the twenty-fourth of this month?'

Mrs Newby immediately became tearful. She looked away for a moment before recovering herself as she faced Hood. She wiped her eyes before answering for her husband who had slumped in his wheelchair and put his head in his hands.

'He would have been here, with me,' she said. 'We never venture out on the twenty-fourth of July. You see, Inspector, that is the anniversary of my daughter's death, back in nineteen ninety-three.'

CHAPTER THIRTY-ONE

'Do you want me just to drive away, sir? Despite what we just heard in there?'

'That's exactly what I want you to do,' replied Hood, adjusting the passenger seat in Bradley's Mondeo and fixing his seat belt in place. He took out his mobile phone and pressed a digit that automatically connected with Wendy Knight's phone. 'Tell me, Bradley, how long have you been in CID?'

'Nine months, sir. I'm really enjoying it.'

'I'm glad to hear it, but you have a lot to learn.'

Bradley took the reproach in his stride. He said nothing further, turned the key in the ignition and concentrated on his driving. But as he reversed, then pulled out of the courtyard on to the road, his frustration came to the surface once more. 'But it must have been his Jag, sir. He wasn't telling the truth. It only went into the garage two days after the murder. That's too much of a coincidence, isn't it?'

Hood did not respond. He checked his watch as Wendy Knight answered. 'Wendy, I'm afraid your visit to the gym will have to wait. I want you to run a check on a specialist garage business in Banbury – on the Southam Road. It's called "Bensons". Get Thames Valley to send an officer over there immediately. There's a Mark Two Jaguar in the workshop being restored and, I suspect, being re-sprayed. All work on it is to stop, understand? Speak with DI Ambler if you have any problems. If the place is closed, the officer is to remain outside until we get the key-holder out. I can't be sure, but I think it's our Mark Two they have in there. See if you can get hold of the garage owner as well. I also want a plainclothes officer here at Stanton Harwood, keeping an eye on the

Olde House' – he spelt out the first word – 'that's what it's called. Get someone sensible. Whoever you choose will have to be ready to spend most of the night there, so it won't be too comfortable.' He paused and listened to Knight's response before continuing. 'No problem in finding the place. Biggest house in the village. You can't miss it. It's occupied by a Mr and Mrs Arthur Newby. I'll be running a check on them too. I'm on my way back to the Grange with Bradley now. One other thing, Wendy. I want you to include a black Range Rover in the questions being asked of the congregation who attend the chapel regularly.' He paused. 'I know. I appreciate it will mean visiting some of them again, but it's important.'

He terminated the call as Bradley pulled out of the lane from Stanton Harwood and on to the main road.

'So you do think this may be the car we're looking for, sir?'

'It may be. On the other hand, young Francis Gilbert might have made a mistake.' He shot a critical glance at Bradley. 'I wasn't going to continue questioning Newby until we are certain it's his Jaguar we are trying to trace. Going in too strong on the say-so of an eleven-year old boy is too risky, as I hope you now appreciate. I also want to do some research on the death of their daughter. The file must be somewhere. You can give that priority tomorrow. Find the file and check who was working on the case. If any of the officers are still around, I shall want to speak to them.'

'Yes, sir. But that can't have anything to do with the priest's murder, can it? The girl was killed nine years ago in a traffic accident.'

'Just do as I say, will you? And put your foot down. We have a lot to be getting on with.'

Bradley increased his speed as the main road straightened out.

'What do you reckon to him being in a wheelchair, sir? Did you notice he was wearing outdoor shoes and he had a shirt and tie on underneath that jumper?'

'You noticed that? At least you keep your eyes open. I noticed it too. Oxford brogues, hand stitched by the look of them. And his wife looked as if she'd been out somewhere. I doubt if she dresses like that just to have dinner with her husband.'

'Do you think that was for our benefit, sir? Coming in pushed by his wife like that. I reckon he was putting it on. The wheelchair looked too small for him too. My grandfather had cancer and he was never in a wheelchair, right up to when he died.'

'You may well be right. Did you notice how Mrs Newby kept interrupting, answering the questions for him?'

'I did, sir. You don't think she could be involved?'

'I don't know, Bradley. We'll have to wait and see.'

'Could I ask a question, sir?'

'Go ahead.'

'Why didn't we search the barns at the back. They could be lying about the Jag being at Banbury. It could be in one of those barns.'

'What, without a warrant? I don't think that would have gone down well at HQ if we'd found nothing, Newby being a magistrate and a future High Sheriff. Besides, all being well, we'll be back there tomorrow or the day after, with a warrant *if* we have grounds. And we'll have someone watching the house in the meantime and making a few inquiries with the locals. If the Jag is there, Newby will have been caught out lying, which will be justification enough for questioning him formally, magistrate or not.'

'He did admit he'd been to the Grange before.'

'Yes, but some years ago, along with hundreds of other people, no doubt. That hardly proves he's our murderer. We need a lot more than that to get a warrant to search the place. Then there's the question of his motive. Why would he want to kill a harmless old priest? There's a long way to go with this investigation, Bradley. Even if he's lying about the car, that won't take us much further in itself. We have no evidence it was at the Grange on the evening in question or who was driving it. Any competent defence counsel would make that perfectly clear in no time. Establishing that Newby's Jaguar was at the Grange on the seventh of this month is only the start. It doesn't prove anything in itself.'

'Wouldn't need a warrant if we'd arrested them there and then, sir. We could have searched the whole place under PACE.'

Hood sighed. 'I'm well aware of that, Detective Constable, but as I hope I have just explained, we don't have sufficient grounds for an arrest, not yet. You just keep your eyes on the road.'

Bradley did as he was told and concentrated on his driving but he couldn't resist asking a further question. 'Bit odd about the date, don't you think, sir? The daughter was killed on the same day in July that Father Dominic was murdered, nine years between the two events, of course.'

Hood gave him a dismissive look. 'Probably just a coincidence. There've been many anniversaries since the girl died. Mentioning the date did appear to upset both of them though, but I think that's understandable in the circumstances.'

'I don't know about you, sir, but I don't believe in coincidences,' said Bradley.

'You don't? Well, you'll certainly come across a few in this job. Look out!'

A small animal ran across the road in front of them as Bradley braked hard. 'What the hell was that?' asked Hood.

'Looked like a muntjac, sir. A small type of deer. You sometimes see them about these parts. No road sense either.'

The remainder of the journey to Easton Parva passed in silence apart from Hood ringing his wife and apologising for his anticipated late return.

CHAPTER THIRTY-TWO

Hood did not get home until well after nine o'clock. His wife was not in the best of moods when he walked through the door.

'You promised Amy you would be here for her party. She's very disappointed.'

'I know, love. I'm sorry, but something came up which I had to deal with. Is she still awake?'

'Yes she is. She's waiting up just to see you. It's a good job the school holidays have started. Really, Harry, you could have made the effort. I thought senior officers were supposed to delegate work, not deal with it all personally?'

'That doesn't begin until Thursday. Anyway, I would have done what I did tonight even if my promotion had taken effect. We seem to be getting somewhere at last. Look, I'll pop up and see Amy, then tell you all about it. She liked her present, I hope?'

'She loved it, but I'm sure she'd have enjoyed it more had her father been here when she opened it.' Hood was racing up the stairs as his wife called after him. 'By the way, your dinner is in the dog.'

'We don't have a dog,' shouted Hood, who was now at the door to Amy's bedroom.

'I was speaking metaphorically. It's ruined anyway.'

'Not hungry,' came the distant response.

'You always say that and I know it isn't true. I'll make you an omelette.'

Fifteen minutes later, Hood pushed his empty plate forward and stretched out his arms. 'That, as always, was delicious.'

Sarah eyed him suspiciously. 'You're not spending enough time with me and the children, Harry. I mean it; this has to change. You spend more time with Wendy Knight than you do with me.'

Hood took her hand and grinned. 'You're not getting jealous are you? I realise she's rather attractive, but as you know, I only have eyes for you.' Sarah pulled her hand away and scowled. Hood tried his best to placate her. 'It will get better, I promise. I'll be working office hours once this murder is solved. The local DCI is away in Australia at the moment and Wendy is filling in for him. When he's back and I've sorted out the division, you'll be only too glad to see the back of me. I'll be under your feet most of the time.'

'You don't expect me to believe that? You'll never change, not even if you made Assistant Chief Constable.'

'Now, that is a desk job. Regular hours, no night duty…'

'It would drive you mad,' smiled Sarah. 'But it's something to think about for the future. ' She hesitated before continuing. 'I've been asked if I'm interested in going back to work. Only part-time. There's a shortage of psychologists at the moment, and the money would help.'

'What about the children?'

'You will have to play your part. I wouldn't go back until Nicky starts at nursery, but it's something we need to talk about – when you have a minute or two to spare for us.'

Hood smiled. Sarah was now her old self, her testiness resolved. 'When will you solve this murder of Father Dominic?' she asked. 'It's still getting massive publicity I see. Amy saw you on the six o'clock news again this evening. At least she still knows what you look like.'

Hood tried to laugh. 'I know, and I have to see the DCC on Thursday. She'll put the screws on. But I have reason to believe that I'll be able to offer her some progress.'

'You said you thought you'd identified the car you're looking for when you rang earlier.'

'I can't be sure. Wendy hasn't been able to raise anyone yet. We probably won't gain access to the garage until tomorrow morning. I have two grumbling police officers sitting outside it at the moment, making sure nothing is removed. I'll be there first thing.'

'That means another early start, I suppose, with Wendy?'

Hood grinned. 'Afraid so. But she's coming to pick me up in her car. We are having lunch with Guy Romney and some top neuro-surgeon from London after we have visited the garage. He reckons Father Dominic couldn't have made his own way to the Long Room. His injuries were too severe. Someone has to have dumped him in there. So that's progress of a sort.'

'What about the owner of the car you hope you've located. Could he be responsible?'

'Two problems with him. First, even if it is his car we are looking for, it doesn't prove he's the killer. Second, when I saw him earlier tonight, he was sitting in a wheelchair. He's recovering from cancer. In remission now, but he'd been given very bad news a few months back. And he says he's had no dealings with the deceased.'

'But you think he's lied to you about the car?'

'If this Jaguar has ever been maroon in colour, yes he has. It's registered with DVLC as midnight blue. If it's been re-sprayed, the details were never altered.'

'Isn't it an offence to fail to amend the details with Swansea?'

'Yes, but punishable only with a fine. Wendy looked it up. He's only owned it for a couple of months, and that's borne out by DVLC, so he may well not be responsible for any failure to file any changes with Swansea. But I keep coming back to the same question. Why would anyone want to kill Father Dominic?'

'Someone who was abused by him, perhaps? You said he used to be a teacher at the Abbey school. There are a lot of such cases emerging these days.'

'No evidence of that at all. I somehow don't think that's the explanation. Why wait until now if it were? He hadn't taught at the school for fifteen years or more. And he was seventy-three.'

'But it can take years for someone to pluck of the courage to make a complaint or to take action. The owner of this car, for example, where did he go to school?'

Hood appeared surprised at Sarah's question. He had never got round to asking Newby about his schooling. 'I don't know. I didn't go into such details with him. I do know he's a magistrate and runs several businesses, or so he says. And he obviously isn't short of money. You should see his house.'

'Wasn't Sir Robert a JP?'

'Yes, but he resigned from the bench after his wife died. I shall ask him about this Newby fellow. He might have heard of him. They don't live that far apart. According to Mrs Newby, her husband is lined up to become High Sheriff next year. And she was very quick to point out that she has friends in high places.'

'Has she indeed? A couple of some influence then. You'll have to take care, Harry. They'll be using their sway with the Chief Constable.'

She smiled broadly. Hood gave her one of his looks. Sarah instinctively knew her husband would not allow such considerations to have any bearing on his investigation. 'So, what have you got on him, assuming it's his car you're looking for?' she asked.

Hood leant back in his chair and placed his hands at the back of his head. 'The car was seen at the Grange immediately after Mass on the seventh of this month. Whoever was responsible for it being there must have attended that Mass. There's no other reason for its presence. And the discovery of the priest-hole was mentioned in Father Dominic's homily that very day.'

'The driver of the Jag would have heard about the priest-hole then?'

'Yes. Unless he'd been asleep, and he'd have known that it was in the Long Room too. Dominic mentioned that. Whoever he was, he didn't leave as soon as Mass was over. Swanson's wife noticed a similar car was still there after she'd sorted out the flowers. And she was the last to leave. Neither was Dominic about. The door from the sacristy into the Long Room was locked. Only he had a key, apart from Sir Robert, of course.'

'That suggests whoever it was might have been with Father Dominic.'

'He might have been, yes. But we have no evidence that he was.'

'But it's a fair inference, isn't it?'

'I agree, but Newby denies having any dealings with him.'

'What about the day of the killing?'

'Assuming as I do that the killing has nothing to do with Philip Southall, a Mark Two Jaguar, maroon in colour, passed him as he was walking towards the farm where he spent the night – a mile and a half out of the village. That happens to be the road you would take from the Grange to get to where Newby lives.'

'Another link, then?'

'But very tenuous. You can also get on to the A45 that way. By the way, the Newby's daughter was killed in a road traffic accident nine years ago to the day Dominic was murdered.'

Sarah took a deep breath. 'That must be a coincidence, surely?'

'I suppose it must. But it's a bit weird, don't you think?'

'One of those unhappy coincidences you seem to attract.'

Hood smiled as Sarah got up from the table. 'I've had an idea,' she said. Where's that old copy of *Who's Who* I bought from the charity shop?'

Hood appeared puzzled. 'It's in the study, but it's a bit out of date. Nineteen ninety-seven, I think.'

Sarah disappeared, then returned with the heavy tome and placed it on the table. 'Just a thought,' she said, turning through the pages. 'This fellow, Arthur Newby, that's his name is it?' Hood nodded. 'He might be in here.'

'I doubt it.'

'Well you're wrong. He is.' She gave her husband a broad smile. Hood stood up and walked round to the other side of the table.

'This must be the right Newby, I think. There's a couple of them.' She started to read, her finger following the small print, difficult though it was to make it out in the subdued lighting of the kitchen. "Newby, Arthur William Henry, OBE, nineteen ninety-four, Chairman and Managing Director of Newby Enterprises PLC, born third November nineteen forty-seven, only son of Henry Arthur Newby and Charlotte Isabelle Newby, married, nineteen seventy-seven, Eleanor Victoria Alexandra Marshall, only daughter of Colonel Sir Ronald Malcolm Brotherton, KBE, MC and Lady Brotherton and widow of Simon Warren Marshall, died nineteen seventy-six. One step-daughter, deceased.' She stopped reading and glanced towards her husband.

'So, Hannah was his step daughter,' mused Hood.

'His step-daughter, yes,' repeated Sarah. 'That was her name, was it?'

Hood sighed. 'Yes. She was not quite seventeen. A real tragedy. Hit and run. Neither of them mentioned she was his step-daughter, though.'

'Understandable, I suppose. He probably treated her as if she were his own child. He could even have adopted her. She can't really have known her real father if he died in nineteen seventy-six. She'd still have been a baby. No other children mentioned.'

'Read on, Sarah.'

Sarah found her place but looked up again. 'I don't believe it.'

'What?' Hood pushed forward but his wife resisted him. 'Don't keep me in suspense, darling.'

Sarah moved aside. 'Look for yourself.'

Hood found the entry and started to read aloud. 'Educated, Melford

College and Exeter University, Batchelor of Science, nineteen sixty-eight.' He looked at his wife. 'That must be the college at Melford Abbey, where Father Dominic was a teacher.'

'Newby must at least have heard of him then.' Sarah frowned. 'He lied to you Harry. There's no other rational explanation.'

'So it appears. Let's work it out, shall we? Newby will be, what, fifty-five in November, so he'd have been at Melford from the age of, er, about twelve or thirteen until he was eighteen.' He checked the entry again. 'That would have been from about nineteen sixty until nineteen sixty-five if he graduated from Exeter in nineteen sixty-eight. I'm not sure when Father Dominic taught at the college, but he must have been there at least some of the time that Newby was a pupil.'

'Why would he lie about knowing Father Dominic?' asked Sarah.

'The inference is almost irresistible. I think I need to have further words with Mr Newby.'

'I suppose it's just possible they never crossed each other's paths. There were some teachers at my convent school whom I never really knew, especially some of the older nuns.'

'But you'd have heard of them, surely?'

Sarah nodded, then smiled. 'Anything else I can help you with, governor?'

Hood grinned. 'D'you know, I don't think I'd ever have thought of looking in *Who's Who*. Mind you we are already checking when Father Dominic taught at the school and I'd certainly have established full details about Newby.'

'Oh, yes?'

'I would. As I said, it's already underway.'

'Hardly need to bother now.' Sarah gave him a superior look.

Hood smiled. 'There is another thing, while you're in detective mode, something the Prior of Melford mentioned. He suggested that I read the Father Brown stories, you know, Chesterton's priest-detective. I don't suppose you have a copy of that hidden away anywhere?'

'No, but Pip has. He has the cumulative edition with all the stories. But I don't want you disturbing him now. It's in his bedroom and he's fast asleep. Why would the Prior have suggested you read Father Brown?'

'No idea. He's suddenly become a little distant with me. I suspect it's something to do with Grantham.'

'You surely don't suspect Grantham; he's a priest.'

'You know me, I suspect everyone. I've only just excluded you.'

She picked up the copy of *Who's Who* and pretended to hurl it at him.

'As if.' She paused. "Do you still think there's a connection between the priest-hole and the murder, apart from the fact that's where the body was found?'

'I'm convinced that Dominic came across something in there, apart from the sacramental we discovered in his hand, but if Newby is involved in the killing, I don't immediately see a link between him and the priest-hole.'

'But you haven't found anything?'

Hood let out a lengthy sigh. 'No, and we've turned the place upside down. I'm re-checking the contents of the safe on Thursday afternoon when the photographer is booked to attend but there doesn't seem to have been anything in there that isn't accounted for.'

'What's in the safe?'

'Sir Robert's collection of chalices, or his grandfather's to be precise. Thirteen of them. They're all still there. Wendy counted them. I intend to get Sir Robert to look at each one individually and compare them with the description in his insurance schedule.'

'Are they valuable?'

'One or two. Worth a few thousand at the most, according to Sir Robert. Nothing in there worth killing for and he has the only key to the safe.'

'Is he still looking for this Powdrell chalice, assuming it exists?'

Hood chuckled. 'Not actively, but he was hoping to find something in the hide.'

'What did the Prior say to you about Chesterton's Father Brown?'

'I didn't understand him. He mentioned something about hiding a leaf. Any idea what he meant?'

Sarah nodded. 'I was reading one of the Father Brown stories to Pip on Sunday afternoon, you know, while you were out and about and ignoring your family responsibilities.' She smiled then spoke slowly and deliberately. 'Where would a wise man hide a leaf?'

Hood grunted. 'That's what Father Milmo said. But why would anyone want to hide a leaf?'

She grimaced. 'You're missing the point as usual, Harry. Listen again and don't interrupt. This is the full quotation as I recall it: "Where would a wise man hide a leaf? Why, in a forest, of course." You see the point? Impossible to distinguish one leaf from another!' She paused and looked at her still bemused husband. This was giving her an excellent opportunity to have a go at Wendy Knight who she secretly blamed for keeping her husband away from his family responsibilities as she continued. 'Where would a wise man hide a chalice? In a forest of chalices.' She beamed at him. 'And where do we have a forest of chalices? In Sir Robert's safe! Wendy simply counted them. She didn't *examine* them. Thirteen were there so no further inquiry was thought necessary. Good place to conceal it, if it really had been found?' She paused and folded her arms. 'You really need to have words with that young woman, Harry.'

The point did not escape Hood for long. 'You think Father Dominic might have put whatever he found in the priest-hole into Sir Robert's safe?'

'It's a possibility, don't you think? He was a wise man, wasn't he? Seems the ideal place to me. He could have removed one of the less valuable chalices and put that somewhere else.'

Hood was not so sure. 'But where? As I said, we've turned the place upside down. There was nothing in his cottage, or in the chapel, or anywhere, unless he buried it somewhere, and why on earth would he do that? Then there's the question of the key. It was kept in Sir Robert's desk in his study.'

'But Sir Robert was away, wasn't he?'

'Yes. He spent Tuesday and Wednesday night in London.' He looked at his wife and smiled. 'I suppose it's worth another look. I'll speak to Wendy in the morning.' He took hold of his wife around the waist and pulled her towards him. 'Sarah, you're a genius. If there is something hidden in that safe which solves this case, I'll take you out to dinner at Hambleton Hall.'

Sarah gave him a doubtful look. 'Promises, promises. Sounds like tomorrow will be another busy day, for you – and Wendy.'

CHAPTER THIRTY-THREE

'Welcome to Benson's of Banbury,' smiled the manager as Hood and Knight entered his office on Tuesday morning. 'I'm Vic Benson. What can I do for you?' Benson, a short, rotund individual with a cheery countenance and what appeared at first sight to be a quite remarkable comb-over, wore a navy suit with a colourful bow tie. A half-eaten bacon sandwich rested on a plate on his desk. Hood glanced at Knight. Having spent well over an hour in her rather cramped sports car passenger seat, he was not feeling quite as full of *bonhomie* as Mr Benson. Knight produced her warrant card. 'I'm Detective Sergeant Knight. This is Detective Chief Inspector Hood. We are from Mid-Shires constabulary.'

The smile disappeared from Benson's face immediately. 'Oh. So you're responsible for that police car sitting across the road from here, are you? It was there when I opened up at eight this morning. Not good for business, you know.' He walked to the window and looked out. 'But it's a Thames Valley car, isn't it?'

'An example of inter-force cooperation, Mr Benson,' smiled Hood. 'Hopefully they'll be gone soon.'

Benson grunted, returned to his desk and sat down. 'What can I do for you anyway?' He swung round in his chair and faced Hood, picking up his bacon sandwich and taking a large bite.

Knight answered him. 'You have a Mark Two Jaguar belonging to Mr Arthur Newby of Stanton Harwood undergoing restoration, I believe?'

Benson nodded and replied as he chewed on his sandwich. 'We have. Been here since Friday. Hardly started on it yet. We are very busy you know.'

'Good. We'd like to see it,' said Hood. When did he book it in?'

'Over three weeks ago. Might I ask why you want to know?'

'I may be able to answer your question once I've seen it. Tell me, what colour is it?

'Colour?

'Yes.'

'Bit non-descript if you ask me. The log book says it should be midnight blue but someone's had a go at re-spraying it to look like the motor used in that TV detective programme, you know, *Inspector Morse*.' He finished his sandwich and wiped his lips and hands on a paper napkin which he then deposited in a waste bin at the side of his desk.

'So it's maroon?' said Hood.

'Most of it, yes. Whoever did it has made a right Horlicks of it. Re-spraying a motor like that requires considerable skill and a hefty bank balance. It's very expensive and can't be rushed.'

'Does it have a black roof?'

'An "Everflex" roof, yes.'

'How would you describe its general condition?'

'We've only carried out a preliminary examination. The engine seems fine; it's only done twenty thousand, according to the odometer, but some of the bodywork restoration is diabolical. Whoever did it should be ashamed of himself. It will be here for a while before it's in perfect condition. But when we've finished with it, you won't recognise it. And it'll be worth a fair bit. Mr Newby got it at a bargain price. He only paid five grand for it, or so he told me.'

'What were your instructions in respect of the colour when you re-spray it?'

'Original colour, of course, midnight blue, but there's a lot to do before we get round to that stage.'

'I'm afraid you will have to defer doing any work on it for the moment, Mr Benson.'

'Oh, yes. And why would that be?'

'I require it to be inspected by forensic experts.'

The manager became truculent. 'Oh, you do, do you? You've got a warrant have you, or Mr Newby's permission?'

'I can get a warrant if you wish, but I was hoping you would cooperate?'

'I will, if Mr Newby gives the OK.' He reached for the phone on his desk. Hood raised his hand and took out his mobile. He pressed a digit and waited. 'Inspector Bannerman? Proceed as indicated will you?' He looked at the manager. 'Do you have a fax number?'

'Yes.' Benson was no longer so disobliging. If anything, he appeared uneasy. He replaced the receiver then handed Hood a card from a container on his desk. Hood recited the number to Bannerman, then looked at his watch. It was six minutes past nine.

'The warrant will be with you, by fax, in under thirty minutes. Until it arrives, perhaps you would simply show us the vehicle?'

The manager hesitated. 'All right. It's round the back, in the yard. We haven't touched it yet other than to give it a quick once over. I shall have to speak to Mr Newby about this, you know. He's a magistrate.'

'So I believe,' replied Hood. 'But that hardly affects the issue. We are investigating a murder which occurred in Northamptonshire last week. I'm sure you don't want to appear obstructive.'

That remark took the wind out of Benson's sails. 'Are you, by God.' He scratched his head. 'Not the one there's been all the publicity about? The priest found in the 'ole? That was on News at Ten last night.' He swallowed as Hood nodded. 'This is serious then, isn't it?'

'About as serious as it gets, Mr Benson.'

The manager's attitude changed dramatically. He stood up and moved from behind his desk and took out a cigarette and lit it. 'Now look, Chief Inspector, I want to make it perfectly clear that we are a respectable business. If there's anything hooky about that Jag, I knew nothing about it; nothing, I tell you. You need to speak to Mr Newby, not to me. I have all the documents here.' He took a long drag on his cigarette.

'Do you know the registered number?'

'Of course; it's 132 AX. I don't want any comebacks. It's all legit as far as I'm concerned. All the paperwork matches, the colour excepted.'

Hood was relieved that his suspicions about the car had been confirmed. Young Francis Gilbert had not made a mistake when jotting down the registration number. This must have been the maroon car seen at Easton Grange on 7 July. It could not have been a different vehicle. Either Newby, or his wife, or both, were lying. He now had sufficient at least to interview Newby formally and as work had not yet commenced on the restoration, there remained the prospect of further evidence emerging. He took a conciliatory approach with the garage proprietor. 'I'm sure that's right, Mr Benson. Your reputation is safe with us. You have nothing to worry about. I'm perfectly satisfied the car belongs to Mr Newby. Now, may we look at it?'

'Follow me.'

Benson stumped out his cigarette in an ash tray and led Hood and Knight out of the office. The Jaguar Mark 2 was parked in the rear yard covered in what appeared to be a heavy duty tarpaulin. Hood looked about him. The yard was secured by a substantial fence at least nine feet high with sharply pointed metal spikes and a line of barbed wire secured over them to deter would-be thieves. There were several other vehicles in need of restoration taking up the available space and a few seriously damaged cars which he surmised were probably used for spare parts. Benson quickly dragged the tarpaulin from the Jaguar. It looked a sorry sight. While it was basically maroon in colour, there were patches on the bodywork where the previous colour showed through intermingled with blotches of rust. It had a black "Everflex" roof, just like the Jaguar in the television series.

'Do you have the ignition key?' asked Hood.

'Back in the office.'

'Could you get it?'

'Right away Inspector. I won't be a moment.' Benson scurried back inside.

'I want to see if its capable of running,' Hood confided to Wendy Knight. 'Then we'll get the forensics team on to it. Could you ring Nigel Mullen and let him know?'

Wendy nodded and produced her phone. 'We'll need a low-loader if it's to go back to Northampton.'

'Nigel can organise that. I've already alerted him. The warrant should arrive before his team gets here. He'll leave a copy with Mr Benson and we'll give Newby a copy when we see him.'

Benson reappeared, keys in hand. He couldn't have been more cooperative.

'Could you start her up, just so we can see how she runs? But please don't touch the steering wheel.'

Benson opened the driver's door, climbed gingerly into the driver's seat and started it up. The engine roared into life as he gently pressed the accelerator. 'Sweet as a nut,' he said through the now open window. 'That's the beauty of a Jaguar engine. Lasts forever.'

'Mileage?' asked Hood.

Benson looked down. 'Twenty-one thousand six hundred and seven, according to the clock. Mind you, it could have been tampered with.'

Wendy Knight noted down the figure.

'You can switch if off now, thank you,' said Hood.

Benson did as he was bid.

'Have you checked the boot?' asked Hood.

'Not yet, no. But I have noticed that someone has had a go at cleaning up the area around the driver's seat. There's quite a difference between this part of the motor and the rest of the interior.'

Hood bent down and looked inside the car. 'So it seems. We'll have to look into that.' He stood up. 'Does the documentation include the MOT certificate?'

'It does. It's in the office. We always insist on seeing the paperwork. Sometimes we have to amend the details. Most customers like us to do all that for them. Saves a lot of bother all round.'

'I'm sure you do it very well Mr Benson. Shall we return to the office and look at the documents?'

CHAPTER THIRTY-FOUR

Hood instructed the two uniformed officers to remain in place until SOCO arrived. They could then go, with his thanks. Nigel Mullen had agreed to send one of his specialist vehicle examiners to supervise the uplifting and removal of the Jaguar to the police garage and workshop in Northampton. Hood and Knight then set off for the Grange. He was now in possession of all the relevant paperwork but was careful to put on latex gloves before he handled any of it. Newby's fingerprints might well be found on the documents and, possibly, his wife's. Hood had said nothing to Benson about contacting Newby but he hadn't the slightest doubt that he would make the call. The chief inspector studied the paperwork as Knight drove into Northamptonshire, noting that whoever had sprayed the car maroon had not notified Swansea of the change of colour. Still, it didn't appear that Newby was responsible for that. It had undoubtedly been re-sprayed before he purchased it. He speculated that Mrs Newby might have indicated that the vehicle was blue in colour because that is what the paperwork stated. Nevertheless, anyone looking at it, if only for a moment, would have described the colour as maroon or dark red.

He also noted that, according to the sales invoice, the mileage had increased since the date of purchase, but only slightly. As it had been moved to Banbury on a low loader, it must follow that someone had driven it on the roads since Newby came into possession. The additional mileage, while small, was significantly greater than the distance between the vendor's address and Stanton Harwood.

The two detectives were close to the Grange when Hood received a call from DC Mark Bradley who had eventually recovered the file from the police archive at HQ relating to the death of Hannah Marshall otherwise known as Hannah Newby.

'Do you want me to start going through it, sir?' he asked. 'I had a hell of a job finding it. It had been misfiled.' Hood could tell from the tone of his voice that he was desperate to do so. He increased the volume on his phone so that Knight could hear the conversation.

'What do you think, Wendy?' he asked. 'Shall we let young Bradley prove what a good detective he is?' Bradley would have been able to hear what he was saying.

'I don't suppose it can do any harm. He might spot something. Fresh mind and all that.'

'All right Bradley, but do you have any idea what you're looking for?'

Bradley said nothing for a few seconds. 'Not really, sir, no.'

Hood laughed. 'That makes two of us. Just go through the file and see if you can spot any inconsistencies. You have all the witness statements there, do you?'

'Yes, sir. There are quite a few and some photographs, and there's an accident reconstruction report.'

'Someone did an accident reconstruction?'

'That's what it looks like.'

'Who was the supervising officer?'

'It looks like it was a DCI Fowler, sir. Not a name that I know.'

'Fowler, eh? All right. Get to it then and leave your thoughts in the file in writing. I doubt if I'll have time to look at it until much later today or tomorrow. If you come across anything you think is potentially significant, give me a bell, OK?'

'Yes, sir. I'll get on with it straightaway. Do you still want me to leave the file in Northampton?'

'Yes. You'd better work on it there. I won't need you back at the Grange today.' Hood terminated the call. 'He's certainly keen enough is Bradley, but he has a lot to learn.'

'We all have to start somewhere, sir.'

Hood nodded. He was in a much better mood. He was beginning to make progress, at last. 'By the way, Wendy, you don't need to keep calling me sir when we are alone. I like to keep up professional standards when other officers are about, but I think we know each other well enough to be on first-name terms, don't you?'

'If you say so, sir.' She laughed. 'I suppose I'll get used to it eventually.'

'Ever heard of this DCI Fowler? Is he still in the job? Doesn't ring a bell with me.'

'There was a Richard Fowler who moved to the Met. I think he ended up as a Deputy Commissioner, if he's the one I'm thinking of. I never met him. He was long gone when I came here, but some of the older officers have mentioned him. Very ambitious they say.'

'Seems they were right, if he ended up as a Deputy Commissioner.'

Knight pulled up outside the Grange. A uniformed officer pushed back the gates and half-saluted as they passed, crunching through the gravel at the entrance. She dropped Hood off at the front of the house, parked outside the chapel then trotted over to him. The front door, unusually, was locked. Hood rang the bell. After a few moments, a uniformed officer opened the door and acknowledged the chief inspector.

'Why is the door locked?' asked Hood.

'Sir Robert's instructions, sir. He's concerned about security, and I don't blame him what with all these journalists and TV people about the place. He found one of them wandering around the stable yard this morning. We are keeping the entrance gates closed as you instructed until they lose interest. The Long Room is locked as well. I'm still keeping an eye on things. I'm the only officer here at the moment, apart from the young probationer on the gate, so it makes sense to keep everything secure.'

Hood agreed. He made a mental note to increase the number of uniformed officers at the Grange. 'Where is young Philip?'

'In his room.'

'And Sir Robert?'

'He's in the library with Father Grantham.'

'Do you know what they're doing in there?'

'No idea, sir. They've been closeted together all morning.'

Sir Robert appeared at the top of the stairs. 'Ah, Mr Hood. Ready to look at the contents of the safe? Your sergeant warned me you were bringing the examination forward. Would you mind if Father Grantham joined us? We've been going through his research together. He may be of some assistance.'

Hood was not altogether surprised that Sir Robert was still on friendly terms with Grantham and he had no objection to his presence while the contents of the safe was examined. There was always a chance he might give something away if anything unusual were found. 'Not at all, Sir Robert. Do you have the key?'

The baronet descended the stairs with Grantham now close behind him. 'In my desk, which you'll be pleased to hear is securely locked.' He went into his study. Grantham remained in the hallway. 'Any progress, Chief Inspector?' he asked.

'Some,' replied Hood, 'but it must remain confidential.'

Grantham nodded. Father Milmo then appeared on the staircase. 'Did I hear you are going to check the contents of the sacristy safe?'

'Yes.'

'Mind if I come along?'

'You're very welcome,' said Hood. He glanced at Knight, raised an eyebrow and whispered to himself, 'The more the merrier.'

'You think there may be something in there from the hide?' asked the Prior.' There was a definite twinkle in his eye.

'Just checking it out – at your implied suggestion, in fact,' replied Hood.

The Prior smiled. 'You've had a look at the Father Brown stories?'

'No, not yet, but someone mentioned to me one of the priest detective's more famous observations.'

The Prior nodded and smiled. 'Where would a wise man hide a leaf? Is that it?'

Hood nodded. 'It is. If Father Dominic did find a chalice in the niche, the safe would have been the perfect place to put it along with all the other chalices that are kept in there.' He looked at the Jesuit. 'What do you think, Father Grantham?'

The Jesuit shook his head but smiled at the same time. 'Logic would suggest that the safest place to leave it was where he found it, always assuming he found something. Your hypothesis is based on the assumption that Father Dominic found an object of historical significance. As no one else knew about the niche, why not leave it where he found it? Where could be more secure?'

'But there was nothing in the niche when it was exposed.'

'Quite; which may suggest he found nothing there, apart from the sacramental. Then again, perhaps Dominic was not always driven by logic?'

'Or possibly he did find something and he moved it elsewhere in case the niche was exposed later?' countered Hood. The chief inspector then led the party, including Wendy Knight, to the Long Room. The uniformed officer unlocked the door and ushered in everyone. Hood quickly checked the hide. The empty niche was still exposed and the priest-hole taped off. Sir Robert produced the first of two keys and inserted it into the lock of the door which led into the sacristy.

'That is your key to the sacristy door, Sir Robert?' asked Hood.

'Of course. I believe I have a key to every door. It is my house, you know.'

'How many other keys to this door are there?' asked Hood

'DC Swanson has the details of all the keys. There are only two for this door that I'm aware of. This one and the key that I entrusted to Father Dominic, but I assume you have that one now.'

'Being checked by forensics, sir,' said Knight. 'We should have them back from the lab later today.'

Sir Robert turned the key, the mechanism of the lock straining and creaking, just as Grantham had said when he was questioned the day before. The deadbolt sprang back suddenly. Sir Robert pushed open the door and entered the sacristy followed by the others. It was not a particularly large room. A wooden cupboard in the fashion of a French *armoire* was fitted against the far wall. Taking up almost the full length of the room on the adjacent wall stood a flat topped mahogany sideboard with a highly polished surface, several drawers underneath, and a large crucifix set above it. Two chairs and a small side table completed the furnishings. There was a small sink and cold-water tap in the corner. Both sideboard and cupboard had already been the subject of a thorough search on the afternoon Father Dominic's body had been discovered. Towards the other side of the room, fixed to the wall, stood a large, old fashioned safe. Sir Robert approached it, his excitement clearly visible. Was he about to locate the Powdrell chalice? He inserted the key. It turned much more easily than the key to the sacristy. Pulling back the heavy metal door, he handed Knight his insurance file and slowly started to remove the items from the safe, one by one. They were placed on the sideboard and checked against the descriptions in the insurance documents. His excitement, alas, started to fade rapidly. After half an hour of intense scrutiny of each object, thirteen chalices or ciboria only were found along with the Pugin designed monstrance. Each one fitted the description set out in the insurance schedule. The Powdrell chalice, if it existed, had not been secreted in the sacristy safe after all. If Father Dominic had found something in the hide, he must have hidden it elsewhere. Grantham did not appear to be surprised in the slightest. Sir Robert appeared dejected.

'Nothing. Another false dawn.' He shrugged his shoulders and sighed. 'Well, there we are. I'm beginning to think that Father Grantham is right. There's nothing more to be found. We'll have to content ourselves with the sacramental.'

No one else spoke as Hood checked the large cupboard. Apart from a number of chasubles and matching stoles in various liturgical colours, he observed a small chalice of no particular intrinsic value sitting on a shelf and an alb hanging from a hook. A box containing unconsecrated hosts and a bottle of altar wine were the only other items present. He pointed towards the chalice.

'That's Father Dominic's,' whispered Sir Robert, the disappointment still evident in his voice. 'He always kept it there. It wasn't considered valuable enough to be put in the safe. Besides, I have the only key and I'm pretty sure Father Dominic would not have removed it from my desk without asking me first. So it was always a bit of a long shot that he would have placed something of significance in the safe.'

'So much for Father Brown,' muttered Hood, eyeing the Prior. He was, it had to be said, a little disappointed himself.

The Prior shrugged his shoulders and spoke defensively. 'I thought it might be worth considering.'

Hood knew his wife would be disappointed too. She liked to think her sudden insights made a contribution to solving his cases. Wendy Knight, on the other hand, seemed relieved. At least she had not missed anything during her earlier inspection of the safe and its contents or any other possible hiding place in the sacristy. As an added precaution, Hood instructed her to search the sideboard a second time.

The Prior remained disheartened. 'Perhaps there never was a chalice or anything of historic interest in the first place? Or if there were, it's long gone by now. Carried away to who knows where.'

Hood shot a glance at Grantham. He was still not convinced that the priest/historian had disclosed everything he knew. Grantham said nothing until he joined in the general commiserations.

'It's a great pity. I would have been proud to have been associated with the discovery of such a historic artefact. On the other hand, the mystery still endures, which is something worthy of note when you think about it. Did such a chalice ever exist? Or was it the product of a fevered imagination or simply wishful thinking? That's what makes it all so interesting, don't you think?' He looked towards Sir Robert. 'The Powdrell chalice will remain an enigma which is arguably a good thing. Like the Holy Grail, it will probably never be found. Historians will continue to research it and perhaps, one day, the truth will emerge.' He then looked directly at Hood and smiled. 'We historians like a good mystery, Chief Inspector.'

Hood begged to differ. He could not avoid showing more than a trace of annoyance. 'As a detective, I prefer solutions to mysteries, and I'm more interested in finding Father Dominic's killer. Searching for something that may never have existed in the first place is fast becoming a distraction.' He turned towards the baronet. 'Could I have a quick word, in your study, Sir Robert? No need to trouble anyone else.'

'Of course.'

'DS Knight and I have an important appointment, and we mustn't be late. Wendy, could you have a word with Father Milmo about the Abbey School while I speak with Sir Robert? You know what to ask him.'

CHAPTER THIRTY-FIVE

'Do you think Father Grantham is being truthful about Father Dominic? I have this recurring feeling that he's holding something back.' Hood spoke privately with Sir Robert in his study having carefully closed the door after checking no one was in the hallway outside.

'About the hide?'

'About what may have been found there, yes.'

Sir Robert seemed surprised. 'I thought I heard you say moments ago that searching for the Powdrell chalice had become something of a distraction?'

Hood smiled. 'I said that purely for the benefit of Father Grantham. And I'd be obliged if you didn't mention what I've just said. I haven't entirely dismissed the possibility of the murder being connected in some way with the priest-hole.'

Sir Robert sat down behind his desk and pondered the chief inspector's question. 'Is Father Grantham being deliberately deceitful or obstructive? No, I genuinely believe if he knew anything he would reveal it. I'm just going to have to accept there was nothing in the hide other than the sacramental. And finding that is reason enough to celebrate.' His voice softened. 'It's very sad, of course, that it had to be discovered in such tragic circumstances. Father Dominic's death rather detracts from the joy of finding it, but Father Grantham seems to agree now that it was probably hidden there over four hundred years ago and that Dominic must have come across it during the excavation.'

'And not told him anything about it?' said Hood, pointedly.

Sir Robert nodded gently. 'That is an oddity, I agree.'

'It certainly seems out of character given what we know about Father Dominic. Why would he keep such an important discovery to himself?

He would certainly have appreciated its significance. It's as if he didn't trust Grantham. It makes me think I shouldn't trust him either.'

'I don't know, Mr Hood. Perhaps the hide isn't linked to the murder after all?'

'There have been developments that suggest there may be another explanation for the killing, but they have to remain confidential for the moment.'

'I understand.'

Hood hesitated. 'I really wanted to ask you about a man by the name of Arthur Newby. He and his wife live in Stanton Harwood, about eleven miles from here. Do you know anything about him?'

Sir Robert paused as if in thought. 'There was a man called Newby who was chairman of the bench for a time when I was a magistrate, not that I ever sat with him, but I came across him a few times at meetings and training events. The County bench was quite large in those days, and I believe he lived out that way.' He paused before continuing. 'We were never on intimate terms, though. My late wife never took to him and she was an excellent judge of character.' He smiled. 'She used to say he was the sort of fellow who would wear a ready-tied bow tie, if you understand my meaning?' He smiled more broadly. 'I also saw his name two years ago amongst those who have been under consideration for appointment as High Sheriff. I believe he has been nominated for next year and he was certainly invited here when I held the position. My late wife and I held a couple of large receptions for the great and good of the county, then another one for the villagers.' He laughed. 'That one was much more fun!'

'Do you think you would recognise him if you saw him again?'

'I think I probably would, but I can't be sure. I retired as a JP nearly three years ago, so I've had no reason to have had any dealings with him of late.' He winked at Hood. 'Rumour has it that he's supposed to be very wealthy, but whether that's true or not, I simply don't know. I do know he has a number of business interests both locally and elsewhere. Is it important?'

'Probably not. It's just something that came up.' He paused. 'I believe that Newby's step-daughter was killed in a road accident about nine years ago. Were you aware of that?'

'Now you mention it, I do believe I was. Yes, it's coming back to me now. My late wife and Newby's wife were on the committee of the same charity for a few years and I recall her mentioning it. My wife thought Mrs Newby had something about her, unlike her husband. She was helpful and a very good organiser. Poor woman was very cut up about her daughter's death even years afterwards. I seem to remember it received widespread publicity at the time. I believe the person responsible was never found.'

'That certainly seems to be the case.'

'Is her death connected in some way with Father Dominic? Surely not?'

'I don't think so. At the moment it's just a question of excluding Newby from the inquiry.'

'Is he under suspicion in some way? Now that really would cause a scandal in the county. I can see the headlines now!'

Hood shook his head. 'I wouldn't go as far as that. He has a maroon Jaguar. A maroon Jaguar was seen here on the seventh of July, when Father Dominic celebrated Mass. We are checking all such vehicles, not just his.' He pulled a chair up and sat down opposite Sir Robert. 'It was the first Sunday in the month. I wondered if you might have noticed him or his car?'

'I was here that week-end and the congregation was larger than usual. It always is on the first Sunday in the month; it's the Latin that attracts them, not that I would have recognised many of them if they were not regulars. Interestingly, I do recall Father Dominic's sermon from that Sunday. He mentioned the discovery of the priest-hole; one of his more interesting homilies.' He smiled. 'He was not a natural when it came to preaching, God rest his soul.'

'But you didn't notice a maroon Jaguar parked outside or Arthur Newby in the congregation?'

'No, I didn't. My place is always at the front of the chapel. I didn't go outside. I went straight back into the house, through the sacristy door. You'll recall I have my own key.'

'So the door was locked?'

'Oh, yes. Father Dominic always kept it locked as did I if I used it. He had disrobed and was leaving the sacristy as I went through the door. I locked it behind me. He was heading through the chapel to greet the congregation outside. I had emphasised the importance of security when he first came here. I didn't want people wandering into the house, you see.'

'Father Grantham tells me that after they had eaten together on Wednesday evening, Father Dominic went into the chapel through the door in the Long Room.'

'That doesn't surprise me. He was a creature of habit. He usually prepared for his morning Mass the evening before.'

'Yes, Grantham mentioned as much.'

'It only took a couple of minutes. I know because I was with him on one occasion. He would take two or three hosts, many more for a Sunday, from the box you saw earlier. He would place them along with his chalice and paten and cruets of wine and water on the small table next to the altar, ready for the morning.'

'Now that is interesting.'

'Really?'

'Yes. If he had done that last Wednesday evening, why was his chalice still in the cupboard in the sacristy? But the two cruets were on the table next to the altar.'

Sir Robert nodded. 'That is intriguing, Mr Hood. He must not have followed his usual practice. I wonder why? And I didn't notice his paten in the cupboard in the sacristy. He usually kept it there. I wonder what happened to it? He probably intended to say Mass on Thursday morning, had he survived, but I could be wrong.'

'Unless someone removed his chalice from the chapel and put it back in the sacristy? The cupboard, unlike the safe, is not kept locked.'

Sir Robert frowned. 'I can't see the murderer, whoever it might have been, doing that. And why leave the cruets by the altar? Furthermore, what happened to the paten? Whoever killed him would have to have known Dominic's routine and what would have been the point? Much more likely that, something occurred that prevented him from completing his usual preparations.'

Hood did not dismiss what Sir Robert said but the presence of Dominic's chalice in the sacristy cupboard continued to trouble him. 'I shall have to give that some thought, but if Father Dominic was in the grounds when he was attacked, as seems to have been the case, why would he not have completed his preparations for his Mass as usual before he left the chapel?'

'Can Father Grantham not help? He seems to have been the last person to have seen Dominic alive, the murderer apart. He would surely know if Dominic was intending to say Mass on Thursday morning?'

Hood scowled. 'He hasn't been of much assistance so far. Tell me, was Father Dominic in the habit of inviting members of his congregation into his cottage?'

'I don't think so, but he might have made an exception if the circumstances demanded it. As I told you last week, he was a very private person. He was certainly not one for socialising, but if an individual had a problem, he could well have taken him there so they could talk in private. But he always refused social invitations of which I know there were many. Not like some priests I've heard of who have a better social life than me.' He laughed.

'Your son told me that Father Dominic once heard his confession in the Gatehouse.'

'Did he? There is no confessional in the chapel, so that doesn't surprise me and I know Father Dominic sometimes heard confessions in the sacristy. One only had to ask him. He was very obliging in that respect.'

'I noticed, too, on Sunday, that there is no sanctuary lamp in the chapel.'

'That's right. The Sacrament is not reserved here, Mr Hood. The Bishop has never given his consent, not in my time here anyway, though the truth is I've never asked him. Father Dominic would consecrate sufficient for the congregation at each Mass. The Prior will do the same tomorrow, as you will see for yourself, if you attend. It's the feast day of Saint Ignatius Loyola you know. Grantham will be attending.'

'As he's a member of the Society that does not surprise me.'

'I don't know about you, Mr Hood, but I have noticed that he seemed much more at ease with himself today. It seems as if a burden of some kind has been lifted from him. He was very engaging when we were together in the library this morning. And much more relaxed.'

Hood could not cast off his doubts about Grantham. 'I don't know about that. He seemed almost pleased that we found nothing of interest in the safe. Did you notice?'

'That was not my impression, Mr Hood.'

Hood did not respond but looked at is watch. 'Now, if you will excuse me, I must find my sergeant. Thank you for your help.'

'I have been of assistance then?'

'Certainly. By the way, how is Philip getting on?'

'So far so good. My worry is that he will become bored. I'm trying to find a few jobs for him to do around the estate, well away from the old chapel grounds, of course. He's been working in the wood at the boundary of our land. There's a lot that needs to be done there. I've rather let it go in recent years. It should keep him busy. Idle hands and all that.' He smiled. 'The sooner you solve this murder the better for all of us.'

CHAPTER THIRTY-SIX

'That was a wonderful lunch. Thank you, er, Harry.' Knight was still not used to addressing the chief inspector by his first name. She would have much preferred to continue deferring to his rank, especially as he would soon be promoted to Detective Superintendent.

'My pleasure.'

'I can't let you pay for me, though.'

'That's not a problem. Egerton was willing to pay for all of us. No doubt he can afford it, but as he's a potential prosecution witness now I didn't think it appropriate. Anyway, you hardly ate anything, and I did promise you lunch.'

'The sea bass was delicious. I just didn't fancy any of the starters. And I never have a dessert.' Knight changed into fifth gear as the Mazda emerged onto the A43 and picked up speed. 'He was very impressive, Mr Egerton. I can't see anyone disagreeing with what he said.'

'No, neither can I. He certainly knows his stuff.'

'And all from a few photographs.'

'Plus Professor Romney's findings, of course.'

'We can take it as a fact now, can we, that Father Dominic did not make his way to the Long Room under his own steam? Someone must have transported him there, then dumped him in the hide.'

'That's about it. What does that tell us, Wendy?'

'Whoever it was, he must have known about the priest-hole and where it was situated. He was unlikely to have come across it by chance.'

'And?'

'The killer had to have some means of access and must have either carried the body or used something in order to get it to the priest-hole. If

Father Dominic had locked the door from the chapel into the Long Room, the killer must either have come in through the front door, which would have been very risky, or used the priest's own key and come through the chapel. Didn't you say that the door was locked when you arrived at the Grange on Thursday morning?'

'It was,' replied Hood. 'I checked all the doors in the Long Room. But I gather that Father Dominic didn't usually lock the public entrance in summer until he had completed his office. It could still have been open at the time he was attacked.'

'Whoever it was must have had a key to lock it afterwards. Father Dominic's presumably? And only Grantham was in the house.'

'Quite. We keep coming back to Grantham, don't we?'

'We do. Father Dominic's keys were not on him when he was found.'

'No, his keys were hanging up in his cottage by the back door. If they were used, someone must have put them back there.'

'Someone who knew where he kept them.'

'But who would know that?'

'Anyone who'd been to his cottage with him.'

'Such as?'

'Philip Southall, the housekeeper, Grantham, Sir Robert, even?'

'What about the driver of the maroon Jaguar?'

Knight nodded. 'Him too, always assuming that's where he was after Mass on the seventh. But we don't know that for sure.'

'No, we don't. And if an outsider were responsible, would he have known that Grantham was in the house? Remember, not even Helen Swanson knew about Grantham's presence until after the killing, and not much gets past her.'

Knight did not reply for a few moments. She was thinking through the possibilities. 'Of course, Grantham didn't arrive at the Grange until the ninth, so Father Dominic could not have mentioned him in his homily on the seventh when whoever drove the Jaguar would have heard about the priest-hole being discovered.'

'That seems to be the position, unless the driver visited again before the twenty-fourth.'

'We have no evidence that he did,' said Knight.

'No, two sightings only. The seventh and the twenty-fourth. And the sighting on the twenty-fourth by Philip Southall could be argued away by any competent defence counsel. He didn't get the index number like young Francis Gilbert.'

'It's a bit of a coincidence though, isn't it? An identical Mark Two in Easton Parva on the evening the murder occurred?'

'It is. Let's hope something comes of the examination of the car to bolster the likelihood of it being the same vehicle.' He paused. 'When will we have the information about the period Dominic was teaching at the college?

'We should have it by tomorrow morning at the latest,' said Knight. 'It will be faxed through to Northampton as soon as it's available. The college keeps excellent records, apparently. Father Milmo is pretty certain that the deceased was teaching at the college in the sixties. He was also a housemaster for five years or so. I don't see how Newby could not have heard of him.'

'I'd like it confirmed in writing all the same.'

Knight's mobile phone buzzed. 'Could you answer it for me? I shouldn't really, not while I'm driving.'

Hood picked up the mobile from the tray by the gear lever. 'Hello.' He paused and seemed surprised. 'Mr Benson? Chief Inspector Hood here. Tell me, have you told Newby that we have taken his car?'

Benson replied in the negative. He told Hood that Newby had just telephoned him asking when the re-spray would be completed. When Benson told him that no work had yet started Newby became angry and said he would have the job done elsewhere if the restoration did not begin immediately. Benson was to ring him by close of business on Wednesday confirming the work had started or he would make arrangements for the car to be removed.

'What did you tell him?' asked Hood.

'I said I would see what I could do. I didn't tell him the police had taken the car.' He paused and let out a deep breath. 'I'm afraid I lied to him Mr Hood. I told him the Jag was safely under lock and key in the yard here. But he'll be ringing tomorrow. I'll have to tell him the truth then. That's why I'm calling. Your sergeant gave me her card.'

Hood considered the position and came to a rapid decision. 'You won't need to tell him anything, Mr Benson. You won't be troubled, I assure you. He'll know before Wednesday that we have his Jaguar because I shall tell him myself. And thank you for the information. Best not to

270

mention this call if he does ring again before tomorrow.' He terminated the call then related to Wendy Knight what Benson had told him.

'Change of plan. We are going to have to see Newby later today after all. We can't put it off any longer if he's pressing Benson about the Jaguar. Let's pray Nigel and his boys really do have something for us before we question him.'

Wendy Knight shook her head. 'Nothing so far. I've asked Nigel Mullen to get in touch if anything is found, no matter how minor. And it's probably for the best if we do see Newby today. I didn't like to mention it, but we really should serve that warrant on him. There'll be a copy waiting at Campbell Square.' She smiled. 'You see, Harry, I've always tried to adhere to your example of following procedure to the letter.'

'I'm glad to hear it.'

Knight smiled. 'Where to? Northampton or straight to Stanton Harwood?'

Hood looked at his watch. 'We have plenty of time. We'll call in at Campbell Square and pick up the warrant then head for my home. I need to pick up my Saab. There won't be room in your car if I decide to arrest Newby. I must also have a word with Martha Morton before we tackle Newby and I want you to ring Nigel again. Emphasise the urgency. I'll meet you back at the Grange after you drop me off. We'll then drive out to Stanton Harwood. Hopefully we'll be there by five o'clock at the latest.'

CHAPTER THIRTY-SEVEN

Hood and Knight drove into the courtyard of the Olde House, Stanton Harwood just before five o'clock in the afternoon. Hood had briefly questioned the housekeeper at the Grange and was in possession of the fax from Melford Abbey detailing Father Dominic's period in the Abbey school. It had arrived just as he was leaving Campbell Square. He'd also had a brief conversation over the phone with Detective Constable Swanson who had spoken again to the previous owner of the Jaguar Mark 2. The chief inspector was looking forward to questioning Arthur Newby. Real progress was now anticipated.

Eleanor Newby was standing at an upstairs window and saw the two detectives getting out of Hood's Saab 9.3 SE. Mrs Newby recognised Hood immediately and called to her husband who was lounging on his bed reading *The Times*.

'It's that black police inspector again, Arthur. I thought he said he'd been misinformed and wouldn't trouble us again?'

'He'll have checked up on the Jag,' Newby replied, casually, putting down the newspaper. 'Why on earth did you tell him it was dark blue?'

Eleanor Newby turned on her husband. 'That's what the paperwork says. Remember, I was going on the details in the log book when I rang the brokers to insure it for you. Why you ever bought the damn thing in the first place, I simply don't know.'

'It was an investment and a way of celebrating the good news about my cancer. I've always wanted a classic Jaguar. It wouldn't have mattered if Bensons had got on with it and re-sprayed it. I assumed they'd have had things underway by now.'

'You can't be sure about that. The manager said when it was booked in it would take at least a fortnight, given its condition. It depends what it is that triggered their interest in the thing. I can't imagine what it could be. No doubt we're about to find out. You're sure that the interior was thoroughly cleaned?'

'The parts you told me that mattered, yes. Not that I had much help from you and I didn't get round to finishing it.'

She glared at her husband. 'If that's why Hood has returned it will be entirely down to you. I told you to clean the whole of the interior.'

Newby looked far from comfortable. He hesitated before continuing. 'I'm sure I have no idea why they're interested in it, but it can't be because of that. No one will remember the car anyway, and if they do, we can just deny it. They won't be able to prove anything.' He paused. 'What'll I say to them?'

The bell rang before Mrs Newby could answer. The dog started barking and rushed out of the kitchen into the hallway. Eleanor Newby took firm control of the situation. 'You'll say nothing to them. I will see what they want. You are too unwell to be disturbed. I suggest you get undressed and get into bed. The inspector may ask to come upstairs.' She gave her husband a disdainful look. 'At least try and look the part.'

'But I'm feeling fine. A bit tired, but that's all.'

'You think so? I suspect that any celebrations about your recovery are premature. It was tiredness that led to your initial examination last year if you remember?' She did not wait for an answer, left the room and headed for the stairs as the bell rang a second time.

'I'm coming, I'm coming,' she muttered to herself as she descended the stairs and rushed into the hallway, grabbing the still barking springer spaniel by the collar. Opening the front door, she acknowledged Hood but held on to the dog. She smiled towards Wendy Knight who already had her warrant card to hand. As she raised it towards Mrs Newby, the door was pulled back farther and both she and Hood were invited to come inside. Mrs Newby pointed them towards her drawing room then dragged the still excited dog into the kitchen. 'Quiet Monty,' she insisted. She turned her head towards Hood. 'I won't be a moment. I'll just get the dog out of the way.' A minute later she returned and entered the drawing room. 'What is it now, Chief Inspector? I thought you had finished with us?'

'I'm afraid not,' replied Hood, producing the warrant authorising the detention and inspection of the Jaguar Mark 2 motor car. 'Your husband's car is presently undergoing forensic tests in Northampton.'

Mrs Newby took the warrant. She appeared quite shocked and sat down in an armchair. She started to read. 'I can't think why you should be interested in my husband's car. I hope you haven't gone to all this trouble simply because I got the colour wrong. I'm not very familiar with the vehicle you see and I was basing what I told you on the paperwork. I sorted out the insurance for him. I deal with all the household administration. For a businessman, Arthur is perfectly hopeless when it comes to dealing with such matters. Our other cars are insured through the business but not this one. The accountant wouldn't allow it.'

'That's what I thought must have happened,' said Hood, raising an eyebrow. 'Could I ask where your husband is?'

'He's upstairs resting. He's not feeling at all well. It's one of his off days. He's on the mend, at least I hope he is, but he has them now and again.'

'I really do need to speak to him, quite urgently.'

'What? Because I got the colour of his car wrong?'

Hood shook his head. 'That's hardly to the point, not now we have established it is maroon in colour. But it is the colour that makes the car a matter of interest to us. As you are aware, we are investigating the murder of Father Dominic Renville at Easton Grange on the twenty-fourth of this month. We have reason to believe your husband can assist us with our inquiries.'

'Arthur? I doubt that very much. He's hardly left this house in the last nine months other than to attend hospital appointments. And I've already told you neither of us went out on the twenty-fourth.'

Hood was firm. 'I still require to speak to him, Mrs Newby.'

Mrs Newby replied in kind. 'I'm afraid that's out of the question, Chief Inspector. He can't possibly see you today. He's simply not well enough. I suggest you come back when he's feeling better.'

'I'm afraid I must insist, Mrs Newby. If he won't speak to me here, I shall have to consider inviting him to Northampton police station.'

She stood up and took a step towards Hood. 'Arresting him? You can't do that. He isn't involved in any murder. The whole idea is preposterous.'

'It isn't a question of arresting him, certainly not at the moment. We just want to speak to him. As a magistrate, I'm sure he would want to give us whatever assistance he can.'

Mrs Newby did not reply. She was undoubtedly a formidable woman but Hood's implied threat of removing her husband to Northampton seemed to be having the desired effect. The chief inspector looked at Knight. She handed him the fax from the monastery. 'You told me yesterday that your husband had had no dealings with Father Dominic, and he agreed with you, remember?'

'What if I did? That's the truth.'

'We have established that your husband was educated at Melford College which is attached to the monastery, Father Dominic's monastery. He was a history teacher at the college when your husband was a pupil there.'

'And what is that supposed to prove? That was years ago. How is he supposed to remember someone from so far back? He left there over thirty years ago.'

'Father Dominic was also housemaster for over five years at St Benet's, one of the boarding houses at the college. Arthur Newby was the head boy at St Benet's in his final year. Your husband was the only Arthur Newby in the school. It's not a common name.' He looked intently at Mrs Newby. 'Father Dominic was still the housemaster. They must have known each other quite well.'

Her expression changed immediately. 'I wasn't aware of that. I knew he was at Melford, that was all. Anyway I still don't know what it's supposed to prove.'

'You were very quick to interrupt yesterday evening, Mrs Newby, and to inform me your husband had not had any dealings with Father Dominic.'

'I suppose I was, but where he went to school is hardly a major topic of conversation these days and I can't think how that can have any relevance to your inquiry. And, for what it's worth, I'm sure my husband has had no dealings with this priest or any priest from Melford in recent years. I'd have known if he had. We have no secrets from one another, Chief Inspector.'

'Then there's the question of the Jaguar.'

'I don't understand what that has got to do with anything, whatever colour it might be.'

'Your husband's Jaguar was seen at Easton Grange on the seventh of this month – a Sunday. The index number was noted down by a witness.'

Mrs. Newby took this information in her stride. 'There must be a mistake. My husband was not well enough to go out at the beginning of this month. He was very tired. I was getting quite worried about him again. He'd had difficulty sleeping.'

'Another of his off days? Tell me, do you have a driving licence, Mrs Newby?'

'Yes, of course I do. There's no public transport around here as you must know.'

'Someone must have driven that vehicle to Easton Grange. Have you ever driven it?'

Knight watched carefully as Mrs Newby replied. 'No, I have not. I have my own car, a Mercedes. It's an automatic. I always drive an automatic. It's in the main barn if you wish to see it.'

'No, that won't be necessary, at least not at the moment.' He turned and looked into the mirror over the fireplace. He could see Mrs Newby in the reflection, twisting her fingers together. Despite her attempt to disguise it, she was clearly worried about something. Hood turned and faced her. 'Your husband told me last night that he road-tested the Jaguar before he purchased it. And that was nearly two months ago. He was plainly well enough to drive it then.'

'I don't know about that. His condition varies a lot, although I am hoping he's getting better.' There was more than a touch of doubt in her voice. 'Look, Chief Inspector, I've lost one husband to cancer; I have no intention of losing another. I won't have you badgering him when he's not well.' She turned and sat down again, folding her arms and glaring at Hood who simply pressed on.

'Some two hundred and forty miles have been added since the paperwork was completed at point of sale. Someone has driven that Jaguar since it was purchased.'

'If you look at the sales invoice, you will see the previous owner lived in Kidderminster.' Mrs Newby plainly knew more about the purchase of the Jaguar than she had initially indicated.

'I appreciate that,' replied Hood, 'but it doesn't explain the total mileage. We have checked the distance between Kidderminster and here.'

'The rest must have been caused by the test drive then, as you have just suggested.'

'I don't think so. I may have misled you slightly. We have already checked with the previous owner. The mileage stated in the paperwork was written in *after* the test drive had taken place. That can't account for the additional miles. The journey from Kidderminster, perhaps, in part. But it doesn't explain the two hundred and forty miles, not in full.'

Mrs Newby appeared a little shaken. 'I can't help you, then. But I'm sure my husband will have a perfectly acceptable explanation.'

'You may well be right. But I would like to hear it from him. Now, is he going to speak to me here or in Northampton? If he does have a perfectly acceptable explanation, it would be in his interests for him to give it here rather than at Campbell Square, don't you think? I'm very mindful of his condition. I don't want to appear heavy-handed but...'

Mrs Newby stood up, sighed deeply then headed for the drawing room door. She turned and gave Hood an icy stare. 'I'll see what he says, but I shall hold you personally responsible if this intrusion affects his health. Have no doubt about that. I shall also be contacting the Chief Constable. Pursuing a ridiculous allegation against a sick man like this. It's quite outrageous!'

With that she flounced out of the room and disappeared up the stairs.

'Phew,' said Knight. 'She's a one. I think we need to question Newby in her absence.'

'I agree. Perhaps you could have a word with her while I speak with Mr Newby. Take her out and look at her Mercedes or something, anything. Just get her out of here. Check that the Mercedes is an automatic like she says. It will give you the chance to look around the barn.'

'Don't you want me with you when you question Newby?'

'You will be. I have a feeling we're all going to end up at Campbell Square. Not necessarily tonight, but at some point. That's where the real interview will take place. Mrs Newby will have alerted him to what I said to her. He'll probably clam up so I'm going to have to arrange for him to come to Northampton. He'll want to have a solicitor with him I should think.'

'I did wonder why you told her what you did. She's bound to tell him.'

'I want her to. I didn't tell her everything, though. Just enough for her to get him worried. I bet she's giving him what for as we speak. I think she's definitely the dominant one in that relationship.'

Knight's mobile phone rang. She answered it quickly. It was Nigel Mullen. She listened intently, then thanked him.

'That was Nigel. They've found a tiny trace of blood in the boot of the Jaguar. They're getting the blood group checked as fast as they can.'

Hood's eyes lit up. 'Anything else?'

'He says that someone has given the boot a really good clean and the carpet is missing. Someone obviously didn't do as good a job as they thought if they left a trace of blood. It struck the examiner as odd that the rest of the car is pretty dirty, with the sole exception of the driver's compartment. No attempt to clean the other seats or footwells. They've also got a good set of prints from the steering wheel; they're not on record. Could well be Newby's. Now why would someone make the effort of cleaning the boot and the driver's side but not the rest of the interior?'

'Presumably because something had been in the boot and they didn't want to leave any trace of it.'

'Or someone? Father Dominic, perhaps?'

'Now that would simplify things, but it's not very big, the boot of a Mark 2, is it?'

'Big enough if he were dead or dying. And it would explain how the body got from the old chapel grounds into the house and then into the priest-hole. No need to use the wheelbarrow.'

'How long to get the blood group?'

'Assuming there's enough and it hasn't been contaminated, a couple of hours. The sample is already on the way to the lab.'

'And no blood in the interior?'

'Not that they've found so far. Of course, if the killer had driven the Jaguar shortly after the murder, he would have had blood on him which might well have contaminated the driver's seat and footwell.'

'That would certainly explain why that area had been cleaned.'

'Bit careless not to clean the rest of the interior, though. It makes that part of the car stand out from the rest.'

Knight looked towards the door and nudged Hood. Mrs Newby had returned She shot a sharp look in Hood's direction.

'My husband is on his way. As I said, this is not one of his better days. I trust you will bear that fully in mind. I don't mind telling you, Mr Hood, his health seems to be deteriorating again. I'm getting very worried about him.'

Hood nodded. 'Of course, I'll keep that fully in mind, but this is a murder inquiry, Mrs Newby.'

She did not reply. Arthur Newby then walked slowly into the room in his dressing gown and slippers. No sign of the wheelchair.

'I hope this won't take long, Chief Inspector. I'm feeling very tired. Not one of my good days.'

He slumped into the armchair his wife had previously occupied. Hood took a couple of steps towards him, then addressed Mrs Newby. 'I'd like to speak to your husband alone, if you don't mind. Perhaps you could show Detective Sergeant Knight your Mercedes in the barn?'

'What on earth for? What has my car got to do with any of this? I think I should be here. I won't have you bullying my husband.'

Hood sighed. 'I'm afraid I must insist, Mrs Newby. And you offered to show it to my sergeant only a few minutes ago.' He glanced towards Knight. 'Would you accompany Mrs Newby into the kitchen or somewhere, anywhere?'

'It's all right, my dear,' said Newby. 'I shall be fine. It's only procedure. The inspector's only following procedure.'

If looks could kill, Hood would have been struck down. Mrs Newby sneered and spat out her response. 'Very well. But I shall be ringing our solicitor. And I shall be back in ten minutes.' She stormed off. Knight followed her out of the room.

'I suppose you want to know about the Jaguar, Chief Inspector?' said Newby after his wife and Detective Sergeant Knight had left the drawing room.

'I do. You presumably knew it was maroon in colour when your wife indicated yesterday that it was dark blue.'

Newby appeared quite relaxed as he answered. 'Of course, I did. I asked her afterwards why she had said that. She explained that the log book says it's blue, midnight blue I believe. She didn't want there to be any inconsistency between the colour of the vehicle and the paperwork.'

'So why didn't you correct her?'

Newby smiled but remained relaxed, 'Are you married, Chief Inspector?' Hood nodded. 'My wife doesn't appreciate being corrected, especially in front of other people. And I hardly thought it mattered. It's being restored to its original colour at Bensons in Banbury. My wife did tell you it was there, didn't she?'

'She did.'

'Hardly needed me to say anything then. I presume you've seen it?'

'We have it in the forensic workshop in Northampton. I showed your wife the warrant.'

'I know. She told me. Seems a bit extreme. I can't think why you want to examine it.'

'Did she tell you anything else?'

'That you know where I went to school.'

'Yes. You were at Melford College in the sixties.'

'A long time ago.'

'Over thirty years; but when Father Renville was teaching there.'

'That's right. He was my housemaster for a couple of years. I was in St Anselm's House until I entered the sixth form, then moved to St Benet's. St Benet's was for pupils over sixteen; lower and upper six.'

'So you knew Father Dominic?'

'I suppose I did. But I don't really remember him, not after all this time.'

'They do say we remember our teachers, especially those who made a very real impression on us. I, for example, still remember my English teacher and always will. Did Father Dominic ever teach you?'

Newby shook his head. 'Not while I was in St Benet's, no. I studied only science and maths at A level. If my memory serves me, he taught history, religious knowledge and Latin. I think we had him in my first year but I gave up history before my O levels. Kept up the Latin though as far as O level. Got a good grade too.'

Hood was not impressed. He too had studied Latin, although over the years he had forgotten much of what he had learnt. 'You were head of house as well, weren't you?'

'In my final year, yes. But I was studying most of the time. I had to get two As and a B to get into Exeter. I saw Dominic around and had a couple of sessions with him to organise the leaving celebrations, but that's about all.'

'He'd have been a much younger man, then, of course?'

'I suppose he would. Younger than I am now. But all the monks looked the same to us. We never thought about their ages.'

'Tell me, Mr Newby, how were you known at Melford?'

'What an odd question. It was all surnames back in those days. I believe I was the only Newby in the college.'

'And the other pupils? What did they call you?'

He smiled. 'It was Newby with most of them, I suppose. A few friends called me Harry. I thought Arthur was a bit old fashioned. I preferred Harry. My wife, however, likes Arthur. So I'm definitely Arthur these days.' He chuckled to himself.

Hood recollected the initials H N on the sacristy calendar. *Could they have stood for Harry Newby?*

'You were a practising Catholic then, presumably?'

He frowned. 'We had no choice in the matter. None of this freedom of religion nonsense in those days, Mr Hood.'

'When did you stop practising.'

'Completely? After I married Eleanor, I suppose. I went to Mass occasionally but after Hannah was killed I stopped altogether. But I suppose I remain culturally Catholic.' He smiled. 'It's never crossed my mind to join my wife in the C of E. But as to going to Mass, I couldn't see the point of it anymore.' He raised his voice. 'How could God, if he exists, have allowed such a thing to happen? Tell me that. She was such a beautiful girl. I often think what she would have become, had she lived.' He became quite emotional.

'I don't pretend to know the answer to that question Mr Newby, but I am interested in your relationship with Father Dominic. Bit of a coincidence that he was living only ten or eleven miles from you, don't you think?'

'How was I supposed to know that? I have nothing to do with the church these days.'

'Then why did you deny knowing him?'

'I didn't. I said I had had no dealings with him, which is the truth.'

Hood had to concede the distinction, but Newby's failure to volunteer when first asked that he knew Father Dominic remained highly suspicious.

'Your Jaguar was seen at Easton Grange on the seventh of this month. That was a Sunday. It was there during the time Father Dominic was saying Mass in the chapel.'

'Not my Jaguar. I was here. I slept late that Sunday, as I do most Sundays. I had taken something to help me sleep the night before. I'd had little enough for a couple of nights. Must be a mistake. Who is this witness of yours?'

'That must remain confidential for the moment. A Maroon coloured Mark Two was also seen on the evening we believe Father Dominic was murdered.'

'At Easton Grange?'

'No, but passing through the village shortly after the time we believe he was attacked.'

'I know nothing about that. There must be hundreds of other maroon Mark Twos. It's a popular colour.'

'You deny you have been to Easton Grange recently?'

'I most certainly do. I haven't been there for several years. I told you, I went to a reception there when Sir Robert Southall was High Sheriff. That was many years ago. Although he was a fellow magistrate, we didn't see a lot of each other. We certainly never socialised. He always sat in Wellingborough and Towcester; I only sit in Northampton.'

'Can you explain the mileage on the Jaguar?'

'What do you mean?'

'Two hundred and forty miles have been added since you purchased it.'

'I don't see how you can say that.'

'The mileage at the time of purchase is stated on the paperwork.'

'Is it? I can't say I took much notice of that. I test drove it over quite a distance, but I told you that yesterday. That apart, I have no idea.'

'The previous owner says he inserted the mileage on the paperwork after the test drive.'

'Again, I didn't notice one way or the other. The precise mileage was not of great moment. It was the car that mattered.'

'Have you driven it around these parts at all?'

'Once or twice. But only over short distances.'

'In the direction of Easton Parva?'

'Not that I recall. I drove it to Northampton once. That's in the opposite direction. I had two new tyres fitted to the front. I have an invoice somewhere.'

'Can you help me about the boot? The carpet seems to be missing? The boot of a Mark Two is usually carpeted. My sergeant is a bit of an expert on Mark Twos. Her father used to own one.'

'Is she? Can't say I recall much about the boot. I must have looked at it I suppose. Perhaps Bensons removed it?'

'I don't think so. They've not done any work on it at all. Not yet.'

Newby grunted. 'I know. I was a bit annoyed with them about that. They promised they'd start straight away. I rang them earlier today.'

'So I understand. Were you in a rush to get it finished?'

'Not particularly. I just like people to stick to what they say, that's all. They've had it since last Friday. There's a classic car event on the other side of Oxford in early September. I was hoping it would be restored in good time for me to take it there. Not much chance of that now, I suppose, if the police have got hold of it. When will I get it back?'

Hood did not answer. He paused and stroked his chin. 'The vehicle examiners found a bloodstain in the boot. Can you account for that?'

Newby drew in his breath. 'A bloodstain? Now, listen Inspector, I know nothing about that. Where was it exactly?'

'I don't know. I've only just received the information. But I'll have full details soon enough.'

'Well, it's nothing to do with me, I assure you. It must have been there before it came into my possession.'

'We will be checking the blood group and the DNA, of course. It's amazing how a tiny sample can sometimes reveal quite interesting results.'

Newby was no longer as confident as before. He appeared rattled and sat back in his chair. After a few moments he leant slightly forward, smiling. Something had obviously occurred to him. He appeared more relaxed.

'I know something about bloodstains, Chief Inspector. I remember trying a case in the Magistrates' Court a couple of years ago where we had an expert witness. It was a commercial burglary. The expert said that while a DNA result had been obtained from some blood which matched the defendant's profile, he couldn't say when the sample from the crime scene got to where it was discovered. On a window sill, as I recall. I believe that's still the position. A blood sample cannot be aged. Am I right?'

Hood nodded. 'I believe that is still the position but advances in science are being made all the time. One day, I fancy it will be possible, at least in respect of recently shed blood.'

'But not yet, eh? Not in two thousand and two.' He sat back in his chair. 'As I thought. Well, it must have got there before I bought the car; I can't explain it otherwise.'

'I've also been informed that the area immediately around the driver's seat appears to have been cleaned, but not the rest of the interior.'

Newby smiled. 'That was me. I decided to start cleaning the interior before it went to Banbury, but I only got as far as the driver's seat. I didn't have the time or the energy to complete it. Nothing suspicious about that. I just didn't get round to finishing the job.' He paused, a determined expression on his face. 'And I'm saying nothing more without my solicitor present. I'm not having you trying to tie me to a murder, especially the murder of a priest that's attracted huge national publicity. I'm not having it I tell you.'

He tried to get up from the armchair but was unable to do so. He fell back, grabbed the arms of the chair a second time and called for his wife. She was back in the room in less than a minute, Wendy Knight following at a safe distance. Newby looked at Hood and then at his wife. 'The Chief Inspector will be leaving now. Any further questioning will take place in the presence of my solicitor or not at all.'

Hood frowned. 'I do have further questions for you Mr Newby, several in fact. Perhaps we can arrange a mutually convenient appointment – at Campbell Square police station in Northampton.'

Newby grunted his agreement. 'If you please. I can't do tomorrow. I have an appointment with my oncologist in Milton Keynes. My three monthly check-up. I can't miss it.'

'I wouldn't want you to miss that, of course. Your health has to be given priority. Thursday afternoon then, shall we say four o'clock? I shall be at police HQ in the morning.'

'Assuming Mr Sewell is available,' interrupted Mrs Newby. 'I've telephoned his office. He's not there at the moment. Hardly surprising given the time.' She looked at her watch.

'If you let my sergeant have his number, we'll liaise with him and find a suitable time. It shouldn't take more than an hour. Hopefully, I should be in possession of more evidence by then. That bloodstain, for example. It shouldn't take long to group it.'

Mrs Newby glanced towards her husband. What was this about a bloodstain? Although her expression remained indifferent, Knight thought she detected just a flicker of nervousness at the mention of blood.

'Our solicitor is Mr Gerald Sewell of Sewell & Underwood,' she said. 'You've no doubt heard of him.'

'Can't say I have,' replied Hood, casually, 'but I haven't been in this county for very long. I look forward to meeting him.'

CHAPTER THIRTY-EIGHT

'You decided not to arrest him, then,' said Wendy Knight as she and Hood drove away from Stanton Harwood in his Saab. She had said nothing until they were out of the village but there was just a hint of criticism in her voice.

'No; do you think I should have? I doubt if we have sufficient grounds at the moment. If Nigel comes through with something definite, things will change. We'll treat Thursday as a voluntary interview to begin with. If he chooses to leave or clams up, then I may be forced to arrest him. The time has come to take a bit of a risk and kick the investigation forward.'

'Did you ask him about his Range Rover? I saw a photograph of it in the kitchen. It's black and fairly new. I got the index number, too. 190 AWH.'

'AWH? A personalised number, then?'

'Yes. Might make it stand out from other Range Rovers?'

'It might. To answer your question, I didn't get round to it, but I will take that up with him on Thursday. He's already confirmed that it's his usual mode of transport. I did ask him how he was known at school, though. It was all surnames formally, but some of his friends called him Harry rather than Arthur. Remember the initials on the sacristy calendar? H N? Could be a reference to him?'

'You think he'd arranged to see Father Dominic on the Friday?'

'Could be.'

'It could also refer to Hannah, of course.'

Hood nodded. 'True. Perhaps Newby had asked Dominic to remember her in his Mass on the Friday, although her anniversary was on the twenty-fourth?'

'More than a coincidence that, isn't it? Both she and Father Dominic dying on the twenty-fourth of July, although years apart.'

'But we have no evidence that it's anything other than a coincidence.' He paused. 'Tell me, what do you make of Mrs Newby?'

Knight scoffed. 'She definitely wears the trousers in that relationship. She's very fit for her age, too. She attends a gym twice a week and goes in for a couple of hours of Pilates as well. I hope I'm in as good condition as her when I hit fifty.'

'Is that how old she is?

'She will be, come December. They have a big party planned. Not that we are invited, of course.' She grinned broadly.

Hood was impressed. 'How did you find out so much about her?'

'After she calmed down – she has quite a temper on her – we got talking. I mentioned I'd missed my appointment at the gym last night and she just came out with it. There was quite a lot of other stuff pinned to the notice board in the kitchen too. That's where the photo of the Range Rover was. There were a few invitations as well. She seems to have a hectic social life despite what she said to you yesterday. By the way, sir, she's extremely ambitious for her husband. She seems to regard his becoming High Sheriff as the culmination of her efforts at social advancement.'

'Really? Is it such a thing then, to become High Sheriff?' He smiled. 'I suppose as the daughter of a knight she sets great store by such things. Being High Sheriff is purely ceremonial these days, and I've heard it costs a small fortune. It's unpaid, and you're expected to foot the bill for all the social engagements yourself.'

'That doesn't seem to concern her.'

'I suppose they can afford it. Did you ask about her Mercedes?'

'She confirmed it was an automatic, but I didn't get the opportunity of checking it out. She wasn't at all keen taking me to the barn and when we first went into the kitchen she was busy on the phone trying to speak with their solicitor.'

'Ah, the solicitor. She obviously regards him highly. Have you heard of this Sewell chap at all?'

'I have, yes. He's got quite a reputation in this area. I've come across him before. He managed to get one of DCI Saunders' fraud cases thrown out before it even got to the Crown Court. He certainly knows what he's doing and he is, incidentally, perfectly straight. He wins his cases through attention to detail and natural ability, at least that's what I've heard. A very smooth operator.'

'We'll have to be very careful with him, then. Make sure we are well prepared and that anything we suggest is soundly based. Bradley mentioned that the Newby's solicitor was very much to the fore in the investigation into the death of the daughter. I suppose that must have been Sewell?'

'It will have been. She said his firm has acted for them for years.'

'Bradley is still going through the accident file. He can't have found anything relevant yet or he'd have mentioned it. I suppose it was always going to be a bit of an ask, establishing that the daughter's death might be connected with our present investigation.'

Knight was equally pessimistic. 'I can't see how it can be. It was a long time ago. And I'm the one who usually goes in for thinking outside the box, not you.'

'I just didn't want any loose ends, not where Newby is concerned. I want to know as much as possible about him. I want to know what makes him tick. It occurred to me that the investigation into his step-daughter's death might give me a bit of a steer. The accident obviously hit him hard. He got quite emotional when I mentioned it.' He sighed. 'But there's something about him that doesn't quite add up. I can't put my finger on it, but I have the impression he's holding something back, something significant. I'm convinced he knew Father Dominic much better than he's letting on. If only we could prove he'd been to Mass at the chapel. Those initials on the calendar may prove to be important.'

'His Range Rover hasn't been spotted at the Grange, so far as we know.'

'No, but it's worth pursuing. As you said, it might stand out with its personalised number. Have we got anywhere with re-interviewing our witnesses?'

'Not yet. No one has mentioned seeing a black Range Rover apart from Sir Robert's somewhat ancient looking four by four. Do you think Newby might have been at the Grange before the seventh of this month, then?'

'It's a possibility. Proving it though, that's not going to be easy. But if he visited Father Dominic before he acquired his Jaguar, it presumably would have been in his Range Rover.'

'Or his wife's Mercedes. But what makes you think he may have visited earlier?'

'Just a thought I've had. If he'd lost his faith and was facing up to his death, he might have wanted to speak to a priest. Such things do happen.'

'You'd understand that more than me. Could it have been just a social visit?'

'I don't think Father Dominic did social visits, not even from former pupils. No, if Newby was there, he must have had a reason and a good one.'

'He was quite unwell back then, wasn't he?'

'Yes. In March it looked like it was all over for him. He thought he was dying. He'd been told his illness was terminal. The chemo was the last chance saloon as far as he was concerned.'

'Seems to have done the trick, though?'

'He's in remission, but still not a well man. And cancer has a nasty habit of biting back. I don't think he was necessarily putting it on tonight. He's still got a long way to go before he's out of the woods.'

'It might explain why he sought out Father Dominic, I suppose?'

Hood nodded. 'It might. As I said, looking death in the face may well make a man think about what he really believes. I remember an old priest I used to know saying that a man on his death bed never regrets being a baptised Catholic, however he may have lived his life. It would be helpful, though, if we could establish if he discovered Dominic was living at the Grange. He'd been there for about eighteen months in March, but how would Newby have known that? At the moment we have no evidence he'd set foot in the place, apart from what he's admitted.'

Knight considered what the chief inspector had said then had a sudden thought. 'Does Melford College have a school magazine or an old boys' association?'

Hood braked harder than he needed to as he came to a junction. 'That's it, Wendy. It does. Father Milmo mentioned it in passing.' He dropped into first gear, pressed the accelerator and turned on to the Easton road. 'Get on to it. The Prior should be able to help. Check if Newby's on the list of recipients. And see if you can find some back copies. They usually provide updates in respect of staff and the like as well as old boys. Father Dominic might have got a mention. And most public schools like Melford have an old boys' association if only to attract funds from former pupils who do well in the world.'

'Like Newby.'

'Exactly. He's done very well for himself. He'd be a prime target.'

'What next then?'

'I'll drop you off at the Grange, then I'm off home. Give Sarah a surprise. I can't remember when I last got home when the kids were still up. I'll be working in Northampton in the morning, going through the accident file with Bradley. You work on getting copies of the college magazine and find out about the old boys' association. I'll see you in the afternoon back at the Grange. We also need to check Father Dominic's keys and see which doors he was able to access.'

'I contacted the lab when the keys hadn't been returned to Campbell Square as they promised. They assured me they'll be there first thing tomorrow. They didn't find any prints and we'll have to wait for the DNA analysis of course.'

'I'll pick them up and bring them with me. And see if you can make contact with Mr Sewell. Don't let him put you off with that silver tongue of his either. I want Newby questioned at Campbell Square by Friday at the latest, but Thursday afternoon if possible. Don't forget, I'm seeing the DCC at HQ on Thursday morning. And it won't be just to congratulate me on my promotion. She'll be applying considerable pressure. She's understandably anxious we should make progress.'

'Will do.'

Silence.

'Father Milmo is saying Mass tomorrow at five. Grantham will there. I propose to join them,' said Hood.

'Grantham is still not in the clear then?' She laughed. 'The housekeeper didn't think much of being asked if there was anything between the two of them. Her face was a picture when you asked her!'

'Yes. And I think she was probably telling the truth. We were a bit off beam with that idea. But like you, I wasn't entirely happy with her. Something seems to be worrying her and it's linked to Dominic's death, I'm sure of it.'

'You haven't given up on Grantham though? He's not out of the frame yet?'

Hood glanced at Knight and chuckled to himself but said nothing.

CHAPTER THIRTY-NINE

'Have you got anywhere with that file, Bradley?' asked Hood after he arrived at Campbell Square early on Wednesday morning. He had gone straight into the squad room. It was deserted apart from DC Mark Bradley. The young detective constable looked up from the papers strewn across his desk.

'I'm not sure, sir. I've prepared a timeline...'

'A what?'

'A timeline, sir. It's a sort of chronology which I've constructed from the statements. But there's a bit of an inconsistency when it comes to the arrival of the girl's step-father at the place where the party was being held.'

Hood sat on the edge of the desk and examined Bradley's hand written document, replete with numerous crossings out and arrows going in all directions. He tried not to sound too sceptical. 'This is supposed to help, is it?'

'It's a bit rough and ready, sir, but I'm in the throes of making a fair copy for you on the computer. I'll print it off when I've finished.'

'Remind me, where was this party taking place?'

'Lonsdale Hall. About three and a half miles north of Towcester. It's a country house owned by a Mr Lawson; well it was then. It's since been sold. Part of a golf course now. Must be one of the most luxurious club houses in the county, judging from the photographs.'

'I wouldn't know. Golf has never appealed to me. Spoils a good walk as someone once said. What's this apparent inconsistency, then?'

'Well, sir. Newby says in his statement that he set out from his home just after eleven thirty. According to him, his daughter was supposed to have phoned home before eleven so he could pick her up. This place is no more than fifteen minutes or so from Stanton Harwood. I've driven the route to make sure.'

Hood raised his eyebrows. 'Well done, Bradley. That shows initiative.'

'Thank you, sir. But I've come across a statement from a young guy by the name of Charles Buchanan. He saw Hannah getting into a vehicle at about five past eleven. It seems he'd been chatting her up, but she said she had to go. He said she was a bit upset about something but he doesn't say what.'

'Does he identify the vehicle?'

'He thinks it was a four by four, but he's not sure. He only saw it from a distance in the dark and there were several cars blocking his view. Newby says in his statement he was driving a four by four that night.'

'Don't tell me, a Range Rover?'

'Yes, sir. But he says he didn't get to Lonsdale Hall until almost a quarter to twelve. Hannah never phoned home. That's why he set out when he did. And plenty of people saw him after he'd arrived. The party was still in full swing. He was going around asking if anyone had seen her. Several witnesses say he sounded very upset and concerned as to where she might be.'

'Was the vehicle she got into ever identified?'

'It appears not. Only this Buchanan fellow noticed her leave.'

'How old was Buchanan at the time?'

Bradley handed over Buchanan's statement. 'It just says over eighteen.'

'Any chance of locating him?'

'The telephone number he gave is no longer in service. I tried to ring it yesterday.'

'And his address?'

'It's his parents' home. He was living there at the time of the party, during the summer vacation. He was studying law at Cambridge, Jesus College. His mother is still alive, but he no longer lives there. He's a barrister in Birmingham now. Commercial lawyer. She's very proud of him.'

'So you've seen Mrs Buchanan? Been to the address?'

'Yes, sir. Only thing I could do in the circumstances, the telephone number having changed and they're ex-directory now. His mother thinks he was nineteen going on twenty at the time of the party.'

'She told you where her son's chambers are?"

'Yes, sir. I looked him up to confirm what she told me. Fountain Court Chambers. I telephoned them first thing this morning. Unfortunately, he's on holiday in Portugal. Not due back in chambers until Friday morning.'

'You have been busy. Commercial barrister, eh? Well I suppose he must be nearly thirty now if he was in his late teens nine years ago. Does his clerk not have a number for him in Portugal?'

'No, sir. And he hasn't contacted his chambers since he's been there. But he has an important conference on Friday afternoon. They are expecting him to be there first thing on Friday morning. More papers have come in for him to read. He's travelling back tonight.'

Hood looked again at the timeline although he, personally, would have described it as a schedule. He went through the bundle of photographs of the scene of the accident then glanced very quickly at the *post-mortem* photographs shaking his head as he lingered for a moment over the images of the dead girl's body. 'What heartbreak and what a waste! Although she wasn't quite seventeen, she could easily have passed as older. Perhaps Mr Buchanan was keen on getting to know her better?' He looked up. 'Did he have a car with him?'

'He says in his statement that he'd never met her before but he did have a car with him, yes. He drove to the party in his mother's Volvo. It was still there when the police arrived. Hadn't been driven for some time. The engine was quite cold. He'd already booked a taxi to get home.' Bradley paused. 'He'd been drinking it seems.'

'How very responsible of him. Who contacted the police?'

'Mr Newby. The call was logged at twenty-three-fifty-nine. He telephoned from the Hall.'

'Cause of death?'

'Multiple head injuries. Wholly consistent with being hit by a vehicle at some speed.'

'And the road she was on?'

'Not much more than a track. She was heading towards Stanton Harwood. It's an unclassified road, a short cut, not much used. She was less than a mile from home when she was run down.'

'No suggestion that the body was moved?'

'No sir. Only by the impact.'

'And the vehicle that hit her was travelling from the opposite direction?'

'Yes, sir. That much is clear from the report. She was struck head on.'

'Who found her?'

'Police officers. Several mobile units were sent out looking for her. She'd been dead for a couple of hours when she was found, according to the PM report.'

'We'll visit the scene later if necessary. Now, what makes you say there's an inconsistency in the evidence?'

'It occurred to me, sir, that it might have been her step-father who picked her up, that's all. If he'd arranged to meet her at eleven, why would he want her to phone home? What would be the point? He knew where the party was being held. He and Lawson were well known to each other. They were both directors of the same company at one time. Why not just turn up there and pick her up? And Buchanan says she left the party at about eleven, as if she was expecting to be taken home by someone.'

'He didn't offer to drive her, then?'

'No, sir. As I said, he'd been drinking.'

'So why Newby?'

'Why not?'

'You do have a suspicious mind, Bradley. Did she have her mobile phone with her?'

'Not with her, no. She'd apparently left it at home. It was found in her bedroom. It was checked, Nothing relevant.'

'So how was she supposed to ring home?'

'The landline at Lonsdale, presumably? Or using a friend's mobile. But there's no evidence that she did. Not many of her friends had mobile phones. They weren't that common back in ninety-three. Everyone seems to have one now.' Hood looked at his own mobile phone as Bradley continued. 'And we only have his word that there was any arrangement for her to phone home. There's no mention of it in his wife's statement. And she made her statement several days later.'

'Probably too upset to make one earlier. But from what you say Hannah was clearly expecting to be taken home by someone.'

'That must follow, sir. The DCI's report concludes that someone she met at the party must have offered her a lift home. Whoever it was, was never identified.' He paused. 'It was some party. They catered for over a hundred and fifty. And there were a few who got in who were not invited;

friends of friends if you know what I mean, so not everyone who attended was identified.'

'You're seriously suggesting it could just as easily have been Newby who picked her up?'

'Yes, sir. Her mother's statement is pretty clear that she was to leave at eleven. She wasn't at all keen on her daughter attending the party in the first place. She thought Hannah was too young. It was only because it was her school friend's seventeenth birthday and the summer holidays that she was allowed to go. Mrs Newby was out herself at a meeting of a charity she chaired, a local women's group. It was the AGM. She left it to her husband to collect Hannah.'

'So she can't alibi him.'

'No, sir. She got home about five minutes before midnight. Newby had left by then, even on his own account. I just got the impression from reading the other witness statements that there was something odd about the way he was going round asking everyone about the girl, as if he was trying to make sure they all remembered him. And he kept mentioning the time.'

'I don't know about that, Bradley. If my daughter had gone missing, I'd have reacted in exactly the same way. You do realise what you're suggesting?'

'Yes, sir. That he picked her up, that something happened to make her get out of the vehicle and then someone ran into her as she made her way home. Perhaps she was trying to thumb a lift, then in desperation took the short cut. Not much traffic even on the main road at that time of night. And I don't suppose anyone driving down such a deserted track would have expected to meet a pedestrian.'

'Doesn't prevent them acting like a decent human being after the event and seeking help. Was Newby's Range Rover checked?'

'That's the other thing, sir. I can't find any evidence that it was.'

'Any indication of the type of vehicle involved?'

'Nothing definite, sir, but it looks to me that it must have been a four by four or similar. The accident reconstruction report suggests she was thrown up in the air and propelled over the vehicle. It must have been moving at some speed. She was found some distance from the likely point of impact half in a ditch on the other side of the road. Both her upper legs were fractured as well as the head injuries, so it must have been a vehicle with a higher road clearance than usual. It's pretty plain where the collision must have occurred although there's no sign of the vehicle braking.'

'Sounds like a boy racer hit her and just carried on.'

'It looks that way, yes. But the leg injuries are certainly consistent with being struck by a four by four.'

'Like a Range Rover.'

'Exactly, sir. There's no street lighting and according to the weather report, it was cloudy. Not much of a moon either. It's possible that whoever hit her didn't realise he'd hit a person at all. Could have thought it was an animal. She was wearing a black dress and a black coat. Very difficult to spot her in the darkness.'

'I don't know about that. Too scared of the repercussions, more likely. But whatever vehicle hit her, it would have suffered impact damage – even a four by four.'

'You would have thought so. Though no broken glass or debris was found at the scene and no paint flakes or anything. A shoe and her handbag were found on the side of the road.'

'No debris of any kind? That's certainly unusual. And yet Newby's Range Rover was never checked?'

'No, sir. No indication that it was.'

Hood sighed. 'It's all very speculative. Did Newby's Range Rover have bull bars fitted by any chance?'

'I don't know. But I'm not saying he ran into her, just that he could well have picked her up from the party and then let her out on the way home.'

'So nothing solid to implicate him, your theorising apart.'

Bradley dropped his head. 'No, sir.'

'If she were picked up by Newby he would have had to stop his vehicle for her to get out. Does your theory run to what could have caused him to do that?'

Bradley hesitated before he replied. 'Perhaps they had a row and she insisted that he stop and let her out? She wasn't very pleased about having to leave at eleven. She'd made that clear to her friends earlier in the evening. She wanted to stay until the end. The party was due to go on until two in the morning. Her friends also say she was a very confident young woman despite her comparative youth. Perfectly capable of speaking her mind.'

Hood had his doubts that she would have chosen to get out of the car in the circumstances unless something very serious had happened. 'Why would she get out in the middle of nowhere? She wasn't quite seventeen. Hardly in a position to insist on anything.'

Bradley had got the bit between his teeth. He was not for giving up on his theorising. 'Depends what the row was about. And she could have got out earlier in the journey while they were still on the main road and still close to Lonsdale. Her shoes were quite muddy. It had rained heavily the day before and had started again in the early hours. She could have been walking for some time before the collision occurred. The short cut was pretty mucky and she wasn't found until gone one-thirty. There'd been another heavy shower by then.'

'You think she could have got out of the vehicle long before she reached the short cut?'

'Yes, sir. It's possible. I doubt if someone heading towards Stanton in a car would have bothered with the short cut. You'd understand why if you saw it. Only used by farmers in the main. The verges were quite cut up by heavy machinery. It shortens the journey for someone on foot but it's probably as quick to stick to the main road in a car. The only advantage is that the track avoids the traffic lights at the junction with the Towcester road and there seems to be a gated road off it that leads to the rear of Lonsdale, but that has been closed since it became a golf club.'

Hood mused on what the young detective had said. Had Bradley's enthusiasm got the better of him? Hood pointed out a logical flaw. 'If it were as dark as you say, why would a young girl go that way at all? Surely she'd stick to the main road. Have you really thought this through?'

'The report suggests that whoever gave her a lift went that way precisely because it was quiet and dark. He parked up and tried it on with her. She protested and got out then started to walk home. That's the thrust of the report.'

'Sounds a more likely explanation than implicating her step-father in the matter. If she were in his motor, what could have prompted him to stop and let her out so close to home? His wife would have given him a roasting if he'd come home without her. You've seen her; have you thought how she would have reacted?'

'But I think it's possible that he didn't go home.'

'What do you mean?'

Bradley hesitated before explaining what he meant. 'I reckon it's perfectly possible that he went back to Lonsdale Hall looking for her. Perhaps he thought she'd headed there?'

'But you've just told me she was heading towards Stanton when she was struck. And he'd have seen the direction in which she was walking, wouldn't he?'

'Yes, sir. But he might have remained stationary on the main road in case she relented and returned, then lost sight of her. It depends where she got out of his motor. If she'd objected to coming home so early while the party was still going on, he might well have thought that she'd doubled back there. And we know for a fact that he ended up at Lonsdale Hall. He doesn't seem to have got home until after the body had been found.'

Hood glanced again at the bundle of photographs, then started to read the accident reconstruction report. Bradley interrupted. 'She was a very good looking girl, sir. Very well developed for her age.'

Hood looked slightly shocked. 'What *are* you suggesting?'

'Well sir, he wouldn't be the first step-father who was unable to keep his hands off his attractive step-daughter. Such things do happen, as we both know.'

Hood rolled his eyes and shook his head. Bradley had gone too far with his speculating. 'Not in Stanton Harwood, they don't. And not when he had to face that wife of his. You saw what she was like on Monday. She's the one in charge in that relationship.'

'Perhaps it was different nine years ago? I noticed when you were questioning him, he left it to Mrs Newby to give the details surrounding the accident. He couldn't face talking about it.'

'That doesn't prove anything, Bradley. A tragedy like this will inevitably evoke painful memories, especially around the anniversary of the girl's death.'

'Same day and month that the priest was murdered, too. Still think that's a coincidence, sir?'

'We have no evidence to the contrary, not at the moment. And you have to bear in mind that Newby's been very unwell.'

'I wouldn't know the details of that, sir. What I do know is that DCI Fowler doesn't seem to have considered the possibility that it was his Range Rover she got into after she left the party. It seems to me that was something that should have been followed up. That's all I'm saying. It should have been looked into.'

Hood took a deep breath then stood up. He had to acknowledge that Bradley had a point, but after all the time that had passed since 1993, there was little chance of retrieving the situation.

'Perhaps, like me, the DCI proceeded on the basis of evidence, not speculation.' He paused and gazed at the disappointed detective constable for a few seconds then gave him an encouraging look. 'Leave the file on my desk. I'll go through it later. Oh, and let me have your schedule when you've completed it.'

Bradley screwed up his face. 'Schedule, sir?'

'Yes. You know, your *timeline*.'

Bradley nodded then smiled. 'Yes, sir. It will be with you in twenty minutes.'

CHAPTER FORTY

'Mr Sewell can't do Thursday, Harry. He says he can manage Friday afternoon at a push, but not until half-past three. He assured me his client can also make it then.'

Hood had arrived back at the Grange. He and Wendy Knight were walking towards the Gatehouse to check Father Dominic's keys. Hood had signed them out from the property store at Campbell Square. The grouping of the blood stain found in the boot of the Mark 2 Jaguar had also come through. It was the same group as Father Dominic's. Hood was delighted. If the DNA analysis came up trumps as well, there would be sufficient for Newby to be arrested and charged.

'So he's obviously spoken with Newby. You fixed it for Friday afternoon, then?'

'Yes. Three-thirty, like he requested.'

'At Campbell Square?'

'Yes.'

Hood nodded. That the blood stain found in the boot of Newby's car was the same group as Father Dominic was more than encouraging, but he was not jumping to conclusions until the DNA profile came through, and that would take a few more days. He remembered what had happened with Philip Southall's coat. He wasn't building up his hopes, not yet. He was also still waiting for the scientists to report back on their examination of the sacramental and the debris samples taken from the niche.

'Remind me, Wendy, what percentage of the population has the same blood group as the deceased?'

'He was A negative. I think it's about eight per cent of the population.'

'That's still a lot of people. Can't we get a quicker result on the DNA?'

Knight did not hold out much hope. 'I did push them, but it's going to take a week even if we are placed close to the head of the queue. We are already fast-tracked.'

'I suppose the delay might work to our advantage.'

'How?'

'I want you to have a quiet word with a Mr Charles Buchanan. He's a barrister in Birmingham. I've written the details down for you. He was in conversation with young Hannah before she left the party, not long before she was killed.'

'Is he a suspect?'

'Not at all. He's in the clear; no doubt about that. It's a theory that young Bradley has come up with. Bright young lad is Bradley, but a bit over enthusiastic. When he calms down a tad he should do well.' Hood stopped and looked directly at Knight. 'He feels that Hannah's death was not properly investigated and that Newby should have been looked at with greater scrutiny by DCI Fowler, as he then was.'

'Deputy Commissioner of the Metropolitan police as he is now.'

'Quite!'

'What do you mean by looking with greater scrutiny into Newby?'

'I've brought it all with me.' He tapped the file under his left arm. 'You have a look at it and see what you think. Bradley reckons that Hannah could have been picked up from the party by her step-father. He reckons she must have got out of his car and started to walk home before becoming the victim of a nasty hit-and-run traffic accident. While it seems a bit of an ask, it's just about plausible on what I've read. Bradley has prepared a schedule – what he calls a timeline – pretty accurate too. It will help you to understand everything if you look at that first. This Buchanan chap saw her leaving. He was speaking to her immediately before she put on her coat and walked out of the marquee. Of course, it all happened nine years ago, but I want more details about their conversation. Whoever took his statement doesn't seem to have pressed him about it.'

Hood handed Knight the file. The Detective Sergeant opened it as they reached the Gatehouse. The statement in question was on top of the file but the space where the name of the officer taking the statement should have been written was blank. 'Will he remember anything after all this time? Nineteen ninety three is a long time ago.'

Hood remained hopeful. 'I don't know Wendy, but these lawyers are supposed to have good memories, aren't they? See what you can get out of him. He'll be in his chambers first thing Friday.'

'You want me to go all the way to Birmingham to see him?' Knight did not sound at all keen. 'Won't a phone call do?'

'No, I want you to see him in person and let me know what you make of him. You're good at getting things out of people, especially when you see them face to face. It's not the same over the phone.'

'So you think there might be something in Bradley's theory?'

Hood shrugged his shoulders. 'I haven't reached a final view. And I haven't examined the file as thoroughly as I should. That's another reason I want you to take a look at it. Bradley may have missed something. I was thinking of sending him, but this needs a more experienced hand. I want to clear up any possibility that Newby may have played a part in Hannah's death, inadvertently or otherwise, before we question him on Friday afternoon.'

'But if he did have a role, would that have any relevance to Father Dominic's murder?'

Hood smiled. 'I have a little theory of my own which I intend keeping to myself for the moment. What you make of both Bradley's ideas and Mr Buchanan may well be important.'

'I'm flattered, but you're not going to share this theory of yours with me?

Hood smiled and shook his head. 'No, not yet. I want to give it a little more thought. It's still a work in progress.'

Knight paused before she replied. She wasn't going to push the matter. She knew Hood would reveal his theory when he was good and ready. 'OK. I'll ring Buchanan's clerk and make an appointment. Now, what about these keys?'

Hood took the exhibit bag from his pocket and removed the set of keys. He selected the most modern-looking of the four, a Yale, as he approached the front door of the cottage. It turned easily in the lock. He gave it a cursory examination. It was identical to the key Sir Robert had given him to gain access to the cottage. He walked around the side to the back door and tried the smaller of the two mortice keys. Again, the key turned in the lock without a problem. He looked at the older and largest of the set, very similar to the key Sir Robert had used to open the sacristy door in the Long Room. 'This must be the key to the entrance to the chapel as well as the one which opens the sacristy door. Sir Robert relied on Dominic to keep the chapel secure so he would need a key that fitted both doors. It was always locked in the evenings.'

'There is a fourth key, of course,' said Knight.

'Doesn't look like the sort that would operate a heavy door. A very elaborate design, don't you think?' He held up the smallest key of the set. 'Looks more like the key to a trunk or box. Let's try it in the trunk in the bedroom, then we'll go over to the chapel. I want to check that the sacristy key really does open the main door to the chapel. If it doesn't, it must follow that there's a key missing.'

The two of them went into the Gatehouse, climbed the little staircase and entered the dead priest's bedroom. The trunk Hood had noticed previously was still at the end of the bed. He took the smallest key, bent down and tried to insert it into the lock. It did not fit. He twisted it, this way and that, but couldn't even get it into the key hole.

'Not the key to the trunk, then,' he said, standing up and scratching his head. 'I wonder what it opens?' He looked round the room, then walked into the tiny bathroom, checking if there was a lock on the door. There was a bolt on the inside but no lock that required a key. 'Can't see anything this would fit,' he called out. 'And there's nothing downstairs.'

'Perhaps Sir Robert can help,' suggested Knight.

'He didn't mention an additional key when Swanson took a statement from him. But we'll show it to him all the same. It's always possible that it's a key that was personal to Father Dominic, of course. Perhaps it's for something back at the monastery?'

After leaving the Gatehouse, Hood and Knight strolled over to the main entrance to the chapel. As Hood had anticipated, what he took to be the sacristy key opened the chapel door with comparative ease. It seemed to fit the lock better than Sir Robert's key had fitted the door in the Long Room. The two detectives then headed for the sacristy. Like Sir Robert's key, the large key that had opened the main chapel door with comparative ease seemed to have difficulty in turning in the lock of the sacristy door. With some persistence, Hood eventually managed it.

'Could do with oiling,' commented Knight.

'It could certainly do with something,' replied Hood, looking at his watch. It was nearly half past three.

'I'd better get on reading this file,' said Knight. 'I'll need to be familiar with it before seeing Charles Buchanan on Friday. What will you do?'

'I'll have a word with Father Milmo, then seek out Sir Robert.'

'Sir Robert's not here at the moment, sir,' interrupted the uniformed officer on duty in the Long Room. 'The housekeeper tells me he lost a filling at breakfast this morning. He's gone to see his dentist but expects to be back just after four.'

Hood thanked him then turned to Wendy Knight as they walked through the corridor and out of the front entrance. 'That was good news about the Melford College Magazine, by the way. When will the copies arrive?'

'Adrian Swanson's gone to get them. It's a bit of a hike but he should be here shortly. They keep a full set in the college library, apparently, right back to nineteen hundred and three. I've asked him to fetch copies for the last five years, just to be on the safe side. Father Milmo thinks the deceased had been back at the monastery for over two years before he came here. And he did write the occasional article for the magazine, usually on a historical topic.'

'Good. That was excellent thinking on your part, Wendy. I must confess I would never have thought of it. You get off to the Gatehouse and examine that file. I will certainly value your take on it. You saw that I left the front door unlocked?'

She nodded. 'Shall I take charge of the keys?'

Hood nodded and handed them over. 'If Sir Robert's not here, you may as well have the keys. Lock up when you're finished. I still want to show the mystery key to Sir Robert, but I'll do that after Mass.' He glanced at the file. 'It will take you well over an hour to go through that lot. Don't rush it, though. There's an outside chance it might be useful. It'll certainly give young Bradley a fillip if you come to the same conclusion he has.'

'But what do you think?'

Hood smiled. 'I'm remaining wholly neutral for the moment. I don't want to influence you more than I have already. I'll see you just before five at the chapel.'

CHAPTER FORTY-ONE

Hood spied Father Milmo heading for the chapel. He caught up with him and the two men walked through the porch and then sat together at the back of the little church. Hood had never really examined the style of the building before. It quickly became apparent that the Prior of Melford had been doing some research of his own on its history and construction.

'It was planned by Sir Robert's great-grandfather but only completed well after his death,' he explained. 'It's really a mortuary chapel, somewhere for the Southalls to bury their dead. There are three generations already buried here in that small annexe on the left, behind those ornamental iron gates.' He pointed to where he was referring. 'Sir Robert's wife, however, is buried immediately in front of the altar. You've no doubt seen the inscribed marble slab in the floor? Very sad business that. She was taken from him quite suddenly.'

Hood nodded. 'Nearly three years ago, now, isn't it?'

'Yes,' sighed the Prior. 'She was only fifty-seven. Not that her funeral was held here, of course. Far too small for the large numbers expected. Her Requiem Mass took place at the Cathedral in Northampton and she was buried here afterwards. Very well attended too. The cathedral was full to bursting, according to young Philip. Do you know, he still has the order of service and he's kept all the cards completed by those who attended? He obviously misses his mother very much.'

Hood recalled what Sir Robert had told him about Philip. 'You've spoken to him, obviously?'

'Yes. He told me all about the funeral. There was a reception for the mourners in the Long Room, but I believe the burial itself was limited to family members and a few close friends. That this is Lady Southall's resting place is really what drives Sir Robert to try and keep the chapel open, but I suspect it's a forlorn hope. Philip, too, is very keen it should remain a functioning church.'

'Is Sir Robert minded to close it then?'

The Prior sighed more deeply. 'Well, you see the state of the place. It bears little resemblance nowadays to what was originally proposed. Gothic revival, that's the style. I discovered that the original drawings were prepared by Edward Pugin, the son of the famous architect, Augustus Welby Pugin. They were both involved in the design and extension of the Cathedral in Northampton too. Alas, Edward never saw this chapel completed. He died in eighteen seventy-five, in debt and concerned for his own sanity.'

Father Milmo expanded on what he had discovered, informing Hood how Edward Pugin had engaged in a war of words with the architect Charles Barry which was the beginning of a downward path ending in a serious deterioration in his mental health and his being close to bankruptcy. The chapel was only finished several years later with much of the originally planned decoration excised on the grounds of cost. Both the house and chapel were listed in 1966, grade two★. The main house was generally in good order, the roof having been renewed ten years ago but the chapel was a different matter altogether. The roof was in need of urgent attention and would require a considerable sum of money to repair it. Sir Robert didn't have the necessary funds. He had considered selling his Reynolds but was loath to do so. An application to Historic England for financial assistance was still under consideration. The only realistic option was to close it until the required work could be done.

'Health and safety, you understand?' added the Prior.

'I quite like it,' said Hood. 'It's very simple, austere even, but there's a nice atmosphere in here. It would be a pity to lose it.'

The Prior smiled. 'Yes. A still point in our turning world. But it has few architectural pretensions.' He laughed. 'The Rosslyn chapel it isn't. Unlike the house, it's actually brick-built, you know. The stonework on the exterior is only cladding, to give the impression that it is as solidly constructed as the old priory. Unfortunately, it isn't. And the interior walls are simply plastered.' He glanced towards a large window to his left. 'The only stained glass apart from the little rose window in what in a larger church would be described as the narthex is the one on the south-east side; a memorial to Sir Andrew Southall, Robert's grandfather.' He smiled. 'The decoration that did exist was painted over just before the war. Then of course, further vandalism occurred after Vatican Two. I can't really explain why there was such a surge in re-ordering the layout of so many of our churches. The destruction wasn't quite on the scale as the reformers in the sixteenth century, but I believe we will eventually come to regret what occurred. Take the altar, here, for example. You see how the original stone one has been pushed back into the rear wall and replaced with that brutal wooden structure.' He smiled. 'Cranmer would certainly have approved! Nothing more than a communion table really.' He paused, shook his head and pointed. 'Odd, though, that they preserved the tabernacle which is never used these days. The Sacrament is not reserved here any longer, you see. That would require the Bishop's approval.'

'I was aware of that, but at least it's still here.'

'Yes, but not in its original place.' The Prior spoke with emphasis that did not disguise his disapproval. 'We should, I suppose, be grateful it wasn't removed altogether, as has happened in some churches. The tabernacle has been relocated in a side chapel in some places, you know. It should be the centre piece of the sanctuary not pushed almost out of the way.' He paused and looked about him. 'We avoided most of this at Melford, thank God.'

'What will happen to the chapel if it closes?'

'As it is listed, it would be difficult to get permission to demolish it, but quite a few Pugin buildings have gone over the years. At least it's not standing in the way of any proposed development. Not like the Bishop's House in Birmingham; that was demolished to make way for the new ring road. Can you imagine such a thing? I suspect this place will simply deteriorate unless a financial miracle occurs.'

'Is that why Sir Robert is so preoccupied with finding the Powdrell chalice?'

'It's discovery would certainly have helped and would have boosted the chances of success with Historic England. If it were displayed here, it would certainly bring in the visitors, especially if it were established that it had originally come from Glastonbury. Anything to do with Glastonbury still reverberates with the English; it's not just the famous festival that fascinates people. There's a lot of interest in the legends that seem to owe their origins there. Poor Dominic; he was quite the expert on Glastonbury, you know. He wrote an article about the last Abbot and the suppression of the monastery by that scoundrel Thomas Cromwell. You'll find it in one of our magazines.'

'Do you think Dominic knew about the story of the Powdrell chalice before Grantham raised it with him?'

'I don't believe he did, not according to Grantham, but I can't remember the details of his article; it was written some years ago.' He paused. 'I'll look it out if you wish?'

'If you would; you never know, it may help. I have built up a fairly comprehensive back story about Father Dominic, but if you could lay your hands on it, I'd be grateful.'

'I will see what I can do. It may take a day or two.' He paused and gave Hood a curious look. 'You haven't entirely dismissed the possibility of a connection then, between what may have been secreted in the hide and Dominic's death?'

Hood remained circumspect. 'I never dismiss anything, Father. I just follow the evidence.'

'I don't know, Mr Hood. I think Sir Robert is reconciled to the fact nothing more will be found, not now. And no one was more enthusiastic than he about finding an artifact of historic importance. But do I detect that you've not quite abandoned all hope of discovering something?'

Hood frowned. 'It's not a major line of inquiry at present. There may well be no connection at all. In fact, some recent developments suggest that to be the case. But it would certainly help if we could determine one way or the other if Father Dominic did find anything in the hide apart from the sacramental. Pity he didn't leave us any better clues.'

The Prior nodded. 'Like you, I was very disappointed nothing came of the search, especially when the niche was uncovered behind the panelling, but I'm driven to conclude it's unlikely now that anything more will be found.'

'Is that Father Grantham's view too?'

'Now, Mr Hood. You know I have to be discreet about saying too much about Father Grantham. But I'm sure you noticed that he didn't seem too surprised on Monday when nothing was found in the safe. If Dominic did find something of interest, he obviously didn't hide it there.'

Hood smiled. 'Forgive me, I thought your previous prohibition no longer applied.'

The Prior smiled. 'It is true that Grantham seems to have resolved whatever was worrying him and I hope I helped him in that regard. I remain more than willing to assist in every other way, I assure you. I'm as anxious to find Dominic's killer as you. It would be fitting if it were all settled before his funeral.'

'We have established he did keep a diary. Father Grantham saw him with it once, but we have not found it. His killer must have removed it.'

'So Grantham has been helpful?'

'More than he realises.' Hood smiled then changed the subject.' Tell me, what use was made of the chapel before Father Dominic came along? Sir Robert told me they didn't have a chaplain as such, not since his father's time.'

'That's right. When his father inherited their previous priest was a retired Dominican friar, the chaplain at the convent in Northampton. He was paid a small stipend to come here on Sundays, to cover his travelling costs and the like, but the convent closed many years ago and he returned to their house in Leicester. He'll be long dead by now I expect. The chapel was only used on family occasions thereafter.'

Hood stood up and walked slowly along the nave. He soon came upon Lady Southall's grave, set into the floor immediately before where the altar rails had once stood. He gazed up at the tabernacle set into the wall above the original stone altar. The small marble pillars still guarded it, the tiny brass doors covered in what appeared to be peeling gold leaf. Father Milmo followed him, standing behind him and lamenting the condition of the sanctuary.

'I've seen a photograph of what the altar looked like over sixty years ago. It is much changed. Some beautiful iron-work altar rails stood here in those days, but they were removed long ago in the mistaken belief that the second Vatican Council rendered them redundant.' He shook his head then his mood lightened. 'But the important thing is that Mass is still offered here, at least it will be today. Remember, Mr Hood; five o'clock. No homily, so we should be finished by half-past. We shouldn't delay your investigation for very long.'

Hood heard a loud cough. He turned and looked behind him. DC Swanson was standing there with a small package in his hands.

'That will be the copies of the Melford College magazine I asked for,' said Hood. He called to Swanson. 'Am I right?'

'Yes, sir,' replied Swanson. 'For the last five years.'

'Sergeant Knight didn't disclose why you wanted them, Mr Hood,' said the Prior. 'I don't immediately see how they will help with your investigation.'

'I simply want to establish whether Father Dominic's residence here at Easton Grange was generally known. The college magazine seemed a good place to begin.'

'I can certainly help you with that. Any significant changes in the lives of the monks at the Abbey and the staff at the college are carefully detailed in the *Melford Recorder*. There's a special section along with marriages, baptisms and deaths of old boys.' He took one of the magazines from Swanson, flicked through it and pointed to the section in question, towards the back of the magazine. 'There we are, Mr Hood. If we find the appropriate edition, we should find Father Dominic's move mentioned. We usually publish in November each year, so his coming here should have been mentioned in the millennial issue. It would have missed the publication date the year before.'

Hood looked in the year 2000 magazine. The Prior was right. On page fifty-nine, a small black and white photograph of a much younger Father Dominic appeared with a caption stating that he was leaving the Abbey for a period to work as chaplain to Sir Robert Southall at Easton Grange in Northamptonshire.

'That means the recipients of this magazine would know he was here,' said Hood.

'They would, if they bothered to read it,' agreed the Prior. 'I believe we print about fifteen hundred copies every year, but how many readers would notice that announcement, I couldn't say. It's twenty years since Dominic taught in the college, you know.'

'It may well be a blind alley, but I would like to see a list of the old boys who receive the magazine.'

'I already have it, sir,' said Swanson, producing an envelope from his inside pocket. 'It's all computerised at Melford. I was quite surprised they were so up to date at a monastery. One of the monks gave me a print-off.'

'Don't look so surprised,' smiled the Prior. 'We may be an ancient order, but we are quite up to date in many ways.'

Hood's eyes lit up. 'Well done, Adrian. If you'll excuse me Father, I'll see you at five o'clock.'

'I hope it assists Mr Hood,' said the Prior. 'But I doubt if it will help you narrow down your list of suspects. I should tell you, the magazine is sent out to all the members of the Old Boys' Association. I believe there are about thirteen hundred who have kept up their subscription. That's an awful lot of potential suspects.'

He walked off still smiling in the direction of the sacristy. Hood was not, of course, concerned about the numbers. He was looking for only a single name as he perused the list quickly. There it was: "Newby, A. W. H. (1965)". He could not resist a look of triumph.

'What does the nineteen sixty-five mean?' asked Swanson.

'That, Adrian, is when our suspect left school; thirty-seven years ago.'

CHAPTER FORTY-TWO

'Any sign of Sir Robert?' whispered Wendy Knight as she met up with Hood at the back of the chapel. It was just after a quarter to five. Father Grantham walked past them, acknowledging Hood with a slight bow of his head. He walked towards the altar and knelt down in the front pew. Only half a dozen others, scattered around the chapel, had gathered for the service.

'No, and if he doesn't get here soon, he'll be late for Mass. That will never do. What did you make of Bradley's theory? Do you think it holds water?' He indicated to Knight and the two of them left the chapel and went outside where they could speak more privately. Knight looked down before she answered, keeping her voice as low as she could.

'I have to admit, it's a bit of a stretch. I came across a statement which he may have missed in his eagerness to make his mark; a Mr Stansfield. He's lived in Stanton Harwood for forty years, probably the same person Adrian Swanson spoke to the other day. On the night in question, he couldn't get to sleep because of the heat. He decided to take his dog for a walk. He says he saw Newby's Range Rover driving *out* of the village just after eleven thirty, which supports what Newby said at the time.'

Hood heaved a sigh. 'Do you think that undermines Bradley's theory completely?'

'It depends. It's just possible this was Newby's second trip, of course.'

'His second trip?'

'Yes. Suppose Hannah got out of the car somewhere as Bradley suggests, Newby then drove home arriving before his wife got back. Hannah didn't return so he had second thoughts and went out again looking for her. That might explain Stansfield seeing him when he did.

It would also fit in with his arriving at Lonsdale Hall at about a quarter to midnight.'

A pained expression appeared on Hood's face. 'That opens up another possibility, remote though it may be.'

'What do you mean?'

'I hesitate to mention it. Not even Bradley has gone this far.' He paused and swallowed hard. 'What if Newby didn't just let her out of his car; what if he ran her down when he went back to look for her?' Hood explained what he meant to the shocked detective sergeant. 'Just suppose you're right and that he drove home without Hannah and panicked when she hadn't returned as the time drew near for his wife to get back? He'd know he'd be in for a tongue-lashing if she hadn't got home by the time his wife returned. So, he went out looking for her, but took the short cut along the unclassified road. Suppose she had taken that route and was walking home; he could have been the person who ran into her, not deliberately of course. I'm not suggesting he did it on purpose.'

Knight gasped in astonishment. 'But he would have stopped, surely? He wouldn't just have left her there, dying, his own step-daughter?'

'That would suggest a degree of heartlessness, I agree. But perhaps he didn't realise who or what he had hit? You noticed Bradley's tentative suggestion that he could have sexually assaulted her on the way home, which might explain why she insisted he let her out of his vehicle.'

'I did. But that couldn't be proved, not now. And the PM report indicates she was still a virgin.'

'Many sexual assaults don't go as far as actual intercourse.'

'I know, but suggesting he sexually assaulted his step-daughter? Come on, Harry. Without any evidence to back it up? We can't build a case on something so speculative, can we? Imagine his reaction and that of his wife, and, more to the point, his solicitor. I can just imagine what Mr Sewell would say if that were put to his client.'

'I agree. Without more we can't go there, especially after all this time. But if he did pick up his daughter, there'd have to be some very compelling reason for her to get out of his vehicle. It would have to be pretty serious for a young girl like that to force him to stop and for him to let her out. I can see where Bradley's coming from.' He paused at length and noting Knight's reaction, turned to a different topic. 'How are we getting on investigating the housekeeper's background?'

'Bill Renfrew has been looking into that. He got back to me fifteen minutes ago. He's made some progress too, which I think will surprise you.' Knight looked around before she continued and stepped closer to Hood. 'As we know, Martha Morton's last post, before she came here, was as deputy manager of a Hospice in north London. She was there for over five years. Glowing references.'

'Go on.'

'It's a previous position that's of interest. One she didn't mention to Sir Robert and is not included in her CV. She worked in Milton Keynes as PA to the chairman and managing director of a subsidiary company of, wait for it, Newby Enterprises PLC. A company called Dowlas Logistics.'

Hood was taken aback. 'Who was in charge at Dowlas?'

Knight smiled. 'It gets even better; Arthur Newby. According to Renfrew, he's chairman of all his subsidiary companies. They're all linked. Newby Enterprises PLC is simply a holding company. Renfrew's getting a print-out from Companies House. We should have it first thing tomorrow.'

Hood shook his head almost in disbelief. 'That's too much of a coincidence. We need to speak to Martha Morton again, and quickly. When was she actually working for him?'

'Between nineteen ninety and nineteen ninety-three. She became the company secretary for a period between ninety-two and ninety-three.'

'She'd have been quite young back then and even more attractive than she is now. Late twenties, I would guess.' He paused. 'And she came here, what, seven months ago? To work as a housekeeper? Something doesn't add up.'

'I agree. Two months after Newby was diagnosed with cancer she arrives in Easton Parva.'

'Do we know why she left her employment with Dowlas?'

'Not yet, no. She worked for quite a time for another unrelated business before she started at the Hospice. That is mentioned in her CV. It was a long time ago, of course. Bill Renfrew's trying to make contact with some people she worked with at Dowlas.'

'This must be what she's been keeping from us. What reason could she have for coming here?'

Knight shrugged her shoulders. 'I don't know, but my antennae are telling me she may have come here to be near to Newby. I reckon she was very close to him when she worked for Dowlas, and not just in a professional sense.'

'You think so?' He reflected on what Knight said. 'Why has she never mentioned it, then? Embarrassment? Or something more sinister?' He sighed. 'There is a downside, though. It means if Newby came here to the Grange, he may have come to see her; although she lives in the village, not in the main house.'

'That's always possible. Does that undermine your little theory? You know, the one you have declined to disclose to me?' She tilted her head and smiled.

Hood grinned and shook his head. 'Possibly.' He became serious. 'Of course, if there were something between them, the last thing Newby would want is his wife finding out about it, especially as he's lined up to be High Sheriff in a few months.' Hood mused on the possibilities. 'I suppose if he admitted to an affair with Martha he could use it as an explanation for why he lied about being here on the seventh?'

'You mean he didn't come here to attend Mass or to see Father Dominic?'

Hood nodded. His disappointment coloured his response. 'Exactly. Ideal opportunity, when you think about it. Everyone else in the chapel for an hour or so. No one about.' At the same time, he noticed that Knight was still smiling. Did she have something else to tell him?

'Except for one thing?' said Wendy, her smile broadening. She obviously did have something else to say. She took out her note book and checked it. 'That's the week-end she told me that she was away; you know, when I first questioned her last Friday. Visiting her sister in London. She only got back on Sunday evening. I asked her about her movements for the whole month. That was the only week-end in July she was not here.'

The relief was immediate. 'So my theory still stands, just about.'

'I wouldn't know, Harry,' whispered Knight as she noticed Philip Southall approaching the chapel door. 'I don't know what it is. Are you going to tell me now? If I've kept it alive, surely you can at least give me a clue?'

'Later. And you already know the first part of it. See if you can work it out for yourself.' Hood looked at his watch. It was approaching five o'clock. Philip Southall nodded to Hood as he passed by and took his place in the chapel. Still no sign of Sir Robert. Hood then whispered his instructions to Knight. 'You speak further with Renfrew. See if you can get more details from him – and locate Martha – but don't speak to her, not yet. I'll see you after Mass, unless you want to stay?'

'I don't think so. Not really my scene. I'll catch up with Bill and see you immediately afterwards.' She looked around. 'I see Swanson and his wife are on their way.' Hood acknowledged the couple as they approached and walked into the chapel. He turned again towards Knight.

'Have a word with Philip, too, when you get the chance would you? I understand he has kept the cards completed by the mourners who attended Lady Southall's funeral. I want to see them.' Sir Robert's four by four drew to a halt outside the chapel. 'Must have been longer in the dentist's chair than he anticipated. Could you let me have the keys to the Gatehouse, Wendy? I'll ask him about the mystery key when I speak to him after Mass.'

CHAPTER FORTY-THREE

Hood had difficulty concentrating during Mass. He stood, sat and knelt out of habit but he was hardly listening as Grantham read the lesson. The various threads of his investigation into the murder of Father Dominic constantly intruded into his thoughts. *Could Newby really be the murderer?* He was now satisfied that the wealthy businessman had lied to him about his relationship with the priest. *But why?* The chief inspector's theory, which he had so far declined to disclose to Detective Sergeant Knight in its full detail, seemed too shocking to contemplate, but the pieces of evidence were increasingly pointing him in that direction. The more he tried to concentrate on the liturgy, the more the doubts and questions engulfed him.

As Father Milmo had promised, there was no homily. Hood was still deep in thought when the Sanctus bell rang. He automatically knelt and attempted to follow the priest's words without further distraction. Moments later, the most sacred part of the Mass was upon him; the Liturgy of the Eucharist. He listened as Father Milmo uttered the words he had heard a thousand times before; *This is my body which will be given up for you.* Hood raised his head and watched as Father Milmo elevated the host, then genuflected. He bowed his head as the priest paused for a moment before picking up what had been Father Dominic's chalice. Hood knew the words which followed off by heart, but this time they struck him as never before. *When supper was ended, He took the chalice…* Hood almost gasped. The words hit him like a lightning bolt. It was as if Father Dominic were speaking to him directly. His eyes were opened. Everything suddenly fell into place. The legendry chalice did exist. It had been found in the niche and removed after supper a week ago. *But who had taken it? Grantham or Dominic? And what had become of it?* He looked up. Father Milmo raised Dominic's chalice and Hood's eye caught sight of the tabernacle, the gold leaf reflecting the sunlight coming through the stained glass window. *The tabernacle! Of course! The mystery key! The mystery key was the key to the tabernacle. Why had he not thought of it before? How could he have been so blind?* He could hardly wait for Mass to finish. He felt in his pocket, reassuring himself he still had the key with him.

Father Milmo was as good as his word. Just after five-thirty he pronounced the blessing and made ready to leave the altar. Hood waited until most of the tiny congregation had vacated the chapel before approaching Sir Robert.

'Could I ask you to wait, sir,' he asked. 'Something has occurred to me, and I would like you to witness what I am about to do.' He then addressed Philip Southall. 'Could you ask Father Milmo to come back. I would like him here too.'

Philip did as he was asked and returned moments later with Father Milmo, now in his monk's habit. Grantham remained where he was, intrigued by Hood's announcement. Adrian Swanson, sensing something significant was about to occur, kept his place alongside his wife. He intended to witness whatever was about to unfold. 'What is it, Mr Hood?' asked the Prior, his look of curiosity shared in the faces of the others.

The chief inspector removed two latex gloves from his pocket and produced Father Dominic's keys. He held up the smallest key, the key he had intended to speak to Sir Robert about. 'I have a feeling this key will open the tabernacle. It's just something that came to me during Mass. I should have realised it before, of course.' He stepped forward on to the sanctuary, pulling on the latex gloves. 'I suppose it's nothing more than a hunch, but I think it's worth investigating.' He approached the old stone altar, closely followed by Father Milmo. Sir Robert also moved forward, his eyes full of anticipation.

'We haven't used the tabernacle in over forty years,' he said. 'I'd forgotten that we still had the key. It must have been on the key ring I gave to Father Dominic.'

Hood took the small, elaborately designed key and inserted it into the lock in the tabernacle door. It fitted perfectly. He turned the key clockwise and everyone present heard the click as the lock was released. There was absolute silence. Hood turned round before he opened the brass doors and glanced at Grantham whose attention, like everyone else's, was concentrated on the tabernacle. Hood opened the brass doors slowly. This time he was not to be disappointed. Inside, covered with a white cloth, was an object about eleven or so inches in height. He removed it with great care, turned and placed it in the centre of the altar at which Mass had been celebrated. All eyes were upon him. He looked first at Father Milmo, then at Sir Robert before removing the cloth. A gasp of astonishment passed round the assembled group. All eyes were fixed on the object now revealed; a golden chalice of the most sumptuous design.

'Holy Mother of God,' whispered Father Milmo. He moved closer to Hood in an attempt to touch it. Hood raised his hand.

'I must ask that no one touches it,' he instructed. 'It will have to be examined by the forensic scientists. It may be linked in some way to Father Dominic's death.' The others looked at each other as Hood removed the paten which rested on the chalice and placed it to the side. He then picked up the chalice in his gloved hands. He gently turned it in a full circle, so that everyone could see it, then examined the underside of the base, looking to see if there were any marks that explained its origins. Etched into the circumference of the underside were six words which the chief inspector initially found difficult to make out. He rotated the chalice slowly, then read aloud what he had been able to discern: *"RETURN MEE TO GLASTON IN SOMERSETT."* More gasps of astonishment followed.

'The Powdrell chalice,' exclaimed the still shocked but delighted Sir Robert. 'Don't you see? Glaston is shorthand for Glastonbury. This has to be it. But how on earth did it get into our tabernacle?'

Hood, his feet now firmly on the ground, had no intention of mentioning what he had imagined were Father Dominic's words during Mass. He knew it's being where he found it was anything but miraculous. Someone must have put it there, but who? He looked directly at Grantham. 'I don't think it's been there for very long, do you?' Grantham smiled as Hood continued. 'Forgive my inexpert opinion, but it looks like someone has polished it. If it came from the hide, as I suspect it did, it's in remarkably pristine condition.'

'It's beautiful,' said Mrs Swanson. 'Absolutely beautiful. Just look at those precious stones. Are they genuine?'

Hood placed it again on the altar as the others drew close to gaze at it. No one said anything for well over a minute. The silence was broken by Grantham. 'Are there any other marks?' he asked, practical as always.

Hood looked again at the underside. 'Yes. I can't interpret it, but there is what appears to be an animal head – not a lion – and two other marks including the capital letter "A" over the creature's head.'

'Pre-reformation, possibly,' said Grantham, in a matter of fact way. 'Probably a leopard's head with a Lombardic capital above it. Am I right?' Hood held the base towards him. The Jesuit nodded as he scrutinised it, but without touching it. 'As I thought. It predates the lion passant which is still in use today. We must have it looked at by experts, Mr Hood. But, I have to admit, the reference to Glastonbury on the underside strongly suggests that this is the so-called Powdrell chalice.' He turned towards Sir Robert. 'Those words must have been engraved many years later, after it had been removed from the Abbey, probably by a member of the Powdrell family who knew where it had come from.' He smiled broadly. 'Congratulations, Sir Robert; this is a most remarkable discovery.'

'So you agree that this must be the Powdrell chalice?' said a still stunned Sir Robert.

Grantham nodded. 'It is certainly consistent with the available evidence. I can't think of anything that would suggest the contrary.' He smiled broadly and patted Sir Robert's shoulder. 'It seems your search is over.'

It would be explained three weeks later by an expert from Sotheby's that the chalice, which stood some eleven and three-quarter inches high with a wide and deep bowl seven and-a-half inches in diameter, was formed for the most part of gold mixed with silver with four rubies the size of pigeons' eggs located in the foot. The stem was engraved and hexagonal, the plates at the joints filled with emeralds. A crucifix engraved between flowering plants on a hatched background separated two of the precious rubies. The other two were divided by an engraved image of the Virgin and Saint John kneeling in prayer. The markings strongly suggested it dated back to the beginning of the reign of Henry VIII. No attempt was made to value it. It had no comparator in the United Kingdom according to the expert. It's size alone distinguished it from other chalices of the period. It's value, in material terms, could only be determined at auction. Sir Robert, who did not hesitate to assert ownership, had no intention of testing the market in that or any other form. His conscience was quite clear. The Abbey at Glastonbury was long gone and he doubted if anyone could assert a better claim to an antiquity that had been concealed in his home for hundreds of years. He now possessed what both his father and grandfather had coveted but never found; a pre-reformation chalice. And what an example! A chalice that had been kept out of the grasp of the rapacious Thomas Cromwell by the courage of a humble monk, Aidan Powdrell, whose family had once resided at the Grange and held fast to their faith during the years of persecution. This was the treasure they had guarded and preserved at huge personal cost, now revealed in all its glory. At least that is what Sir Robert believed and in the years that were to follow no one would ever shake him from it. His excitement and gratitude knew no bounds. He would, of course, eventually report the find to the Coroner for the county, but he hoped and prayed it would fall outside the definition of treasure trove. He was quite determined to prove his title. Happily, his deeds clearly showed that all and everything conveyed to his ancestors belonged to the estate, whether identified or not, and he doubted if the Crown would assert ownership given the circumstances of Glastonbury's dissolution. His only concern was the request he received a few weeks later for two experts from the British Museum to examine it. He felt unable to refuse but was resolutely opposed to it being put on display in a museum. He was determined to keep it at Easton.

Hood, of course, had other matters on his mind. He had still to solve the murder of Father Dominic and his reservations about Grantham remained. That the chalice was found where it was suggested the killing of the priest was unrelated. If getting hold of the chalice were the motive for murder, it would have been taken by the killer. Hood's dreadful but as yet unspoken theory was gaining traction by the minute. He asked to speak to Grantham in private in the sacristy.

'How do you think the chalice ended up where we found it?' queried Hood, settling into one of the two chairs in the small room, well away from the others who had been invited by Sir Robert for a celebratory drink in his drawing room. Grantham initially remained standing, his arms folded, but he eventually took the other chair and faced the chief inspector. His manner betrayed not a hint of unease or trepidation. The discovery of the chalice seemed to have induced a sense of exhilaration in him.

'I can think of only one explanation, Mr Hood. Father Dominic must have put it there.'

'Without mentioning it to you? You had supper with him that very evening, didn't you? Am I to discount the possibility that you put it there.'

Grantham smiled broadly. 'How could I? Why would I? And remember, Dominic had the only key.' He paused. 'Oh, I understand your suspicions about me, Chief Inspector. They have not gone unnoticed, I assure you. But I forgive you.' He raised his hands in mock blessing and laughed. *'Ego te absolvo!'* He them became more serious. 'After all, that is your trade, is it not? To suspect everyone?' He smiled again and repeated the words that had so affected Hood during Mass implying he knew only too well the impression they had made. *'When supper was ended, He took the chalice* – you think that could have been me? Am I right? You think after Dominic and I parted on Wednesday evening that I had somehow gotten hold of this priceless antiquity and hidden it where no one would dream of looking?'

Hood shifted in his chair but did not respond. Grantham now became deadly serious. 'Well, I'm sorry to disappoint you, Mr Hood, but I assure you I never saw it before you produced it, and in such a dramatic fashion too. You must tell me how you worked out it was there. It had honestly never occurred to me, for the simple reason I was unaware Dominic had found anything. Do you think if I had known about it I could have kept it to myself?'

'It seems Dominic managed to do so.'

'Ah, I suppose he did. But you must appreciate that Dominic and I are quite different characters. Had I found it, I would have been as delighted as he but would have felt in conscience bound to tell Sir Robert of the discovery immediately. I would have contacted him at his London club. Dominic obviously felt under no such obligation, at least not immediately. Perhaps as a Benedictine he thought his order had the better claim. It undoubtedly belonged at one time to the Benedictines of Glastonbury Abbey.'

'I doubt if such a proprietary claim would be upheld today.'

'I agree. His order never recovered any of their monasteries, nor did they try to.'

'He presumably would have told Sir Robert at some point?'

'I have no doubt he would; but I think I know why Dominic put it in the tabernacle and kept its discovery to himself, just for a little while.'

'You do?'

'It's only supposition on my part, you understand, but it makes sense if you consider Dominic's likely response to finding it, especially if he saw the words engraved on the underside, which I'm sure he did. He'd have examined it very closely and is probably responsible for its present pristine condition.' Grantham leant forwards and lowered his voice as he explained. 'Having located the niche behind the panelling in my absence, I suspect he removed the chalice and the sacramental. He took the chalice into the chapel, again in my absence, cleaned and polished it and placed it in the tabernacle. It would be safe there, of course, as he had the only key and no one would suspect there was anything there anyway.'

'You suggested yesterday that anything he found would have been safe if he'd left it in the niche behind the panelling.'

'So I did. Perhaps he thought I might discover the niche if I continued working in the hide in his absence as I sometimes did. But there was another reason why he placed it in the tabernacle, now that I come to think of it.'

'There was?'

Grantham sat back in his chair. 'I can't be one hundred percent sure, but I think he intended to use it to celebrate Mass on Thursday morning before he revealed its discovery to Sir Robert, and perhaps, to me. To sanctify it, if you understand my meaning? That could, I suppose, be interpreted as a selfish act on his part, but I suspect many a priest with a sense of history would have done the same. Think of it, Chief Inspector. He had found something of quite outstanding historical significance that had been lost for centuries. And what better way to make it holy once more after all that time than by celebrating Mass with it? It's first encounter with the Lord for over four hundred years. That the paten was also there supports my contention he intended to celebrate Mass with it.'

Grantham paused as Hood reflected on what he had suggested. The chief inspector was not convinced Grantham's theory was correct until the Jesuit pointed to another feature of the evidence which had always puzzled Hood.

'It also explains why his own chalice was still in the cupboard in the sacristy. He would normally have taken it the evening before and placed it in the chapel. As he intended to use the Powdrell chalice, there was no need for him to do that.' He paused and let out a deep sigh. 'Unfortunately, he was murdered before he had the opportunity. Utterly tragic when you think about it.' He paused again. 'But it now seems his murder was nothing to do with the chalice at all. You were following a wrong lead Mr Hood, understandable in the circumstances, but wrong nevertheless. There must be another explanation for his death.'

Grantham's theory certainly explained why Father Dominic's own chalice was still in the cupboard in the sacristy. 'That might explain the chalice being placed where we found it, but what of the sacramental? Why not secure that in the tabernacle too?'

'I can't say for sure, but I suspect Dominic was still in the process of verifying it. He must have had it with him as he completed his daily office in the grounds of the old chapel. Nothing on this earth would have prevented him from saying his office. You need to understand, Mr Hood. Dominic's prayer life was not restricted to his breviary. When he had finished praying his office, he would usually pray again. In that respect he was an example to us all.' He smiled then continued. 'As the sacramental fitted into his pocket, there was no particular reason why he shouldn't have kept it with him.'

'He'd have known what it was?'

'Of course he would. No doubt about it.'

Hood sighed. 'At least it was there to comfort him at the end.'

'Do you think so, Mr Hood? I've been giving some thought to that myself since we last spoke. Please don't misunderstand me. I hope it was a comfort to Dominic, I really do, but it occurs to me there was another reason it was in his hand.'

Hood leant forward. 'Another reason? I'd be obliged if you would enlighten me.'

'We must go back to first principles. What was the function of such a sacramental in penal times? Remember, Dominic was a trained historian and well informed about the period.'

Hood recalled his conversation with Grantham and Sir Robert when the sacramental was first examined. 'As we discussed last week, it may have been employed as a way of indicating that someone was a priest. The authorities would certainly have used it as incontrovertible evidence that a man found in possession of such a thing was a priest or a recusant.'

'Precisely. More than one priest was executed for that very reason. And Dominic would have known that. Have you considered, Mr Hood, that by clasping it in his hand as he did, Dominic was trying to provide you with a clue?'

Hood was at a loss. He was having difficulty following Grantham's train of thought. 'Provide me with a clue? I don't understand. We already know he was a priest. And the sacramental hardly tells us anything about his killer.'

Grantham shook his head. 'You misunderstand what I'm saying. That's not what I mean. I'm suggesting he was trying to tell those whom he knew would investigate his death not *who* attacked him but *why* he had been attacked. He could hardly identify his killer before he died, but by holding the *agnus dei* in his closed hand he was, perhaps, trying to tell you, or whoever was assigned the case, that he'd been attacked *because* he was a priest.'

Hood did not reply. Such a subtle distinction had never occurred to him but Grantham's words were advancing his as yet unspoken theory. He allowed the Jesuit to continue. 'And what does a priest do, Chief Inspector? As you know, he celebrates Mass and administers the sacraments, including the sacrament of penance or reconciliation as it is sometimes called these days.' He continued in a confidential tone. 'If I were you, I'd be looking for someone who had dealings with Dominic in his role as a priest; someone who had, perhaps, sought advice or absolution from him and revealed something about himself which, on reflection, he wished he'd kept to himself. Something that could cause him irreparable damage if it became generally known.'

Hood swallowed hard. Grantham was pursuing the very line the chief inspector had already identified. He said nothing but listened carefully as the Jesuit continued. 'And Mr Hood, don't imagine that confession these days has to be conducted in the traditional ritualistic way you are probably used to. My confessor back in the States usually begins the proceedings by opening a bottle of single malt. We sit in comfortable chairs and discus matters. We have, I hope, moved on from just reciting our sins, real and imagined, in the fashion of a shopping list like children. There is more than one route to achieving reconciliation and absolution.'

Hood frowned. 'I doubt if Father Dominic followed such a progressive style. But he would never break a confidence. He'd have died first.' Hood caught his breath as he realised what he had just said.

Grantham did not dissent. 'Exactly, Mr Hood. I suspect he died for that very reason. He may have been rather fixed in his ways, but he would never have broken the seal. Someone obviously thought he might. And it cost poor Dominic his life.'

Hood reflected at length on what Grantham had said. He had to concede it made perfect sense, but Dominic's failure to tell Grantham that he had found what he must have suspected was the Powdrell chalice still vexed him. And Grantham himself might well fall into the very category he had described, although there was, as Hood well knew, a more likely candidate.

'I still don't understand why he didn't tell you what he'd found, you being a priest and a historian too. He could still have said Mass using the chalice after informing you what he had discovered.'

'He could have, I suppose, yes. But I swear to you he did not say anything to me before we parted on Wednesday evening.' He smiled. 'I think it would have appealed to Dominic to do things the way he did. He had a very dry sense of humour and was in some ways a little eccentric. He could be quite prickly, too, when he felt like it. Finding the chalice would have completely dominated his thoughts and, of course, Sir Robert was not here to be told about it last Wednesday. It probably explains why Dominic was so uncommunicative but at the same time rather excited when we had supper together. I suspect he must have been bursting to say something. But I assure you, he didn't.' Grantham pushed back his chair and smiled. 'You mustn't fall into the trap of thinking we priests are all uncanonised saints, Mr Hood. We are subject to the same temptations as you and everyone else. And when it comes to historic artifacts like the Powdrell chalice we historians can be just as vain as the next man.' He laughed. 'I don't blame Dominic in the slightest, please don't get me wrong. I guess he didn't tell me what he had found for the simple reason he wanted to reveal this treasure to Sir Robert and then to the world. Of course, had I attended his Mass on Thursday morning, I would have seen it; that could not have been avoided.'

'I suppose that must be right,' said Hood. 'Perhaps that's what he intended to do?'

Grantham continued. 'But by finding it in the tabernacle and revealing it as you have, you have stolen his thunder – and mine. You do realise you will get the credit for its discovery?'

'I doubt that very much,' insisted Hood. 'I merely located where Father Dominic had placed it. He discovered it in the niche. The prestige of finding it will be his. Very appropriate too; a Benedictine finding an antiquity originally given to a Benedictine monastery. He will get the recognition he deserves in my report and, presumably, elsewhere.'

'That's very modest of you, Mr Hood. My only consolation is that you discovered it on the feast of Ignatius Loyola, our founder. So we Jesuits will have something to celebrate once the find is made public.'

'That won't be for a while yet. I have to solve his murder first.'

'Let's hope it remains a secret for a little longer then.' Grantham paused. 'I've had another thought too, Mr Hood, if you're interested?' He smiled broadly.

'You have?'

'Yes, although you've probably considered this already. It was perfectly understandable for you to link Dominic being found dead in the hide with the search for the chalice, but I suspect whoever dumped him there did so deliberately, intending to mislead and hoping you would follow a false trail. Had the killer been after something like the Powdrell chalice, it would have been removed and disappeared for good. That much is clear. Now, why would the killer want to muddy the trail to the truth? He must have had other options. His killer would have to be someone who knew that Dominic was hoping to find something in the hide – and that must reduce the list of suspects somewhat, don't you think?'

Hood nodded. 'As you said, Father, I have been thinking on similar lines.' He gave Grantham a shrewd look. 'You of course could be included in such a list.'

Grantham laughed. 'Don't waste your time on me, Mr Hood.'

'We have some evidence that Dominic spoke of his hope of finding something in the hide in his homily on the seventh of July, nothing specific, just a passing remark. That was before you arrived here. So the list remains a fairly long one, although I think I can delete you from it now.'

Grantham stood up and gave a slight bow. 'I'm pleased to hear it.'

Hood gave him a long and curious look. 'You seem much more relaxed than previously, if I may say so? Whatever was troubling you has been resolved, has it?'

Grantham smiled. 'My brief crisis of faith has passed, thanks in part to Father Dominic's example. And I found speaking with Father Milmo very helpful too. Surprisingly beneficial discussing issues with a priest who is not a Jesuit.' He paused, smiled again, then became deadly serious. 'Pray you are never put to the test, Chief Inspector.' A troubled expression passed over the Jesuit's face. He said nothing for several seconds. When he did speak his voice was much softer. 'Have you ever been weighed down with doubt, Mr Hood? Ever endured what is sometimes called the dark night of the soul?' He did not wait for a reply. 'I have always envied those who have a simple faith. No room for doubt with them. Nothing can shake them. But for some of us, doubt is, I suppose, a privilege, something we have to work through.' He sighed deeply. 'It is sometimes necessary, I think, for us to walk for a time in the wilderness, until the Lord takes us by the hand. And when he does, and we have endured, despite the pitfalls and the snares, I think we are the better for it.' He gave Hood a kindly look. 'I think you guessed I'd been talking to Father Milmo?'

'Not from anything Father Milmo said to me.'

'I'm glad he was discreet, as all priests should be.'

Hood smiled more broadly. 'But your inheritance? Does that not remain a problem; you having taken a vow of poverty?'

Grantham nodded. 'Ah, one of the snares that was presented to me.' He re-took his seat before continuing. 'That should not prove too difficult a problem to resolve. The Jesuits have access to expert legal advice, both here and in the States. And there's a considerable sum in the funds, which always helps.' He smiled then became more serious. 'But I really do wish Dominic had told me what he'd found. I would have loved to have discussed the chalice and its provenance with him. I don't suppose we shall ever know for sure why he didn't tell me about it, not now. But please believe me, he said nothing to me, nothing at all.' He looked towards the door as he stood up. 'Now, shall we join the others for that drink Sir Robert promised us? I suspect he will be breaking open some rather good champagne.'

CHAPTER FORTY-FOUR

'So, I missed all the drama!' exclaimed Wendy Knight. She looked directly at Hood. 'When can I see it? You must let me see it.'

She and the chief inspector were sitting in the kitchen of the Gatehouse reviewing the case file. Hood had restricted himself to a single glass of 1988 *Veuve Clicquot* in Sir Robert's drawing room, then begged leave to depart. He still had work to do.

'Tomorrow, after the forensic boys have examined it. I don't expect to find anything other than Father Dominic's DNA, but we have to follow procedure.'

'Where is it?' asked Knight.

'It's secure enough.'

'Aren't you going to tell me?'

Hood grinned. 'It's in Sir Robert's safe, to which I have the only key, I might add.' He held it up for her to see. 'I've reached a compromise arrangement with him and agreed the chalice can stay here as long as I retain the key. Nigel can examine it tomorrow afternoon when I get back from HQ. Handy that we have the photographer booked for tomorrow. And as it's looking increasingly likely that the chalice is quite unconnected with the murder, it means we can't really justify seizing it. Besides, it's probably priceless; no one is likely to put a value on it at less than tens of thousands. In such circumstances I think it's better if Sir Robert continues to assume responsibility for its safety.' He laughed. 'I don't want to risk it getting lost in our police property store.' He paused then spoke softly. 'It's a magnificent thing, though, Wendy. Probably dates back to the beginning of the reign of Henry the Eighth, according to Grantham. Just think about that for a moment. And it's clearly linked to Glastonbury. There's an inscription on the base to that effect. It really is likely to be the mythical Powdrell chalice. What was thought to be the stuff of legend is now as real as you or me.'

'And it's been here all those years? It's hard to take in. I wish I'd been there to see it exposed. High drama indeed.' She hesitated. 'Swanson's told me what happened. I pulled rank and insisted he told me, by the way. I really had to force it out of him. I'm also extremely jealous that I wasn't there.'

'You were invited.'

She appeared indignant but smiled all the same. 'And fancy you finding it rather than Sir Robert or Grantham. I suppose you'll get the credit, won't you? Your name will appear in learned academic journals, I shouldn't wonder.'

Hood smiled modestly. 'You are beginning to sound like Grantham. The glory, if there is any, belongs to Father Dominic, not to me. I might, if lucky, be mentioned in a footnote.'

'And the DCC will want a photograph. I bet Sir Robert's over the moon.'

Hood nodded. 'He's certainly very pleased, and I must say, I'm pretty excited about it myself, but I've asked everyone who was there to keep it to themselves for the time being. I don't want any publicity about its discovery overshadowing our investigation into Dominic's murder. I would have told you, of course if Swanson hadn't and I've agreed that Sir Robert can instruct an expert from Sotheby's to look at it in due course, but for the time being, no publicity is the order of the day.'

'I don't know whether that will stick, Harry. These things always leak out. Better not to say anything to the press office.'

Hood scowled. 'No chance of that!'

'But I'm intrigued. What made you look where you did? I thought the chapel had been thoroughly gone over by Nigel's team? And our search officers also must have missed it.'

'No one searched the tabernacle, which is understandable. They probably, didn't understand what it was or even notice it was there, and without the key they couldn't have gained access anyway without breaking it open.' He shook his head and let out a deep sigh. 'I have to admit it wasn't great detective work on my part which led it its discovery. It just came to me, during Mass I'm ashamed to say. I really should have thought of it before. We've had that key since the outset of the inquiry. We just didn't realise its significance. And the tabernacle is a sort of safe when you think about it.'

'Ah, the mystery key!'

'Exactly. Not a mystery any longer, thank God. I don't know why I didn't make the connection before. It seems so obvious now. There it was all the time, right under our noses, in plain sight.'

'At least you'll have some good news for the DCC tomorrow.'

'That's true enough, but it doesn't really advance our investigation into the murder of Father Dominic. In fact, it removes one of our principal suspects.'

'Grantham's out of the frame then?'

'I think so.'

'You're probably right. I had a message from Inspector Ambler while you were at Mass. He's spoken to the porter who was on duty on Friday night at Christ Church. Grantham was definitely there. He saw him walking across the quad late on Friday evening and again well before eight on Saturday morning.'

'It couldn't have been him who Helen Swanson saw leaving the housekeeper's cottage, then. We'll double check with Martha's husband when we find him, of course, but she's already given her explanation. Sounds like she was telling the truth.'

'So, we're left with Newby.'

'Yes. Grantham's actually come up with something that may help in respect of him.'

'He has?'

'Yes. He thinks that Father Dominic wasn't just holding the sacramental in his hand merely to comfort himself. He thinks it's possible he was trying to convey a message.'

'About Newby? I can't think what?'

Hood shook his head. 'Not about Newby specifically, no. He thinks Dominic was killed not because he'd found the chalice or because of anything to do with the priest-hole. He reckons he was murdered precisely because he was a priest, which I'm bound to say advances my little theory somewhat. He thinks we should be looking for someone who'd told Dominic something in confidence and then thought better of it.'

'And killed him? Because of what he'd told him? It would have to have been something pretty damning. And if it had been disclosed in the confessional, Father Dominic couldn't or shouldn't have said anything. Even I know that.'

'The murderer may not have understood the position. There is no confessional in the chapel and words exchanged in the priest's cottage might not have been understood as binding the confessor, especially to someone like Newby who had not practised his religion for many years, which is where my theory concerning our Mr Newby comes into play.'

Knight stood up. She took a couple of paces away from the table then turned and looked at Hood. 'I wouldn't know, Harry. I don't know what your theory is. Are you going to tell me?'

'I've as good as told you, but before I elaborate, let me ask you something, have you any more information for me? Have you spoken with Philip?'

Knight nodded and retook her seat. 'Yes. Straight after Mass, while you were with Grantham. Good news. The Newbys did attend Lady Southall's funeral. I have the card one of them completed. Do you know, Philip still has most of them? I was quite touched. He's kept them all this time. I think he really misses his mother. There were over a hundred completed. It must have been an impressive turnout. I've been through them carefully. Of course, I didn't let him know we were looking for anyone in particular.'

She handed Hood a small white card from her bag bearing the funeral director's printed invitation for the mourners to indicate their presence printed across it. In the prescribed place, the words, *"Mr and Mrs A W H Newby"* had been written in a flowing hand. She paused as Hood examined it. 'They've both lied to us, Harry. The funeral was on the twenty-second of November nineteen ninety-nine, less than three years ago. They've both been here more recently than they're letting on.'

Hood looked up. 'But this only proves they attended the requiem at the Cathedral in Northampton, not that they necessarily came here afterwards.'

Knight handed over a copy of the order of service. 'Look at the back page. All who attended were invited back to the Grange for refreshments after the burial in the chapel. I can't see the Newbys missing out on that, can you?'

Hood nodded. 'You're probably right. Tell me, has Bill Renfrew got any further checking on the housekeeper's possible liaison with Newby?'

'Not yet, no. He won't have anything until tomorrow at the earliest. By the way, she's available now if you want to speak to her. I've asked her to come here to the Gatehouse for seven, but I can go and find her if you like. She seemed pretty nervous when I saw her half an hour ago.'

Hood looked at his watch. 'It can wait. I hope she doesn't know about the chalice.'

'She knows something's happened but she doesn't know what.'

'Good. But I don't suppose Sir Robert usually doles out champagne on a Wednesday evening. He told her it was a welcome home party for Philip.'

'I doubt if she believed him. Especially with Swanson and his wife in attendance. It's the not knowing that's worrying her, I suspect. But there's no chance of keeping this under wraps Harry. It's bound to come out.'

'Let's hope not. Of course, if she were in some form of relationship with Newby back in the early nineties, it may well be relevant, not to the discovery of the chalice, but to Father Dominic's death.'

'I don't see how. It's nine years ago. Any relationship must be long over by now. We already know she wasn't dismissed from Dowlas; she resigned. No more relevant than the nine years separating the step-daughter's death and Father Dominic's.'

'Do you think we're right treating that as a mere coincidence?' asked Hood. 'Young Bradley, for one, doesn't believe in coincidences. And both of them dying on the twenty-fourth of July does seem decidedly uncanny.'

Knight frowned. 'There can't be a connection, surely? Not even in the circumstances of this already bizarre case.'

Still, Hood couldn't quite get it out of his head that the coincidence of the dates might be significant. He thought about it again, then dismissed it as a quirk of fate. It hardly affected the theory he was about to expound.

'Think about this for a moment, Wendy. Don't be afraid to shoot me down but I would value your opinion.' He paused as he prepared to articulate his thoughts, bowing his head as he contemplated how to formulate what he wanted to say. 'Newby was given what amounted to a death sentence earlier this year. Agreed?' The detective sergeant nodded as Hood continued. 'We'll get hold of his medical records in due course so we should be able to be precise when it comes to dates.'

'He also said he'd more or less given up his religion following the death of young Hannah, didn't he?' said Knight

'Yes. If not earlier. He'd had nothing to do with the church or any priest for many years. But as I suggested before, coming so close to death may have re-awakened something within him. In that frame of mind, suppose he sought out Father Dominic whom he knew from his schooldays? He probably got on with him very well back then, despite what he now says. He could have discovered from the college magazine that Dominic was living here, a few miles from Stanton Harwood.' Hood looked up and smiled. 'He probably regarded that as some sort of portent.'

'But you've already mentioned this before. The problem is proving it.'

'I haven't finished yet, Wendy. Bear with me. Let's suppose he visits Dominic, seeking spiritual consolation. Perhaps he confesses some dark deed from his past. Later, he unexpectedly gets the news that he's probably not going to die after all. He's going to live, at least for the immediate future. The chemo has worked. His condition is in remission. But he's already disclosed something to Dominic that might well ruin him if it got out. He revisits the priest, perhaps on the seventh of this month. Words are exchanged. He leaves, but returns on the twenty-fourth when he thinks no one will be about. An argument breaks out as Dominic is saying his office in the grounds of the ruined chapel. Newby loses his temper and attacks him, using the spade that Philip Southall had unfortunately abandoned nearby. Newby panics. What to do with the body? Thinking Dominic is already dead, he covers the body in a rug or something similar which he obtains from the Jaguar, then dumps the body in the priest-hole and throws whatever covering he used into the boot. But he leaves behind that tell-tale trace of blood.'

Knight interrupted him. 'But why go to all the trouble of dumping him in the priest-hole?'

'He'd heard about it at Mass on the seventh or perhaps from Mr Hitchens. Remember Hitchens had mentioned it to him when he quoted for some work. And his object was to distance himself from the murder and to mislead us by putting us off the scent. Pretty well succeeded too. He wanted us to think that the killing was connected with the hide, which is why I think we should regard where the body was found with a jaundiced eye. Don't forget, the excavation was completed by the time of the killing.'

Knight did not seem convinced. 'Bit speculative, isn't it?'

'Let me finish. He then drives away in his Mark Two Jaguar. A day or so later, it's taken to Banbury for restoration and a re-spray, the boot having been cleaned and the carpet removed and destroyed beforehand.' Hood looked at Knight. 'What do you think, Wendy? Too far-fetched?'

Knight waited until she had fully considered what Hood had said 'It's arguable; you can just about get the evidence to fit, but proving it beyond a reasonable doubt in the face of a complete denial by Newby? That's a different ball game altogether.'

Hood nodded. 'I take your point. But what do we know for sure? First, Newby has lied to us. His car was definitely here on the seventh. Young Francis Gilbert has not made a mistake. Secondly, Newby, and probably his wife, are familiar with the Long Room. They've been there, at least twice in recent years, probably more frequently. Third, Newby knew about the discovery of the priest-hole and its location. He also knew that Dominic was hoping to find something in the hide of historical significance. Dominic mentioned it in his homily on the seventh. Fourth, both he and his wife lied about the colour of the Jaguar. Fifth, Newby can't explain the inconsistency over the mileage recorded on the odometer. Sixth, there is blood in a crevice in the boot of the Jaguar which is the same group as Dominic's. Seventh, the boot and the driver's area, but not the rest of the vehicle, has been carefully cleaned and the carpet which lined the boot disposed of. Eighth, the Jaguar was at the garage in Banbury when we found it in order for it to be restored to its original and officially registered colour. Just think; if we hadn't made the connection, it would eventually have been re-sprayed and no-one would have been any the wiser.'

Knight stood up. She breathed out slowly as she arranged her thoughts.

'Too many holes and too many assumptions, Harry, unless we get a DNA match on the bloodstain. If we secure that, we may get somewhere. Without it, he'll wriggle free.'

'Go on,' said Hood. 'I'm listening.'

'In the first place, suppose Newby had some other reason for visiting on the seventh? Aren't we assuming he was here to attend Mass? We know the housekeeper was not here that week-end, but he may not have appreciated that. Seeking her out would explain both his presence here and his lies. And I'll lay even money that wife of his will back him up if it comes to it. If he thought he was dying, he's probably already admitted his relationship with Martha to her. She'll have forgiven him too; she won't want to prejudice his becoming High Sheriff or lose her present lifestyle or social position. Secondly, what misdeed from his past would have prompted him to seek out Father Dominic? That he'd had an affair with Martha, nine years ago? I don't think so. It would have to have been something much more serious than that. Third, why take the risk of going into the house and dumping the body in the priest-hole? The chance of being seen was surely too great, even if he didn't know Grantham was there. He could have dumped the body anywhere anytime or left it where it was. Fourth, was he physically able to move the body? Father Dominic was fairly light, but you can guarantee Newby will make what he can of his ill health. Fifth, and this creates a fundamental problem when you think about it, he may be a lapsed Catholic, but he was brought up in the faith as you like to call it. You know what they say? Once a Catholic…' Hood nodded and completed the saying, '…always a Catholic.'

Knight continued. 'Exactly. But if he had confessed something so terrible that he was later prepared to kill because of it, he would surely have known that, as a priest, Dominic could not have revealed it. And I doubt very much if Newby would have confessed to anything really serious unless he knew he had the protection of the confessional.'

Hood had to agree. 'I see what you mean. Confession may be good for the soul, and Newby may have started to recover his faith, but there's no way he would have risked disclosing something that could have ruined him if there were any chance of it getting out. That's what you're saying?'

'Exactly. And Dominic's obligations as a priest should have guaranteed whatever it was would remain a secret. That seems to me to be the real stumbling block. There would be no need for him to do anything if he trusted the priest.' She sat down in the chair with a flourish and crossed her legs.

Hood sighed. 'And you think he trusted Dominic?'

'Why shouldn't he?'

'I take your point. For an agnostic, you're quite the theologian, Wendy. You may have holed my theory below the waterline.'

'Well, you did ask for my take on it.'

'There is one possible factor I haven't included thus far,' cautioned Hood. He hesitated before continuing. 'Suppose the terrible deed he confessed was his running over his own step-daughter, something he had covered up all these years?'

Knight's face was a picture. Hood had mentioned such a possibility when they spoke outside the chapel, so she was no longer shocked at the suggestion, but she had difficulty accepting it as something that could be proved. 'And how, after all this time, do we establish that?'

'I don't suppose we can, unless he were to admit it.'

'Can't see him doing that, can you? Not with Mr Sewell sitting next to him in the interview room at Campbell Square.'

'I don't know, Wendy. If this is the reason he approached Father Dominic, he's somehow managed to ease his conscience for the last nine years, but he's obviously not been able to shake it off completely. Old sins cast a long shadow. He still feels guilty. That may give us an edge; something to work on when we interview him.'

But the detective sergeant remained doubtful. She put a further question to Hood that caused him again to question the viability of his theory. 'But surely, if he felt compelled to confess something so egregious as killing his step-daughter, why has he lied about so much since? Why doesn't he admit to us what he did? Doesn't sound to me that he feels genuine remorse. And isn't that what's required, in religious terms I mean?'

Hood let out a deep sigh. How could he explain the concept to an agnostic like his sergeant? 'The opposite of sin is not virtue, Wendy, but freedom. We still have the freedom to do what we want, even to sin again. If Dominic had persuaded Newby to come to us on the twenty-sixth and confess responsibility for Hannah's death, it's always possible that he had a fundamental change of heart, especially if he no longer thought he was at death's door. He would be risking a great deal, even imprisonment, if he came to us. If he panicked and changed his mind, that is precisely what may have led to a confrontation with the priest.'

'That's as may be, but as I've pointed out before, we presently have no evidence that Newby confessed anything to Father Dominic.'

'And we never will,' agreed Hood, 'unless he makes a further confession, this time to us.'

A knock on the door interrupted further discussion. Wendy Knight got to her feet and answered it. Martha Morton was standing there. She appeared to be very nervous as she acknowledged the chief inspector. 'You wanted to see me again, Mr Hood?'

Hood asked her in and invited her to take a seat at the kitchen table. 'Just a couple of things, Mrs Morton. Nothing for you to concern yourself about unduly.' He glanced at Knight, who took out her notebook and pen from her bag, pulled up the remaining chair and sat down as Hood began his questioning.

'I was hoping you could enlighten me as to why you accepted your present job with Sir Robert. Given your previous employment, you seem somewhat over qualified to work as a housekeeper, even in a household like Sir Robert's.'

'What do you mean?' There was more than a hint of apprehension in her voice.

'Well, you were deputy manager of a large hospice in north London. Was there a particular reason why you came here? I don't suppose it would have meant an increase in salary?'

'You've been checking up on me, have you?'

'We have been checking up on everyone, not just you.'

Mrs Morton hesitated before she replied. 'I've already given Sergeant Knight my explanation. I don't see why it is necessary to repeat what I said.'

Hood then asked her about her employment in Milton Keynes. 'But before the hospice, you worked as a PA and company secretary, did you not? Dowlas Logistics? A job you left out of your CV.'

The housekeeper's expression changed. She seemed uneasy that this aspect of her past life was being raised. 'That was a long time ago, Mr Hood. It can't have any bearing on your investigation.'

Hood did not agree. 'We know that the chairman and managing director was and is Arthur Newby. That's correct, isn't it?'

The housekeeper blushed slightly. 'He always called himself Harry to me.'

'Did he?' Hood shot a knowing look at Knight. Those initials on the sacristy calendar came instantly to mind. 'How well did you know him?' he continued.

She sat up straight in her chair. 'What do you mean, exactly?'

'Let's not beat about the bush, Mrs Morton. We are all adults here. Your relationship with him went well beyond the professional, didn't it?' Hood appreciated he had no real evidence to support what he was suggesting. He was taking a punt. Would it prove successful? The housekeeper looked down. She shifted in her chair and mumbled her reply.

'I don't see what that has to do with anything. It was all a long time ago.'

Hood had hit home. He glanced towards Knight then looked directly at Mrs Morton. 'Indulge me, please. I have no wish to embarrass you. But I need to know.'

She looked up. There was a hint of defiance in her tone. 'All right; we had an affair. I was twenty-nine at the time and unmarried. He promised he would leave his wife, but he never did, of course. I was warned about him, but, of course, I thought I knew better. It seems I wasn't the first. So I resigned and went to work for a rival company in Bedford. That's where I met my husband. Another blunder on my part.' She paused then half-smiled. 'I'm certainly very good at choosing Mr Wrong.'

'Mr Newby lives quite close to here. Are you aware of that?'

She did not answer.

'It's very important Mrs Morton. Do you know he lives – with his wife – in Stanton Harwood?'

She struggled to answer. 'What if I do?'

'Have you had any contact with him since you came here?'

She picked up her bag and searched for a cigarette but found none. 'Neither of us smoke,' said the chief inspector. He had no intention of letting Martha Morton off the hook. She released her hold on her bag, leaving it on the table.

'I suppose I have no option but to tell you.' She put her hands together and breathed out heavily before she continued. 'I was in Northampton in early March. My car was being serviced and I had a bit of time to kill so I caught a bus into the town centre to do some shopping. I was near the County Hall when I stopped at a nearby café for a coffee. It was full inside so I sat at a table outside. It was quite sunny and dry, but cold. As I was waiting for my coffee, a couple approached and sat down at an adjacent table. I didn't recognise the man, not at first, but I recognised the woman immediately. It was Mrs Newby.'

'You knew what she looked like?' queried Hood.

'I'd never met her, but Harry Newby had a photograph of her on his desk in the office. She hadn't changed. It was the expression on her face that I recalled more than anything else and those ice-cold blue eyes. He, on the other hand, had changed markedly, but not for the better. As I said, at first I didn't recognise him. If he hadn't been with his wife

338

I would probably never have made the connection. She grew impatient when the waitress didn't appear and went into the café, presumably to order something. It was only then, when I noticed he was staring at me, that I knew for sure who he was. He looked dreadful. Much thinner and very haggard. He'd lost a lot of hair, too.'

'What did you do?'

'He was only a few feet away from me. My coffee arrived and I spoke to him. I asked him how he was and he told me he was very ill. He didn't expect to last much longer.' She looked down. 'He said he had terminal cancer. I don't understand why, but it really upset me. He told me not to distress myself and asked where I was living. I couldn't see any reason not to tell him. He then asked for my phone number. I wrote it down on a bit of paper and handed it to him. I can't think why I did that, but I did. He said he realised he had treated me badly and wanted to make it up to me.'

'Did anything else happen?'

'Not really, no. His wife came back carrying two coffees. She must have seen me talking to him. She gave me a very icy stare. I'm not sure if she recognised me. I drank my coffee in silence then left and went to finish my shopping in Marks and Spencer.'

'Did you hear from him again?'

She hesitated. 'Yes. He telephoned me and I met him for lunch, once and only once. That was, what, a few days after he telephoned. He repeated that his cancer was not getting any better. I felt so sorry for him and he still looked quite dreadful. And he hardly ate anything. He'd lost so much weight l could still hardly believe it was him.'

'Your coming here to Easton Grange had nothing to do with him, then?'

She answered immediately. 'Absolutely not. I had no idea when I came here that he still lived at Stanton Harwood. It was just a coincidence. I was never invited to his home when we we're seeing each other.'

'But you knew he lived in the area when you came here?'

'Yes, but I didn't think it mattered. I never expected to see him again. Back in ninety-three he always kept personal things from me. He was very careful about keeping his wife and family out of our relationship. I never even knew his home telephone number. He was ex-directory back then and he made it a rule that he was never to be phoned at home, so no one in the office knew his number. We always met in a hotel or in my flat just outside Milton Keynes, occasionally in the office after working hours.'

'Did you re-kindle your affair?' asked Knight. The detective sergeant's question was not solely prompted by the investigation into Father Dominic's death. She simply wanted to know.

Mrs Morton gave Knight a hard look. 'No we did not. He didn't ask, not then anyway, and I wouldn't have agreed had he done so. And he was hardly physically capable of playing the role of the unrequited lover. It's all in the past, as far as I'm concerned.'

'Did he phone you again?'

'Yes. He said he wanted to see me again. I told him I didn't think it was a good idea. He also wanted an assurance that I hadn't told anyone about our affair. I thought it was an odd request after all this time.' She paused and looked down. 'I promised him I wouldn't tell anyone, although one or two people at Dowlas must have known about us.' She looked up and smiled. 'Harry wasn't always as discreet as he thought he was. He was always phoning me at work which drew the attention of colleagues. And he didn't come to Milton Keynes very often before the affair started. That all changed. There were also a few comments – not very nice ones – when I was made company secretary.'

'Had you seen him or heard from him in the ensuing years?'

'Not until I saw him in Northampton, no. Our parting back in ninety-three was anything but civilised. I was very angry with him at the time. I thought he'd been using me and I told him exactly what I thought of him. He even used the death of his daughter as an excuse. He said he couldn't leave his wife because of what had happened to Hannah.'

Hood and Knight looked at each other.

'You knew about the accident?'

'Oh yes. We all did. He was really upset about it. He said it was all his fault.'

Hood was now very interested. 'What do you mean?'

'He was late picking her up, or so he said. She'd been at a birthday party. I remember the details from reading about the inquest a few months later in the *Chronicle and Echo*. There was quite a gap in time between the accident and the inquest.'

'That's not unusual,' said Hood. 'The investigation would have taken some time.'

'Had you ever met his daughter?' asked Knight. 'Actually, she was his step-daughter.'

The housekeeper looked away. 'Well, did you?' persisted Knight.

Eventually Mrs Morton replied. 'I can't see how it's relevant, but I did meet her, yes. And I thought she was his daughter. He never mentioned her being his step-daughter. He brought her into the office during her school holidays. Work experience. It was all the rage back then. She was very bright and very good looking. Quite beautiful in fact.'

Hood intervened. 'You saw her more than once, then?'

The housekeeper nodded. 'She came in for three days. That meant he came into the office for the whole day, which was unusual. We saw quite a lot of her during that period.'

'He was in the office too?'

'Yes. He brought her in each morning and took her home in the afternoon, apart from the Friday.'

'What happened on the Friday?'

She sighed. 'It was all very embarrassing. He had booked a taxi to take her home on the Friday because he was seeing me that evening. He told his wife he was working late, or so he claimed. We thought Hannah had gone, but she came back unexpectedly because she had left her phone behind. She saw us together in his office.' She looked away.

'And?'

'There was a large couch in his office. She saw him being, er, quite intimate with me. Everyone else had gone home.'

'What was her reaction?'

'She was shocked and screamed at him, turned about and rushed out of the room. She even forgot to take her phone. He chased after her. I didn't see him again that night. He phoned me later to apologise, but that was the beginning of the end for us.'

'She had a mobile phone of her own?'

'Yes. They weren't as common as they are now and quite expensive. Harry bought it for her; the latest model, a Motorola. I remember she showed it to me. I was thinking of getting one myself so he could contact me more easily. I'd had to rely on him phoning me at my flat or the office to keep in touch. As I said, I was not allowed to phone him.'

'Can you remember when this was?'

'Oh, yes. The week before she was killed. That's what finished us. He said it couldn't go on. Not after his daughter died. That's why I handed my notice in. There was a bit of a complication because I was the company

341

secretary, but I'd gone by the end of August. He paid me quite a generous leaving package, more than I was entitled to; he obviously didn't want any comebacks.'

Hood reflected on what she had said. 'Why did you agree to meet up with him for lunch after the way he'd treated you?'

She sighed then gave Hood a rueful look. 'Because I'm too bloody soft, I suppose.' She paused, relaxed a little and gently shook her head. 'He told me he was dying. He thought he only had a few weeks left.' Her eyes now filled with tears. 'He sounded so frightened. He was quite terrified at the prospect, you know, absolutely petrified. I suppose that opened old memories. I was very much in love with him back then.'

'Have you ever seen him here?' asked Hood.

'At the Grange? You mean to speak to?'

'Not necessarily, no. Just caught sight of him, perhaps?'

'You know that he's been here, do you?'

Hood pushed her hard. 'That's what I'm trying to establish.'

'No, I haven't seen him here. And he's never been to my cottage in the village. But I did see his Range Rover once. I wondered what it was doing here, but I didn't see him and I didn't speak to him. He had parked right outside here – outside the Gatehouse. I thought he might be seeing Father Dominic. It was in the late afternoon. I walked past on my way to my cottage but I didn't catch sight of either of them.'

Hood gave Knight a knowing look.

'You've never mentioned this before,' observed the detective sergeant. 'Are you sure it was his Range Rover?'

Mrs Morton showed a flash of irritation. 'Yes, of course I'm sure. He has a personalised registration number; his initials. I teased him about that when we had lunch together.'

'Why did you not mention this yesterday?'

'I didn't think it was important. No one asked me anything about Newby or his Range Rover.'

Hood continued to press her. 'When did you see the Range Rover? Can you remember? It may be important.'

'It was a few days after I'd had lunch with him. I can certainly tell you when we met for lunch. I made a note in my diary.' She searched through her bag, produced a small diary and flicked through the pages. 'It was March the twenty-seventh, the Wednesday before Easter. The Range Rover must have been here the following week. I went to my sister's in London over Easter.'

'So, if anyone rang you over the Easter week-end, you would not have been there to answer?'

'Not before I got back on the Sunday evening, no. And it was fairly late when I arrived home.'

'Early April, then, when you saw the Range Rover?'

'I believe so, yes.'

'Thank you. Have you ever seen a maroon Jaguar parked here?'

'No, I was asked about that before. I haven't noticed one, not here.'

'Anywhere else?'

'I don't think so.' She looked directly at Hood. 'What is this all about, Chief Inspector? I'm not involved in any way with Father Dominic's death and I'm sure Harry Newby isn't either. He was a louse with me; an absolute bastard, but I can't imagine him killing anyone. He wouldn't have it in him. He couldn't even pluck up the courage to tell his wife about us.' She hesitated, as if a sudden thought had struck her. 'You're not going through all this with me because he's died are you?'

Hood shook his head. 'No, he's very much alive, Mrs Morton. When did you last hear from him?'

'Three weeks or so after I'd seen his Range Rover here. Towards the end of April. He phoned me at my cottage. That would have been the second or third time, I can't really remember. He certainly wanted to see me again but I refused. I asked him what he was doing here a few weeks before. He was reluctant to tell me. I asked him if he was seeing Father Dominic but he didn't reply.'

'But he didn't deny being here?'

'No, he didn't, not in so many words. He seemed a bit shocked at the suggestion when I told him I'd seen his Range Rover parked outside the Gatehouse, but I didn't pursue it. I thought it was none of my business. I told him in no uncertain terms that I didn't want him coming here. I didn't want my affair with him to come out any more than he did. I haven't heard from him since.' She gave Hood a wry smile. 'He also asked me not to mention to anyone that I'd met up with him.'

'That may be helpful, thank you. I understand you were away the week-end of the sixth and seventh of July?'

She checked her diary again. 'Yes. I went to London to see my sister. My husband had been giving her grief. I got back on Sunday night.'

Hood glanced towards Knight. 'Anything else, Sergeant Knight?'

Wendy Knight shook her head. 'Oh, just one thing, sir. Could Mrs Morton confirm that her maiden name was Goring, Martha Elizabeth Goring?'

The housekeeper nodded. Knight looked at Hood. 'I'll take a further statement from Mrs Morton. If anything else occurs, I'll make sure it's recorded in her statement.'

'Do I have to make another one?' moaned the housekeeper. 'I really don't want my relationship with Harry Newby to come out.'

'I'm afraid so, Mrs Morton. Detective Sergeant Knight will not keep you over long and we will be as discreet as we possibly can.'

CHAPTER FORTY-FIVE

Hood arrived at Mid-Shires police headquarters in Leicester early on Thursday morning. The chief was in London attending an important ACPO meeting. He had left his apologies and his congratulations. Hood was not put out. He'd waited long enough for his promotion. The absence of the chief constable hardly worried him. He was photographed, smiling, with the deputy chief constable, who congratulated him and seemed delighted when he told her about the discovery of the Powdrell chalice. She suggested that after the forensic examination had taken place later in the day, Hood should be photographed with it and a copy sent to her. That a senior officer had found such an important historical artefact was something she thought should be celebrated, publicly. She was convinced the chief constable would agree. Hood was not so sure. He hoped he had persuaded her to keep any such photograph under wraps until he had solved Father Dominic's murder. The last thing he wanted was a media frenzy about the discovery of the chalice.

'And please don't say anything to the press office,' he had said. 'I don't trust them an inch after they disclosed we had probably found the murder weapon.'

The DCC was not so pleased when it came to the murder investigation. It had only been a week since the body of the deceased had been discovered, but she was under immense pressure. The media had made the investigation its number one story and were demanding another press conference. While the press conference arranged for Friday morning would be taken by Chief Superintendent Coupland, Hood, as SIO, was to make sure he attended. Any developments were to be discussed with Coupland beforehand.

Mrs Newby, too, had been as good as her word. She had complained by telephone to one of the assistant chief constables alleging that her very sick husband was being harassed by Hood and his team of officers. When Hood fully explained his dealings with Mr and Mrs Newby, the DCC nodded sagely and simply repeated her advice about the overriding importance of discretion, especially when dealing with someone of Newby's standing. Discretion was her middle name, and it had certainly stood her in good stead. She would, no doubt, make chief constable one day having carefully avoided anything too controversial throughout her years of service. Hood merely smiled and assured her that he would arrest Newby only if the results of the DNA examination of the blood found in the boot of the Jaguar came back with a match, unless, of course, some other solid piece of evidence emerged before then.

He then returned to Easton Grange and met up with Nigel Mullen and DS Knight in the sacristy. As he had anticipated, both Milmo and Grantham requested permission to be present while the chalice was examined. Anything to get a second look at it. Hood gave his permission. Sir Robert, as the chalice's custodian and probable owner, insisted he should be there too. Hood nodded his approval. Wendy Knight, who was seeing it for the first time, gasped in amazement as the chalice was removed from the safe, uncovered and placed on the polished top of the sideboard.

'Are those stones real?' she asked, echoing what Helen Swanson had said when the chalice was first unveiled. 'They can't be. Look at the size of those rubies.'

'Quite real,' insisted Grantham, who could hardly take his eyes off the chalice. 'And the hallmarks tell us approximately when it was made. It's ironic, isn't it? This chalice may well have been given to the monastery at Glastonbury by that old monster Henry the Eighth himself. Of course, great things were expected of him in fifteen hundred and nine when he came to the throne. His egoism and cruelty developed later.'

'Do you think he could actually have presented it to the Abbey?' asked Father Milmo. 'Would there not have been something engraved upon it if it came from the King?'

'Not necessarily,' replied Grantham, adopting his usual didactic tone. 'There may not have been time, especially if it were a sudden whim on Henry's part to make a gift of it. It could originally have been made for his own Chapel Royal; it probably was. I can't think of another pre-reformation chalice as large or as fine as this which strongly suggests it has a royal pedigree. Henry often acted on the spur of the moment, both when in generous mood and when wrathful. If it were a gift from the King, it would probably have been intended to mark his coronation. He liked to appear a generous sovereign in those early days and as a great supporter of the church; Defender of the Faith and all that. I doubt if anyone else could have afforded such a magnificent gift.'

'But his title from the Pope came much later didn't it?' said Sir Robert.

'It did, but he liked to believe he was a loyal supporter of the church well before then.'

'But why Glastonbury? Why not present it to Westminster Abbey? That's where his coronation took place.'

'Why not Glastonbury?' replied Grantham. 'It had associations with the Kings of England going back centuries, right to the time of the mythical Arthur and before. I suspect it was that which appealed to him.'

'I've certainly never seen anything like it,' whispered Nigel Mullen, as he swabbed the chalice. 'It must be worth a king's ransom. There, finished. You can put it back in the safe now, after the photographs have been taken. I certainly don't want the responsibility of looking after it.'

Hood went back to the Gatehouse with Detective Sergeant Knight after reluctantly having his photograph taken standing next to the chalice with Sir Robert. He gave strict instructions that the prints and the negatives were to be returned to him. He didn't trust the DCC to keep the story of the chalice's recovery out of the press. But he appreciated that because the find had to be reported to the Coroner, there was a risk of its discovery becoming known, possibly before the murder of Father Dominic was solved.

DC Renfrew appeared minutes later with the print-out from Companies House, promised from the day before. Hood perused the documents quickly. They fully supported what Martha Morton had told them. She had officially ceased to be company secretary of Dowlas Logistics on 31 August 1993. David Howarth, who was also a shareholder, had taken over. He was to turn out to be a cousin of Mrs Newby. Although he had subsequently retired as an employee in 1999, he had retained his shares which represented 3 per cent of the share capital. He was now living abroad in the south of France. Renfrew had not yet managed to contact him or any of the other employees who had worked with Martha Goring (as she then was) back in 1993. The print-out also showed all the changes in the management of the company, including in 1992 the introduction of Mrs Newby as a director. But Arthur Newby remained the majority shareholder; he owned 50 percent of the shares. His wife held 40 percent of the stock of the holding company and a pension fund the remaining 7 percent. Newby and his wife remained as directors along with an accountant who had been put on the board at the insistence of the pension fund. The Newbys, assuming they acted together, retained complete control of the business. Renfrew had totted up the debts of the various subsidiary companies and assessed their profitability. All the businesses operated profitably, but on very fine margins. A significant amount was owed to the bank, secured as it was on the Newby's home and other assets owned by Mrs Newby alone. But the value of the company was considerable. If Newby were to sell his shares, he would have become immensely rich.

'We need to see some of the employees who worked with Martha,' said Hood. 'I want to know everything that was going on there back in ninety-three. Let's get on with it.'

CHAPTER FORTY-SIX

After attending the press conference on Friday morning at Wootton Hall, Hood returned to Campbell Square and spent the rest of the morning preparing for the interview with Arthur Newby later in the day. He was pleased with Chief Superintendent Coupland's handling of the press briefing, despite the demands made by some of the journalists present. Nothing had been disclosed about the finding of the Powdrell chalice or the police interest in Arthur Newby. Coupland had handled the questions with consummate professionalism, much to the annoyance of many of the reporters. They took exception merely to being told that progress was being made. The only new information they were given was that Philip Southall was not considered a suspect in the murder of Father Dominic. A further press conference was promised for the following Wednesday. Any significant developments would be disclosed before then if considered appropriate.

Alone in his office, Hood read and re-read the witness statements, in particular, when it eventually arrived, the helpful statement Knight had obtained earlier that morning from Charles Buchanan. Buchanan's hand written account was more than he could have hoped for. The barrister certainly had a good memory. He vividly recalled his conversation with Hannah Newby before she left the birthday party on 24 July 1993. She had not only told him that she did not want to leave as early as she had been instructed, but also revealed she was still angry with her step-father because of what she had witnessed at his office the previous week. She had gone into considerable detail. Buchanan also recalled that Hannah had said she had not told her mother what she had witnessed because she did not want to upset her, but she was weighing up in her mind whether she should do so. Neither did she want her step-father to drive her home. She had spent the previous week trying her best to avoid him. He had begged her more than once not to tell her mother what she had seen. She had told Buchanan that he was picking her up at eleven o'clock. Desperate to avoid being alone with him, she had asked Buchanan if he would drive her home instead. He felt he had to refuse; he did not think he was safe to take charge of his mother's Volvo because of the champagne he had consumed earlier in the evening. Interestingly, he had no recollection of Hannah saying that she had to ring home to remind her step-father to collect her.

Over the years that had passed, it had crossed his mind more than once that if he had taken Hannah home, she might still be alive. When asked why he had not mentioned the details of their conversation before, he emphasised how upset Newby had seemed when he arrived at Lonsdale Hall at a quarter to midnight. He was almost in tears, desperately seeking information about his daughter. He hadn't the heart to mention what Hannah had said to him and he had assumed that she had found someone else prepared to give her a lift home. He didn't think what Hannah had told him was particularly relevant and the officer taking his statement had never asked him for any details of their conversation. He repeated that he could not definitely identify the vehicle which Hannah had got into five minutes or so after she'd left him, although he had the impression it was a four by four. He added that he had not seen her step-father before a quarter to midnight.

'How do we play it, sir,' asked Knight when she joined Hood in the basement at Campbell Square, forty minutes before the interview was due to take place.

'I'm not sure,' replied Hood. 'I intend to mention the accident in which Hannah was killed just to see his reaction, but I'm in two minds how far we should go with it.' DC Bradley was with her. Hood had agreed he could sit in providing he remained silent. It would be an interesting learning experience for him.

'What about Swanson? He's in the station and is anxious to see Newby being interviewed.'

'I can understand why, but four officers in the room at the same time will be too much. It might cause Newby to go "no comment." I want to tease his account from him, not intimidate him. What's Swanson doing here anyway? He's on leave today, isn't he?'

Knight shrugged her shoulders. 'Waiting for his wife, sir,' said Bradley. 'She's having a driving lesson in Northampton. He's driving her home.'

'Well, I'm sorry, but he'll have to miss out this time.'

As half past three approached, Gerald Sewell, Newby's solicitor, asked to see Hood in private. Hood hesitated but agreed to the request. He asked Knight and Bradley to leave the room. After congratulating Hood on his promotion, Sewell then raised an issue which he asked should remain confidential.

'I'm not sure I can agree to that. It very much depends what it is,' said Hood.

'I understand your reaction, Superintendent, but it concerns my client's health. I suppose I shall have to disclose it anyway. I think you're aware he saw his oncologist on Wednesday?'

'Yes. Have there been developments?'

'Unfortunately, yes. The news he was given some months ago was, how shall I put it, over optimistic. There are indications that his cancer has returned. Arrangements have been made for him to undergo a new type of scan. It will mean him attending a private hospital in London. These new scanners are very rare in hospitals at the moment.'

'A new type of scanner?'

'Yes. Positron Emission Tomography. I'm not sure how it works but it uses radiation to show activity in the body on a cellular level. It should confirm whether his cancer has returned, and, if it has, to what extent. His blood tests were not particularly encouraging, and there have been other indications. I have noticed myself that his health seems to have deteriorated over the last few days. His wife, incidentally, is blaming it on what she describes as your harassment of him.'

Hood frowned. 'I've heard that suggestion before from her. In fact, I have been very restrained in my dealings with your client because of his illness, but what you have said doesn't sound hopeful.' He hesitated. 'I never asked him where his cancer is located. I suppose that's confidential is it?'

'There's no reason you shouldn't know,' replied the solicitor. 'Oesophageal; not one with a particularly high success rate, I'm afraid, but he remains hopeful. Mr Newby has always been one for playing the long odds. And these are very long odds, especially if it has metastasised.'

'Are you asking me to postpone the interview?'

'No. My client feels he can deal with things today and satisfy you he had nothing to do with the homicide you are investigating.'

'Does he now? You appreciate he's not been particularly truthful with me so far?'

'You think so? I believe he'll explain everything, now that you know about his previous relationship with Martha Goring. By the way, Mr Hood, he believes his wife still doesn't know about his affair and she's here in the police station with him.' He grimaced. 'You will appreciate the delicacy of the situation. She seems to think she can sit in on the interview. I have explained the position to her and told her that is not how things are done. I have suggested she should go home, but she insists on staying. She's not one for listening to advice.'

'When is this scan due to take place?'

'It was organised yesterday, but the first available date is next Tuesday. It's not easy to get an appointment. It's also quite an expensive procedure which has to be paid for, but that isn't a problem for Mr Newby. He's a private patient, although he usually sees his oncologist at the hospital in Milton Keynes.'

'Next Tuesday is when I expect to get the DNA results on the blood trace found in the boot of the Jaguar. I'll bear what you say in mind, but I'm afraid I can't keep this from my immediate team in the longer term. It wouldn't be in your client's interests for me to do so. I will keep it to myself for the moment and if I need to mention it to DS Knight, I can assure you it will go no further than her. It would also be helpful if your client would agree to disclosure of his medical records. If you want me to bear his health in mind, I need to know what he says is supported by his doctors.'

'I'm grateful. But I doubt he would lie about such a serious matter. I'll take instructions and let you know.'

'There's more disclosure too, Mr Sewell. It's being typed up at the moment. It concerns the accident which involved your client's step-daughter in nineteen ninety-three. You may wish to discuss it with him. I'm prepared to let you see the entire statement my sergeant took from the witness this morning – after it's typed.'

Sewell appeared surprised. 'That can't be relevant, can it? I'm familiar with the details. I acted for the family at the inquest. It quite devastated the both of them, you know. I don't think Mrs Newby will ever get over it.'

Hood did not immediately reply. When he did, he thought he discerned a slight look of apprehension on Sewell's face. 'We may have to disagree about that, sir. The witness spoke to your client's step-daughter just before she left the party. Shall we say four-fifteen to begin the interview?'

CHAPTER FORTY-SEVEN

It was almost five o'clock when the interview began. Hood switched on the tape machine but emphasised that Newby was not under arrest and could leave at any time. He nevertheless cautioned him and made sure he understood his rights in full. He began in a conciliatory tone. 'I'm aware of the developments in respect of your illness, Mr Newby. If you need a break at any time, you just have to ask.' Newby nodded his appreciation as Hood continued. 'I'm also grateful for your signing the consent form so I can see your medical records. I will also require a sample from you for DNA purposes. Nothing to it, just a buccal swab.'

Newby looked slightly alarmed. 'I don't know about that. I shall have to speak to Mr Sewell before I agree to have my DNA all over your systems. How do I know what you'll do with it?'

Hood smiled. 'In the event of no charges being brought, it will be destroyed.'

'Charges? I certainly hope there will be no charges.' Newby paused and shot a glance towards his solicitor who nodded. 'All right then. Subject to anything Mr Sewell advises, I'll do it. I have nothing to hide.'

'Don't feel you have to volunteer,' said Hood, adopting a slightly less friendly tone. 'In the event of a refusal I might have to consider arresting you. You'd have no choice in the matter then.'

Newby raised his voice. There was more than a trace of ill-temper in his response. 'I've just said I'll do it, damn you. What more do you want? Now, can we get on with it?'

Hood noted the sudden outburst of anger. Newby sighed and apologised. 'I'm sorry, Superintendent. I'm not feeling too well. I had some bad news earlier this week. I don't want to be sitting here all night.'

He glanced towards his solicitor and grinned. 'And the meter's running you know. I'm not on legal aid.'

'Don't forget if you need a break...'

'I'll be fine,' he interrupted. 'I'm not going to let this beat me. Never give up; that's my motto.'

Hood nodded. He noticed the determination in Newby's voice and there was what seemed to him to be real hope in the suspect's eyes. Newby was obviously not one for giving up.

'Now, I want to begin by asking you about events in nineteen ninety-three. I'm sure Mr Sewell has been through the disclosure with you. What was the nature of your relationship with Martha Goring in nineteen ninety-three?'

Newby glared at Hood then looked to his solicitor to intervene.

'Is this really relevant, Superintendent?' asked Sewell. 'Mr Newby is prepared to admit he had a brief affair with this woman, but I fail to see how it has any bearing on your present investigation.'

Wendy Knight cringed at the solicitor's use of the phrase "this woman," but she bit her tongue and said nothing.

'I'd be grateful if you would bear with me,' replied Hood. 'I don't want to appear intrusive, but I believe it may have some relevance. It ceased in the late summer of nineteen ninety-three, didn't it?'

'It did,' replied Newby. 'And has not been resurrected. I want that clearly understood. I'm hardly fit enough for that sort of thing at the moment.' He grinned, indulgently.

'I understand that your step-daughter came across you and Martha Goring indulging in precisely that sort of thing – some very intimate behaviour. Hannah was attending your office in Milton Keynes as part of her work experience programme, I believe?'

Newby appeared concerned. 'Who told you that?' He seemed more than a little anxious. 'Oh, you've been talking to Martha; you've located her, have you?' He paused. His anxiety turned into annoyance. 'Anyway it wasn't that intimate. I was fully clothed. If Hannah hadn't burst into the room...'

'But Hannah was very upset, wasn't she?'

Newby took a deep breath. 'I suppose she was. It was the shock. I followed her out and calmed her down. I dismissed the taxi and took her home myself. She agreed not to tell her mother; I agreed not to see Martha again. That was the bargain we struck.' He heaved a sigh. 'You need to understand, Mr Hood. Eleanor and I were going through a difficult patch at the time. I couldn't afford a divorce; the financial consequences would have been ruinous. I was mortgaged up to the eyeballs and Hannah was fully aware that her mother and I were not getting on. She had the good sense not to want to make matters worse.'

'You kept to the bargain, did you?'

'More or less. Martha was the company secretary so I had to see her once or twice, but the affair definitely came to an end. She resigned not long afterwards as I recall and had gone before the end of August.'

'Did your wife have any suspicions you were sexually involved with Martha Goring?'

Newby's anxiety returned. 'No, not as far as I know. We were very discreet. And she still doesn't know about it. I don't want her finding out either. Not now; not when I need her support during my illness. I can't face this thing on my own, I really can't.'

Newby's distress was now palpable, but Hood continued with his questioning. 'You made contact with Martha earlier this year, didn't you?'

Newby paused and looked to his solicitor.

'My client will be answering no further questions about his relationship with Martha Goring, or Morton, as she now calls herself.'

'I'm not particularly interested in their relationship,' replied Hood, sharply. 'Martha Morton says she saw your client's Range Rover at Easton Grange three months before the priest was murdered.'

'So, she has been talking, has she?' interrupted Newby. 'I hope you're not going to fall for anything she says. She's hardly a disinterested witness you know. She has it in for me for obvious reasons.'

'We have spoken to Martha and taken a full statement from her. In the event of a charge it will be disclosed in full. She works for Sir Robert, but you already know that, don't you?'

'I didn't, but that explains a few things. That's the connection with Easton Grange is it? What did she say? I want to see her statement now.'

Hood ignored the demand and pressed on. 'All in good time. You told me when I saw you at your home you had not visited Easton Grange recently. I would remind you that we have cogent evidence that your Mark Two Jaguar was seen at Easton Grange on the seventh of July while Father Dominic was saying Mass in the chapel.'

Newby slammed his hand down on the table. 'The evidence of an eleven-year old boy taking down car numbers? That's what you're relying on? Give me strength, man.' He shook his head. 'He must have made a mistake. I wasn't there and my wife can confirm it.'

'Are you still saying you have not visited Easton Grange this year?'

'I have not been there for ages. I told you, I went with my wife to a reception when Robert Southall was High Sheriff and that was it.'

'I think you've been there since then, Mr Newby.'

A look of astonishment crossed Newby's face. 'Oh, I don't think so.'

'Didn't you attend Lady Southall's funeral?'

Newby seemed taken aback for a moment. 'What if I did? That was at the Cathedral in Northampton.'

'You went, with your wife, to the reception afterwards at the Grange, didn't you?'

'Did we? He paused, breathed out and nodded. 'You're right, we did. I'd forgotten. We only popped in for form's sake. Robert was a fellow magistrate. Stayed for about a quarter of an hour to give our condolences. We then left.'

'The reception was held in the Long Room I believe?'

'I think so, yes. There were a lot of people there.'

'So, you are familiar with it? The Long Room, I mean.'

'If going there twice in six years is being familiar with it, I suppose I am, yes.'

The solicitor interrupted. 'When was Lady Southall's funeral?'

Hood looked towards Knight for the exact date. 'Twenty-second of November nineteen ninety-nine. Less than three years ago.'

'You are aware that Father Dominic's body was found in the Long Room, in the recently discovered priest-hole?' continued Hood.

'Of course I am,' replied Newby, angrily. 'It's been all over the bloody media. The world and his wife knows that.'

Hood moved on. 'You were educated at Melford College, were you not?'

Newby nodded. 'I've already admitted that when I saw you earlier this week.'

'But you denied having any dealings with Father Dominic, despite the fact he was housemaster of St Benet's House while you were a pupil there. Head of house weren't you?'

'I told you the truth. I knew him back then, but I've had no dealings with him in the last thirty odd years.'

'You take the college magazine?'

'What if I do? I usually only skip through it. I'm not over interested in goings on at my old school. I've only been back there once and that was twenty years ago.'

'But you still pay your subscription, obviously?'

'It's only ten pounds a year. I pay it by standing order. I've never got round to cancelling it. I certainly will after all this nonsense.'

Hood produced the millennial edition. 'Would you look at page fifty-nine? For the benefit of the tape, I am showing the suspect a copy of the *Melford Recorder,* Exhibit AS03.' Newby flicked through it. 'You will see there's a brief report that Father Dominic was coming to Easton Grange as Sir Robert's chaplain.'

Newby shrugged his shoulders. 'Never noticed it. And if I did, why should that concern me?'

'Are you telling me you did not know that Father Dominic was living only ten or eleven miles from Stanton Harwood?'

'That's exactly what I'm telling you. I don't read this from cover to cover you know.'

He threw the magazine on to the table. Hood produced the sacristy calendar from his file, contained as it now was in a transparent protective covering. He handed it to Newby, opened for the month of July.

'You see those initials for the date of the twenty-sixth of July?'

'Yes.'

'H N? Harry Newby perhaps?' Had you made an appointment to see Father Dominic that Friday?'

'Certainly not. They could refer to anyone. Anyway, I'm known as Arthur Newby, not Harry.'

'But you've already told me Mr Newby, when you were at Melford College, you preferred Harry to Arthur. Did Father Dominic know you as Harry? Martha certainly did.'

Newby did not reply. Hood turned to the question of Newby's vehicles.

'You have a black Range Rover with a personalised plate?'

Newby sighed. 'Yes, my initials, 190 AWH.'

'When did you acquire it, the personal number plate, I mean?'

'Years ago, why?'

'Has it been on more than one vehicle?'

'Yes.'

'How many?'

'Two, I think. Both Range Rovers.'

'What were you driving in nineteen ninety-three?'

'Ninety-three? A Range Rover. I've had Range Rovers for years.'

'With that registration plate?'

'No, I didn't get the plate until about ninety-six. Cost a bomb too.'

'How come Mrs Morton was able to tell me the registration number on your current Range Rover?'

'No idea.'

'She says she saw your Range Rover outside Father Dominic's cottage in early April, a few days after you had taken her out for lunch in Northampton. She's told us you bumped into each other there some days earlier.'

'Bumped into her? Taken her out for lunch? What is all this? She's lying. Trying to get her own back on me for giving her the push. I've neither seen nor spoken to her since nineteen ninety-three. And I had no idea she was working at Easton Grange.'

'It seems she's waited a long time to get her own back. We are checking calls to her phone.'

'Check away. I never called her. You'll not see a call from my phone in Stanton Harwood to wherever she lives. I guarantee it.'

'You have access to other phones? At your places of work?'

'What if I do. I've hardly been anywhere in months. I've been very ill you know.'

'Do you have a mobile phone?'

'Yes. I can let you have the number if it helps, for exclusion purposes.'

'Only the one?'

'Only the one. I'm not a drug dealer you know.' He laughed. 'Why would I want more than one cell phone?'

Hood ignored the remark. 'She also says you asked her not to divulge to anyone that you and she had an affair.'

'I told you, she's lying.'

'Why did she resign her position at Dowlas Logistics?'

'I don't know. Presumably because I finished my relationship with her. I didn't go into the office in Milton Keynes very often, anyway. You should have heard what she called me when I told her it was all over between us. And she said she would have her revenge on me. You need to remember that Mr Hood. It may be nine years ago, but she definitely threatened me.'

'You gave her a generous leaving package, very generous indeed?'

'Did I? I left that sort of thing to the accountants.'

'You must have signed it off, surely?'

'I don't remember.'

'Let's return to the seventh of July. Where were you that Sunday?'

'At home, with my wife.'

'Your maroon Mark Two Jaguar was seen at the Grange during Mass that very morning. It was still there at twelve noon.'

Newby shook his head and smiled. 'Who says it was? Got any witnesses apart from this boy? He could have got the number anytime or mixed them up.' He sat back in his chair, seemingly satisfied with his explanation.

Hood produced the boy's original note, now in its protective transparent cover.

'For the benefit of the tape, I'm showing Mr Newby exhibit WR 01, the note made by Francis Gilbert on the seventh of July this year.'

Newby took it in his hand for a moment then scoffed. 'He could have done this anytime. And it isn't dated.'

'But it's in the middle of a list of other numbers. All the others have been checked out. They all relate to cars which were at Easton Grange that Sunday during Mass. How could the lad have noted your number otherwise? On your own account, you've hardly taken the Jaguar out on the road since you acquired it.'

'I can't explain it, then. But, of course, I don't have to, do I?' He smirked.

'After Mass had finished, your Jaguar was the last to leave. We also have another witness, the wife of one of my officers actually, who saw a maroon coloured car on its own in the car park. All the other cars had departed by then.'

'Did she get the registered number too?'

'No, she didn't.'

Newby scoffed. 'She doesn't even know the make. I've been through the disclosure with Mr Sewell, you know.'

'I believe you were in the Gatehouse with Father Dominic.'

'You have some evidence to support that statement, Superintendent?' asked the solicitor. 'If you have, I don't think it's been disclosed.'

'At present, it's an inference I draw from the presence of the Jaguar after everyone else had gone. And the fact that Father Dominic was nowhere to be seen either. He occasionally saw people in his cottage. That is a fact.'

'You'll have to do better than that,' said Newby, his confidence growing. 'Let's face it, Mr Hood. All you have is an eleven-year old boy's jottings and my former mistress, who has every incentive to lie. Revenge is a dish best served cold. Isn't that what they say? Not much on which to build a murder case.'

Hood responded quickly 'The blood in the boot of your Jaguar matches Father Dominic's blood group or are you overlooking that?'

Newby swallowed hard before recovering his confidence. 'But is it his blood? And if it isn't, what does that prove?'

'We'll have the DNA results soon enough. What will you say if it is shown to be Father Dominic's blood? If it is, it can't have got there before you owned the vehicle, can it?'

'No comment.'

'Exactly,' interposed the solicitor. 'It's not for Mr Newby to answer hypothetical questions. When you have the DNA results, I'm sure he'll answer for himself, if he needs to.'

Hood continued. 'The forensic experts also noted that the boot had been carefully cleaned and the carpet removed.'

'Can't have been that carefully cleaned if you found some blood,' replied Newby.

'It was in a little crevice. It had clearly been missed by whoever cleaned the boot.'

'Not by me. If I clean something, I do it properly.'

'And the driver's seat and its immediate area had been subject to a similar process, but not the rest of the interior.'

'I've already explained that. I didn't have time to finish the remainder of the interior before it went to Banbury.'

'Why start with the driver's area?'

'Why not?'

Hood shuffled the papers in the case file. He was not making the progress he had anticipated. He decided to change the subject. 'When I saw you earlier in the week, your wife complained about the performance of the police investigation of your step-daughter's death.'

'She was right to do so. I agree with her. They never got anywhere. No one was ever prosecuted.'

'It's because of what she said that I retrieved the file and examined it in some detail. Tell me, was the vehicle you were using at the time examined by the police?'

Newby took a sharp breath. 'How the hell should I know? I told them what I was driving that night and it was always available for them to inspect. It's hardly down to me if they didn't get round to it.'

'Did you have bull bars fitted to it?'

'I certainly had them on one of my Range Rovers. I can't recall if they were on that one. I told you, I've had several over the years. I usually change them after three years. I do a high mileage, at least I did.'

'There's one thing I don't quite follow from my inspection of the file. Perhaps you can help me? Your wife insisted that Hannah left the party at eleven o'clock.'

'That's right. She wasn't over keen on her going at all. I didn't mind one way or the other. She was too cossetted was Hannah, but her mother thought the world of her. She was her mother's daughter all right. What she said went.'

'You say in your witness statement made in nineteen ninety-three that Hannah was supposed to ring you just before eleven?'

'That's what we arranged, yes.'

'Why?'

Newby appeared puzzled. 'What do you mean?'

'You knew where she was. Lonsdale Hall was owned at the time by a friend of yours. You were fellow directors at one time.'

'Larry Lawson, yes. We don't speak these days. He persuaded me to invest in his hotel in Northampton and I had to buy him out of Dowlas to get rid of him. One of the worst financial decisions I ever made, that hotel. He had to sell Lonsdale Hall when his own finances collapsed. He could have taken me down with him if my wife hadn't stood by me.'

'Why not just turn up there and pick her up at eleven?'

Newby began his explanation. 'Eleanor was out at a meeting. I'd had a long day on the golf course. I think I fell asleep. And Hannah didn't ring anyway. She'd left her phone at home. She was always leaving it about the place. He paused and returned to events on 24 July 1993. 'It was about eleven thirty when I set out. I seem to recall from the inquest someone in the village saw me. Mr Sewell reminded me, you have a witness statement to that effect.'

The solicitor nodded his agreement. 'Yes, Superintendent. Mr Stansfield. He recalled seeing Mr Newby driving out of the village around that time. That was clearly established at the inquest.'

'Which way did you go?'

'Along the main road, why? It wasn't that far.'

'In a bit of a rush, were you?'

'I don't think so. I remember there wasn't much traffic about.'

'There's an unclassified road which runs close to the main road. Cuts off the wide bend and avoids the traffic lights.'

Newby's confidence started to dip. He hesitated. 'I know it. Not much more than a farm track. That's were Hannah was found.' He looked sharply at Hood. 'What are you getting at?'

'The accident report concludes that someone must have given Hannah a lift, probably because you were late picking her up.'

Newby sighed. 'Don't remind me. I blame myself. I have done for years. If I'd been on time she'd have been safe. It didn't go unnoticed by my wife either. We nearly parted over it.'

'She blamed you, did she?'

'You can say that again. She felt she needed to blame someone. My wife has quite a harsh side to her character, you know. She doesn't forgive easily and she will have her own way. And seeing as your lot never made an arrest, I copped for it. She hardly spoke to me for months after the funeral.'

'But were you as late as you say? Charles Buchanan says he noticed Hannah getting into what he originally thought was a four by four about five minutes or so after she had left the marquee. That was just after eleven. He'd been talking to her. She was very angry with you and didn't want you picking her up. Had you had another row?'

'Charles Buchanan? Who is he?' Newby looked towards his solicitor.

'Someone at the party. He was speaking to Hannah, just before eleven.'

'Where is this going?' interrupted the solicitor. 'I haven't had time to go through that statement with my client. I've only just received a typed copy.'

Hood did not answer him. He simply pressed on. 'Is it possible, Mr Newby that you did pick her up? That you and she had a row shortly afterwards as you drove back towards Stanton Harwood? Probably about your relationship with Martha. She then insisted on getting out of your vehicle and started to walk home?'

'Absolutely not. What are you suggesting?'

'You drove off and left her. That's what I'm suggesting. You got home. When she didn't turn up and as the time drew near for your wife to get back, you went out looking for her. Your wife would have had something to say if she'd got home before Hannah, wouldn't she?'

'Are you suggesting I ran her down? That I took the short cut, ran into her and left her there to die? How dare you!' He became emotional and started to breathe rapidly.

'I'm not suggesting that at all, Mr Newby. Why have you jumped to that conclusion? I'm suggesting, as you've just admitted, that you felt considerable guilt for her death, not because you were late picking her up but because you had let her out of your vehicle which resulted in her being run down by someone who has never been apprehended.'

Newby appeared quite shell-shocked. Hood had seemingly touched a nerve. His solicitor intervened. 'I thought we were here to be interviewed about the killing of this priest, not the accidental death of Mr Newby's step-daughter? This really won't do Mr Hood. If you persist with this line of questioning I shall have to call a halt and speak to my client in private.'

The solicitor pushed back his chair and folded his arms. Hood did not react; he continued calmly. 'But I think it may be relevant.'

'How?' asked the solicitor.

'Let me explain,' said Hood, softly. 'Earlier this year, Mr Newby was told his condition was thought to be terminal, agreed?'

'Yes,' replied the solicitor. 'Actually, I think it was at the end of last year. Late December, I believe, when he was warned his condition was probably terminal, just before Christmas. He'd already had his second operation. It did not prove as successful as was hoped.' He glanced towards his client who nodded his agreement then suddenly appeared lost. His features became contorted and he was fast losing the colour from his cheeks. He looked around the room and shifted in his seat. His breathing became irregular. He was taking shortened breaths and started to sweat. Hood shot a glance at Knight before continuing.

'I'm suggesting it's possible that having been given such dreadful news, Mr Newby went in search of spiritual consolation. He lost his faith some years ago, or so he told me. Sometimes, when a man is staring death in the face, it makes him think about what he really believes. Coming close to death can have that effect. We all like to think we're immortal, but of course we're not. We all have to die.'

He paused and looked directly at Newby, whose expression seemingly confirmed what Hood had said. The Superintendent continued, leaning towards Newby, narrowing his eyes. 'I'm suggesting you made contact with Father Dominic. You would have seen from your old school magazine that he was living close by. Having renewed your acquaintanceship with him, you disclosed something serious; something that was affecting your conscience; something that may even have required formal absolution. Perhaps a feeling of guilt about Hannah's death? Perhaps something else?' Hood paused again to let what he had said sink in before continuing. 'When you later received much better news that your cancer was thought to be in remission, the prospect of your demise no longer seemed so imminent. Now, I don't' pretend to know what passed between you and Father Dominic, but with your life no longer in the balance, I believe you had second thoughts about what you had disclosed. I suspect you felt the need to make sure whatever it was should never see the light of day. I'm not saying you went to the Grange intent on murder. I suspect an argument of some kind ensued and you lost your temper, picked up the spade which had coincidentally been left nearby and struck out wildly. Whatever you intended, it silenced Father Dominic – permanently. Your secret was now safe.'

Hood paused and looked intently at Newby, then added. 'A maroon Mark Two Jaguar passed through Easton Parva that very night, after the killing had taken place. We have a witness who saw it.'

Newby did not respond other than to look down. Was that panic in his eyes? Not so his solicitor. He seemed almost amused. He shook his head then challenged Hood. 'A witness whom you arrested on suspicion of this very killing, I believe. His credibility will be very much in issue if you persist in this highly speculative theory of yours, Superintendent, which is supported, I emphasise, by no hard evidence at all.'

Newby's increasing distress had not gone unnoticed. 'Your client doesn't seem to think it's so speculative. Look at him.'

Wendy Knight intervened. 'I think Mr Newby is unwell, sir. Perhaps he would like a break?'

Newby looked up and shook his head. He grunted his response. 'I want to get this over with. If Superintendent Hood has any other wild theories, I'd like to hear them. I would like some water though.'

Hood nodded to Bradley who left the room, returning, moments later with a plastic cup of cold water. Newby grabbed it and sipped at it repeatedly. Bradley remained standing. It was clear he had something to say. Hood looked at him pointedly and shook his head. 'It's not a question, sir. It's DC Swanson.'

'What about DC Swanson?' Hood did not hide his irritation at Bradley's intervention.

'He's outside. He has something urgent to tell you.'

Hood let out a deep sigh. 'I'd better hear what he has to say, I suppose. We'll take a short break. Give Mr Newby a chance to recover.'

Detective Sergeant Knight, looked at her watch, stated the time and switched off the tape machine.

CHAPTER FORTY-EIGHT

'Well, what is it Adrian? It had better be important. We'd reached a rather crucial stage in the interview.'

'You can say that again, sir,' said Wendy Knight. 'I think you've got him rattled. On the ropes even. He's got quite a temper on him too.'

'It could be his illness that's playing him up. I think he's in pain from time to time.'

'I don't think that explains everything,' said Knight. 'I think you've put your finger on it. He obviously thought we'd never work it out.'

'Oh, it's "we" now, is it?' He smiled. 'Well Adrian?'

'It's my wife, sir.'

'Your wife?' Hood rolled his eyes. 'What is it this time?'

'She's just walked through reception to meet up with me. She's been having a driving lesson here in Northampton, you know, getting used to heavy traffic. I'm giving her a lift home.'

'Never mind that. What is this important information?'

'The woman in reception, sir. She recognised her. Straight away. No doubt about it.'

'Your wife recognised someone in reception? Recognised her from where?'

'The chapel at Easton Grange. She was there on the seventh of July when Father Dominic said Mass. She doesn't recall whether she was on her own or with someone, but it's definitely her.'

Hood and Knight looked at each other. 'How does she remember her? There must have been several people there that Sunday she didn't know.'

'It's the pearls she's wearing round her throat, like a choker. She's wearing them now. The wife admired them when she saw them on the

367

seventh. She also remembers the woman's very fashionable two-piece suit. Jaeger she thinks and very expensive. It's the same one she was wearing that Sunday.'

'Anything else she remembers?' asked Hood.

'She says the woman was wearing a fairly large spider brooch on the lapel of her jacket; it had what Helen thought was a ruby in its centre. But she's not wearing that today.'

'She's never mentioned this woman before?'

'No, sir. Not to me. But suddenly coming across her like that brought it all back.'

'Mrs Newby,' whispered Knight. 'Now there's a turn up for the books.'

'Is she still sitting in reception now?' asked Hood

'Yes sir,' replied Swanson. 'As far as I know.'

'Waiting for her husband, no doubt,' said Knight.

'Where's your wife now?' asked Hood.

'Upstairs in the squad room. I've advised her not to go back through reception.'

'Good man.' Hood turned and looked for Bradley who was lurking at the end of the corridor.

'Bradley, I want you to go upstairs and take a witness statement from Mrs Swanson. Think you can manage that? This relates to a possible identification, so make sure you go through all the usual criteria.'

'Yes, sir,' enthused Bradley. 'Right away, sir.'

'You go with him, Adrian. Introduce Bradley to your wife, but you must keep apart while the statement is taken. And don't let her go through reception or see the woman again. When you leave, go out the back way.'

'I will, sir.'

The two junior officers disappeared up the stairs. Hood and Knight walked slowly back towards the interview room.

'So, he had an accomplice, did he?' said Knight.

'Not necessarily. Let's not jump to conclusions. But it means we shall have to interview Mrs Newby.' He smiled. 'I think I'll let you handle that.'

'Thanks very much. Supposing she supports her husband's account and says she wasn't there? I'm sure Helen Swanson wouldn't make a mistake, but why would Mrs Newby go to Mass with or without her husband at Easton Grange?'

'I don't know. She's C of E, but happily we live in more ecumenical times. She could well have accompanied him. And if she was with him that Sunday, both of them must have been with Father Dominic in the Gatehouse. There was no one about when Helen noticed the maroon car on its own in the car park.'

'Then she may well know what it is that her husband confessed, not because of anything Father Dominic said, but because Newby may have told her.'

Hood shook his head. 'I don't think he's told her everything that he confessed. Had he told her he had run down her daughter, she would have undoubtedly thrown him under the bus. We'd be investigating his murder not Father Dominic's.'

'But by the seventh, he'd had the good news that his cancer was in remission. He'd have known that for several weeks. Why would he want to see Father Dominic, and more to the point, why would he take his wife with him? Perhaps she was the one who was more worried about his secret getting out?'

Hood nodded. 'You may well be right, Wendy. She wouldn't necessarily know or understand anything about the seal of the confessional. Mind you, if she does support her husband and lie about being there on the seventh, we really will have to put our thinking caps on. I think we may have to make it official and arrest both of them.'

'Helen Swanson doesn't remember anyone being with her, not as far as we know. That's what Adrian's just said. She doesn't appear to have mentioned seeing Newby.'

'Newby wouldn't stand out, not like his wife. He's not exactly memorable in his appearance, is he?'

'Doesn't do anything for me,' smiled Knight. 'She, on the other hand has something about her. A bit of charisma. She'd be noticeable in any company, dressed up to the nines or not. I'll go and take a quick look.'

'Don't let her see you,' Hood called as Knight rushed up the stairs. She returned two minutes later to find Hood pacing the corridor.

'Very smart,' said Knight. 'And Helen's right, she's wearing a pearl choker and what looks like a *very* expensive two-piece suit.'

'She was wearing something like that when I first met her with Bradley but not when you and I saw her subsequently. She was much more casually dressed then.'

'Do we mention what Helen Swanson says when we go back in?'

'Let's play it by ear. We don't know the precise details of what Helen will say, so we can't be too specific. This is going to be very interesting.'

Hood and Knight re-entered the interview room. Newby was still sitting in his chair, his head in his hands. His solicitor was standing close to him. He looked up as Knight closed the door.

'Mr Newby is not at all well, Mr Hood. I think we will have to postpone further questioning. I think he needs a doctor.'

Newby looked up and growled. 'I don't need a doctor. I want to get this over with. I have more important things to worry about at the moment than your screwball theories.'

Hood looked at Knight who shook her head. 'He's not fit, sir. We'll have to suspend the interview.'

Hood said nothing. He switched on the recorder and named those in the room. He repeated what he had said at the outset of the interview. Mr Sewell re-took his seat. Knight sighed, walked around the table and sat next to Hood. She made it clear by the expression on her face that she didn't think the interview should continue. Hood's first words removed her concerns.

'I think Detective Sergeant Knight is right, Mr Newby. I am going to postpone this interview until next week, Wednesday at noon would be convenient, but before I do, I want to deal with one matter that has just come to light.'

The solicitor intervened. 'I've had no disclosure about this, Superintendent.'

'Hardly surprising,' replied Hood. 'The witness is making her statement to DC Bradley as we speak. I don't know the full details myself.' He turned towards Newby. 'Could I ask, is your wife waiting for you in the foyer of this police station?'

'Yes,' said Newby. 'She's driving me home. Mr Sewell has another appointment in Northampton this evening.'

'Then I think you're entitled to know this. Your wife has been identified by a reliable witness as being present at Easton Grange when Father Dominic said Mass on the seventh of July.'

Newby's eyes widened. He seemed stunned.

'Rather demolishes your alibi, don't you think?' continued Hood. 'If you and she were together as you say, you must have been with her. You, I suggest, saw Father Dominic in his cottage afterwards together with your wife.'

Newby shook his head. 'I don't know where your getting this from Mr Hood, but it isn't true. I was at home. Your witness has got it wrong. My wife was at home with me. Why would she attend Mass at Easton Grange? She's not even a Catholic.'

'Does the witness say Mr Newby was there?' asked the solicitor.

Hood hesitated. 'Not so far as I am aware, no. But I propose to invite your client to attend an identification procedure in due course.'

'I'll discuss that with Mr Newby, Superintendent. Now, I think this interview really should be suspended, unless you propose to arrest my client?'

'Not at this stage, no. But I would like Mr Newby to return here next week when the DNA results comes through on the blood found in the Jaguar. I would still like him to give a sample for DNA purposes before he leaves today and it would be helpful if he would agree to have his fingerprints taken. Detective Sergeant Knight will arrange it. It won't take long.'

Newby stood up and nodded. 'If Mr Sewell advises me to do so, I have no objection. I have nothing to hide. I had no involvement in the murder of this priest. I never had any contact with him on the twenty-fourth; I neither saw him nor spoke to him on the seventh of July.' He sighed and held his hand to his lower abdomen, as if he were in pain. 'Until next week, Mr Hood. I hope we can get this sorted by then.'

CHAPTER FORTY-NINE

'He seems very confident,' said Knight as she and Hood spoke in the Superintendent's room half an hour after Newby had left the police station with his wife. He had given a saliva sample for DNA purposes and his finger prints had been taken. Wendy Knight smiled, knowingly 'But I suppose he's used to bluffing his way through difficulties?'

Hood finished reading Helen Swanson's detailed witness statement before he answered. Bradley had certainly made a good fist of it. Mrs Swanson made it clear that she had not seen the woman she recognised sitting in the reception area at Campbell Square in the body of the chapel on 7 July. She had only noticed her outside in the car park after Mass was over, but she had not the slightest doubt it was the same woman. She had particularly noted the pearls around her throat and the spider brooch with what appeared to be a ruby at its centre. Hood ordered a print to be taken from the CCTV in the reception area. It was definitely Mrs Newby who had been sitting waiting for her husband. The CCTV showed the two of them walking away together. Hood looked up, pensively.

'Do you think she was involved with her husband in killing Father Dominic?' asked Knight.

Hood shook his head. 'What would be her motive? As I said before, if she knew about her husband's transgressions in full, she'd surely be more likely to have despatched him than an elderly priest she didn't know.'

He stood up and put his hands in his pockets and sighed. Helen Swanson's evidence, while potentially squashing Newby's alibi, introduced an unwanted complication into the investigation.

'Who knows the evil that lurks in the heart of man?' he murmured, looking at the detective sergeant.

'And woman,' added Knight. 'She may not have been involved directly in the killing but Newby's not physically strong, is he? And she looks as fit as they come. It might explain, I suppose, how the body was moved into the priest-hole. Two of them would have made handling it much easier.'

'That's a possibility, I suppose,' said Hood.

'Odd, though that he didn't admit being at the Grange in April and seeing Martha Morton in Northampton when she said he did,' observed Knight. 'He admitted he'd had an affair with her back in the nineties. He didn't try and cover that up. He could easily have accepted seeing her as she says. It would go a long way to explaining her version of events. By denying he's had any recent contact with her, he's left himself wide open.'

'That could be the mistake which brings him down. Let's hope so.'

'I must say, I'm rather disappointed with him,' added Knight. 'I thought he'd be a bit smarter. He's making it far too easy for us if the DNA comes through.'

DC Renfrew knocked on the door before Hood could comment. He was invited into the room.

'How have you got on, Bill? asked Knight. 'Made any progress?'

Renfrew addressed Hood rather than the detective sergeant. 'I've completed the check of the phone traffic at Martha Morton's cottage, sir. BT were being a bit difficult identifying the callers. I had to get a production order this morning from Judge Mowbray at the Crown Court. DS Knight authorised it, while you were at HQ yesterday and Inspector Bannerman signed off the application.' He acknowledged the detective sergeant with a nod of his head and a grin. 'I'll have the schedule ready for Monday when I get the rest of the information from BT.'

'Anything of interest so far?'

'There's a mobile number ending eight nine seven that called on four occasions during the period under review. BT were persuaded to let me have a schedule of calls this morning. It more or less fits with what the housekeeper told you on Wednesday.' He checked his notebook. 'The number first appears on the nineteenth of March, a Tuesday, then again on the twenty-fourth. On the thirtieth of March there's what seems to be a missed call. There's a bit of a gap, then it appears finally on the twenty-fifth of April. I'll have the precise times the calls were made and how long they lasted by Monday when BT cough up the rest of the information. I should have an updated list of calls by then as well.'

'No later calls?'

'No, sir."

'Do we know who's phone it was that made the calls?'

'No. It looks like it's an unregistered cell phone, but I may get more info from BT about that. But all the calls were between the same two numbers. The land line number is definitely the housekeeper's. And all one way; cell phone to landline.'

'That's why Newby sounded so confident we wouldn't be able to tie him to Martha's phone,' said Knight. 'He used a mobile that can't be linked to him.'

'Unless we find it. There are definitely four calls are there?'

'Yes, sir.'

'Correct me if I'm wrong, Wendy, but didn't the housekeeper only mention receiving three calls from Newby?'

'Two, possibly three is what she said, sir.'

'One of them wasn't answered, of course. She did say she was away over Easter didn't she?'

'She did,' nodded Knight.

'We'll have to wait for further information about that. Anything else, Bill?'

'Yes, sir. DS Knight asked me to make a few inquiries into Mrs Newby. I haven't approached her directly, of course, but I have been checking up on her charitable activities. She's been the chair of the Northampton Women's Support Group for the last six years as well as a couple of other worthy causes. And the patron of the Support Group, for three years, until nineteen ninety-nine, was none other than Lady Southall, Sir Robert's late wife.'

Hood nodded his appreciation. 'So, she knew Lady Southall. Sir Robert told me that his wife took her charitable work very seriously and that she may have known Mrs Newby. Lady Southall wasn't just a figurehead. Mrs Newby could well have been to the Grange several times.'

'Yes, sir,' continued Renfrew. 'Until Lady Southwell died, a few meetings were held at Easton Grange. I've spoken to the police liaison officer who attended some of the later ones. It's quite definite that at least three took place at the Grange when Mrs Newby was there.'

'Another lie, then,' said Hood. 'She must be very familiar with the set up.' He paused. 'If the two of them are involved, it must be one hell of a secret they were trying to preserve if Newby felt the need to silence Father Dominic in such a brutal way.'

'Did you ask about the AGM on the twenty-fourth of July nineteen ninety-three?' asked Knight.

'I did, but WPC Mason was not the liaison officer back then – she was still at school – and Lady Southall did not become the patron until ninety-six. I'll have to make further inquiries, but some of the meetings from ninety-seven until the end of July ninety-nine were definitely held at Easton Grange. She still has the copy minutes.'

'You do that, Bill,' said Hood. 'See what you can uncover. Mrs Newby is certainly becoming a person of interest.'

'Have you got anywhere with the housekeeper's former colleagues at Dowlas Logistics? asked Knight.

'Yes. I've made contact with a Rosemary Carrington. She's retired now, but she remembers Martha Goring very well. Mrs Carrington was the office manager there until just over two years ago. I'm seeing her tomorrow. It will mean a trip to St Albans. That's where she lives now.'

'Good. Let me know if anything comes of it,' said Hood. 'I'm taking the weekend off but ring me at home in the evening if you think it necessary, after seven o'clock, mind, but only if it's something that can't keep. I've promised my wife the week-end will be hers and the children's.'

'Thank you, sir. I will.'

'One other thing before you go. Did we get anywhere with the ANPR cameras, now we know the registered numbers of the Jaguar and Newby's Range Rover?'

'Nothing for the twenty-fourth, sir. But the Range Rover was picked up in Northampton on the day he had lunch with the housekeeper.'

'That should help. Thanks Bill.'

DC Renfrew departed.

'He's done well,' commented Knight. 'But I still don't understand all the lies. Surely, they must have realised we would look into their backgrounds?'

'Let's wait and see what emerges, shall we?' Hood looked at her and smiled. 'I think you could do with a week-end off too, Wendy. You've been over doing things on this inquiry.'

'I'm fine. I have nothing planned for the next two days so I'll be able to have a bit of a rest. I'll see you bright and early on Monday morning.'

CHAPTER FIFTY

After a highly enjoyable but tiring day with his wife and family, Hood was settling down in his favourite armchair to continue reading Charles Dickens' *Barnaby Rudge*. Not his favourite Dickens' novel but there were parts of it that appealed to him. It was only one of two historical novels the master story-teller had penned, the other being *A Tale of Two Cities* which he had recently re-read for the umpteenth time. The children were asleep in bed and he and Sarah had enjoyed a delicious supper and a bottle of excellent Burgundy. The telephone rang. Hood looked up from his book but did not otherwise stir until Sarah called him. She brought the cordless phone into the sitting room.

'Really, Harry, you promised. No police work this week-end.'

'Must be important,' said Hood. 'Whatever it is, it won't affect tomorrow.'

'It better not.' Sarah gave him one of her looks as she thrust the phone into his hand.

'Sorry, to disturb you, sir.' The caller was DC Renfrew. 'But I think you need to know this. Mrs Carrington, who I saw this afternoon, reckoned that Martha Goring was about three months' pregnant when she left Dowlas Logistics. She thinks that Newby must have been the father. She and a couple of other members of staff suspected they were having an affair.'

Hood whistled in disbelief. 'Is she sure about this?'

'Absolutely, sir. She says Martha told her the day before she left Dowlas that she was pregnant but didn't name the father. Rosemary Carrington is quite certain about it. She tried to keep in touch with Martha after she left because she was so concerned about her, but lost contact pretty quickly.'

'Does she know what happened to the baby?'

'No sir. She doesn't know whether Martha had it or sought a termination.'

'You've taken a statement from her?'

'Yes, sir. It will be with you first thing on Monday.'

'Thanks Bill. You've done well. Enjoy the rest of the week-end. I'll see you on Monday.'

Hood returned the cordless phone to its station in the hallway. His wife was waiting for him when he sauntered back into the sitting room, her hands on her hips.

'Well, Detective Superintendent Hood, off out are we?'

Hood shook his head and smiled. 'No. I promised you I would be here for the whole of the week-end, and as you know, I always keep my promises.'

Even he could not keep a straight face. He had broken so many similar undertakings over the years, he had lost count.

'That's a first,' replied Sarah. 'Can't have been very important then?'

'Actually, it was very important. But not much I can do about it until Monday.' He picked up his book as if he intended to continue reading. Sarah looked at him suspiciously before stepping forward, removing the book and putting her arms around him. 'Aren't you going to tell me, then?'

'I thought you wanted this week-end to be entirely free of police work?'

She frowned. 'That telephone call breached the protocol. You can't keep it from me, now. You never know, I might be able to help. Save you calling Wendy.'

'I have no intention of calling Wendy. I told you, it can wait.'

'Come on, Harry. Don't be like that. You've said before how helpful my little insights can be.'

'You were wrong about the chalice being in the safe.' He smiled broadly.

'You never told me there was a locked tabernacle. I'd have suggested searching there if I'd known about it, especially if you had told me it was covered in gold leaf.'

'Of course you would!' He smiled again and tried to take back his book.

Sarah resisted. 'And remember, I want to see this magnificent antiquity.

That's another promise you've made and which I will make sure you keep.'

'You'll get the opportunity. Sir Robert has given permission for it to be used at Father Dominic's requiem a week on Wednesday at Melford Abbey. We are both invited. Let's hope we've solved his murder by then.'

'Tell me, what was said in that phone call?' She handed the book back.

Hood sighed. 'All right. If you must know, it was about the housekeeper, Martha Morton, or Goring as she used to be known.'

'Well?'

'She's an important witness in supporting our case against Newby. She saw his Range Rover parked outside the Gatehouse. That was after she'd had lunch with him in Northampton. She even remembered the registration number. It's from her evidence we draw the inference Newby was inside with Father Dominic. But there's something she seems to have kept from us. That's what Bill Renfrew has just discovered.'

'This is the woman who had the affair with Newby years ago?'

'Yes.'

'Does it matter?'

'It might.' He paused for effect. 'Apparently, she was three months' pregnant when she left her employment with Newby's company in Milton Keynes.'

Sarah drew in her breath. 'Did she tell him?'

'That's what I need to find out.'

Sarah sighed. 'You said yesterday that he gave her a generous severance package.'

'Yes. And I know what you're thinking.'

'Not hard to work out is it? He abandoned her, pregnant and jobless. He probably wanted her to have a termination, the louse. That's what the generous financial settlement was for. All tax deductible too. You men really have it easy.' She paused. 'But this was years ago. How can it be relevant to Father Dominic's death?'

'It may not be. But the fact that she didn't mention it could affect her credibility. Newby said she told him she would have her revenge on him. This could be her way of exacting it, even after nine years.'

'Nursing her wrath to keep it warm, eh? It's understandable she didn't mention it, though Harry. It's not the sort of thing you shout from the rooftops, not even these days.'

'What if she had the child? Imagine Newby's reaction if he discovered he had a son or daughter.' He paused. 'She could have had it adopted, I suppose?'

'Never mind his reaction. What if his wife found out about it? I wouldn't want to be in his shoes if she did. And they had no other children. How old would it be now if it survived?'

'The child? About eight, I suppose.'

'If she did have the child and he or she were adopted, it's the sort of thing that could affect the birth mother psychologically for years. I've come across many examples in my work. Anniversaries of the birth can be particularly traumatic. Thinking back all the time, wondering how the child is. Guilt about giving it up for adoption. It can lead to all sorts of distress, even serious mental illness. Not something I could ever have done, but her circumstances are not my circumstances.'

'She did marry subsequently, but it was not a success. Her husband was unfaithful and addicted to gambling. She's divorcing him at the moment.'

'That could make matters even worse, don't you think? Especially if for whatever reason she couldn't have any more children. Poor woman. Go easy on her Harry.' She paused. 'She's leaving Sir Robert's employment, isn't she?'

'Yes, at the end of next week?'

'Why?'

'I'm not sure. I think Father Dominic's death has affected her, but she hasn't given any particular reason. Perhaps she wants to get well away from Newby, now that she knows he lives so close to Easton Parva. Perhaps he wants to renew their relationship?'

'But she knew he lived close by before Father Dominic died, didn't she?'

Hood hesitated. 'On her own account of matters, she did, yes.'

'But didn't feel the need to resign her position then?'

'No, she didn't. I wonder why? We really are going to have to speak to her again.'

'Tread carefully, Harry. Giving her child up for adoption would have been traumatic. Then there's Mrs Newby to consider; she could be vulnerable on that score too, losing her only daughter and never getting pregnant again. If he fathered Martha's child, there's obviously not a problem with him. And if she were to find out about his child...?' She shook her head gently. 'The anniversary of her own daughter's death could well be a challenging time for her too which would not necessarily get any easier with the passage of time.' She paused and gave her husband a concerned look. 'This sort of thing can be very stressful, Harry, and lead to all sorts of unforeseen consequences, especially if it's been hidden away for years.'

Hood pondered on what his wife had said. 'Even to murder, do you think?'

CHAPTER FIFTY-ONE

'There you are, Wendy. I was wondering where you'd got to.'

Hood checked his watch. It was almost ten o'clock on Monday morning.

'I'm sorry, sir. I overslept this morning. I must have been more tired than I thought. I've had difficulty sleeping all week-end, which is very unusual for me.' She suppressed a yawn. 'I really am sorry.'

'Is there something worrying you?' asked Hood. He was genuinely concerned. In truth, he was very fond of Wendy. 'Is this investigation getting you down?'

She dropped her voice and whispered her reply. 'You'll think I must be losing it, but I kept dreaming about Father Dominic.' She appeared suitably embarrassed.

Hood raised his eyebrows. 'You did?'

'Yes. I don't know why, but I couldn't get him out of my head. Nothing like this has ever happened to me before. It's not as if this is the first homicide investigation I've been involved in.' She sighed. 'I just kept seeing him lying there in that priest-hole. It was the look on his face that distressed me. His eyes were open, giving me a reproachful gaze. It really disturbed me. I was almost afraid to go back to sleep.'

Hood was sympathetic. 'I wonder what brought that on? Perhaps it was your attending the *post-mortem*. I suppose I really should have gone.' He then smiled in an attempt to lighten the atmosphere. 'I don't suppose Dominic gave you any clues as to what happened to him?'

Knight responded with a grin. 'No, he didn't. It was all very weird. He just looked at me in a very critical way, as if we were taking the wrong path in our investigation.'

'The wrong path?' remarked Hood. 'How very interesting.'

Knight paused and pulled herself together. 'You must think I'm hallucinating or something. Anyway, it's not like me to turn up late whatever the circumstances. I really am sorry.' She watched for Hood's reaction. He remained supportive.

'As I said on Friday, Wendy, you've been over doing it. But we do need to get on with this investigation. I want to reach a resolution this week if possible. Now that we have a credible suspect.'

Knight was relieved and anxious to get back on track. 'Anything to report?' she asked, taking a seat. She'd already noticed that neither Swanson nor Renfrew were in the squad room.

'Bill Renfrew's at the Magistrates' Court, hopefully getting a search warrant from the District Judge. I drafted the application myself late last night. He's also come up with something that may surprise you.'

'He has?'

'Yes. Apparently Martha was about three months' pregnant when she left Dowlas Logistics. She admitted as much to the office manager. Here, look for yourself. This is the statement Bill took from Rosemary Carrington on Saturday afternoon.'

Knight read the statement quickly. 'Why didn't she tell us about this?'

Hood shrugged his shoulders. 'Embarrassment, perhaps? As my wife said, it's not the sort of thing you shout from the rooftops.'

'Did she keep the baby?'

'I don't know. We are going to have to find out though.'

'We?'

Hood grinned. 'Correction, *you* are going to have to ask her. The question may come better from a woman.'

'Thank you very much. But is it relevant? It's nine years ago.'

'It could be. If she had an abortion because Newby left her in the lurch, it could spell trouble for us when it comes to her credibility. Newby said she would have her revenge, remember?'

'But nine years later? What if she had the child?'

'She told Sir Robert she had no children. If she gave birth to Newby's child, I suppose she could have arranged to have had it adopted.'

'Newby could always deny it was his.'

'He could. If the child is alive somewhere, it may not be straightforward to trace it. Adoptions are highly confidential. She may not have revealed

382

who the father was, but we should still be able to find out who adopted the child if she didn't have a termination. It will take time, though.'

Knight sighed. 'It will take time, I agree. Time we don't have.' She paused. 'She will need to be spoken to as you say. Is this why you've asked for a warrant to search Newby's home at Stanton Harwood?'

'Not really, no. I reflected on matters over the week-end. Having a short break from the investigation gave me the opportunity to do some thinking. We can't keep waiting for something to turn up. The possible involvement of Mrs Newby means we need to speed things along. I want you, Swanson, Renfrew and Bradley to join me for the search. Find a uniformed female officer too. You can ask Mrs Newby a few questions at the house. Whether you arrest her, I shall leave entirely up to you. If you do arrest her, she'll need a different solicitor than her husband.'

'No Mr Sewell for her, then?' Knight smiled.

'Quite. If the warrant comes through, I shall telephone Sewell and inform him of our intentions. He may want to be there.'

'We're not obliged to do that, are we?'

'No, but in the circumstances I think we should. You never know, he'll probably be too busy to come himself. And I need to speak to him again about Newby's medical records. The sooner we get hold of those the better.'

'What about the housekeeper? I'm not looking forward to questioning her about an alleged pregnancy.'

'She can wait until after the search. But it will have to be done. By tomorrow at the latest.'

'And Newby himself? He won't be expecting a visit after what you said to him on Friday.'

'That can't be helped. If they are both involved, the two of them have had plenty of time to get rid of anything incriminating. We really should have searched the house before.'

'But we had no grounds,' said Knight. 'They were a bit slow with the Jaguar, so we might still find something incriminating.'

Hood smiled. 'Let's hope so. And I have to bear in mind Newby's hospital appointment tomorrow. I've promised the DCC to defer any arrest of him until the DNA comes through. On second thoughts, it might be better to keep any arrest of his wife until then too.'

'The DNA results won't be with us before tomorrow evening. And even that's not guaranteed.'

'I know,' sighed Hood. 'I spoke with the lab earlier. They are very busy, but they promised to continue to give us priority. That bloodstain in the boot of the Jag is going to be crucial. If it doesn't match the deceased, we're in trouble. But I'm fairly confident it will.'

'I know one of the scientists who works there.' said Knight. 'She's a DNA specialist. I could have a word.'

'You do that. Anything to move things on.'

The door was rapped and DC Renfrew came in, a file in his raised hand.

'Got it, sir! The deputy DJ was not over keen to begin with but she came round in the end. She's heard of Newby but fortunately does not know him personally. I've had copies made.' He took a document out of the file and handed the search warrant to Hood, who glanced at it then gave it to Knight to peruse.

'Right, let's get to it. Has Bradley appeared yet?'

'Yes, sir. He's waiting downstairs with Adrian Swanson. Sergeant Harris has laid on a WPC to accompany DS Knight.'

'I'm putting you in charge of the search log, Bill. Anything that's found is to go through you and must be carefully and accurately recorded. OK? I don't want any cock-ups.'

'Yes, sir. Are we looking for anything in particular?'

'Well, there's the carpet from the boot. That was definitely there when the Jaguar was sold to Newby. It's not there now. The deceased was also probably wrapped in something when his body was smuggled into the house. We are still awaiting information from the scientists, but there must be some prospect that whatever was used to wrap the body will have resulted in fibres transferring to the priest's habit. I suspect that whatever it was has probably been destroyed along with the carpet but keep a lookout for anything that fits the bill. The barns will need a thorough going over as well and Mrs Newby's Mercedes. If an attempt has been made to destroy evidence, they may have been as careless as they were with the bloodstain in the boot of the Jag.'

'Shall I check Mrs Newby's jewellery as well,' asked Knight. 'If we find a spider brooch that would certainly support any identification Mrs Swanson may make.'

Hood glanced at the warrant. 'I think we are covered although we will be concentrating on Newby rather than his wife. But have a look anyway.'

'The fingerprints from the steering wheel have also come through, sir. They're Newby's. No doubt about it.'

'That's hardly surprising. He admits he's driven the Jag more than once. Only his?'

'Yes, sir. But no sign of blood around the driver's area of the car.'

'Someone did a better job there than with the boot. Be on the lookout for bloodstained clothing too, although I suspect he'll have got rid of it by now.'

'And the phone schedule?' asked Knight.

'All completed, sarge. It's in this file.'

Renfrew placed the file on Hood's desk and explained in full what he had established. All the calls were fairly short, except the second one. The others varied in length. The first lasted 22 seconds, that was on 19 March. The second call on 24 March was longer; it lasted 5 minutes and 27 seconds. As Renfrew had previously indicated there was a missed call on 30 March which was when Martha Morton was away for the week-end. There was a further call much later, on 25 April, which lasted just under two minutes. He then explained he had checked the phone was still live.

'I called the number earlier just to check if it's still connected. It rang. I then terminated the call.' He paused before revealing something further which surprised Hood. 'Interestingly, the further information shows another call using the same phone. On Saturday last. And it wasn't a missed call. It lasted six minutes and twenty-three seconds. That's what prompted me to check if it was still connected to the system.'

'Newby called her after his interview on Friday? ' said Hood. 'We will definitely have to speak to the housekeeper again.'

'No, sir. She called him. At least, that's what it looks like. When I say him, I mean she called the same phone.'

Hood looked at Knight whose eyes widened. 'She called him?' he repeated.

'There's no doubt the call was made from her landline to the same number as the earlier calls.'

'And the mobile phone that was used? Any joy with that?' asked Knight.

'Unregistered as we thought. It can't be linked with Newby at the moment, but we have the I/D for the phone. We could get DS Oliver to do a cell-site analysis, once we have all the necessary information.'

'Cell-site analysis? How would that work?' asked Hood.

'It's fairly new, sir. With his box of tricks, he should be able to tell which phone mast picked up the calls when they were made. They're all recent enough. A mobile phone is like a radio transmitter. It connects with the nearest cell on a mast. I suppose that's why they were originally called cell phones. I still prefer that description. If a call were made or received in or around Stanton Harwood, there's probably only one mast that could have handled it. In a more urban area it gets a little more complicated. The masts are much closer together and the volume of calls more numerous. The various providers tend to share masts but not always, and calls can bounce off more than one mast depending how busy they are, and whether the phone is moving, but they're usually within close proximity to each other in a town or city so the information can still be helpful.'

'All this is recorded somewhere?'

'Yes, sir. Mobile phone data records are all kept on the computers of the providers for at least six months, sometimes longer. Putting that information together with a survey of the available masts in the area usually does the trick. It's not generally known at the moment that this can be done.' He grinned. 'DS Oliver reckons he can trace the movements of a cell phone even if the user doesn't make a call or receive one. The phone will continue to connect with the nearest mast, apparently. I don't fully understand it myself, but he's the expert so I assume he knows what he's talking about. We'll probably need another production order to get the details from the phone companies, but that shouldn't be too much of a problem.'

'He can do this without having the phone or the Sim card?'

'Yes, sir. The International Mobile Equipment I/D remains constant, even if the Sim card is removed. It connects with the mast and is recorded.'

Hood was impressed. 'So, although we don't know who's phone it is, we might be able to pin point where the individual was when the calls were made?'

'Not the individual sir, the phone. But the location of the phone can frequently suggest who was using it at the relevant time. I think it's worth a go.'

'I agree. Get DS Oliver on to it. Where is he based?'

'Nottingham, sir.'

'Organise it before we head off for Stanton Harwood. Let's see if he can do what he claims. I have a couple of calls to make before we leave.' He picked up his phone.

'Yes, sir. There's something else, too.'

Hood put down his phone. 'Something else?'

'Yes, sir. As I checked the calls from Newby's landline, I notice a call made on the night we think the priest was killed.'

'Is it relevant?'

'I don't know, but it might be. At nine seventeen and thirty three seconds, there was an unanswered call to the ex-directory number at Easton Grange.'

Hood and Knight looked at each other. 'The call that Father Grantham heard but didn't answer, perhaps?' suggested Knight.

'So Grantham was telling the truth.' Hood smiled. 'Well done, Bill. Is that call contained in your schedule?'

'It is. I've marked it in green. The other calls are marked in yellow.'

'Good, you get on to DS Oliver. Tell him from me he is to give this priority. I want to know whether the calls to and from the mobile were made from Stanton Harwood or received there.'

Renfrew nodded and left the room.

'Interesting, don't you think, Wendy?'

'Yes. Pity Grantham didn't answer the phone. It must mean that either Newby or his wife were at home at Stanton Harwood. But which of them?'

'Possibly both of them. Father Dominic must have been attacked by that time.'

Knight continued to mull over the recent information about the housekeeper. 'Now, why would Martha have spent seven minutes talking with Newby last Saturday?'

'You can ask her when you see her,' replied Hood. 'We need to follow this up. There may be more to all this than we presently appreciate.'

CHAPTER FIFTY-TWO

'He's here again,' said Eleanor Newby as Hood's Saab pulled slowly into the gravelled courtyard of the Newby's home in Stanton Harwood closely followed by an unmarked van carrying the rest of the search team. Mrs Newby pressed her face to the bedroom window as the occupants of the van started to alight. 'There's more of them too. Several officers are getting out of a van. They must be going to search the place just like Gerald Sewell warned us. I'd better get down there.'

'Let them. They'll find nothing. At least I hope they won't. You're sure we got rid of everything?'

'Of course. I, unlike you, know what I'm doing. I assume you did what I told you?'

Newby looked away. 'To the letter.' He gave a wry smile as he adjusted his position on the bed. 'I still don't understand why you insisted I lie about the priest. I don't see the harm in admitting I saw Dominic. It was months before he was killed when I rekindled our relationship.'

She glared at him. 'Do I have to explain this again? We don't want them to be able to prove any connection with him. Surely you can see that? Anyway, it's too late to change things now. How could you become High Sheriff if it were known you had lied to the police in a murder investigation? I've put a lot into getting you that position. Don't you let me down now.'

Newby grunted. 'I never wanted it. I only allowed my name to go forward because you insisted. Why, I have no idea. And it will cost a small fortune; just so you can hob nob with the great and the good. Anyway, the way I feel at the moment, I doubt if I'll be up to it.'

She intensified her glare. 'You'll be feeling better soon. I'm sure of it. There's the royal visit to look forward to next year. You haven't forgotten I hope? As High Sheriff, you and I will get to meet the Queen.'

Newby let out a lengthy sigh. He had more immediate concerns than meeting the Queen. 'What about the blood in the boot? How the hell do we deal with that? I don't understand how it could have been left there after hosing it down and destroying the carpet.'

'We'll worry about the blood when we have to. I don't know how it got there. I thought you had cleaned it thoroughly, but as usual you can't be trusted to do anything properly. Hopefully, there won't be enough to produce a DNA profile. That's what Gerald Sewell thinks.'

'Does he? But it's the same group as the priest's. They've already established that.'

'Along with a few hundred thousand others. It's not enough to prove the Jaguar played any part in this priest's death or that you had any contact with him. There are no witnesses.'

Newby sighed. 'But I didn't have any contact with him on the twenty-fourth, not while he was still alive. I only said what I did because you told Hood I'd had no dealings with him. Why did you have to say that?'

'You should have told me the truth. You kept it from me, just like you've kept other things from me.'

'What are you talking about? I did tell you I'd seen him and that I'd been to confession with him.'

'Too late though, as usual. And you never told me everything about Hannah. I had to find out for myself. You left me with no alternative.'

He paused and shook his head. He sounded bewildered. 'I still can't believe Dominic betrayed me. Telling you all that. Confession is supposed to be wholly confidential. A sacred trust. And I trusted him absolutely.'

'More fool you. How you could go in for that nonsense, I simply don't understand. I had to find out what you were up to somehow. It was the only way. You told this priest what you were not prepared to tell your own wife.'

Newby raised his voice only slightly. 'And if I had told you the whole truth at the time? What would that have achieved? ' He paused and looked away briefly. 'You'll never understand me.' He then turned and faced his wife as he started to get out of bed, raising his voice in anger. 'For God's sake woman. I thought I was dying. Can't you see that? I needed absolution. I couldn't die with that on my conscience, even though it was an accident.' His voice dropped. 'And I knew I would never get forgiveness from you.' She glowered as he continued. 'I told you all you needed to know at the time.' His voice softened almost to a whisper. 'And what does it matter now? The poor old boy's dead. He can't say anything to anyone.'

She gave him an even sharper look. 'Exactly. Whatever you told him; it will never come out. What's done is done.'

He heaved another sigh as she approached him and gripped him by the shoulders. 'Look, we have to stick together over this. Don't forget, I know about you and that Goring woman and her bastard child. I knew about you and her from the outset.' He bowed his head as she continued her rant. 'You'll never learn. You should realise after all these years Arthur Newby that you can't fool me. I know all about your other affairs too.' She paused. Mentioning her husband's child brought memories of her own dead daughter flooding back. 'If you had brought Hannah back here like I told you, she'd still be alive. How could you have kept what really happened from me all these years?' Her eyes filled with tears.

Newby bowed his head. 'I'm sorry. I truly am. If I had my time over again I would act differently. But it wasn't only my fault. You know what she was like. I had little option. She wouldn't stop screaming at me. I just couldn't cope with it. I had to stop the car and she just got out.'

'But you left her there; in the middle of nowhere. And at that time of night. My beautiful daughter. And then…' She was unable to continue. When she eventually did, her tone had altered. 'Being sorry isn't good enough, Arthur Newby. You brought this down on us. You will do as I say if you want to get out of the mess you've created.'

'I've created? I gave them my DNA and fingerprints because there's no way it can be proved I was even there.' He paused. 'But I lied to them about Martha. I regret that now, but you would have it that way. Suppose they prove I've seen her? Suppose they believe her and not me?'

Eleanor Newby spoke dismissively. 'That hardly matters. Why should anyone believe what she says? She's a nobody. We are part of the establishment; the establishment looks after its own. Have you ever heard of a High Sheriff standing in the dock?'

She walked back to the window and saw that Hood and Knight had finished speaking to the officers from the van and were almost at the front door. She turned and continued to instruct her husband. 'As long as they don't have any evidence for the twenty-fourth nothing can be proved. Suspicion is not enough. You should know that as a magistrate. Now, get back into bed. They'll probably come up here. At least try and look the part. Just stick to what I told you to say. Play dumb. You're good at that. They'll get round to interviewing me eventually.' She sounded suitably defiant. 'I'll do the explaining. Leave everything to me.'

She headed towards the door. As she reached it he called after her. 'I know you haven't been in the house on occasions when I've been resting. And Hood's started to work things out. He's on to us, I tell you. And he's not going to give up.'

She ignored him and swept out of the bedroom and rushed down the stairs as Hood rang the bell. The door was opened and pulled back rapidly. Hood and Knight were standing together, the other officers hanging back a few yards.

'What is it now, Chief Inspector,' said Mrs Newby, making no attempt to hide her irritation. 'If you want to speak to my husband, he's in bed. He's not at all well this morning.'

Hood produced the warrant, handing a copy to Mrs Newby. 'Actually, it's Detective Superintendent now. Didn't your husband tell you about my promotion?' He did not wait for a response. 'I intend to search the house and the outbuildings, Mrs Newby. You will see the details set out in the warrant. I hope it won't be necessary to disturb your husband. My officers will be thorough but professional. If you wish to accompany any of them during the search, I will have no objection providing you do not interfere.'

'Interfere indeed. What are you hoping to find? There is nothing in this house or the outbuildings of any possible relevance to your investigation.'

'I'll be the judge of that, if you don't mind. DS Knight will stay with you. If you have any questions, she will do her best to answer them.'

Mrs Newby's attitude did not change. 'The idea that my husband is involved in the murder of this priest is quite ridiculous. I shall be making a further complaint to your superiors, I assure you.'

Hood ignored her. 'That is your privilege. Now, does your husband have a study? If he does, we'll make a start in there.' He turned to the officers standing behind him. 'Bradley and Swanson will search the barns with PC Johnson.' He then addressed Renfrew. 'Bill, you're with me.' He turned back to the others. 'Let's get on with it and, please, as quietly as possible. Anything you uplift, you report to DC Renfrew. He's keeping the log.'

'Monty is in the smaller barn,' warned Mrs Newby. 'You remember him, Mr Hood?' She started to calm down, just a little. 'He's friendly enough, but for God's sake, don't let him get out. He hasn't been for his walk yet.'

'Do you hear that?' said Hood. 'Watch out for the dog. You'd better search the larger barn first.'

'Yes, sir.'

'Anything else my officers need to know, Mrs Newby?'

She grunted and turned on her heel. 'The study is this way, Superintendent.'

★ ★ ★ ★

The search was completed in under three hours. Several items were uplifted. Hood and Knight returned to the Superintendent's office at Campbell Square. The seized items, bagged and marked with exhibit labels, were resting on his desk as they discussed the outcome. Two SOCO officers had remained at Stanton Harwood examining the Mercedes and areas inside the barns.

'Well, I wasn't expecting we would do as well as that, Wendy.'

Knight shook her head. 'Me neither. He must have been very confident that he wouldn't come under suspicion, either that or his illness has affected him more than we imagined.'

Hood could not disguise his concerns. The ease with which potentially incriminating items had been found worried him. None of it seemed to make sense. 'But why keep the phone?' he said. He pointed to one of the exhibit bags. 'There it was, as bold as brass, sitting in the back of his filing cabinet. There's no doubt about it; this is the phone that was used to telephone Martha. It was switched off, but Renfrew has checked the sim card. He's also checked the other phone that's registered to Newby. He's had it for years. It's hardly been used.'

'He lied to us, Harry. He distinctly said he only had one mobile. Why he kept the one he contacted Martha with doesn't make sense.'

'I agree. Then there's the college magazines, still on his bookshelf in date order. The report about Father Dominic moving to Easton Grange has a circle drawn round it in black ink. I know we rely on suspects making mistakes, but for an intelligent man like Newby, this is verging on the ridiculous.'

Knight then referred to perhaps the most damning evidence that the search had revealed. 'That piece of carpet looks like it came from the boot of the Jaguar. If you were going to burn something, why not do the job properly?' She picked up the transparent exhibit bag containing about two square inches of carpet with burnt edges and examined it. Another bag contained ashes removed from the brazier. 'Swanson could hardly believe it when he found this in the ashes. I'm only surprised that we didn't locate the rug or whatever Dominic was wrapped in.'

'I suppose Newby must have thought he wouldn't come under suspicion? Let's hope he survives long enough for us to charge him and get him to trial.'

Knight did a double take. 'I thought he was on the mend?'

'I'm not so sure. You saw his condition on Friday. We'll have to wait for the results of this new type of scan he's having tomorrow, but his health has obviously deteriorated. It certainly doesn't look good. But if the DNA analysis proves the blood came from Dominic, there'll be more than enough to charge him.'

Knight was worried about waiting for the DNA to come through before interviewing Newby again. 'His wife is bound to tell him what we seized. We really should see him again, before he thinks up some innocent explanation.'

'That's not possible until he's had his scan tomorrow,' insisted Hood. 'I promised the DCC to hold fire for the present. And if the DNA analysis proves the blood from the boot to be Dominic's there won't be room for an innocent explanation.'

Knight nodded but like Hood she could not hide her unease in respect of the other recently acquired evidence. 'It all seems to have fallen into our laps rather easily, don't you think? Almost as if he wants us to prove the case against him. Perhaps he feels so guilty he just wants to get it over with?'

'He didn't give that impression last Friday, though. He denied everything. Very confidently, too. But I agree with you Wendy, it all seems just a little too neat and tidy and altogether too convenient.' He paused. 'How did you leave things with Mrs Newby?'

'She knows we have a witness who says she was seen at Easton Grange on the seventh of last month. No doubt her husband told her, but it didn't seem to bother her. I didn't disclose who the witness was, other than it was not the eleven-year old boy. All she said was that she and her husband were at home on the seventh. She refused to say anything else in the absence of a solicitor, so following your advice, I left it.'

'So, they're alibiing each other?'

'That's what it looks like. I gave his Range Rover a quick going over too. It wasn't locked. Nothing of relevance, but I did notice it's an automatic. His wife's Mercedes is also an automatic, just like she said.'

'She could have driven the Range Rover then,' said Hood. 'It could have been she who visited Father Dominic back in April?'

'Possibly. But why would Eleanor Newby visit a Catholic priest, on her own? Even I would hesitate to do that.'

'Really? They don't bite you know. It's possible she wanted an explanation about confession. Perhaps both of them were there?'

'Oh, you think my earlier suggestion might have something to commend it then?'

'I always listen to your views, as you know.' Hood smiled, then continued. 'Did you look for the spider brooch that Helen Swanson remembers?'

'I did. Mrs Newby showed me her jewellery, but no sign of a brooch meeting that description. Helen Swanson produced a good sketch of what she says she saw, but I found nothing like it amongst the jewellery. And she has a hell of a lot of stuff. She could open a shop with the amount of clothing and jewellery she has.'

'What do you think? Do we arrest her too if the DNA comes through?'

'I think so,' said Knight. 'They were probably acting together at some point. She may well have taken part in the attempted cover up.'

Hood sighed, stood up and walked towards the open window. 'Probably isn't good enough. Even if she's lying about being at Easton Grange on the seventh, that doesn't really prove anything in itself and we have no proof she ever spoke to Father Dominic or that she drove the Range Rover to the Grange in April. I'll be speaking at length to Fiona Morrison from the CPS on Thursday. Let's see what she thinks about the wife's possible participation. You may well be right. She may just have assisted her husband after the killing had taken place by attempting to get rid of the evidence.'

'She didn't do a very good job, then.'

Hood smiled. 'That, happily, is not a defence.'

'And the housekeeper?'

Hood turned and faced Knight. 'Go and see her again. See if she'll make another statement. And ask her about that call on Saturday. That does concern me. Newby knew we were investigating telephone calls to the housekeeper's number. I made that very clear when we interviewed him. For him to call her again would have been reckless in the extreme; but for her to call him? That makes no sense at all.'

'Unless she was asking him to lie for her? Perhaps they've become closer than she admitted?'

Hood had his doubts about that. 'Why should she lie? She's hardly under suspicion. No, what worries me is that she was seemingly prepared to speak to him for so long and then he leaves the phone where we were bound to find it.' He sat down at his desk and opened the case file. 'The pieces of this jigsaw seem to be fitting together far too easily all of a sudden. There can't be any other explanation for it all, can there?'

Knight smiled and gave Hood one of her looks that usually indicated she was about to start thinking outside the box. 'Unless someone is trying to frame him, of course.' That was said flippantly, but Hood did not dismiss it.

'Good God, Wendy. Do you think that's a possibility? It had crossed my mind that Mrs Newby and the housekeeper might have been in contact with each other, but to frame Newby? That can't be the case. Neither would it explain why Father Dominic was targeted.'

'I don't mean frame him in the sense that he's innocent. Perhaps they're just trying in their own little way to make sure he's convicted. Perhaps Mrs Newby knows about Martha's child?'

Hood raised his eyebrows. 'Now that is a thought, Wendy. But how could she have known? Surely Newby wouldn't have dared tell her?'

Knight continued to speculate. 'Perhaps Mrs Newby is in league with the housekeeper? If she's discovered that Newby killed her daughter and Martha has told her about her pregnancy, both women might have reason to want to punish him and get him out of the way?'

'Hold on there,' said Hood. 'What are you suggesting?'

Knight began adding substance to her theorising. 'The housekeeper knew about the excavation of the priest-hole. In fact, she'd have known everything that was going on in the house, including the presence of Grantham and where he was likely to be at any given time. She'd also knew that Sir Robert was away on the Wednesday when Father Dominic was killed. She'd be a useful source of information.'

Hood didn't like what he was hearing. He returned to his desk and sat down. 'You think that Martha might have told Mrs Newby about her pregnancy and told her what was going on in the house? She seemed to want to keep her relationship with Newby secret when we interviewed her.'

'She did,' continued Knight. 'But if she has disclosed it, Mrs Newby would have reacted in some way. She has quite a temper on her; she can more than match her husband in that department. I saw that for myself. And I can't see her simply ignoring something like that, especially if there's an eight-year old child fathered by her husband somewhere in the world while her daughter lies cold in the ground. And suppose she's somehow discovered that her husband killed her daughter, accidentally or otherwise? Newby himself said that Hannah was the apple of her mother's eye. The combination of the two might well have unhinged Mrs Newby.'

Hood shook his head. 'But how does all this impact on Father Dominic's murder? Only Newby would have any reason to have contacted him. Eleanor Newby wouldn't have known him from Adam.'

Knight did not reply for several seconds. She could see that was a problem. It certainly didn't provide either the housekeeper or Eleanor Newby with a motive to murder the elderly priest. 'Perhaps it doesn't?' she conceded.

Hood stood up, approached her and patted her arm. 'I'm not dismissing what you say, Wendy. If Martha gave birth to the child and Mrs Newby knows about it, we may well have to revise our ideas, no matter how inconvenient. It would certainly complicate matters but we must follow where the evidence takes us.'

Knight faced Hood and smiled. 'I can raise this with Martha if you like? Always assuming you really want me to ask her about her pregnancy. It's very personal.'

Hood thought for a moment. 'She's very vulnerable, and I don't want to make her situation worse, but if we are to get to the truth, we have no choice in the matter. It all has to come out in the open. Things have been hidden away for far too long. I'll leave it up to you, but if you think it wise, you might introduce Eleanor Newby into the conversation and see how Martha reacts.' He glanced at his watch. 'It's getting late. Arrange to see her tomorrow. We should also have the DNA results by close of play.'

'I hope so. I had a word with Dr Irwin. She promised me we would have them by tomorrow evening at the latest, but I don't suppose they work the sort of hours we do at the forensic science lab.'

CHAPTER FIFTY-THREE

'I think it's time you told us the whole truth, Martha,' said DS Knight as she sat herself down at the kitchen table in the housekeeper's cottage. It was just after three o'clock on Tuesday afternoon. Mrs Morton had made a pot of tea and appeared perfectly calm on the surface as she poured out two cups. Although she didn't like the fact that she was being questioned yet again by a police officer, she had no intention of displaying her true feelings. She was used to repressing her emotions. She'd become quite adept at it over the years, but there was always the risk that one day the damn would burst and her heartache exposed in all its bitter rawness for all to see. Would she be able to keep control? She dreaded that the traumatic events which she had kept so well hidden were about to be revealed.

'I'm sure I don't know what you mean.'

She took a seat opposite the detective sergeant, picked up the milk jug and offered it to Knight. 'Milk?'

'Just a drop. No sugar.'

Knight took a sip of her tea then opened her notebook. She got straight down to business. A sixth sense told Martha that her secret was about to be exposed.

'You didn't tell us about your pregnancy back in nineteen-ninety-three. We have obtained a statement from Rosemary Carrington, remember her? She was the office manager at Dowlas Logistics where you used to work.'

The housekeeper sighed deeply. She did not reply for some time. 'So you know about that? I suppose I always knew you'd find out about it, eventually.'

'Why didn't you mention it before?'

Her reaction was fierce. 'Because it's highly personal, and it can't possibly have anything to do with Father Dominic's death. It was years ago.'

'May I ask, did you go through with the pregnancy?'

Martha's face betrayed the pain which was beginning to overwhelm her as the memories returned. She nodded. 'Yes. I gave birth to a son early in nineteen ninety-four. He was adopted. I've had no contact with him for over eight years.' Her eyes filled with tears as she continued. 'But I don't see that has anything to do with your investigation into Father Dominic's death.'

Knight looked her in the eye. 'Was Newby the father?'

Martha hesitated before replying, nodding her head as tears flowed down her cheeks. Despite her best endeavours she could no longer maintain her composure. She blurted out her response. 'Yes. Harry Newby is his father.' She wiped her tears with her hand. 'Not that I ever disclosed that during the adoption process. I refused to say. I can hardly believe it now. I was still protecting him despite everything.'

'Does he know about the child?'

'He does now.'

'You told him?'

She nodded. 'He knew I was pregnant, of course, before I left Dowlas. I hoped that when I told him it would make him think seriously about leaving his wife, but I was proved wrong. It had quite the opposite effect. He was absolutely furious with me. He insisted I should arrange to have an abortion. He accused me of getting pregnant deliberately to put pressure on him; as if it were nothing to do with him. He treated me in such an off-hand and cruel way when we broke up, I couldn't have stayed there. I simply couldn't. If I'd continued working for Dowlas he would have forced me into having a termination. I know he would.'

'You didn't consider a termination, then?'

Her reply was immediate and forceful. 'No, I didn't. I couldn't have lived with myself if I'd done that and I don't regret it. We have to take responsibility for our actions, don't you think? Getting pregnant isn't like catching the flu, you know. I knew the risks I was running, as did he.' She half-smiled. 'He was a lovely little boy. I just hope he tries to get in touch with me when he comes of age. I read somewhere that sometimes happens, doesn't it?' She looked away for a moment. When she settled her gaze once more on Knight, the detective sergeant noticed a desperate pleading look in her eyes. 'It's a long time ago, but it doesn't get any easier, you know. I think about him every day.'

Knight wanted to be sympathetic but she needed to make progress. 'Did Newby ask about the child when you met up with him?'

Martha shook her head. 'No. He assumed I'd had a termination. He didn't know I'd actually given birth to his son; that's what he said anyway. I suppose it explains why I was handed such a generous severance payment.' She adopted a cynical tone. 'He told me it would help me make a fresh start, with no incumbrances. Can you believe it? That's how he described his own son; an incumbrance. It was quite obvious what he meant.' She paused. When she continued her tone became less strident. 'But when we met for lunch and I saw how ill and frightened he was, I couldn't help myself. I told him he had a son who had been adopted.'

Knight bore in mind what Hood had said to her about Martha's vulnerability. She hesitated before asking her next question although she appreciated it had to be asked. 'How did Newby react?'

Martha looked up. She was now in control and almost smiled before replying. 'I thought he'd be angry, but actually he wasn't. He seemed delighted. His eyes lit up and he took hold of my hand. It seemed a relief to him that I hadn't had a termination. He became quite emotional. He said he wanted to help me and his son to make up for the way he'd treated me back in ninety-three.'

Knight was not impressed with Newby's apparent change of heart. 'Guilt, I suppose. Very late in the day too.' She paused then asked the question to which she knew Hood needed an answer. 'Have you been in contact with Mrs Newby at all?'

The housekeeper hesitated then nodded.

'This may be very important Martha, so I want you to consider your answer very carefully. Why have you been in contact with Mrs Newby?'

Martha became defensive. She wiped her eyes and sat up straight in her chair. 'It wasn't my doing. She contacted me, out of the blue. I didn't contact her. She's the last person I wanted to speak to.'

'When did she contact you?'

'I don't recall exactly when, but it was well before Easter.'

'Before Easter? How did she contact you?'

The housekeeper lowered her eyes and did not reply.

'You must tell me, Martha.'

Martha looked up. Tears began forming in her eyes again. 'She telephoned me. Look, I didn't tell you the whole truth before. The first call I received was from Eleanor Newby, not from her husband. It was after I'd seen them together in Northampton but before I met Newby for lunch.'

She dropped her head. Knight tried her best not to react and completed her note before commenting further. 'So, you didn't tell the whole truth when you made your witness statement?'

'I suppose I didn't. I was too scared to mention Mrs Newby, especially after what she said.'

'What did she say?'

'She said she knew about me and her husband. It scared me. She sounded so angry.'

'How did she know your telephone number?'

'I'm in the phone book. I assumed she got it from there, or from directory enquiries. But I have no idea how she knew where I was living.'

'How did she find out about you and her husband?'

Martha shook her head. 'I'm not sure. I asked her who had told her such a thing, but she refused to say.'

'What was your response?'

Martha swallowed hard. 'I denied it. I said I had no idea what she was talking about. I didn't want to have anything to do with her.'

'And?'

'She said there was no point denying it because her husband had admitted everything to her. She said she had chapter and verse. But I couldn't be sure if she was telling me the truth or bluffing. I put the phone down on her. It was a very short call.'

'Did you believe her?'

'I didn't know what to believe. When I saw Newby later, he looked so weak and pathetic. He told me his condition was terminal. I thought he might have said something to her, a final confession sort of thing before he died, something like that. So she might well have known about us.'

Knight pressed on. 'Did Newby confirm what his wife had told you when you eventually met up with him? I'm assuming you were telling the truth about having lunch with him in Northampton?'

'Oh, yes. I met him after I'd seen them together in Northampton and after she had phoned me. He rang later. That was the main reason I agreed to see him. I had to know what he'd said to her. I asked him why he had told her about us after all this time. He seemed shocked. He didn't seem to have been aware that she had spoken to me. He denied that he had said anything of the sort to her. That really confused me. I didn't know what to believe. He got into a right state when I told him what his wife had said to me.'

'Tell me, did you mention the child to Mrs Newby?'

'No, of course not. I wouldn't have dared.' She paused. 'And what good would it do bringing that up now? It was all so long ago.'

'Were you telling the truth when you said you had seen Newby's Range Rover at Easton Grange parked outside Father Dominic's cottage?'

'Oh, yes. That's the God's honest truth. I definitely saw it there like I said in my statement. It was only the phone call from Mrs Newby I failed to mention.'

'You also said in your second statement that you hadn't actually seen either Newby or Father Dominic on that occasion.'

'That's right. I didn't see either of them, just the Range Rover.'

'And you recognised it as Newby's?'

'Of course I did. It had his personalised number plate; his initials. It couldn't have been anyone else's. I had seen the same Range Rover parked opposite the café when I saw them together in Northampton. It was parked on the yellow lines by the side of the church.'

'And you associated the Range Rover you saw in Northampton with the Newbys?'

'Yes. I saw him and his wife getting into it when I was walking back from Marks and Spencer. That's when I first noticed the personal registration number.'

Knight removed Martha's second statement from her file. 'If you recall, you also said in this statement that Newby telephoned you later and more or less confirmed he had been with Father Dominic on the occasion you saw his Range Rover at Easton Grange.'

'Well, he certainly didn't deny it when I suggested that's where he had been.'

'I believe from the information we have assembled that call must have been made on the twenty-fifth of April.'

Martha lowered her eyes. 'That sounds about right.'

'Did it occur to you that Newby might not have been driving his Range Rover that day?'

She hesitated. 'You mean in April? No, it didn't. Why should it have? It was his car.' She paused as if she were casting her mind back. 'Oh God, I've just remembered something. When I saw them getting into the Range Rover as I walked back from Marks and Spencer in March, it was Mrs Newby who got into the driving seat.'

'Why did you not mention this before?'

'I've only just remembered. I'm sorry. Is it important?'

Knight did not answer her. 'It follows that Mrs Newby could have been driving it when you saw it at Easton Grange?'

'I don't know. I'm sorry. I thought he usually drove it. He was driving it when we met for lunch in Northampton.'

'Have you spoken to either of the Newbys on any other occasion?'

'Why do you ask?'

Knight frowned. 'We have evidence that a call was made to a mobile phone which is central to this investigation from your land line number early on Saturday morning last, the third of August.'

The housekeeper gasped. 'How can you know that? I thought phone calls were supposed to be private.'

'We obtained a court order to examine calls to and from your phone over a six month period. It's very important you tell me the truth.'

Martha swallowed hard. 'I see. You're allowed to do that are you, without saying anything to me?' She looked down before answering. 'That was me. I was hoping to get hold of Harry, but she answered.'

'Where did you get the mobile number from?'

She closed her eyes. 'Newby gave it to me when we met in Northampton. He said if I wanted to phone him I was to use that number and not the landline.'

She stood up and walked across the kitchen to an easy chair where her handbag was lying. She picked it up, searched through it and produced a printed business card bearing Newby's name and a mobile telephone number.

'Is this the number you mean?' she asked, handing the card to the officer.

Knight checked the number. 'Yes. I shall keep hold of this for the time being. Why did you want to speak to him?'

Martha hesitated. 'He'd told me he wanted to do something for his son when we had lunch in Northampton. He said he would leave him a substantial sum in his will that he could access when he was eighteen or twenty-one. I was worried that he might have changed his mind when I refused to see him again.'

'But Mrs Newby answered?'

'Yes. It rather took me by surprise.'

'Why didn't you just put your phone down and cut her off, like you did before?'

'I was going to, but she knew it was me. She made that clear enough. I just knew she would keep contacting me if I didn't speak to her. I don't know why, but I got the impression she'd been waiting for me to call. She insisted on meeting me. She told me she knew everything. She went on about it for ages. I couldn't get a word in.' Martha was becoming increasingly distressed as she continued. 'She said if I didn't agree to meet her she would see to it personally that her husband would not leave my son a brass farthing.'

'So, she knew about the child and the promise her husband had made?'

'She did by then. Newby must have told her, because I certainly didn't.'

The detective sergeant finished her note. 'Did you actually meet with her?'

Martha shook her head. 'No.'

'And that's the truth, is it?'

She nodded. 'I told her I would think about it. But I have no intention of seeing her. I wouldn't dare.'

'And Newby? Have you spoken to him again?'

She shook her head. 'No. I decided not to contact him. I felt betrayed all over again; him telling his wife about our son. I'll be gone from here in a few days. I just want to get away from all this. I don't want to have anything more to do with him or her. She frightens me.'

Knight closed her notebook and pushed back her chair. 'That may not be possible, I'm afraid, Martha. I'm going to have to ask you to come with me to the police station. This interview will have to continue there, if necessary, under caution. My superintendent will want to see you. Your relationship with both Mr and Mrs Newby is going to have to be carefully examined.'

'Under caution?' There was panic in her eyes. 'What if I refuse?'

'Then I suppose I shall have to arrest you. This is a murder inquiry you know. And you've admitted you have not told the whole truth in your witness statements. That you have been in contact with Mrs Newby may well have consequences for our investigation into the murder.' She paused. 'Attempting to pervert the course of justice is a serious offence.'

Martha appeared shocked. 'But I haven't attempted to pervert anything. I can't tell you anything else. And I've told you the truth. I haven't tried to mislead you. I didn't have anything to do with Father Dominic's death. Honestly, I didn't.'

'Let's hope for your sake that proves to be the case.'

Tears filled the housekeeper's eyes again as Knight stood up and ushered her towards the door.

CHAPTER FIFTY-FOUR

'I've told you everything,' said Martha between sobs. 'It never occurred to me that my relationship with Harry Newby could have anything to do with Father Dominic's murder. And I still don't see how it does.'

The housekeeper was sitting opposite Hood and Knight in interview room 3 in the basement of Campbell Square police station. The tape machine was running and she had been cautioned, but not arrested. Hood glanced towards the detective sergeant. He was beginning to doubt a connection himself.

'So, you had the child without Newby knowing that you had continued with the pregnancy?'

Martha nodded. She wiped her eyes. 'I did. And I don't regret it. Not even after all these years. He made it quite plain he wanted nothing more to do with me. Staying with his wife was all he cared about, especially after what happened to Hannah. He was terrified of his wife finding out about our affair.' She paused. 'There was also the question of his business.'

'His business?'

She dropped her voice. 'He was in financial difficulties before I was made company secretary. There had been several redundancies. We were all worried about our futures.' She paused. 'Things must have been pretty bad because his wife had to bail him out. She could have ruined him had she wanted to. That proved more important to him than me or his child.'

'How did you know this?' asked Hood.

'When I became company secretary I was involved in the new share issue.'

'When did that take place?'

'The year before. His solicitor was involved too, and the other director.'

'Who was the other director?'

'A Mr Lonsdale, but he resigned when the new shares were issued to Mrs Newby.'

'Who had control of the business after the new shares were issued?'

'It was still Harry, at least I always assumed it was. He was still the majority shareholder, but I had a suspicion that there was some secret arrangement with his wife.'

'What arrangement?'

'I don't know. It was just a feeling I had. And I was aware that she had loaned a substantial sum to the company apart from what she had invested in the new shares. Harry always seemed to do what she wanted even when he didn't agree with her proposals.'

'Do you know how much she invested?'

'From the number of shares issued, it must have been a hell of a lot. He did tell me once that it was over three quarters of a million.'

'And when you told him you were pregnant?'

'As I told Sergeant Knight, he insisted I had an abortion. He claimed he couldn't risk his wife finding out because of the effect it would have on the business if she withdrew her support. I wasn't prepared to do what he asked.'

'And your son was born on the sixteenth of January nineteen-ninety four, is that right?

She nodded. 'Yes. He was two weeks' premature.'

'And there's no doubt in your mind that Newby is the father?'

She glared at Hood. 'Of course not. It couldn't have been anyone else,'

Hood nodded. 'There's something I have to tell you. Newby admits he had a relationship with you back in ninety-three, but he denies that he'd ever seen you recently in Northampton or anywhere else. He claims he's had no contact with you since you split up.'

Martha appeared shocked. She responded angrily. 'He said that did he? Well, he's a liar. He paid for lunch in cash, so there may not be a record, but I could take you to the restaurant. It's still there. Harper's in Gold Street.'

'That won't be necessary, not at the moment.' Hood cleared his throat. 'He also denies speaking to you over the phone.'

Tears formed in Martha's eyes. 'But he did, And more than once. How did I get hold of his business card if he never met me?'

Knight, who was noting down what Martha was saying, put her pen down and changed the subject. 'You decided to leave your job with Dowlas in the summer of nineteen ninety-three.'

'Yes.'

'When did you hand in your notice?'

'About a week or so after Hannah was killed.'

'In writing or orally?'

'Both. I had to put it in writing because I was the company secretary. There should be a copy somewhere.'

'How much was your severance payment?'

Martha paused and looked down before she answered. 'Seven thousand five hundred pounds.' She looked up. 'He also gave me an excellent reference.'

Hood glanced at Knight. 'That was a considerable sum back in ninety-three. Was the payment by cheque?'

Martha nodded. 'Yes. He signed it himself. He had to because of the amount. No one else was authorised to issue a cheque for as much as that, apart from his wife, of course. Only a director could authorise a cheque for so much.'

'And she was the only other director?'

'That's what I understood, although a pension fund that was thinking of investing in the business wanted to have a representative on the board. I had left before that was resolved.'

'Did you tell anyone else you were pregnant?'

'Not anyone at Dowlas, no.'

'How did Rosemary Carrington find out?'

'I don't know. I'm sure I never discussed it with her while I was still at Dowlas, not that I can remember anyway, but she was quite shrewd was Rosemary. She had expected to be made company secretary when Harry gave me the job. Our relationship was strained as a result, but we were on quite good terms by the time I left. I suppose she must have noticed something. She certainly knew about the cheque. I told her how much it was for. She was amazed at the amount.'

'Did you have any contact with her after you left?'

'We kept in touch for a while, so I suspect she must have picked up something. I suppose I might even have let it slip; I was very upset at the time. I wasn't always in full control. When I moved to Bedford we lost contact. I had the baby after I moved there.'

Knight picked up her pen. Hood continued the questioning. 'Did you have any suspicions about Hannah's death back in ninety-three?'

Martha seemed surprised by the question. 'No. I thought it was just a tragic road accident. And Harry Newby was really cut up about it. I saw him in tears more than once.' She paused and her tone changed. 'It did cross my mind later that he knew more than he was letting on, but I wasn't thinking straight by then. I was hardly a disinterested party after the way he treated me.'

'What do you mean, exactly?' asked Hood.

'I remembered something about his car.'

'His car?'

'Yes. He had a black Range Rover, just like he has now, but a different model. He booked it into the garage not long afterwards. The bull bars had been removed when he got it back. I noticed that. I thought nothing of it at the time, but later, when I was feeling really angry with him, I started to think it was a bit more than a coincidence.'

Hood was now very interested. 'There were bull bars on his Range Rover?'

'Oh, yes. Stainless steel as I recall. But they'd gone when he got it back.'

'Did you ever ask him what had happened to his vehicle?'

'I did. But It was just a casual inquiry on my part because he was taking it into the garage. He said he'd hit a muntjac or something and his Range Rover had sustained some slight damage. I think he mentioned replacing a headlight too.'

Hood cast a knowing look towards DS Knight. 'And this was around the time Hannah was killed?'

'Around that time, yes.'

'Can you remember the garage he used?'

'Yes. It was the main dealer in Northampton. I picked him up from there after he'd dropped off the Range Rover. It was only in for a couple of days, but for some reason he didn't borrow a courtesy car while his was being repaired like he usually did. That's why I had to pick him up. But he wouldn't let me drive him home. He was quite insistent about that. He took a taxi. I didn't see him again until the Range Rover was returned.' She smiled cynically. 'This was just before he told me it was all over between us.'

'Do you recall the date his car went in?'

She shook her head. 'No. But it was a Wednesday. We usually met up on Wednesdays and Fridays and this occasion was during the week. I'm certain of it.'

'What makes you so sure?'

'It was the week after Hannah was killed. And only a few days before he told me we were finished. He didn't come in on the Monday and Tuesday, which is understandable in the circumstances. I felt really sorry for him; he was quite beside himself with grief.' She looked away for a moment. 'Believe it or not, I'd only just discovered for sure that I was pregnant. I'd done one of those tests a few days earlier but the result was unclear so I went to see my GP on the Monday. It turned out I was nearly three months gone. I didn't say anything to him until the following week-end.'

'Why did you not mention any of this before?'

'I didn't think it had anything to do with Father Dominic's death, and I still don't. I can't believe Harry Newby had anything to do with it. He's a weak man controlled by that wife of his; I realise that now, and I don't like talking about what happened to my child – his son.' There was bitterness in her voice. 'I also assumed the police would have checked out his Range Rover. Didn't they do that?'

Hood cleared his throat again but did not answer Martha's question. Knight looked down and concentrated on her note taking.

'But you thought the accident with his Range Rover might have had some bearing on what happened to his step-daughter?' asked Hood.

'I didn't think anything until much, much later and there wasn't really any other evidence to support my suspicions. I just didn't made the connection at the time, I suppose. Perhaps I still thought too much of him and believed that he would have said something if he'd been responsible. It was only after my son was taken from me and I read about the inquest that I started to have second thoughts about the damage to his Range Rover. It had crossed my mind before, but the inquest wasn't until the end of January ninety-four. I didn't know the full details until then.' She looked away for a moment. 'I still think he's a coward but I can't believe he's capable of deliberately harming anyone. If he was responsible, I'm sure it must have been an accident.'

'Has he ever admitted responsibility for Hannah's death?'

'Not in so many words, no. At the time, he just said he felt guilty about not picking her up when he should have done. And as I said, I didn't make a connection between her death and the damage to his vehicle until later. And I'm not sure about it even now. It could have been a coincidence. By the time I became suspicious, I thought there was little point in raising it.

I was about to give birth, so I had other things to worry about and I had no real proof. After my son was born, I just let it go.'

'Have you ever mentioned your suspicions to anyone else?'

Martha dropped her head. 'No. Who would take any notice of anything I said?'

'Not even after you read about the inquest?'

'No.'

'Mrs Newby, for example?'

She shuddered. 'Mrs Newby? No, definitely not.'

Hood decided to disclose the discovery of the mobile phone which had received the call made by Martha on 3 August when she had spoken to Eleanor Newby. 'We have seized the mobile phone that was used to accept your call last Saturday which must also be the phone which you say Newby used to contact you.'

Martha appeared unsettled by the information. 'You have the phone?'

'Yes.'

'I don't understand.'

'What don't you understand?'

'How you found the phone? If Newby had it, why did *she* answer when I rang? I thought it was his personal phone that he'd used to contact me. How could she have access to it?'

'A good question,' replied Hood, 'and one we shall be asking Mrs Newby, rest assured.' He sighed. 'We'll also keep possession of Newby's business card for the time being too, if you don't mind.' He took it from the file and held it up for her to see.

Martha shrugged. 'I don't want it back. You can keep it as far as I'm concerned. I won't be contacting him again.'

Hood exhaled. 'Tell me, have you had any other contact with her, Mrs Newby I mean?'

Martha shook her head. 'No, and I don't want to have any contact with her. She scares me.'

'What is it about her that scares you?' asked Knight.

Martha hugged herself. 'I don't know, but she does. She seems to be very manipulative, very controlling.'

Both Hood and Knight would not have dissented from that opinion.

'Can you confirm where you were on the evening of the twenty-fourth of July?' asked Hood.

411

'That's when Father Dominic was murdered.'

'It is.'

'I had nothing to do with that, I promise you.'

'It was your day off the next day, wasn't it?'

'Yes. I left the Grange at about five on the Wednesday afternoon. Sir Robert was away in London and I'd prepared a meal for Father Dominic and Father Grantham. I left it in the fridge. A cold collation; Scottish salmon, mainly. Father Grantham had asked me to prepare something special. I don't think they'd ever had supper together before. Father Dominic rarely ate in the house.'

'Did you go back to your cottage afterwards?'

'Yes. And I didn't go out again that night other than into the garden. It was very warm that evening, if you remember?'

'You didn't hear anything untoward while you were in your garden?'

'No, it's quite a way from the Grange to my cottage. There are several nearer houses.'

'You didn't go back into the grounds of the Grange or back to the house?'

'No. I was still at home when Father Grantham rang me the next morning to tell me he'd found Father Dominic in the priest-hole. I rushed back and called the police.'

'Did you go into the Long Room yourself?'

'No, I didn't. I was in shock. I couldn't believe what had happened. I stayed in the kitchen. You saw me there. But I told the young officer all this at the time.'

'You did, of course. Had you seen the priest-hole previously?'

'Yes, Father Dominic showed it to me two or three days earlier after the excavation had been completed. It wasn't that impressive; just a hole in the floor as far as I could see. I didn't understand what all the fuss was about.'

Hood stood up. 'Well, if there's nothing else?' He shot a look at Knight.

'Nothing from me, sir.'

'Right. Detective Sergeant Knight will take a further statement from you, in a few minutes then run you home. Don't miss anything out, no matter how trivial you think it may be. Let me judge whether anything you recall is relevant. I don't want to have to bother you again.'

'So, you're not going to arrest me?' Martha seemed relieved.

Hood smiled and glanced towards Knight. 'No. Whatever gave you that idea?'

CHAPTER FIFTY-FIVE

'It's a match,' said Knight with an air of triumph after she returned to Hood's office. Her excitement was palpable. She had left Martha in the interview room with a cup of tea and a WPC. 'I've just received a call from Dr Irwin at the laboratory, Jennifer Irwin. I know her quite well – remember? I told you we attend the same gym – when I can get there.' She smiled broadly. 'The blood from the boot of the Jaguar Mark Two is definitely from Father Dominic. One billion to one it was shed by someone other than he. She's faxing the full report over first thing tomorrow after it's been typed. I think we've got him.'

Hood looked at his watch and nodded. He did not seem in the least surprised. 'So they do work late on occasions?' He glanced at his watch again. 'It's almost ten to six.'

Knight realised Hood was being sarcastic. 'They knew this was very important.'

'I would have thought everything they do is important,' countered Hood, beaming. 'Still, it's great news. Some solid and indisputable evidence at last. We'll arrest both Arthur and Eleanor Newby tomorrow.'

'Mrs Newby, too?'

'Oh, yes. Mrs Newby too. It wouldn't surprise me if she put Newby up to this. We'll arrest the wife for attempting to pervert the course of justice. We'll proceed on the basis that she was at least involved in the cover up. Of course, if she did put him up to it and we get the evidence, we can charge both of them with murder.'

'And the housekeeper?'

'I doubt if she had any involvement. What she said about the business is confirmed by the information from Companies House. Interesting, though, what she says about Mrs Newby answering Newby's mobile phone. I wonder how it got into his filing cabinet? And if Newby did have the bull bars removed from his Range Rover after Hannah was killed, it advances my theory about how she died. I want Mark Bradley to get over to the main Northampton dealers now before they close for the day and do some digging.'

'I'll organise that before I take Martha's further statement,' said Knight, 'but we might be a bit on the late side. If they're closed he'll have to go there first thing tomorrow.' She gave Hood a curious look. 'You're sure she's telling the truth? She never mentioned any of this before and it may be significant that she's spoken to Mrs Newby since she made her last statement.'

Hood shook his head. 'No, on balance, I don't think Martha is involved. If the garage has kept its records from ninety-three, we should be able to confirm her account of Newby's Range Rover having the bull bars removed.'

'But revealing that now might suggest she is in cahoots with Mrs Newby? Think about it. Supposing she told her what she's just told us. The two of them acting together to do Newby down would make a powerful combination.'

Hood smiled. 'I don't think so. I don't believe Martha thought any of this relevant to the investigation. If Eleanor Newby knew for sure her husband was responsible for Hannah's death, she'd have done something about it before now. I can't see her standing by and doing nothing if she believed he had killed her beloved daughter, even if it were in an accident.' Hood noticed a look of disappointment on Knight's face. 'But you keep that theory of yours alive, Wendy. The way this investigation has twisted and turned, I wouldn't be surprised at anything.' He grinned broadly. 'Take a further statement from Martha then run her back to Easton Parva. We'll treat her as a witness for the time being; we can review the position after we've spoken with both the Newbys and the CPS.' He paused. 'Now, I have a lot of preparation to do for tomorrow's interview and I must finish my report and fax it to Fiona Morrison. I shall be working late tonight, with my wife's permission I might add, and I don't want to be disturbed. We should crack this case by tomorrow, if all goes well. I'll see you here when I return from the press briefing at Wootton Hall.'

As Knight departed, Hood settled down at his desk and started to go through the material that had been building up during the day. He made a quick note of the DNA analysis of the blood from the boot of the Jaguar then started to read the statements that had come in earlier comparing the dust and debris from the niche discovered behind the panelling in the priest-hole with the sacramental found in Father Dominic's hand. The scrapings from the *agnus dei* and the samples from the niche were stated as having a high match probability, certainly sufficient to established that it was likely that the sacramental had been hidden there. As Hood had expected, there was no blood found on the swabs from the Powdrell chalice and no sign of any fingerprints. If Father Dominic had polished it, as seemed likely, he must have removed any evidence of its being touched, even by him. DNA results from the swabs Nigel Mullen had taken were still awaited but were not expected to reveal anything of significance.

Hood now considered it was safe to conclude that the discovery of the priest-hole and the murder of Father Dominic were not directly connected. The full report from Nigel Mullen detailing the results from SOCO's examination of the old chapel grounds and the priest-hole clearly demonstrated where the priest had been when the fatal blows were struck. Hood was satisfied that the body had been removed, smuggled into the house and dumped in the hide, but he was still intrigued by the absence of a bloody trail. There was no evidence that any blows had been struck in the Long Room or inside the priest-hole. He was perfectly satisfied that however it was done, the object of leaving the body in the hide was to divert the inevitable police investigation away from the truth.

The tiny glass fragments found on the spade along with the traces of blood confirmed that the same implement which had been employed by Philip Southall to break the window in the Long Room had been used to kill Father Dominic. The full profile from the blood on the blade of the spade identified only Father Dominic's DNA. Hood was still waiting for the results of the examination of the remains of the carpet from the boot of the Jaguar, but he had no doubt about its provenance. He had extracted a promise from the senior scientific officer at the laboratory that the comparison between the exhibit and the interior carpeting of the Jaguar would be carried out immediately and an oral report telephoned through as a matter of urgency. He was also awaiting the result of the examination of Father Dominic's habit. It was always possible that fibres from whatever was used to cover the body and remove it into the house might be found on the fabric of the habit. There was also an outside chance of the killer's own DNA being detected.

The full report from the forensic pathologist, with the addition of the statement from Martin Egerton, now contained the photographs taken during the *post-mortem*. Hood, who never relished looking at such images, forced himself to examine the impression made by Father Dominic's cowl on one of the wounds towards the back of his head. The photograph of the injury and the impression in the blood had been enlarged several times. Even to the inexpert eye, the evidence was clear. The cowl must have been over the priest's head when he was struck by at least one of the blows which killed him. The two threads removed from one of the wounds appeared to have come from his Benedictine habit although confirmation was still awaited.

Hood then concentrated on the timeline prepared by DC Bradley in respect of the investigation into Hannah Newby's death. The file now contained a copy of the order Bradley had obtained from the County court showing that Newby had adopted Hannah in 1985. A thorough examination of the accident file from 1993 by both Knight and Bradley had shown no evidence of Newby's Range Rover being subject to any kind of examination by those investigating Hannah's death. No mention of his Range Rover being the subject of even a visual inspection. *A significant oversight, that, on the part of the investigating team.* Hood crossed his fingers that Bradley's visit to the Northampton main dealers would confirm what Martha had said about Newby's vehicle.

The telephone on Hood's desk rang. He initially ignored it, then as the ringing persisted, he glanced at his watch and picked up the receiver. It occurred to him the call might have been from Bradley.

'Hood,' he barked. He was annoyed at the interruption but relaxed when he recognised the voice as that of Newby's solicitor.

'Ah, Superintendent. I'm sorry to disturb you. Gerald Sewell here. I was hoping I might catch you. I thought I'd ring you in advance of our meeting tomorrow. I'm afraid the news about Arthur Newby is not good.'

'Not good?' repeated Hood. It took him a moment to focus on what Sewell was talking about.

'I'm afraid so. The scan he had this morning and his latest blood tests have confirmed that his cancer has returned. More to the point, it has spread to his liver. They're suggesting the possibility of more chemotherapy, but the prognosis is very poor. He's given me authority to disclose this to you. As you can imagine, it has hit him very hard, but he still wants his interview tomorrow to go ahead. I've advised him that it could be postponed, but he was very insistent. He wants it over with, one way or the other.'

Hood reflected on his response. 'You're satisfied he's fit enough to be interviewed under caution? I don't want any admissions he may make being compromised later by his claiming he was too sick to be questioned.'

'I'm not anticipating Mr Newby admitting anything, Superintendent. I have my doubts about his fitness, but not his determination to put this matter to bed. His instructions are clear. He wants to go ahead.'

'I shall need to see something confirming the result of the scan and I might also point out I'm still waiting for his medical records.'

'I shall make them available tomorrow afternoon. I should have a full report from his oncologist by then too. Dr Freeman appreciates the urgency and as Mr Newby is a private patient the report is being prepared overnight, for a fee, of course. Good job he's not reliant on the NHS.' He paused for a moment. 'It will not make happy reading, I assure you.'

'Will his wife be accompanying him to the police station as before?'

'I suspect she'll drive him into Northampton, yes.'

'Good. My sergeant will have a few questions for her. I don't suppose you can represent both of them. I doubt if she'll say anything though without a lawyer at her elbow.'

'I thought you would want to speak with her after the search of their home. I have arranged for a partner in another firm to be available should you wish to question her tomorrow.' He paused and cleared his throat. 'My client still feels he can explain the evidence that was seized in the search satisfactorily.'

Hood has his doubts about that. 'There will be some further disclosure in the morning Mr Sewell, which I don't think he will be able to explain satisfactorily or at all. The DNA analysis has just come through on the blood found in the boot of the Jaguar. It's definitely Father Dominic's. I should have the full report tomorrow morning. I will make that available for you as soon as I can.'

The solicitor did not respond immediately. When he did, he sounded surprised. 'That is not what I was expecting to hear Mr Hood. It seemed to be such a tiny bloodstain. But I suppose advances in DNA techniques are being made all the time. I shall have to take further instructions and we may well need to get our own expert to review the findings. I shall also require to see the scientific working file in due course. I'll see you at noon tomorrow.'

Hood could not resist a smile as he replaced the receiver.

CHAPTER FIFTY-SIX

'Where's Harry the Hood,' asked Bradley as he rushed into the incident room just before noon on Wednesday morning. He had several pieces of paper in his hand and looked anxiously around him. 'Is he back from the press briefing yet?'

'Don't let him hear you calling him that,' advised Swanson, looking around the room. 'He's been back over an hour and about to start interviewing Arthur Newby.' Swanson continued to concentrate on his computer screen. 'He was asking whether you had got anywhere at the dealers before he went downstairs.'

'Oh, have I got somewhere,' replied Bradley, a broad grin on his face. 'I had to wait for it, but I've only managed to get copies of the invoice which relates to the servicing of Newby's Range Rover in nineteen ninety-three. Look.' He held up the papers in his hand. 'Newby had the bull bars removed shortly after Hannah died, just as I always suspected. I've also got a call coming in any time soon about Mrs Newby's previous motor. She hasn't only driven automatics in the recent past.'

Swanson stood up and walked towards his colleague. Bradley pointed to the documents in question. 'See what I mean?'

Swanson looked through the paper work. 'We've got him,' he said, 'This, along with the DNA, will do for him. And he traded his Range Rover in shortly afterwards too. You'd better get this down to the Super before he starts. He's using interview room number three with the DS. Take this with you.' He handed Bradley the full DNA report on the bloodstain found in the boot of the Jaguar that had just been faxed through from the laboratory.

'Where's Newby now?' asked Bradley as he grabbed the fax.

'He's with his solicitor in the room off the front desk. His wife is in there too. DS Knight will be asking her a few questions later.'

'Rather her than me,' said Bradley as he made for the door and rushed downstairs. He knocked on the door of the interview room. Hood invited him in. He could tell from Bradley's face that something of interest had been found. He took the papers from him, handed the fax to DS Knight and started to digest the paperwork from the garage. Bradley could not resist commenting on what he had discovered. 'It's all there, sir. Bull bars removed and off-side headlight replaced. Minor service carried out.'

Hood looked up. 'So it would appear. Well done, Bradley. I suppose you'd like to sit in on the interview?'

'Yes sir!' exclaimed the young detective. 'I can't wait to see his face when you show him that invoice.'

'Well, you're going to have to be patient. There are other matters to deal with first, but this copy invoice will certainly come in very useful. But don't get too excited. We don't want to give too much away too quickly.'

'Shouldn't we disclose the copy invoice?' queried Knight.

'We shall,' said Hood with a broad grin. 'During the course of the interview. Now, have you checked over the DNA analysis?'

'Yes, sir. It's all there. Exactly as I was told last night.'

'Let's have him in then. Would you like to go and get him, Bradley? He's in the waiting room just off the front desk with his solicitor. And I don't want his wife brought along if she's there, not yet. DS Knight will be having a word with her later. And say nothing to those reporters hanging round outside. They know an arrest is imminent – they were told about the DNA at this morning's press conference. Newby's name is to remain confidential until he's charged, though. I don't want any leaks.'

★ ★ ★ ★

'I'm sorry about the news concerning your illness, Mr Newby,' began Hood in sympathetic mode. 'You must tell me if you need a break at any time.'

Newby did not reply; he simply nodded. He appeared gaunt and pale. His solicitor intervened.

'Mr Newby feels that he must continue with the interview, Superintendent. I have given him certain advice, but the decision is his.'

Hood nodded then shocked both the suspect and his solicitor by arresting Newby on suspicion of the murder of Father Dominic. He cautioned him fully.

'So, you're arresting me, are you, for murder? Because of that damned bloodstain I suppose?'

'That and other evidence,' replied Hood. He tapped the file in front of him. 'I take it Mr Sewell has told you the result of the DNA analysis of the bloodstain in the boot of your Jaguar?'

'He has. There must have been some kind of mistake. That's all I can say. I have no idea how it got there.'

Hood looked towards Knight who handed the fax to the solicitor. 'No mistake,' she said.

The solicitor examined the document then looked up. 'You'll let me have a copy of this, will you Superintendent?'

Hood nodded. 'Along with one or two other documents that I've just received.' He glanced towards Bradley who maintained a poker face.

'You're surely not suggesting that this priest was bundled into the back of Mr Newby's Jaguar? I imagine a Mark Two has a very small boot,' said the solicitor.

Hood had not formed a definite view. 'While I don't discount that possibility, I suspect the blood came from whatever was used to cover the body as it was taken to the priest-hole and dumped there. Microscopic examination of all possible routes has not revealed any blood at all. As the deceased bled profusely, it follows the body must have been wrapped in something and that something must have been placed in the boot afterwards.'

'Speculation,' grunted Newby. 'Where's your evidence? Where is this something?'

Hood looked directly at the suspect. 'It's your vehicle, Mr Newby. It seems a reasonable enough question for me to ask how the blood of a murdered priest came to be found in the boot of your Jaguar motor car a few days after the killing, a vehicle you had owned for only a few weeks.'

Newby did not reply. Hood stared at him for half a minute then removed an exhibit from his file.

'I want to begin by showing Mr Newby this copy of the *Melford Recorder*, which was seized from his study earlier this week, Exhibit WR 04. In particular, I'd like his comment about the circle drawn in ink around the announcement of Father Dominic's move to Easton Grange.'

He handed the open magazine to Newby, still in its protective cover. Newby, glanced at it then returned it to Hood.

'I suppose I must have done that, but I have no recollection of doing so.'

'It confirms that you knew Father Dominic was coming to Easton Grange, doesn't it?'

'I suppose it does, but I have no recollection of making that mark. If I did, it must simply have been because I remembered him from my schooldays and because Easton Grange is close by. I have to admit that I do tend to circle things when I note something of potential interest. It's a habit of mine. My wife can confirm it. But I paid no heed to it afterwards. And it was all some time ago. Before my illness developed.'

'I've been through the whole magazine, Mr Newby. You don't appear to have circled anything else.'

'I'll take your word for it. Nothing else interested me, I presume.'

'Do you wish to add to or revise anything that you told me about your relationship with Father Dominic?'

Newby looked away for a moment. Hood was almost expecting a change of position, but it did not come. 'No, I don't. I didn't have a relationship with him.'

'I want to turn now to your former employee, Martha Morton.'

Newby's reaction was fierce. 'I've told you already, I won't discuss her. She's out to get me.'

'And her child? asked Hood. 'Is he out to get you too?'

'What child?' replied Newby. But his tone suggested his ignorance was feigned.

'The child she gave birth to on January the sixteenth nineteen-ninety-four. The child she had adopted; the child she says is your son.'

Newby hesitated. 'No comment.'

'The son she told you about when you met up with her in Northampton on the twenty-seventh of March.'

'No comment.'

'You did meet up with her, didn't you?'

'No comment.'

'We are checking the CCTV from Gold Street in Northampton. That's where the restaurant is situated where the two of you had lunch. I wasn't too hopeful the tape would still be available, but fortunately, it is.

It's been preserved for another unrelated investigation. There's a lot to go through, but I think we should be able to prove you were with Martha that lunch time.'

'No comment.'

'Does your wife know about the child?'

Newby looked towards his solicitor who did not intervene.

'No comment.' He shifted in his seat.

Hood produced Newby's business card from the file.

'You gave Martha this card when you had lunch with her which bears the mobile phone number you asked her to use if she rang you. We are awaiting the result of DNA analysis of a sample from the card.'

Newby hardly glanced at it. 'I probably gave her that years ago. The fact that she's kept it proves she's out to get me. Can't you see that?'

'I don't think so, Mr Newby. The phone number printed on this card did not exist back in ninety-three. We've had it checked. It wasn't assigned until nearly two years ago. That number was also used by Martha to phone you last Saturday, but the phone was somewhat surprisingly answered by your wife. The two of them spoke for over six minutes. We have the record from BT. I assure you, there's no doubt about it. During that conversation your wife told Martha that she knew about her affair with you and that she was aware of Martha's pregnancy.'

A look of panic crossed Newby's face. 'I don't believe you. That can't be true. Eleanor's never mentioned that to me. You've met my wife, Superintendent. Do you think she's the type not to mention my having an affair if she knew about it?'

The solicitor intervened. 'Are you saying you have a recording of the conversation, Superintendent?'

'No, I'm not saying that at all. But we have the time, duration and both numbers used from the computers of BT and the air-time provider.'

'So, apart from what this woman says, you have no evidence to support what you have just suggested?' said the solicitor. He gave his client a reassuring look.

Hood looked directly at Newby before he answered. 'That phone was also used by your wife earlier this year to call Martha Morton before you and she met for lunch in Northampton. That appears in the phone schedule too. The calls marked in yellow.'

The solicitor started to look through the disclosure package.

'I don't understand,' said Newby. 'Why would my wife want to contact Martha in March?'

'Why do you say March, Mr Newby? I didn't say the call was in March. I said earlier this year.'

Newby leant forward and spat out his reply. 'Because it's marked in yellow on the schedule, Mr Hood, and dated. I've been through it with my solicitor, you know.'

Hood half-smiled. He had to give Newby that one. Despite his illness, he still had his wits about him. Hood moved on. 'According to Martha, your wife called her at her cottage.'

'No way. I don't believe it. There must be some mistake. I know nothing of any such call.' Newby seemed very much on edge. It seemed that what Hood had told him about his wife had come as a shock. He looked anxiously towards his solicitor.

'The disclosure package states you have seized the mobile phone,' said Mr Sewell.

'Yes. We found the phone in the back of the top drawer of Mr Newby's filing cabinet. DC Renfrew's statement deals with it. But Mr Newby already knows that. His wife will have told him. She was there when it was seized. Who, I wonder, put it there?'

Hood gave Newby a harsh look. The response was matter of fact. 'I know you found it there. My wife informed me and I've seen the disclosure. That's where it was kept. I've hardly used it recently. It proves nothing.'

'The Sim card has been checked and a cell-site analysis has been carried out. That call on Saturday was received via the closest mast to Stanton Harwood.

'I have not received any notice of that,' interrupted the solicitor.

'I'm sorry about that Mr Sewell. I only got the bare bones of the report this morning. The examination was only carried out yesterday.'

The solicitor tried to cast doubt. 'Cell-site analysis is in its very early days, Mr Hood. It's possible there has been a mistake or perhaps there's a quite innocent explanation.'

'A copy will be made available to you in the event of a charge. And I don't myself see much scope for an innocent explanation. There's no doubt about it. And if you recall, Mr Newby, you have previously stated you only had one mobile phone.'

'I'd overlooked that. I haven't used the other one for ages.'

'And your wife? Has she used either of them?'

'No. She has her own phone. And my wife has said nothing to me about any telephone calls to or from Martha Goring.'

'I don't suppose she has. I suspect there are a few other things your wife has not mentioned to you. But we have Martha's recollection of what was said. Detective Sergeant Knight will be speaking to your wife immediately after this interview. Hopefully, we'll obtain her account then.'

'Good luck to you with that,' said Newby, with a measure of sarcasm. 'You'll get nowhere with Eleanor.' He almost smiled.

'Of course,' added Hood. 'That interview will include asking your wife about Martha Morton's child.'

'No doubt it will,' replied Newby, showing signs of irritation. 'If you're still taking what Martha says seriously. Happily, I don't.'

'You knew she was pregnant when she left your employment, didn't you?'

'No comment.'

'That's why you gave her such a generous settlement.'

'No comment.'

'You hoped she would have a termination?'

'No comment.'

'The child has to be yours, doesn't he? You and she were in a sexual relationship at the time the boy must have been conceived. She wasn't in a relationship with anyone else.'

Newby took a deep breath. 'No comment.'

'We are taking steps to trace the child. We can then do a DNA check.'

Newby sighed but did not answer. Hood waited then looked at Knight. 'Perhaps you should speak with Mrs Newby now. If Mr Newby continues to exercise his right of silence, we shall make little if any progress. We may do better with his wife.'

The solicitor interrupted as Knight pushed back her chair. She hesitated as the solicitor spoke. 'Mrs Newby will not say anything in the absence of a solicitor. I have made an arrangement with another firm as I promised, but Mrs Dangerfield – she's the solicitor who will be dealing – will not be able to attend until later. And, if I may say so, Superintendent, I fail to see what Martha Morton and her child, assuming she has one, has to do with the killing of this priest.'

Knight pulled her chair in and resumed taking a note.

'We'll be coming to that, I assure you. Now, perhaps Mr Newby can explain what his Range Rover was doing parked outside Father Dominic's cottage back in April?'

Newby seemed puzzled. 'No idea. I was not at all well in April. Better than I had been and in remission, but I was very tired and hardly ever went out. And this all comes from Martha, doesn't it? I've told you already, she's out to get me.'

'Your Range Rover is an automatic, isn't it?'

'What if it is?'

'Does your wife ever drive it?'

Newby seemed surprised by the question. 'She has her own car, a Mercedes. I suppose she might have driven the Range Rover when I've been laid up.' He paused. 'Why are you so interested in my wife?'

'As you already know, she's been identified as being present at Easton Grange on the seventh of July. That was the same day the Mark Two Jag was seen there. Our witness does not say that she saw you with your wife on that occasion but that doesn't mean you were not there. Although no one was observed with it, I can't at the moment exclude the possibility that it could have been your wife who was driving it.'

Newby scoffed his reply. 'What would my wife be doing there? Look, I'm not going through all this again. While she might have driven the Range Rover, my wife couldn't have driven the Jag on the seventh of July. She only drives an automatic. She's already told you that. Anyway, she was at home with me. I was in bed. I'd taken some pills prescribed by my doctor to help me to sleep.'

'Which means, if true, that you can't alibi your wife, not if you were asleep.'

Newby reacted angrily. 'She was there. I'll swear to it if I have to. I heard her downstairs in the kitchen and saw her when she brought up my lunch, which means she can't have been where you say she was.'

'Is that what your wife has asked you to say?'

Newby appeared furious. He slammed the palm of his hand on the table. 'My wife hasn't asked me to say or do anything.'

Hood continued to push. 'Hmm. I shall certainly have to consider the possibility that it was Mrs Newby who visited Father Dominic in April and again on the seventh of July.'

Newby sat back in his chair then placed his hand to his abdomen. 'You leave my wife out of this. She has nothing to do with it.'

'Well, one or other of you is certainly involved. Tell me, does your wife own a ruby brooch in the shape of a spider?'

'A spider?' He looked blankly at Hood. 'No idea. I know she has a lot of jewellery. Her first husband was very generous in that direction, but I don't recall a piece like that. ' He smiled. 'My wife is terrified of spiders. Hates them. I doubt if she'd wear a brooch of that design.'

'And we mustn't overlook the bloodstain in the boot, must we?' said Hood.

Newby looked away. The bloodstain seemed an insuperable problem. Hood then removed the garage invoice from his file and handed it to Newby. He glanced at it and placed it on the table.

'We have recently established that you took your Range Rover into the Northampton main dealer in late July, a few days after your step-daughter was killed. You had the bull bars removed and a front headlight replaced. Why was that?'

Newby looked again at the invoice and swallowed hard. 'Where did you get this from?'

'DC Bradley recovered it this morning.' Hood acknowledged Bradley with a nod. 'The garage still had it in their computerised records, which is fortunate. This is a print-off. As you can see, it clearly refers to the vehicle you owned in nineteen-ninety-three.'

Newby looked up. 'What are you suggesting?'

'I'm not suggesting anything at the moment. I'm simply asking you why you took your Range Rover in for the bull bars to be removed and the headlight replaced at that particular time?'

'It's a long time ago. There must have been a reason. I'll have to think about it. Late July nineteen-ninety-three, you say? Oh, I remember, I'd hit a muntjac on the A43. Bloody nuisance they are. They may be small but they're quite stocky. Damaged the bull bars and broke the glass on one of the headlights, well cracked it really. I decided to have the bull bars removed while it was in.'

'Stainless steel weren't they?'

'Don't recall.'

'It's written on the invoice.'

Newby looked again. 'So it is. That must be the case then.'

'Badly damaged were they?'

'Slightly. Bit bent as I recall, but spoiled the look of the vehicle. Expensive to replace, and the garage had none in stock, so I got rid of them.'

'Relevance, Mr Hood?' asked the solicitor, raising his eyebrows.

'It lends some support to Martha's account of matters. She picked up Mr Newby in her own car after he dropped off the Range Rover. And it also supports what I suggested in the last interview. That Mr Newby had some involvement in the death of his step-daughter.'

Newby became agitated. 'How dare you suggest that!'

The solicitor remained calm and touched his client's arm to reassure him. 'In the absence of any check being carried out on the Range Rover in nineteen-ninety-three immediately after the accident, this remains mere speculation, Superintendent, as you well know.'

'Does your wife know about this, Mr Newby?' asked Hood. 'Because she will shortly.'

'I've told you, my wife has nothing to do with any of this. Leave her out of it. I don't want you bothering her. And I'm answering no more questions. Either charge me or I'm out of here.'

'Not yet, Mr Newby. As Mr Sewell will advise you, I can keep you here initially for twenty-four hours. You remain under arrest.' Hood pushed his seat back. 'In view of your poor health, I won't detain you in a cell at the moment. You can remain here in the interview room with your solicitor, after you have been booked in. I'm sorry, but there is no question of your leaving until after your wife has been questioned.' Hood stood up. 'You might like to think about that piece of burnt carpet we found at your premises.' He paused, smiled, then took a photograph from his file and held it up. 'For the benefit of the tape, this is a photograph of the exhibit in question which is presently at the forensic science laboratory undergoing examination. It appears to have come from the boot of your Jaguar. It certainly seems to match the carpet in the rest of the vehicle. Now, why would anyone want to remove the carpet from the boot of your Jaguar and burn it?' Newby looked down as Hood continued. 'Because it was bloodstained, perhaps?'

Newby did not reply. He gradually started to hyperventilate and looked towards his solicitor who glanced at his watch.

'It will be almost another hour before Mrs Dangerfield gets here, Mr

Hood. I am concerned about Mr Newby's fitness to remain in the police station for much longer. And I have a brief appointment elsewhere later today.'

Hood noticed Newby's condition was continuing to deteriorate. 'The FME is in the station at the moment. I shall ask her to take a look at Mr Newby.' Hood glanced towards the suspect. 'He could be here for some time yet.'

'And Mrs Newby?' asked Sewell.

'I propose to arrest her and to go through the booking-in procedure before Mrs Dangerfield gets here. Detective Sergeant Knight will do the honours. It will save time. I assure you, she will not be questioned until Mrs Dangerfield arrives. As I said, Mr Newby will have to be processed too, now that he is no longer attending here voluntarily.' He nodded towards Newby who dropped his head. 'The FME can see him after he has been officially detained.'

Newby looked up. He seemed more concerned about his wife than his own detention. 'You're arresting my wife?' His eyes betrayed panic. He shook his head then slumped in his seat.

'That's what I intend to do, yes.'

Newby appeared at a loss.

'Perhaps your wife will be more forthcoming?' continued Hood 'Mind you, she didn't tell me the truth about the colour of your Jaguar did she? Then we have the evidence about her being at Easton Grange on the seventh. And given your poor health, someone must have burnt that carpet, don't you agree?'

Newby did not reply. He placed his head in his hands.

'And remember, Mr Newby,' added Hood before he made for the door, 'there can be no absolution without true contrition.'

Newby grabbed his lower abdomen as if in pain. DS Knight leant forward, stated the time and switched off the recording machine.

CHAPTER FIFTY-SEVEN

Hood determined to take a bit of a gamble with Mrs Newby. Wendy Knight, he decided, would interview her alone. He thought the detective sergeant would make more progress if he were not present. Wendy, on the other hand, was not so sure. She hated to admit it, but she liked the reassuring presence of Hood when questioning potential suspects in such a serious investigation.

'I don't know, Harry. She's likely to be much trickier than her husband, especially if you want me to put your theory to her about how her daughter died? I think it would come better from you.'

Hood reflected for a moment. He certainly wanted to gauge Mrs Newby's reaction to the suggestion that her husband was responsible in some way for the death of her daughter. But he thought this could be achieved more effectively if he were not in the room.

'You're fully on board with it now, aren't you, Wendy? You saw Newby's reaction for yourself. No reason why it shouldn't be put to her.'

Knight nodded. 'I still think it would come better from you.'

Hood spoke reassuringly. 'You'll be fine. I'll watch the proceedings on my computer. I can always come and join you should it prove necessary.' He noted Knight remained apprehensive. 'I'll tell you what, you raise it with her; I'll then join you and deal with the implications of her husband's confession to Father Dominic. I'd like to see how she reacts when you first mention it to her, though. We really need to establish if she and her husband are singing from the same hymn sheet. If she departs from what he has said in any significant way, we may have to put on our thinking caps again.'

'Always assuming she doesn't go "no comment." That's always possible, isn't it?'

Hood was certain that would not happen. 'She won't do that, whatever advice her solicitor may give her. I guarantee it. She'll want to have her say. She won't be able to resist it. It's in her nature to argue her corner. But whatever she says, I'll get a better impression watching it on screen. After all, that's why this expensive equipment was installed.'

Hood was referring to the video camera that had recently been introduced into interview room number 2. It enabled a senior officer to observe an interview as it took place. It meant that the reaction of the suspect could be assessed with greater objectivity. It was not provided, as junior officers sometimes suspected, for senior ranks to assess the capabilities or otherwise of their interviewing techniques.

'No pressure then,' sighed Knight as she headed out of the Superintendent's room. She would give it her best shot whatever her forebodings.

Hood called after her. 'Give a nod towards the camera if things get too much for you. It might well make a greater impact if I join you after you have dealt with the preliminaries. And you never know, she might reveal more to you than she would to me.'

Knight turned briefly and smiled sweetly, but did not reply. Three minutes later she walked in to the interview room carrying the now bulky case file. Eleanor Newby and her solicitor were already sitting on the far side of the table, the camera to their right. Knight dismissed the uniformed constable and took her seat on the opposite side and placed the file in front of her.

'No Superintendent Hood?' sneered Mrs Newby. Hood's absence seemed to increase her self-confidence.

'He's otherwise engaged,' replied Knight as she switched on the tape machine and the camera. 'Evidence is still coming in. He may be joining us later.' She pointed out the video camera to her left and made it clear that the interview would be recorded both audibly and visually.

The solicitor intervened. 'Mrs Newby will be exercising her right of silence, Detective Sergeant. You'll be wasting your time, I'm afraid. You may as well release her now.'

Knight frowned. 'That, of course, is her right, Mrs Dangerfield. But I need hardly remind you it's also my duty to question her nevertheless, certainly during the next twenty-four hours. Whether I will be wasting my time we will have to see. She may prove more amenable when she hears what I have to say. Some up-to-date information has just reached us.'

Mrs Newby glanced towards her solicitor. A worried expression crossed her face. Was DS Knight intending to keep her at the police station overnight? And what was this new material?

The solicitor reassured her client. 'And after this interview has finished, she will be permitted to see her husband I presume? I assume his interview has concluded?'

Knight was not diverted. 'That will be a matter for Detective Superintendent Hood to decide. Mr Newby is likely to be interviewed again after we have finished here. We were not able to complete his interview. There are number of issues still outstanding but a break was considered necessary.'

'What do you mean? How is my husband?' asked Mrs Newby. 'He's not at all well. He's not fit enough to be held in a police station. He's had some very grave news about his health. I was against him coming here at all.'

'He's fine. And we are aware of his health issues. There is a doctor in the police station at the moment who can be called upon if necessary.'

Mrs Newby scowled and sat back in her chair, but said nothing further.

'And my client? You will bail her or release her unconditionally at the conclusion of this interview?' asked the solicitor.

'Mr Hood will make a decision about her precise status when we have finished. As I said, he will hopefully be joining us later.' She turned slightly to her left and looked at the camera as she spoke. Up in his room, watching the proceedings on screen, Hood smiled and settled back in his chair. He was looking forward to this encounter. He had every confidence in Wendy Knight's abilities and had no doubt she would be able to carry it off. After all, he was the person who had taught her how to go about questioning a suspect. The usual preliminaries completed, and all present having identified themselves, the detective sergeant then turned towards her prey.

'Eleanor Newby,' she began, 'As you are aware, you have been arrested on suspicion of doing acts tending and intended to pervert the course of public justice arising out of the murder of Father Dominic Renville on the twenty-fourth of July this year. You are not obliged to say anything but it may harm your defence if you do not mention when questioned something which you later rely on in court. Anything you do say may be given in evidence. Do you understand?'

Mrs Newby gave Knight a derisive look. She then glanced towards her solicitor who shook her head, but as Hood had anticipated, the suspect was unable to remain silent. She just couldn't help herself. And with Hood absent, she was confident she could deal with any questions Knight might ask her. She would have no problems bossing a mere detective sergeant, or so she thought. She immediately went on the attack.

'I understand that you and Detective Superintendent Hood must have taken leave of your senses. What, precisely, am I supposed to have done? I thought it was my husband you were harassing, not me. I have nothing to do with the death of this priest. And, so far as I am aware, neither has he.'

Knight was not distracted. But she noticed the "so far as I am aware." 'You have been arrested because we have reason to believe that you have interfered with evidence in an attempt to assist your husband who, as you know, is detained here on suspicion of the murder of Father Dominic.'

'Absolute nonsense. My husband has not murdered anybody. The idea is simply preposterous. Arthur wouldn't hurt a fly. And as for me, I repeat, what exactly am I supposed to have done?'

'Perhaps we can begin with your motor car?' said Knight.

'What has my motor car got to do with anything?'

Knight consulted the file, focussing on the information recently provided by DC Bradley. After checking the details of Arthur Newby's Range Rovers, it had occurred to him that a similar inquiry into Mrs Newby's motoring history might produce a similar dividend. His hunch had proved correct.

'You implied when you were spoken to at your home that you could not have driven your husband's Jaguar Mark Two because you only drive an automatic?'

'My Mercedes is an automatic, yes.'

'And your previous Mercedes? The one you part-exchanged for your present model in November of last year? Was that an automatic too?'

She did not reply.

Knight took a document from the file. 'I have a copy of the sales invoice.'

She handed it to Mrs Newby who gave it a cursory glance but remained relaxed and unruffled. 'You have been busy. And what has this to do with the death of this priest or my so-called interference with the evidence? I happen to prefer driving an automatic, that's all. They are not exactly uncommon these days.'

'You owned your previous Mercedes for just under three years. Which means you are perfectly capable of driving a non-automatic motor car, like your husband's Jaguar.'

Mrs Newby smiled but not in a friendly way. 'I think, Detective Sergeant, there's quite a difference between my previous Mercedes and my husband's ancient Jaguar. Hardly comparing like with like, is it?' Her smiled broadened.

Knight remained focused. 'It was the Jaguar in which a trace of Father Dominic's blood was discovered in the boot. You appreciate we now have the result of the DNA analysis. The blood matches that of the priest. Is that why you are distancing yourself from the Jaguar?'

Mrs Newby swallowed and looked towards her solicitor who shook her head.

Mrs Newby responded quietly 'No comment.'

Up in his room, Hood smiled and made a note. The discovery of sufficient blood in the boot of the Jaguar for a successful DNA analysis to take place was a game changer. It provided an unchallengeable link between the murder of the priest and the Jaguar motor car. Arthur Newby had not been able to explain its presence. It looked like his wife was similarly handicapped. If anything were likely to cause a split in their respective accounts, it was that bloodstain.

Knight continued to press Eleanor Newby about the Jaguar. 'The vehicle I suggest you or your husband drove to Easton Grange on the seventh of July, the Sunday morning Father Dominic was saying Mass in the chapel.'

'Nothing to do with me or, so far as I am aware, my husband. We were both at home that Sunday, like any other Sunday. My husband has been very ill, you know.'

There was that "so far as I am aware" again. Knight continued. 'The Jaguar was seen at the Grange on the seventh of July at around noon. Its registered number was noted.'

'By a boy of eleven, I believe. I think he is wrong about what he imagines he saw. And whatever he says, I know nothing of it.'

'As you are aware, we have a witness who identifies you as being there at the same time.'

Mrs Newby remained completely calm. She answered quietly. 'Your witness must be mistaken. I was not there.'

'Are you prepared to cooperate with an identification procedure?'

'If you insist and my solicitor advises, yes.'

Knight made a note and changed the subject. 'Your husband usually drives a Range Rover, doesn't he?'

Mrs Newby hesitated before replying. 'Yes. What if he does?'

'Has he always driven a Range Rover?'

'He has had several models over the years, yes.'

'Did he have a Range Rover back in nineteen ninety-three?'

'Yes, I believe he did.'

'At the time he was having an affair with Martha Goring, now known as Martha Morton.'

'No comment.'

'You have since discovered that he had an affair with Martha, haven't you?'

'No comment.'

'And that your husband is the father of her son?'

Mrs Newby was unable to restrain herself. She ignored her solicitor's silently mouthed advice to make no reply. 'I fail to see what this woman's son, assuming she has one, has to do with the death of a priest at Easton Grange earlier this year.'

'Let me enlighten you. Your daughter, Hannah, was killed in a road traffic accident towards the end of July that year?'

Mrs Newby's eyes involuntarily filled with tears at the mention of her deceased daughter. Her solicitor intervened.

'I fail to see the relevance of that question, Detective Sergeant, unless you are deliberately trying to upset my client. If you are, you have clearly succeeded.'

'Not at all, Mrs Dangerfield. Superintendent Hood and I have studied the evidence in that case. We both agree with Mrs Newby and her husband that the inquiry could have been pursued with greater vigour.'

Mrs Newby's response was heavy with sarcasm as she quickly recovered herself. 'Well, at least we can agree about something.'

'Yes. The *post-mortem* report suggests very strongly that Hannah was struck by a vehicle with higher than usual ground clearance, probably a four by four.'

'That's what we were informed at the time,' said Mrs Newby. 'But it hardly tells us who ran her down.'

Knight continued. 'One of the features of the case I don't quite understand is the arrangement made for picking up Hannah from the party at Lonsdale Hall. I have read the statement you made at the time. You don't really deal with it.'

The solicitor intervened again. 'Relevance, Detective Sergeant?'

Mrs Newby waved aside her solicitor. 'No, I don't mind. My husband and I were never satisfied with the way the investigation was handled. If DS Knight has further information, I would like to hear it.'

Knight nodded her gratitude and took a quick glance at the video camera. 'I asked about the arrangements for picking up Hannah?'

Mrs Newby paused before she answered, weighing her words very carefully. 'I was out at a meeting. Anticipating as I did that I would not be home until late, I asked Hannah to ring my husband just before eleven. He was then to collect her and bring her home.'

Knight then asked the same question which had earlier been asked of Mr Newby. 'Why was it necessary for her to call home? You both knew where she was. Why did your husband not simply collect her at eleven.'

Mrs Newby sighed. 'You need to understand my husband, Detective Sergeant. The phone call was to make sure he did what I asked. You must know what men are like? They are generally quite unreliable. My husband is no exception. Arthur was in the habit back then of falling asleep when he'd been out all day playing golf. All that fresh air to say nothing of the Scotch he'd have consumed in the club house. It seems that Hannah didn't ring because she left her mobile phone in her bedroom. He told me he had nodded off and was late arriving to pick her up. She must have accepted a lift from someone else who abandoned her on the way home. If Arthur had been on time she would still be alive today.'

'So you blame him for what happened?'

'I did. No one was ever prosecuted, of course, thanks to police incompetence. I suppose I felt the need to blame someone. I realise now, of course, that the only person really to blame is whoever ran her down. If I could get my hands on him…'

Knight removed another document from the file but retained possession of it.

'Your husband had a range Rover at the time, as you have said?'

'Yes.'

'Were you aware it had been damaged about the time of your daughter's accident?'

Mrs Newby reacted with what seemed to be genuine surprise. 'No. I never noticed any damage.' A suspicious look appeared on her face as Knight passed her the document. She took it and examined it carefully. The Detective Sergeant was quick to press her advantage. 'I think you'll agree this relates to the Range Rover your husband owned in the summer of nineteen ninety-three?'

'Yes. But, as I said, I know nothing about any damage.'

'The invoice shows that the bull bars were removed because they were bent and a cracked headlight was replaced.'

'So I see.' Mrs Newby checked the date on the document. 'This is five days after Hannah died.' She furrowed her forehead and more than a touch of incredulity coloured her tone. She handed the document to her solicitor who scrutinised it before placing it on the table. Knight retrieved it and replaced it in the file before continuing.

'The vehicle went into the garage the Wednesday following Hannah's accident. Do you recall seeing your husband's Range Rover after Hannah was killed but before it was taken in for repairs?'

Mrs Newby now seemed bewildered by what had been revealed. 'No. I was in no condition to notice anything.' She raised her voice and allowed the tears to run down her cheeks. 'For God's sake, Detective Sergeant, my daughter had just been killed. My only child. I was in a dreadful state. I was sedated and in bed for three days before I made my statement. Look at the date on it.'

Knight took a moment to examine the file which gave Mrs Newby the opportunity to pull herself together. She then continued. 'I appreciate that and I fully sympathise. I am not criticising you. It must have been quite soul destroying for you.' She paused for a few seconds then cleared her throat. 'We were also informed by the dealer that your husband took delivery of a new Range Rover in September of the same year. He part-exchanged the vehicle he'd owned at the time of Hannah's death.'

The response was swift and accusatory. 'What are you suggesting? He changes his vehicles every two or three years, There was nothing unusual about that.'

'But on this occasion, he part-exchanged his vehicle for an identical model when it was only fifteen months old and only a month or so after Hannah's death.'

Mrs Newby appeared slightly flustered. 'Perhaps he didn't like it. He is very fussy about the cars he drives.'

'And he never told you he'd been involved in any sort of collision?'

'No.' A look of horror crossed Mrs Newby's face. 'Good God, you're not suggesting he ran down my daughter?'

She fell back in her seat. Knight raised an eyebrow, turned, and gave a cynical look towards the video camera. Was Mrs Newby really as shocked as she appeared? She was surely far too intelligent not to have considered previously the *possibility* that her husband had accidently killed her daughter? She slowly gave the impression of recovering her composure, but appeared traumatised as Knight resumed her questioning. 'Your husband told us he'd hit an animal on the A43, a muntjac.'

Mrs Newby did not initially reply. When she did, she sounded at a loss. 'He never said anything to me.' The look of horror was gradually turning into something approaching barely controlled fury. Her breathing became louder and faster and the colour in her cheeks intensified.

The solicitor intervened again. 'I'm sorry, Detective Sergeant. What has this to do with the murder of this priest? Can't you see you are upsetting my client?'

'That is not my intention, I assure you. The reasons for raising this will become clear later.' Knight then deliberately changed the subject. 'Now, Mrs Newby, we have evidence that you telephoned Martha Morton on the nineteenth of March this year using the mobile phone we found in your husband's filing cabinet. Was it about then you discovered that your husband had had an affair with Martha when she worked for him in nineteen ninety-three?'

The suspect did not reply. Her mind seemed to be elsewhere. Fully a minute passed before she said anything. Was she calculating her response?

'Well, Mrs Newby?'

Eleanor Newby looked down then seemed to come to herself. Her breathing returned to normal. There was a sharpness in her tone as she looked at Knight and scoffed her response. 'Detective Sergeant Knight, do you think I'm the sort of woman who wouldn't realise her husband was having an affair? I didn't discover Arthur's infidelity earlier this year; I knew about it back in nineteen ninety-three.'

'You did?' Knight did her best to conceal her astonishment. Hood, who was not subject to such restraints as he viewed events up in his room, whistled through his teeth. That was something he had never contemplated. That Mrs Newby knew of her husband's affair while it was going on potentially altered the landscape of the inquiry. Another series of questions immediately entered his head. Did she know about the pregnancy too? Why had she departed from the account given by her husband? Had she realised that his denial of any recent contact with Martha Morton could no longer be sustained? He pulled nearer the screen, impatient for the interview to proceed as Mrs Newby continued with her account.

'Of course, I did. Please don't take me for a fool, Detective Sergeant. I own forty percent of the shares in most of my husband's companies, including Dowlas Logistics. It was my family money which kept him afloat in the early nineties, otherwise he'd have gone under. With nearly all of the money I inherited invested in his companies, I made it my business to keep in touch with what was going on. I am a director of the holding company you know. Besides, the man who took over from his mistress as company secretary, David Howarth, is my first cousin. Until he retired eighteen months ago, he kept me informed on an almost daily basis.' A wry grin played on her lips. 'My husband is not as clever or discreet as he thinks he is. I also knew this woman was not the first. He'd had a fling with a secretary from the Northampton office three years before.'

'Did you challenge him about any of this?' asked Knight. She was still trying to get her head round what Mrs Newby had revealed.

Eleanor Newby's response was emphatic. 'Never.' She paused and shifted in her seat. 'We'd have ended up in the divorce courts if I had, which is the last place I'd want to be seen. I could not have coped with that. Divorce may be common but it is never respectable, whatever others may say these days. It may sound old-fashioned, but till death us do part – that's what we both signed up to. And I meant it; Arthur was obviously ambivalent.'

'Was he aware that you knew about his disloyalty back in nineteen ninety three?'

'Of course not. But he would have appreciated that I would never allow him to have his way and he had the good sense not to push it. He never even hinted about leaving me or wanting a divorce. As I effectively controlled the purse strings, he had sufficient intelligence to realise he would have no say in the matter.'

'Is that still the position? He doesn't know you knew all about it almost from the outset?'

'I suggest you ask him. We never speak of such matters.' She continued in her disdainful manner. 'I also regard my social standing as of the utmost importance, Detective Sergeant. My father was knighted by the Queen at Buckingham Palace, you know. People in my position do not rush to the divorce courts over something as trivial as an affair with a minor employee.' She paused. 'I thought he would tire of her eventually. He usually did. I left them to it.'

Knight then asked the very question Hood was silently urging her to raise 'Were you aware of Martha's pregnancy?'

Again, Mrs Newby's reply was not what Knight was expecting. 'I suppose I was, yes. David told me. And about the cheque Arthur wrote for her. But I have to admit, I assumed she'd had an abortion. She was paid enough when she resigned. I only discovered she'd had the child recently.'

'How did you find out?'

A look of utter contempt crossed Mrs Newby's face. 'My husband told me in late March, after he'd met up with the woman. He told me he was intending to leave his son' – her voice trembled with the words – 'a substantial legacy. He was proposing to change his will to that effect.'

'What was your attitude to that?'

'I didn't agree with it. In fact I forbade it. I reminded him it was my family's money that had built up his little empire. Without it he'd have lost everything. In many respects my husband can be very foolish, but not when it comes to his financial security. He knows I could bring him crashing down in an instant if I were minded to. The child's been adopted. Better to leave things as they are; better for all concerned.'

'But you have spoken to Martha, haven't you?'

'I might as well admit it. Yes, I have. I saw her by chance while I was in Wellingborough in February.'

'February?' echoed Knight.

'Yes, I think it was about then. I wasn't sure it was her to begin with. Then I saw her again in Easton Parva as I drove through the village. A visit to the village shop was all it took to find out she was working for Sir Robert. When I rang her, she put the phone down on me after only a few words had been exchanged. I then saw her by chance in Northampton when I was with my husband. It was obvious to me that they recognised each other.'

'How did you identify her when you first saw her in Wellingborough? You'd never met her, had you?'

'I told you, Detective Sergeant, my husband is not as discreet as he thinks he is. I found a photograph of her in his study years ago when I was looking for some papers; a very revealing photograph I might add. I ripped it up, but I remembered her all right. She had hardly changed. I have to admit she has certainly kept her looks.' She paused and cleared her throat. 'I obtained her number from directory enquiries. That she was living so close to Stanton Harwood naturally made me suspicious.'

'Were you aware your husband had seen her for lunch in Northampton?'

She shrugged her shoulders then smiled broadly. 'Of course. In fact, I suggested it.'

Knight swallowed hard. The disclosures just kept on coming. What would Mrs Newby say next? Nor had any of this ever crossed Hood's mind. He continued to watch the proceedings on his computer screen with intense interest. Here was Mrs Newby describing events in flat contradiction to what her husband had said earlier in his cautioned interviews. What was going on? Was she trying to undermine her husband's case? What was her object? What was in it for her? He had a sudden thought. *My God,* he said to himself. *Have we been looking at this case from entirely the wrong angle?* He pushed his chair back from his desk. He needed to speak to Knight urgently. He was minded to rush downstairs and bring the interview to a temporary halt, but Mrs Newby's continuing revelations caused him to wait.

'I told him to telephone her and arrange to take her out for lunch or meet her for coffee. He was initially reluctant to do so. But he did as I asked; he generally does. That's when we discovered she had not had a termination. Arthur, being as naïve as he is, was delighted; I, on the other hand, was furious.'

'He told you all this after he'd seen her?'

'He did. He sounded quite proud of himself. Not a thought for how I felt about it.'

'Did you do anything?'

She shook her head. 'No, I did not. What could I do? You must understand that in late March we thought Arthur was dying.' She paused and took a deep breath. 'I wanted him to resolve whatever outstanding issues he had with this woman. I could see he was fretting after we had first seen her in Northampton which was affecting him and aggravating his condition. He became almost uncommunicative and very depressed. It was obvious to me that she was all he was thinking about. I thought it best that he should see her on his own and get whatever it was out of his system.'

'Go on,' said Knight.

'I was not, however, expecting to discover Arthur had a son. That was the last thing I imagined when I suggested he should meet up with her. And I'm sure you can picture for yourself how I felt when he started to pick up after he'd spoken with her. Seeing her after all these years and discovering he had a son by her seemed to give him a new lease of life.' She paused and added resentfully, 'We never had any children together, you see. Arthur adopted Hannah, but she always regarded him as her step-father, not her father. She was told the truth about her birth when she was about nine or ten. Arthur always resented the fact that she would not accept him as her father. He always felt very hurt when she made it clear he was not her real father, which she had a habit of doing when she was angry with him. She never knew my first husband, of course. He died before she was one-year old.' She looked down. 'Arthur and I have not had a physical relationship for some years, and, if anything, his obsession with his former mistress just made our relationship worse.' She looked up. 'Not that I'm the jealous type, of course. Nor am I a sentimentalist. Life has to go on.'

Knight was almost beginning to feel sorry for Arthur Newby. There was a coldness about Eleanor Newby which she found deeply unattractive. She continued with her questioning. 'Was it shortly after he met up with Martha that he got the news that his cancer appeared to be in remission?' Knight tried to sound sympathetic, but was not really succeeding. Eleanor Newby's indifference discouraged empathy of any kind. She answered in a matter of fact way.

'Yes it was. A remarkable coincidence, don't you think? But with a clear warning, of course, that it might return. Arthur seemed like a new man and, once I got used to it, it suited me, especially as he was due to become High Sheriff of the county next April.' She smiled then sighed as she reflected on recent events. 'Not that that will happen now. His cancer has returned and is much more extensive and aggressive than before. He was very low this morning at breakfast.' She took her handkerchief and wiped a tear from her eye. 'He has written to indicate that he will not be fit enough to take up the position. Someone else will have to assume the role.' She paused briefly. 'Very regrettable, after all the effort and time I put in to advance his prospects. And there is a Royal visit to the county arranged for next June.' She paused. 'I was looking forward to that very much.'

Knight pressed on, wondering what next Mrs Newby would reveal. 'Martha Morton, or Goring as you knew her, called your husband on that same mobile phone on Saturday August third, but I believe you answered?' Knight was expecting a straight denial. Mrs Newby's reply surprised her and confirmed that Martha Morton was telling the truth.

'Arthur was asleep on the couch. I heard his mobile phone ring. I found it underneath him and picked it up and answered it. I had no idea it was his former mistress on the line until I recognised her voice moments later.'

'I'm told you demanded to meet her. You told her you would see to it that neither she nor her son would benefit from your husband's estate if she refused?'

A cynical smile passed over Mrs Newby's face. 'What if I did? Arthur is showing all the signs that his health is deteriorating again. I've seen it all before, remember. I fail to see how his former mistress or her child should benefit from his death.'

'It's as serious as that is it?'

'It's every bit as serious. He had a scan yesterday which confirms it.'

'And if he dies, who will inherit the business?'

'I don't think there's any "if" about it, Detective Sergeant. Not that Arthur has given up. He's a fighter. He'll not give up without a struggle.' She paused for a brief moment before answering Knight's question. 'As things stand, I will inherit. We have made mutual wills. It's a common enough arrangement with married couples, especially where there are no children. As far as I am aware, he has not taken any steps to alter his will in favour of that woman's child. Not yet.'

Knight moved on. 'I want to ask you now about Father Dominic Renville. Have you ever met him?'

Knight had hardly finished the question when the emphatic denial came. 'No.'

'But I believe you are more familiar with Easton Grange than you indicated previously?'

'Am I?'

'Officers have investigated your charitable activities, Mrs Newby. You are, or were, a trustee of the same charity as Lady Southall, Northampton Women's Support Group. Some of the meetings which you attended were held at the Grange up until the time of Lady Southall's death. I have seen the minutes.' Knight tapped the file in front of her.

Eleanor Newby said nothing, then turned and whispered to her solicitor. The solicitor nodded. She turned back and faced Knight. 'So, you know about that? Not much point in my denying it if you've seen the minutes.'

'I suppose not. Tell me, why did you lie?'

Mrs Newby breathed out then gave Knight a weary look. 'Absolute honesty is a greatly overrated virtue, Detective Sergeant. I wouldn't say it was a lie, exactly. I suppose I didn't want my limited connection with the Grange to be known in case people jumped to the wrong conclusions about my husband. I was only thinking of him. But I'd only been there a few times and not recently. The meetings took place elsewhere after Lady Southall died.'

'Those meetings at the Grange were in the Long Room weren't they?'

'On occasion, yes. But the last meeting there was held in the converted barn that was sometimes used for wedding receptions. It was the AGM. More people than usual attended including a junior government minister, I might add.' That superior smile again. 'The barn was considered more appropriate and refreshments were served afterwards. I had quite a lengthy conversation with the minister, actually.'

Knight suddenly changed tack. 'How do you explain the blood in the boot of the Jaguar?'

Mrs Newby was hardly phased. 'I can't. It's my husband's car, not mine. You should ask him. But no doubt you already have?' She raised an eyebrow and gave Knight a quizzical look.

Knight ignored her and continued. 'How often did your husband go out in the Jaguar, before it was taken to the restorers in Banbury?'

'I don't know. I suppose he used it on occasions after his health improved. He always wanted a classic Jaguar. As far as I was concerned, it was a complete waste of money. I warned him against it but he wouldn't listen. He used his own money to purchase it – as an investment.'

Knight then put the question Hood had been waiting for. The same question he had put to Arthur Newby. 'It must have been driven by someone on the twenty-fourth of July, Mrs Newby. Otherwise how did Father Dominic's blood get into the boot? It must follow that one, or both of you, had been in contact with him while he was bleeding. We know for a fact he bled heavily both during and after the attack on him that evening. There is a clear forensic link between his murder and your husband's Jaguar.'

Mrs Newby was not put out for a moment. She had clearly anticipated being asked to account for the bloodstain and although she had answered "no comment" when first asked the question at the beginning of the interview, she now placed the blame, by implication, elsewhere.

'That is a question better put to my husband. As I said, it is his car. Whatever he may have said to you, it has nothing to do with me.' She then indicated to her solicitor that she would like a short break.

'Very well, 'said Knight. 'Will ten minutes suffice?'

CHAPTER FIFTY-EIGHT

Up in his room, Hood smiled. Neither Eleanor Newby nor her husband had been able to work out a credible explanation for the presence of the blood. She clearly thought had no option but to distance herself from having any contact with the Jaguar. Hood was now certain she was going to abandon her husband in order to protect herself. The solicitor must have had a similar thought. When the interview recommenced, she pressed Knight to reveal what Arthur Newby had said when interviewed.

'Are you prepared to disclose Mr Newby's response to that question which must surely have been put to him?'

'No. Not at the moment,' insisted Knight, with a shake of her head. 'Anything Mr Newby may have said must remain confidential at this stage. It is essential that Mrs Newby's account is not influenced by anything her husband may have disclosed.'

'So, he has said something has he?' said Mrs Newby. Her eyes narrowed as she spoke and drilled into Knight.

'And what if he has?' replied the detective sergeant.

The expression on Eleanor Newby's face did not change. It now seemed permanently fixed. She was intelligent enough to realise that her husband could not have said anything which implicated her. If he had, she would have been asked about it. Hood, viewing the proceedings from his office, sat back in his chair. Watching DS Knight conduct the interview on screen was giving him a quite different perspective on the whole investigation. Tempted as he was to intervene himself, he decided to let the questioning proceed. Wendy was making considerable progress; perhaps more than he would have achieved had he been conducting the interview. It was now obvious that Mrs Newby was no longer using

447

her best endeavours to protect her husband. Quite the reverse. Knight's questions were gradually pushing her to look solely to her own interests. As Hood had always appreciated, the discovery of the bloodstain in the boot of the car and the subsequent DNA analysis proving it was Father Dominic's blood really was a game changer. There was no getting away from it. Whoever was in that Jaguar on 24 July must have been directly involved in the killing of the priest. In addition, Mrs Newby had been seen at Easton Grange on 7 July on the same day and at the same time that the Jaguar had been there. Helen Swanson was not mistaken; neither had young Francis Gilbert got the registration number wrong. Eleanor Newby had to be lying. But why was she lying? Neither she nor her husband would have gone to Easton Grange other than to see Father Dominic, would they? Certainly not if they had been together. Neither of them would have any other reason to be there. Hood remembered DS Knight's major reservation about his theory. Even as a lapsed Catholic, Arthur Newby would have known that whatever he confessed to Father Dominic would have remained confidential. Perhaps it really was Mrs Newby who feared whatever her husband had confessed becoming generally known? And if Newby had accompanied Father Dominic to the police station on 26 July and admitted he was responsible for Hannah's death, everything would have become public knowledge – the accident, his unfaithfulness, the cover-up. There'd be no appointment as High Sheriff then. And the public humiliation would have been unavoidable and intense.

Hood silently urged the detective sergeant on. It was essential that Mrs Newby explained where she was on the evening of 24 July. He had no need to worry. Wendy Knight moved seamlessly to the very question he would have asked. As he continued to watch, the telephone on his desk began to ring. He at first ignored it, then reached out for the receiver without taking his eyes from the screen. He indicated for the caller to wait.

'What were you doing on the evening of the twenty-fourth of July?' asked Knight.

'That is when you believe this priest was killed?'

'Yes. That is the evening Father Dominic was *murdered*.'

Hood continued to watch the proceedings as he listened to the brief message from the FME about Arthur Newby's condition. It was not what he wanted to hear. In interview room number 2, Mrs Newby continued with the details of her alibi for 24 July.

'If my memory serves me, I had a bad migraine that evening. I went to my bed early. My GP will confirm I suffer from severe migraine headaches. He advises me to lie down and rest when they come on. That is what I did.'

'Where was your husband?'

'As far as I am aware, he was in the rear courtyard tinkering with that damn Jaguar of his, preparing it for the garage in Banbury. It had been booked in three weeks before. As you know, it was, coincidentally, taken there a couple of days later.'

'Your husband could have gone out in it then?'

'I don't know. I was hardly in a position to monitor his activities. I suggest you ask him.'

'Were you aware that a priest-hole had been discovered at Easton Grange?'

'Not on the twenty-fourth of July, no.' She hesitated as if she were considering whether to say anything more. 'But I believe Arthur had heard about it.'

'You do?'

'Yes. From Mr Hitchens, Sir Robert's gardener. Arthur wanted some landscaping work doing in our rear garden back in early July. We have used Hitchens from time to time over the last few years. I believe from what Arthur told me later, that Hitchens mentioned that some sort of hiding place had been discovered at the Grange when he gave us an estimate for the work.'

'When did your husband tell you what Mr Hitchens had said?'

'The day after the priest died. I didn't even know what a priest-hole was before then. Of course, I have since read all about them in the newspapers, but that was after this priest was found dead.'

Upstairs in his room, Hood pushed his chair back and got to his feet. Mrs Newby was now using every opportunity to imply that responsibility for the killing lay with her husband. He cursed himself as the truth dawned on him. How could he have got it so wrong? Why had he not seen it before? *Newby didn't kill Father Dominic; she did!* Time for him to join Knight and stop the interview. He needed to speak to the detective sergeant urgently. The basis of further questioning would have to be revised. He left his computer running and rushed down the stairs to the basement where the solicitor had just interrupted Knight again.

'You indicated, Detective Sergeant, that you would inform us of the relevance of events in nineteen ninety-three to the death of this priest. Time is getting on. We are still waiting.'

'You're absolutely right, I did.' Knight paused and glanced again at the camera. She would have much preferred Hood to have been present in the room before raising this aspect of the investigation. She was by no means sure she could articulate it as well as he would. After all, it was his theory. She was much relieved when there was a knock on the door and Hood walked in.

'For the benefit of the tape, Detective Superintendent Hood has entered the room,' said Knight, glancing at the clock on the wall and stating the time.

'Good afternoon, Superintendent,' said Mrs Newby in that supercilious way of hers. 'I take it you have come to bring this little pantomime to a conclusion? Do you have news of my husband? I am very concerned about him. He's been detained here for several hours now. He's not a well man, you know. As I have just informed your sergeant, he was very low at breakfast this morning.'

Hood took the remaining vacant seat and addressed Mrs Newby and her solicitor. 'I regret to inform you, Mrs Newby, that your husband has been taken to hospital. He became suddenly unwell after his interview and appeared to be in considerable pain. I immediately arranged for him to be seen by a doctor who thought he should go to hospital as a precautionary measure.'

Mrs Newby stood up. Her eyes flashed with anger. 'This is what happens when you place a sick man in a cell. I demand you allow me to see him. This is quite intolerable Superintendent. My husband's health is obviously deteriorating as a result of your continued harassment of him. I have a right to be with him.'

Hood was unimpressed with Eleanor Newby's pretended hysterics. 'In due course, Mrs Newby, in due course. His condition is by no means critical and I assure you, he was not placed in a cell. He became unwell in the custody suite while going through the booking-in procedure. I repeat, his going to hospital is merely a precaution. No reason to put off the remainder of your interview. I suspect it has some way to go.' He glanced at Knight who smiled in response.

The solicitor intervened. 'I request that you note my disquiet, Superintendent. Mrs Newby is understandably concerned about her husband's condition. You are, I hope, now fully aware of the unfortunate recent changes in his circumstances. I assume you have read the medical report that was sent over to you earlier this afternoon? Surely, the rest of this interview can be postponed until my client has seen her husband?'

Hood reflected on the situation. He had read the report, the contents of which merely added to his concerns. He was fast revising how and why Father Dominic had been murdered. He was now convinced Arthur Newby was not the actual killer. But his part in events remained unclear. Hood needed to speak to Knight in private before Mrs Newby was asked any further questions. He also needed to speak to Arthur Newby again. Mrs Newby's understandable desire to see her husband offered the perfect opportunity for a brief postponement. But he didn't want to give the impression that it suited him for the interview to be temporarily halted.

'Yes, I have seen the oncologist's report,' he replied. 'But I'm afraid it is not possible to interrupt Mrs Newby's interview at this stage.' He addressed the suspect. 'In view of the answers you have given to Detective Sergeant Knight, which I have been following on screen for the most part, there are further questions that must be put to you before I can allow you to speak with your husband. Please bear in mind you are both under arrest on suspicion of involvement in the death of Father Dominic.'

Mrs Newby was incandescent. 'This is outrageous, Mr Hood. I have answered everything I have been asked. I did not rely on my right of silence as I could have done and as I was advised to do. Whatever my husband may have done, I was not involved. Whatever you suspect him of, he is a very sick man. I am his wife. I am entitled to be with him.'

'That's right, Superintendent,' said the solicitor. 'Surely some credit can be given for Mrs Newby's cooperation?'

Hood had made his point. Time to appear generous. He said nothing for half a minute then addressed the solicitor. 'The best I can do, Mrs Dangerfield, is to postpone the remainder of this interview and allow Mrs Newby to see her husband, but subject to stringent conditions. Mr Newby is still under arrest on suspicion of murder and Mrs Newby, too, remains under caution. A police officer will have to be present and note anything said between them.'

'Is that really necessary?' asked the solicitor. 'Surely a degree of privacy is appropriate?'

Wendy Knight's expression betrayed her concerns. She plainly wanted the interview to continue. *What was Hood playing at?*

Hood answered the solicitor's question. 'I'm afraid so. In the ordinary course of events, a person in custody on suspicion of murder would not be allowed to see anyone other than his lawyer, especially in these unusual circumstances where his wife is suspected of some involvement and her interview has not yet been completed. That Mr Newby is in hospital does not alter his present status. I am only making an exception in this case because of his state of health. And I must emphasise that Mrs Newby's interview must continue after she has seen him. She remains under arrest.'

The solicitor continued to make her objections until Mrs Newby raised her hand and cut out any further intervention by Mrs Dangerfield. 'Very well, Superintendent. I accept your conditions. I want to see Arthur as soon as possible. I will return here for my interview to continue after I have seen my husband.'

CHAPTER FIFTY-NINE

Arrangements were made to escort Mrs Newby to Northampton General Hospital where she was permitted to visit her husband under strict supervision and subject to the requirement that anything said between them was to be noted. She was spirited discreetly out of the rear of the police station and into an unmarked vehicle in order to avoid the reporters camped outside the main entrance. DC Adrian Swanson was given the task of monitoring any conversation between the Newbys and organising her return to Campbell Square within the hour.

'How is Mr Newby?' asked Knight when she saw Hood in his office a few minutes after Eleanor Newby had left the police station. The detective sergeant was extremely disappointed that her interview had been cut short and try as she might was unable to hide her displeasure. She was delighted with the way her questioning of Mrs Newby had gone and was convinced further revelations would have been made had it been permitted to continue. She, of course, had not seen nor read the oncologist's report recently delivered by Newby's solicitor to Hood. The content had not come as a surprise to him but he recognised that Knight was upset as he answered her question.

'Not at all well. He's barely conscious at the moment and heavily sedated, but they're expecting him to improve shortly when the medication he's been given kicks in. Unfortunately, he'll not be fit for interview for some time, certainly not before tomorrow. I also think our chances of getting him to court are fast receding.'

'She was telling the truth then, about his state of health? I thought she was possibly exaggerating.'

Hood sighed. 'I'm afraid not, Wendy. Not this time. Mr Sewell sent over the oncologist's report earlier. Read it for yourself.' He pointed to the slim blue file on his desk. Knight picked it up and turned immediately to the final paragraph on the third page.

'This couldn't have happened at a worse time,' she groaned. 'Just when we were getting somewhere.' She looked up and bit her tongue. It was not for her to question a senior officer's judgment but she couldn't help herself. 'I don't want to be over critical, Harry, but shouldn't we have carried on with Eleanor Newby's interview? Breaking off like we did will hand her the advantage. It interrupts the flow. We may lose momentum with her now.'

Hood smiled. He understood Knight's frustration but he had no doubt he had done the right thing. But she deserved an explanation. 'I don't think so, although what she'll say next is anyone's guess. This break can be used to our advantage. Watching your very professional interrogation has caused me to reconsider our approach to the entire case.'

Knight appreciated the praise but appeared taken aback. 'It has?'

Hood nodded and sat on the edge of his desk. 'I believe we were right in thinking they were in this together, at least after the event, but we've got it the wrong way round when it comes to the actual killing.'

Knight remained puzzled. 'The wrong way round? Mrs Newby has undermined almost everything her husband told us. We can now prove he was lying. And she may well have gone further if we hadn't broken off when we did. He was toast!'

Hood smiled. 'I agree that she's only just got going. Like you, I'm convinced there's more to come from her.' He paused and shot a knowing look at Knight. 'She's obviously gone back on the arrangement they'd come to.'

'Arrangement?'

Hood explained. 'Yes. I think they'd done a deal; she was keeping to herself what he must have recently admitted to her about her daughter, although it must stick in her craw, and in return, he has agreed to alibi her over the death of Father Dominic. They thought they could get away with it if they stuck together.' He smiled. 'You see, Wendy, Arthur Newby didn't kill Father Dominic; *she* did.'

Knight did not react other than to sit down. She then became doubly serious. 'As you know, I've always thought that she could be implicated in the cover up and that she's guilty of skulduggery in respect of some of the evidence, but proving that *she* killed Father Dominic? Can we do that?'

She shook her head. 'It's highly speculative, isn't it, Harry? We have no hard evidence to back it up. Absolutely nothing to put her at the scene of the murder on the twenty-fourth; no forensics, no DNA, no witnesses.'

Hood was quick to elucidate. 'I agree, but it's the only thing that makes sense. Let's take a step back and think about it. You said yourself Newby must have appreciated that whatever he may have confessed to Father Dominic, it would remain wholly confidential. He had no need to do anything, however grave his sins, let alone commit murder. Father Dominic would have carried Newby's secret to his grave.'

'As he did,' replied Knight, solemnly.

Hood exhaled. 'Indeed he did, poor man.'

He stood up and approached Knight. 'Don't get me wrong, Wendy. I don't think Newby told his wife everything about Hannah's accident. I reckon he only admitted allowing her to get out of his car, not that he actually ran her down.'

'She'd be furious even about that, wouldn't she? And I gained the distinct impression when questioning her that she'd worked out for herself how her daughter came to be killed. And what's more, she'd worked it out before I mentioned the damage to her husband's Range Rover. I think she's had a strong suspicion for some time that her husband ran down her daughter. The damage to his Range Rover merely confirmed it.'

'You may well be right. She suspected him, but I don't think Newby has made a full confession to her. He wouldn't have dared, not after all this time. But she undoubtedly believes that he confessed all to Father Dominic. *That's* why the priest had to die.'

'But without an admission, we can't actually prove he confessed anything to Father Dominic, as you have said before. The most damning evidence we have is the bloodstain in the boot of the Jaguar, but that implicates Newby more than her. It's his car.'

'I know. But the person with the most to lose, who probably would not understand the nature of the sacrament, is the wife. She's not a Catholic and she's the social climber, not him. I don't suppose he was bothered one way or the other whether he became High Sheriff, ill as he is. But she was. She's been working towards it for years. Now, just as it's within her grasp, it's been taken away. She's lost it. And not just because of this murder investigation' – he hesitated before continuing – 'because Newby is dying.'

Knight gave him a troubled look and picked up the report again. There was a cynical tone to her response. 'Is that definite this time? Shouldn't we get him looked at by an independent medical expert? You know, just to be on the safe side. And she did tell me her husband had withdrawn his nomination anyway.'

'That's why he's withdrawn. He's too ill to take on the role and probably won't live long enough even to be sworn in next April. I really don't think that an independent assessment is necessary. She wouldn't have let him withdraw unless there was no alternative.'

Knight sighed. 'I suppose that must be right.'

Hood continued. 'This new-fangled PET scan he underwent makes his position very plain. I'm sure the Newbys believed his cancer was in remission, as it was for a few months, but now?' He shook his head. 'As things stand, he'll probably die before we get him to court. I think she was telling you the truth about that. Oh, she's very clever. She mixes the truth with lies and I have to admit, she does it very well. She's given a lot of thought to what she's about. His cancer has certainly returned and with a vengeance. I've studied the oncologist's report as should you. You need to read all of it, not just the conclusion. It's very clear. His cancer has spread to his liver. No further treatment, save chemo, is thought appropriate and that comes with a warning that it may advance his demise. Palliative care only is what is recommended.' He sounded appropriately subdued. 'I'll be surprised if he lives beyond Christmas.'

'So he may escape justice for his part in all this, whatever his role may have been?'

'He may well, but she won't, not if we play it right. We've always proceeded on the basis that the killing wasn't planned; and I think we were right about that. It was done on the spur of the moment. If that spade hadn't been so handy it may never have happened. Fate can be so very cruel.'

'But Guy Romney is surely right when he says the priest was struck several times?'

'Of course he is. I'm speaking about the first blow. That was done in temper as Dominic turned away. I suspect she had visited him unexpectedly. Dominic may have counselled Newby to go to the police and open up about Hannah's death. Remember those initials on the calendar? Perhaps it was going to be that coming Friday. Eleanor Newby would have been wholly opposed to that.'

'Would she? She seemed very keen that someone should be prosecuted for her daughter's death.'

'Yes, but not her husband. Not now. Not when his prosecution would destroy his reputation and expose his infidelity to public scrutiny. She'd have been furious, of course, but couldn't have lived with the inevitable embarrassment. Just imagine how she'd feel about him being the subject of a story on the front page of the *News of the World*. She couldn't cope with that. She's an unusual woman, I grant you, but her social standing means everything to her. Nothing is more important. And it would look to the world that she had covered up her daughter's death as much as he, especially when the tabloids had finished with it. Who would believe she hadn't worked it all out long ago and joined him in covering it up?'

Knight remained sceptical. 'I don't know, Harry. She didn't seem that bothered about his adultery. And if you're right about her, it will all come out now anyway. Everything she's tried to hide will be revealed. And the publicity will be massive because of the murder of Father Dominic. So what would she have gained?'

'She obviously hoped it would never be disclosed. That's why Dominic had to die. With him gone, she thought nothing could be proved. But now she's caught up in this investigation she's had to change her tactics. The death of Father Dominic is already the number one story in the media. She has now recast herself in the role of the victim. The desolate mother lied to by her conniving and murdering husband. That's the narrative she's now anxious to adopt and promote.'

'But why kill the priest? If it meant so much to her, why not do in her husband?'

Hood smiled. 'Isn't that exactly what she's doing by gradually implicating him in Dominic's death? But she's doing it in a way which she thinks will gain her sympathy and understanding and divert the inevitable publicity away from her. Newby must have realised his illness had returned and told her what he was going to do. Imagine her reaction if he'd said he was going to come to us and admit what had really caused Hannah's death? She simply couldn't risk that happening. She had to act quickly. I think she went to the Grange on the Wednesday evening and spoke with Dominic as he was saying his office in the grounds of the ruined chapel. He probably listened to what she had to say until her questions became too intrusive, eventually turning away from her after refusing to tell her anything about her husband's confession. She

457

picked up the spade in temper and struck him, probably a glancing blow. He turned towards her and raised his arm to protect himself. The other blows which followed were to make sure he couldn't identify his assailant; namely her. Panic had set in. Those further blows were clearly intended to kill.'

Knight mused on what Hood had said. 'She didn't go there intending to assault him then, let alone to kill him?'

'No, I don't think so. She wanted to know what her husband had disclosed to Dominic. That temper of hers got the better of her. I don't think she anticipated anything like this happening. But her attack on Dominic changed everything. She then needed her husband to protect her from the consequences of her own actions.'

'You think he had no part in it?'

'I suspect he knew nothing about it until after the event. Remember what Martha said about him? He couldn't harm anyone, not physically. He's a weak man. That's what she told us and I think she's right. Even his wife told you he wouldn't hurt a fly. He may have gone back to the Grange with her to check on what she had done; to see if Dominic was really dead, perhaps. Then she embroiled him in the cover up.'

Knight, as always, looked for logical flaws in what Hood was suggesting. 'Why did she drive to the Grange in the Jaguar if she had no intention of attacking the priest?'

'For the same reason she drove it there on the seventh. Because she knew we would associate the Jaguar with her husband, if we found out about it. She's been very cautious. She didn't want any evidence of her contact with Dominic to remain. She probably had this fall-back position in mind from the beginning.'

Knight said nothing for some time. When she spoke she still sounded unconvinced. 'How the hell do we prove she's the one responsible, especially if she blames her husband after he's died? There won't be a trial before next year at the earliest.' She frowned. 'She's going to walk Harry. He'll get the blame.'

Hood stuffed his hands in his pocket and returned to his seat behind his desk before continuing. 'That's certainly what she hopes will happen. The pieces of this jigsaw were starting to fit too easily. We both thought as much, remember? Having thought about it further, I think that's because Mrs Newby has been helping to put those pieces together – to create a wholly misleading picture, as you hinted at some time ago.'

'A very risky thing to do, don't you think?' She smiled. 'I wasn't far off, then, with my speculating? If only we had some evidence that implicated her alone; but we don't. The visit to the Grange on the seventh doesn't prove anything in itself.'

Hood placed his hands on the desk in front of him and played with his wedding ring, twisting it around his finger. 'I agree. But whatever she may say, she now believes her husband's illness is terminal. She probably reached that conclusion before the doctors, possibly before even him. After all, she lives with him; she sees him every day. No one is better placed to notice the gradual deterioration in his health. And remember, her first husband died of cancer. She's been through it all before. She knows the signs. The prize of Arthur Newby becoming High Sheriff and covering up his infidelity is no longer what motivates her. She's now concentrating on her own survival after he's passed on. It's all been deliberately staged. She now realises that the original plan will no longer work. She's implicating her husband simply to save her own skin. All done with great subtlety, of course, while still appearing to support and protect him. That's why she wanted to see him. To assess for herself how much he has deteriorated; how close he is to dying.' He looked at Knight and smiled. 'So I accommodated her.'

Wendy Knight gasped. 'That's why you interrupted the interview!' She now understood Hood's tactics. She shook her head. 'I'm sorry I was so slow on the uptake.'

Hood smiled. 'You hadn't seen the medical report; I had. But it makes sense, don't you think? Why should she go down for murder when he's available as a fall-guy who'll be dead before she gets to trial? To put it simply, he's her get-out-of-jail card, or she thinks he is. And, if he dies, which I suspect he will, well before any trial takes place, it will give her a potentially unbeatable defence by allowing her to claim he was the killer. He won't be around to contradict her.' He paused and added cynically, 'there is no way either of them can get round the bloodstain in the boot; not when the science proves it's Dominic's blood.'

Knight said nothing for some time. 'And you think he doesn't know what she's up to?'

'The poor sap hasn't a clue, but he must be beginning to cotton on since we searched the house and after we revealed his wife had been speaking to Martha. I think that came as quite a shock. He's not that much

459

of a fool. He's gone along with what his wife says so far because she's in charge of the narrative and she's effectively blackmailing him about Hannah's death. She's the one calling the shots. Our job now is to change that narrative or she may well get away with it. We need to get him to tell the truth.'

'He's not shown much inclination so far.'

'I know. But if I get the opportunity of pressing him further, I think he might crack, especially if we disclose to him what his wife said to you in her cautioned interview. That's another reason why I wanted it videoed. I intend to let him see his wife in full flow.'

Knight still had doubts. 'You think there was more than one journey in the Jag on the twenty-fourth? That Newby went back to the Grange with her?'

'I do. Having killed Dominic, or thinking she had, she drove home, told Newby what she had done, then returned with him to remove the body and dump the priest where we found him.'

'But why? They'd be taking one hell of a risk moving the body into the house. Supposing they'd been seen?'

'Do you think so? I believe I was right about why the body was placed in the hide. I reckon they took a chance in order to mislead us and put us off the scent. And, as a precaution, one of them telephoned first. When there was no reply they assumed there would be no one in the house, so the coast was clear. They'd have had access to Dominic's keys and didn't know about Grantham's presence. They were simply lucky he didn't see anything.'

'I suppose no one seems to have known about him being there – apart from Mr Hitchens. He knew about him; he'd helped with the heavy work. He mustn't have mentioned Grantham when he spoke with the Newbys.'

'Remember what she said about Mr Hitchens visiting her husband and telling him about the priest hole? If you have a look at Hitchens' statement, you'll see he thinks that both of them were present when he disclosed not only the existence of the hide, but the fact that Father Dominic was hoping to find something hidden there.'

'He says he *thinks* they were both present. Mrs Newby was in and out of the kitchen. Will he stick to that in court? Perhaps we should see him again?'

'Yes, we need to firm up his account,' replied Hood. 'But it all fits. Eleanor Newby used that information to confuse the issue. Having panicked initially, she was now thinking logically. She calculated we would associate the hide and the search for an artifact from way back with the killing. It was the obvious way to mislead us. She needed to involve her husband in covering up what she had done in order to make sure he didn't give her away. The truth is they both knew about the priest-hole, well before Dominic's death received any publicity. They hoped we'd be misled, as we were at the outset.'

Knight frowned then smiled. Hood nodded towards her. 'All right. I was misled. You were always more inclined to the view that there was some other motive.'

Knight beamed her gratitude. 'Good job you located the chalice; that should put the kibosh on that little theory of theirs. We may even have to disclose how you found it. Now, that will be interesting!' But she remained doubtful about proving Mrs Newby was the killer as she continued to pick away at possible flaws in the evidence. 'Odd, though, that Newby told those stupid lies about having no contact with Martha. Once he admitted to the affair in ninety-three, it couldn't have harmed him if he'd agreed he'd met up with her recently. Would we have linked his affair with the murder? I suspect not if he'd told the truth.'

'He's probably said what he has on his wife's instructions. Dancing to her tune. She's the one in charge in that relationship. She's also much brighter than he is. He's still doing what he's told.'

Knight nodded. 'But his lies would make him look very guilty if she were suddenly to expose him.'

'As she has. Clever, eh? The penny will drop with him eventually. Let's hope it does so soon. I think we have enough now to charge both of them. We'll have to speak to her again before she's charged with murder, of course and I will have to get approval from the CPS. I don't think he's likely to expire in the immediate future. If it comes to it, they can fight each other over who actually killed Dominic.' He gave Knight a reassuring grin. 'The time has come to make it quite clear that we know exactly what happened. I'd lay even money that Mrs Newby will place the blame squarely on her husband when we recommence her interview.'

CHAPTER SIXTY

Eleanor Newby returned to the police station 55 minutes later. She had spent 10 minutes speaking with the doctor who had assumed responsibility for her husband's treatment in Northampton in the absence of his regular oncologist. Dr Lingard was disinclined to question the views of the distinguished consultant who had treated Newby since the discovery of his cancer. Lingard had seen the report and studied the results of the PET scan which had been faxed over from Milton Keynes. He shook his head and offered Mrs Newby little hope of her husband surviving for very long. There was nothing medical science could do for him other than pain relief. That was the gist of what he told her. The cancer had spread and was seemingly aggressive. Mrs Newby reacted in the way she thought appropriate, her handkerchief prominently displayed. She then asked to be taken to see her husband in the private room where he had been placed under police guard. No words passed between husband and wife, at least that was what DC Swanson reported when he telephoned Hood from the hospital. She had, he informed the Superintendent, sat in silence, placing her husband's hand in hers at one point and she'd kissed him before leaving the room. A police officer accompanied her back to Campbell Square in the unmarked police vehicle. She was joined there by her solicitor.

'My client wishes to make a statement, Superintendent,' said Mrs Dangerfield as soon as Hood and Knight re-entered the interview room, nearly an hour later.

'Does she?' said Hood. His eyes met Knight's as if to say, "I told you so." He indicated for her to switch on the tape machine. The detective sergeant then made the usual introductions, after which Hood took charge of proceedings.

'Before Mrs Newby says anything, there is some further evidence which has just arrived from the lab. I think it is appropriate for me to disclose it now. It concerns that tiny piece of carpet recovered from the brazier in the larger of the two barns at Stanton Harwood. We are still waiting for the written report, but the scientist has spoken with Detective Sergeant Knight some twenty minutes ago. The examination was fast-tracked at my request. I shall ask her to give you the gist of what the report is expected to say.'

Both Mrs Newby and her solicitor appeared only slightly apprehensive. Knight cleared her throat. She looked at her notebook and revealed what had been reported by the scientist. 'We now know for certain that the piece of carpet, Exhibit AS04, came from the boot of Mr Newby's Jaguar Mark Two. It matches exactly the samples taken from the interior carpet in the car – the rear passenger area and the front passenger footwell.'

Hood produced a photograph of the Jaguar boot from the file and handed it to Mrs Dangerfield. Knight then continued. 'There is no doubt that the exhibit formed part of a larger piece of carpet that lined the boot. What remains is burnt at the edges, which proves that an attempt was made to destroy the whole thing. It must have had Father Dominic's blood on it. That's why, we infer, it had to be destroyed. Someone, it seems, was very careless in failing to destroy all of it.'

Mrs Newby remained perfectly calm. Her solicitor whispered something to her. She nodded her head.

'In addition,' added Hood, 'my officers have located and viewed the CCTV which shows Arthur Newby outside Harper's restaurant in Gold Street on the twenty-seventh of March together with Martha Morton. I can arrange for you and Mrs Dangerfield to see it if you wish.'

Mrs Newby scoffed. 'I've already told you about that. There is no need for me to see it. The last thing I want is to see the two of them together.' She narrowed her eyes and glared at Hood.

'But you suggested he should meet her, didn't you?'

'What if I did? It doesn't follow I want to see them together.' There was real bitterness in her tone. Knight detected more than a touch of jealousy.

Hood paused and glanced towards Knight before addressing the solicitor. 'Very well. Now, you indicated Mrs Newby wishes to say something.

The solicitor nodded and opened her notebook which contained several pages of recently completed handwriting.

'Mrs Newby and I have been in discussion while we have been waiting. I have made some notes to assist her in what she proposes to say. I don't pretend they are complete. She wishes to help you with your enquiries as much as she possibly can and I hope you will note her cooperation and assistance when it comes to any decisions you may make as to her immediate future.'

Hood did not reply. He nodded to Knight who cautioned Mrs Newby, again in full. The solicitor then handed the notebook to her client. Mrs Newby took her spectacle case from her pocket, opened it, removed her glasses, and put them on. She then started to give her account, glancing from time to time at the notes.

'On the evening of the twenty-fourth of July, I had a bad migraine, as I told you earlier today. It was the anniversary of my daughter's death which I always find difficult to get through. I was resting in my room. My husband and I have separate bedrooms. We have not slept together since Hannah's death. Sometime around a quarter-to-nine, my husband came into my room and disturbed me. I'm sure of the time because I looked at the digital alarm clock by the side of my bed. I also noticed my husband had blood on his shirt; a lot of blood as I remember. He was in a terrible state and said there had been an accident. I asked him where he had been and what had happened. He said he'd driven to Easton Grange to see the priest who was residing there. That was the first time he had ever mentioned this priest to me.'

Mrs Newby looked up as if to check how her account was going down with Hood. His expression gave nothing away. She then grabbed a plastic water beaker to her left and took a drink before continuing. 'My husband then explained that he and this priest had argued about something and tempers had risen on both sides. The priest turned away and my husband lost his self-control and lashed out at him and injured him. Arthur then panicked and drove back home.'

'Did he say which vehicle he was driving?'

'Not then, not immediately, but when he went back to the Grange, I went with him, in the Jaguar. It was the only car outside the house, so I assumed he'd used it on his earlier journey. The Range Rover and my Mercedes were locked in the barn.'

'He went back?'

'Yes.'

'And you went with him?'

'Yes.'

'Why did you go back with him?'

'To check on this priest, of course, in case he needed help. I insisted. My husband wasn't making much sense. I could hardly follow what he was saying. I first rang Sir Robert thinking he could help if he were there, but regrettably there was no reply. He must have been away. Arthur was hardly forthcoming whether the priest was seriously hurt or not, but the blood on his shirt suggested he could have been very badly injured. Arthur had a quick shower and cleaned himself up, changed his shirt and trousers, then we set off. He was driving. When we got there, he showed me where he and the priest had argued, but there was no one about. I assumed the priest hadn't been as badly hurt as I had first thought and must have made his way to his cottage or into the main house.'

'Where did your husband say they had argued?' asked Hood. 'We have a pretty solid idea where the assault took place.'

'In the grounds of the ruined chapel.' She paused for breath then continued. 'There was no one about at all. It was almost dark when we got there. My husband then directed me to the cottage where he said the priest lived, but he wasn't there either. It was unlocked, but there was no sign of him or anyone.'

'Father Dominic was found dead in the priest-hole the following morning.' said Hood.

'I know, but I never went anywhere near this priest-hole. I never went into the house. Arthur thought that the priest might have got up and staggered inside and sought assistance then collapsed.'

Hood frowned. 'That would not have been possible.'

'Oh, why not?'

'Because the injuries he received were too severe. He could not have moved of his own accord after he received the final blow. The pathology shows he was struck several times. There is no doubt about that. And we know for certain he was attacked in the grounds of the ruined chapel. He could never have made it into the house. Neither could those injuries be considered by any stretch of the imagination to have been inflicted accidentally.'

465

Mrs Newby gave Hood another of her looks. 'Superintendent, I am only repeating what my husband told me.'

Hood gave Knight a cynical glance then continued. 'Did your husband tell you if he had used a weapon of any kind?'

'Yes, a spade that had been left nearby.'

'Was your husband injured in any way?'

'I don't think so. He never said he was.'

'Which means the blood on his shirt must have come from the priest?'

'I suppose it must.'

'Where is the shirt now?'

She answered in a matter-of-fact way. 'Destroyed. He burnt it that night, along with the trousers and the casual shoes he'd been wearing.'

'Where was the spade he'd used?'

'I don't know. I never saw it.'

'A spade was found in the stable block. It had Father Dominic's blood on it. How did it get there?'

'My husband must have put it there. I never saw it.'

'Was your husband wearing gloves by any chance?'

'I believe he was, yes.'

'And yourself?'

'No, of course not. It never occurred to me to wear gloves. I only went to see if I could help.'

'This account you say your husband gave you does not explain how Father Dominic's blood got into the boot of the Jaguar or the removal of the carpet and the attempt to destroy it.'

'I'm coming to that if you'll bear with me. I won't be rushed.' She paused and glowered at Hood before continuing. 'My husband had a bit of a bonfire when we got back. He didn't realise I was watching him from a window at the rear of the house. I saw him remove the carpet from the boot of the Jaguar along with something else that looked like a large rug or blanket. He burnt them in the brazier along with his shirt and trousers. He then hosed down the boot with a high-pressure hose.'

'Did you ask him why he did that?'

'I did not. It was obvious why he did what he did. He was too upset to say anything sensible when we got back. He seemed to be in shock. He was acting like an automaton. I left him to it until the next day. He took something to help him sleep. I didn't see him until the following lunchtime. I then heard on the afternoon news that a priest had been found dead at Easton Grange. I realised then that things were now deadly serious. I wanted nothing to do with it and I told him as much. He begged me not to say anything. Thinking, as I did, that a wife could not give evidence against her husband, I said nothing. Now, of course, I know differently. Mrs Dangerfield has explained the position, I assume accurately.'

The solicitor nodded in agreement as Hood disputed her client's comment.

'But, Mrs Newby, you actively supported what you now say were your husband's lies when I visited your home. There's a distinction, you know, between giving evidence in court and lying to police officers investigating a murder.'

She gave Hood a contemptuous look. 'I did my duty by him as his wife. And, by the way, you have me to thank that a piece of that carpet survived. I made sure of that when he left the brazier unattended to answer a call of nature. I recovered a tiny piece of the carpet and kept it safe until you searched the house and grounds. You would not have found it otherwise.'

'You mean you put it back in the brazier?'

Mrs Newby's expression remained fixed. 'Yes I did. Before you came to search the house I pushed it under the ashes. I'm glad you found it, Mr Hood. I was beginning to worry that you were not going to search the place. You were rather slow in doing so, if you don't mind my saying so.'

Hood exhaled loudly. He was finding Mrs Newby's account and criticism of the police investigation not only incredible but offensive. He also thought it odd that no attempt seemed to have been made to dispose of the ashes from the brazier. If Newby had burnt incriminating evidence, surely he'd have got rid of the remains? He made it plain he did not accept what she was saying. 'I find that very difficult to believe. Why didn't you mention it before now?'

'I did it so you could find it without my saying anything to incriminate my husband. I thought that was the only thing I could do in the circumstances.'

'How very public spirited of you,' said Hood. 'It's a great pity you didn't volunteer this information earlier. You've had several opportunities. And you are certainly doing your best to incriminate him now.' She bowed her head as Hood continued. 'Your husband will support all this, will he?' He couldn't help sounding sceptical.

She raised her head. That fixed expression was still there. 'It depends how desperate he is, but what I have told you is the truth. I will swear to it. Anyway, from what I saw and from what I was told, he's in no condition to say anything at the moment.'

'Some may think that's very convenient, Mrs Newby.' Hood glanced at the solicitor as he spoke. Neither woman said anything in response. Hood moved on. 'On your version of events, it must follow that your husband managed to get Father Dominic into the house and then into the priest-hole entirely without assistance before he returned to Stanton Harwood.'

The response from Mrs Newby was full of rancour. 'Unless his mistress helped him, of course.'

Hood gave Knight a cynical look. She simply raised an eyebrow. 'Did you see Martha Morton while you were at the Grange that evening?' he asked.

'No, but she lives nearby, doesn't she? I'm sure they've been in contact with each other more than he has let on. I know for a fact he couldn't get her out of his head after he'd seen her in Northampton. It was all he talked about. And I don't believe for a moment that her presence in Easton Parva was a coincidence. She obviously moved there because she wanted to be near my husband.'

A bitter look crossed her face as her solicitor again intervened. 'I think the telephone schedule supports what Mrs Newby says, doesn't it? And the call Martha Morton made on the third of August was obviously intended for Mr Newby. For all we know they could have seen each other again after they had lunch together.'

Hood was firm in his response. 'We have found no evidence to suggest Martha Morton is involved.' He paused then looked directly at Mrs Newby. 'But surely, given your husband's state of health when I saw him at your home, he would not have had the physical strength to move a body, not alone? Are you sure you didn't help him?'

'You mean when he appeared in his wheelchair?' Mrs Newby shook her head and hardly resisted a smile. 'That was entirely for your benefit, Mr Hood. It wasn't even his wheelchair. It belonged to my late mother who came to live with us a year or so after the death of my daughter. Mummy died three years ago. Surely you noticed it was far too small for him?'

Hood recalled he had thought exactly that on his first visit to Stanton Harwood, but he said nothing and allowed Mrs Newby to continue.

'Arthur was certainly capable of moving a body on the twenty-fourth. Perhaps he put him in the boot of the Jaguar? That would explain the blood you found there.'

'Very careless of him to leave that microscopic trace of blood there, especially if he'd hosed it down as you say?'

Her eyes drilled into Hood. 'I suggest you take that up with him, Superintendent.'

Hood had a sudden thought. *Was it carelessness? Or was it placed there deliberately to implicate the husband?* He decided to keep such thoughts to himself and returned to the narrative. 'Did he say why he had struck out at the priest?'

Mrs Newby paused and received a nod from her solicitor. Again she weighed her words carefully. 'He told me he had changed his mind about accepting whatever advice this priest had given him. He believed he was getting better and had decided not to see him again. I assure you, I knew nothing about his contact with this priest before. That's why he went to see him on the twenty-fourth apparently; to tell him he wouldn't be seeing him again and would not be keeping an appointment he had with him on the twenty-sixth.' She let out a deep sigh. 'I also suspect he had plans involving the Goring woman and I don't just mean leaving her money in his will. I think he was thinking of leaving me for her, and after all I have done for him.' A pained expression appeared on her face.

Knight intervened. 'When did you first realise that your husband might have been responsible for the death of your daughter?' The detective sergeant's directness seemed to take Mrs Newby by surprise. She did not answer immediately. Looking towards her solicitor, who nodded her approval, she again chose her words carefully before replying.

'Arthur told me he had picked up Hannah from Lonsdale Hall as we had arranged. He also admitted that they had argued on the way home. Hannah apparently told him she intended to tell me what she had witnessed in the office the previous week. She'd seen him being very intimate with that woman.' A tear formed in Mrs Newby's eye, which she quickly brushed away. 'You see, Hannah wasn't aware I already knew about his mistress. If I hadn't been so committed to keeping the affair a secret, she would probably still be alive today, so I blame myself as much as my husband.' She wiped her eyes again.

469

Knight pressed on. 'When did your husband tell you this?'

'Not until after he'd met up with this Goring woman. Not that long afterwards, as I recall. Just before we heard he might be in remission. A sort of dying declaration I suppose. I had no idea he'd picked Hannah up before he admitted it to me. He'd always denied it previously.'

'You had suggested he'd let her out of his car before, had you?'

'It had certainly crossed my mind and I had asked him more than once. Hannah was very independent and spoke her mind. She took after me in that respect. It would not have surprised me had she caused him to stop during an argument.'

'Did you husband ever confess to you that he had run her down himself?' asked Hood.

Mrs Newby did not react immediately. Her expression remained the same. Again, she looked towards her solicitor before replying. 'No, but I worked that out for myself earlier today after your sergeant told me about the damage to his Range Rover. I hadn't been aware of that before. I realise now that he purposefully kept that from me. I'd had my suspicions, of course, but no proof. Had the police examined his car as they should have done, the truth would have emerged long ago. Another failure on the part of your predecessors, Mr Hood.' She gave him a severe look.

'That is unfortunate, I agree,' conceded the Superintendent.

'Unfortunate? Incompetence would be a better description. Arthur had always shied away from discussing what had happened. He would get terribly upset if I ever mentioned it. You saw that for yourself the other night.' She looked down. 'Perhaps part of me didn't want to know either.' She turned away then placed her head in her hands. 'I suppose I have always known he wasn't being wholly truthful with me.'

'Is that why you are disclosing all this now? Because you now believe he killed your daughter?' It was Knight who asked the question. Her bluntness surprised even Hood. Mrs Newby looked up before collapsing in tears and sobbing uncontrollably. She could hardly get her words out.

'What do you expect me to do? He's not only been repeatedly unfaithful and fathered an illegitimate child, he killed my beautiful daughter. My Hannah.'

The tears flowed freely. Hood and Knight said nothing; they simply sat and waited until Mrs Newby seemingly recovered the ability to speak. As she calmed down, she screwed up her face, her anger manifest. 'And he

470

kept it from me all these years. He ran her down and left her to die alone in that ditch. He didn't even stop.' She curled her lip and with a rasp of contempt revealed what she thought of her husband. 'He deserves all he gets.'

'Then why did you insist on seeing him earlier this afternoon?' asked Hood, quite unmoved by her hysterics.

She spat out her reply. 'So I could tell him that I knew what he had done before he died. That's why I wanted to see him and that is all I said to him when I leant over and *pretended* to kiss him.'

'Were you aware your husband had been to confession with Father Dominic?'

She hesitated then replied, her tone suggesting the point had never occurred to her. 'No. Has he told you that?'

Hood did not reply. She continued, angrily. 'I don't go in for all that Papist nonsense and my husband had not practised his religion for years. Are you suggesting he confessed he had run over my daughter?'

Hood did not answer her. 'But he told you he had an appointment with Father Dominic on the twenty-sixth, did he?'

'He only told me about that after the priest was dead as I told you earlier. Arthur was in a terrible state when I saw him on the Wednesday evening. He couldn't believe what he'd done. He begged me not to say anything to anyone. It was an argument with the priest about the appointment on Friday which had caused him to lose his temper, or so he told me, but not until later.'

Silence.

'Do you know why he had arranged to see Father Dominic on the twenty-sixth?'

'I have no idea.'

Hood paused. 'There is an alternative explanation, of course.'

'What do you mean?'

Hood gave her a long and challenging look. 'Mrs Newby, I am now arresting you on suspicion of the murder of Dominic Renville.' Hood started to caution her, but she interrupted him.

'How dare you! I haven't killed anyone. What are you suggesting?'

Hood completed the words of the caution, then continued. 'I'm suggesting that it was you who killed Father Dominic. All this is merely an elaborate charade; an attempt to place the blame on your very sick husband, knowing as you do, that he'll probably be dead before any trial can take place. He told you about the appointment with Father Dominic *before* the killing took place, not afterwards, didn't he? You couldn't, of course, allow that to happen.'

'What on earth do you mean? Why would his seeing a priest be of any concern of mine? Is this what he has told you?'

'What your husband has said must remain confidential, for the time being. I suggest you believed he was intending to come to us with Father Dominic on the twenty-sixth in order to admit he was responsible for your daughter's death. You'd calculated that he'd probably confessed as much to the priest. You couldn't have lived with that becoming generally known; not with the embarrassing, all-consuming publicity that would follow. Your family's reputation dragged through the mud; the effect on the business. That's why, I suggest, *you* went to Easton Grange to see the priest to make sure the appointment on Friday was not kept. It was you who lost your temper and you who attacked him.'

She gave Hood a bemused look. 'Do go on, Superintendent. You tell a good story. I have already informed you that my husband told me about that arrangement only *after* the priest was dead. Tell me, if my husband was so overcome with guilt, why has he never handed himself in and admitted he was responsible for Hannah's death? Why did he lie to you when you asked him about this priest? Remember, he told you in my presence he'd had no dealings with him.'

Hood was quick to respond. 'Actually, it was you who said that to me Mrs Newby, when we first met.'

'My husband did not attempt to correct me though, did he? He agreed with what I said.'

'Because you persuaded him that the two of you could get away with it, if you stuck together. You agreed to cover for him in respect of your daughter's death and in return he agreed to alibi you for the evening of the twenty-fourth of July. And you might have got away with it until we received the DNA analysis of the bloodstain in the boot of the Jaguar. That changed everything. There's no way around it.'

Mrs Newby shook her head. 'Why would I want to kill a priest I have never met? Why would I want to stop my husband confessing he had run down my daughter if that's what he intended to do? I've been desperate to learn the truth about what happened to her for nine years.' She glared at Hood. 'I had nothing to do with this killing and, more to the point, you have no evidence that implicates me, nothing at all. Where is your proof?'

Knight gave Hood a knowing look. She recognised there was some force in what Mrs Newby was saying, but Hood pressed on. 'You say you never met Father Dominic, but why did you go to Easton Grange on the seventh of July? Too see him, I suggest.'

Mrs Newby did not reply.

'You were there that day, were you not?' insisted Hood.

That look again accompanied with a cynical smile. 'I was not. Your witness is mistaken. If the Jaguar was there, it had nothing to do with me. My husband must have driven it there.'

'But you have said previously your husband was at home with you that lunchtime,' said Hood.

She hesitated and appeared for the first time to be slightly ruffled. 'You're right, I did. I must have been mistaken. He was usually at home with me on a Sunday as he was most days. You have to understand Mr Hood, every day has been the same since my husband has been ill. They seem to merge, one into another. It's surely understandable how I could get one Sunday mixed up with another? It's easily done.'

Hood gave her a cynical look. 'What happened to the spider brooch you were wearing that Sunday?'

Mrs Newby raised her eyebrows. 'So, that's what Sergeant Knight was looking for when she went through my jewellery? I could have saved her the trouble if she'd only said. I have never owned or worn a brooch of that description. And I have kept the receipts for all my jewellery, for insurance purposes, you understand? My solicitor will let you see the schedule if you wish.'

Hood declined the offer and moved on. 'If your husband had taken the unusual step of going out on a Sunday without you in his Jaguar you'd have remembered it? Or is this another attempt to push the blame on to him?'

She narrowed her eyes. 'It is nothing of the kind. I am not his keeper. He can decide to do things for himself. He certainly went out on his own on occasions when he was in remission. He'd even been to the office in Milton Keynes when he was feeling well enough.' She paused. 'I am trying the best I can to help you get to the truth. Surely you can see that?'

'One last question, Mrs Newby. If you went to Easton Grange to check on the priest, why didn't you do so?'

'Because I assumed my husband was being truthful when he said the priest must have managed to make it into the house and seek assistance. I thought he was not as badly hurt as I first imagined.'

The Superintendent glanced at Knight. 'I think we'll take a break. I need to consider what you've told us.'

Knight stated the time and switched off the tape recorder. She noticed a self-indulgent smirk on Eleanor Newby's face as she left the room.

CHAPTER SIXTY-ONE

Hood decided to bail Mrs Newby despite the strongly expressed contrary view of DS Knight. The detective sergeant thought a night in the cells would at least wipe that smug expression off the suspect's face. Hood took a more measured and proportionate approach. He was content for Eleanor Newby to think she had persuaded him that the evidence against her was insufficient to justify charging her. But, in reality, his view had not changed. If anything, he was more convinced than ever that she was the prime mover in events leading to the death of Father Dominic. He just needed one piece of solid, unchallengeable evidence to justify re-arresting her. As for her husband, Arthur Newby's role remained obscure; Hood needed to speak to him again before deciding to seek approval to charge one or both of them with murder.

He imposed strict conditions on Mrs Newby's bail, of course. She was to have no contact with her husband and to spend every night at her home in Stanton Harwood. One telephone call a day to the hospital was permitted, but she would not be allowed to speak to her husband. Hood agreed that she was entitled to know how he was progressing but such information as was thought appropriate to be disclosed by the hospital would be passed to her through Sister Norris or one of the other senior nurses. Mrs Newby was furious when informed of these restrictions. At first, she continued to demand to visit her husband and it was only when she was told she would otherwise be kept in custody overnight that she reluctantly agreed to Hood's terms. Hood emphasised it was as much in her interests as those of her husband that there should be no contact between them. She was warned that a police officer would visit her at home twice every 24 hours and she would be expected to present herself on the doorstep when he called. She was also required to return to the police station on Friday morning to attend an identification procedure.

The next morning, Hood telephoned Fiona Morrison at Regional CPS. He had already faxed her a copy of his interim report which included a brief summary of the oncologist's opinion on the progression of Newby's cancer. Her advice could prove critical as the investigation moved to its conclusion. He had previously despatched DS Knight to see Mrs Gilbert and her son and to speak further with Mr Hitchens. He wanted to firm up the evidence that it was definitely 7 July when young Francis had noted the registration numbers of the vehicles parked outside the chapel at Easton Grange. Knight was also to get confirmation from Mr Hitchens that Mrs Newby was definitely present when Sir Robert's gardener revealed the discovery of the priest-hole when visiting the Newby's at Stanton Harwood. The lengthy telephone call with the regional head of the CPS began just after 10 o'clock.

'You've eliminated Sir Robert's son, have you?' Morrison asked. 'Despite his fingerprints being on the murder weapon.'

'We have. He's responsible for the broken window but I'm sure he had no further involvement. That bloodstain in the boot of the Jaguar means the Newbys are the only real suspects. And whoever did this would have been covered in blood. No sign of anything like that on Southall's body or clothing.'

Morrison paused. Hood could tell from her tone that her advice was not going to be what he wanted to hear. 'This is a difficult one, Harry. I see where you are coming from in thinking that Eleanor Newby is the killer: it's an interesting theory. But I have to consider the evidence from the point of view of a jury, in other words, what can be proved and what can't. We have to meet the threshold test. I'm far from sure that we can, not in respect of her alone. Not on a charge of murder.'

'You don't think there's enough to charge her?'

'Not at the moment, no. You were right to bail her. The problem as I see it is the survival of her husband, even if he comes clean about what really happened. With the state of the lists at the moment, I can't see a trial getting before the Crown Court this side of Christmas, even if it were given priority. And the chances of Arthur Newby living that long do not look good. Unless he's in the dock with her or available as a witness, how will we get in whatever he may say about his wife's part in all of this? And

I need hardly point out, he's not said anything yet to implicate her, quite the opposite.'

'I'm hoping that when I next speak to him and disclose what his wife has said about him, he'll cooperate and tell me the truth. I can't see him continuing to protect her in the longer term.'

Morrison laughed. 'You're hoping they'll cut each other's throats? A worthy ambition, but even if he does implicate her, the chances of getting his account before a jury after his death are pretty remote. Whatever he may say to you when you next speak to him will be treated as hearsay and under the present law, will be difficult to get in. On the other hand, the defence will have no problem adducing his lies. I can't see a judge excluding them. But if he were to point the finger at his wife and we were to seek to rely on what he says after his death, we'd hit the hearsay barrier full on.'

'Even if we recorded what he said on video?'

'That might help. It would certainly get our application off the ground and remove any argument about the accuracy of the record, but if he's no longer with us when the trial takes place, which seems highly likely, it stands to reason that he won't be able to be cross-examined. That means there's every prospect we'll fail the interests of justice test under the nineteen eighty-eight Act as well as section seventy-eight of PACE.'

Hood hesitated. 'We could charge both of them with murder, couldn't we? Reading between the lines of the oncologist's report, he's likely to live at least a few more weeks or perhaps longer. Let them fight it out between them who did the actual killing.'

'I doubt if he'll live long enough to get him to trial,' said Morrison. She paused at length before continuing. 'That's the dilemma as I see it, Harry. There's a draft bill about to be presented to Parliament following work by the Law Commission. It will make the introduction of hearsay evidence much easier. I'm not sure where it's got to at the moment, but it's been hanging around for years waiting for Parliament to grapple with it. It will help in future, but it won't apply to this case. We have to work within the law as it is now.'

Hood exhaled loudly. 'Sounds like there's little point in my speaking to him?'

Morrison sounded more optimistic. 'I wouldn't give up on him, not yet. If he's feeling more cooperative, he may alert you to some other evidence, always assuming he reacts as you hope to his wife dropping him in it.' She paused ominously. 'But there's always the chance he may say nothing. As he's dying and probably knows it, he may just choose to say nothing and save his wife from receiving a life sentence. You shouldn't overlook that possibility.'

Hood could not hide his disappointment. 'Can we at least do her for perverting the course of justice? She's admitted planting that bit of carpet in the hope that we would find it.'

'We can certainly try. Replacing that piece of carpet in the brazier arguably amounts to the offence, but if a jury were not sure she was involved in the actual killing and that she did what she says she did in order to implicate her husband because she believed he killed the priest, would they convict? I'm not convinced I would, not if I were sure she took no part in the murder. We would have to consider whether it would be in the public interest to prosecute her at all in such circumstances. And she does come across well in those video interviews. I watched them on screen. A jury may well be sympathetic.'

Hood frowned. 'Yes, an Oscar winning performance. I have to concede she's no mean actress.' He scratched his head. 'You know, I'm beginning to think it wasn't just that bit of carpet she fitted him up with. That bloodstain in the boot, for instance. How did that survive if the boot was cleaned with a high-pressure hose after the carpet had been removed?'

'You think she could be responsible for that?' Morrison sighed. 'That would be a high risk strategy, Harry. If it wasn't for that blood matching the priest's, the case against both of them would be much weaker.'

'I know. That's why I thought they'd done a deal. You know, she was protecting him in respect of her daughter's death and he's helping her out by covering up the killing. But the more I delve into things, I think she might have taken the risk of leaving a bit of blood there just to rid herself of her husband having worked out for herself long before now that he killed her daughter.'

Morrison drew in her breath. 'I'll have to think about that one. The evidence that he killed the daughter, without an admission from him, is not at all strong. As you point out in your report, the failure to examine his Range Rover at the time was a serious oversight. And we mustn't overlook the lies he told about his relationship with Martha Morton. Why should a jury take any notice of anything this guy says? We would have to concede he lied his head off in interview. That isn't going to help to convict his wife.'

'That has not escaped me, I assure you. That's why I'm convinced she told him to say what he did so that she could expose him as a liar when it suited her. I'm now thinking she has some kind of hold over him that goes beyond what she knows about his part in her daughter's death.'

'Any idea what that might be?'

'Could be financial. Her family money rescued his business back in the early nineties.'

'Would Newby be prepared to help with that? He will presumably know the truth of it.'

'He knows the truth about a great deal more than that, believe me.'

'But shows little sign of revealing anything about his wife. We have to be realistic, Harry, and deal with the case on the evidence we have.'

Hood paused for some time then returned to his earlier suggestion. 'Could we not pursue them both for murder – and hope he manages to hang on for the trial?'

'When the investigation is complete, I'll certainly consider that, but we would still have to make a decision as to how we put the case.' But Morrison remained sceptical about pursuing the wife alone. 'We really need some independent evidence that puts her at Easton Grange at the time of the killing. I've been through your report with a fine toothcomb; we don't have anything substantial. Not even a piece of bloodstained clothing. And whoever despatched this priest must have been covered in blood.'

Hood had to agree. 'I think we can safely assume if they got rid of the carpet from the boot, that any clothing that would have compromised whoever did this will have been put in the same brazier and destroyed, just like she says.'

'It's not just the absence of clothing, Harry. No forensics, no DNA, no witnesses.

Hood smiled. 'That's exactly what DS Knight said only yesterday.'

'Bright cookie, that one. What's more, the evidence we do have is more supportive of Newby being the killer than his wife. There's certainly enough to charge him. After all, the critical bloodstain was found in his car.'

Hood harrumphed. 'And rely on what his wife says? No way.'

'I think we have enough without his wife. We'll have to think about it Harry. A decision will have to be made soon.' She paused, noticing the disappointment in Hood's voice. 'Look, you see if you can get anywhere with him. If he's prepared to tell what you think is the truth, you can at least challenge his wife with it.'

Hood sounded downcast. 'Always assuming I get a chance to speak to him again, of course.'

'You will. He's not about to pop his clogs, not yet. Do your best. If you can't persuade him to tell the truth, no one can.'

CHAPTER SIXTY-TWO

'Some good news, Harry.'

Wendy Knight returned from seeing Mrs Gilbert and her son. Hood looked up from his computer. He had been reviewing Mrs Newby's second interview.

'It had to be the seventh of July when young Francis noted the registration numbers. The family went on holiday the next day – to Blakeney in Norfolk. They stayed there until Monday the twenty-second. Father Dominic was dead before they next attended the chapel at Easton Grange.'

'And the Sunday before the seventh?'

'That was the thirtieth of June. They went to a special service at the Cathedral in Northampton that Sunday. Young Francis was confirmed by the Bishop. So they weren't at Easton Grange. It all checks out.'

Knight noticed that Hood was not his usual self. He seemed quite low. Pleased as he was with the information she had gathered, he did not react as enthusiastically as she had expected.

'How did it go with Mr Hitchens?' he asked.

'I telephoned him. He's confident they were both present when he mentioned the priest-hole. He checked his records. He was at Stanton Harwood on the sixteenth of July. Mrs Newby had made him a cup of tea and they were sitting together at the kitchen table when he told them what Dominic had said. He even remembers the slice of fruit cake she offered him, home-made apparently.'

Hood almost smiled. 'Who took his statement?'

'PC Barry. He was helping out during the first few days of the investigation.'

Hood frowned. 'Pity he didn't get that sort of detail out of him when he spoke to him. How many times do I have to tell these young officers that background is very important when taking a witness statement, especially in a murder inquiry?'

'Bill Renfrew is seeing Mr Hitchens later today to take a further statement. He'll get it right.'

Hood looked down and sighed. His mood had not changed.

'Anything wrong?' asked Knight. She was not unfamiliar with Hood's occasional bouts of despondency. 'How did it go with Fiona Morrison?'

Hood let out a prolonged sigh. 'Not as well as I anticipated. We may have difficulty getting in evidence anything Arthur Newby may say if he dies before we get to trial with the wife. Anything he says to us will be treated as hearsay in such circumstances, with the possible exception of the lies he's told. They'll go in. No problem.'

'Hardly seems fair. All or nothing, surely?'

'That's the law, according to Fiona. The defence, in practice, are given more latitude. Understandable I suppose if the witness is dead so can't be cross– examined.'

Knight said nothing for a moment. 'Do we know how he is today, Newby I mean?'

'He was asleep when Bill Renfrew phoned first thing. Adrian Swanson took over at the hospital at twelve. We should be hearing from him soon.'

'And Mrs Newby? She hasn't done a runner?' Knight smiled broadly.

Hood recalled her objections to granting Mrs Newby bail. 'Still at Stanton Harwood. She was checked at eight last night and again at ten o'clock this morning. She's keeping to her bail conditions, at least so far. There's been no contact with her husband. But she'll want to know how he's progressing.'

'More likely how he's deteriorating. I bet she can't wait to start arranging his funeral.'

'You are becoming almost as cynical as me, Wendy. I hope she'll have to wait some time for that. I shall be going to the hospital later to see him. I've obtained a twelve-hour extension from Chief Superintendent Coupland but that will expire just after one-thirty tomorrow morning. I shall have to make an application to the Magistrates' Court to detain him further unless we charge him of course.'

'Even with him in hospital?'

Hood nodded. 'That makes no difference.'

'Will you charge him with murder, despite your views about his wife?'

'Fiona Morrison reckons there's enough evidence to do so, but you know what I feel about that. I'm by no means sure he did it.'

'What are the chances of interviewing him again?'

'His oncologist, Dr Freeman, is due there at two. He's coming over specially. I'm hoping to have a word with him about Newby's prospects. Hopefully, he'll be well enough to be interviewed later this afternoon.'

'And if he isn't?'

'Let's cross that bridge when we come to it.'

Hood's mobile buzzed. 'Ah, Adrian. Any news?'

'He's out of bed, sir, sitting in a wheelchair. Sister Norris says he's been stabilised. They've sorted his medication apparently. She says there's no reason for him to remain in hospital, certainly not after today. His consultant is on his way. He'll have the final say.'

'Anything else.'

Swanson hesitated. 'There is one thing, sir.'

'Yes.'

'He's asking for a priest.'

'Is he, indeed? Did he say why?'

'I didn't ask, sir. I assumed it's because of his condition. But he didn't want to see the C of E chaplain. He turned him away. He's still in a bit of pain some of the time and he doesn't look well but he was insistent. He wants to see a Catholic priest.'

'There's a Catholic chaplain on call there isn't there?'

'Usually, yes. But Sister Norris says Father Lorimer is on holiday and the other priest they call on in his absence is with a dying parishioner. He won't be able to get here until later. Newby was very upset when I told him. I phoned the Grange to see if Father Milmo could help, but he wasn't there.'

'I know. He's accompanying Father Dominic's body back to Melford Abbey. The Coroner released the body yesterday. There's always Grantham, I suppose, but he's a potential witness in the case. Has anyone else spoken to Newby today?'

'Only Mr Sewell and another lawyer, a Miss Randall. DC Renfrew told me they were here for some time this morning. I understand Mr Sewell will be returning later. I believe the other solicitor is a civil practitioner.'

He dropped his voice to a whisper. 'It looks like Newby is altering his will.'

'Another lawyer? Now that is interesting. Perhaps Newby accepts he won't be with us for much longer. Look, I'm on my way, Adrian. No one is to see Newby, medical staff apart, before I get there. I'll see you in ten minutes.'

Hood turned to Knight, his mood suddenly lifted. 'Come on, Wendy. I'll explain on the way. We're off to Northampton General.'

CHAPTER SIXTY-THREE

Hood and Knight met DC Swanson outside Newby's room at the hospital.

'How is he?' asked Hood.

'Fully conscious, sir, stable, but still in some pain. Shall we go in and see him?'

'I'm waiting for DC Bradley to get here. He's bringing a tape recorder and a portable video player; a camera too. I need to make sure that anything Newby may say to us is accurately recorded. And I want him to see his wife's video interviews. We must also wait for his solicitor to return. If he does say anything useful, I don't want it ruled out later because of a procedural breach. We'll have enough trouble as it is with the hearsay rule.'

'I don't know when Mr Sewell will get back. He didn't give a time.'

'I think I'll speak to Sister Norris while we are waiting.' Hood turned to Knight. 'See if you can contact his solicitor, Wendy. Stay here and let me know when Sewell plans to return. Adrian, you come with me.'

Hood headed along the corridor with DC Swanson. He noticed Sister Norris talking to a nurse at the entrance to an adjacent ward. She dismissed the nurse and approached Hood. The three of them walked in the direction of her office.

'This police activity is becoming a bit of a nuisance, Superintendent. While I appreciate the circumstances are unusual, I can't have my office used as a waiting room and canteen by your officers, you know. They've been making coffee and tea in there. I have work to do. And all these police officers about the place is upsetting our routine. If you need somewhere private, I can let you have the use of the room next to Mr Newby, for the next day or so anyway. The patient who was occupying it went home this morning. I really do need my office back.'

Hood acknowledged her cooperation. 'If the room adjacent to Mr Newby is available, that should be sufficient for our purposes. We'll vacate your office now. DC Swanson will remove whatever we have in there.' He indicated to Swanson and the DC disappeared inside. 'I'll need to set up some equipment in the room next door to Newby's if that's all right with you?' continued Hood

Sister Norris nodded her approval. 'You mean to interview him while he's here?'

'Yes, assuming he's fit enough. Tell me, how is he doing?'

'The diamorphine has done its job as expected, but he remains very unwell. He'll be on pain relief for the duration, I'm afraid. But there is no need for him to remain here after tonight, unless there is a sudden deterioration in his condition.'

'No further treatment?'

She shook her head. 'I managed to speak to Dr Freeman at Milton Keynes late yesterday. I don't think he's particularly optimistic. Realistically, pain relief is all we can offer at this stage. And that can be organised at his home or in a hospice.'

Hood frowned. 'He is under arrest on suspicion of murder, you know. I'm not at all sure he'll be going home.'

'I wouldn't know about that. He should be well enough to answer your questions if he is minded to do so, but I don't think much of your chances of getting him to court in the longer term.'

Hood appeared suitably concerned. 'How long has he got?'

'Difficult to say. He seems very determined to live. I've seen many people die, Superintendent, but this man won't contemplate the possibility.' She sighed. 'Three months, four months, perhaps longer, perhaps shorter. It's impossible to say. You had better speak to Dr Freeman when he gets here. He's more familiar with Mr Newby's case than anyone else, but I doubt if he'll say anything different. Dr Lingard was very pessimistic when he spoke with Mrs Newby yesterday, but it's really anybody's guess. Incidentally, Mr Newby asked for a priest – a Catholic priest. Did your colleague mention that?'

'He did, yes. I've given instructions that no one is to see him yet, other than his solicitor and medical staff, of course. But if he is as ill as you say, it would seem churlish to prevent him from seeing a priest. What arrangements have been made?'

'Nothing definite at the moment. We usually ask Father Lorimer from St Joseph's, but he's away and I couldn't raise his curate. Father Cotton, who we've used before in an emergency, is with a sick parishioner. It will be some time before he can get here but he's agreed to come as soon as he can. Your colleague suggested a priest from Easton Grange. Mr Newby was so insistent he saw a priest today I thought we had little option. DC Swanson telephoned but I don't know the outcome. Mr Newby was getting himself very worked up. Something is definitely bothering him; something quite unrelated to his illness. Is there a particular problem you know about?'

Hood glanced towards the uniformed officer standing by the office door. He had a good idea what was causing Newby grief but had no intention of disclosing it. 'I'm not sure, but it certainly sounds as if something's upsetting him. But before he sees a priest, I must at least attempt to interview him further. I shall do my utmost to find out what it is that is worrying him, though. Thank you, Sister. You've been very helpful.'

CHAPTER SIXTY-FOUR

'How are you bearing up?' asked Hood, as he and Wendy Knight sat down in the room made available by Sister Norris immediately adjacent to Arthur Newby's hospital room.

'Apparently, I'm not long for this world, Mr Hood,' replied Newby. 'That's what they tell me and to be honest, I don't feel at all well. I think I have to accept that I'm no longer in remission.'

Newby appeared pale and gaunt and was obviously in some pain but otherwise reasonably alert. But he presented a sorry sight, slumped in the wheelchair in his hospital issue pyjamas and dressing gown. An attempt had been made to do something with what hair he had left and he had shaved. A needle had been placed under the skin of his left arm connected to a syringe driver which enabled a small amount of diamorphine to be dispensed when necessary to relieve his pain.

'This thing helps,' he added, as he half-raised his arm. 'I suppose I'm stuck with it now.' He then gave Hood a cynical look. 'I don't reckon much to your chances of getting me to court, if that's what you're still after doing.'

His solicitor was sitting next to him and immediately expressed his concerns about his client being troubled by further questions while detained in hospital. Hood assumed the solicitor's anxieties would have understandably increased after he and Newby had been afforded the opportunity of privately viewing Eleanor Newby's recorded interviews. Would what she had said persuade Newby to be more forthcoming? Hood had already spoken with Dr Freeman while he waited for DC Bradley to set up the recording equipment brought from Campbell Square. The consultant oncologist had not been any more optimistic than Sister Norris as to Newby's prospects. Further chemotherapy remained an option but was not advised.

Hood continued sympathetically. He looked at Sewell then at Newby. 'I understand that you've asked to see a priest?'

'What if I have?'

'May I ask why?'

'You can ask, but don't expect me to tell you.' He turned away and dropped his head, then after a lengthy sigh, looked up. 'Why do you think? A man should be able to see a priest if he's dying. After all, that's what they're for, isn't it?'

No one said anything for several seconds. Hood eventually broke the silence. 'I'm sorry about your condition, I really am, but you're still under arrest you know, despite your being in hospital.'

Newby gave Hood a sharp look. 'I'm aware of that, Superintendent. I suppose I should be grateful you haven't chained me to my bed!'

'There's no question of that, I assure you. You haven't been charged with anything, not yet. But I would like to know if you have anything to say about your wife's allegations.' He nodded towards Knight and she reminded Newby of the words of the caution having first pressed the start button on the recording equipment and stated the date and time.

Newby tried to laugh as the words of the caution concluded but did not succeed. 'I shall soon be appearing before a much higher tribunal than any court you can put me before, Mr Hood, according to my doctors, that is. But I've not given up, not yet. Not by a long chalk. They've been wrong before. I've told Dr Freeman I'm willing to repeat the chemo although he doesn't recommend it. All or nothing. That's me. I've always been one for backing an outsider.'

His face told a different story. The glimmer of hope that had been present in his eyes when Hood had first interviewed him was much reduced, almost extinguished. Newby squeezed the syringe and released some diamorphine, closing his eyes briefly as his pain was alleviated.

'You've seen the recordings of your wife's interviews, I take it?' continued Hood.

The solicitor intervened. 'I can confirm that Mr Newby has seen both of them. I have taken his instructions. He is not proposing to make any further comment, not at the moment, not while he's in hospital. I would welcome a transcript, though, when one is available.'

Hood nodded. 'Of course, but I think I can do better than that, Mr Sewell. I'm prepared to let you have a copy of the actual recordings.' He paused. 'I was hoping Mr Newby might wish to comment on what his wife has said. She makes no bones about it. She's saying in terms that he murdered Father Dominic.'

Newby sighed. 'No comment.'

'She's also implying that Mr Newby killed her daughter, by running her over in his Range Rover, very much as I suggested in his last interview.'

Tears formed in Newby's eyes. 'No comment. I'm saying nothing until I see a priest. And I don't want anything I say recorded.'

'What do you mean?' asked Hood. 'I have to follow the rules, even here in the hospital. You are under caution as I'm sure Mr Sewell will advise you. And arrangements are in hand for you to see a priest.'

Mr Sewell intervened. 'I think a break would be in order, Mr Hood. I need to confer with my client, in private. And I remain very concerned about his being interrogated in his present circumstances.'

'I'm not proposing to interrogate him,' replied Hood. 'I'm merely giving him the opportunity to comment on the very serious allegations his wife has made. It would not be fair otherwise, would it? If, of course, he chooses to say nothing, as is his right, I shall have no alternative but to proceed on the basis of the evidence we have, including his wife's account of events at Easton Grange on the twenty-fourth of July and immediately afterwards.'

'I would still like that break,' insisted Sewell.

Hood looked at Knight, sighed, then nodded. She stated the time and switched off the recording equipment. The two detectives then left the room.

'What's happening, Harry?' asked Knight as they paced the hospital corridor and Newby was wheeled back into his own room. 'Is he saying he's prepared to comment on his wife's account if we don't record it?'

'It's looking that way,' said Hood. 'But any outside chance of using it will vanish if it isn't recorded.'

'We could make a note of what he says afterwards?'

Hood heaved a sigh. 'And get him to sign it? That won't help overmuch. Interviewing him outside the police station in his present circumstances we can just about get away with. But a proper recording is essential. Fiona Morrison has made that perfectly clear. PACE applies even in a hospital.'

'What do we do?'

'Wait. There's not much else we can do. Newby will be discharged from here in the next twenty-four hours and you never know, Mr Sewell may be able to persuade him to cooperate. Eleanor Newby will make a damning witness against him if he remains silent, whatever our views as to her credibility. His solicitor is bound to realise that. I'm hoping he'll persuade Newby to say something. And he won't find a prison hospital quite as comfortable as Northampton General. He can't go home, not while his wife is there.' He paused briefly. 'I'm sure Sewell won't want him saying anything unless it's fully recorded. What worries me is it rather sounds like he doesn't want him saying anything at all to us at the moment.'

'In which case he'll probably clam up altogether. We'll have no option then but to charge him and get him remanded. Time is against us.'

Hood hesitated. 'Let's wait a little longer, shall we? I'm not for giving up on him yet.'

DC Swanson approached. 'Excuse me, sir, but Father Cotton has turned up. He's with Sister Norris at the moment in her office.'

Mention of Father Cotton gave Hood an idea. 'Newby has asked to see a priest. He's just said he wouldn't say anything until he'd seen a priest. Suppose we allow Father Cotton to speak to him in private then have another go at interviewing him? His attitude may change after he's got off his chest whatever it is that's worrying him. Sister Norris mentioned he was upset about something other than his illness. And I have a good idea what it is now that he's seen his wife's interviews.'

Knight shrugged her shoulders. 'Worth a go, I suppose.'

'Would you ask Father Cotton to meet me here, Adrian?' asked Hood. 'I need a quick word with him. He needs to understand Newby's position before he goes in there.'

CHAPTER SIXTY-FIVE

Almost an hour passed before Father Cotton emerged from Newby's room. Hood was not expecting him to reveal very much. He appreciated that whatever had passed between priest and penitent would remain confidential. He approached Father Cotton cautiously.

'How is the patient, Father?'

Father Cotton, a slim, athletic-looking man in his late thirties, smartly dressed in a well-cut traditional black suit and sporting a clerical collar, smiled his response. 'I think you will find him in a much better frame of mind, Mr Hood. I believe he is beginning to accept his situation and he appears to be reasonably settled. As you will appreciate, I can't say anything more, but I am grateful for your allowing me the opportunity of speaking with him. It was a wise decision on your part, if I may say so. He has asked me to return tomorrow before he is discharged from hospital and I have agreed to do so.'

'Do you think he is now inclined to help with my investigation into Father Dominic's death?'

The priest smiled. 'I think I have already said more than I should.' He then smiled more broadly as he prepared to take his leave. Was that a twinkle in his eye? 'How is your Latin, Mr Hood?' he asked. *'Nemo moriturus praesumitur mentire.'*

Hood did not react as the priest made to leave. 'Well, I'll be off. Duty calls. God bless you.' Father Cotton then went on his way with a cheery wave.

'What does all that mean?' whispered Knight, a puzzled look on her face. 'As you know, I'm no Latin scholar. Was Father Cotton trying to tell us something? Why did he have to be so obscure?'

Hood did not answer. His Latin was, as he would be the first to concede, a little rusty; he recognised a couple of the words but did not understand what the priest meant until Gerald Sewell, who was also waiting in the corridor and had heard the priest's remark, came to his rescue.

'Forgive me for interrupting, but I think a loose translation is along the lines of *"a man will not meet his Maker with a lie in his mouth."* If I remember my university evidence lectures correctly, it's the basis in law of allowing a dying declaration in evidence as an exception to the hearsay rule. It's not something one comes across very often these days.' He smiled before continuing his explanation. 'It's based on the proposition, common enough in more religious times, that a victim of a deadly attack who is at the point of death is unlikely to lie in identifying the person who assaulted him. Not that it would apply to Mr Newby, of course.'

'It wouldn't?' Hood raised an eyebrow.

'You can say that again,' added Knight, cynically. 'He's hardly been truthful with us so far.'

'I can't comment on that, Detective Sergeant, but that's not what I mean,' insisted the solicitor. 'First of all, he isn't at the point of death, not at the moment, but more importantly, he isn't the victim here, not of a violent assault anyway. Now, if Father Dominic had named his attacker before he died, and had realised he was dying when he did so, that would have fulfilled the legal essentials comprehensively. But, unfortunately, as far as we know, he didn't.'

Hood appreciated the point but was not solely concerned with the legal principle. 'Perhaps Father Cotton meant it in a religious sense? After all, he's a priest, not a lawyer. I'm sure Mr Newby wants to get something off his chest and soon. I suspect that's why he wanted to see a priest.'

The solicitor smiled but remained non-committal. 'Perhaps he does. But he's not one for giving up on life, not yet, and I think I should speak to him before you see him again. I don't know what he said to Father Cotton or what the priest said to him, but I have a professional duty towards him as his solicitor. I don't want him misunderstanding the situation, especially given his position as the major suspect in a murder inquiry.'

Hood looked at his watch then agreed to the solicitor's request. 'I would appreciate it if you could make it brief, though. Time is getting on. I have to make a decision about charging Mr Newby in the next few hours or apply to the Magistrates' court for a further extension. And I don't want to be making an application to a JP in the middle of the night.'

'I understand,' replied Sewell. 'I shan't be over long. Mr Newby will make up his own mind about what he proposes to say, if anything.' He gave Hood a knowing look and shrugged his shoulders. 'He listens to what I advise but he doesn't always follow my guidance. He takes an independent line as you may have noticed. I shouldn't be longer than fifteen minutes.'

'So he isn't actually dying?' said Knight as the solicitor disappeared into Newby's room.

'Not at the moment, no,' replied Hood. 'He should survive for some time yet, but if I've grasped what Father Cotton was trying to convey to us, I think he might prove more cooperative than before, always assuming we get the opportunity to speak to him again.'

CHAPTER SIXTY-SIX

'You have to understand, Mr Hood. Although I didn't kill Father Dominic, I feel some responsibility for his death.'

Hood had eventually relented and agreed to speak with Newby without their conversation being recorded. Arthur Newby had also insisted that there should be no one else present other than his solicitor. DS Knight advised strongly against such a course, reminding Hood of his invariable practice of following procedure to the letter. But the Superintendent was hoping Newby would reveal something that would help him get to the truth about the death of Father Dominic. Time was running out. He had to take a chance, whatever the consequences, although he realised he would not be able to use anything Newby might say as evidence in court, certainly not if he died before any trial of his wife could take place. He sent a disappointed Knight back to Campbell Square to monitor evidence that he was expecting to arrive from the forensic science laboratory.

Newby spoke slowly and carefully, glancing occasionally towards his solicitor. 'Where shall I begin?' he asked.

'It would help me if you told me about your relationship with your wife, given what she has said about you.'

Newby took a few deep breaths as he prepared to give his account. 'My marriage was not exactly made in heaven, Mr Hood. Neither was it a love match. It was more of a business merger than anything else.' He attempted a smile. 'Eleanor's first husband, Warren Marshall, was a good friend of mine. He was a few years older than me and about ten years older than Eleanor, but we all got on very well together. He was a decent golfer too. He and I spent many happy hours on the golf course and in the bar afterwards, not that Eleanor approved of our drinking.'

He smiled to himself as he recollected happier times, then, realising he was straying from the subject in hand, turned again to the narrative. 'Warren and I went into business together. Dowlas Logistics was our first venture. Very successful we were too, but we probably expanded too quickly. It was all very exciting and we undoubtedly got carried away with our initial success. Then Larry Lawson joined us.' He paused and grunted to himself. 'Not a wise decision on our part as it turned out. Larry was of a reckless disposition, if you know what I mean? Bit of a gambler. Lucky to begin with, but things eventually started to turn very sour. We took on too much debt; leased too many lorries and took on far too much warehousing space, just as Warren went down with lung cancer and the economy turned downwards. And he never smoked in his life, poor bugger. He liked his whisky, but I never saw him with a cigarette.' He shook his head. 'He made a fight of it, of course, but succumbed pretty quickly. Marrying his widow seemed the right thing to do. She inherited his shares and I couldn't afford to buy her out. I never thought of myself as the marrying type before then and I wasn't quite thirty, but the opportunity seemed too good to miss. And she seemed keen enough. We waited for what Eleanor thought was a suitable period of mourning then married quietly in a register office in London.'

'You didn't marry in church?'

'No. Eleanor wouldn't marry in a Catholic church; she was dead against that, so we compromised and chose a civil ceremony.'

'And her family? Both her parents were alive then, were they?'

'Oh, yes. We only informed them after the event, which proved a serious mistake. Her father was very hurt he was excluded from the wedding. He had wanted to make a big thing of it, apparently. My wife came from a wealthy family, Superintendent, but her father didn't take to me at all. He certainly seemed to resent the fact that I came from a Catholic background; he always regarded Eleanor as his daughter rather than my wife, understandable I suppose. She was certainly in awe of him, especially after he was knighted, and Hannah, of course, adored him. He spoilt her rotten. Although I adopted her, she never regarded me as anything other than an interloper, although I tried my best with her, I really did. Eleanor told her I wasn't her real father when she was about eight or nine, a year or so before I adopted her. I thought adopting her would help, but if anything it aggravated the situation. Her attitude

496

towards me changed markedly. She was her mother's daughter all right was Hannah.' He let out a prolonged sigh. 'But you have to understand, Mr Hood. I needed Eleanor's family money to keep the business afloat so I maintained a relationship of sorts with her father. After he died, about nine years into our marriage, relations between Eleanor and me deteriorated rapidly. I always felt she blamed me for her father's death, because of the financial worry she said I caused him, but he was well into his late seventies and crippled with arthritis. Not a well man at all.' He sighed again. 'Her mother came to live with us afterwards, which didn't help. After she died, Eleanor inherited all her family's estate – like me she was an only child – and became a director of the holding company. We bought Lawson out and issued new shares.' He paused and let his head drop. 'Then Hannah was killed. Nothing was the same after that.'

His head remained bowed for some time. He was quite overcome with emotion. He pressed the syringe driver and waited for the diamorphine to take effect before continuing. 'Confession time.' He looked up at the Superintendent. He was on the verge of tears. 'You were right, Mr Hood. I was responsible for Hannah's death. I did pick her up, I did let her out of my car and I did go back looking for her when she didn't arrive home. I also took the short cut. I was driving too fast and wasn't paying as much attention as I should. I hit something, but I didn't see what. I hoped and prayed it was some animal – a muntjac or something – but later, the circumstantial evidence made it highly likely it must have been Hannah. I tried to convince myself it couldn't have been her. I've worked to get it off my conscience ever since but have never succeeded. It's always been there. An indelible mark.'

'You didn't stop?' queried Hood. He sounded both surprised and critical.

Newby shook his head. 'No, it didn't occur to me until hours later that it could have been Hannah that I'd hit. Not until I'd been at Lonsdale Hall for some time and was told where her body had been found. I still can't understand what she was doing on that road. She was an intelligent girl and it was almost pitch black that night. Why she took that route, I simply don't know.'

'It is slightly shorter on foot than the main road,' said Hood.

'But it isn't lit. The main road is much safer. I only went that way because I thought she'd gone back to Lonsdale and in those days you could get into the grounds from that road through a little-known rear entrance. It's all changed now since Larry sold up.' A pained expression clouded his features and his voice weakened. 'When the police found her body in the ditch, I went completely to pieces. As for Eleanor, well, she collapsed when she was told Hannah was dead and had to be sedated for about three days. I didn't dare tell anyone what had really happened. I'd only just got the business back on an even keel after the Lawson farrago. If I'd said anything and gone to prison, we would have lost everything. No one else knew the ins and outs of the industry like I did. All Eleanor's money had been invested in the expansion of the business. And it wasn't just going to prison that concerned me. If I'd confessed to the police what had happened, she would have destroyed me anyway. It's no excuse, I know, but she's a hard woman, entirely without compassion for anyone or anything, herself excepted. I've lived with her for over twenty years. No one knows her better than me. No wonder I started having an affair.'

'Why did Hannah get out of your car?'

'We had a terrible row. It started because she didn't want to leave the party, but that was entirely down to her mother. She didn't want Hannah to go in the first place. Hannah turned on me as soon as she got into my Range Rover as if it were my fault that she was leaving early. Then she started going on about Martha and me. As you know, she'd seen us together in the office when she came back for her phone. She went on and on about it, screaming and shouting. She even started to hit me. I had no option but to stop or I'd have gone off the road. She then got out and marched off, in the direction we'd just come from. That's why I assumed she was heading for Lonsdale Hall – back to the party. I was on the main road and I considered going after her, but then thought better of it and carried on home. There was no arguing with Hannah. She always insisted on having her own way. I thought I could go back later and persuade her to come with me after she'd calmed down a bit. She knew her mother would be back around midnight and expect her to be at home.'

'Had she threatened to tell your wife what she had seen back in the office?'

'She had, yes. But I'd already spoken to her about that during the previous week. I thought we'd reached an understanding. As I told you before, I'd promised not to see Martha again and she'd undertaken not to tell her mother.'

'And you thought at that time that your wife knew nothing about your affair?'

'I did back then, yes. But now I know different, of course. She told me she had known about us all along when I eventually admitted the affair to her just before I was told I was in remission. That part of her interview was true, I'm afraid.'

'But you never told your wife what had really happened to Hannah?'

He looked down. 'Not then I didn't. You have to understand, Mr Hood, my wife is as unforgiving as the southern sun. She'd have ruined me and everything connected with me if she'd found out back then what had really happened, whatever the consequences for herself. Hannah meant more to her than anyone or anything, certainly more than I did. I said very little, half expecting the police to investigate me, but they never did. Never even checked my Range Rover, which surprised me. I had the bull bars removed then sold it.' He looked up before continuing. 'But what I'd done was always there, niggling away at me. It haunted me on a daily basis. It destroyed what little was left of my relationship with Eleanor. She always blamed me anyway for not getting to Lonsdale Hall on time. I let her think that's what had happened, you see. Seemed the lesser of two evils. If she'd known the truth? Well, I don't know what she would have done, but it would not have been pleasant, I assure you.'

'And Martha?'

His eyes lit up. 'Oh, Martha! She was *so* different from Eleanor. I never could understand what she saw in me, but she must have seen something I hardly knew was there. I was a different person when I was with her. I thought that once the business was re-organised and the pension fund on board, I could dispose of most of my shares and leave Eleanor and start a new life with Martha. The pension fund was keen to acquire more shares and I was quite prepared to walk away.' He heaved a sigh. 'Then her getting pregnant coincided with Hannah's death, and I lost my nerve.' He sighed again and looked into Hood's eyes, pleading for understanding. 'It was all too soon, you see. I couldn't risk it financially and I couldn't take the chance of Eleanor finding out what really happened to Hannah.' He paused and looked away. 'Martha called me a coward. She was absolutely right. That's exactly what I was. I even continued to lie to her when she told me I had a son when I met her for lunch in Northampton. She asked me if Eleanor knew about us, and I told her she didn't. On my wife's instructions, of course.'

'And Martha didn't know the truth about Hannah?'

'No, of course not. I told no one.'

'And when you discovered you had cancer?'

'Well, I thought that was a judgment from on high. I did what I could to fight it, then I was told around Christmas time that it was looking very bad. I thought I was dying, just like Warren Marshall. There was an outside chance of a period of remission if I completed a second course of chemo, which I did, but the doctors were pessimistic. I became very depressed.' He gazed into the middle distance and said nothing for some time. Hood waited patiently. When Newby continued it was plain he had his illness and his likely death very much to the forefront of his mind. 'You're a Catholic, I think, Mr Hood. You know how important it is, even to a lost sheep like me, to make a good death. No man can cut himself off from God's mercy and forgiveness. That's what they say, isn't it?' Hood simply nodded. 'That's certainly what we were told at Melford by the monks. It's always stuck in my mind. That's why I went to see Dominic. I knew he was living at Easton Grange.'

'From the announcement in the college magazine?' asked Hood.

'Yes, I'd seen it a couple or so years before and remembered it. I always got on well with the Dom as we called him at school, and the fact he was so close seemed a happy coincidence. He remembered me when we met, too. I had to get Hannah's death and the other thing off my conscience.'

'The other thing?' queried Hood. 'You mean your relationship with Martha?'

'Not just our relationship.' He paused at length and when he spoke the words almost died on his lips. 'I paid her to have an abortion. Seven and a half grand. Can you imagine that? I paid her to dispose of my own son. I must have lost my moral bearings altogether. You see, while I discovered recently that my wife knew about the affair, neither Eleanor nor I knew about the child. I'd always assumed Martha had opted for a termination. You can imagine the relief when she told me she'd hadn't, and that my son had been adopted and is still alive.' Tears welled in his eyes. 'I don't suppose I'll ever see him, not now, and I don't deserve to. That's why my Range Rover was seen at the Grange in April. I went to see Dominic to tell him that the abortion hadn't taken place.'

'What did he say?'

'He was delighted, of course, but he couldn't resist pointing out that my intentions at the time were both dishonourable and sinful. He was a kind man, but he didn't mince his words.'

'How did your wife react to discovering you had a son by Martha?'

Newby grimaced. 'She was absolutely furious. It was she who had insisted I should see Martha, but she wasn't expecting to find out I had a son any more than I was.'

'You said Martha told you she'd had the child when you met for lunch in Northampton?'

'Yes. I'm sorry I lied to you about that. It was particularly stupid of me. It was all Eleanor's doing. She said no one would believe anything Martha said and it was important there should be no link between Martha and me because of the child. She said she couldn't forgive me about the boy and she was worried that if he were traced, it might be proved I was the father.' He shook his head and sighed. 'We never had any children of our own, you see.' He paused again and swallowed hard. 'She never stopped going on about him. So I did what she told me. Took me for a complete idiot, didn't she? I realise now it was all part of her plan to set me up. Thank God you found out the truth when you did.'

'You seemed surprised when I interviewed you previously that your wife had spoken to Martha on the phone on third August.'

'I didn't know about that, honestly I didn't. Eleanor never mentioned it.'

'But you're sure you never told her you were responsible for Hannah's death?'

Newby shook his head vigorously. 'No. I wouldn't have dared.' He paused ominously. 'In fact, she'd accused me of being responsible several times over the years by not picking her up. And recently, I have gained the distinct impression she had worked out what had really happened.'

'I don't understand. What did she say to you?'

Newby paused and took several deep breaths. 'I'd better explain. I told her I had seen Father Dominic at Easton Grange and had been to confession. That was in March before I was told I was in remission.' His eyes filled with tears. 'I thought I was on the way out. I admitted to her that I had picked up Hannah and let her out of my car, but nothing more. Believe it or not, we were discussing my funeral arrangements at the time, not that we could agree even about that.' He sipped more water. 'I had, in fact, confessed everything about my part in Hannah's death to Dominic and sought absolution, but I didn't tell my wife that, only that I had stopped and let her out of my car after we had quarrelled.' He looked away briefly before continuing. 'Dominic spoke to me afterwards – after my confession had concluded. He was very careful to make that clear; that the seal no longer applied. It was then that he urged me once more to go to the police and tell them what had happened, but I never did. I was too scared. And I said nothing further to him. I certainly didn't repeat what I'd told him in confession. He was unbelievably kind and understanding but it was months later when I saw him again that he advised me once more to go to the police. He even said he would come with me. He thought it would show real remorse for what I had done if I were to come clean about it.' He tried to smile. 'You were right about the initials on the calendar, Mr Hood. That was the day I had reluctantly agreed to go with him to turn myself in. I'd taken some persuading and put it off and put it off, although I have to admit I was still having second thoughts about it as the twenty-sixth drew near. I'd only agreed to do what he suggested because I was beginning to realise that my cancer had probably returned.'

'And you told your wife about the arrangement to go to the police, did you? Even if you didn't tell her why?'

Newby did not reply immediately. When he did, he took Hood by surprise. 'No, I didn't; not until after Dominic was dead. She knew nothing about it before then.'

Hood sat back in his chair. He had theorised that Mrs Newby had visited Father Dominic on the twenty-fourth because her husband had told her about the appointment on the twenty-sixth. That she had been informed about the appointment only after the priest's death didn't quite fit. Was Newby telling him the truth? Hood pressed him further. 'What do you mean then, when you say she told you she knew the circumstances of Hannah's death? How could she have known if you hadn't told her. Dominic would certainly not have revealed what you had confessed.'

Newby caught his breath, took a sip of water, then breathed out slowly. The effort of speaking at length about past events was having its effect upon him. He seemed to be tiring fast but he explained what he meant in a voice full of self-disgust. 'She tricked me, Mr Hood. She led me to believe that she had spoken to Dominic and that he had told her what I had confessed – that I was responsible for Hannah's death. And like a fool, I believed her. She was bluffing – I know that now – but I fell for it and confirmed I had run Hannah down, accidently, of course. I just couldn't fight it any more. I was too tired and overcome with guilt. I thought she'd started to work it all out anyway. She was guessing, of course. It was only when I saw her interviews with you and Sergeant Knight that I fully grasped that she had lied.'

'When did she tell you this?'

'When she returned from Easton Grange on the Wednesday night and told me what she had done.' He heaved a sigh. 'She told me she had lost her temper with Dominic after he'd told her what I had confessed. She killed him, she claimed, in order to make sure none of this came out. It was all for my benefit, apparently. She told me she thought Dominic might reveal what I'd confessed by going to the police himself. As he'd told her, why would he not repeat it to the police? Then I would be exposed with all the consequent embarrassment for her and the business. More to the point, it would also prejudice my chances of becoming High Sheriff.'

Hood gave Newby a serious look. 'I didn't know Father Dominic personally, Mr Newby. But I've learnt a lot about him during this investigation. From what I know of his character, I don't believe for one second he would have breached the seal of the confessional. It would have been contrary to everything he believed in.'

Newby nodded. 'Neither do I, Mr Hood, not any longer. After talking with Father Cotton I realise I was wrong, but I did believe her that Wednesday night. I didn't want to, but it seemed the only logical explanation. It's obvious now why she said what she did. She had to get me on board to help cover up what she had done.' He paused and half-smiled. 'Do you know, until this morning I was actually considering saying nothing to you at all?' He shifted in his wheelchair and looked at his solicitor. He found it difficult to continue for several seconds. Mr Sewell passed him a fresh beaker of water. He took several sips through a straw then cleared his throat. When he continued, he spoke softly. The tears returned. 'I'm dying, Mr Hood. I think my time in this world is fast running out. Oh, yes, I know what I said about fighting on, but I'm not expecting a miracle. I have to accept reality.' He leant forward. 'I thought it would be a noble gesture on my part to allow Eleanor to get away with what she'd done and for me to take the blame. She'd made it look like I was the killer anyway.' He paused and wiped the tears from his eyes. 'I thought I owed her that much.' He tried to smile and looked into Hood's eyes. 'You see, I know you'll never get me to court. And even if you do, a dead man can't serve a prison sentence, can he?' He looked wistfully towards the window. 'She, on the other hand, would never survive it. The humiliation. The embarrassment. Her social standing torn to shreds. Imprisonment. It would all be too much for her. I thought saying nothing might act as some sort of reparation, some amendment for my failure to acknowledge my responsibility for Hannah's death. It all originated with me, you see. It's my fault really.'

He shifted again in the wheelchair and tried to adjust his position. His solicitor placed an additional cushion behind him. Newby then continued.

'Hannah's death must have deranged Eleanor. You may not realise it but she is very vulnerable, despite the impression she gives.' He paused and looked about him, then attempted to lean forward, as if to whisper something to Hood. 'There's something you should know. I tell you this in confidence, not to be repeated. My wife not only took to her bed for three days when she was told about Hannah, she required continuing support and treatment for months. She started self-harming. That's one of the reasons she always wears a high neckline. There are scars on her neck and other parts of her body, particularly her arms. I became very worried about her. She was put on some sort of medication – I can't remember what – and had a very discreet series of meetings with a consultant at St Andrew's in Northampton – all very hush hush and paid for privately. I drove her there myself to begin with. She didn't want anyone finding out about it.'

Hood concealed his surprise. 'Do you know the name of the doctor?'

Newby nodded. 'Dr Anna Russell. I can't remember whether she was a psychiatrist or a psychologist, but she seemed to do Eleanor some good. She gradually got back to something approaching normal, except so far as I was concerned. That hardly changed.' His voice strengthened. 'But telling such a lie about Dominic?' He shook his head. 'He deserves better than that. He deserves justice; he deserves the truth.'

Hood reflected on what Newby had said. That Eleanor Newby had a history of suffering with her mental health introduced a wholly new and unwanted factor into the equation. He remembered what his wife had said to him about the distress that can arise on the anniversary of a death or other traumatic event. Perhaps Dominic dying on 24 July was not a coincidence after all? He continued with his questions. 'How did she manage coping with the anniversary of Hannah's death this year? You must have noticed that it was on Hannah's anniversary that Father Dominic was killed.'

Newby nodded before replying. 'Yes, I appreciated that from the outset. I realised it wasn't just a coincidence. Eleanor was coping very badly. I'm sure that had something to do with her actions that day. She was very depressed that morning as she always is at that time of the year, but she usually gets over it pretty quickly. Not on this occasion though.'

Hood pressed him gently. 'I'm still having difficulty understanding how she found out the truth about Hannah if you didn't tell her? How did she work it out? You'd manage to keep it a secret for years. And you accept, now, that Dominic didn't tell her.'

Newby shook his head and let out a deep sigh. 'You managed to work it out, didn't you Mr Hood? That was obvious from your questions when you interviewed me before. Eleanor must have worked it out too. I'm not sure how. But she's very clever, and usually very insightful. On reflection, I think I gave it away by revealing I had been to confession; it must have got her thinking. She must have worked out that I was in some way responsible for what happened to Hannah beyond failing to get to Lonsdale on time. She also knew I hadn't been to confession for decades and must have speculated why I'd chosen to see Dominic, but please believe me, I never told her what I had confessed, not until she tricked it out of me. And poor Dominic was dead by then. I suppose she had always been suspicious about my account of what happened. I invariably changed the subject when she mentioned Hannah's accident, which she did on a regular basis.' He sighed.' I wish to God I had never told her that I'd been to confession or seen Dominic. If I hadn't said anything, he'd probably still be alive. And Mr Hood, for God's sake don't tell her what I've told you about her mental health. I promised her I'd never mention it to anyone. If you look at her medical records it should all be recorded there. Let that be your source rather than me.'

'What really happened on the twenty-fourth?' asked Hood.

Newby took a deep breath then exhaled loudly. 'As I said, Eleanor was not coping that day. She'd had no breakfast and was very despondent and moped about the house all morning. She kept mentioning Hannah. I found her weeping in her room in the late afternoon. She's never been one for emotional accessibility. I tried, but nothing I could do or say had any effect, so I left her to it and went to bed very early, at about seven-thirty, which was not that unusual. I took something to help me sleep. I was awakened by her at about nine o'clock. I was still half asleep, I suppose, but I noticed she had blood on her blouse. She wasn't her usual self either. She seemed almost intoxicated, but as she's always been teetotal, that can't have been the explanation. She told me she had seen Dominic and wheedled out of him what I had confessed. As I have said, I didn't believe her at first. I couldn't accept that Dominic had said anything to her, not about my confession, but Eleanor is a past master at getting information out of people. She convinced me he had told her what I had confessed. She seemed to know all the details. She then went on to tell me that an argument had broken out and she had lost her temper. She had hit him, repeatedly.'

'I think it more likely that she attacked Dominic in temper because he wouldn't tell her what you had confessed.'

'You're undoubtedly right about that Mr Hood. I should have realised that at the time. I'll never forgive myself for thinking Dominic broke the seal. And it was only then that I admitted to her what I had done. There seemed no point in concealing it any longer.' He continued his account. 'She then insisted I had to go back with her to move the body from the grounds of the ruined chapel.' He paused and gave Hood a wry smile. 'She'd had this marvellous idea, you see – her phrase not mine – of placing him in the priest-hole to confuse the investigation and to put you off the scent.'

'You knew about the priest-hole?'

'Oh, yes; Mr Hitchens told me about it when he came to give me a quote for some landscaping work Eleanor wanted doing.'

'And your wife knew about it too?'

'She was there part of the time, yes. And I'm sure I talked to her about it afterwards.'

Hood pressed on. 'You agreed to go back with her after she told you what she had done?'

He nodded. 'Yes, I'm ashamed to say, I did. But I had to know if what she was saying was really true. I couldn't believe she had actually killed

Dominic; not at first. It all sounded so surreal, then I became concerned when I realised how much blood was on her blouse. She had a shower and changed. All the clothes she'd been wearing, including her gloves, she put to one side for me to destroy. I even called the Grange before we set out. I had a note of the ex-directory number from the days when Sir Robert was a fellow magistrate. I found the number and rang it, but there was no reply. Eleanor had already told me there was no one about, but I wanted to confirm it. She even had the foresight to take a torch with her before we drove there. It was beginning to get dark.'

'How did the two of you move the body.'

'We simply carried him. He was surprisingly light. I think she could have moved him on her own had she wanted to. I got the impression she had already been in the Long Room because I asked her whether the priest-hole had been fully excavated. It hadn't been when Hitchens told us about it. We wrapped the body in a blanket or rug that she'd brought along; it was usually kept in the boot of her Mercedes. She wanted to make it appear that he had been attacked near the priest-hole.'

'Did you see a weapon of any kind?'

'You mean the spade you mentioned in my earlier interview? The one she said I had used?'

'Yes.'

He shook his head, 'No, I never saw it. She must have put it where you found it before she returned home the first time. I never touched it.'

'How did you travel to the Grange?'

'In the Jaguar. She's driven it before, despite what she told you. She could handle it quite easily. It was due to go into Banbury in a day or two. I suspect that's why she used it.'

'And if it was seen, as we now know it was, she may have thought it would be associated with you rather than her.'

Newby appeared surprised. 'That had honestly never occurred to me. My God, she has been careful.'

'Who drove on this occasion?'

'She did. I didn't feel up to it. As I said, I'd taken some medication to help me sleep and I still wasn't fully awake. It all felt like a dream, a very bad dream.'

'And when you got there?'

'She had some keys, Dominic's I supposed. We went in through the chapel which was not locked and then through the sacristy – that door was unlocked too.' He paused and looked directly at Hood. 'It was in the sacristy that Dominic heard my confession.' He then continued with the narrative. 'There was nobody about. She showed me the priest-hole. We then went back into the grounds and wrapped the body in the rug and carried Dominic into the Long Room. He was dumped in the priest-hole. He was obviously dead.'

'Did you go down into the hide and check on him?'

Newby shook his head. 'No, and neither did she. We just dropped him in there. She pulled back his cowl first. That's when I saw the wound to his head; it looked a mess and he wasn't breathing as far as I could see. I thought he must be dead. There was no point in checking for a pulse. We left the Long Room the way we went in. She locked the sacristy door behind us. I remember the lock was difficult. Eleanor put the keys back on the hook in the Gatehouse then removed the gloves she'd been wearing. I put the rug in the boot and we drove home. I burnt that second pair of gloves and the rug later along with the carpet.'

'Why didn't you call for help? Dominic might still have been alive. We believe he didn't die until sometime after he was dumped in the hide.'

'Is that right?' Newby sighed, a guilty expression crossing his face as he continued. 'She convinced me he was already dead. She was already working out how to distance us from the killing as we left. On the way home, she had a real go at me; she said it was all my fault for not telling her the truth about Hannah. She reminded me that I could still go to prison if the police discovered I had run into her and not stopped or reported it. And I knew that causing death by reckless driving usually resulted in a hefty prison sentence. She even went so far as suggesting it wasn't an accident; that I had run Hannah down deliberately, to prevent her revealing the truth about Martha, which is nonsense. As we now know, she already knew about the affair. Other people at Dowlas probably knew about us too, including that cousin of hers. He'd tried it on with Martha but had got nowhere. Eleanor then said we had to protect each other. I was to alibi her and, in return, she would say nothing about Hannah to the police. That surprised me, but I suppose she needed me to alibi her for the time of the murder. No one would suspect us, she said. Why should they?' He adopted a cynical tone. 'We were far too important to come under scrutiny.

That's what she said. She hoped you'd think his murder was associated with the priest-hole.' He sniggered. 'I realise now she was setting me up. That bit of blood in the boot, for example. I've always wondered how that got there. I hosed it down with a high-pressure hose. She must have put it there afterwards, deliberately. There's no other explanation. Just like that bit of carpet she preserved. Well she's not getting away with it. I had nothing to do with Father Dominic's death.'

'But you helped her cover up what had happened, didn't you?'

He dropped his head. 'I suppose I did, yes. There's no denying that. I could go to prison for that I suppose, if I live long enough.' He gave Hood a cynical smile.

Hood did not respond. He continued with his questions, concerned that the solicitor would intervene because Newby was clearly flagging. 'Did you notice anything in Dominic's hand?'

Newby seemed surprised. 'No, was there something?'

'When he was found, yes. An *agnus dei*.'

'What's that?'

'A small oval wax object of religious significance.'

Newby shook his head. 'Never heard of such a thing. How did it get there?'

'We believe Dominic found it in the priest-hole on a previous occasion. He may have taken it into his hand to comfort himself as he lay dying.'

Newby sighed deeply. 'I hope it did, comfort him, I mean.'

'It also provided me with a clue as to why he was attacked.'

'It did?'

'Yes. It told me he was attacked because he was a priest, a priest who had probably heard someone's confession. That's why you came under suspicion. I thought that someone was you after I examined the circumstances of Hannah's death.'

'So you worked it all out from the circumstances of Hannah's accident?'

Hood nodded then moved on.

'What time was it when you left the Grange?'

'Getting on for ten, I think. I didn't check the time. It was quite dark. She took over when we got back. I just did as she told me.'

'I think you implied your wife had seen Father Dominic before the twenty-fourth?'

'She must have. She certainly went out in the Jaguar on the seventh July, despite what she told you. And she knew where the priest's keys were kept. I noticed that when she put them back. She must have been in his cottage before. I'd been there on a couple of occasions, but never with her and I never noticed where he kept his keys. I swear to you, I was at home that Sunday. I didn't go out.'

Hood stood up and walked to the window and looked out. While he was inclined to believe Newby, he needed something solid in the way of evidence. Newby had to allow his account to be recorded. Whether Hood would be able to use it in evidence, the lawyers could squabble over later. Hood turned and looked at him, then returned to his seat. 'Unless you agree to put all this on tape, what you're telling me will be of little practical use, you know. She may well get away with it.'

Newby attempted a smile. 'You won't need me, Mr Hood.'

'I won't?'

He smiled. 'No, I'm not quite the fool my wife takes me for. I suspected she might do something along these lines, so while I did what she wanted for the most part, I took some sensible precautions in case her plan fell apart.'

Hood became quite animated. 'What precautions?'

Newby grinned. 'Mr Sewell has all the details. I told him this morning.'

'What precautions?' repeated Hood.

Sewell placed his hand on Newby's right arm and nodded. Newby took a deep breath. 'She thinks I burnt the blouse and trousers she was wearing when she killed Dominic. Oh, I got rid of the carpet from the boot, or thought I did, and the rug we wrapped the body in. She made sure of that. But I still have her blouse, covered in what must be Dominic's blood, and her trousers as well as the gloves she was wearing when she killed him.'

Hood narrowed his eyes. 'We never found anything like that when we searched your home.'

Newby smiled. 'They're not there. She'd have found them and got rid of them if I'd hidden them at home. She had the entire house cleaned by a professional cleaning company, you know. I made a bit of a performance of burning one of her other blouses. I have the clothes she was wearing carefully hidden. Mr Sewell knows where they are. I have made a sworn statement to him.'

Sewell nodded. 'That's right, Mr Hood. I have a lengthy affidavit that Mr Newby swore this morning. I would be grateful if you would make a note that it was sworn before he had sight of his wife's interviews. His original instructions were that it was to remain confidential. But viewing his wife's false account has caused him to change his mind. And if you recover the items he has mentioned, that should be more than enough to establish what he has told you is the truth.'

'He wasn't changing his will this morning?'

'No, that is in hand, but we were working on his affidavit. That's why Miss Randall was here. I didn't think it proper for me to swear him myself in the circumstances. I believe Mr Newby is now prepared to disclose his affidavit to you at an appropriate juncture.'

Newby nodded his agreement. Hood was more concerned with recovering what could amount to damning evidence against Eleanor Newby.

'Where is this clothing? I have to retrieve it.'

Newby hesitated and waited for his solicitor's signal before answering.

'Separately bagged and carefully hidden in the large drawer on the left-hand side of the desk in my office at Milton Keynes. You'll find the key on the bunch you removed from me when I was arrested. The Chub key; you can't confuse it. It's the only one of its type.' He smiled to himself. 'I'd love to see my wife's face when you put all this to her.'

CHAPTER SIXTY-SEVEN

Helen Swanson had no difficulty in identifying Eleanor Newby on Friday morning. She picked her out immediately despite the suspect having turned up wearing very casual clothes and a noticeably different hairstyle. No Jaeger suit, no pearls, and no high heels, but she had a silk scarf nonchalantly placed around her neck. All to no avail. Helen was certain she was the woman she had seen outside the chapel at Easton Grange on 7 July. Hood immediately re-arrested Mrs Newby and lodged her in the cells until he was ready to interview her again. The protests from both she and her solicitor were loud and indignant but had no effect on either him or Knight.

The clothing Newby had told the Superintendent about was retrieved from the office in Milton Keynes by Nigel Mullen and DC Bradley. The several items were removed from the plastic supermarket bags in which Newby had deposited them and placed in brown paper exhibit bags and carefully labelled. The supermarket bags, slightly bloodstained, were dealt with in a similar fashion.

At 12 noon, Mrs Newby was brought to interview room number two. Her solicitor was already present and had previously spent over an hour with her client in private. After Knight had cautioned Mrs Newby and named everyone present in the room, Mrs Dangerfield continued to protest the basis upon which her client had been re-arrested.

'You had already relied on the so-called identification when you first arrested Mrs Newby. A subsequent confirmatory identification – which we dispute – hardly amounts to fresh evidence, as you must surely appreciate, Superintendent.'

Hood smiled. 'I'm not relying on the identification to justify your client's re-arrest, helpful though it is. We have some further evidence which radically alters the situation. I have been speaking to Mr Newby, who has been very helpful and decided to cooperate.'

Eleanor Newby scoffed. 'I hope you are not going to be so foolish as to rely on anything my husband says, Mr Hood. He's obviously desperate to avoid being prosecuted for running down my daughter and killing this priest. He'll say anything. And he may not survive to give evidence or to stand trial. He is very ill, you know.'

'I don't have to rely on what he says,' responded Hood. 'We have received further evidence from the laboratory. The fibres found on Father Dominic's habit have been matched to several fibres discovered in the boot of your Mercedes. We believe they are from the blanket or rug in which the priest's body was wrapped as he was carried into the Long Room at Easton Grange before being dumped in the hide. I can let Mrs Dangerfield have a copy of the report as soon as it comes through.'

'What is that to do with me?' sneered Mrs Newby. 'My husband must have removed the rug from my Mercedes before he went to Easton Grange. I would have thought that such an obvious explanation would have occurred to you before now. My car was not locked when parked inside the barn.'

'Do you know, I thought you'd say that,' said Hood, unable to keep a straight face. He then became deadly serious. 'We have also recovered further evidence which is not so easily dismissed.' He indicated to Knight who rose from her seat and went to the door. When she opened it, DC Bradley was waiting outside. He walked in carrying three brown paper exhibit bags.

'For the benefit of the tape, DC Bradley has entered the room,' said Hood, noting the time.

Bradley placed the bags on the table, then withdrew.

'What have we here?' asked the solicitor. Mrs Newby's face fell.

'DC Bradley has now left the room,' continued Hood. He smiled towards Knight who looked away. She knew only too well what was coming.

Both detectives then made quite a show of putting on latex gloves. The superintendent checked the exhibit label on the largest of the three bags, then tore it open. He withdrew a pair of folded dark blue trousers, watching Mrs Newby as he did so. She gasped involuntarily as he lay the trousers out on the table, carefully placing the exhibit bag under them. 'Recognise these, do you, Mrs Newby.'

Eleanor Newby looked at her solicitor who shook her head. 'No comment,' replied the suspect.

Hood picked up the trousers in his gloved hands, holding them at the waist. He then raised them up so everyone could see them. 'They look quite a neat fit for you, Mrs Newby, don't you think?' Hood pointed to an obvious bloodstain on the front close to a pocket. Mrs Newby did not reply. She was clearly taken aback and while she did her best to hide it, remained stunned.

'I don't think we should have any problem proving these have been worn by you, and no one else,' emphasised Hood. 'They'll be submitted to the laboratory for DNA analysis. It's usually very easy to obtain a DNA profile from the waistband of an item like this, especially when it's been worn recently. I'm also sure that bloodstain will be shown to be from Father Dominic.'

'Where has this exhibit come from?' asked the solicitor. 'I've received no disclosure about it or the other items on the table. There must be hundreds of women who could get into those trousers.'

'It's not just the trousers,' replied Hood, as he replaced them in the exhibit bag and initialled the label. 'Shall we have a look in the other bags?' He examined the label on a second bag, then opened it and produced a white linen blouse, with several marks on it in a spray pattern across the front. The marks were obviously in blood. There were several smudges on the sleeves and the outside of the collar.

'I don't think there can be any argument that this blouse belongs to Mrs Newby. We'll have it checked by the scientists, of course, but there are initials embroidered just below the inside of the collar. Specially tailored for her I suspect, no doubt at some expense. He read them out slowly – 'E. V. A. N. Now, I wonder what those initials stand for? Eleanor Victoria Alexandre Newby, perhaps?' He gave Mrs Newby a severe look then continued. 'This blouse also matches several identical garments hanging in Mrs Newby's dressing room, all with the same initials in exactly the same place.'

'You've been searching my home again?' said Mrs Newby, her voice much weaker than before, 'without consulting me.'

'We have, yes. We are entitled to do that following your being re-arrested this morning. Your solicitor will confirm it.'

Mrs Dangerfield nodded. 'I'm afraid that's right,' she said. 'Section eighteen of PACE gives them the authority.'

'And the blood on the front of the blouse and the sleeves will, I am sure, prove to be Father Dominic's,' continued Hood. 'The spray pattern is exactly what one would expect to find if someone had been repeatedly struck while he was bleeding by someone wearing such an item of clothing.'

Mrs Newby's face was a picture of incredulity. 'Where did these items come from?' she asked, repeating her solicitor's earlier question. She could hardly get out the words.

Hood could not resist a smile. 'You thought your husband had burnt them, didn't you? Well, as you can see, he didn't. He's not quite the fool you took him for.'

'You got these from him? Then he must have contaminated them in order to try and blame me for his criminal actions.'

'I don't think so, Mrs Newby. It would be impossible to replicate that spray pattern in Father Dominic's blood. Shall we let the scientists determine how these marks got on to your clothing? You do accept these items are yours, don't you?'

'No comment,' snapped Mrs Newby. Hood replaced the blouse in its bag then opened the smaller third package and produced a pair of black ski gloves, stained with what appeared to be dried blood. He held them up. 'Yours, I believe?'

Mrs Newby looked away but did not reply.

'You were wearing these items when you attacked and killed Father Dominic on the twenty-fourth of July, were you not?'

The solicitor cleared her throat and interrupted. 'I would like to speak with my client in private, Detective Superintendent, before she says anything further. I did not have the opportunity to discuss this new evidence with her before this interview began because I knew nothing about it.'

Hood frowned. 'Very well. I can give you thirty minutes, but please be under no illusions. I will give Mrs Newby one final opportunity to account for these items. I am fully prepared to listen to any explanation she may wish to give. Otherwise, if she declines to answer, she is likely to be charged with murder before the day is out. I shall not be waiting for the scientists to report, by the way. I don't think there can be any doubt what they will find when they do.'

Mrs Newby said nothing. For the first time she appeared seriously rattled. Hood continued. 'In the event of a charge, she will be placed before the Magistrates' Court tomorrow morning. Until then, she will be detained in the cells at this police station. In view of the evidence we have discovered, and her husband's account of events, I take the view there is a significant risk of further interference by her with the course of justice. Any application for bail will have to be made to the Magistrates' Court.'

He paused briefly. 'Subject to the views of the CPS, any such application will be vigorously opposed.'

CHAPTER SIXTY-EIGHT

As Hood anticipated, Mrs Newby declined to answer any further questions when given the opportunity. On the advice of her solicitor, she exercised her right of silence. Hood then charged her with murder and attempting to pervert the course of justice. Eleanor Newby said nothing in response before she was returned to her cell, but she was visibly shaken. The position of Arthur Newby was postponed for further consideration. He was bailed for two weeks and permitted to return home to Stanton Harwood after being discharged from Northampton General. A Macmillan nurse was engaged to take care of his medical requirements.

Hood organised a short briefing for the press late on Friday afternoon. He resisted pressure from the numerous media representatives to identify either Mrs Newby or her husband, despite their names being repeatedly put to him. His statement was brief and to the point.

"A forty-nine-year old woman from Stanton Harwood has been charged today with the murder of Father Dominic Renville on the twenty-fourth of July. She will appear in court tomorrow. No further details will be given until her court appearance. A fifty-four-year old man from Stanton Harwood has also been arrested and bailed in connection with the death of Father Dominic but has not been charged."

Hood emphasised that the person charged was entitled to receive a fair trial and that further comment was therefore inappropriate. Given the nationwide interest in the case, the Attorney-General's London office issued a statement warning the media about the perils of contempt of court. Not that it stopped them. It didn't take much for the journalists

517

present to work out who had been charged. That Mrs Newby and her husband had been arrested was already a hot topic of conversation in Stanton Harwood, Easton Parva and beyond. The gates of the Olde House had been closed and a uniformed police officer stationed outside. That alone told the media all they needed to know. Most newspapers led with the story the following morning stating that "local sources" had named Eleanor Newby as the individual who had been charged with the murder of the priest.

A special hearing at Northampton Magistrates' Court was arranged for 10 o'clock on Saturday morning. Fiona Morrison, who had authorised charging Mrs Newby, decided to leave the question of the admissibility of Arthur Newby's account of matters to leading counsel to consider. Harold Cronshaw QC would be briefed to prosecute the trial, but she handled the first appearance before the District Judge herself. Mr Sewell released Newby's affidavit to Hood and agreed to his client being interviewed under caution in a few days' time when he was feeling more settled after leaving hospital.

Northampton Magistrates' Court was packed. Hood and Knight almost had to fight their way through the crowd that had assembled outside. Mrs Newby looked a forlorn sight sitting in the dock as the case was adjourned for one week. Her anguish and embarrassment were plain for all to see. She rarely raised her head and when she did, in order to answer the few questions that were put to her by the clerk, she studiously ignored the disdainful looks from the overflowing press benches and the chock-full public gallery. She spoke only to confirm her name, address, and date of birth. To her obvious distress, she was remanded in custody to Holloway prison, Mrs Dangerfield's application for bail and the offer of several sureties having been firmly rejected by the District Judge. Hood nevertheless shared the concern expressed for the accused's welfare and safety in custody, not that he disagreed with Morrison's decision to oppose bail. He had no doubt that were she at liberty, Mrs Newby would continue to interfere with the evidence and try and cast further suspicion on her husband. Hood had received confirmation from her medical records that she had indeed suffered mental illness in the past and supported the suggestion that additional precautions should be taken to monitor her safety at Holloway in order to guard against the risk of self-harming or worse. Mrs Dangerfield was already in the throes of commissioning a psychiatric report and had expressed similar fears during her unsuccessful submissions for conditional bail. The last thing Hood wanted was Mrs Newby avoiding a trial by harming herself.

Photographers vied with each other to get a shot of the distraught and now handcuffed prisoner as she was led from a rear door of the court building into a waiting closed custody van. Several of them pursued the vehicle along the road in an attempt to take photographs through the darkened windows, their cameras flashing against the opaque glass.

Hood and Knight returned to Campbell Square. Greatly relieved as they were that the investigation was almost complete, Knight raised a feature of the case which continued to trouble her. 'There's one thing I don't quite understand,' she said as the two detectives relaxed and enjoyed some coffee in Hood's office. 'If Newby never told his wife about the appointment he had made with Father Dominic for the twenty-sixth until after Dominic's death, what prompted her to go to Easton Grange on the evening of the twenty-fourth?'

'That threw me for a while,' confessed Hood. 'As you know, I thought that was the trigger for her visit. But I was wrong. She must have calculated that Newby going to confession related in some way to her daughter's death. Newby had told her he'd sought out Dominic to confess something that was troubling him, but he didn't say what. She'd always been sceptical about his account of his movements the night her daughter died. I think she went to Easton Grange to get confirmation of what she suspected before the twenty-fourth, probably on the seventh, and it was no coincidence that she chose to go back on the anniversary of her daughter's death. Her grief may well have contributed to her actions. Young Bradley was right after all. I'm sure now the date is significant. When Dominic refused again to reveal what her husband had confessed, she must have lost her temper and struck him with the spade. Her husband had taken something to help him sleep that evening so he wouldn't have been aware she had gone out and I suspect she'd become quite obsessed with finding out what he wouldn't tell her. I also think she was getting more anxious about Martha, after she discovered she'd given birth to Newby's child. Perhaps she thought her husband might leave her and go off with Martha. I think she'd become quite unbalanced and I fancy was heading for some sort of breakdown. She'd covered it up quite successfully, but that couldn't last. That's why I am still worried about what she might do to herself in custody. Holloway is a quite dreadful place for someone like her.'

Knight was not so convinced. 'She's not the type, surely? She was as cool as they come when we visited her home and she's gone to a lot of trouble to implicate her husband. None of that would suggest she was under acute mental stress at the time. It could all be a bit of a show.'

Hood shook his head. 'You never can tell, Wendy. Whatever may happen at trial, the fact remains she's lost everything she regards as making life worth living. Her only daughter is long gone. Her reputation has been dragged through the mud and has all but disintegrated and it can only get worse. You've seen this morning's papers I assume? And they'll have a field day once the trial gets underway. I doubt if she can live with all that.' Hood took another sip of coffee.

'I suppose attempting to frame her husband will form part of the case against her?' said Knight.

'That will be up to the lawyers, but she certainly did the best she could and I have to admit she went about it with some aptitude; once she started thinking straight, of course. But I still think the first blow was struck in temper.'

'I don't understand why Newby went along with it for as long as he did.'

'I think he was genuinely terrified of it getting out that he'd killed Hannah in that accident after his wife had worked out the truth. When she lied about Dominic revealing his confession he fell for it. I don't believe it occurred to him that he was helping build a case for murder against himself, not until recently. She certainly made intelligent use of our suspicions about him and turned them to her advantage.' He paused for a moment before continuing. 'I also think Newby felt considerable guilt in respect of Hannah's death. He may well have thought it was the right thing to do to try and protect his wife. His conscience had certainly troubled him for many years. He still blames himself for setting the whole thing in motion. Remember, he'd always understood how Hannah's accident had affected his wife and how she was unable to cope on the anniversary of the girl's death. Not that she reciprocated.'

'What do you mean?'

'It's crossed my mind more than once that she may have gone on to kill Dominic deliberately after her first strike in temper; just to set her husband up for murder. She was probably more vengeful and deranged than even I anticipated.' He sighed. 'I think she wanted him to suffer more than he already is with his cancer. I was wrong, too, when I said they'd done a deal. Newby may have thought they had, but I think she always intended to expose him as the likely killer. I'm pretty sure now that she planted that blood in the boot of the Jaguar deliberately.'

'Do you think so? She was taking a hell of a risk; it might have bounced back and implicate her, as it has.'

'I agree, but it's the clothing that proves what she did, more than the bloodstain in the boot. She acknowledged in her interview that Newby hosed it down after removing the carpet and the rug. How could it have got there otherwise? I think she's always had in mind that he'll be dead before any trial takes place to counter any suspicion falling on her.'

Knight finished her coffee. 'Do you think she'll admit responsibility, now that the evidence against her is piling up?'

'I doubt it, but we'll have to wait and see. There's a long time to go before any trial takes place. She may well think of something, or she may try and plead diminished responsibility. She won't be one for giving up, not yet.'

CHAPTER SIXTY-NINE

In the weeks that passed after Eleanor Newby's first court appearance, her mental health deteriorated significantly. It was reported to Hood that she had started to self-harm in prison and had become isolated, aggressive and delusional. The Secretary of State, eventually, issued a warrant under the Mental Health Act 1983 transferring her from Holloway to a medium secure unit in a mental hospital in a London suburb where she could receive treatment. Her trial was fixed for early December, but concerns were beginning to be expressed that she might be unfit to plead. Hood hoped that the treatment she was receiving would enable a full trial to take place on the due date. Talk of a possible adjournment caused him considerable anxiety. He needed the trial to be underway before Arthur Newby died. As for Newby himself, he repeated his admissions to Hood under caution. A full recording was made on video. The DPP decided not to prosecute him for assisting an offender or attempting to pervert the course of public justice. Nor was it considered in the public interest to bring proceedings in respect of Hannah's accident. Newby would prove more useful as a witness, always assuming he survived long enough. And, much to Hood's astonishment, he continued to defy his doctors, living on, despite a gradual and continuing decline in his condition. He subjected himself to a further course of intensive chemotherapy which detracted from what quality of life remained to him. His prognosis, however, remained poor. It was not anticipated he would live beyond the spring. But all this was for the future. Hood had other priorities including attending the funeral of Father Dominic at Melford Abbey.

Grantham deferred his return to the States so that he, too, could attend and Sir Robert, true to his word, allowed the Powdrell chalice to be used at the Requiem Mass. He arranged beforehand a private viewing to which Hood and his wife were invited. The Superintendent felt a trifle self-conscious as the ancient chalice was scrutinised by the more distinguished guests which included two archbishops, the Abbot President of the English Benedictine Congregation, and the Bishop of Northampton in whose diocese the monastery stood. The Apostolic Nuncio was also present, anxious as he was to hear directly from Hood a detailed account of how the chalice had been found.

Afterwards, as Hood and his wife made their way into the body of the Abbey church accompanied by Grantham, the Jesuit couldn't help noticing that Hood appeared somewhat overawed by the reaction of the distinguished ecclesiastics all of whom had congratulated him on his investigation into Dominic's murder and the discovery of the legendary chalice.

'Don't take them too seriously,' the Jesuit advised. 'Never forget, Mr Hood, the most powerful individuals in the Church are not the cardinals and bishops, not even the Pope, important though they are. Those who follow the hard path of solitude, silence and prayer, hidden from the world – they are the ones we should look up to. Cistercians of the Strict Observance and other religious, praying for us constantly in their cells; cloistered nuns in their Carmel; Carthusians in their hermitages; *they* are the real powerhouse of the Church.'

'And the rest of us? Don't we count for something?' asked Hood.

Grantham nodded. 'Of course. We are all called with equal dignity to make our contribution.'

'That, I suppose, would include the Jesuits?' quipped Hood, an impish grin on his face. Grantham responded with a wry smile.

★ ★ ★ ★

The funeral of a monk is both simple and solemn. But the circumstances of Dominic's death added a layer of unlooked for grandeur as the various dignitaries took their places on the sanctuary. The Abbey church was packed to capacity as the great bell of the monastery began to toll. Many old boys from the college who had been taught by Father Dominic attended, but not Arthur Newby. He remained at Stanton Harwood where he was now cared for by Martha Morton who had agreed to remain with him until the end, Newby having altered his will, ensuring she and their son would want for nothing after his death.

The small community at Melford was augmented by several monks from other Benedictine houses. Together they sang the **Suscipe me Domine**, always sung at a monk's solemn profession and again at his funeral. At the Mass itself, the Abbot of Melford presided after which Father Milmo would preach the panegyric. When the Liturgy of the Eucharist was reached, Hood heard again the words that had made such an impact upon him in the chapel at Easton Grange, *"when supper was ended He took the chalice…"* The Abbot raised up the Powdrell chalice immediately after the words of consecration were spoken, so everyone could see it in all its glory. But it was not the chalice itself that now held meaning for Hood. Something of much greater significance had come about. As the Abbot held the chalice aloft Hood whispered to himself the words of the Apostle Thomas when he saw for the first time the risen Christ, 'My Lord and my God.'

At the burial which followed, the monks alone processed behind Dominic's simple oak coffin as it made its way to the Abbey's cemetery, chanting as they went, the words of the *In Paradisum*.

May the angels lead you into paradise
May the Martyrs receive you at your coming
And bring you into the holy city, Jerusalem.
May the choirs of angels receive you
And with Lazarus, who once was poor
May you have eternal rest.

ALSO BY MICHAEL GT STOKES

Blackmail
A Private & Convenient Place
The Harman Brief
The Tinkerman

Visit the author's website:
michaelgtstokes.com